THE EARTH REMAINS

a novel

SHELLEY BURCHFIELD

Relax. Read. Repeat.

THE EARTH REMAINS
By Shelley Burchfield
Published by TouchPoint Press
Brookland, AR 72417
www.touchpointpress.com

Copyright © 2021 Shelley Burchfield

ISBN: 978-1-952816-92-5

Editor: Jenn Haskin

Cover Design: Colbie Myles
Cover Images: Peach tree- vintage engraved illustration – "Dictionnaire encyclopedique universel illustre" By Jules Trousset - 1891 Paris by lynea (Shutterstock); Watercolor Pattern with peaches and flowers by Knopazyzy (Shutterstock); Watercolor hand drawn botanical illustration with summer fruit whole peach with leaf by Lelakordrawings (Adobe Stock)

Visit the author's website at https://www.shelleyburchfield.com/

First Edition

Printed in the United States of America.

To Sam, who knew I could do it.

Generations come and generations go, but the earth remains forever.

Ecclesiastes 1:4

Prologue

September 1922

THE WOUND HAD TURNED SEPTIC, and neither homemade salves and tinctures nor the doctor's hasty amputation of her right hand had slowed the old woman's raging infection.

Curtains fluttered gently at the window as soft rain fell outside. Thunder rumbled in the distance and she stirred in her sleep. A cool breeze brushed her skin and raised goose flesh. With her left hand, she tried to pull the quilt close around her tiny shoulders. Old bones refused to warm.

So it comes to this, she thought. When she had avoided so many more interesting ways to go. The irony made her smile. A snapping turtle was hiding in the rhubarb, nowhere near the muddy pond. Its crushing bite had nearly severed two fingers, and the bacteria in its mouth quickly colonized her bloodstream.

"Ma'am?" murmured the young nurse, rising sleepily from her rocking chair in the corner. "Miss Polly, do you need something? Are you chilly?" She crossed the room to close the open window and returned to lay a dark hand on the woman's forehead. Damp wisps of snow-white hair clung to the old woman's fevered brow, and perspiration beaded her upper lip.

"Miss Polly? I'm Elizabeth," the nurse leaned close and whispered. "I'm here to help you. Remember?"

Polly opened her eyes, confused. It was the remembering which frustrated her. The memories came unbidden now; the good mixed up with the bad. She felt as if she was seeing her life from outside her own skin, hovering just close enough to watch it happen all over again, with a softness over it, like a veil. She longed to call out, to keep the little girl safe. To warn the young woman of danger ahead. But it was too late.

"No need to worry yourself, Ona. I just had a bad dream . . ." Her shaky voice drifted off as she turned in her bed. She had no regrets. She had atoned for her sins, at least the deeds she credited as sin. Some of the things that had been done she would never ask God to forgive.

Polly tentatively touched the bandaged stump with her left hand, willing the ghost of her right hand to flex and bend. To feel. She squeezed her eyes shut tightly and tried to think on happy times.

Whitehall. There was Mother, fussing around the lawn, the roses her pride and joy. The view looked far to the north, to hazy green hills folding into the mountains of the Blue Ridge. Pink roses climbed over the veranda railings in profusion and sweetened the summer breezes. The veranda was always swept clean and welcomed visitors with comfortable rocking chairs and a ceiling painted pale blue to keep the "haints" away. Bright orange daylilies lined the long drive. Every evening, Ona rang the brass bell on the post to call the children in for supper. Polly's brothers always beat her home, stiff boots and ankle-grazing skirts no match for their own bare feet and long legs.

Father raised cotton, although his heart was elsewhere. He was an entrepreneur of sorts, working to bring the railroad further into upstate South Carolina. His dream of a tunnel through the Blue Ridge Mountains kept him away much of the time. When he came home, his warm embrace smelled of fine tobacco and leather. He always brought Polly a paper sack of penny candies after lengthy trips to Columbia and Charleston.

The old woman clambered after another recollection. Perfect summer days, corn fields waving emerald green. Cotton was high. In the distance, the men stooped to their hard labor. Polly balanced precariously on the split rail fence post, eating a ripe peach with childish abandon. Sweet juice dribbled down her chin as she lifted her face to the warm sun.

She blinked and saw Duke, ebony arms and torso glistening with sweat, hard at the plow with the mules, slicing furrows in the rich bottomland. She lifted a sticky hand to wave and he waved back. She tossed the peach pit towards the mules and the nearest animal flicked his ear in irritation.

The overseer rode up, tall in the saddle. With a wink and a smile, he told her to get on home. "A young lady doesn't exactly belong in the fields when the slaves are picking," he'd said. As if that were where the danger lay.

The clear creek where she waded with her brothers on hot August afternoons tumbled over smooth grey rocks on its way to the river. Barefoot, dark braids undone, she remembered wading in the icy water, her eyes alert for the smoothest stones. Mother chastised her for spoiling another good dress; creek mud and peach juice stained her smock front a dull brown.

Another memory. She watched with satisfaction as Ben kissed his bride. Ah, she had done a fine thing then. But my, how she missed him still.

And there was her beloved husband, long gone. His handsome face was so hard to summon. Their time together wasn't long enough, but it was fair, she supposed. A life for a life. God's idea of justice confounded her.

The hot summer morning at the trading post, the most vivid image in a lifetime of memories, brought her fully and instantly awake. It wouldn't stay down. It was less painful now, more than seventy years later, but no less unjust. Why was that picture clear as day? Why not the kiss of her husband or dear Father's smile?

Elizabeth bent to offer her a sip of water, which Polly took gratefully.

She lay back, exhausted from the effort. At the edge of sleep, John's blue eyes followed her, wide and questioning. Not angry really but surprised to find Polly capable of her own crimes.

Her rheumy eyes closed. Nothing would stay down anymore. The memories seeped out of her very marrow and into her blood and breath. With every exhalation, she released another fragment of her life into the ether. Here was her last chance to have her say and set things right before she left this earth. She tried to speak but no words came from her dry throat.

Chapter One

"POLLY CAROLINE, BE STILL!" MARY BURGISS, straight pins between her lips, pushed her daughter's arms down at her sides. "How can I fit this dress if you won't be still?"

Polly squirmed. It was hard for an eight-year-old to be so still when the world outside beckoned on this late summer day. Her mongrel pup scrambled around at her feet, yipping and jumping.

"I want to go to the creek with Joshua and Caleb. I don't need a new dress anyway. Can I go please?" Polly whined.

"Polly, you know I have to have this dress finished. Your father wants his family to look fine for the Senator's visit. He is bringing very important men with him. You will look respectable and you will behave like a lady. Now hold still! You may catch up to your brothers in a while."

Polly stopped fidgeting. She thought of the licorice twist, a secret gift from her father, wrapped in her handkerchief and stashed in the pocket of her skirt. Her mother tucked the last bit of fabric into a dainty pleat and pinned it with the final straight pin.

1

"There, let me get this dress off you before you tear it, and you may go. And take that dog with you. I am tired of having it under foot." The pup thumped his tail against Polly's legs.

Polly wriggled free of the party dress and quickly stepped into her skirt, fingering the licorice in the pocket. She let her mother button up her smock, barely able to keep still.

Mary smoothed the little party dress and laid it aside. She brushed a wisp of hair from her damp forehead and sighed, "Law, I don't get a moment's peace with you children and your animals always in my path—and with your father bringing Senator Calhoun to Whitehall tomorrow. Stay in shouting distance, you hear me?" Mary called after her daughter. But the little girl and the pup were well out the door.

— • —

MARY PICKED UP THE TREASURED daguerreotype of her husband and smiled. The upcoming visit from Senator Calhoun, once the Vice President, was proof enough that her young husband was moving in the right direction. Meeting the right people. His father's connections had proved invaluable.

She looked around at the home she had created with her husband. For thirteen years now, she and James had worked to make Whitehall their own. Theirs was not a large plantation like the Senator's vast estate at Fort Hill, just a few miles up the road. It certainly was not like the grand plantations down on the coast, with hundreds of slaves; many outbuildings; and broad fields of cotton, rice, and indigo as far as the eye could see.

The Burgiss land was a share of "bounty land" that had once belonged to the native people before the Indian Removal. The Cherokee had ceded most of this territory to the state, shortly after the end of the Revolutionary War.

In recognition of heroic service to his country during the War of 1812, Major Joshua Burgiss, of Richmond, Virginia, had been given a large piece of property in this up-and-coming district, a grant of land extending from the Keowee River to the Big Generostee Creek. It included a few outbuildings, and an existing log house set on a gentle hill, with a winter view of the river to the west and the rolling Blue Ridge Mountains far to the north.

Burgiss gifted the land to his second son, James, on the occasion of his marriage to young Mary Kent in 1835. Not long after their wedding, James set off with his bride for their new home.

— • —

LIKE SO MANY FAMILIES IN THOSE DAYS, the newlyweds came down the Great Wagon Road, a well-traveled thoroughfare running from Philadelphia to Augusta, Georgia. James hired a seasoned guide named Jenkins to take them down the length of the busy road. The couple traveled in a shiny new phaeton drawn by two black horses, followed by two mule-pulled wagons loaded with goods. The phaeton was wildly inappropriate for the Wagon Road, but Mary had insisted on taking the carriage, as it was a wedding gift from her parents.

Four slaves traveled behind the young couple in the heavily loaded wagons. Martin, a gifted blacksmith, and three field hands, Ezekiel, Duke, and George, accompanied their young master ever deeper into slave country. James allowed the men to ride in the wagon unchained by day. Clear nights found them shackled to the wagon bed under blankets. Rain found them under leaky oilcloth tarps, while their white owners slept soundly inside local inns.

Caravans of settlers' wagons moving south passed wagons full of farm produce heading north. Every so often, the group had to move completely off the road for hours at a time as northbound herds of bellowing cattle or squealing hogs plodded past their wagon. Near Charlotte, swarms of flies and the stench of dead animals lying along the roadside made Mary ill. Two months pregnant, she heaved and retched as the phaeton bumped and rolled through miles of manure, nearly ankle-deep in some places along the road.

When the broader road ended in Augusta, Georgia, Jenkins parted ways with the weary group. They followed a lonely, backcountry U-turn of a path into upstate South Carolina. Mary spent those final two days sheltered inside the carriage with her hands inside her cloak, clutching a small Deringer. Slight of build and of nervous temperament anyway, she was nearly frantic about being overcome by the slaves, afraid that they would turn on her on this lonely stretch of the road should James nod off. The Nat Turner rebellion back home was still fresh in her mind.

The Burgisses arrived in the South Carolina upstate on a near-perfect Indian summer day. The couple set about making the place their home. James commissioned extensive work on the house. The sturdy logs were covered with whitewashed pine boards and a new two-story wing was added. Glossy black shutters framed the windows. Ezekiel and Duke unloaded finely upholstered settees, cherry tables and chairs, and crates of fine china and glass. They unrolled beautiful Oriental carpets across heart pine floors.

Mary planted the popular pink Baronne Provost climbing roses along the front porch railings. Gardenias were tucked under windows to perfume the summer breezes. Mary exhaled and christened the place Whitehall.

An attorney by profession, James was quickly hired to assist state leaders and investors with a new railroad venture. Most travelers or goods coming from the Midwest at the time traveled east to New York, before heading down the coast by ship to Charleston. Land speculators in the Carolinas were eager to expand a rail line from Anderson, South Carolina to Knoxville by tunneling through the granite heart of the Blue Ridge Mountains. James was eager to head the effort to build the tunnels and cash in on the enormous opportunity that this shortcut promised. It would make its investors wealthy men.

Burgiss's reputation as the son of a famous war hero was widely circulated prior to his arrival. This granted the Burgiss family some immediate status with other residents, old and new. The Carolina upcountry served as a haven for wealthy Lowcountry planters attempting to escape steamy, mosquito-filled summers on the coast.

Mary had been delighted to find out that several prominent families had plantations nearby, including former Vice President and South Carolina Senator John Calhoun and his family. There was the promise of parties and dinners and church socials. Mary aspired to the hope that one day a Burgiss child might marry into an important South Carolina family such as the Calhouns and make a fine match indeed.

The backcountry also called to many a nouveau-riche businessman from the Northeast with its promise of abundant land and mild winters. A former merchant from New York, Sam Stone was one such man. Stone and his wife hosted a weekend of festivities at River Wood to welcome the young couple to the district. He gave them a pregnant house slave, named Ona, as a generous welcome gift. Acquiring her was a double blessing to the young Burgiss family as her child would also become Burgiss property. No one mentioned the baby's father, or whether Ona had a husband.

Immediately, Ona had fallen for Martin, and he with her. Martin asked his master's permission to marry the young woman and James readily agreed. A wizened old slave from nearby Fort Hill, who was considered a preacher in the slave community, came out to Whitehall, and married the two in the slave way of "jumping the broom."

Only months later, a terrified Mary helped Ona birth her baby boy on the crude floor of a slave cabin, before she was even a mother herself. He was born healthy, skin the color of coffee with a good splash of cream, like his mother.

Now, that baby boy, Ben, was a tall and skinny thing of twelve, a fine slave himself. Ona had gone on to have three baby girls by Martin, all stillborn.

5

— • —

MARY RANG THE SILVER CALL BELL she kept on the parlor table.

"Ona!" Mary called, ringing the little bell again with some irritation. One house slave simply did not give Mary the amount of help she needed with three growing children and such a large home. And now, a visit from the great Calhoun himself. She made a mental note to speak to James about adding another girl.

Ona appeared in the parlor doorway, wiping her hands on a rag. She wasn't a pretty woman. Her bulging eyes reminded Mary of an insect's: lashless and too large for her small face. Tight cornrows tinged with early gray were only partially hidden under a blue gingham headscarf. Over a faded brown cotton shift, a stained apron was tied tightly around her waist. "Yes'm?" Her wide eyes looked at Mary without emotion.

"Ona, you're filthy," Mary wailed. "I have Senator Calhoun and his party coming here for dinner tomorrow! It is hard enough to keep after the children and think about what to serve the men without worrying about the appearance of my house girl."

"Yes'm," Ona replied obediently. "I was cleanin' them dirty fireplaces." Thin lips set, she lowered her head and stared at the floorboards. Her face was haggard and pinched for her young age.

Mary continued. "Now, to this dress of Polly's. Hem it for me. You see I have already pinned it for you. It must be finished tonight." She thrust the little dress toward Ona. Ona nodded again and reached for the dress.

"Oh, never mind. You cannot take it now!" Mary wailed, snatching the garment back. "Look at your dirty hands. Wash up at the pump and then come and get it." Ona nodded and turned away, chastened.

— • —

THE AFTERNOON SUN PRESSED HARD ON the land as James Burgiss stood watching the cotton harvest from a nearby ridge. The heat shimmered like ocean waves across the fields. His field hands bent low in their rows, long sacks thrown across stooped backs, picking the fluffy white fiber from each open boll.

In the beginning, wheat, corn, and a little tobacco had been planted. New soil never took well to cotton. King Cotton was only planted in succeeding years as the soil became tired and poor. He remembered the first year that he had planted cotton. On a frosty February morning over a decade ago, he had watched as the hands prepared the beds for that first crop. Harrows combed the soil free of debris. Slaves followed behind, picking up any sticks and rocks left behind. In April, the soil was built up in long rows, and the seed was sown by hand. In May, the new plants were thinned and continually swept and hoed to keep the weeds down. In June, the tiny plants bloomed, and the fields surrounding Whitehall appeared to passersby as carpets of pale pinkish blossoms. When late September arrived, he remembered the swell of pride as his slaves set out to pick the final product of their six months of hard labor.

Upland cotton was not nearly as valuable as Sea Island cotton, grown in the coastal Lowcountry. Sea Island cotton merited three to five times the price of its inland cousin. However, upland cotton was still a valuable commodity, and James was ready to claim his share of the cotton boom. He had 200 acres under cultivation by the time his third child, daughter Polly, was born.

The years turned round and round. Now it was late summer again and the snowy fields signaled the bounty of another successful year. Burgiss owned eight field hands. Each man could be counted on to plant and tend ten to twelve acres of the finicky cotton along with the other crops. With long strides, he descended the ridge and stopped at the edge of the field. He leaned over to inspect a plant. He pulled the fluffy white cotton from the boll and combed it with his fingers. Minimal seed and good color. It looked to be a fine year. He grinned and stood, gazing out at the broad fields and the hazy Blue Ridge Mountains to the north.

"Whew! Another hot one!" Tom Roper called out as he approached, hat in hand. He wiped his forehead with the back of his sleeve and firmly replaced the damp hat. Roper was a young man of twenty-three, tall, dark-headed, and thin as a rail. He was an honest, hard-working man, a trusted employee for the last few years. He had no young family of his own and spent all of his time working to make Whitehall a prosperous farm.

James raised his hand in return. He gestured toward the line of mountains in the distance. "Do you know what the Cherokee call those mountains? The Blue Wall. That's what the railroad will have to tunnel through. The Blue Wall."

"Yes sir. I can see why the tunnel takes all your time." Tom nodded.

Time . . . Burgiss had so little time at home. The railroad was of primary importance and continued to take him away to Walhalla, Charleston, and Columbia frequently. The dream of tunnels through the Blue Ridge toward Knoxville lured investors from as far away as Washington, D.C., and New York, and they clamored constantly for news of their investment.

Burgiss clapped his overseer on the back. "You have done a fine job as always. The cotton looks good."

"Thank you kindly." Tom smiled proudly. "We could sure use a few more days to get this crop in. That storm on the coast might head inland. I can see about borrowing a man or two from River Wood to speed things up. The overseer, Wilkins, says he'd like to have Martin make two new wheels. Says we can borrow a few men in return for as long as we need."

Burgiss frowned at his overseer. "I am not lending out Martin, especially to Sam Stone's overseer." James was protective of the slave he had known since their boyhoods together in Virginia. "Although to put River Wood hands in our fields for a day or two would surely better their own lives temporarily," he added good-naturedly. "What are slaves going for at auction these days?"

"At Anderson, field hands were going for $1000 apiece. Cotton has driven slave prices sky-high. We could surely use more men in the growing season, but then I barely have enough work for them in the winter," Roper said.

James let out a low whistle as he looked out over the fields. Mature cotton needed to be picked and ginned quickly, baled, and sent off down the Savannah River to market. It was a laborious process at best, and terribly slow with so few slaves. Sudden storms and insects were a constant threat. Yet, he hadn't lost a crop in all his years at Whitehall.

He crossed his arms defensively. "Trading Martin is out of the question, and I am not in a position to buy more slaves until we make some real progress on the railroad. Not at those prices. Nor am I in charge of the weather."

Tom slapped a mosquito on his arm. "I have an idea. What if you hire from those immigrants coming in to work on the railroad? You said that half the time those men sit idle waiting for blasting to commence."

James looked at his overseer incredulously. "Paid labor? For cotton? White men will not pick cotton. The work's too hot." He snorted, loosening his tie. Slaves were expensive, but they were a necessity in the cotton business. "We can't pick cotton without slaves, Tom." Burgiss shook his head.

Tom cocked his head. "We could find out."

James nodded, acutely aware of the sweat trickling down his back under his shirt and jacket. He clapped Tom on the shoulder. "Very well. I will humor you. If George has the men under control, ride up to Tunnel Hill tomorrow, early. I have five Irishmen in mind, the group that arrived in the spring. Ask for their crew boss, Mr. Carey. See if any would like to hire on here for a few days." He shrugged. "They are subsistence farmers at this point and have families to support. Maybe you could get a few takers. We won't blast again until late next week anyway. Pay out a little cash and give them hunting and camping privileges on the land around the river while they're here. Tell Mr. Carey I'll make it worth his while, too."

Tom grinned. "What shall I offer to pay them?" he asked.

9

"Offer a dollar a day," James said. "Three days."

Tom's eyes widened. "That's damn good money. I'm sure I can get a few men with that."

James pointed a finger at his overseer. "But mind you, they bring their own food, bedding, and canteens. It'll be hot work. They won't be loading rocks in the cool dark." He looked out at the hands in his fields. Several men had stripped to the waist, their shirts tied around their heads like turbans. The broiling sun baked their necks and shoulders. He wondered what would happen to fair Irish skin.

James nodded towards the men in his fields. "Cheaper to crack the whip over these boys, but I'll give your idea a try, Tom."

Tom studied his employer's face. "Mr. Burgiss, sir, if you think I can get more work from these men, well, I sure as hell don't know how. Some are picking three to four hundred pounds a day. I am working them six days now, sunup to sundown and we're only halfway through the acreage. They're good men. Reliable. I won't whip them unnecessarily."

Burgiss scanned the fields once more, glanced at the azure sky overhead, and turned to his overseer impatiently. "Calm down, Tom. I have faith that you can get this crop in on time. You always do. Use whatever method seems appropriate. Just get it in. I have a very important meeting with Senator Calhoun and some new investors tomorrow. I do not have time to argue."

James touched the brim of his hat and turned to go.

Chapter Two

POLLY RAN TOWARD THE CREEK, PETTICOATS FLYING. She found her older brothers Joshua and Caleb midstream, pant legs rolled to knobby knees. She pulled the licorice twist from her pocket and bit off a small piece. She carefully wrapped the rest and put the handkerchief back in her pocket before her brothers noticed.

"Can't find tadpoles today, Polly, but the crawdads are whoppers!" Caleb thrust a pair of crayfish out towards his sister's face, their small claws snapping open and closed. Twelve years old, his dark curls and pale skin gave him away as being his mother's child, while ten-year-old Joshua had the fair hair and ruddy complexion of his father. Polly favored her brother Caleb in appearance and looked up to him as any sister would her elder brother.

Polly swallowed the candy, hands on hips. "Caleb Burgiss, I am not afraid of no crawdads." She lifted her skirts and began wading down the slippery bank toward her brothers. Jack followed, splashing happily. Suddenly the little dog began to bark furiously. Polly stopped and stood still, looking with wide eyes past Caleb and Joshua to the tree line on the opposite bank. The boys turned to follow her stare.

Caleb dropped the crawdads with a splash. Standing on the steep bank above them was a strange man, partially hidden by a mountain laurel thicket. Dark and tall, his head was shaved except for a long black braid that fell from a central topknot. A single hawk feather was woven into the braid. He wore tattered pants under deerskin leggings and an open shirt made of settlers' homespun. A short string of fish and a mud turtle were threaded onto the spear he carried in one hand. He raised his other hand and nodded at the children.

The two younger children had never seen a Cherokee man before. Caleb vaguely remembered a young Creek couple who had stopped at the river's edge when he was a small boy, near the time of the Removal. Seeking permission to hunt deer on Burgiss land, they had moved on after his father gave permission to hunt only near the river. Caleb knew his mother was frantic about Indians and wanted them gone. He remembered that his father had prevailed, telling his mother that the gaunt couple were clearly starving and in need of food. Caleb remembered feeling sorry for them.

"*Osda sanalei*," the man said with a nod. He put down his catch and pulled a leather pouch from his waist. He looked at the three white children before pulling a beautiful, beaded necklace from the pouch. He held it out to them. Jack barked furiously and splashed around at Polly's ankles.

"Jack, stop it!" Polly said sharply. She was mesmerized. The man did not appear threatening, but she placed her hand protectively over the sweet delicacy in her pocket.

All her young life, Polly had heard terrible stories from her mother about the Indian menace in the area. The children were instructed never to leave Burgiss property unescorted and to always stay within the sound of the old bronze dinner bell on the front porch. Sometimes, as children are wont to do, they failed to heed their mother's words. Polly yearned to go closer and touch the beads, but the creek and the steep muddy bank prevented it. Still, she pulled her wide blue hair ribbon from her braid and held it in her extended hand.

The man nimbly leaped the width of the creek across slippery rocks and grabbed the ribbon. A thrill of electricity jolted through Polly's arm. He thrust the necklace toward her, nodding his head. She reached for her prize.

Caleb shook his head and said loudly, "Polly, no! No trade, Indian! Go away!" Polly jerked her hand away from the necklace. The man nodded again and put the beads back into the pouch. He picked up his spear of fish and passed Polly's quivering body, before vanishing into the woods. Collectively, the children let out their breath.

"Caleb, what'd he want?" Joshua asked, spellbound. His gaze did not leave the spot where the man had been standing.

Caleb shrugged casually, false bravado a disguise for his knocking knees. "I think he wanted us to buy something or trade with him. We don't need no stinkin' Indian beads." Caleb tried to appear nonchalant but was beside himself with excitement. He had spoken to an Indian. He puffed out his chest and put his hands on his hips proudly. "He should have paid us for the fish he caught. This here's our creek."

"I thought there were no Indians 'round here anymore. You think he came by way of the trading post?" Joshua asked his older brother excitedly.

"He did just come from that direction," Caleb said with authority. "We can't tell Mother and Father. They will forbid us from coming to the creek."

Joshua scrambled atop a large rock in the stream and exclaimed, "How about we go see old Mr. Kemp? We can cut through the orchard. Maybe he knows the Indian."

The Kemp place abutted the Burgiss land along the main road and through the orchard, but the families were nodding acquaintances at best. Alexander Kemp had come from North Carolina in 1830 with his wife, Nancy. For the past 18 years, they had run a general store and tavern of sorts. Kemp sold his corn liquor to anyone with a coin or something to trade. Now well into his seventies, he sat in a front porch rocker, smoking his corncob pipe, and regaling occasional customers with tales of the Indian Wars.

13

Kemp specialized in Indian tales, which assured a rapt audience of local children, unbeknownst to their parents. Alexander Kemp had fought alongside Indians and against Indians in several skirmishes as a young man. Rumors were rife that Kemp had a hidden fortune in gold coins and jewelry taken in Indian raids during the wars. The Kemps were known to be friendly with the few remaining Cherokee who hadn't been driven out years ago. They would appear from tiny holdings in the backwoods to trade several times a year. Their deerskins were in demand by local farmers for making breeches, gloves, and other sturdy work clothing. Their herbs were wanted by white women as remedies for everything from snake bite to stomach ailments. In return, the Indians were happy to receive cloth, wheat flour, guns, and ammunition for hunting. Indian troubles had been over in the South Carolina backcountry for years, and Kemp long defended the Cherokees as a peaceful people, unlike the war-mongering Creek of earlier days.

There wasn't much real business now that white folks were able to get their mail and supplies at the fancy new general store in town. Ladies, especially, preferred the civilized Pendleton General Mercantile. With its tinned food, bolts of pretty fabric, ribbons, newspapers, and magazines, it was where townspeople shopped. It was well away from Kemp's, with its propensity to invite the worst of the local citizenry to come forth. Still, Kemp's place was at an important crossroads in the community for travelers, backwoods farmers, and hunters alike. Any good frontier stories coming down the pike always came to Kemp's first.

Polly toyed with her braid, now bereft of decoration. "Joshua, Mother said to stay nearby," she chided. "I'm telling on you. We aren't allowed to go that far."

Caleb frowned and put a hand on Polly's shoulder. "Polly, you go on back now with your pup. You don't want to tattle on us like some baby. Think about how much trouble you'll get into, yourself. You gave him your hair ribbon! Don't tell her we went to Mr. Kemp's, and we'll not tell her

14

you touched an Indian. We'll be home before dark. Deal?" Without waiting for an answer, they took off at a trot up the path that led through the woods towards the trading post.

Polly would not be left behind. She called after them as she laced her boots, but the boys raced ahead of her toward the Kemp place, cutting through the small woods at the edge of the property. Short-legged and tripping over her skirts, she slowed to a walk and urged Jack along the dusty deer path. The puppy was in no hurry to race ahead when there were intriguing scents to smell along the way.

Polly began to dawdle, too. She finished the melting licorice and wiped the inky blackness from her face with the handkerchief. In the orchard, she paused to gather fallen peaches in her pinafore. Then she crouched to make a daisy chain from the bright yellow fleabane that grew along the deer path. It took nearly an hour for her to cut through the woods to the clearing where the little trading post stood.

Trees still obscured a clear view of the trading post. Polly suddenly heard a woman's scream and instinctively dropped to the ground and froze. From behind a patch of dog hobble, she peered out. In the dirt yard ahead lay Mr. Kemp, his body splayed, head at an impossible angle, mouth agape in agony. Polly had never seen a dying man, but she knew her neighbor could not be alive much longer. His skull was exposed, hairless and red with blood.

Standing on the wide porch, a blonde, young man sprinkled a jug of what smelled like kerosene across the brittle floorboards. His nose and mouth were well covered by a red bandana. He backed up and touched a match to a branch and tossed it onto the floorboards. The old and dry planks soon leaped into flame. The man whooped and hollered his excitement. He lowered his handkerchief just enough to raise a bottle to his mouth. He took a long drink of its contents and then replaced the disguise over his face.

Polly could not call out. She felt frozen in place, her legs unable to move. The puppy stayed crouched by her feet as if it knew not to make a sound.

Caleb and Joshua burst from the smoke-filled cabin, hacking and coughing, blinded by acrid smoke. They were quickly followed by wizened old Nancy Kemp, held at knifepoint by a burly and rough, red-bearded man, his large face only partially obscured by a stained handkerchief.

Nancy frantically shouted at the boys to run away. She appeared to be pleading with her captor as if she knew the man. When he grabbed her by her hair, she slapped him hard. The man let out a stream of expletives and pushed her back inside the building. The younger man quickly pulled the wooden door shut and used a leather strap to tie it closed.

Caleb bounded up the steps and tried to untie the door handle but the bearded man used a meaty fist to punch the boy in the face, knocking him down onto the front porch. Polly heard Nancy scream from inside as the flames crept up the eaves to the roof. The cabin had but one window, its shutters barred tight with a piece of lumber.

Caleb stood up slowly, his nose streaming blood. Joshua ran towards the blonde man and bravely pummeled him with his boy fists. He jumped on the man's back and tugged at his hair, reaching for the handkerchief covering his face. The man wildly grabbed at Joshua's legs. Joshua screamed and tried to hop off but was scooped up by the red-bearded man and hurled down the steps to the ground with force, where he lay still.

Yelling his brother's name, Caleb launched himself at the big man, but the man was too strong for him. He swung his rifle butt hard at Caleb's head. There was the sickening thud of the weapon connecting with bone. Polly opened her mouth to scream, but no sound came out. She felt everything go silent and dark.

— • —

KATYDIDS BUZZED IN UNISON. The puppy whimpered and licked Polly's pale cheek, as she lay huddled in the thicket. She tried to crawl away, but briars scratched her skin and hooked her clothing. The heat of the day faded, but acrid smoke from the cabin fire burned her eyes and her lungs. Mosquitoes hovered over her exposed arms and face, but she dared not stand and run.

Finally, a cool evening breeze brought some relief from the smoke. Polly dozed, in and out of the nightmare in her mind. Curled in the fetal position, she lay with her dog deep into the night. The shouts of men calling her name in the dark only made her cringe and squeeze her eyes shut. Wispy clouds drifted over a crescent moon, and the familiar hoot of a barred owl comforted her.

The twisting column of black smoke over the Kemp property led the search party to the grisly scene at sunup the next morning. As the sky paled to pink and blue, Polly heard the voices of men again, and shrank back under the cover of the dense scrub. Someone called her name but she would not answer. She tried to get up and run but found that her cramped legs would not move. Jack began to bark. There was a gentle tap on her arm, and Polly opened her eyes in terror.

"Miss Polly. Miss Polly." A familiar voice quieted her mind only a bit. "It's me, Ben. I'm gonna take you home now." She felt the young slave lift her up. She heard him call out to the others searching. Polly could only stare at him before she sank back into unconsciousness.

— • —

A BRIGHT SUNRISE REVEALED THE extent of the carnage. The store had burned to the ground with Nancy Kemp trapped in the smoking rubble. The broken safe lay in the charred weeds, door broken off the hinges, and nothing left inside. Flies swarmed over the corpse of Alexander Kemp. The sheriff's deputy directed George and Martin to bury the remains of Kemp and his wife in simple graves away from the smoldering ruin of their store.

James Burgiss knelt and carefully wrapped his dead sons in linen sheets and carried each one to the waiting wagon. He kissed Polly on the forehead and took her from Ben. He cradled his daughter in his lap on the wagon ride home.

— • —

MARY PACED THE LENGTH OF THE VERANDA, her Bible open to the Psalms. She silently begged God for mercy, praying that He would deliver her children back to her whole and sound. When her husband's search party returned, Mary hurried down the steps; her wild eyes quickly took in the scene.

James Burgiss eased down from the wagon bench, carrying a trembling Polly. He came towards his distraught wife, his eyes brimming with tears. The bodies of their sons, wrapped in shrouds, were carefully taken from the wagon bed, and placed in the parlor. In agony, Mary sank to the ground, keening into the dirt, Rachel weeping for her children.

— • —

WHITEHALL'S PORCHES AND WINDOWS WERE draped in black and white. Ona threw sheets over mirrors and portraits. Ben made sure that windows were shuttered before the wake. Mary dressed in heavy black bombazine and James wore a hastily acquired mourning suit. Dozens of neighbors came to Whitehall to pay their respects while Mary and James sat at the feet of the boys' caskets. The funeral the following day was held at the First Presbyterian Church of Pendleton, and the brothers were laid to rest under a spreading white oak tree in the church cemetery.

Mary took to her bed soon after the funeral. Ona tended her mistress and young Polly, who was still in shock and not able to speak of what she had seen. The sheriff could only surmise that a band of thieves had killed the four victims in a botched robbery. It was not even clear if valuables had been removed from the safe. Until Polly Burgiss could speak, no one would know more about the crime.

One week later, a haze of tobacco smoke clouded the air in the Burgiss parlor as pipes were filled, smoked, and refilled. Senator Calhoun's postponed trip from Washington to discuss the progress of the railroad through the upstate had taken a decidedly different turn. Voices were raised in despair and anger. Local men were up in arms about the seeming reappearance of Indian troubles after a long and peaceful time without incident.

The sheriff shook his head and looked at Burgiss. "I'm sorry, Mr. Burgiss. We just don't have any real leads. If your daughter comes to her senses and can tell us what she saw, that will help. Right now, we have no suspects."

James turned to Senator Calhoun, who was quietly puffing on his pipe. "What do you think, Senator?"

Senator Calhoun stood to speak but was interrupted by angry voices.

"Senator, we heard what they did to the boys and the Kemps. They took Alex's damned scalp clean off!" barked one man. "They were butchered by Indians."

"It was thieving, dirty Cherokee. Mark my word," shouted a red-faced Sam Stone. "The store safe was found empty, wasn't it? We have to rid this district of the Cherokee rabble following the river. The whole lot of them should have moved on out west anyway. I'll pay any man, in gold double eagles, who'll bring me a dead one!" There were murmurs of approval.

"We have the right to protect ourselves," said another man loudly. "Kemp traded with Indians. He got too comfortable with those savages— and look what happened. Everyone around here knew he had a safe on the property. He bragged about how much gold he had." There were murmurs of agreement.

Stone continued, "Several folks say they saw Cherokee traders headed to the post that very morning."

"Gentlemen, gentlemen," Burgiss said calmly from his overstuffed chair near the fireplace. The men quieted and looked at the grieving man. Seated, his slumped shoulders and haggard face reflected his deep and profound loss. He paused to light his pipe and inhale the rich tobacco into his lungs.

"Senator Calhoun is my guest today. He has come to Whitehall despite his very full calendar, at my request. He brokered nearly forty treaties with the Indians. He created the Bureau of Indian Affairs, almost single-handedly. No one here is in a better position to know the Indian mind." James pointed to the statesman with the stem of his pipe. "And we are honored to call him our neighbor, so hear what he has to say."

Calhoun nodded his wild gray head. "Thank you, James. Gentlemen, we all grieve with this family. We all want answers. As he said, I have some experience with the Indian populations. There has not been any trouble with the Cherokee in the Pendleton District in years, not since the Removal." Men began to protest. He raised a hand to silence them. "The few Cherokee left behind are mixed-bloods, and in good standing with us."

"Senator, we mean no disrespect," said Sam Stone sharply. "But you are a politician. You live in Washington. This had to be an Indian raid. Everyone in the district remembers that it was Cherokees fighting alongside the Tories during the wars. Kemp talked a blue streak about how he was still trading with Cherokee. How are we supposed to farm this land and take care of our families, let alone push your railroad through, if we still have Indians killing innocent women and children?"

Stone turned and pointed a shaking finger at his host. "James, I promise that we will clear these savages out of the district once and for all. And if we find the Indians responsible for this awful crime, they will be shot on sight." Again, men murmured their approval. "We aren't waiting for the law to catch up," Stone growled, staring at Calhoun. "We take care of our own."

Calhoun's dark eyes bored into Stone's. "I would stake my name and reputation on this—the murders are not the work of the Cherokee. I have spoken to Chief Thomas. He is adamant that his people are innocent of this crime. They keep to themselves across the river and make a little money as scouts for hunters in the mountains. In fact, I know several of them were instrumental in helping us find the best railroad route northwest. They are neither thieves nor murderers."

Calhoun paused, ready to argue again, but no one spoke. "With Cherokee knowledge of the mountains, and immigrants coming in to do the hard work of blasting through granite, we will soon have tunnels in place before the Georgia & Western begins to blast through Chetoogeta Mountain into Tennessee. South Carolina's upcountry is poised for an economic boom, gentlemen, one that everyone in this room can profit from in some way, if we do not scare off the investors. Or murder any remaining scouts." He scowled behind bushy eyebrows.

Stone gave a derisive snort. "Are you saying that scalpings aren't evidence of Indian attack, sir?"

Calhoun shook his head. "I am not saying that at all. The savage nature of this attack leads us to suspect a desperate raid by a murderous band of Indians; that is true." He paused. "The killers wanted you to blame Indians for our neighbors' deaths. And so you have."

The senator put a hand on his friend's shoulder. "James, Major Edwards at Oconee Station dispatched riders west to the border and north to the fort. No one has reported Indian activity to speak of along the Keowee Trail or on the rivers."

He puffed on his pipe and looked down at Burgiss. "If there is any new information, our garrisoned men will track in the direction they were headed. But I believe that our best chance of finding the culprits will be from information from your little girl when she awakens."

Burgiss sighed and rubbed the back of his neck. "Thank you, Senator. And gentlemen, thank you all for coming out tonight. Let's remember that we should neither say nor do anything that might further jeopardize the tunnel project. A project we can all benefit from. We don't need an irrational fear of Indians in the area to cost us further."

As the men adjourned the meeting, they clapped each other on their backs, finished their whiskeys, and tried to give some comfort to their grieving neighbor. Justice was all but hopeless, and the men knew it. They tried to console themselves with the knowledge that Alexander Kemp had been an Indian lover, a damned fool who got what was coming to him for trading with Cherokee. Nevertheless, an innocent woman and two children were brutally murdered as well. A family was destroyed. As each man left Whitehall, he made sure that his sidearm was at the ready for the trip home.

— • —

As Burgiss's guests were downstairs saying their goodbyes to Senator Calhoun, Ona tucked a quilt snugly around Polly. The girl dozed fitfully. Ona's thoughts were on Ben, and the horrific tale of the grisly scene the search party discovered at the Kemps' store. Just a boy himself, she wondered how he managed to cope with what he had witnessed. Ona was startled by a noise behind her and turned to find Ben standing there.

"Ben, what you doin' in the big house?" Ona hissed at her son. "You ain't supposed to be in here." She crossed the floor and closed the bedroom door behind him quietly. "What you want?"

Ben stood with his hands folded across his chest. "Ma," he whispered. "I followed after her that day. I wanted to see where they were going. I caught up to them at the creek. I have to tell Mr. Burgiss," he rambled. "I keep seeing it in my mind. It wasn't Indians. It was white men. I saw them trying to use an ax to break into Mr. Kemp's safe, in the yard. One of them pushed Miss Nancy inside. The other one killed Caleb and Joshua. Mr. Kemp was dead . . . his head was split open when I got there."

Ona sat down slowly on the bench near Polly's bed. She glanced at the girl, who was asleep under the quilt, curled in a tight ball. She looked at Ben, his face twisted in sorrow. "You was there?" she whispered, her lower lip quivering.

Ben nodded. "I disobeyed Pa, I know. I'm sorry. I left my chores and followed Miss Polly to the creek. I hid behind a tree. There was an Indian man at the creek, that's true." Ben's brown eyes grew wide. "But he seemed friendly and just wanted to trade. Caleb told him to go away and he did.

22

Caleb and Joshua wanted to see if Mr. Kemp knew the Indian. I followed behind Miss Polly. She didn't see me. But she was dawdling. When we finally got there, I saw them close enough to be sure, Mama. They weren't Indians," he whispered. "It was Mr. Stone's overseer, Mr. Wilkins, and . . . Johnny Stone. He was standing there with a firebrand. He started the fire. He pushed Miss Nancy inside the store and lashed the door shut."

Ben glanced at the sleeping Polly and knelt at his mother's feet, his brown eyes wet with tears. "Mama, no one saw me. I was hiding off the path. I wanted to run for help right away but I didn't want them to see me. And Miss Polly wouldn't move." His words tumbled out. "I couldn't get her to answer me or to stand up and run. She just closed her eyes and froze. If I had carried her or shouted at her, they would have seen us both. I think they killed Caleb and Joshua because they surprised them, coming through the orchard woods instead of by the road. The boys must have seen the robbery. I need to tell Mr. Burgiss."

Ona shook her head in disbelief. Her eyes were wide with fright. "Ben, you got to be wrong," she whispered. "That Wilkins is a bad man, real bad to slaves. . . . But ain't no reason for those men to do such a thing to neighbors, to a old white woman and babies. Johnny Stone is just a boy hisself. He's not but sixteen."

Ona twisted her apron in her hands. "If anyone hears you was there, they'll say you was one of the killers. No one gonna believe a slave boy. They come and take you away from me. . . . And if you tell 'em you left Miss Polly in the woods and came runnin' back here, they hang you fo' sure."

Ben nodded, his brown eyes wide. "I knew they'd kill me if they saw me, so I waited. When they ran off, I cut back through the woods and stayed off the road. I never run so fast in my life. I thought I was gonna scream when I got back here, thinking about what they did to those folks. I know the men would have killed Miss Polly and me like they killed Mr. Kemp. His head was about pulled free of his body, Mama."

Ben wiped his eyes and nose with his sleeve and continued, "No one saw me go after Miss Polly. I was fixing the loose shingles on the smoke house when I saw her follow her brothers toward the creek. I thought I just might have a swim, to cool off. No one saw me leave. I need to tell Mr. Burgiss! When Miss Polly wakes up, she can tell what she saw. Her daddy will listen to her and know I told the truth." Ben dropped his head into his mother's lap and cried.

"Sshhh . . ." Ona exhaled slowly and looked first at the sleeping girl and then back at her boy. She helped him up off the floor. Closing in on thirteen years old, he stood taller than his mother by inches, but he was still just a boy. She clasped Ben's face between her brown hands. "You listen to me, son," she whispered. "You and I is goin' to our graves with this secret, you hear me? Don't tell your Pa. An' don't you ever set foot off this land again, you understand? Folks liable to think you a runaway. Your place is doin' yo' work with your Pa and the other men. If someone hear you tell this tale, you gonna end up accused. Mr. Burgiss is a good white man, but if you tell this to anyone, they hang you, son. They hang you!"

— • —

WHITEHALL'S COTTON CROP WAS PICKED and ginned and finally shipped down the river to Savannah after the boys' funerals that September. The late harvest was likely saved by the fact that the coastal hurricane did not hurl inland as Tom Roper expected, and the damaging rain and wind stayed away. Only one Irishman had responded to his trip to Tunnel Hill, and that man quit when he realized he would be working in the same fields as slaves.

In October, a local farmer and his son out hunting deer spotted a Cherokee man near the river. The farmer shot the Indian at point-blank range. They hauled the dead man's body into Pendleton by wagon and proudly showed off the victim, the man wearing a homespun shirt given in trade long ago and a curious bit of blue silk ribbon wound through his hair. The farmer received his double eagle from Sam Stone. The last Indian in the Pendleton area was surely gone, and town folk were relieved. The Kemp tragedy was deemed a cold-blooded Indian massacre, a case closed. Life could go on as usual.

News of slave uprisings across the state had Tom on edge. He was certainly not an ardent slaver, nor was he an abolitionist, just a man who had a job to do. He knew people on both sides; people who would chase down a slave for reward and people who were opposed to slavery and would readily help runaways passing through toward the mountains.

Late one Sunday afternoon in November, Tom crossed the yard toward the house, his mind lost in thought. Dry leaves crunched under foot and a chill west wind blew off the river. He shoved cold hands into his coat pockets as he walked. Nearing the house, he noticed that the lamps were already lit against the early dark. With numb fingers, he removed his hat and knocked on the front door of the house.

After a few moments, Ona opened the door and peeked out. "Yessuh, Mr. Roper?"

Tom smiled. "Ona, I want to speak with Mr. Burgiss, if he is free."

Ona opened the door wide for the overseer. Tom was grateful for the warmth in the room. His own cabin was small and badly in need of extra chinking to keep out the cold. Ona stepped to the library and knocked on the open door. "Mr. Roper to see you, suh. And supper be ready in a hour." She came back into the foyer and motioned for Tom to go on in.

Burgiss was seated at his desk, his pipe smoldering in the ashtray and a finger of whiskey in cut crystal nearby. Across the room, a fire blazed in the hearth. He was pale and thinner, no doubt. Although his suit was pressed and sharp as always, it hung on his frame. "Come in, Tom. Have a seat. Is this about that cotton report?" he asked with a frown.

Roper took the offered seat and shook his head. "No sir. I wanted to discuss something else with you though. Won't leave my mind. I hope you'll indulge me."

"Of course. Join me in a whiskey, then." Burgiss stood and retrieved a second glass from the sideboard. He poured his young overseer a drink and sighed. "What's on your mind?"

Tom smiled and accepted the whiskey. "River Wood had another slave run off. A woman this time. Clay Wilkins wants to head up a posse to hunt her down and he asked me for help. I'd rather not, if that's alright with you, sir." He shifted in his seat uncomfortably. "Wilkins thinks there may be a runaway stop just over the river, a way station of sorts. It is easy to ford at the shoals near the north property line. With all the patrols that Senator Calhoun's ordered, though, I doubt they could hide for long, but Wilkins says he aims to clean it out."

"A posse?" Burgiss asked. "This isn't the Nebraska territory. I have had enough of vigilante justice in these last months. It makes us all look like rubes. And I think you have enough work to do here. I will send a note to Sam to that effect." Burgiss eyed Tom and leaned back in his chair. "Is that it?"

Roper shifted in his seat. "Has your daughter spoken?" Tom asked hesitantly. "About what she saw?"

Burgiss glared at Tom. "She has not recovered," he muttered. "I will not bring the matter up until she is well." He picked up his pipe and clamped it between his teeth.

"Of course." Tom nodded. "I am sorry."

Burgiss cocked his head and asked, "What's any of this got to do with my Polly?"

Tom leaned forward. "Wilkins let slip that River Wood also had three runaways in August, at the time of the . . . when your sons were killed. A small family. They took a horse. Stone sent Wilkins out to scout around— quietly. He said he took Johnny with him. No one else. Sam did not alert Sheriff Cane."

Burgiss puffed on his pipe. "And you think Sam's runaway slave family killed my boys?" he snorted. "Is that more likely than rogue Indians?"

Tom shook his head. "I don't know," he admitted. "Something is just off.

26

Why didn't Sam order a patrol in August when three slaves stole a horse and ran away? Why just send his sixteen-year-old son out with the overseer?" He sipped his whiskey. "And why would the sheriff be so quick to close your case?"

James puffed on his pipe and waited.

Tom leaned forward. "Sam Stone was so anxious to pin the crime on the Cherokee. Why? To get the law to look the other way for some reason?"

The men sat in silence for a time before Burgiss spoke. "Tom, I doubt I will ever know the truth of what happened to my boys. I cannot force Polly to speak of it. My wife lies in a stupor. No one else witnessed the crime. Truth be told, I find that I no longer have the stomach for the search." He removed his pipe and blew a cloud of smoke into the air. "And Sam Stone is a friend."

"I understand." Tom tipped his glass and finished his drink. "But Sam is in ill health, and he has allowed Clay Wilkins to run River Wood into the ground. The entire district knows they treat slaves harshly. And Wilkins leads John around by the nose."

Burgiss sighed. "It is none of our concern. If Mr. Wilkins wants to scour the countryside for horse thieves, savage Indians, and missing slaves, that is his business, not ours. Sam Stone has been a good neighbor to us."

"Very well, sir," Tom said.

Burgiss swirled the whiskey in his glass. "Here I am trying to convince investors to blast a commercial railroad tunnel through a mountain, to move Southern cotton and supplies through to the Midwest. And yet it seems we still live on the damned frontier. I'm walking a fine line, Tom. A fine line, indeed."

Chapter Three

MARY BURGISS LANGUISHED AS HEAVY DOSES of laudanum smoothed the edges of her grief. She wandered, ghostlike, through the upstairs rooms of the house, unwashed and unkempt, her mourning black soiled and wrinkled, cuffs soon frayed. Some days, Ona found her curled up in one of the boy's beds asleep. Other days, she didn't bother to dress at all, but sat on the edge of her bed, furiously crafting mourning jewelry from locks of her sons' hair.

Gradually, her few friends stopped knocking on the door with their cards of inquiry, for which she was grateful. Perched on the edge of sanity, laudanum became the friend Mary could rely on to take her away from the pain. It assaulted her at midnight and again at dawn, when she would wake briefly, having forgotten her sons were gone.

Ona was ordered to keep mirrors covered and windows shuttered, the rooms darkened. Many a time Ona had barked her shins on furniture as she stumbled in the stuffy blackness, attending to housework.

James wrote and asked for a noted specialist from Charlotte to visit his wife. After the briefest of examinations, the diagnosis was hysteria. Ona watched from a corner of the room, horrified, as the doctor applied his leeches. The writhing black creatures affixed themselves to Mary's legs and abdomen. They quickly swelled and turned purple, engorged on the mistress's blood.

The doctor sat impatiently flipping through the pages of a book while the worms sucked toxins from Mary's bloodstream. When the last leech had gorged itself and dropped off of Mary's pale limbs, he finally consulted his pocket watch, stood, and advised James that his wife should be sent away to an asylum for further treatment. Burgiss summarily dismissed the physician and turned to Pendleton's Dr. Adger, who knew his family well. Indeed, he had brought all three Burgiss children into the world.

After examining Mary, Dr. Adger stood in the foyer, putting on his coat. "Jim, she will come out of this catatonia. You must give her time. She grieves two sons. It has only been a few months. Keep up the laudanum. Increase the dose even. I will check on her every week. If Ona can make her eat and can bathe her, eventually she should come around." He paused. "And what of Polly?"

Burgiss shoved his hands in his pockets and shook his head. "Ona tends to both of them. Polly will get out of bed, take meals, and play with her dolls. She has not said anything about the day . . . the day of the murders."

"Do not force her to speak of it," Dr. Adger advised, buttoning his heavy coat. "She is a child. It is best if she does not have to remember that awful day. Maybe you can take them both on an outing? Christmas is in a week. Perhaps a shopping trip in Anderson or even to Columbia?"

"My work keeps me quite busy . . ." Burgiss's voice trailed off. "It would be difficult."

"I see," Dr. Adger conceded. "Well, I will be going now. Send for me if something changes." He pulled open the heavy front door and stepped out of the darkened foyer into the bright winter sunshine.

— • —

WHEN BEN TURNED THIRTEEN THAT FEBRUARY, his workdays immediately grew longer. He left the care of his mother and moved under George's authority. He was still expected to feed and water the stock, groom the horses and turn them out to pasture at dawn. But now, once those chores were done and if nothing in the barn needed his attention, he was expected to join Martin at the forge. Already acquainted with the hearth and the bellows, tongs, and poker, the water trough for cooling fiery metal, he would need to learn the tools and the process of shoeing Burgiss horses and repairing metal work around the farm.

Early spring found Ben in the smithy, learning the art of melting and bending iron to create spokes, handles, nails, and other hardware required to run the farm. He quickly became familiar with the contents of the shoeing box—the knives, rasps, and heavy files necessary to prepare a horse's hooves, and the hammer and special nails to attach new shoes. The constant ringing of hammer on anvil did not make for conversation, but Ben admired the beautiful pieces Martin made and enjoyed being near his father. He was thankful that the horrible events of September seemed well behind him.

Ten-hour days, six days a week were tough in the hot smithy, but Ben was a quick learner. His arms and legs grew longer and well-muscled. He was proud to be considered an apprentice blacksmith, the most valuable of slaves after his father. In fact, when Ona asked Mr. Roper for new boots to fit the boy's large feet, they were procured right away. Burgiss rewarded Martin's diligence and loyalty with extra food, muslin cloth, and even a small jug of corn liquor.

As his mother had instructed, Ben did not speak to anyone of what he had witnessed. Ona was thankful to have him in the smithy and away from the house and lawns. There was little chance of Miss Polly seeing him and triggering a warped memory of that gruesome day.

— • —

APRIL BLEW IN WITH GUSTY NORTH WINDS and renewed cold weather. Defiant Lenten Roses that emerged from the warming ground in February soon found their pale blooms frozen solid under sheets of freezing rain.

James buried himself in his work away from Whitehall. He traveled more frequently to Columbia, Charleston, and Atlanta on railroad business. In Washington, D.C., Senator Calhoun took ill. Though sick, he wrote many letters to Burgiss, regarding states' rights and slavery's role in southern commerce, particularly the new railroads. He sent letters of invitation to the titans of business, suggesting they invest in his friend's railroad project. He also offered James the use of his opulent home in Charleston to conduct business on his behalf. Burgiss made a temporary home away from home there for several weeks at a time and was quite comfortable. He disliked coming home to a depressed wife who fell into fits of histrionics at every departure. He preferred that Mary sleep through her spells in a laudanum-induced fog while he conducted business in the Lowcountry. It was much easier for everyone.

Polly gradually came back to the living thanks to Ona's tender ministrations. The woman obeyed her master when it came to the heavy dosing of his wife with medication but took great pains to get Polly up and outside on warm spring mornings. She led Polly to an oak rocker on the front porch each morning and wrapped her charge in quilts. Sunshine played across the little girl's face. At first, Polly just sat and stared straight ahead blankly, clutching a china doll. Small breezes ruffled her hair and smelled of damp soil and new life.

"Sit an' listen to the world wakin' up, Miss Girl." At first, Ona sat and rocked next to her, speaking to the little girl of good times on the farm as she shelled peas or darned socks. She was careful to speak only of the living, never of Polly's dead brothers.

"Dem buttercups by the fence line is real purty," Ona said one morning as she swept the wide front porch. "Why don't we go pick some after I sweep?" She lifted Jack up towards Polly, and the neglected dog eagerly licked his mistress's little face. When Polly laughed, Ona's heart warmed.

By early May, the color had reappeared in the girl's cheeks and she would laugh readily as she hoisted Jack into her own lap. Ona eventually gave her simple tasks to do, and Polly reveled in being useful. Pulling carrots in the garden, collecting fresh brown eggs, and learning to darn her own stockings seemed to give Polly life again.

— • —

ON A BRIGHT SEPTEMBER AFTERNOON, James Burgiss's carriage pulled into the front drive and came to a stop amidst a shower of golden maple leaves. In the distance, men in the cotton fields stooped to their work. As Burgiss stepped from the carriage, Polly leaped off the front steps and ran to her father.

His eyes brightened, and he bent to regard his pink-cheeked daughter as she eagerly approached him. "Well, this cannot be my little girl. I see you have a new tooth where weeks ago you had a gap in your pretty smile." He smiled. "A lady of nine years old, I believe?"

Polly grinned and laughed. "You came home!" She rushed into her father's arms, and he lifted her up. Polly leaned into her father's chest and inhaled the familiar scent of tobacco, leather, and whiskey.

"Did you bring me something, Father?" the little girl asked eagerly.

Burgiss hugged Polly and said, "I did indeed, but I think you should wait and open it tonight at supper. Can you wait?"

Polly nodded. "Ona made an apple cake! Do you think Mother will come downstairs and eat with us?"

Before he could answer, Burgiss noticed Tom Roper approaching from the outbuildings, greeting his employer with a wave of his hat.

Burgiss squeezed Polly's hand and stooped to put his daughter back on solid ground. "I will talk to your mother. Leave it to me," he said with a wink. "Now run along. I must speak with Mr. Roper." Polly smiled and turned, skipping up the front steps and into the house.

"Mr. Burgiss, sir." Tom removed his hat and wiped his face with a handkerchief. "I saw you coming up the road. Welcome home. Your little girl looks well."

"Thank you, Tom. She does indeed." Burgiss nodded, removing his hat. "I trust that you have good news."

Tom stretched his arm toward the far fields. "Those Irish and German folks who came in from Charlotte this spring? I had a man approach me in town to see if we were hiring again this year. Your tunnel construction can't use all of them. Well, sir, I got six men to come out. They didn't care as to who was in the fields next to them this time. I told them they could use that acreage near the river to camp and trap. The ginning I bartered out as well, so the slaves could work that wheat and cut the corn down for fodder. We'll be done and loaded to Savannah by Thursday next, a whole week before anyone else around here."

Burgiss smiled and clapped Tom on the back. "Ah, Tom, that is good news. Your novel idea seems to have had some merit. Come inside and have a drink. I want to hear more before I see to my wife." The two men climbed the steps and went into the parlor. Ona scurried to light the oil lamps to dispel the room's gloom and then exited quietly.

"Well, sir," Roper began, as Burgiss poured two shots of whiskey. "Like I said, I was able to hire six immigrant men to pick. With land prices so high right now, it doesn't surprise me that some of the poor folks coming down can't afford land once they get here. I paid ten cents on the bale and an extra penny a bale if it's clean through. Your slaves are picking 250 pounds a day each man. The white men are getting about 200. Several places nearby may not get their cotton and wheat in before the first frost, while we're ahead of schedule."

Burgiss seemed pleased. He sipped his whiskey thoughtfully. "I have always been told that slaves are better at the hard work of cotton picking, and it seems to be true. But the white men have an incentive to pick. They're being paid."

Roper drained his glass. "I don't think the field hands want to let the whites pick faster than them. I have a feeling your hands are taking it personally. I never thought I would see such a thing." He chuckled. "You'll come out ahead, sir. Mark my word. Slave labor was costly this summer. The Columbia auction last week saw young hands about Ben's age going for $1200."

"How old is Ona's boy now?" Burgiss asked. "$1200 is a great deal of money."

"Thirteen, sir," Tom said. "He's a hard worker. Coming along fine in the smithy. I don't expect you'll want to sell him, sir. I surely do not. And I'm not one to break up families. I'm sure you agree."

James eyed Tom warily. "I suppose you're right about that."

— • —

AFTER TWO WEEKS AT HOME, Burgiss found himself in the midst of preparations for another extended trip. As Ona was cleaning the last of the cutlery after supper, he called her into his study. She steeled herself and went to the warm room lined with books, praying to God that Mr. Burgiss had not discovered Ben's secret. She had not told anyone what Ben had seen, not even Martin. Yet she lived in fear that someone would find out and blame Ben for the murders.

Burgiss was seated in his favorite leather chair, a book in hand. Behind him, the fire crackled cheerfully. "Ona," said Burgiss, leaning forward. "Come in." He sighed and put the book down. "I have been thinking about my daughter. Miss Polly is growing up quickly."

"Yessuh, she is gonna be quite a beautiful lady someday." Ona smiled nervously.

"Thank you for seeing my girl through . . . a difficult time. And now I need you to do something else for me. And for Polly." Burgiss looked up hopefully. He handed Ona what looked like a children's book. She took the book and looked at her master cautiously.

"I cain't read, suh," Ona said guardedly. "Slaves ain't allowed."

"Ah, of course." Burgiss nodded gravely. He took the book from Ona's extended hand, unsure of how to continue. "Polly has regained her strength, thanks to you. I realize that she is well past the age when she should begin her formal education. There is no school as yet in the county for girls."

Ona nodded. "Is you sendin' her away?"

Burgiss shook his head, frustrated. "No, Ona. She must learn here." Until the railroad paid off, an expensive hired tutor was out of the question. Boarding school in Columbia was beyond his ability to pay. He knew that educating his girl child should fall squarely on his wife. Mary's medicine-induced fog would have to end if Polly was going to begin an education. His wife had been educated at one of Virginia's finest girls' academies. She would have to tutor Polly.

"We need Miss Mary to teach Polly to read. Her education should have commenced by now, but with the boys . . ." His voice trailed off. Ona waited without saying a word.

"I am going to dispense with my wife's laudanum. I fear it has become a crutch and is interfering with her recovery. Her mind is dull." He sighed.

Ona appeared confused so he tried again. "That means that she will not get any more of the medicine from Dr. Adger. She seems to sleep all the time. I want you to pour out the bottle she has. Help her get her strength back so that she can tutor Polly," he said. "You make tinctures and herbals for the men when they're ill." He shrugged. "Use one of your remedies if she needs pain relief."

— • —

ONA NODDED SLOWLY. "YESSUH." Questions came to her mind but she knew better than to ask.

Burgiss stood and crossed the room. He pulled a cotton sheet from a large mirror. "And take down these damned sheets over the mirrors. Throw open the drapes. I cannot abide this tomb-like atmosphere anymore when I am home. I despise it, and it isn't good for Polly."

His temper flared, and he pointed a finger at Ona. "When I return in a fortnight, I expect my wife to be clear-eyed and sound, ready to undertake Polly's instruction. I will leave written instructions for her to read, apprising her of my decision. I've purchased children's books and primers while in Charleston." He gestured to the stack of thin books on his desk. "Your job is to make my wife ready for the task." With those brief but firm instructions, he stormed from the room.

Ona swallowed hard and wrung her hands. Mr. Burgiss had never spoken to her like that and it frightened her. She climbed the stairs slowly, her shaking hand on the banister. She knocked on Mary's door softly, but the woman was deep in sleep, snoring evenly. Ona crossed to Mary's bedside table and quietly opened the drawer. She lifted the small brown bottle of laudanum and put it in her apron pocket, before padding silently out of the room.

At dawn the next morning, Burgiss rode off toward Walhalla yet again, leaving Ona to tend to Polly and her mother.

— • —

LATER THAT NIGHT, MARY THRASHED VIOLENTLY, in and out of consciousness. Her nightdress had wound around her legs, and she kicked furiously, trying to free herself. Her addiction was powerful in its withdrawal, and she craved the morphine-based droplets on her tongue more than life itself.

Two babies had died in the womb since the woman had started taking the potent medicine. Ona reckoned this poison was tied to the bloody miscarriages even if Dr. Adger had claimed that laudanum was a healthful tonic that many white women took regularly to get over their monthly pains.

"Ona!" Mary whined, slapping at the slave woman with her palms. "Give me my medicine. Damn it, give it to me—now."

"Please, Miss Mary," begged Ona tearfully. "Mr. Burgiss ain't buying no more. You have to believe me. Read the note he left you. I ain't got none to give you. He threw it all out." She bent near the woman's face. "We gonna get you better a different way."

Ona felt the flat of Mary's palm sting her cheek. Out of the corner of her eye, she saw Polly standing in the doorway, teary-eyed and trembling. "It's alright, Miss Polly. Yo' Mama sick, but she gonna be better soon. Please go and bring some of that cool water in the pitcher downstairs on the sideboard, you hear? Go on now." Her soothing voice sent the little girl away obediently for the water. Ona cursed under her breath at both the crazy woman in the bed and her no-account white husband too afraid to deal with the mess in his own home.

— • —

DOWNSTAIRS, A SHAKING POLLY LIFTED the heavy pitcher and poured a tall glass of cool water for her mother.

"She will be fine," said a voice behind her. Polly startled and knocked the glass over, spilling the water across the table and onto the floor. As she stood staring, Ben knelt down at her feet and began to wipe up the spill with the bandana he had untied from his neck. "You don't have to worry, Miss Polly. Mama says your mother will be just fine once she is off that poison."

"I thought she was dying." Polly looked down at Ben, tears in her brown eyes.

"Nah." Ben chuckled. "She isn't dying. Don't you worry. Mama takes good care of her. Soon Miss Mary will be taking care of you again like a mama should. She is just sad. Now go on upstairs and give her this drink." Ben smiled and poured another cup of water.

Polly had never heard a slave speak such fine English, or tell a white person what to do, ever. But she was comforted by Ben's words and tone, so she took the cup from him and smiled in return.

"Are you allowed into our house?" she asked innocently. Ben's smile vanished and he set the pitcher down softly on the table. He turned and walked out the door.

— • —

WHEN MARY FINALLY LAPSED INTO sleep after a particularly violent outburst, Ona gently tied the woman's hands to the bedposts to keep her from hurting herself until the poison was out of her system. Not knowing how long it would take for the laudanum to leave Mary's body, she bathed her mistress's damp forehead and remembered Mary's good care of her during Ben's difficult birth. She emptied the chamber pot regularly, brought food and water, and tried to keep Mary clean and comfortable.

After several more days of screaming and retching, Mary woke up early one morning, sweat-drenched and shaking, but clear-headed for the first time in more a year. She looked around the room and saw Ona drowsing on the pine floor near her bed.

"Untie me, Ona." Mary's voice was calm.

Ona startled and sat up. She hurried to her feet, too frightened of her mistress not to obey. "Yes ma'am." She loosened the ties that had bound the woman's wrists and quickly backed away. "Law, Miss Mary, I know you was in pain from the medicine. I know you wasn't in yo' right mind. I was afraid you was gonna hurt yo'self or Miss Polly." Ona's voice trembled. "Mr. Burgiss, he told me to watch you. He threw away yo' medicine. There's a paper he left here explainin' everything." Ona crossed to Mary's vanity to retrieve the note.

"I'm so tired," Mary's voice wavered and she closed her eyes. "I'll just sleep a while longer. Please let me be." She rubbed at her wrists and rolled over onto her side.

Ona placed the paper on the nightstand with a shaking hand and quickly left the room.

The next morning, Mary descended the oak staircase fully dressed in her gray satin. Pale and shaking, she stopped in the hallway to pat her wild hair into place and check her reflection in the glass.

Ona appeared from the dining room. "Miss Mary, you sho' look well today. It's good to see you up and about." She fumbled nervously with her apron.

Mary turned to look at Ona with cold eyes. "Where is my husband?"

"He gone fo' another week, ma'am."

After a few moments, Mary sighed. She fingered the embroidered edge of her collar and said, "Bring my daughter to see me."

— • —

ONCE MARY WAS WEANED FROM THE addictive laudanum, Ona felt the lifting of a great burden. She had done what Mr. Burgiss had asked—she'd healed the mistress. And to her great relief, there had been no punishment beyond the stinging slap that first day. Now she watched hopefully as her mistress attempted to tutor Polly in reading and sums. Perhaps Mary would finally take charge of her own daughter and train the child in the way she should go. While Ona dusted furniture and polished silver, she listened. As she stoked fires and served meals, she watched. From the outset, she saw that Mary had little interest in the task despite being an intelligent, well-read woman.

Ona knew that Polly was eager to learn. She saw that the girl ached to spend time with her mother once again. But when Polly asked too many questions or gave an incorrect answer, an impatient Mary snapped at her, or ended the lessons, leaving the room abruptly without explanation. After only a week, she complained to Ona that she was weary of the task she had been charged. She left her daughter with the primers to look over, but little guidance in understanding them.

Mary still summoned her daughter to tea in the afternoons to work on her beloved samplers and other quiet needlework—which Ona knew Polly hated. After a while, the ruse faded and neither mother nor daughter sought each other's company. By the time that Polly was ten years old, her mother had taken to her bed again and given up the illusion of educating her daughter. Ona wasn't sure how she felt about the matter. On the one hand, she was relieved that Mary stayed out of sight. But on the other hand, it meant that Ona was in charge of Polly's days once more.

— • —

THE IDEA OF SHAPING POLLY INTO A well-educated young lady was something James Burgiss also put out of his mind when he received word that his friend and business partner John Calhoun died of tuberculosis in March 1850. As the south mourned the defender of states' rights and slavery, and the nation mourned a former vice president, James reeled from the loss of his greatest friend and ally in the push to extend the railroad.

Investors grew nervous. The project was fraught with delays and no longer had Calhoun's backing. The Columbia and Greenville railroad, with its route between the two named cities, had veered away from Anderson toward the northeast, taking many investors with it. The idea of a Blue Ridge Railway to Knoxville and beyond seemed to slip further away.

James spent more time in Walhalla, to be near the locus of activity. His absence further angered his wife, but he reasoned that if the railroad was to receive a charter, at least one tunnel would need to be constructed.

One afternoon in late spring, he sat wearily at a table in his rented rooms in Walhalla, penning yet another letter to a potential investor.

He dipped his pen in ink and continued his plea.

A spur line now runs to Greenville. Rail lines have been completed from Anderson into Pendleton, soon to West Union and Walhalla. The upstate tunnels will be blasted through the mountain rock only a day's ride from Anderson. When the tunnels are finished, the railroad line through to Tennessee and the Midwest can proceed at a rapid clip, and investors shall reap huge rewards.

With Calhoun's death so recent, he dared not ask for help from the largest landowner in the district, the widow Floride Calhoun. He would need more money soon or the whole project would grind to a halt. He sat with his head in his hands, worried that the rail line through the Blue Ridge would fall apart without Senator Calhoun's patronage, taking everything he owned with it.

He sighed and put down his pen. His thoughts drifted to his wife and daughter a half-day's ride to the south. He could make it home that evening with a fast horse. But there were other letters to write. He hoped to be through the mountain in a year or two and home for good.

Chapter Four

September 1853

MORNING SUN STREAMED THROUGH THE LONG dining room windows as Polly and her mother ate breakfast in silence. The light in Mary's eyes was gone. She carried with her the weight of two dead sons and a family broken. She spent her days rocking quietly on the front porch, staring off into the distance. Despite James' admonishments, she did not have the strength to tend to her home or her child. The roses growing over the front porch languished and would have died had Ona not pruned and fed them. Mary's long hair showed streaks of grey, and her pale cheeks had a hollowness to them. Only recently had she shed the dull greys and lavenders of half-mourning. James had returned from Charleston weeks ago with beautiful ready-made silk dresses for her in the latest colors and fashions, but she stashed them in trunks unseen and unused.

Polly took a bite of the biscuit on her plate and chewed slowly. She considered asking her mother the important question on her mind but knew the time was not right. There was no need to further distress her. She swallowed, blotted her lips with her napkin, and pushed back her chair.

Polly planned to spend her day the way she usually did, following Ona as she worked. Later, she would help polish silver and brass in the dining room or work in the kitchen garden. Polly loved to tend the garden, flicking aphids off tomato plants and checking for cutworms and grubs.

She routinely fed the chickens, even killed a hen herself once, bravely wringing its neck the way Ona taught her. She had learned to cook meat over the spit and put up vegetables. Ona taught her how to make biscuits, how to darn her own stockings and hem a skirt, and where the best herbs grew for tinctures and salves.

She listened to Ona speak of the city she frequently remembered, called Charlotte, where she had lived before River Wood and Whitehall.

"Yes'm, Charlotte be a fine place. I was born there." Ona smiled, beads of sweat dotting her forehead. The two were in the kitchen house. It was an unusual fall day, hot and sultry. The kitchen was always steamy but heat this late in the year seemed almost unbearable. The girl was trying to spoon cooked apples into a jar, but the sweet fruit dribbled down the outside of the jar and over her hands in a sticky puddle.

"Miss Girl, you is the messiest child I ever did see." Ona clucked affectionately. Polly liked it when Ona called her "Miss Girl."

"My ma and pa were slaves on a fancy estate. We had our own rooms over the stables. Pa was in charge of the stables. He was the head coachman. And we kids would get to he'p him curry the horses. They was beautiful horses, too. So shiny and smooth."

Ona stared out the window, dreamily. "We had enough food to keep our stomachs full. The master never beat us or treated us bad. I had three little brothers and a big sister, June."

"Then why did you want to leave?" Polly asked innocently, licking the sticky syrup from her fingers.

"Land sakes, chile." Ona shook her head, her eyes downcast. "I didn't want to leave. My family was there. But Missus jus' up and sold me when I turned fifteen. Said I was too pretty a nigra to stay. Now you look at me, Miss

43

Girl. I ain't pretty. She jes' wanted me gone. That's all." Ona chuckled and sealed a jar of fruit and wiped the rim with a rag. "I got sold down here to River Wood." She paused. "Mmm-hmm, that was a bad time," she whispered.

Polly put her wet hand on Ona's arm. "Ona, you're my only friend. I don't like it when you're sad."

— • —

ONA WIPED HER HANDS ON HER APRON. She did not resent the girl's presence while she cooked in the kitchen or cleaned in the house. Polly's own parents ignored her. The poor girl had no one to talk to or care for her. Ona saw that all the Burgisses grief and anger over their sons' deaths was heaped on top of Polly. They didn't exactly blame her for the boys' absence but having her around reminded them of their loss. Ona knew that it was the only way her parents could cope, but she wasn't sure how long Polly could manage so much neglect.

"Yo' mama needs to see that you meet some young people yo' own age. No slave women should be yo' only friend," she grumbled. Ona looked at the skinny girl. The child was growing so fast that her arms were too long for her sleeves and her collar was frayed in places. Ona tried to keep up with the sewing, but Polly was changing and would need new clothes as winter approached. The faintest beginnings of a bust line showed through the bodice of her summer dress. How could the Burgisses not see?

"Ona, may I ask you a question?" Polly's demeanor grew dark and worried.

"Miss Girl, you can ask ol' Ona anything." She wiped the sweat from her forehead.

"Well, I . . . I think I'm sick. And I sure don't want Mother to worry about me. I mean, she is already sick with worries. I declare I don't want to make her mad," the girl confided.

Ona snorted. "Sick? What makes you think you sick? You look fit as a fiddle to me."

Polly reddened and whispered, "I'm bleeding—and it won't stop. It's been two days!" She continued, "I have gone through my knickers something fierce. I thought maybe you had noticed—from the soiled laundry. I've been frightfully worried. I'm not even grown up yet . . ." She trailed off. "It doesn't hurt, but I'm scared that I am dying."

Ona smiled. "Miss Girl, you ain't dyin'. That's yo' woman's monthly time. It means you is growin' up. I get you some rags from the rag bag. And that's all I has to say 'bout that. You ask yo' mama and she explain it all to ya. Now run on and git back to the big house befo' she finds out you in this hot kitchen." She playfully swatted at Polly with her dishrag. "You as healthy as a horse."

Polly sighed and picked up a jar of apples. "I'm so glad. I thought I was very sick. I will take some apples to Mama. Maybe she'll make me a cake like she used to do . . ." Her voice trailed off.

"Well, that's an idea, Miss Girl," Ona said absentmindedly. "Although yo' mama ain't likely to want to get out here in the hot kitchen."

"Yes, well, I hoped she would make it for me today. It's my thirteenth birthday." Polly fumbled with the jar in her hands.

Ona put down the plates she was carrying and looked at Polly tenderly. "Well, happy birthday, Miss Polly. I forgot it was yo' birthday. You thirteen years old today, is that a fact?" Ona asked.

Polly beamed.

"Tell you what, go on up to the big house and I will make a cake. You and yo' mama can have a fine birthday party tonight. And you can celebrate you is a growin' woman, too. I'll even clabber up some cream to top it off!"

"Oh, Ona! Thank you! I'll let her know that we're having a celebration tonight!" The girl hugged Ona tightly. Ona was surprised at the emotion it conveyed and at the way it touched her own heart.

— • —

SEVERAL DAYS LATER, ONA STOOPED near the front porch railing, cutting fragrant pink roses for her mistress. Mary had not offered gloves, and Ona had already stabbed herself twice with the nasty thorns. Sweat trickled down her back and soaked her dress. She glanced up to the shaded front porch and saw Polly gazing out at the dusty front lawn and the dry, withered fields as she absentmindedly brushed her mother's hair. It looked like this year would go down in the record books as the driest one in decades. The long drought had taken its toll on the Whitehall landscape. Rain had not fallen in two months, and the creeks had dried to a trickle. The wells brought up muddy water if anything at all, and the slaves had to tote drinking water in barrels all the way from the river.

When the tin pail was filled with long-stemmed blossoms, Ona wiped her face with her apron and climbed the porch steps wearily. She paused and watched Mary Burgiss, asleep in her rocker, wrapped in quilts despite the heat. Polly sighed and ran the brush through her mother's unpinned hair in long strokes, watching as Ben and George unloaded the heavy barrels from the wagon.

When Ona noticed Polly's eyes on Ben she said softly, "Miss Polly, you want to help me dig up dandelions? I show you how to make that tea."

Polly shook her head.

Ona fretted about Ben spending time around Polly. There was always the chance that something would remind her of the murders and of what she saw at the Kemp house. It was best to keep the horrible mess buried and over with—best for Polly and especially for Ben. Polly was a healthy young woman now, and the memories could come roaring back at any time.

Ona had given Ben strict instructions to avoid the big house and keep to the fields or smithy during the day. As time passed, Ben had grown from a lanky boy into a strong young man of seventeen. He was also learning a good deal from Martin about blacksmithing, and he had made horseshoes and repaired wheels on his own. He had even fashioned a beautiful piece for the front gate Mr. Burgiss eventually wanted to erect. Ben had stayed true to his word and had not divulged to anyone the identities of the men he had seen at the Kemps' years earlier.

—— • ——

"POLLY!" MARY SNAPPED, AS THE BRUSH snagged in a tangled knot of hair. "Stop woolgathering and pay attention. You're hurting me."

"Oh, I'm sorry." Polly's attention reverted back to the brush and her mother's unpinned tresses. She began to brush Mary's hair with gentle strokes. "Is that better?"

Mary closed her eyes again and tilted her head back. She enjoyed the sensation of the boar bristle brush on her scalp. She wondered if her husband would be coming home soon, but it was a passing thought. He only disrupted her household. Her days were dull and easy now and ensured as little emotional pain as possible. She seldom went into town unless Polly begged and pleaded. She sighed. She did not deserve this sad state of affairs. Any woman in her shoes would have been vanquished as well, she reasoned. She had only one lazy house servant and one child. A daughter. Guilt poked at the edges of Mary's mind, but she pushed it away. Of course, the house was in need of attention, her daughter uneducated. Calls no longer made. But did it matter? Mr. Roper had mentioned a new girls' school in Anderson, but it was a half-day's ride just to get there. Perhaps she should try again with the primers . . . She turned these things over in her mind, unable to relax.

She opened her eyes enough to see Ona snipping the stem of each rose before plunging it back into the pail of cool water as she'd taught her. Suddenly, the sound of a carriage approaching, along with clouds of orange dust, signaled that visitors were headed to Whitehall. James was in Walhalla and not expected back for days. Mary shielded her eyes against the bright morning sun and she tried to make out who might be coming up the long drive.

— • —

POLLY LEANED OVER THE RAILING AND CALLED, "Who is it, Mother? Can you tell?" She put a hand to her forehead and squinted into the sunlight as a lovely brougham pulled by two beautiful black horses approached. She glanced back to the porch and saw the empty rocking chair still rocking, but her mother had vanished. Polly swallowed hard and watched as the carriage slowed upon approach to the house. The brougham was the finest carriage that Polly had ever seen. The horses were tall and well-muscled, their glossy black manes and tails brushed to perfection.

"Lan' sakes and I do declare!" Ona exclaimed. The carriage stopped in front of them.

A single dark coachman, in deep scarlet livery with gold brocade, stepped down from the seat and opened the passenger door with a bow. A tiny silver-haired woman wearing a lavender silk mourning gown stepped down from the carriage. The gown had such an enormous skirt that Polly could hardly believe it had come through the tiny carriage door. It was the most beautiful dress that Polly had ever laid eyes on, outside of *Godey's Lady's Book*, which her mother faithfully read. A matching lavender silk bonnet and a tiny, jeweled purse completed the ensemble.

"Hello, my dear." The woman smiled. "You must be Polly." Polly returned the woman's kind smile but couldn't speak.

"I daresay you don't remember me. You were just a babe in arms at one of my Christmas parties years ago. I believe that you spent most of that evening squalling in the nursery with a nasty bout of colic." She chuckled. "I am Floride Calhoun."

Polly gulped and dropped her knees in a shallow curtsy. Was she to curtsy? Or to bow? Oh, why didn't she know what to do in front of such an important lady? "Yes ma'am, so nice to have you here, ma'am," she stammered.

Mrs. Calhoun threw her head back and laughed. It was such a hearty and strong laugh, coming from such a tiny woman. It surprised Polly and set her at ease. "You don't need to grovel, my dear. Just invite me inside."

Polly quickly stood up, feeling self-conscious in her faded gingham dress and messy braids. "Yes ma'am, please come inside." Polly led the grand dame up the stairs and into Whitehall. Ona dropped her clippers and headed around to the back door of the house.

It wasn't long before Mrs. Calhoun was seated in the parlor on the comfortable settee. She adjusted her voluminous skirts patiently. Ona quietly appeared with a pot of tea and a tray of cookies and placed them on the low table in front of Polly's guest.

Polly sat across from her in awe, watching as the woman removed black lace gloves and her feather-trimmed bonnet. The woman set them down beside her. Polly yearned to reach out and touch the lace gloves and stroke the shimmering silk gown. She could hear the grandfather clock tick off each second and wondered what could be keeping her mother from this most wondrous guest.

"I should have announced my call. I daresay I have caught your mother unawares," the woman commented without apology, looking around the room. "Polly dear, will you pour?" Mrs. Calhoun nodded toward the tea tray. Polly was jolted out of her distraction. "I like mine with cream, please." Mrs. Calhoun smiled.

Polly gulped and picked up the pot. This pot was not the chipped ceramic pot in which Ona served tea to her mother. Where did Ona find this one? It was delicate bone china, tiny blue flowers painted all over it, fine and lovely. Polly tried to steady her shaking hands as she poured tea for their guest.

The double doors opened and Ona appeared, her eyes downcast. "Mrs. Calhoun, ma'am, Mrs. Burgiss say she ain't feelin' up to visitors." Ona dipped her head towards Mrs. Calhoun. "She sends her 'pologies, and asks you to maybe call another day, ma'am. She real sorry." The woman silently backed out of the room, closing the parlor's doors behind her. Polly looked after Ona, dumbstruck.

Her gaze returned to Mrs. Calhoun, who sat calmly, sipping her tea.

"I'm sorry, Mrs. Calhoun. My mother just hasn't been herself since . . . since my brothers died."

Floride appraised Polly's appearance over her teacup and raised an eyebrow. "Yes, and that was how long ago? Five years?"

Polly reddened and tried to still her shaking knees. "Yes ma'am." She looked down at her faded skirt and dirty fingernails. She suddenly felt protective of her mother. "We were out enjoying the sunshine, planning the flower beds, but Mother is quite shy of visitors still. I was hoping she would come down."

Mrs. Calhoun sipped her tea and then set the cup down gently. "We have been neighbors for a long time. Your mother is a delicate one, isn't she?"

Before Polly could reply, the woman continued, "I remember my Christmas party, years ago. You were a screaming infant, and your mother was beside herself at leaving you in the nursery. Just distraught. Your father had to pull her away."

A trace of a smile played at Polly's lips. Mrs. Calhoun continued, "The children of our guests had been invited to come along, as the nursery was decorated with a festive tree, lights, and presents for all. In fact, the older children put on a Christmas play for the adults. It was lovely. Your brothers . . ."

"Caleb and Joshua." Polly smiled broadly.

The woman nodded. "Yes. Caleb and Joshua were just toddlers themselves at the time, but in awe of the beautifully decorated rooms and the merriment. You, my dear, screamed the entire time."

Polly laughed. "I did?"

"I recall my exasperated nurse upstairs finally sending your mother a message that nothing, absolutely nothing would make her baby stop crying, not even a sugar tit. She would have to come upstairs and nurse her wailing child. Oh dear, Mary had been so relieved at the time. She rushed up the stairs. She clearly was not at ease leaving you." Floride gazed at Polly warmly.

Polly sipped her own tea and crossed her ankles the way Mary had shown her. "But she was so happy and lively before . . ." Polly regretted the words as they left her mouth.

Mrs. Calhoun sighed and changed the subject. "I am sure that you are wondering why I came calling unannounced today. It isn't a social call. I wanted to discuss some business and your schooling with your mother." She looked at Polly expectantly. "You are thirteen, yes?"

Polly looked at Mrs. Calhoun defiantly. "Mrs. Calhoun," she began. "My mother has tutored me—a bit—in sums and reading. I'm making progress in the primers. And I sew. Ona taught me to darn stockings and mend my own clothing. And how to put up preserves and make biscuits."

Floride Calhoun pursed her lips thoughtfully. "Ah. Did she now? Young lady, when I was your age, I was proficient in three languages, had traveled extensively, and played the organ quite well. My granddaughter in Belgium is almost your age and she has had a comprehensive education. She is proficient in four languages and plays the piano beautifully. When they return to the United States I expect her mother to enroll her in a superior finishing school." Chastened, Polly blushed and dropped her gaze.

Floride sipped her tea, looking across the rim of her teacup at Polly with a glint of conspiracy in her eyes. "Have you heard of Miss Munson's Seminary for Young Ladies, in Charleston?"

"No ma'am," Polly admitted.

"It is a lovely school, run by a friend of mine. I think you would benefit from attending. I had written to your father about that very thing and offered to cover the boarding fees for the first year."

Polly shook her head vehemently. "I can't leave my mother! She'd have no one. My father is rarely home."

Mrs. Calhoun held up a hand. "Oh Polly, calm yourself. Your father wrote back the very same thing. As much as I think the school would do you good, it isn't my place to insist. I am known to have strong opinions, but I am not your kin. Do you have any friends, my dear? Other young ladies with whom you may socialize?"

Polly's shoulders sagged. "Until my mother is recovered, my place is here."

Floride shrugged. "Very well. You know your own mind. But you aren't a child anymore, Polly. If your poor mother isn't able to run her household, you may have to step up."

The woman began to pull on her lace gloves. "Your mother shouldn't make things worse by continuing this perpetual mourning. It isn't healthy, nor is it good for the appearance of business at Whitehall. It causes your father to struggle even more so. Despite having received the charter for the railroad company last year, what investor would be heartened by such a mess?"

Polly stared blankly at her guest.

"So—you should know that the whole district is talking about your family's continued use of white pickers instead of slaves. Do your slaves sit idly, while the fields swarm with white men?" Floride drew an elaborate silk fan from her bag and fanned herself furiously. "It's outrageous!"

Polly sat still, unsure of what to say. Her father had never discussed his business in her hearing. And she was not allowed outside anywhere near the cotton fields when picking took place.

Mrs. Calhoun stood and began to gather her belongings. "It wouldn't hurt you to become acquainted with his business, Polly. I sense a good head on those pretty shoulders. Your father has several large investors close to backing out of the Blue Ridge Railway project. Perhaps you can help your mother see that even she plays a role in this effort."

"The railroad tunnel is my father's dream," Polly said. "If his tunnel fails . . ." Her voice trailed away.

"It will not fail on my watch. I plan to buy more stock in the venture," said the older woman confidently. "I wrote to him with this very news. I have several interested businessmen who are eager to invest, as well. It might save this project."

"Mrs. Calhoun!" Polly exclaimed. "Oh, thank you! This will surely make him so happy."

"Nonsense. I'm not doing it for James Burgiss's happiness. I am doing it for myself. For South Carolina. Extend the railroad quickly, and we can bring in new industry and merchandise. I have cotton to ship north to the Ohio River Valley. When it is finished, a railroad through the Blue Ridge will be the fastest way to get it there, and we'll all make money on the venture. Let us show the rest of the country that it is a good investment, captained by an able and prosperous local family—the Burgisses of Whitehall."

Polly smiled, and a feeling of hope quickened her pulse. Maybe this news meant that her father would be home more. "I am so glad that you called today, Mrs. Calhoun."

"One more thing." Floride leaned toward Polly conspiratorially. "I would love to have you and your mother visit me in Charleston. You would have a fine time there and you would both be able to get some new clothing and see the sights. It appears you are practically dressed from the ragbag."

The grand lady turned to go. "I trust you will relay my sentiments to your mother."

"Yes ma'am." Polly followed Mrs. Calhoun to the front porch where they said their goodbyes. She watched Mrs. Calhoun's beautiful carriage roll down the drive and back toward Fort Hill.

— • —

ON A SUNDAY MORNING WEEKS LATER, Polly woke early to find that autumn had finally decided to paint the sourwood outside her open window a brilliant ruby red. The morning air held a crisp chill and sent ghostly swirls of fog across low places in the fields. She shivered with cold and threw back her quilts, crossed the room, and closed the window. She poked the glowing embers in her fireplace and stirred the fire back to life. She found her chamber pot, then dressed quickly and headed downstairs on silent feet, not wishing to wake her mother. She headed toward the kitchen house, stomach growling. The kitchen was still dark and quiet. She looked out toward the row of slave cabins and noticed grey smoke curling from Ona's small chimney.

With some trepidation, she decided to visit the woman and ask about an early breakfast. As she neared the cabin, she heard an unfamiliar voice.

". . . I shall not want. He leadeth me beside still waters . . . ," a man's deep voice intoned. The smooth bass mesmerized Polly, so calm and assured. She crouched down under the shuttered window and listened for a while. ". . . and I will dwell in the house of the Lord forever."

The man was quoting scripture from the Bible. Polly's family had not taken her to church since her brothers' funeral five years earlier, but she recognized the Psalmist's words. A slave had been praying the same words just now.

Polly's curiosity got the better of her and she stood on tiptoes to peek through a crack in the shutters. She saw Ona, her husband Martin, and Ben sitting together at a small table in the dim light of a single candlestick. Martin held a thick book open in front of him. Polly was astonished to see that he was reading the Bible. A slave—reading! In her haste to back away quietly, she tripped over a pail and it clattered noisily away.

As she struggled to get to her feet, Ona flung the door open, one hand on her hips. "Miss Polly, what in tarnation you doin' here at this hour?"

The woman looked around to see if Mr. Roper was outside anywhere. "This is our private time. I ain't up to the big house till noon dinner time." Ona looked both shocked and angry at the same time. "It Sunday mornin'."

"Oh, I forgot today was Sunday," Polly murmured.

Martin appeared beside his wife in the doorway. Polly had not been so near the blacksmith before. He stayed busy well away from the house. She stared wide-eyed at Martin. He appeared much older than Ona, very tall and thin, well-muscled, and so black that he was almost blue. Polly thought his skin was beautiful. His dark eyes stared her down.

"I—I didn't hear anything," Polly lied. She felt guilt wash over her and immediately apologized. "I'm sorry. I mean, I did hear him reading." She stammered, "I didn't know slaves could read. I thought only whites could read." Her cheeks burned with shame for spying on the slaves, for forgetting it was Sunday, and because she herself, a white girl, could not read.

Ona's eyes darted around the yard. "Miss Girl, you go on now, before yo' mama catches you here. I come up directly to the kitchen to fix yo' breakfast. If you get me some eggs, I make you hotcakes. We can try that apple butter you he'ped me put up the other day. Please—go on now."

Polly brightened. Ona's hotcakes were delicious. Her stomach rumbled at the thought. She turned to go and then paused to look directly at Martin. "Can you really read?"

— • —

MARTIN STARED AT THE SKINNY, BROWN-EYED GIRL. She looked so like her grandmother back in Virginia. "Yes, Miss Polly, I can read," he said proudly, in a voice smooth like honey. "Your grandfather hired a teacher for his own children, a Miss Patchett. She was a good white woman. She taught me to read when I was about the age of Ben here. She gave me this Bible." The man pointed to an inscription written inside the leather cover.

"Mother told me once about a slave who had his eyes gouged out when his master saw him reading a newspaper!" Polly exclaimed.

"Martin." Ona touched his shoulder with her hand to stop him from speaking further.

Martin pushed Ona's hand away gently. He was too old and tired to worry about what the little white girl might tell her parents. He could read and quite well. He had read many of the books in Mr. Burgiss's expansive collection because Ona would slip in and out with volumes for him to borrow while Burgiss traveled. *So be it*, he thought. How could he be punished for reading the Bible to his family? But he half expected the girl to run off and tell her mother about slaves reading books when they should be working the fields. "Child, you run on now. I expect that your mother would be disappointed that you have come to the slave cabins on the Lord's day."

— • —

POLLY KNEW MARTIN WAS RIGHT, but she was mesmerized by his deep voice and by his perfect English. No wonder Ben spoke so well, so differently from his mother. She looked at both of them pleadingly and pointed to the Bible in Martin's hands.

Polly mustered her courage. "Teach me to read the Bible. Please." She looked at Ona's worried face and added, "I will not tell my parents that you can read. I promise. I have no one else to ask. I want to read well. My mother is no help. Mrs. Calhoun all but threatened to send me away to a boarding school!"

Martin regarded the child, the daughter of the man who owned him, and shook his head. He held the Bible against his chest. "We do your family's bidding from dawn to dusk. We break our backs for your family. But this, this I do not have to do." He glared at Polly. "You should go now, Miss." The proud man handed the tattered Bible to Ona and walked past them and out toward the smithy shed.

Polly felt color rise in her cheeks. She was so ashamed. What had she been thinking, coming to the slave quarters? This wasn't the kitchen house. This was Ona's home, early on a Sunday morning. She turned to leave as Ona went back inside the cabin.

"I will teach you." Ben's voice made Polly stop. He hopped down the steps, hands in his pockets.

Polly turned and looked up at him hopefully.

Ona opened her mouth to speak, but Ben cut in. "I will teach you to read—if you'll help Mama make Sunday dinners for the duration. Meet me in the kitchen house on Sundays at daybreak. I'll give you thirty minutes before I tend the stock. Then you help her with the Sunday cooking. No one else is to know about it. Especially not Pa. You promise?" He pointed a finger at her. "And you fix your own breakfast."

Ona stepped into the yard quickly and tugged on her son's arm. "Stop your foolin', Ben," she snapped. "Miss Polly, don't pay no mind to Ben. He jes' don't know when to shut up." She glared at the boy.

But Polly broke into a wide smile. "I will be ready next Sunday morning at sunup. I'll get breakfast for myself and tea for Mother. I will light the fires. I will empty my own chamber pot, Ona. I will help make Sunday dinner, and I promise I won't tell a soul." Polly turned to leave but paused to look back at Ben. "Thank you, Ben."

— • —

ONA CLOSED THE DOOR AND SAT DOWN heavily on the sagging cot. She covered her face with the Bible and began to cry.

"Ma, what's wrong?" Ben asked, surprised. He sat next to his mother and gathered her into his arms. She had grown so thin. Sometimes Ben felt like he was the parent and she was the child. "Why are you and Pa so upset about her wanting to read? Remember how happy I was that Pa could teach me? She just wants the same thing."

"It's nothing like you or me!" Ona snapped. "How can you be so blind? She white, she ain't a slave. Her daddy is yo' master. And when Mr. Burgiss told me she needed schoolin', I didn't say nothin' about yo' Pa and you readin'. It's against the law, Ben. Fo' years, that woman been lyin' in the bed . . . didn't teach that girl nothin.' If she find out a slave boy teachin' her daughter, you have no idea what Miss Mary gonna go and do. She crazy, that one. You likely to be lynched, boy!"

"Mama, you can't read! You didn't lie to Mr. Burgiss," Ben blurted out. Ona pulled free. He looked at her and shrugged, exasperated. "Why would she get mad at us for helping Polly with something the girl begged us for?"

Ona slapped Ben's face hard with her open palm. The young man stared at his mother, stunned into silence. She had never hit him before.

"You listen to me and listen good," Ona said through gritted teeth. "You ain't never to talk about white folks out loud that way ever. You ain't white. You ain't free. You ain't Miss Polly's friend, and you certainly ain't gone teach that chile to read, sittin' together every Sunday while her mama sleeps away the mornin's not knowin' what's goin' on. You is a slave, Ben. Behave yo'sef. Do yo' work and keep yo' head down. Don't cause no trouble for yo' Pa and me. We seen how bad it can be other places. Whitehall ain't so bad, Ben. You jes' as soon remember that, 'cause you ain't never leavin' here."

Ona wiped angry tears with the back of her hand and continued, "Do yo' work and keep away from Miss Polly. Don't you think that she'll start to remember one day? About you bein' there when her brothers died? There are so many bad white men around here. Bad places like River Wood we could be sent to. I could tell you stories to make yo' eyes pop. I pray every day we ain't ever leavin' here. Don't go and get us separated—or your Pa whipped. You hear me? Jes' behave," Ona admonished.

Ben rubbed his cheek, angry and humiliated. He stood. "I hear you, Ma. But I am not a child. I told Miss Polly I would teach her to read, and I will. And Ma, one day I will leave this place. I won't be a slave all my life like you . . . like Pa. I won't. No white man will own me forever." Ben stormed outside, slamming the cabin door behind him.

— • —

ONA ROCKED BACK AND FORTH ON THE BED with her eyes closed, waiting for Ben to be well away from the cabin before she let out a long low moan. She buried her face in the straw mattress to stifle her sobs and began to pray. She knew the day would come when her headstrong boy would try to make good on his promise. Like so many others, he would run.

Chapter Five

FOR WEEKS, POLLY MET BEN IN THE KITCHEN house early on Sunday mornings. Mary Burgiss slept late, not interested in seeking any comfort in the church service in town. She was free to sleep until late morning at which time she would awaken to tea and biscuits served proudly by her own daughter.

Ona made sure that she was always in the kitchen house with Ben and Polly, bustling about on her one morning off, as Ben patiently taught Polly how to string together vowels and consonants. When each lesson ended, he got up and left the kitchen house. Sometimes Polly tried to engage him in conversation after lessons were over, but she always caught the look between Ona and Ben that said Ben must leave. Martin was never around, and Polly didn't have the courage to ask whether he knew what his son was up to every Sunday morning. After lessons, Polly would make the coffee or tea and mix biscuit dough, knead, and bake biscuits for herself and Mary. She learned to roast venison and make rice pudding, her mother's favorites for Sunday dinners.

By early December, Polly could read advanced primers without error. By the time that her father was expected home for the Christmas holidays, Polly had eagerly begun to work her way through her father's small library.

Lessons ended abruptly on a frosty morning two weeks before Christmas. Ben sat listening to Polly read from Ephesians. The heat from the wood stove and the smell of Polly's apple cake cooling on the hearth made the kitchen feel especially warm and cozy.

"That's real nice, Miss Polly." Ben nodded as she finished the passage. "You read the Bible well. I guess we are done."

"Are we finished already today?" Polly looked surprised. She had come to look forward to her weekly sessions with Ben as much for the company of someone close to her age, as well as the instruction.

Ben reached his hand tentatively toward Polly's face and she jumped.

"You have a smudge of flour on your face," he said sheepishly.

"Oh," Polly murmured, embarrassed at her reaction. She brushed at her cheek until Ben nodded.

"I think we are finished—for good." He closed the Bible and glanced toward his mother.

Ona stood at the wood stove, hoisting the heavy lids off the burners. She did not look up but nodded in agreement. Ben knew she too had mixed feelings about the lessons ending. She did not want Ben around Polly unnecessarily, even though she told him she had come to enjoy the cozy Sunday mornings in the kitchen with the two of them reading nearby.

"You're a quick learner. You read as good as me, and you got a house full of books to start on," Ben said.

"As well as me," Polly corrected. "And I have a house full of books." She felt a pang of sadness at the thought of the isolation she knew only too well in the big house. "It was nice of you to help me, Ben. Your English is fine. Ona speaks like a slave." As soon as the words left Polly's mouth, Ben could see that she regretted them. Ona did not appear to hear the comment.

"I'm sorry. I meant that your English is almost as good as mine. When I heard your father speak, I realized where you had learned," Polly clarified.

Ben glanced past Polly to his mother, busy at the hearth. "She's a smart woman, but she won't learn to read," he murmured under his breath. "It's against the law. She doesn't want to do anything that might get us in trouble—with your parents."

Polly reddened. "Thank you again." She turned to Ona and spoke up. "I think I will surprise Father and read the Christmas story to him when he comes home." She saw Ona's face cloud with worry. "Don't fret, Ona." Polly rolled her eyes in amusement. "I'll tell him that those Charleston primers did the trick."

Ona sniffed and pointed a spoon at the girl. "At least you learnt to fix up yo' own breakfast. But don't go tellin' him that either." She chuckled.

Ben stood. "I wouldn't mind some of that apple cake you baked, Miss Polly." His wide smile showed even white teeth.

Ona shook her head. "No suh. You ain't about to eat Miss Polly's cake. This fo' her mama. Git on to your chores now," she barked. "That cow don't milk herse'f"

"Yes ma'am!" Ben winked at Polly playfully and started out the door of the kitchen house, rubbing his arms briskly against the cold. Polly followed him into the yard.

"I almost forgot! I have a Christmas present for you." From her cloak, she brought out a slim volume and handed it to Ben. Her excitement was palpable.

Ben glanced down at the book. "*Uncle Tom's Cabin*," he murmured.

"Father brought it home when he came back from Charleston last time. It's new. He tucked it away on a shelf, but I found it. I haven't read it yet myself. Just have Ona pass it back to me before Father comes home for the holidays. Maybe we can discuss it, like in a grand Paris *salon*."

She smiled innocently and added, "Merry Christmas, Ben."

— • —

POLLY SOON FORGOT ABOUT THE BOOK when Mr. Burgiss arrived home earlier than expected for the Christmas holiday. He had good news to share. The incorporation of the Blue Ridge Railroad was official. The

Calhoun family had reinvested in the railroad project, and construction was resumed to connect Anderson to Knoxville, Tennessee, through the Blue Ridge Mountains. Their little town would soon become a bona fide railroad hub, James announced, with a spur line into neighboring Abbeville and into Greenville further northwest. He planned to be home for some time. Polly reveled in the idea of having her father at Whitehall.

Christmas morning dawned cold and clear. A rare Christmas Eve snowfall had dropped several inches in the night and left a crystalline glaze on the fields and trees around Whitehall. The sun reflected off icicles hanging from the front porch. Deep in the woods, trees groaned and cracked under the weight of snow and ice.

The little family sat together in the warm parlor on Christmas morning, a crackling fire cheerfully burning in the fireplace. Later, there would be a Christmas service at the small Presbyterian Church in town, if Mary felt up to it. They were invited to Floride Calhoun's new home, Mi Casa in Pendleton, for a small party that evening, and Polly could hardly wait.

At some point, she wanted to tell her father about Mrs. Calhoun's visit, to ask about his white laborers, but for now, she was content to spend the morning with both of her parents for the first time in months.

"I love my new gown," Polly exclaimed, pressing the yellow silk dress to her chest, and then twirling in front of her parents. "I feel like a princess." She laughed. "A dress all the way from Charleston!" She paused to consider the snowy scene outside their windows. "You don't suppose the snow will be too much for our carriage tonight, do you? I would pull it myself if it meant we would get to Mrs. Calhoun's." Instantly, she seemed like her parents' little girl again. "I'm desperate to get out."

"Good gracious, Polly!" exclaimed her mother. "Please calm down."

James laughed. "You should have seen the snowy winters we had when I was growing up in northern Virginia. I think the horses will manage, daughter. Maybe later we'll venture outside for a winter walk. That is, after we eat our fill of Ona's roast turkey."

— • —

HE PUFFED ON HIS PIPE AND SMILED at his wife and daughter. Mary looked beautiful. Color was back in her cheeks, and her eyes were bright once more. She wore one of the ready-made dresses that he had purchased for her in Charleston, a stunning green silk with an enormous hoop skirt.

"Mary darling, I have another Christmas present for you," James smiled and pulled a small box from behind the settee cushions.

"James Burgiss, what have you done?" Mary clapped her hands together like a child. Having her husband home for an extended holiday seemed a tonic like no other.

"There is a small shop in Charleston that I pass frequently. I saw this in the window, and knew it was destined for my lovely wife." James beamed at Mary and then winked conspiratorially toward Polly.

Mary opened the velvet box and gasped. Nestled inside was a lovely cameo brooch, encrusted with pearls and tiny diamonds. What took Mary's breath away was the cameo itself. It was the silhouette of Polly. "James . . . How . . . ? When . . . ?" She could not speak.

"Our Polly helped me with this present. Remember when I had the portrait maker come to the house last summer to paint Polly? He sketched one picture of her in profile. I took it with me to Charleston, and the jeweler made this cameo to fit the brooch."

"Do you love it, Mother?" Polly asked.

Mary looked at her husband and her daughter with tear-filled eyes. "This is the most wonderful Christmas present I think I have ever received." She pinned the brooch to the bodice of her gown and stroked it lovingly.

Polly laughed. "Now it is my turn. I have a present for both of you. Close your eyes." While her parents closed their eyes good-naturedly, Polly scanned the bookshelves and soon returned to the sofa. "Open your eyes, please."

She sat with her mother's family Bible in her lap and beamed at her parents. "I would like to read the Christmas story from the Book of Luke." Polly began to read the story of the birth of Jesus. She read it beautifully and with great passion because she believed the truth of what she read.

James squeezed Mary's hand as their only child read from the Bible. He was so proud of his wife and daughter. Resilience. They had overcome the tragedy that threatened to overwhelm the little family. Things were surely looking up for the Burgisses of Whitehall.

— • —

JANUARY 1854 BLEW IN WITH STRONG WINDS and ice storms and bitter cold. Old-timers nodded at the expected weather, for the mast had been especially heavy that fall and the wooly worm's brown stripe a wide one. The livestock refused to leave the shelter of their barns and stables. The slaves were amazed to see the Seneca River, a tributary of the warm and lazy Savannah, frozen hard enough in places for folks to walk across its surface. Yet they still had chores to do despite the sub-freezing temperatures.

Bundled in her warmest shawl and stockings, Ona crunched across the snowy ground, the iron soup pot heavy in her hands. The sky was a brilliant blue, and the crisp air was scented with wood smoke and pine. A grey squirrel, holding a walnut in his mouth, scampered across her path and into the woods. Her eyes scanned the tree line, where tall evergreens were bent low but held tightly to their prickly cones. In the distant woods, trees groaned and cracked under the weight of ice on their limbs. She paused to dab at her runny nose with a bare hand and sighed at the wonder of it all. Her breath condensed in the frosty air and became a swirling plume of vapor carried away on the slight breeze. She hoisted the steaming pot of soup up the steps and into the small cabin where Martin lay sleeping.

Only a week later, Ona lost Martin to influenza. He had suffered for weeks after Christmas with a fever, labored breathing, feeling hot and then cold to the touch for days, despite bone broth and onion poultices to his feet. That morning Ona woke and sensed that the body beside her in the old bed was no longer her husband. She lay still, tears streaming down her face and soaking her pillow while Ben slept soundly nearby.

No one from the Burgiss family assisted with his burial. Several of the men dug a new grave in the plot of land behind the slave cabins, where Ona's stillborn babies rested. Now she stood in a cold drizzle at the edge of the muddy hole and watched Mr. Roper, Ben, and two other slaves lower Martin's pine box into the gaping earth of the little cemetery, near his stillborn daughters. From the corner of her eye, she saw Polly standing in the distance, watching the little funeral from behind a pine tree.

Tom had graciously given Ona and Ben two full days to mourn the dead man before resuming work. Ona rocked by the hearth, saying prayers and singing hymns that did nothing to ease her pain. It was as if she had lopped off half of her own body and soul and thrown them into the ground forever. The cold and dreary days dragged, and evenings found her stretched across Martin's grave, silent prayers drifting into the leaden sky.

— • —

AFTER SEVERAL WEEKS, MARY MADE IT clear that Ona had grieved long enough. She snapped at Ona on several occasions and complained incessantly to James that she was unhappy with the slave woman's work. Privately, the pain that Mary saw in Ona's eyes reminded her of her own loss. It made her sharp with her slave instead of sympathetic.

James Burgiss's response was to buy a River Wood house girl for his wife, a woman named Cissie, who would have been sent to April auctions if Sam Stone had not found a local buyer. Burgiss expected that she would be of additional help around the house and with the cooking. She was young and healthy and had cost him a pretty penny, but Burgiss knew that he would get a good return on his money.

The slave boss, George, quickly asked Burgiss's permission to marry Cissie. The pair jumped the broom that same month, and the woman immediately found her place in the kitchen, cooking for the hands, and tending the gardens and the chickens. Cissie was indeed a help if only because her arrival reminded Ona that any slave was expendable. She would need to keep her mistress content and do her work well.

— • —

MARY AND POLLY WERE COMFORTABLY ENSCONCED in the parlor, enjoying a warm fire on a chilly March afternoon. Spring was nowhere to be found outside the windows. A dark sky hung low and promised more snow. Mary stitched a sampler while Polly sat with the farm ledgers, studying forecasts and reports.

"Didn't you say that cotton futures are up, Polly?" Mary asked hopefully.

Polly did not look up. "Sea Island cotton. I saw nothing of our grade."

Mary sighed. "You're right, of course. You seem to understand this business better than I do." She put down the sampler in a pout. "And you enjoy reading those papers."

"I do enjoy it," Polly smiled. "It's more interesting than stitching samplers. Why are you so cross today?"

Mary frowned. "I have much on my mind." She mentally ticked off the lengthy list of smithy work that had gone undone. Several metalworking projects had fallen by the wayside after Martin's death. Who would forge a gate for the front lawn or keep the horses shod? And the new girl, Cissie, seemed a sassy little thing. The household worries twisted her gut and made her even more upset. She had seen a spot of blood in her handkerchief after a cough—twice now. She sighed heavily and stared out the window at the snow beginning to fall in fat flakes.

Polly looked up from her papers. "We could take a walk."

Mary dismissed Polly's comment with a wave of her hand. "I have things to resolve indoors. Apparently, I must remind Ona how to properly polish that silver," she said wryly. "And your father needs to find a new blacksmith. The smithy work is adding up without Martin."

"The man's casket was just lowered into a gaping hole in the earth, Mother," Polly said, shaking her head. "I watched the whole affair. Poor Ona."

"Why would you do such a thing? How horrid. A slave's personal affairs and feelings are not our concern," Mary snapped. She pointed her sewing scissors at Polly. "Indeed, Ona is lucky that Cissie came along and took some of her chores. Although this Cissie seems irresponsible and brash. Ona should tell her how I like things to be done."

Polly shrugged and looked down at her newspaper. "She lost her husband, Mother. That must be awful. And what about putting Ben back in the smithy? He worked with his father there the past few years."

Mary looked askance at her daughter. "He makes me nervous. He seems such an angry young man. Why would I put him in charge of pikes and axes? He's better out in the fields this spring when crops go in."

Polly rolled her eyes. "He apprenticed with his father and knows how to do the work. Ona brags on him all the time. And I am sure he would prefer it to field work," she added. "Wouldn't you?"

"Don't be crude." Mary frowned at her daughter's disrespectful tone and changed the subject. "I declare, this is the longest winter I can remember."

"Seems like there should at least be a crocus or two out there somewhere. I may go out and take a walk. Join me?" Polly asked.

Mary picked up her sewing. "No. Spring will come, daughter. Until then, you have time to sew and read here with me. It is too cold and wet to go out. We will ruin good shoes and catch our deaths."

Polly put her reading aside, stretched, and stood. "Then may I ride to see if there is a newspaper or any mail in town?"

Mary shook her head. "I will send Mr. Roper."

Polly crossed her arms and cleared her throat dramatically. "I simply cannot stay inside any longer. I am not a hothouse flower that you can keep in a vase on the table. Since I cannot wander outside on my own, may we at least pay a call on Mrs. Calhoun later this week? She did say that her niece would be visiting from Newport. It would get us out of the house."

Mary perked up. "Hmm, there are some things I would like to discuss with Floride, and I am sure that her niece is as bored as you are. I will send her a note."

Polly leaned over and planted a kiss on her mother's head. "Thank you, Mother. I don't like to sit inside all day."

Mary studied her daughter's face. Would she ever be comfortable with Polly out of her sight again? Polly was sixteen, nearly grown. She had looked into sending her to a finishing school at Mrs. Calhoun's suggestion, but the Upstate had nothing like the Virginia academies Mary remembered. The cost of boarding school in Charleston was prohibitive. And if Polly left, Mary would be truly alone.

Mary was tired and blamed the cold weather for her fatigue and malaise. She coughed into her handkerchief and was alarmed to see a spot of bright blood. She studied the stained fabric for a moment and then folded and pocketed the square.

— • —

UPSTAIRS, ONA MOVED SLOWLY AS SHE pulled sheets taut on Miss Mary's four-poster bed. Rheumatism was taking its toll on her shoulders and back, and she winced as she stood. She straightened up and gripped her lower back with both hands. Her aches and pains made it difficult to get her work done. Why wouldn't that woman let Cissie into the house? Cissie was young and strong and could be of such help in the house. Ona massaged her aching lower back and sighed. After her long workday, she would make up a potato poultice and lie down.

She missed Martin terribly, but her thoughts were on her son, now a man of twenty. Martin's death made him even more lonely and angry. She knew it was time for Ben to find a woman, and Cissie's arrival and quick marriage to George only made Ben angrier.

Ona briefly entertained the idea of asking Mr. Burgiss about a wife for Ben but quickly realized the folly. Why would he spend more money on another house slave when they were always short field hands in the summers? It would call undue attention to her son anyway. Mr. Burgiss might just as soon sell a valuable young slave man away for cash than spend good money to buy him a wife.

— • —

AFTER ANOTHER WEEK OF SPITTING SLEET AND SNOW, Polly fairly wanted to explode from boredom. The visit to Mi Casa had been a disappointment as Polly found Floride's niece to be haughty and dull. They did not make plans to visit again while the girl stayed there.

She sat in the parlor stitching on her sampler while Mary sewed nearby. With an exaggerated sigh, Polly stood and laid the sampler aside. Wandering into her father's library, she decided to look for a book to read. As she perused the collection, mostly legal volumes and works of poetry, her eyes locked onto a familiar title, Uncle Tom's Cabin, by Harriet Beecher Stowe. She let out a small gasp. There it was! She had forgotten all about the little book that she loaned to Ben years earlier and hastily pulled it from the shelf. She settled herself on the settee under the tall window and began to read.

Polly read late into the afternoon. As the shadows lengthened and then darkness outside closed in around Whitehall, she continued to read. She skipped supper. She lit a lamp and carried it, torch-like, up the staircase to her bedroom, where Ona had just stoked her fire with extra logs. She read deep into the cold winter night. She pictured the protagonist, the young runaway slave Eliza, crossing the frozen Ohio River, carrying her child in her arms, trying to escape a merciless slave trader. In her mind, she pictured Ona as Eliza. She thought of the evil Simon Legree and wondered how someone could be so vile. She imagined herself as Little Eva.

Early the next morning, the hands ate their meager breakfasts of corn pone, yams, and watered-down coffee. Wearing their threadbare coats and worn shoes, they prepared to brave the bitter cold to tend to the needs of her small family and their property. Polly closed the book, placed it on her bedside table, and buried herself under her thick quilts. Covering her face with her warm pillow, she began to weep.

Down the road, across the nation, and around the globe, over one million copies of this little book written by a northern preacher's wife fanned the flames of an ongoing battle that would soon become a war.

Chapter Six

August 1858

POLLY WAITED FOR THE TINY MOSQUITO TO LAND on the back of her hand before she smacked it with her other palm. She was bored and restless. The late summer humidity made her irritable. She stood and walked to the veranda railing, hoping for a breeze. Fanning herself with a political magazine, she wiped her brow and squinted at the sunbaked lawn. The land everywhere she looked was baked and dry. Leaves hung limp on fading trees. With the drought, the streams and creeks in the woods had all but evaporated, leaving muddy trickles in their wake. In the distance, Ben fitted a new wheel on the wagon and Duke stood by, ready to load the wagon with empty barrels for water. Their feet kicked up clouds of red dust.

Polly sighed deeply. Her mother did not notice. Mary sat in a rocker and perused an older issue of *Godey's*. "This heat is withering, Mother." She stood behind Mary and put her arms around the woman's shoulders. "May we go into town later? Maybe there is a letter from Father. We could get the latest issue of *Godey's*?"

Mary coughed and nodded absentmindedly but did not look up from her reading.

Polly tried again. "Did you write to Father about my idea?"

Mary sighed and put down her magazine. "No, Polly. I don't think I should bother him right now. When he returns home, I will broach the subject."

"Those girls are about my age. I envy them their chance to work and be useful," Polly said sullenly. "I've been reading a Betsy Chamberlain article, Mother. You would be amazed at what she writes about northern women in the textile mills. They are so independent and hard-working."

"Then you should be thankful that you are not a northern woman."

Polly ignored her mother's jibe and turned her attention back to the view from the veranda. She had grown into a beautiful young woman, nearly eighteen. Her dark curls and long-lashed brown eyes were striking. She had the tall bearing of her father and her mother's ivory skin. She was desperate to meet other young people and go to parties and church outings, but her mother was still reluctant to let Polly out of her sight.

She gathered her thick hair and twisted it up off her shoulders. The breeze on her neck cooled her only a little. Polly's gaze lingered on Ben. His arms were powerful and well-muscled, and she marveled at his ability to turn molten iron into a wagon wheel. There was something else about Ben, something in the far corner of her mind that nagged at her whenever she saw him. He had not spoken to her since she loaned him the book years earlier—not a word. His eyes never met hers. She knew that he must hate her for giving him such an incendiary book. What must he have thought? That she was taunting him about his lot in life? Suggesting he behave like Uncle Tom and accept inferiority, pleasantly serving his white masters? All she wanted to do was lend him a new book in thanks for teaching her to read. *A fine way to behave*, she thought. *How vulgar of me.* How could she tell him that she did not condone his lot in life? That if it were up to her, he wouldn't kowtow to her family at all.

These thoughts frightened her and she shifted from one foot to another restlessly. A bead of sweat trickled down between Polly's breasts. She decided to sit on the shaded front steps where she could catch at least some of the small breeze as it blew across the lawn. She plopped onto the bottom step and smoothed her skirts, her head propped in her hands. She watched a mosquito buzz near her ankle and swatted at it irritably.

She suddenly remembered running across the meadow with her brother, Caleb, tugging a homemade kite through bright blue summer skies. The thought made her wince, and she redirected her attention. She glanced at Ben again. She was exasperated. She really wanted to talk to him about the book. Maybe she could go to him in the smithy some time. She wished that she could invite Ben to sit with her on the shaded front porch and have a glass of lemonade. Abruptly, she stopped herself, embarrassed to have such thoughts towards a slave.

Polly stood to stretch when she heard the rumble of horses coming up the main road toward the farm. She put her hand to her forehead and squinted into the bright sun. As two riders turned into Whitehall's front drive, she glanced down at her sweat-soaked calico dress and put a hand to her messy hair.

"Who is it, Mother?"

"Go inside the house, Polly," her mother ordered sharply.

A bewildered Polly quickly ducked past her mother and into the house. She closed the wide front doors as two men rode up the drive.

— • —

THE CLATTER OF HORSES' HOOVES STIRRED UP clouds of red dust as they pulled to a halt near Ben and Duke. The slaves coughed and covered their mouths with their handkerchiefs.

"You boys!" Wilkins' voice made Ben's skin crawl. "Go git your master," he barked.

"He isn't here," Ben mumbled and turned to call his mistress when he heard the leather strap of a horsewhip lightly snap behind his back. Ben wheeled around, instinctively grabbing the whip in his hands. He jerked it hard.

Clay Wilkins leaned far off his horse and pulled Ben, still clutching the whip, towards him. His sour breath nauseated Ben. "Whoa there, boy! Don't you turn away from me. John, it looks like they got a uppity one here."

Ben froze where he stood, still holding the whip. Duke dropped to the ground in fear.

"You plan on doin' somethin' with my whip, nigger?" Wilkins growled, sliding from his horse.

"That's enough, Mr. Wilkins." Mary Burgiss was standing, clutching her shawl around her thin shoulders, pale as death. "Mr. Stone pays you to oversee his slaves. You have no business with mine," she called.

Ben scrambled out of Wilkins' reach.

"Mrs. Burgiss, I did not see you there. I do apologize for my overseer," John Stone smiled disingenuously at Mary from atop his horse. "Mr. Wilkins isn't one to allow any nigger sass, as you can see." He dismounted and walked toward the steps, hat in hand, but with a confident swagger that Mary found presumptuous in someone so young.

"One is always responsible for one's employees, Johnny," Mary stared down at John Stone, without acknowledging Wilkins at all. "I take it your father is not recovered from his illness or he would be here to apologize for the rude behavior."

Sam Stone was an old man now, bed-ridden, and sick. Mary had heard from Mr. Roper that he left decision-making to young John and the overseer. It was well known in the community that things at the Stone farm were not going well under John's youthful inexperience. John was their neighbor's only son. He seemed hell-bent on destroying his father's once-prosperous place before he turned thirty. Tom Roper had also apprised Mary of the abusive treatment of River Wood slaves, the poorly managed land, and the way John let Wilkins' decisions override his own father's wishes.

Mary's tone made John tense up with wounded pride and she stared at the young man with a level gaze. His smile quickly evaporated. "Mrs. Burgiss, is your husband home? We have some business to discuss with him. Slave problems."

She studied John, once an older playmate to her own boys long ago. Would they have grown so tall? Would their smooth baby faces have developed the same rough stubble as on John's chin? The thought of her boys as handsome young men nearly dropped Mary to her knees, but she recovered.

She lifted her chin and said firmly, "You'll have to wait for another time, Johnny. Mr. Roper has gone into Anderson. And Mr. Burgiss is in Walhalla on railroad business today."

"We can wait here for Mr. Roper to return," John said smugly.

Mary wrapped her shawl around her shoulders tightly, despite the heat. "That is out of the question. You may speak with me now if it is urgent or you may come back another time."

Neither man spoke. Mary stared down at the young man fiercely. "Then I am sorry that you rode all this way. Good day, Johnny."

Wilkins leaned and spat a stream of tobacco juice. "Mrs. Burgiss, I don't know if you have heard, but slave revolts are happenin' all over the state. We got a runaway at River Wood and reason to believe one of your slaves knows his whereabouts. They could be planning something here. They're like as to slit yer throats in the night. I think we could get some information from Cissie, the gal Mr. Burgiss bought from our place recently. Maybe we could take it up with her, ma'am . . . or with these ones here." Wilkins nodded his head towards Ben and Duke, who were standing quietly by the wagon. "You don't need to worry yourself over this ugly business. It ain't a woman's place."

Mary Burgiss again ignored Wilkins, turned to Stone, and said firmly. "Johnny, I am the mistress of Whitehall, so tell your hired man that it is indeed my place. I will not allow you to harass my slaves."

She glared at John. "I find that this heat has me quite fatigued, so I will ask you again to leave. Please give my regards to your father. I pray for his recovery." She touched her temple delicately with her veined hand. The thought of her slaves turning on her, perhaps murdering her in her own bed, sent shivers down her back, but she would not reveal her fears to this . . . this boy and his hooligan of an overseer.

As she turned to go inside, she came face to face with Polly standing in the doorway. Polly had changed into a pale pink day dress. Her hair was brushed and coiled into a soft chignon at the nape of her neck. Mary could swear her daughter had pinched her cheeks to get a rosy glow.

John smiled past Mary Burgiss, nodding his head slightly.

"Hello, Miss Polly," he said. He looked at her appraisingly and said, "I was going to ask your mother how you are faring in this heat wave, but I can see for myself that you are quite well."

Polly's cheeks reddened even more and she dropped her head.

Mary grabbed her daughter's arm stiffly, turned and pulled her inside the house, slamming the doors behind them. She heard Wilkins guffaw and John let out a long and appreciative whistle.

— • —

BEN WATCHED AS BOTH MEN MOUNTED their horses and rode down the dusty drive. He could barely keep from pounding on the front door and screaming out the truth of what he had seen so long ago at the Kemp place. He pictured Mary Burgiss taking his hands in hers and thanking him for saving her daughter. He imagined Polly, so beautiful in her pink dress, wrapping her arms around him in gratitude. He thought of her smiling up at him, finally remembering that he was the one who rescued her all those years ago. He imagined riding to the Stone farm with James Burgiss and telling Sam Stone that he'd seen his overseer and only son, John, murder the boys and the Kemps in cold blood. He knew that Mr. Burgiss would take his revenge on the men who had done such horrific things. Then he would grant Ben his freedom as a reward.

Freedom. Ben could think of little else since Polly had given him the book so long ago. Why did she want him to read it if not to let him know his cause was a just one? Did she secretly despise slavery like the abolitionists? Did she want to help him get to freedom?

To think that Miss Mary might contemplate turning Wilkins loose on Cissie and the others was frightening indeed. At supper that night, Duke told the hands about Stone's visit. The slaves shook their heads and collectively took it as a bad sign. Cissie had recounted stories of the terrible treatment that slaves endured at the Stone place, but no one ever thought that Wilkins might wreak havoc at Whitehall.

Duke chuckled. "Lawd, you shoulda seed Ben grab that whip. I could see the whites of his eyes, he was so mad. I thought that he was gonna pull Mr. Wilkins off his horse!"

— • —

ONA QUIETLY SEETHED AT THIS NEWS. There was no purpose in Ben aggravating the River Wood overseer.

"Lawd, y'all," Cissie murmured. "It were bad over there. If Wilkins come back, we in trouble. If it were my cousin, Franklin, that's done run off, he gonna get me killed fo' sure. We best start prayin' and stay outta the way." She caressed her belly nervously with her hands, soothing the unborn infant she carried.

George patted his wife's shoulder. "Mr. Roper don't like Mr. Wilkins any more than you do, Cissie. He ain't gonna let that man back onto Whitehall land."

Duke shook his head. "Mr. Roper may say one thing, but Miss Mary . . . who knows what she likely to do?"

Ona stayed silent, her eyes closed as she remembered her own private horrors at River Wood. She shivered and brought her mind back to the present situation. She tried to comfort the group. "Hush now, y'all. You got no cause to think Miss Mary or Mr. Roper gonna turn Wilkins loose on us. You heard what Ben said. She tol' him no. She a good woman at heart."

Cissie snorted. "She ain't a good nuthin'. Don't know why you so fond of her anyway."

Ona bristled. "She he'ped birth Ben. I woulda died otherwise."

Cissie ignored Ona and continued, "I see'd young'uns go off with Mr. John and Mr. Wilkins, and they didn't come back. Either they was sold or worse, but they didn't come back to their mommas again. How is a woman to live after her babies is taken away like that?" Cissie moaned dramatically and drew her apron over her head.

Ona understood the horrific depth of this news and worried for her son more than ever. She knew that Wilkins had a dark soul and was capable of the worst a body could imagine but stirring a pregnant Cissie into a frenzy wouldn't help anyone. Calm thinking and a smart plan were necessary if Wilkins came back to Whitehall to rile things up again. She missed Martin so much. He would have known what to do.

— • —

MARY WOKE THE FOLLOWING MORNING with new resolve. If anyone was going to oversee Whitehall in her husband's absence, it would be its mistress, and it was past time to begin. The confrontation with John Stone and his overseer had infuriated her. If John thought he was going to be allowed to call on Polly, Mary would see otherwise. And as for that foul Wilkins ever laying a hand on her slaves at Whitehall, she knew where James kept a pistol, and she knew how to use it.

Mary called Roper to the house after her breakfast. The day started out warm again, but the stifling humidity held the hope of a passing thunderstorm later in the afternoon. She fanned herself with a book as the pair sat together on the front porch. A cool pitcher of tea sat on the table between them. The condensation trickled down the table leg into a puddle near Polly's dog, Jack. He laid at their feet, panting heavily, his grey muzzle and rheumy eyes a testament to his old age.

"I shall not have Mr. Wilkins on this property again, Mr. Roper. I detest that foul man. Will you see to it that Sam Stone knows this?"

Roper nodded. "Yes ma'am. I will go over there directly and pass your instructions on to John. Sam is quite sick. I don't expect him to make it through the summer." He paused tentatively. "I don't think their place will last. Besides the drought, they've got some big debts and real poor soil conditions. Soil won't even grow cotton."

"Is it true, Mr. Roper, that Johnny Stone drinks in town with Mr. Wilkins?" Mary asked. Tom looked surprised to see that Mary was aware of local gossip. He nodded.

Mary shook her head. "That boy had no kind of proper upbringing after Lena Stone died." She stood and leaned over the porch railing, studying her roses. They needed attention, like everything at Whitehall. "It really is a shame," she said absentmindedly. "Johnny must be twenty-six years old now . . . My darling Caleb would have been twenty-two this year."

Tom smiled at her. "Is that right?"

"Yes, Mr. Roper." Mary felt herself drift for a moment but caught herself. "It's a sad situation. John's a grown man. He should be able to reign in Clay Wilkins."

"They can get quite rough with their slaves. The last one that ran away? I say Godspeed," Tom said.

Mary sniffed. "You sound like an abolitionist, Mr. Roper." She flicked a beetle off a rosebush. "An overseer condoning runaways is not in the best interest of Whitehall."

Tom nodded, chastened. "Yes ma'am. But you don't need to worry about your slaves, Mrs. Burgiss. They aren't going to cause you trouble."

Mary sat down again wearily and closed her eyes. "So you say."

He changed the subject. "You know, there's also talk of Wilkins buying River Wood after old Sam passes."

Mary shook her head. "I don't like that man. And where is an overseer getting that kind of money?" She reddened in embarrassment. "I'm sorry. That was rude of me."

Tom smiled. "He bragged all over town the last time he had too much to drink. Said he had a deal with John."

Mary gripped the arm of the rocking chair so hard that her fingers went pale. She steadied herself and turned to Tom, smiling. "How we do need the rain, Mr. Roper. I daresay there isn't much left of the corn crop this year. Tobacco either."

Roper sipped his tea. "No ma'am. We're feeding hay to the stock already. The grass is dead. We've got mud in the wells again."

He looked out at the sere landscape. "Thank God, August is about gone. Cotton is soon ready. The hands will start soon in the east property. We will hopefully have it done in a few weeks' time if the weather holds. I wish we could pick it more quickly . . ."

"Pull Ben from the smithy," Mary ordered. "I don't like him so near the house anyway."

Tom looked at his boots before replying gently, "He's a good blacksmith. A good man. We have some tool repairs he needs to finish, ma'am, with all due respect. I'm waiting on two wheels and more nails. We're down to one working harrow." He paused and added, "If Ben is a problem, it would help me to know what he has done."

Mary stared up at her overseer and snapped, "Polly seems to have an inordinate interest in him, and I don't like it."

"I'll make sure he stays away from the house, Mrs. Burgiss. When the repairs are made, I'll put him in the fields with the other men if you like. He's a fast picker. Every year it seems that we barely get cotton picked before the storms return. Hopefully, our luck will hold out again this season."

Mary shook her head and gazed out at the brown lawn. "Mr. Roper, if there is one thing we are not, here at Whitehall, it is lucky." She stood and crossed the porch to the front door and turned back to Tom. "My husband wrote to you that his Irishmen cannot help us this year. Is that correct?"

Tom nodded as he stood. "That's right, ma'am. They are clearing blasting debris."

"There may be another way." Mary hesitated. "I may have a solution to our dilemma. Rather, my daughter suggested this. But you might think her idea has merit. The whole community thinks our hiring of white laborers is odd, but this could save us."

Tom narrowed his eyes and waited.

Mary began slowly. She paced back and forth across the front porch, explaining to her overseer Polly's bold idea for the cotton-picking season about to begin. For thirty minutes, Tom and Mary Burgiss debated the plan. She had the last word. He turned to go, hat in hand.

"There is one other thing, Mr. Roper. I want to give a party after the cotton is in. A belated birthday party, a debut of sorts for my daughter. She will turn eighteen. Have some men see to the gazebo across the lawn. It needs to be repaired and whitewashed. And these loose floorboards here need to be repaired."

Hands on her hips, she looked around as if seeing Whitehall for the first time in years. "Have Cyrus see to the roof leak over the kitchen house. Ona said it has ruined some of the staples. He did a fine job on the smokehouse roof. And find out what clothing Ezekiel and Duke might have that will work for helping at such an event. I would need them to see to the guest carriages and horses. I trust them. If they do not have anything without holes, I shall have to go to town for fabric."

Mary smiled and said, "I know this is a tall order out of the blue. Thank you, Mr. Roper. That's all for now unless you have other business to discuss." She coughed delicately into her handkerchief.

Despite her frailty, Tom Roper had not seen this much life in Mary Burgiss in years. "No ma'am. I believe you have made yourself clear."

"Very good. Then our meeting is adjourned." Mary nodded, before retreating into the cool of the dark house.

— • —

TOM SHOOK HIS HEAD AS HE STEPPED off the veranda. He reached into his waist pocket and withdrew a twist of tobacco, which he plugged into his cheek.

"Women . . . Good Lord and God Almighty," he muttered under his breath. He hoped Mary didn't expect him to dress up in livery and silver-buckled shoes, taking coats and serving guests at her gala. Still, he mused, it was nice to see the woman up and around, taking an interest in her own farm. He patted his horse's flank and stepped into the stirrups. "Looks like things are about to get real interesting around here." He spat a stream of tobacco juice onto the ground, clicked his tongue, and wheeled the horse toward the back acreage.

The hot sun continued to bake the land as Tom rode out to find George. The humidity was a thick blanket thrown over the countryside, and he took a long drink from his canteen. He thought of his conversation with Mary and cursed under his breath. James Burgiss had wanted to increase the planted acreage in cotton, so successful was his use of paid white labor, but white workers were soon unreliable when other work became available, and there was still cotton to pick. The plowing, planting, and harvesting took up the slaves' days from dawn to dusk each summer. Old Duke was getting up in years but did his best with tending to the livestock and making small repairs.

And this drought was taking its toll. It took two men going to the river twice a day and filling barrels just to keep enough water on hand for the people and the animals, with the wells drying up. And now he was supposed to hire white women? He would be made a laughing stock.

George and Duke were hauling debris toward a brush pile when Tom rode up. George lifted a hand in greeting. While Tom was a paid white overseer, he was fair and just and had an easy way with the slaves. They knew they were luckier than most. The hands were doing the best they could with the Burgiss land, and Tom knew it. Mr. Burgiss was an important man in the district, but he didn't seem to understand running a cotton farm. Tom knew that the men were having a tough time tending to a place the size of Whitehall, but they were not punished for it.

"Howdy, boys," Tom said amiably. "How long you got left on this clearing? I got a new list of chores you'll have to get on soon."

"Yessuh." George nodded. "We about got it all hauled. Don't expect you want us to burn it yet?" He wiped his sweaty face on his shirtsleeve.

"Hell, no." Tom chuckled. "The whole place is turning to a tinder box." He shifted in his saddle and looked at his foreman. "But tell Ben to get that harrow repaired and get on those nails. He needs to repair the kitchen door hinge next. Miss Mary has plans. Have someone repair those loose floorboards on the front porch of the big house and in the gazebo. You'll need to send Cyrus to repair a roof leak there too, so let me know what supplies he will need. Duke, see to whitewashing the gazebo, and I mean get it as clean and white as a wedding chapel. The Burgisses are throwing a party right after we pull in the cotton."

The men looked at each other and then Tom.

"Miss Mary?" asked George. "A party?"

"Damn straight," answered Tom. "And after you get those chores done, I'm sure we've got a lot more to tend to. George, tell the women to be up at the big house at her teatime. Miss Mary wants to discuss a menu." He turned his horse and then stopped. "And don't be surprised if she sends Cissie to take your measurements for some clothes. Something to wear up to the house on party night."

Tom sighed heavily and cursed under his breath. He kicked his horse and trotted off toward the Anderson road.

— • —

POLLY WAS BESIDE HERSELF. "A party? Really? Oh, how wonderful!" Polly clapped her hands. "Here at Whitehall?"

Mary smiled. "There is so much to do. There is a guest list to consider, a menu, and of course, new dresses to order." Mary patted the spot next to her on the settee. "Come and sit, Polly. We have a great deal to decide."

Polly could barely contain her excitement. A new gown, musicians, young people to meet, and a chance to dance with that handsome John Stone were almost too much to think about. Just remembering the way he had looked at her the day before made her cheeks flush.

"When?" Polly asked. "Certainly not during cotton picking?"

"Next month, after the cotton is all in. A little late, but we will celebrate your birthday in style," Mary said. "I'm sorry that it cannot be a true debut, dear, but—"

"I don't care about being a debutante, Mother," Polly interrupted. "That was always your dream—not mine."

Mary ignored Polly's comment and continued, "We will invite Floride Calhoun and the Clemsons, of course." She leaned in conspiratorially and added, "That should set the tone for the evening. The Pickens, the Jones family summering from the coast, and the families along Pendleton Road. I believe there are three new places along that road since the boys' . . ." Her voice trailed off.

Polly was unwilling to lose the moment. "Oh, Mother, thank you. It will be wonderful! Will Father be home? Can we have musicians? And what about the Stones? Of course, they're invited."

Mary looked at Polly. "Your father returns at the end of the month. I will get a letter to him and tell him of our plans." Mary continued, "I do not think Sam Stone is up for traveling. I heard he is on bed rest and does not have long." She shook her head.

Polly looked down and smoothed her skirts nervously. "But we should ask John Stone, shouldn't we?"

Mary saw her daughter's blush and was firm. "Polly, I don't think Johnny Stone should be invited. He is crude and disheveled, and I hear he has taken to drinking with that overseer of his in town." She continued, "There will be other young men who may attend, closer to you in age, to be sure. Why, I believe the Calhouns' son-in-law will be entertaining house guests from Europe at Fort Hill at that time. It would be perfectly stylish to have European guests at our party!" Her attempt at redirecting the conversation was obvious to her daughter. "And Dr. Adger's son, Ward, may be home from medical school then."

"I am so glad to have a party that I don't even care who comes!" Polly laughed. She would certainly miss the handsome young John Stone, but clearly, seeing him would make her mother uncomfortable. After all, he had run around with her brothers years ago. His presence would no doubt remind her mother of the boys. Besides, a party at Whitehall, whether or not John was invited, was a rare and exciting possibility, and one that she would not jeopardize for the world.

Mary scanned the list in her hand. "Now go find Ona. She knows what we have in the springhouse and cellar, and I need an accounting."

Polly hurried outside, smiling. It was so nice to see her mother in a cheerful mood. A party! The thought thrilled Polly, and she fairly bounced toward the kitchen despite the oppressive heat.

As she rounded the corner of the house, she collided with someone coming from the other direction. Tin buckets and tools went flying. "Oh!" Polly shouted as she landed on her hands and knees, a small cut already oozing on her wrist.

"Miss Polly, I'm so sorry." Ben stooped to help the girl up. "Are you hurt? I didn't see you coming."

"No, I realize that," Polly said sharply, as she straightened her skirts and swiped at her dirty cuffs. She examined her wrist and blotted it with her sleeve.

"Ma'am." Ben nodded and touched his hat. He began to gather up his tools. The pair began to walk to the kitchen house, awkwardly trying to avoid each other despite the same destination.

Finally, Polly broke the silence as they walked. "Ben, is there something you need?"

Ben shook his head and kept going. "No ma'am, Miss Polly. I'm headed to the kitchen to fix the door hinge."

Polly felt her cheeks warm. "Oh. I am going there for Ona."

Ben nodded silently.

"Ben," Polly blurted. "When I gave you that book, *Uncle Tom's Cabin*, years ago, I had no idea what it was about. And I was so young. I only read it recently myself."

Ben didn't say anything but quickened his pace. Polly stepped in front of him and blocked his path. "I apologize. I would not have given you something like that had I known the subject. I . . . I am sorry."

Ben shrugged and walked around her. "No need to apologize, Miss Polly," he said glibly over his shoulder. "Mama took that book right back to the big house when she saw I had it. So whatever you're apologizing for, no need." He looked straight ahead and adjusted the buckets and tools in his arms as he walked.

"It was about a heroic slave named Tom," she began. "He saved a little girl."

Ben kept walking, eyes forward.

"It was about slavery," Polly continued, scurrying to catch up. "And how it is a bad thing. I honestly thought you were angry about the book. I thought maybe it put notions in your head."

Ben stopped abruptly and wheeled around. "Notions in my head?"

"Y-yes," Polly stammered. "You know, ideas about running away or . . . worse." *Why on earth did I bring this up?* she wondered helplessly.

Ben looked at Polly, stone-faced. "Miss Polly, I don't need a book to put notions in my head. I already have all kinds of notions. About how it isn't right for one man to own another man. About how if I could just get myself north, I could be a free man and live the way I wanted. Earn my own money. Do you know how hard it is to work from sunup to sundown every day in someone else's barn and smithy and get nothing for it? And watch my mama work her fingers to the bone for white folks who don't pay her no mind? Oh, Miss Polly, yes ma'am. I have some notions."

Polly was surprised at the anger in his voice—and surprised that it didn't worry him at all to be speaking to his master's daughter this way. Polly stared at him, wide-eyed.

"Now, if it's alright with you, I have to fix a door hinge and see your mama about a bent garden gate." He stomped toward the kitchen, leaving Polly, mouth agape. Angry tears welled in her eyes. Her first instinct was to run and tell her mother what had happened, but guilt and shame at the truth of Ben's words quickly overshadowed the hurt.

— • —

THAT EVENING, TOM KNOCKED ON THE front door of the big house. Ona hurried off to find Mary, who returned just as quickly. "Yes, Mr. Roper. Do you have news?"

"Yes ma'am. I went to Mr. Sloan's new mill in Anderson, like you told me. Craziest thing I ever saw. Women and young girls are living in cabins out behind the factory, just waiting on mill work."

"Did you speak to Mr. Sloan himself?" Mary asked cautiously.

"Yes ma'am. They spin and weave from October until spring, and Sloan'll need everyone then, he said, but your hunch was right. There's not much going on now over a daily six-hour shift and he can't use them all quite yet. But he wants to keep them close. I was surprised at how many takers I had. And for less than those Irishmen, them being women. At least eight Pendleton Manufacturing women will be out here at dawn Monday to work the mornings. Sloan liked the idea of buying all your ginned and baled cotton direct if his own girls are the pickers. You made him a good deal."

"And they know to come with sun bonnets and canteens?"

Tom nodded.

"Splendid, Mr. Roper. We will surely spend less on labor than with the immigrant men. They're busier than ever with the railroad anyway. There will be a fine bonus in it for you." Mary's eyes were bright with excitement.

Tom grinned. "How in the world did Miss Polly think to ask about the mill women?"

Mary shook her head. "Mr. Roper, you wouldn't believe what ideas Polly gets from her newspapers and periodicals. She would be out there herself if I'd allow it."

Chapter Seven

IN HER CABIN, ONA BENT OVER THE FIRE, preparing cornbread for the evening meal. Her cornbread and cracklins were one of Ben's favorite suppers, and after his day of hard work, she knew he was famished.

"Ma, I think I could just about eat the whole skillet tonight. Miss Mary has us getting the grounds ready for her grand party. Seems every outbuilding needs work and the big house is falling to pieces, in her mind." He leaned back in the hard chair and sighed. The old chair creaked and groaned in rebellion.

Ben had grown into a handsome man. No mother could be prouder. Ona ached for him. She knew he should be married and living in his own cabin. At 22 years old, he should have started a family of his own by now. She saw the way his eyes glanced up and down at Cissie when no one else was looking.

Ona patted the golden crust, satisfied that the cornbread was done. She carefully took it from the fire and set the hot skillet on the hearth. "Let's give that a few minutes to cool, and then we eat."

Outside, there was a far rumble of thunder. Ona pulled a chair close to the table and looked toward the ceiling in prayer. The only other pieces of furniture in the room were the two beds, and they would need to be moved before the rain came because of the leaky roof. There was never any free time for Ben to repair it.

Thunder rolled outside the cabin. "I hope that rain is coming this way. I'm about fed up with running the forge and hauling water from the river twice a day," Ben said. He picked up a piece of wood he had been whittling on, a small rattle for Cissie's baby. Martin had shown him how to whittle all manner of whimsical figures and Ona knew he still had a collection of them under his bed.

She frowned. "I been prayin' fo' rain. Mebbe a gully-washer of a storm will put this party off a while. Miss Mary has me doin' all the cookin' fo' it. An' Cissie's baby is comin' any time now . . ."

"What's troubling you tonight, Ma?" Ben asked. He looked at Ona fondly. "You worried about John Stone coming back? He isn't going to cause problems for you, I promise."

Ona sat down next to Ben and stared into the flickering fire. To the end of her days, she would regret what she was about to say, but she was bound and determined to say it. "Ben, I have to tell you somethin' important."

Ben stopped whittling. "What is it, Ma?"

"You ain't gonna like it, but it been weighin' on me a long time." Ona inhaled and paused to gather strength. She exhaled a lengthy breath. "Martin wasn't yo' real daddy." Ona put her small hand over Ben's. "I married Martin when I came as a new slave here at Whitehall. I loved Martin. An' he raised you as his own son. We couldn't have no babies together. But I was 'spectin' you before I met him—when I was at River Wood."

Ben jerked his hand away. "What do you mean—Martin wasn't my father? Was it one of the River Wood hands?"

Ona saw the rage building behind her son's brown eyes.

"Is it that toothless old man who brings Mrs. Calhoun in her fancy carriage? I've seen him looking at you. Does everyone know his name but me, Ma?" Ben spat angrily.

She reached for him but he pulled away and stood. He leaned against the hearth with both arms, his back toward Ona. Outside, rain began to fall on the parched ground.

"No, no, son. He wasn't no slave." Ona swallowed hard. "It was Sam Stone. I was so young, and he took whichever slave girl he fancied, any time he wanted to. He was the master. It's why I am so afraid now. Cissie is right about what goes on there. Miss Mary tol' me Mister Sam is dyin.' Who's to say what could happen if he tells his boy John about you, an' John decides to take you back as his slave." Ona could not stop the tears spilling down her cheeks.

Ben turned back to his mother. He pointed the sharp blade in her direction menacingly. Ona could see so much anger and betrayal in his eyes. "How could you have kept this from me all this time?" he asked.

Ona dropped her head to the rough wooden table, crying out in a hoarse whisper. "Oh, Lawd, please help us. I'm so sorry, Ben. Martin was a good father to you." Her voice trailed away as sobs wracked her body. She finally looked up. "Can you forgive me?"

Ben brought the knife down hard, driving it into the table to its handle, so hard it made Ona wince. And then he began to cry. He eased down onto the floor next to his mother's chair and leaned against her lap. Ona draped her thin arm across Ben's shoulder and watched the tears flow from her grown son's face.

The rain outside began to come down harder, as lightning flashed and thunder clapped. Rain dripped through the leaky roof. It ran in rivulets through holes yet to be patched, splashing down to the floor, God's tears washing away the dust and the heat and the punishing drought.

— • —

THE NEXT MORNING WAS SUNDAY, and Ona woke early to the sound of someone hammering on her roof. She wrapped the thin blanket around her shoulders and stepped outside. Last night's rain had washed the air clean and fresh. There was just a hint of the autumn to come on the breeze. It would be a beautiful morning to rest.

Ben was crouched on the roof, patching holes with strips of tree bark. She silently thanked God that he had not run away and hurried back into the cabin without saying a word. She set to work scraping last night's corn bread out of the skillet. She would save the stale bread for lunch, but a fresh pan for breakfast would make Ben happy. She put two strips of salt pork in the bottom of another pan and set them both on the fire. The hammering stopped and soon Ben appeared in the doorway.

"Ma, I'm sorry." The young man stood in front of her, head bowed. "I had no right to treat you like that."

Ona wrapped her arms around the young man. She sighed, "Son, you have every right. I shoulda told you years ago. But how do you tell a boy somethin' like that?" They sat down at the tiny table where they had shared meals together since Ben was barely able to walk. "Martin was yo' Pa from the day you was born. He loved you like his own. We was blessed to have him."

"I know. He'll always be Pa. But . . ." Ben looked unsure of how to proceed. "Sam Stone? Does he know I'm his son?"

Ona nodded her head and declared, "I hated that man. He had his eye on me the moment I came to River Wood. I was just a girl. I tried to stay away from him. He liked the young gals. Everyone knew it . . . But as bad as Stone was to take slave girls to his bed, that Wilkins is a much worse man. The things that happened to other slaves while I was there . . . he attacked little girls. He did things to boys. He tortured people just out of pure meanness. Ben, I was desperate. The only way for a young girl to avoid Wilkins was to . . . to be with Mr. Stone. Wilkins wasn't no fool. He knew better than to go after me because Mr. Stone favored me."

Ben looked down at Ona, his mouth set in a hard line.

His mother scowled. "I know it was wrong, but I did it to get through that horrible place. And then when I got pregnant, I was so stupid. I thought that Mr. Stone would take care of me, would see to it that you had good things like his white son did. Naw, he sent me over to Whitehall as soon as I tol' him I was havin' his baby. Made a present of me to the Burgisses. Didn't matter to him—he was on to the next gal. Didn't need Mrs. Stone to find out. I wasn't sorry to go. I was lucky I got to leave before Wilkins heard. Whitehall is a heaven on earth compared to River Wood. I got away from Mr. Wilkins and Mr. Stone, and I got you as my baby boy. An' best I can tell, no one else know who yo' daddy was."

Ona smiled and touched Ben's cheek. "But you see why I was afraid to tell you. After what you saw at the tradin' post all those years ago, I couldn't let that story get out. Wilkins woulda killed us. I know it. Mr. Stone mighta thought I was tryin' to get at him. I'm sorry, Ben. I'm real sorry."

— • —

BEN CLINCHED HIS JAW AND THEN RELAXED. He understood that the lives of so many slaves were so much worse than his own. A girl could be raped, a boy whipped to death, a mother could watch as her child was ripped from her arms and sold away, a wife could watch her beloved husband die for lack of medicine easily available to white folk. He would forgive his mother for hiding the truth of his paternity, but the truth made the secret inside so much harder to bear.

He thought back to the book that Polly had loaned him years ago. He had indeed read it. He hated it. Did she expect him to behave like saintly Uncle Tom? To bow and scrape and befriend his young mistress? Was she telling him that she believed slavery a great moral wrong? Or that he should accept his lot in life?

They ate their meager Sunday breakfast in silence. After they had eaten, Ona pulled the worn Bible from under her bed and handed it to Ben. Their Sunday morning routine had seemed strained after Martin's death, but today both mother and son looked forward to reading scripture together. It seemed like the right way to bring them some peace and renew their strength as a family

— • —

MONDAY DAWNED HOT AND HUMID. Tom Roper stood outside his cabin and looked up at the sky. Off to the west, he noticed clouds already building. It would rain again later today. The creeks were up following the weekend rainstorm, and Roper hoped that the wells would be bringing up fresh water soon. The drought might be over, thank God. Getting water from the river had cost several hours of labor every day for weeks.

George called out to Roper as he approached from the slave quarters. "Mr. Tom, it's a good mornin' for pickin' cotton. We can be off and pickin' in the east patch. Bolls are open and ready to go. It lookin' like a good crop, yessuh," He stood in front of his boss, hat in hand. "You wanted to tell me something about the new workers, suh?"

"George, I want you and the boys to stay on that south end today. We've got some new pickers coming . . . white ladies . . . headed out here this morning. To pick. Give them the east." He seemed to stumble over his words as George stared at him, slack-jawed.

"Suh?" George didn't understand. "White women?"

"Mrs. Burgiss hired women from Pendleton Manufacturing Company to come out and pick. Got about a dozen of 'em coming today on a hay wagon. Now you hear me. You boys stay on that south end and let those women work the north and east fields today. Stay clear. I don't want a one of you near those women." Tom pointed his finger at George. "If there's trouble, I want all of you boys as far away from those gals as possible, you hear me?"

George nodded. "Yessuh."

"Dammit, I wonder how many will make it the full week?" Tom muttered, as he stepped past George and headed toward the front gate, grumbling to himself the entire time about cotton, women, and their bull-headedness.

— • —

SEVEN DAYS IN, TOM ROPER SAT STUDYING a ledger at a table near the barn, after paying the last of the women their wages for the week. He watched as the wagon of exhausted pickers pulled away and rumbled toward the road.

Moments later, Mary came riding toward him on Polly's horse. Despite riding sidesaddle, she appeared at ease and comfortable with the animal. Before Tom could stand to assist her, she had neatly dismounted and strode toward him. Her cheeks were rosy and her eyes bright. She looked at him expectantly. "Well?"

Roper sighed and shook his head. Mary looked downfallen. Seeing her expression, he laughed. "Oh no, ma'am. You misunderstand me. Mr. Sloan's girls . . . ," he stammered. "Those gals picked cotton faster than I expected and made you money."

He extended the large brown ledger. He opened it and pointed to a page of neatly written figures. "The field hands average two hundred twenty pounds a day over the course of a season. The women are picking about eighty on average, clean as a whistle. Since you promised them a cash bonus for speed, and because there are so many of them, they are moving through the cotton fast. They need the money. I've never seen such a thing. They've got small hands, and they pick it clean. Just talking away the whole time! So I put Cyrus and some boys on the gin." He closed the book with a slap.

Mary smiled. "Mr. Sloan has been very happy with what has come to the mill so far."

Tom nodded. "Pendleton Manufacturing is buying our cotton at two cents less per pound than slave-picked cotton is getting at market. And we aren't shipping it down the river, so we're actually doing fine. You may have the fastest picking in the district for the acreage, and the cleanest cotton. You'll come out ahead of last year, I think. Your daughter was smart to recommend those gals."

Mary nodded proudly. "I admit that I am surprised, Mr. Roper. My Polly has some wild ideas. She will be pleased to hear it has been a success. She so wants to be useful. And it does seem a balm for my own nerves." She put a boot into the stirrup and easily hoisted herself into the saddle. She smiled at him warmly and kicked at her horse, urging the mare back toward the barn.

— • —

SEVERAL DAYS LATER, TOM HEADED TOWARD the big house with mail he had picked up in Anderson. He looked forward to discussing farm business with Mrs. Burgiss, for she was proving herself a savvy businesswoman, and she wasn't half bad to look at now that she was taking care of herself. The cotton crop had come in more quickly than ever before and with a hefty bonus for Tom. The Pendleton Manufacturing women proved to be adept cotton pickers, motivated and eager to work hard, resulting in a contract with Mr. Sloan for the coming year.

Tom sighed. He knew that this conversation would be about her upcoming party but felt that party preparations were beneath the position of overseer. He removed his hat, smoothed his hair, and climbed the wide front steps to knock on the door.

He heard shuffling feet, and soon Ona was there. She opened the door. "Yessuh, Mr. Tom. Come on in. She be right down."

"Mornin', Ona. How's that rheumatism?"

"Well, it's a little better. Thank you fo' askin'"

He stood in the front hall and watched as the woman shuffled off. He looked down at the floorboards and tested a loose one with his boot. It squeaked and gave a bit. He called after her, "Remind Ben that these floorboards need to be fixed today. He better finish those nails."

Mary Burgiss appeared at the top of the stairs. "Mr. Roper, I have so much to discuss with you about our little party. Oh, I see you have mail." She descended the stairs and held out her hand. For a moment, Tom was too stunned to hand her the worn envelope. She looked like a different woman. Her hair was pinned up and neatly coiffed. Her dress was new and very flattering to her slender figure, and her face was bright and smiling. Silver earrings dangled from her ears. "Mr. Roper, the mail?"

"Oh, I'm sorry, ma'am. You seem to be in good spirits, Mrs. Burgiss." He handed her the envelope. Mary looked at it and exclaimed, "It's from my husband! Do follow me to the parlor, Mr. Roper, while I read it quickly. Then we shall talk." She showed him to a comfortable sofa and passed in front of him to sit nearby, not looking up from the envelope. As she passed, he caught a whiff of perfume and was startled.

Mary opened the envelope carefully and began reading. She read quietly for a minute and then looked up, smiling. "My husband is coming home in time for the party!"

Chapter Eight

October 1858

THE MORNING OF POLLY'S PARTY DAWNED CRISP AND COOL, a perfect October day. The sky outside her window was bright blue and cloudless, surely a good omen for the big event.

Mary had hired several of the Pendleton Manufacturing girls to serve and clean up during the party, and they were busily polishing silver and dusting furniture. Cissie, who could barely walk with the weight of her impending delivery, struggled to prepare all of the dishes her mistress desired. Mary seemed oblivious to Cissie's discomfort and clearly expected the woman to attend to cook and serve alongside Ona and the white women.

Polly lay in her bed, stretching and luxuriating in a new feeling—a young lady awaiting a party in her honor. She gazed at the gown hanging from her wardrobe. It was a beautiful dress from Charleston, six ruffled tiers in pink and white, with tiny rosettes across the neckline and shoulders, and a wide satin sash. The waist was tiny. The skirt required several crinolines and would be the widest skirt at the party if Mary had anything to do with it. Polly smiled. The list of handsome young men who would be attending wasn't long, but she was to be the center of attention. There was a knock on her door and Mary entered, carrying a small velvet box.

"Good morning, dear." Mary smiled and sat on Polly's bed. "I have something for you. This—" An abrupt coughing fit stopped her mid-sentence. She coughed several times into a handkerchief that she carried with her all the time and quickly balled it up after it had touched her lips. "Pardon me."

Polly frowned. "Mother, I am very worried about your cough. You have had it for months. And you're bringing up blood. Maybe you should have Dr. Adger over to see you? You are ill."

Mary waved away Polly's concern and said, "You sound like your father. Hush now. It is the ragweed season, Polly, and nothing will help that until the first frost. As I was saying, this is a little something that I thought it was time to give you."

Polly opened the box and was surprised to find, not jewelry as the lovely box suggested, but a small leather pouch. She looked at her mother quizzically and loosened the strings on the pouch. She poured the contents into her palm and realized she was holding the only money she had ever seen, ten gold coins.

"Mother, this must be a fortune." Polly felt the coins warm in her hand.

Mary leaned forward and closed Polly's hand over the coins. "It is not a fortune, but it is a nice sum, an insurance policy of sorts. I suggest you tuck it away. Hopefully, you will never need it. Whitehall is doing well now and we are comfortable. However, I remember the feeling that everything I needed would have to come from your father, from what Whitehall could produce, and it was frightening in the beginning. When you marry one day, this little nest egg should ensure that you are never completely reliant on the cotton economy, on the whims of a husband with a grand scheme, on weather, and the boll weevil. Lay this by and keep it for an emergency.

And Polly, let us keep this between us. No need to tell your father. A woman is allowed to have her secrets."

She smiled and hugged Polly tightly. "My dear, how you have grown. A beautiful young lady in the blink of an eye. I am so proud of you. I neglected you for so long. I was . . . distraught . . . after your brothers died."

Polly delighted in this rare show of affection from her mother and returned her hug. "Mother, I promise to keep this in a safe place. I don't know what I shall ever do with such a sum but thank you!"

Mary smiled and stood. "Perhaps a wonderful trip someday." She coughed again and continued, "I will have Ona draw a bath for you. It will be time to dress for the party before you know it."

Later that afternoon, as early dusk settled over the rolling hills around Whitehall, slaves lit lanterns that illuminated the length of the drive. A stringed quartet arrived by carriage. Mary directed them to set up in the parlor. Furniture had been removed and carpets rolled back for dancing. They began to tune their instruments and the sounds sent a wave of excitement throughout the house. The dining room table was laden with delicious food, and the wines were uncorked to breathe.

While her parents dressed for the party, Polly descended the staircase in her gown, feeling the picture of southern grace and beauty. Her chestnut hair fell in tight ringlets that Ona had fussed over with the hot curling iron. The voluminous skirt was difficult to navigate and she hoped to practice her dance steps prior to the arrival of guests. Her gloved hand shook as she gripped the banister.

As she reached the bottom of the staircase, she heard a chuckle coming from further down the candlelit foyer. She turned around to see Ben, dressed in brocaded livery, covering his mouth with a gloved hand in an attempt to hide his laughter.

Polly's face turned beet red and she faced him, her hands on her hips. "And what, may I ask, is so funny?" she demanded, looking up at him.

Ben's brown eyes crinkled. "You are—in that outfit," he said in nearly a whisper. "That skirt is so big that you could hide two mules under it and not find them for days. And how are you going to eat anything? They've got you trussed up so tight, you may faint." Ben put his hand to his brow and pretended to swoon. There was a playful glint in his eyes that Polly was relieved to see.

She approached the large hall mirror and stared at herself in despair. "Is it such a silly dress? I feel like I'm a decoration on top of Princess Vicky's wedding cake. Mother assured me it is the latest style, but I can barely get through a door! And I cannot take a deep breath to save my life," she confided.

"I have never seen you in such a thing, that's all." He realized he had gone too far and tried to recover. "I'm sorry, Miss Polly." He nodded solemnly. "I just never thought of you all made up, a fancy lady. But you look real pretty. As always." Then he exploded into a peal of laughter and doubled over, tears streaming from his eyes. "You should have seen yourself coming down those stairs! I thought I was going to have to catch you before you hit the last one!"

A humiliated Polly stomped her foot and hissed, "Have you looked in the mirror at yourself, Ben? You look ridiculous, with that gold fringe on your shoulders and those white gloves. You look like a toy soldier." Ben's face fell and Polly stifled a laugh. "See? We both look silly, don't we?"

"Well, your mother—"

"Ben!" Ona's sharp voice interrupted their playful quarrel. "That's enough! How dare you talk to Miss Polly that way. Thank ya for bringin' in the hams. Now git on outside and wait for guests." She poked her finger in his chest and glared up at him. "You hear me, son?"

"Yes, ma'am." Ben turned abruptly and walked away, chuckling to himself.

"Miss Polly, I'm sorry 'bout that boy. He ain't been brought up with house manners and I'm sorry for that." Ona sighed and patted the tiers of ruffles on Polly's dress and exclaimed, "You look beautiful."

"I actually feel less nervous now," Polly smiled. "Ona, I've never seen you in a dress like that." Polly admired Ona's black cotton dress and white lace collar. "We do look fancy."

Ona nodded. "Well, I'm jes' glad to be wearin' a new dress is all I can say. But you—you look as pretty as a picture."

"Is Ben right? Is this pretentious? Will people laugh? I don't even know the guests, for the most part." Polly's nerves began to get the better of her. "It is difficult to breathe and to walk around. I did almost tumble down the stairs!"

"Nonsense, Miss Girl. You is the belle o' the ball and everyone gonna see just how grown up you is tonight. Ben had no right to say hurtful things to ya.' He jes' has a mouth on him and sometimes don't know when to stop talkin', is all." Ona shook her head. "Please don't complain to yo' mama."

"I think he might be right. This just isn't me." Polly sighed and continued to turn and inspect herself in front of the large mirror. "I feel like a bit of fluff, not to be taken seriously. And this skirt is enormous."

"Look at the most beautiful young lady in all of South Carolina." Polly heard a booming voice from the top of the stairs. She turned to smile up at her father as he descended the staircase, dressed in his finest suit of evening clothes. He smiled and reached for Polly's hands. "Let me take a look at you, my dear."

Polly twirled as best she could in the voluminous skirts and curtsied before her father playfully. "And look at you—the most handsome man in all of South Carolina!" She hugged her father tightly and smiled up at him, brown eyes shining. "I think this is the most exciting thing I have ever had happen to me. Thank you for my party."

James took Polly's face in his hands tenderly. "My dear, it brings me so much joy to see you and your mother happy. I know that my business takes me away quite a bit. That has been hard on you both. I promise that things with the railroad will ease soon enough, and I will be able to spend more time here at Whitehall."

Polly patted her father's cheek. "That would be the best present I could receive, Father." It truly was turning out to be the happiest day of her life.

Shortly, the first guests began to arrive. James and Mary Burgiss welcomed their company warmly. Slaves scurried to remove empty carriages and horses to the stable at the back of the home. Several Pendleton Manufacturing girls, in black serving attire, went about with platters of cheeses, meats, and breads. Cissie, who was clearly in some distress, served glasses of wine and champagne while the music from the stringed quartet drifted throughout elegantly appointed rooms of Whitehall for the very first time. As Mary had hoped, Floride Calhoun, the Clemsons, the Adgers, the Lattas, and the Joneses arrived with well wishes and small gifts for Polly.

Polly was introduced to several young ladies from town and neighboring plantations. She stood in a circle of women trading local gossip and chit chat about the latest fashions. Ben stayed outside, assisting George with guests' horses and carriages. Once or twice, as she saw departing guests to the door, Polly looked for him in the dark, but to no avail. He could have been any of the bowing and scraping slaves outside assisting her guests, not the proud and sharp-tongued young man she knew him to be.

Polly watched her mother weave through the crowd expertly, seeing to it that introductions were made and that drinks and small plates were filled and refilled. In her burgundy silk, Mary was breathtaking. James Burgiss stood with a group of men, discussing politics and the cotton markets but watching his wife proudly as she moved around the room.

The evening progressed and the guests continued to imbibe in Burgiss champagne and other spirits. One man began to accompany the stringed musicians on the grand piano. A rollicking Virginia reel soon had the young people taking up partners to dance, and Polly found herself a partner to young Ward Adger, the local doctor's son home from the College of Charleston. Polly blushed and smiled as he led her through the elaborate steps. She was soon caught up in the dance and whirled around gaily, catching the arm of each man as it was offered. Suddenly, she was standing face to face with John Stone, his hands holding hers tightly, as the reel ended in a burst of applause and laughter.

"John!" She gasped. "Mr. Stone, I mean." He was more handsome than she remembered, tall and sandy-haired, with piercing blue eyes that made her stomach churn.

He smiled at her and chuckled. "You seem surprised to see me, Miss Burgiss." He lifted her gloved hand to his lips.

Polly felt her stomach flip and she pulled her hand away. She knew that her mother had not invited him and wondered at his arrogance in showing up anyway.

"Ah, my daughter." James was before them, placing his arm around Polly. "Have you been properly introduced to our young neighbor, John Stone? His father is an old friend of the family, Sam Stone, of River Wood. Sam gave us Ona, why, I think it was twenty years ago, as a most generous welcome gift." He clapped the young man on the shoulder. "John, I am sorry to hear of your father's continued ill health, but I am heartened to see him here tonight."

Burgiss turned to his daughter. "Polly, the Stones have been good neighbors since your mother and I came down from Virginia. And Sam went out of his way to help us when—when your brothers died."

Polly noticed that John's face paled at the mention of her brothers. He would have been older than Caleb and Joshua, but she knew he would have remembered their grisly deaths. She wondered at her father's lavish praise of the Stone family when her mother clearly disliked young John. Like pieces of a puzzle clicking into place, Polly realized that her mother's disdain must certainly have to do with John being only a bit older than Caleb and Joshua. Seeing him was, of course, a painful reminder of her lost sons.

John regained his composure. "Thank you, Mr. Burgiss, for personally inviting me to your party. I wouldn't have missed this affair." John smiled at Polly before turning back to Burgiss. "When you saw me in town last week and asked if I was coming, I confessed that I must have misplaced any invitation Mrs. Burgiss so graciously extended. My apologies, again. My father's illness has resulted in much disarray in our personal matters."

Polly knew his words were for her benefit. "We would not have dreamt of missing the birthday celebration for this lovely young lady. Seventeen, is it?" When his eyes met hers again, she dropped her head shyly. Why he had this effect on her, she couldn't understand. According to her mother, he was a scoundrel, a drunkard, and a ladies' man. But perhaps her mother was mistaken. Clearly, her father thought highly of the family. Polly was well aware of the other guests staring at both of them, making assumptions about the conversation between the young man and his host's daughter.

"Eighteen," she said softly. She straightened her shoulders and turned to address her father. "Father, I would love to meet the elder Mr. Stone. Will you introduce me?"

"Mr. Burgiss, allow me to make the introduction, please?" John extended his arm.

"Why of course, John. Thank you." James nodded toward Polly and she hesitantly took John's arm. He steered her through the crowded parlor into the smoke-filled library where a group of men stood around an elderly gentleman seated by the fire. The frail-looking man was slumped in his chair and appeared tired and quite ill.

The men quieted their conversations and turned when Polly entered on John's arm. Each man gave a slight bow in turn as she passed. John led her to the old man, who looked up with rheumy eyes that still gave the hint of once being as blue as his young son's.

"Father, it gives me great pleasure to present to you, Miss Polly Burgiss, the belle of the ball."

Sam Stone looked up at Polly and then at John, nodding approvingly. "My dear, forgive me for not standing. My eyes and ears may still work sometimes, but my old legs gave out a long time ago. Will you sit and chat with me?" His warm tone quickly put Polly at ease, and she sat down across from him on the settee. The man continued, "They gave me this stick here, but it doesn't do me any good when I am already sitting down." He shook the ebony cane at his son playfully.

"It is a pleasure to meet you, sir," Polly said. "Thank you for coming to our party this evening."

"You're most welcome, my dear. Although, this isn't the first time we have met."

Polly tilted her head to one side.

"Why, your family came to pick a pup from a litter of hunting dogs. Your brothers ran around the lawns playing at Indians, whooping, and hollering. I remember you sitting on the lawn, maybe six or seven years old, pups crawling all over you like flies to honey. You picked out the runt of the litter." The old man laughed. Polly could see John stiffen.

"That must have been my dog, Jack." She smiled. "He died a few years ago. He was a good dog, a fine companion in my childhood." She sighed and looked down at her hands folded in her lap. The chatter in the room had quieted when Mr. Stone mentioned her brothers.

"Well, you'll have to come to River Wood again and pick out a new pup. John tells me we have a litter ready to wean any day now." Sam looked up at John proudly.

"Thank you, Mr. Stone," Polly said. "I don't know if there is another dog out there that could rival old Jack in my affections. I thank you for your offer, though."

"It would do an old man good to have a pretty young visitor again, so I hope you'll think it over, my dear." Sam blotted perspiration from his upper lip with his handkerchief and closed his eyes. "And now, if you will forgive me, I believe my son and I will depart. Thank you for having us. I haven't been to a party in years. It was lovely to see you again. I wish you all happiness." The twinkle in his eyes seemed genuine. John moved to assist his father in standing.

Polly stood. "It was nice to meet you, sir."

John bowed. "Good evening, Miss Burgiss. If you change your mind about a pup, you have only to let me know. And it really would do my father good to see you again." John turned to look down at Sam, and for a moment, she glimpsed real affection between the two men, despite the rumors.

Polly felt her heart soften toward John. Perhaps her mother was wrong. The man seemed a doting son. He'd lost his own mother as a child. His father was now quite ill. He had no siblings to help him run the farm. She felt the heat of a blush crawl up her throat as she watched him with his father. How would it feel to have John gaze at her so affectionately?

Polly watched from the entrance hall as John assisted his father down the front porch steps to their waiting carriage. He glanced back at Polly and gave her a sly wink that made her cheeks flush deeply. Old Sam was helped into the carriage, while Ben held the horses steady. In the flickering lamplight of the brightly lit porch, Polly could see Ben glaring at both men, nostrils flared. She had never seen such a look of hatred in his eyes before. She had overheard the rumors from Cissie, tales of slave abuse at the hands of the Stone family. Clearly, Ben had heard them, too. *The abuse must have been perpetrated by their overseer,* Polly reasoned, *for John and his father seem so gentle and kind.*

The rest of the evening passed quickly. The last guests, the Chambleys, lingered at the front door chatting with Polly's parents after midnight. Polly stifled a yawn and craned her neck around fat Mrs. Chambley for a view of Ben. He was nowhere to be seen. Only Duke stood quietly by the carriage, calmly stroking the horse's neck, and waiting patiently for its owners or driver to release him from duty.

Polly sighed and turned around in time to see Ona pulling Cissie quickly toward the rear of the house and out the back door towards the slave quarters. She hurried to catch up.

"Ona!" She called from the back porch stoop, watching Ona and

Cissie disappear. "Ona!" Polly could hear Lisbeth Chambley laughing in the foyer at something her father had said.

"Where are you going?" Polly called. "Mama dismissed the Pendleton girls a while ago. You and Cissie must clean up this mess. Don't make her angry!"

"Miss Girl, this ain't no time to clean up yo' party," Ona shouted. "Cissie's done broke her birthin' waters. She havin' this baby now!" The two women ambled off in the night toward the slave cabins, Cissie clutching her belly and gasping for breath.

— • —

LATE THAT NIGHT, JAMES BURGISS SAT IN his library looking over the plantation's books, sipping a glass of whiskey and enjoying his pipe. The ledgers were in order. His daughter's party had been a success. He marveled at his wife's skill in managing the latest cotton crop, at her decision to hire the women who ended up being the fastest pickers in the district. He leaned back in his chair and sighed contentedly.

Suddenly, James clutched his chest in confusion. He grimaced, leaned forward, and shook his head in disbelief about what was happening. He tried to call out, but no sound came from his lips. He slumped onto the desk, knocking over the crystal glass. Whiskey spilled across the Whitehall ledgers, soaking the pages in golden liquid.

One soul left Whitehall in silence, and another arrived with loud wails and cries, as baby Silas announced his presence before dawn the next morning, waking the hands in their small cabins. Cissie and the baby were fine. George was a proud father. The Burgiss family quietly added another slave to their holdings.

Chapter Nine

December 1858

POLLY OPENED HER EYES IN THE DIM LIGHT OF A foggy morning and shivered in the cold. She debated whether to hop out of bed quickly and add a log to the fire but decided to pull the quilts more snuggly around her neck instead. She squeezed her eyes shut again. *This is the worst part*, she thought. Every morning she faced the split-second realization that her beloved father was gone, all over again.

The funeral had been rather grand. Townsfolk and acquaintances from across the state had attended and paid their respects. Polly recognized many of the people who had attended her birthday party so recently. Reverend Davis from the First Presbyterian Church had preached a fine eulogy that extolled her father's many good graces without enumerating his faults and promised that her father was at peace and with his beloved sons. A steady stream of statesmen and business leaders offered their condolences to Mary and Polly after passing the closed casket.

Mary sat stone-faced behind her ebony widow's veil, shocked into the realization that she was alone with a daughter to raise, her husband gone to join her beautiful boys. Polly chafed in her black crepe and bombazine, a readymade hastily ordered from town after the devastating discovery. She held her mother's hand throughout the service, and only released it as mourners began to pay their respects. Known only to Polly, Mary's other hand still clutched the morning telegram from James's father in Virginia, urging Mary to leave Whitehall and come back to Virginia with his granddaughter.

Polly stifled her own cries as her father's casket was lowered into the earth near the grass-covered graves of his two sons. Polly gripped her mother's waist tightly to keep Mary from fainting dead away. Both women scooped handfuls of soil and tossed them into the gaping hole before leaving the gravediggers to complete their task.

Letters and notes of condolence arrived at Whitehall following James's passing. Unbeknownst to Mary, Polly had received a tender note of encouragement from John Stone. He wrote of his sorrow for her loss and of how much he appreciated her kindness toward his father in his own illness. He wrote of offered aid and his hope to be of assistance to the women in the future. He'd asked to call on her when she was ready, and signed it "Yours, John." Her heart fluttered. She read it again, held it to her chest, and then tucked it away in her box of keepsakes.

Now, two months later, Polly still awaited her mother's decision on whether to leave Whitehall. Polly herself was torn. She had never been anywhere else—this was home. But at Whitehall, she was alone, far from town and people her own age. Seeing so many unfamiliar faces at the party had only made Polly realize how isolated she had been as a child at Whitehall. Her father's stories of his boyhood in Richmond had enthralled her. In Virginia, she would have extended family and friends, parties, and city life. She could be far away from the animal smell of the farm and the red dust and heat of sunbaked South Carolina.

But the memory of her mother's gut-wrenching sobs upon finding her husband slumped in his chair, and then the keening over James's dead body as he was prepared for burial, made Polly realize this had to be her mother's decision. How a widow woman and teenaged girl would maintain a cotton farm was beyond Polly's vision. She felt so lost, untethered. A single tear trickled down her cheek and she wiped it away quickly. No matter what Mary decided, Polly would support her decision. She would be strong for her mother. But then, what about John and this friendship that seemed to be the beginning of something more?

There was a timid knock at the door and Polly sat up, expecting Ona with her tea. "Come in," she said, wiping her nose with the back of her hand.

— • —

MARY ENTERED THE ROOM, WRAPPED IN A patchwork quilt and carrying a single candle.

"I wasn't sure if you were awake," she said softly. "May I come and sit with you?" Her long hair was still loosely braided and messy from sleep.

Polly nodded and pointed to the embers in the fireplace. "Will you add a log? I was too cold to get up." She smiled bravely.

Mary returned her smile and placed the candlestick on the dresser. She pulled several small logs from the metal bin near the hearth and added them to the fire. She stirred the embers with the iron poker and watched as the fire flickered to life.

"Ah, that's better. I don't think Cissie is as prompt as Ona was at getting the fires going in the mornings. I will have to speak to her," Mary said crossly.

"I suppose that new baby takes a good deal of her time," Polly suggested.

Mary smiled at Polly's naivety and sighed. "Yes, babies do take up a great deal of a mother's time." She sat on the edge of Polly's bed. "But Cissie also has a job to do."

"I am sorry. I didn't mean to remind you of Joshua and Caleb. It seems I am always saying something to remind you of them." Polly shook her head.

"Polly. No. Your brothers died ten years ago. You cannot be responsible for watching out for my feelings anymore." Mary's brown eyes looked at Polly tenderly. "I admit that it still makes me incredibly sad, but it isn't your job to coddle me. In fact, I need to be strong now for you. You have lost your father, and I know how close you were. After the boys died, I was not available as a mother. I wallowed in my grief for much too long. I simply will not do it again." She leaned closer to Polly. "I am tired of mourning and of wearing black." She chuckled. "Though I will be in widow's weeds for a long time."

Polly was heartened at her mother's attempt at levity. "Maybe we can wear whatever we want here at home and only wear black if we dare go into town," she joked.

Mary waved her hand in dismissal and said, "Enough of that. I want to think about our future. You are a young woman now. Not a child." She touched Polly's cheek with her fingers. "I want to know what you think we should do."

Polly's eyes widened. "What do you mean?"

Mary shrugged. "What should we do about Whitehall? Should we sell everything here and return to Richmond? I have been in prayer about this all night. Your Grandfather Burgiss has offered us rooms in his home. You would have a chance to go to a wonderful finishing school, parties and socials, and there are several aunts and uncles, probably cousins your age. You could make a fine match there. You'll need to marry well."

Polly blushed and Mary continued, "Here there are not as many chances to find a prosperous husband, I'm afraid. Once we thought that South Carolina would hold more for you than, well, than what it has so far. I feel cut off from town folk out here. We just never found our niche. But I learned to love the quiet. I'm not sure I could go back to a city like Richmond. Maybe I could send you to a finishing school in Charleston or Columbia . . ." Mary's voice trailed off. "I've neglected your education, my love, and kept you from making friends your own age."

"I don't know about all of that, but I know that I can read well, and sew, and I can do my sums as well as any girl in town. It was my idea to try the mill workers as pickers. I don't need to go away to school. What would Father want us to do?" Polly asked. "He worked so hard for the railroad tunnels. And Whitehall. What would he want us to do with the land? And the slaves? Where would they go? Should we free them?"

Mary shook her head and regarded her tenderhearted daughter. "I do not know what your father would have wanted for us. And I do not know what will happen with his tunnels. Though, I don't think he would want us to be unhappy, whatever our decision."

Polly nodded. "Didn't we make a good return on the cotton this year? What if I help you more with the accounting? I can read a bit more on crop rotation, too. We can manage the land with Mr. Roper's help. Look what we just did. Shouldn't we try?"

Mary smiled. "Is that what you want, Polly?"

"I honestly think it is," Polly offered. "Caleb and Joshua and Father are all buried here. It is home. I can take over the books. I love to be outside. We have neighbors willing to help us, too." She thought of John's note and continued, "If we try to manage things here for a year, we can see how it goes. Maybe you can tell Grandfather Burgiss that we hope his offer stands should things not go well. But for now, this is home and we will try to make a go of it."

"Well, I declare. You have given my confidence a boost!" Mary hugged her daughter. "I will write to him today to explain—" A coughing fit suddenly overtook her and she held up a hand in pause.

"Mother, I am worried about that cough. Please ask Dr. Adger to come out?" Polly asked fretfully.

"Gracious, no." Mary dabbed her lips. "I feel fine. The dry air just aggravates me." Mary rose from Polly's bed and crossed the room. She opened the heavy drapes to reveal the first bright rays of sunshine slanting through the distant tree line. Frost on the lawn sparkled like diamonds in the early light. "Yes, we can do this, my girl. Whitehall is our home. I confess I am a little scared, but you do give me confidence. Your father loved this land so."

— • —

THE CHRISTMAS HOLIDAY WAS SUBDUED AND MELANCHOLY. Mary's health began to quickly deteriorate. Tom Roper brought the news of Sam Stone's death a few days before Christmas. Ona and the other slaves silently rejoiced when they heard while Polly withheld the news from her mother, visibly ill and weakened. Attending the funeral would be out of the question, Polly knew. She sent a note of condolence to John the following day.

Polly sent Tom for Dr. Adger one February evening when one of her mother's coughing spells brought up so much blood that the woman fainted at the dinner table. Polly screamed for Ona and the two women somehow got Mary to the settee in the parlor.

Polly stood in the corner, twisting her handkerchief nervously as the doctor examined Mary. He listened to her breathing with his stethoscope and then held her wrist, checking her pulse. He tried bloodletting and finally dosed her with laudanum, much to Polly's chagrin.

"Is it consumption, Dr. Adger?" Polly asked.

"I fear it could be, Polly, but let's not rush to any conclusions. And I don't believe she's in any pain now."

Well after midnight, Dr. Adger stood and looked at Polly sadly. "I've done all that I know to do. You can let Ona make up mustard poultices for her lungs as a last resort."

Polly led the doctor toward the door. He laid a hand on her shoulder and said, "You're in my prayers, Polly Burgiss."

Chapter Ten

August 1859

"WAR? JOHN, REALLY, WHERE DO YOU GET THESE IDEAS?" Polly stood in the parlor at Whitehall, pacing the floor and dabbing at her red eyes with a handkerchief. The black silk rustled as she crossed back and forth in front of John. Faded from almost daily wear after a year of mourning her father, the dress seemed to hang on Polly's thin frame.

At first, John had respected Mary's feelings and stayed away. After Christmas, he began to write to Polly almost daily—with prayers for her mother's comfort, offers of help, and plans for his future. Polly had written to him immediately and offered her own belated condolences. John appeared on her doorstep the next day and Polly had nearly fallen into his arms. She was so lonely, and she sensed that he needed her, too.

Now, her mother lay upstairs slowly wasting away from the disease ravaging her lungs. Polly was aghast when Dr. Adger suggested increasing the laudanum to ease Mary's discomfort. She remembered the way the drug had turned her mother into a shadow of her former self. The doctor had assured Polly that Mary's time was limited and that laudanum would ease her mother's tremendous pain. Only when John agreed that the laudanum was necessary, had Polly relented. And indeed, it had been a godsend.

— • —

JOHN WATCHED AS POLLY PACED NEAR the parlor window, twisting her handkerchief in her hands. Days shy of her nineteenth birthday, John found her beautiful, but so naive. Losing her entire family and carrying the heavy burden that was Whitehall was too much for her. She should be grateful that he was there to take charge, to grow Whitehall into a larger and more prosperous place. He sipped at a whiskey near his elbow and glanced again at the document on the table in front of him. Mary's Last Will and Testament, newly written and signed that morning, bore her shaky signature and listed Floride Calhoun and Dr. Adger as witnesses. At Mary's death, it gave Whitehall in its entirety to Polly.

"Polly, if you would only keep up with current events. Abolitionists in the north continue to press us. This Dred Scott case in the courts, for instance. The Republicans are insisting it will be overturned, that slaves are not legal property. There will be war, Polly. It may not be this year, but trouble is brewing. We will never allow the courts to tell us that slaves have the same rights as white men. And if some kind of war comes, we must be ready. Listen to this."

John picked up the newspaper he had been reading and smacked it loudly with his hand. "That Lincoln fellow from Illinois gave a speech. He said that our country cannot endure half slave and half free. 'A *house divided against itself cannot stand*,' he says." John snorted. "He is practically threatening the southern planter! And things have only escalated since then. Rumor has it that he will run for president. We will end up in a civil war. Do you understand?"

— • —

FOR A MOMENT, POLLY'S MIND FLASHED back to a cozy winter morning in the kitchen with Ben and Ona long ago. Ben had opened Martin's Bible to the book of Mark and stabbed his finger at a passage for her to read out loud. She studied the words and began.

"*And he called them unto him and said unto them in parables, how can Satan cast out Satan? And if a kingdom be divided against itself, that kingdom cannot stand. And if a house be divided against itself, that house cannot stand.*"

She had looked up at Ben for approval. "How was that?"

Ben had leaned back on two legs of his chair and asked, "You read it just fine, but what does it mean?"

Polly's brow wrinkled in thought. "A country cannot last if it is at war with itself, just like a family cannot last if the members of the family are fighting all the time."

Ben had nodded and stared at Polly, waiting. But Ona had quickly crossed the room and smacked Ben lightly on the back of his head, so that the chair legs thumped down onto the floor loudly.

"That's enough o' that," she'd said. At the time, Polly had thought Ona was annoyed about the chair.

"Polly!" John called sharply, bringing her back to the present.

"John, the bottom has dropped out of the cotton market. My mother is on her deathbed. Now you tell me there will be war. Is there anything you will not say to frighten me into marrying you? Mother has made it plain that she is not fond of you. I cannot go against her wishes. She has willed me this land in good faith when she could have sold it all and sent me back to Virginia." Polly folded her arms across her chest defiantly. "Mother turned Whitehall over to me and I intend to make her proud. I must do things her way—for now."

A loud knock on the front door startled them both. John looked out the window and then back at Polly, "Are you expecting a caller? I do not recognize the wagon outside." The couple soon heard Ona speaking with an unfamiliar voice at the front door.

Polly shook her head, "No, I am not expecting anyone."

Ona appeared in the parlor doorway and said, "Miss Polly, they's a man here to see the mistress of the house," she said. "I told him she sick, so he wants to see you."

John turned to Polly. "Let me handle this. There has been talk in town of a peddler from Ohio, trying to do business," he warned. When Polly nodded her assent, the two followed Ona into the main hall.

A sharply dressed man sporting a stovepipe hat and a fitted frock coat stood in the doorway. His loosely tied cravat was lacy and too fine. Lengthy sideburns and a clean-shaven chin marked him as someone not familiar with men's fashions in the area.

"Good day, sir and madam!" The man bowed low. "My name is Ezra Gaston. Whom do I have the pleasure of speaking with?"

John stepped forward and said gruffly, "Do you have a license or bond?"

John's manner put the man on guard instantly. "Why, sir, I am a simple country peddler. I offer French-milled soaps and fragrances to ladies of refinement, hair pomades, shaving brushes, and lather bowls to country squires and city gentlemen—"

Before the man could continue his spiel, John took a step forward and interrupted. "Mr. Gaston, you have sixty seconds to quit this property before I shoot. You are clearly not from around here. The state of South Carolina now requires traveling salesmen to have a license, which you do not seem to have. I suggest you take your fancy soaps and get the hell off this property. We shall not see you again here. And if I see you in town, you will be fortunate if you are only arrested." He slammed the door and wheeled around to face Polly.

"John," Polly gasped. "There was no call to be rude. He was only a peddler."

"Polly, that man is clearly a Northern radical. South Carolina passed license laws to discourage these Northerners from coming down, disguised as peddlers, only to incite insurrections among slaves." John looked past Polly to stare momentarily at Ona with cold eyes. He steered Polly back into the parlor and closed the parlor doors firmly.

"I–I didn't know that," Polly murmured. She was going against her mother's wishes in seeing John at all. But he seemed so sure of himself, so capable of shielding her from troubles outside her door. He had been such a comfort after her father's funeral when Polly felt herself falling into a deep sadness. First her brothers. Then her dear father. He had stepped in and saved her, without Mary's knowledge.

"This is why you need me. I can protect you. Make decisions that are best for Whitehall. For us." He paused and smiled. "We are fond of each other. Think of it. We could join our two plantations into one of the largest in the district. You'd want for nothing. And I would be a fortunate man, indeed."

"Someday—maybe. Right now, I need to think about cotton," she said. "Mr. Roper said that we cannot get white labor this season. The girls we used last year have moved on. We will start picking this week and without the mill girls, we don't have enough labor to pick quickly. If my mother finds out, it will worry her."

The entire country was in a financial depression, and South Carolina was no exception. The Burgiss's success with the Pendleton Manufacturing women was short-lived. Millwork had dried up in the bad economy and the young ladies had mostly moved on to Atlanta. Many of the area's poorer white settlers had also moved away toward better opportunities in Georgia and Alabama. There would be little chance of relying on paid white labor in the coming harvest.

"I never understood your parents' schemes to pay white people to pick cotton. Why not add more slaves? Your father was a good businessman. Surely your mother can afford it," John said. "Slaves are meant to pick cotton. They can bear the hot summers. Anyway, white women would not have had a chance in this summer's heat." He swirled the whiskey in his glass and frowned.

Polly wanted to remind him that they had great success with female pickers, but she decided not to argue and took up her sewing. She studied her needlework intently. "Do you really need to drink whiskey so early in the day?" she asked tentatively.

John downed his drink without answering.

Polly sensed she had overstepped and she changed the subject quickly. "I'll write to Mrs. Calhoun in Charleston. I would welcome her advice as a woman running a place alone."

"You don't have to do this alone," John said with a sigh. "Let me prove myself to you. Allow me to bring Mr. Wilkins and some of my hands here tomorrow. You admit you don't have enough slaves to get it in on your own. Your fields are ready now. Mine have a week or more."

Polly was too tired and worried about her mother to argue with John. She felt a headache coming on. Cotton would not pick itself and eight hands were ill-equipped to accomplish it on their own. John's offer of slaves meant that her crop could be picked quickly and cheaply. She had lately come to question the idea of slavery but had no options when it came to picking cotton. Cotton was still king at Whitehall. It would be the only way to save the crop. There was no one else.

"You have men to spare?" she asked hesitantly.

John stood impatiently. "Yes, Polly. Allow me this chance to help. You rest and take care of your mother. I will see to it that Whitehall cotton is picked and ferried to Savannah. She does not have to know."

John's offer seemed a lifeline. Polly preferred to keep him thinking that the Burgiss family had some wealth remaining—that she could be an equal partner if they were to wed. But Whitehall was struggling. Her mother had whispered that her father had put much of his own money into funding the railroad near the end, as a last-ditch gesture of good faith with other investors. But the work had slowed, investors balked, and the mountain tunnel stood unfinished and derelict. Her father's papers, locked in his desk, hinted at deepening financial troubles, even before he died. If John knew how bad Whitehall finances really were, would he disappear?

"Thank you, John. I will leave Whitehall cotton to you—and to Mr. Roper," Polly said, rubbing her temples. "Thank you for that. We have no other options. I will tell Mother about it in my own way. I can only hope that she would approve." She closed her eyes and silently prayed that her words would be true.

— • —

THAT AFTERNOON, POLLY SCANNED THE cotton fields proudly as she headed toward the barn, in search of her overseer. The fields appeared to have been dusted with a thin layer of snow from where she stood. The bolls were almost fully open, and the crop looked to be a good one. It needed to be picked quickly, in case of summer storms or invasion of pests.

The sun beat down hard on her pale skin and she regretted leaving her bonnet inside, but the meeting would be quick. She only wanted to alert Mr. Roper to John's plan. As this was her first decision as eventual owner, she wanted no missteps.

She entered the cool barn and waited for her eyes to adjust to the dim interior. The space smelled of sweet hay, her favorite scent other than her mother's attar of rose perfume.

"Mr. Roper?" she called. Polly paused at a stall and stroked the silky nose of her horse. "Hello, Delightful," she crooned. She offered a carrot and the mare took the proffered snack and nibbled it with her soft lips.

"I'm back here, Miss Polly." Tom stepped out from the stall converted to a business office of sorts. "I'm trying to figure out where to start the men tomorrow. The south field looks most ready. Bolls are completely open there. What can I do for you? It's not your mother—" he began.

Polly shook her head quickly. "Oh no! She is resting. I will check on her after I speak with you." She pressed her palms together nervously.

She inhaled and began. "John Stone will be here with his overseer and some men first thing in the morning. He has offered field hands to help pick since we don't have enough labor." Her exhalation was audible. "And I said yes."

Tom's blue eyes narrowed, and he regarded Polly skeptically. "John Stone?"

Polly watched as Tom's face registered the news. She suspected that Tom wondered at this new alliance between John and his employer's daughter.

"Yes. He offered some men since his fields are not ready yet. We need the help. So I accepted. He will be here early tomorrow. You can tell them where you want the slaves to work and they can start right away, I am sure."

Tom nodded slowly. "Does your mother know about this?"

Polly fairly bristled. "Mr. Roper, I am fully aware that you aren't used to thinking of me as a grown woman." She stood taller and continued. "My mother is unable to make decisions now. When she passes, I inherit Whitehall. This is my decision and I stand by it. We need the labor. The cotton is ready. It costs me nothing."

Tom frowned and crossed his arms. He gazed at Polly with what she took to be sympathy mixed with a new measure of respect. "I'm sorry, Miss Polly. You are right. It is your decision. You have a lot to think about right now. If that is what you want done, then I will be ready to meet with them tomorrow morning and put Stone's men to work. But let me be honest—I know how your mother feels about him—and I'm skeptical about it costing you nothing."

— • —

POLLY SAT UPSTAIRS AT MARY'S BEDSIDE, bathing her mother's face and neck with cool water. The heat and humidity of the early summer evening made the room stifling. Ona had gone downstairs for more cloths. Mary was clearly uncomfortable, and her coughing caused her pain. Her breathing was labored, and the skin on her arms and legs was mottled. Mary coughed violently, and red droplets quickly covered her handkerchief.

"Dear Mother," Polly whispered. She smoothed Mary's forehead with her hand. Mary opened her eyes. Polly pressed the cool cloth to her mother's lips, wiping away crusted blood and spittle.

"Polly," Mary whispered. "Thank you for taking such good care of me." There were tears in her dark eyes. "I know that you will take care of Whitehall, too. Your father had such dreams for this place."

Polly felt tears well in her own eyes again. "I love you," she said simply, bending to kiss Mary's forehead. "I will take care of Whitehall. Don't worry."

Mary reached out a trembling hand and brushed it against Polly's cheek. "I am sorry that I failed you after your brothers died."

Polly shook her head and tried to say something, but Mary put her pale fingers to Polly's lips. "Shhh . . . let me speak. I was in such grief that I forgot that I still had a beautiful daughter who needed me. I wasn't there for you. Can you ever forgive me? I think of all the time I wasted on my lost sons when I should have focused on my Polly." Mary began to cry in gasping breaths.

"Mother, don't cry. You won't be able to catch your breath! Of course, I forgive you. I love you. You'll be well soon enough, and we'll sit out on the veranda near your roses and listen to the honeybees. Maybe we can visit Mrs. Calhoun in Charleston this fall. After the cotton, we'll–" Polly stopped abruptly.

"Are the mill girls picking? It's time, isn't it? I haven't been able to run the plantation like I should . . ." Mary erupted into another coughing fit and closed her eyes.

"Y-yes, Mother," Polly swallowed hard. "The girls will be here. The cotton will be picked on time. A fine crop, too. Please don't trouble yourself. I'll be fine."

"Ask Mr. Roper what to do, Polly." Mary drew in a deep breath. "I found him to be trustworthy and kind. He is a good man . . . He keeps the slaves in line but is not cruel." She coughed. "Take his advice about where and when to begin picking . . ." Her voice trailed off. ". . . so tired." Mary closed her eyes and dozed again.

Polly heard the shuffling of feet behind her and turned to see Ona standing in the doorway, carrying a stack of clean linens.

"Ona! You startled me." Polly stood up and went to meet Ona at the door.

"Mmm hmm . . . I see that. You told yo' mama that them white ladies is comin' to pick her cotton. Miss Girl, that's a lie," the woman whispered.

"It's no concern of yours," Polly hissed. "She doesn't need to hear anything that will upset her right now." There was a knock on the front door and she brushed past Ona and headed to the stairs. "As long as cotton is picked, she will be happy in the end. Now go see about supper."

Polly hurried down the staircase. As she reached the entrance hall, there was another knock on the door. She angrily yanked it open. Standing there was tiny Floride Calhoun, dressed in all her finery. Polly glanced down at her own faded black mourning dress, and gasped, defeat written all over her young face.

"My, my! Are things at Whitehall so bad that the daughter of the home is answering the door herself these days?" Mrs. Calhoun chuckled warmly. Polly practically fell into Floride's arms, and the two women hugged affectionately.

"Mrs. Calhoun, I am so glad that you have come. I thought you were in Charleston. I should have asked you to call sooner. I fear that she does not have long." She led Floride into the parlor and drew the heavy double doors closed.

"Well, I returned today and heard from the Adgers that Mary isn't doing well at all. I do want to visit with her, but I have come primarily to see you, Polly. How are you holding up?"

"You are so good to me, Mrs. Calhoun." Polly sighed as she led the woman into the parlor.

"It is probably time to call me Floride, dear," the woman said kindly.

"I am so tired and worried about Mother. I am completely sick of wearing black. And I do not know a thing about growing cotton or running a plantation," Polly wailed.

"Your cotton looks fine this year. But your parents' hired labor has up and vanished to the wilds of Georgia and beyond." The old woman laughed, and the corners of her eyes crinkled warmly. "Thank God you still have your few slaves."

"I have left everything to Mr. Roper. He is a good man. He knows what to do. Mother certainly puts a lot of faith in him."

Floride nodded. "A good overseer is worth his weight in gold."

"I have also accepted help from John. Our slaves have their work cut out for them with the wheat and fodder alone. He has offered to send some of his hands this way," Polly said. "We have never had enough labor at picking time."

"John Stone?" Floride barked sharply. "You should get help from anyone but John Stone. Why, there are half a dozen planters nearby to beg help from instead of that River Wood trash. Everyone knows your plight. I will ask my son, Andrew, to spare slaves from Fort Hill if you need pickers."

"I would rather not beg," Polly said curtly. Floride's words stung Polly. John had been nothing but kind. "Thank you for the offer, but as a matter of fact, John and his overseer will be here tomorrow to see Mr. Roper. John offered. No one else has. It . . . it was an easy solution."

"Well! I never thought I would see the day." Floride harrumphed. Her pale neck wattle jiggled and she pointed her finger at Polly accusingly. "You know that man has wanted to get his hooks into Whitehall for years. Polly, does your mother know about this?"

"No! Please, Floride, I have to insist that you not say a word." She touched the woman's hand. "The decision was mine to make. You don't even know the man! All I hear from you and Mother are rumors and vague accusations. My father thought the Stones were a fine family. Mr. Roper knows and is ready to put them to work. I don't want to trouble my mother any further. If you are going in to visit with her, I must have your word that you will not tell her that River Wood slaves will be here. I have made the bargain and I will not go back on it." Polly was firm.

"A bargain with the devil! I see that you have made up your mind. I do admire that. I wonder though . . . what else is it that John Stone gets from this new alliance?" The older woman looked at Polly with steely blue eyes. Polly blushed and looked away.

"Ah, I see that there is some new affection between you and young Mr. Stone. I must caution you, Polly. I don't trust that young man. His overseer, Clay Wilkins, is a nasty fellow. He should have been fired years ago. The place is falling apart, I hear. Why he is still employed there is a mystery, but Mr. Wilkins' stench is on everything that goes wrong at River Wood. You make sure that Mr. Roper is in charge of the decision-making during the picking."

"Of course. Do not worry about that," Polly said dismissively. "It does me good to see you. Now, would you like to visit Mother? And then maybe join me for a light supper and a good chat?" Polly took Floride's arm and led the woman up the wide staircase.

— • —

MARY KENT BURGISS DIED LATE THAT NIGHT, Polly by her side. Polly sat with her mother until dawn, weeping and praying over Mary's spent body. Ona padded into the bedroom and draped a quilt around Polly's shoulders. She kissed the top of the young woman's head. "Miss Girl, I so sorry."

"Ona," Polly sniffed in a voice barely above a whisper. "I feel so alone in the world—like I am at the bottom of a deep pit. What do I do?"

"The Lawd'll pull you out, baby. Ask the Lawd—he'll pull you out." Ona squeezed Polly's shoulder affectionately and left the room.

As the sun rose over the tops of the tall pines, Ona bustled around the house, once again stopping clocks, covering windows and mirrors, turning family portraits away, and gathering supplies for her mistress's wake. Lemons were placed in bowls around the casket. Rosemary and mint were strewn again on the wooden floor, to be crushed as mourners walked by, releasing their fragrance. Ona could scarcely believe the number of loved ones that death had snatched from Whitehall, beginning with her own dear Martin. But while Martin was buried in a simple pine box following a short slave service, in a grave close to the cabin where she slept, James and Mary Burgiss were accorded fine caskets, proper wakes, and funerals befitting a white family.

Polly, still in black silk following her father's mourning period, donned the heavy black bombazine that Ona removed from a dusty trunk. The sturdy fabric was in proper form immediately after a parent's passing, but the dress hung on Polly's thin frame and both the cuffs and hem were frayed from wear. She would be expected to mourn her mother's passing in this attire for another full year.

"I've been in black my whole life," Polly sighed, as she smoothed the plain skirt.

"It do seem that way," Ona murmured. She buttoned the tiny black buttons that ran from Polly's collarbone to her lower back. "But you be in pretty colors again befo' you know it."

She picked up a box of stationery on the bureau and handed it to Polly. "Fo' the announcements." Ona knew that Polly would understand the need to send announcements for the funeral right away, for the service must be held soon in the rising heat of an Indian summer.

Polly held the box to her chest. She crossed to the window and peered through a gap in the curtains. "The pickers from River Wood are on their way," Polly said softly. Ona came to stand by her side. Far down the road, wagons were throwing up clouds of red dust in the early morning sunshine.

The sight made Ona's stomach tighten. She turned to fill the washbasin in preparation for bathing Mary's body. She gathered her courage and spoke up. "You could tell 'em to wait, Miss Polly. Until after Miss Mary's funeral. You the mistress now." Polly had the power to turn them back, to delay the picking until after Mary's service, or even send them away for good. Ona feared the River Wood overseer and Ben's reaction to seeing the man. Her gut told her that trouble was coming.

"I could," Polly said. "But the practical side of me knows that the sooner the crop is picked, ginned, and baled, the sooner it will get to market. I need this crop to sell." She turned from the window. "Ona, what would I do without you?" she asked, fresh tears in her swollen eyes. "I want to collapse into your arms as I have so many times when I was small, but I can't. As you said, I am the mistress of Whitehall."

Polly bent to kiss her mother's forehead for the last time. "Goodbye, Mother." Ona gently covered Mary's face with a linen cloth.

Ona felt the monumental shift in their relationship with the passing of Mary Burgiss. "Yes ma'am. You is indeed the mistress now."

Polly moved toward Ona but then stopped. "Ona, I am ashamed of not having said this to you a long time ago . . .. I am deeply sorry that you lost Martin. We didn't do right by you then. Please forgive me. I do know how much it hurts to lose a loved one."

"Thank you, Miss Polly." Ona nodded nervously. "I'll go get some men to he'p carry Miss Mary down the stairs. Duke got the box all ready. It real pretty cedarwood. I know yo' mama would like it." She started down the hallway but turned quickly when she heard Polly behind her. Polly threw her arms around Ona and sobbed like a little girl again, lost without her mother. Ona smoothed the young woman's hair and patted her back gently. "It be alright, Miss Girl. Ona's here. It gonna be alright . . ."

— • —

OUTSIDE, SLAVES MILLED UNDER THE LARGE OAK trees near the kitchen house—River Wood and Whitehall men alike. Together, twenty slaves were preparing to pick Burgiss cotton. The day was already warm, and canteens and gourds were anxiously filled at the pump. Bandanas were soaked in the water barrel and tied around already sweat-drenched throats.

Ben stood apart from the group. He'd been ordered by Mr. Roper to report to the big house when the others headed to the fields, to help his mother with Miss Mary, and he was anxious to leave. He wiped his brow with his bandana and watched as Mr. Roper and Clay Wilkins met up on horseback. Their mutual dislike was evident, even at a distance. Roper gave instructions to the River Wood overseer and the man glowered in return, leaning from his horse to spit a fetid stream of tobacco juice.

Ben squinted in the sunlight and saw John Stone astride his own horse at a distance. He watched Stone pull a flask from his saddlebag and uncork it. He lifted the flask to his mouth and took a long drink of the contents. Ben shifted his gaze back to Mr. Roper. Roper dismissed all hands into the fields with a reminder to refill canteens at the water barrels on designated row ends. He glanced Ben's way and pointed toward the big house before he and Wilkins followed after the slaves, barking orders to their charges as they rode. Ben shook his head and spit on the ground, before heading toward the back door of the big house.

Ona met Ben at the door. "Wilkins and Stone are out there. Following Whitehall slaves all day in Whitehall fields. What kind of hell are we getting into now, Mama?" He glared at his mother as if she were responsible for John Stone being on the property.

Ona hissed, "Ben, you got to rein in that anger, boy. There ain't nothin' we can do about this, 'cept keep outta the way and pray to the Lawd that she don't marry that man. If she do, we all in a heap o' trouble."

She led him toward the staircase. Ben followed his mother up the worn stairs toward the room where Mary Burgiss lay dead. The plush carpets felt strange underfoot and the closed bedroom doors he passed reminded him of the Burgisses who had slept in those rooms and had since died.

It was only the second time in his twenty-two years that he had been upstairs. The memory of sneaking up to Polly's room as a boy to tell Ona what he'd witnessed at the trading post was still fresh. He'd passed Mary's room and heard her keening into her pillow, a horrible sound of loss and anguish. In her own room, young Polly had been curled in a tight ball, lost in terror.

He followed Ona into Miss Mary's darkened bedroom. The mistress of the house no longer grieved her dead sons; she had finally joined them. Now he saw only a pale corpse, dressed in a dark gown that swallowed her wasted frame, her hair loose on the pillow in an intimate way he'd never seen.

His worst fears were coming to pass. Outside, Clay Wilkins and John Stone prepared to have their way with Whitehall land and slaves. Mary Burgiss was no longer alive and able to hold back the coming catastrophe.

"Thank you, Ben." Polly appeared at his side. He nodded quietly and awaited instructions.

— • —

THERE WERE SO MANY THINGS THAT SHE wanted to say to Ben but Ona was in the room and it was not the right time. Polly read his quiet manner as anger, instead of empathy mixed with fear. She quickly composed herself. "Ona, is the casket on the stand?"

Ona nodded. "Yes, ma'am. George has it set up real nice."

"Well . . . She is dressed and ready." Polly sighed. "Ben, can you please carry her to the parlor?" Her tone was cool.

Polly watched as Ben put his arms around Mary's shoulders and knees and lifted her gently from the bed. Ona adjusted Mary's skirts to cover her ankles.

Polly and Ona proceeded down the stairs with Ben behind them. He carried the wasted body with gentleness and dignity, for which Polly was grateful. When they arrived in the parlor, Duke was there in the shadows to aid Ben in getting the body into the casket. Polly waited in the doorway while Ona arranged her mother's dress and fixed her hair. She draped a thin veil over the open casket. All was ready for tomorrow's service. The room was cool and dark, and the fragrant lemons and herbs were a pleasant change from the sickness that clung to every surface of the bedroom where Mary had lain.

"Shut the doors, Ona," Polly instructed. "We must keep it cool." The small group moved into the foyer and Ona quickly closed the heavy parlor doors behind them.

Polly turned to Ben and handed him a stack of sealed envelopes. "Please ask Mr. Roper to deliver these this morning. The funeral is tomorrow." She began to move slowly toward the stairs. All she wanted was to go to her own room and lock the door and be away from death, decisions, and worry. Only her duties as the mistress kept her from collapsing right there in the hallway. She was so alone.

She turned slightly. "Ona, have Cissie drape the house and put out the mourning wreaths. And someone will need to make a funeral cake . . ."

"We doin' it, Miss Polly. We doin' it. Why don't you go on upstairs and rest, now?" Ona patted her arm gently. "We got things taken care of. We take good care of yo' mama. You got a funeral and cotton bein' picked. A rest will do you good."

"The cotton!" Polly exclaimed, putting a hand to her forehead. "Ben, what is happening with the cotton?" At that moment, there was a knock on the front door. Ona moved past Polly and opened the door to find John, hat in hand.

"John!" Surprising even herself, Polly smiled brightly through her tears and rushed forward. She grasped both of his hands in her own. "Your company is so welcome. I know you understand."

"Polly, I am so sorry for your loss." Ignoring the three slaves, he took Polly in his arms and held her. She wanted to melt into his chest and sob. He grabbed her hand and led her into the library.

Polly turned to thank the slaves for helping with her mother and caught the scathing expression on Ben's face as he watched them go. "John, let me have a word with my slaves first?" she said.

"There will be time for that later. Come and sit, my dear." John pulled Polly to the sofa, where she sat uneasily, straining to see into the foyer. He turned back to the library doors. "You boys get to the cotton now! You hear me?"

Polly saw Duke and Ben exchange fearful glances before John abruptly closed the library doors.

— • —

THE NEXT MORNING DAWNED ALREADY HOT AND THICK. Polly awoke dully, confused, and disoriented. It wasn't until she heard the faint calls of workers in her fields and Tom Roper's sharp voice that she remembered. Her mother was dead. She was alone in the world. Cotton was being picked. She rubbed her eyes and turned over, noticing the silver call bell on her night table. The bell had been her mother's way of summoning Ona to her bedchamber for twenty years. The woman must have placed it there, newly polished for Polly, sometime in the night. Its significance wasn't lost on the new mistress of Whitehall. She sat up and stretched, sighed, and reached for the bell. Its clear and bright tone seemed to strengthen Polly's resolve.

She heard the stairs creak while Ona ascended as quickly as her rheumatism allowed. The bedroom door opened. Ona appeared, out of breath but smiling. "Mornin,' Miss Polly. I knew you was probably awake, but that bell sho' he'ps me hear you."

Polly smiled. "Thank you for leaving it. Even as a little girl, the sound of that bell reminded me that Mother was near. I guess I really am the mistress of the house now—but it helps to know, in a way, that Mother is still with me." She stood and began to unwind her long braid haphazardly. "No breakfast today. I will have refreshments at the service. Pull out the black bombazine with the crepe trim. I hung it last night to air."

"That dress you wore fo' yo' daddy's mournin'? Law, you just a tiny bird of a woman since yo' daddy died. That dress looks like a big ol' shroud on you now," Ona chided. "Miss Polly, you don't eat enough. An' it bad luck to wear a dress you wore mournin' another."

"Bad luck?" Polly smirked. "It is the only one that I have that is appropriate. I will visit a dressmaker in town at some point, but not today and not this week. And not for black! The two black dresses I own will have to do. Get the bombazine ready and then leave me alone for a while. I will dress myself." She looked at Ona wearily. "This is hard for me."

Ona dropped her gaze and nodded, chastened. "Yes'm." As she turned to leave Polly's bedroom, the young woman called to her.

"Ona, I do not know what possesses me to be so cross with the one person left that I have loved and trusted since childhood." Polly shook her head. "I am not myself right now. I have so much on my mind. Please stay."

She sat down at her dressing table and looked at her pale reflection in the mirror. "I will get through this. I will not sit around and feel sorry for myself. It killed my mother. I have to think straight. There is a cotton crop to get in and enough repairs to make around here to keep everyone busy for months." She began to unwind her long braid.

— • —

ONA CROSSED THE ROOM AND STOOD BEHIND her young mistress. She picked up the silver hairbrush and began to brush Polly's hair tenderly. "Miss Polly, you is the new mistress. You is strong and brave. And today? You can do this. It all gonna be alright." She expertly coiled Polly's hair into a smooth chignon and pinned it with dark combs.

Polly sighed heavily and put her milky white hand on the wrinkled black one behind her. "Thank you, Ona. You are good to me. I will not forget it again."

Ona looked down at Polly's small hand and gasped. "Miss Polly! What's 'dis new ring you got on? That ain't yo' mama's." She stared at Polly's reflection in the mirror.

Polly slowly turned and displayed her left hand meekly. "John asked me to marry him last night." She looked up at Ona. "Next year, after the mourning period for Mother has ended. You disapprove. I see it in your eyes."

Ona was unsure of what to say next, for fear of offending her mistress. "It ain't fo' me to approve or disapprove, Miss Polly. I jus' think you got a lot goin' on right now. Yo' mama's funeral an' all . . . I get that dress ready fo' you. And you prob'ly be needin' a bite to eat before comp'ny come or you gonna faint with a tight corset on. I bring you a little hot tea and some biscuits. Cissie got the refreshments 'bout ready fo' yo' guests."

Polly didn't argue as Ona left the room.

Chapter Eleven

BEFORE DAWN, THE CLANGING BELL JUST OUTSIDE their shuttered windows awakened Ben and the other hands. For nearly a week, the Whitehall and River Wood slaves had been picking the season's cotton crop. Folks sat up wearily and pulled on frayed pants that had been patched in just about every location. They attended to their regular morning chores before roll call. Ben fed and watered the stock before the sun was even up and silently began to prepare for another full day in the broiling cotton fields. The smithy stayed cold.

River Wood slaves had slept nearby every night, in and around the wagons, for the summer nights were warm and the distance deemed too great to travel home at dark and be in the fields again at sunrise. They crouched around morning campfires, eating meager breakfasts, and then began to fill gourds with water from the pump. They milled around with bandanas over their noses because the single slave privy had quickly been overrun and produced a foul stench that permeated the area.

Each morning, Cissie placed servings of cold fatback and cornbread in kerchiefs tied tight. Both the Whitehall and River Wood hands grabbed lunch sacks and hurried to the oak tree for roll call.

When the day's labor in the fields and barn-turned-weighing house was finished, there was still work to be done. The River Wood slaves were sent to the ginning floor, under Wilkins' watchful eye, and the Whitehall slaves to tend stock and finish evening chores. Wilkins complained to Roper that the slaves should keep picking as long as there was daylight, but Roper drew the line at twelve hours in the fields. Rested slaves picked better and faster, he said.

Tempers flared between slaves from both properties and had Tom Roper on edge. He drew a plug of tobacco from a pouch and shoved it in his cheek. In the weak light of the early morning, he looked over the papers in his hands while the slaves assembled. His own eyes watered from the stench around the outhouse. Nine slaves from River Wood, on loan from John Stone, stood nearby, unsure of this new day's requirements. Tom called each slave's name and waited for a response before he continued.

River Wood slaves were surprised and relieved to find out that the Whitehall overseer was not a harsh man. Their rations had been fair and their workload tolerable. While Roper carried an overseer's whip, he had not used it on any of his men. He rode through the fields daily, giving orders and expecting they be obeyed, but did not lay a hand on anyone.

When Wilkins appeared, however, he cracked his cat o'nine tails often and threatened to administer beatings over offenses he deemed worthy. He kept a cobbing board in his saddlebag, which had holes drilled into it to raise blisters during paddling. Wilkins had been known to give fifty licks for bits of boll in a slave's sack or for broken plants on a row. It was rumored that one poor man was lashed fifty times and then manacled for being caught resting in the field.

Roper had insisted that Wilkins supervise only River Wood slaves. At a distance, though, Wilkins sat astride his horse and glowered at the Whitehall hands as they gathered.

Tom folded the papers and looked at the group. "Right. We got two more hard days' work ahead. Men, I want to see two hundred pounds apiece today.

At least. Gals, I want to see one hundred. If you do that, there's meat for supper and there's a good chance you River Wood folks'll be going home tomorrow night. If you slack off, you're all back in the fields till it's over. Move on out, now," he barked. The first rays of sunlight filtered through the far tree line.

Slowly, the crews set out for their designated fields, already shimmering in the heat. George called out, "Go on, y'all folks. Let's get this day's work done so River Wood workers can get on home soon." He began a quick-cadenced chant as the groups set off. Several folks joined in with the chant and picked up their pace. Wilkins wheeled his horse about and trotted behind his men, cursing, and shouting at them the entire way.

— • —

AT THE BEGINNING OF THE WEEK, BEN HAD NOT been surprised to see two elderly River Wood men, a boy, a teen-aged girl, and a nursing mother picking cotton alongside the men. After Miss Mary's success with the white women, however, he no longer assumed women could not pick. He found it odd that Wilkins did not bother the young mother but harassed the others continuously.

The bone-weary mother dragged her twelve-foot cotton sack behind her and toted her baby on her back as well. Ben admired the woman's ability to tend her infant and pick at the same time. When the infant cried from hunger, she twisted him around in the tiny sling and set him to nursing while she continued down the rows. Ben blushed at the sight but couldn't withdraw his gaze. He was thankful that Ona had escaped cotton harvest and was safely inside the house tending to Polly in the days since Mary's funeral.

The picking was going well and Ben prayed for its quick end. He seethed with rage every time Wilkins stepped onto the property, but he had sworn to his mother not to raise his head or slow his work when the man passed by. Several times, Wilkins had shouted vulgar things at the teenaged girl picking in a nearby row, and it was all Ben could do to keep silent.

The relentless sun crawled higher in the sky. Cicadas hummed and grasshoppers whizzed through the busy fields. The thick humidity made it hard to get a breath. If the stooped pickers felt like their backs would break and their tongues were parched, not one person said a grumbling word. The water barrels had long run dry, and there would be no refilling them until the noon meal. Suddenly, from across the rows, Ben heard a woman's voice begin to sing.

"*Keep on movin', feet, don't stop now.*

Headin' fo' da promise land,

Keep on movin, hands, pickin' it clean,

Gettin' closer to da promise land."

Soon, the other girls joined in and to Ben, it sounded like a chorus of angels. He strained to see which woman had the courage to start the song, and he was not surprised to find that it was the young mother, baby slung around to face her. While the tiny thing nursed, his mother picked the cotton and thrust it in the heavy sack dragging behind her. Her head was wrapped in a bright blue turban, and she wore a flour sack dress of red calico. From what he could see, she looked to be around his own age, slender and small-boned, with large brown eyes and full lips. She picked quickly and with both hands.

"*Keep on movin', feet, don't stop now.*

Jesus is a waitin' fo' me.

Keep on movin,' hands, reachin' fo' my Lord,

Gettin' closer to da promise land."

Ben smiled to himself and quickened his pace, anxious to finish his row and the next before heading to the shade of the big oak tree for the noon meal.

The fiery sun was soon directly overhead. The pickers deposited the last of their morning yields into large row baskets and then lugged the heavy baskets toward the overseer's cabin to be weighed and recorded by the foreman. Ben and a River Wood man named Christmas grabbed the handles of a full row basket and lifted it off the ground. They fell in line behind the young woman who had started the singing. She dragged her sack behind her wearily. Nearly full, it looked to weigh close to what she did, and she carried her infant to boot.

Ben looked around quickly for any sign of Wilkins before he spoke. "It sure did me good to hear you singing out there," he said quietly. The woman did not turn around, but Ben heard her answer him.

"Pickin' a hundred pounds of cotton is like pickin' a hundred pounds of dandelion fluff. Sometimes, if I don't sing, I think I'm just gonna drop dead right out there in the field. And I cain't do that." Her deep voice had a curious effect on him. It was like a tonic that eased the anger threatening to overwhelm him.

"I guess not, with a baby and all . . ." Ben's voice trembled. "How long have you been at River Wood?" She did not answer.

"My name's Ben," he tried again. He watched a bead of sweat trickle down the back of her neck.

The woman still did not turn around but continued to lug her sack a few feet further in the line of pickers heading to the weighing in. Ben sighed and dropped his head.

"I'm Kate." Her voice was deep and smooth.

"Your baby have a name?" Ben asked quietly.

"Solomon."

"Like King Solomon in the Bible." Ben nodded.

Kate turned her head slightly and caught Ben's eye, before resuming her walk, eyes forward. "You know the Bible?" she asked in a murmur. "Then you know that King Solomon was wise. I want my boy to be wise. And it ain't wise to be flappin' yo' mouth when you in line to weigh in, now is it?" Her voice was sweet honey. He chuckled to himself and did not speak anymore.

After the morning's last baskets of cotton had been weighed, the slaves were given forty-five minutes to eat a noon meal and rest in the shade. Water gourds were refilled at the pump, and a few folks managed a catnap.

Kate unwrapped the fussing, sweaty infant and laid him on a blanket under the large beech tree, where the small breeze soothed his chafed and damp skin. The baby soon quieted, watching the play of light and breeze in the tree's branches.

Ben noticed that Kate sat with the other girl and not with a husband. He wondered if her man had been the latest River Wood runaway, a young man called Dell. It was rumored among the slaves that Dell had taken off after being beaten nearly to death for some small infraction. And it looked like he had made it or died trying, for no one had seen him since.

Ben sat down near Christmas, resting against a cart. He took off his straw hat and wiped his forehead and neck with a rag. The old man nodded toward him, closed his eyes, and sighed.

"Whew, it's another hot one," Ben said, trying to make idle conversation. The man opened his rheumy eyes and nodded again. Ben thought that he must be over sixty years old.

"Say, that woman over there in the red dress, with the baby? She someone's woman?" Ben asked. He inclined his head toward Kate casually, but the old man caught his interest. He cackled, showing toothless brown gums.

The man shook his head and looked at Ben like he was dumb. "Yep. She sho' is."

"So who is her man?" Ben asked.

"Kate's man? Damn, you as ignurnt as you sound? Kate ain't got no black man. No nigger come near her once Massa Stone got holt of her. She Stone's woman now, till he through wit' her. An' that baby is his, too! You best not go sniffin' around that one," he muttered. The old man stood up, annoyed, and crossed the swept yard to lie down under the shade of a birch tree and finish his nap.

Ben felt his hatred for John Stone rise again in his chest. Right now, that man was trying his damnedest to win Miss Polly and Whitehall. Ona had whispered that Polly was engaged to the man. John had come to call every day since her mother's funeral. And every day, Ona could see Polly's fondness for him growing. It was only a matter of time until she announced a wedding date.

Ben leaned back against the cart wheel and closed his eyes. *How can I make sure Miss Polly has this bit of information? And what will she do with it when she hears?*

— • —

THAT NIGHT, AN EXHAUSTED BEN SAT watching his mother as she prepared their small dinner. She stirred up the coals in the fire and hoisted the iron cook pot onto the pothook with shaking hands. It seemed Ona had grown old overnight. Caring for Mary Burgiss had been tedious. He knew she missed Martin terribly. Now, the thought of seeing Polly marry John Stone seemed to squeeze the life out of her.

Ben's eyes opened and closed as he dozed at the small table. Then he shook his head to clear his mind and began softly, "Ma, I think it's time I should say something to Miss Polly about what happened at the Kemp place—with her brothers."

Ona wheeled around sharply. "No, Ben! There might have been a time, but that time is gone. She won't believe you, and then Mr. Stone'll get rid of you. Mark my words, son. Get that thought out of yo' mind." She shook the wooden spoon at him angrily. "I forbid it."

"Miss Polly won't marry him if she knows. I found out he already got a slave woman pregnant. She's out picking in the fields with her baby on her back. His child. Her name's Kate. Miss Polly needs to know because he still favors Kate."

Ona cut him off. "Ben, stop it. You think that matters? You know John Stone ain't the first white man to have relations with a slave woman. You forget where you come from?" Her angry eyes glistened with hot tears. "I am fond of Miss Polly. I am. But you my blood, my son, my only chile. I cain't think of what would become of me if you was killed or sold away. I couldn't go on. I couldn't. You the only family I got left. I'm beggin' you. Please git the thought outta yo' mind. Please to God. Leave it!"

Ben sighed and shook his head. "Ma, it's the only chance we have. We'll end up Stone property if things keep going the way they are. You think about that."

Ona reached down and patted her boy's cheek. "I know it's hard. I know it. We has to trust that Miss Polly gonna do right by us. My gut tells me she will . . . I love you, Ben. Thank you for understandin'. My answer is no." She turned back to the hearth and said no more.

The next morning, the sun beat mercilessly on the cotton pickers. The thrum of cicadas and grasshoppers filled the stifling air. Ben stood and wiped his face with his kerchief, scanned the field, and then bent low to pull the fibrous fluff free from the sharp bolls. His hands were rough and bloodied, as the bolls on the last few rows were hard and tight and didn't want to give up the lint. It was slow going. He had to pull the cotton free as best he could to fill his pick sack.

He wondered how the River Wood slaves, especially Kate, were faring in their rows. Wilkins was known to use the lash in the field if he caught someone leaving lint behind in the bolls. Maybe her small hands were more suited to the work, but the heat was withering. And with a baby on her back? Anger simmered in his chest, but he remembered his promise to his mother and bent again to his task.

Ben knew that Duke was picking in the next row north and realized he hadn't seen the man in a while. He stood and looked across the chest-high cotton plants. "Duke? Duke, you there?" he called. He heard a muffled voice and quickly ducked through the row to find Duke crumpled on the hard ground, his cotton sack nearly empty. "Duke! Get up! Can't have Mr. Roper find you here sleeping in the field." Ben tried to pull the man to his feet.

The old man shook his head. "Naw, leave me here, boy. I jes' cain't do it no more." His skin was cold and clammy, and Ben knew enough to suspect heat exhaustion.

Ben stood and cupped his hands around his mouth. "Mr. Roper, sir!"

Far across the field, his overseer sat astride his horse. Tom Roper heard the faint cry and looked up.

"What you want, nigger boy? Git back to work!"

Ben whirled to find Wilkins staring down from the saddle of his horse.

"This Whitehall man is sick," Ben said plaintively. "He is too old to be out here in this heat."

"Don't talk to me about one old lazy nigger. You get back to your row and leave this nigger alone, ya' hear me, boy? Git!" Wilkins barked at Ben.

Ben quickly looked past Wilkins to see if Mr. Roper was headed his way. He saw no sign of his overseer. "This man can't get up. Please. Let me get him back to the water barrel for a cool drink and then he'll be fine. He just needs some water."

A stream of obscenities spewed from Wilkins' mouth as he reached for his lash. "You dirty little—"

"That's enough!" Behind Ben, Roper's sharp voice cut Wilkins off mid-rant. "Mr. Wilkins, you've been told several times to stay with Mr. Stone's hands. You have no business with Miss Burgiss's slaves. I don't aim to argue here. We got one hard day left and then you're free to go back to River Wood and treat slaves as you please."

"Ben, help me get Duke onto my horse." Tom slid off his saddle and bent to help the old man.

Wilkins coughed up a putrid wad of spittle and tobacco juice and spat as violently as possible in Ben's direction. Ben instinctively moved to dodge the vile slime. The angry man wheeled his horse and trotted away, cursing under his breath.

Roper chuckled, "That man's got it in for you, Ben. I'd stay clear of him for the duration if I was you."

— • —

THE COTTON WAS IN. JOHN HAD BEEN TRUE TO HIS WORD. The Whitehall cotton had been picked, ginned, and baled. John and Tom Roper handled everything and Polly stayed out of their way. She was relieved that it was over. From her bedroom windows at night, she had glimpsed the fires from the River Wood slave labor camped out under her trees. She smelled the overflowing privy when the wind was toward the big house. One evening, when she was en route to the kitchen house to speak with Ona after supper, Wilkins had appeared in her path.

"Evenin' ma'am," he had croaked, stepping aside for her to pass. He removed his hat, revealing oily red hair matted to his scalp. His red beard was streaked with ever-present tobacco stains, and his tiny blue eyes bored into her, making Polly quite uncomfortable. He reeked of sweat and alcohol.

"Can I help you, Mr. Wilkins?" She pulled her shawl tightly around her shoulders and forced herself to look him in the eye. She wanted to retch.

"Jes' lookin' for Mr. Stone, ma'am," he smiled, showing brown, uneven teeth. "Got a problem with the niggers. Perhaps John's in the house?"

"No," Polly said nervously. "Mr. Stone is not in my house." She straightened and tried not to appear as nervous as she felt inside. "And do not use that word in my presence. I detest it."

"What? Niggers?" The man chuckled and spit tobacco juice without regard for the hem of Polly's dress. He slowly let his eyes travel up and down Polly's slender frame before speaking. "Well, I reckon I'll look for him elsewhere. You have yerself a nice evenin' now." He chuckled, before turning on his heels and heading into the dark.

Polly had turned and walked quickly back to the house, her heart pounding in her chest.

— • —

JUST TWO DAYS LATER, POLLY WATCHED KEENLY as the last bales were offloaded from the wagon onto the river ferry. The last of her cotton was on its way to market. She twisted John's ring absentmindedly around her finger.

A few years ago, she would have expected that her father's beloved railroad tunnel through the mountains would have carried cotton to markets north by now. How he had longed to see his cotton shipped to the Midwest by train instead of south by the slow river to ports on the Atlantic.

Progress on the tunnel had ground to a halt after his death, in part due to the solid granite at the heart of the mountain and because now the whole state was apprehensive about war. The iron ore and manpower needed to further the construction had evaporated in an eerie portent of what lay ahead. The district buzzed with talk of possible secession from the United States and how an ensuing war would affect cotton prices further.

Polly had followed the wagon on horseback to the ferry, wanting to see the last of her crop off in a fond farewell. She stood near the shore with Tom and Duke, taking in the view. Ben and a new hand, Zadoc secured the last of the jute-wrapped bales. Zadoc was maybe twenty, thin and wiry, but strong. John had given him to Polly as an engagement present. He was good in the fields, but Polly was most grateful to have him on-site to help wherever she needed.

Polly's gaze was drawn to Ben. He pulled the heavy ropes taut to tie down the 500-pound bales of cotton. Despite the creeping chill of early evening, Ben was shirtless. He leaped across one large bale to spread a large canvas tarp over it, his broad muscled back and strong shoulders glistening with perspiration. Polly followed Ben's movements, before sensing Roper's eyes following hers.

She cleared her throat daintily and looked away. It was done. The full barge would shortly pull out into the southbound current of the river and away. She drew her shawl around her shoulders and breathed deeply. Duke strode down the bank to help the other hands secure the bales.

"Were you able to work with John's overseer? I didn't hear of any problems." Polly shifted from one foot to the other nervously.

"That wasn't my first experience with Clay Wilkins. Let me just say that there were no surprises. He is a rough man and treats his hands accordingly." Tom cleared his throat. "I hear that congratulations are in order." He leaned to one side to spit a dribble of tobacco juice into a bottle.

Polly looked up at the overseer, momentarily confused.

"On your engagement to Mr. Stone," Roper offered. "Have you set a date?"

"What a personal question, Mr. Roper," Polly frowned. "No, we have not set any date as of yet. I'm in mourning—it wouldn't be fitting." She glanced down at her faded black crepe and shook her head.

Roper nodded and gazed out toward the river.

Polly continued, "Rest assured, your job is safe. In fact, I will rely on you all the more as I hardly know how my father conducted business. I would like to sit with you at some point and discuss everything. My mother was barely a widow before she took ill herself."

"She had a good mind for business in the end, she did. It's too bad she couldn't snap out of her sadness." Tom leaned away and spit tobacco juice again. When he turned back to Polly, her face could not hide a look of utter disgust.

"Begging you pardon, ma'am," Tom said sheepishly.

Polly turned back toward the river. "Mr. Roper, that is a vile habit. I do wonder why you keep it up."

Amused, Roper looked down at the young woman. "I suppose it is just that, a habit."

Polly turned her brown eyes up to the man. "I do not like it. Have you thought of quitting?"

"What a personal question, Miss Polly." He grinned.

Polly could not help but smile. "Touché." She chuckled.

Tom tried to change the subject. "Do I answer to you? Or to Mr. Stone?"

Polly's smile evaporated. Tom stared at her, waiting for an answer.

"You may put your mind at rest. A wedding is far in the future. Indeed, Mother's will left Whitehall to me. I have not had time to go into town to meet with her lawyer and execute her will, but I am your employer." She sighed. "I never even saw my father's will."

Polly looked out over the slow-moving river and continued, "My decision to marry Mr. Stone has little to do with the state of affairs at home. I don't need a husband to run Whitehall," she said defensively. "Did you know that it was my own idea to try the female mill workers who saved us so much money picking that season?"

Tom looked at Polly with some admiration. "I did. Did you know that it was my own idea to try immigrant Irish pickers from Tunnel Hill years ago?"

Polly turned to look at Tom. A smile played at the edges of her mouth but she ignored his retort. "I suppose that when we marry, Whitehall becomes his property as well as mine." She paused. She had not really considered the idea of Whitehall becoming a Stone property and the thought vaguely disturbed her. "But your position is safe. Right now I need your help to figure out the next steps." She looked up at Tom. "But Mr. Stone's help with this crop was invaluable, don't you agree?"

"If I may be blunt, Miss Burgiss," Roper began formally. He watched the slaves down at the dock and avoided Polly's gaze. "You don't have to marry the man just because he lent you some slaves. Mr. Stone relies too much on Clay Wilkins, and Wilkins isn't good for business."

A fine mist began to swirl in the hollows and low places along the river. Polly pulled her shawl around her shoulders. Fall was finally creeping down the Blue Ridge. The golden sweet gums and ruby red sumacs were brilliant in the last of the light before dusk. Polly watched the mist as it moved over the slow-flowing river. She heard a bobwhite off in the distance and paused to listen. The call of the bobwhite seeking its mate always made her sad. Its call was lonely and questioning. As the hands climbed back up the steep path from the water's edge, they turned to watch the barge move off into deeper water and then south.

"Thank you for loading," Polly called, shielding her eyes from the setting sun.

"Well, Miss Polly. We done it. Ain't ya' proud?" Duke asked. "You was a mite the first time cotton left Whitehall for Savannah. And here you is a growed woman sendin' yo' own crop off. Yo' daddy would be real proud." Old Duke smiled at his mistress with a gap-toothed grin.

"Yes, Duke, I am proud. And thankful. I am not sure we would have gotten it all in without Mr. Stone's help." She sighed and looked out over to the western shore of the river. "But it is finished. My cotton is going to Savannah." She sighed and turned to Roper. "We will talk about how things are going to be handled from here on out, but I expect little to change until after I marry Mr. Stone. Your position here is safe, Mr. Roper, as I said. I hope you will stay."

The slaves looked at each other. Polly caught their downcast expressions and muttered, "That seems to be the reaction, no matter who hears it."

"Congratulations again, ma'am," Tom said. "We best get back. Ready, boys?" He touched his hat, turned, and climbed easily up the grassy bank, trailed by Duke and Zadoc. Ben made to follow, but Polly stopped him.

"Ben, wait. Tell the others. Despite what they may have heard, Mr. Stone is a good man. We could not have gotten the cotton in without him and his—help. He will be a fair master."

A yellow jacket settled on Polly's shoulder and Ben instinctively moved to brush it away. Polly jumped.

Ben frowned. "Fair? Now that's a word I don't hear real often. Miss Polly, forgive me for speaking out of turn, but you can run Whitehall without Mr. Stone's help. You just don't want to try." He smiled ruefully at Polly and turned to follow the others up the hill.

The bobwhite called again in the twilight, but there was no answer.

Chapter Twelve

October 1860

POLLY HELD ONTO HER HAT WITH ONE HAND AND gripped the wagon rail
with the other. She sat next to Ona on the bone-rattling ride into town.
Even John's fine rig, drawn by a beautiful roan, didn't fail to hit every rut
and dip in the hard-packed clay road. Zadoc tried with little success to steer
around the washouts.

"Land sakes, Zee," Polly said sharply, leaning from the window. "I
would like to get to town in one piece, if possible."

"I'm sorry, Mizz Polly," the man called out. "Mr. Stone say the road
was bad after that storm last week. He was sho' right. I'm tryin' to keep to
the smooth parts but they ain't many!" Zadoc shook his head.

Fall had descended in earnest on the South Carolina upstate. The
rains had finally returned and washed the air clean. The sky overhead was
a clear blue and the breeze was fresh and cool. Hickories and dogwoods
surrounding Whitehall surrendered their leaves, brilliant golds and reds
drifting to the earth silently. The early chill was invigorating. Wood smoke
filled the air. The change in the weather lifted Polly's mood after the hard

work of bringing in another cotton crop, again with the help of John's slaves. She inhaled the crisp air and smiled.

Floride Calhoun had invited Polly to visit her in Charleston for the Christmas holidays. To lift her spirits, Polly decided to go into town and visit the dressmaker and milliner. John had insisted she take his good carriage since the rains had washed out much of the roadbed between Whitehall and Pendleton. She was excited to go for new dresses appropriate for a trip to Charleston. She looked forward to the outing and a chance to shop.

John continued to press Polly about a wedding date. Mourning for her mother had given Polly a comfortable excuse to put off making plans. That time had ended. Even now, she felt safe from a decision until after the holidays, but her excuses would soon run out.

She tried to bring up the prospect of divesting themselves of River Wood and its problems. The finances at Whitehall were improving slowly and the land was fertile. The slaves seemed happy and baby Silas had given everyone at Whitehall a bit of joy. The rumors coming out of River Wood involving cruel slave treatment appalled her. And yet, every time she tried to discuss it with John, he put her off. She wished to be rid of River Wood or at least Mr. Wilkins before a wedding, but the hope faded with each passing month.

As the carriage rolled toward Pendleton, Polly couldn't help but notice the bare fields recently stripped of their cotton crop like her own fields at home. Bits of cotton clung to dried stalks, giving fields the appearance of melting snow. It had been a fine harvest, and again, John had handled everything on Polly's behalf. He sent six of his own slaves to pick in her fields. John allowed Roper to oversee his slaves, and so Wilkins did not step foot on her property. She had received a good price at market. There was even a little set aside for this shopping trip, and Polly could hardly wait to get to the dressmaker's storefront on Main Street.

"Ona, I am beyond excited. I need new dresses badly," Polly prattled on. "John wanted me to go into Greenville to shop—on the new train—but

I just couldn't. Not yet. Thoughts of railroads just make me sad," she said, thinking of her father's hard work on the stalled railroad tunnel.

Polly continued, "I am so looking forward to Charleston at Christmas. I suppose it will be expensive, getting all the clothing I'll need, but I think it will do me good. I am twenty years old and I have never even left the district."

She smoothed the faded gown. "I have been a long time in black. "I have lost so much weight. I feel like a scarecrow." Despite her mourning having ended, her thick chestnut-colored hair was coiled demurely at the nape of her neck and a black silk bonnet trimmed in crepe sat atop her head. An ebony satin ribbon was tied crisply under her chin, the black veil at the back, as was the custom.

Ona clucked. "You coulda stopped wearin' that dress a few weeks ago, Miss Polly. I'm fixin' to burn it as soon as you take it off."

Polly dismissed Ona's comment with a wave of her hand. "I hope that Mrs. Batson has that new cage crinoline. It makes the most beautiful full skirt. I know that doesn't sound practical for riding around the fields, but it would be lovely for a Charleston party. I won't need as many petticoats underneath . . . and can you believe what I read in *Godey's*? There are women wearing—pants. That sounds simply awful. Wearing one's knickers for the world to see. Shameful. But what I wouldn't give to see such a thing." Polly chuckled and shook her head.

— • —

ONA SMILED WANLY AT HER YOUNG AND NAÏVE MISTRESS, out and about for the first time in months. She did not dare ask Polly for bolts of cloth for her own new clothing. She would have to broach the subject before winter set in. Ben had no coat, save Martin's ragged one, and the field hands had worn through their pants for the most part and rubbed holes in their thin shirts. She and Cissie were getting by with threadbare dresses but Cissie's baby boy needed clothing and some shoe leather, now that he was toddling around behind his mama all day.

Ona watched the world go by as the carriage bumped toward town. She had not been into Pendleton in years since the children were small and Mary Burgiss needed help as she shopped.

They rounded a bend and Pendleton loomed in front of them. Shops on either side of the road announced their names in words that Ona could not read. White people strolled down the dry wooden sidewalks, while slaves trudged along the muddy streets. The carriage pulled up to the dressmaker's shop. The shingle over the shop read Caroline Batson—Ladies' Dressmaker. Zadoc helped the women down from the rig, loosely tied the horse to the hitching post and waited for instruction.

"Zee, please go on to the post office and collect anything for Whitehall or River Wood. You know to wait outside, and when it is empty of customers, you may go in to see the postmaster." She glanced at Zadoc's mud-caked boots and shook her head. "Try to wipe your feet first. Then, meet us with the carriage at the milliner's down the block in about an hour. There is a painted blue hat on her sign. We will need a few things from the general store . . . I have a list made, so we will do that after."

"Yes'm." The man nodded and walked slowly down the street toward the small post office.

Polly walked into the store, with Ona following meekly behind. A tiny bell over the door tinkled as they entered. The pleasant scent of lavender and crushed thyme greeted them. A plump, greying woman entered from a back room and smiled. "Polly Burgiss?" she asked. "You look so like your mother. I would have known you anywhere!" The two women clasped hands. The woman peered at Ona warily over her spectacles but said nothing.

"Mrs. Batson, I am so happy for the appointment. It is wonderful to think about new dresses."

"It is my pleasure," said Mrs. Batson. "I was sorry to hear of your mother's death. What an awful time you have had. Your entire family is gone. All alone. Still, one must soldier on."

Polly stiffened. "Yes, thank you for your condolences." She tried to recover her cheerful mood. "I am taking a trip to Charleston for Christmas. I will be visiting Mrs. Calhoun there."

"How wonderful!" Mrs. Batson smiled again. "You and the great lady have become quite affectionate."

Polly ignored the comment. "I have several things in mind today, as I am now finally out of mourning."

Mrs. Batson clasped her hands together. "I have paper patterns now. In fact, I have a lovely pattern for a day dress with the most beautiful skirt detail. I assume you want English silk if I can get it. Oh, the pattern has delicate *engageantes* under the sleeves; quite popular in the cities. There is a new red velvet that would look stunning on you and—"

Polly interrupted the dressmaker. "It sounds lovely. However, I wonder if it might be too bold—coming out of mourning, I mean."

The woman shook her finger at Polly. "As a matter of fact, I have been reading lately about the new French mourning customs. In Charleston, it is *au currant*, I believe, to wear brighter shades for mourning now. You have been in black too long, my dear."

"Perhaps you are right." Polly nodded. "I want to take advantage of the very latest in fashion, Mrs. Batson. Really I do. But maybe in a blue or green silk. I feel as if I have been in mourning for most of my life, and red may take a while to get used to. I can at least wear fashionable gowns, if not colorful ones. I am also to be married—later next year."

"Congratulations, Miss Burgiss! A bit of happy news—I had no idea! Who is the lucky gentleman?" Mrs. Batson pulled her tape measure from around her neck and smiled.

Polly met the woman's eyes and said evenly, "Mr. John Stone, of River Wood." She braced for a negative reaction but received none.

Mrs. Batson knit her brows together in thought. "Well, I daresay I do not know the young man from River Wood, but congratulations to you both. I would be honored to help you with your trousseau."

Polly's lowered her defenses. "That would be lovely, Mrs. Batson. I have heard wonderful things about your new patterns, and I cannot wait to see what you can do."

"Ah, Miss Burgiss. You are a woman of taste and forward-thinking." Mrs. Batson beamed. "A wonderful option for you is the new cage crinoline. It will expand hoop skirts to the greatest width possible without those horrible petticoats." She leaned close to Polly and said, "Why, in Charleston, most women would positively swoon in the heat with the layers of petticoats one needs to project a certain image. With the cage crinoline, you will be cool and serene and among the most fashionable ladies anywhere you go." Mrs. Batson clapped her hands joyfully. "And I believe your complexion is the perfect color for the new silk I just received— a beautiful royal blue taffeta. It would be lovely. Oh, what a wonderful gown it will make with bugle beads and frills."

Polly smiled broadly. "It sounds perfect. And do you know about the new bishop sleeve?"

"You must have read the latest *Godey's Lady's Book*," exclaimed Mrs. Batson, obviously thrilled to have this fashionable customer. "Yes, I can make you a lovely dress described in the latest issue, with a closed, full sleeve, gathered into a narrow cuff. The waistline is at the natural waist and the skirt flounced. If you will come with me to the back of the store, I would like to take some measurements. And then we can see to the fabrics I have in mind."

The two women continued chatting as they went through the curtained doorway into the back room.

— • —

ONA STOOD NEAR THE FRONT DOOR AND LOOKED around the room at the bolts of beautiful fabrics and colorful threaded spools. There were silks and velvets, damasks and cottons in every color and print. Ona ran her hand over a rich, navy velvet and shook her head. It was all too much. She was not a woman to pine for things she could not have but being in this dressmaker's shop surrounded by this luxury was painful. She looked down at the threadbare cotton dress she wore. She pulled her moth-eaten shawl tightly around her thin shoulders and continued to peruse the colors and patterns, not sure of what her responsibility to her young mistress was here in this white woman's shop.

The bell over the shop door tinkled brightly and the door opened. In breezed an elegantly dressed older woman with silver hair and a bejeweled cameo at her throat. Following her was a pretty young woman wearing a huge, feathered spoon bonnet, the likes of which Ona had never seen. The women stopped abruptly at the sight of a black woman alone in the shop.

"Where is Mrs. Batson?" barked the older woman, scowling.

"She be in the back, with Miss Polly, I mean, Miss Burgiss," Ona stammered.

"Are you her mammy?" the woman asked abruptly. "Should you not wait outside?"

"Yes'm," Ona answered.

"You should leave immediately," snapped the woman, holding a handkerchief to her nose delicately. "I can smell you across the room. Imagine what your stench will do to these fabrics!" The younger lady reddened behind her gloved hand as if a horrid smell might be contagious.

"Yes'm." Ona darted past the women and opened the shop door.

"Her mammy," Ona heard the older woman snort. "Polly Burgiss brings her mammy with her to go dress shopping? Goodness, Lucinda. How far that family has fallen."

— • —

ON THE BUMPY CARRIAGE RIDE HOME, Polly chattered excitedly about the dresses she had ordered. As the carriage pulled into the turnoff to Whitehall, she noticed that Ona was unusually silent.

"Ona, you are very quiet. What is troubling you?" Polly asked.

"Nothin', Miss Polly. Miss Burgiss." Ona looked away across the bare fields.

"Ona, call me Miss Polly always. You've known me since I was a baby. Now tell me what is wrong? Did I say something to upset you? Was the trip into town too much?"

Ona took a deep breath. "Well, I cain't rightly lie to you. Firstly, we sho' could use some extry cotton or some wool so's I can fix up the men's clothes befo' winter. Cissie an' I is alright, I guess. Naw, but the baby, he growing like a weed and cain't fit into nothin' and the menfolk need pants and such."

"Oh, gracious, Ona. I had no idea. I will ask Mr. Roper to bring some homespun back from town tomorrow. And we can see to some wool and some good yarn so you and Cissie can knit socks and hats. How awful of me. And there you were—surrounded by all those pretty fabrics at Mrs. Batson's shop . . ." Polly shook her head. "I'm sorry. You will have what you need."

"Thank you, Miss Polly." Ona nodded. "Who was those ladies come into Mrs. Batson's while you was in there?"

"Mrs. Davis and her daughter, Lucinda. Captain Davis owns Walnut Plantation east a ways from Fort Hill. I think they must have twice the acreage we do, and three times the fortune, for sure! Why do you ask?"

"I jes' hope you stay clear of folks like them, Miss Polly. Mrs. Calhoun seems like good people, but them ladies was jes' not fine Christian folk." Ona crossed her arms and stuck her lower lip out defiantly. Polly burst out laughing.

Chapter Thirteen

December 1860

POLLY STOOD ON THE SIDEWALK OUTSIDE OF THE stately brick home, surrounded by a collection of trunks and boxes. She closed her eyes and inhaled the sea breeze.

"This is it." She laughed, staring up at the ornate front door, flanked by exotic palms. Warm gaslight glowed behind stained glass windows. The delicate wrought iron work on the gate was a wonder in itself. Polly had never seen such beauty. Despite the fact that the calendar read December, she smelled fragrant blossoms on the breeze. Strange trees lined the street, their branches coming out only near their tops, while their trunks were a collection of spiked protuberances all around.

"What is those trees?" Ona asked.

"I believe those are palmettos." Polly stared at the odd trees.

"Miss Polly, they's the ugliest trees I ever did see." Ona looked around nervously and continued, "We at the right place?"

"Yes, Ona. Her own driver knows where she lives." Polly was elated. She felt as if she knew the city already. Everything was as her father had described years ago, from the narrow brick homes with their secret courtyards and the busyness of the nearby wharf to the cobblestone streets alive with the sound of horse hooves. She longed to walk the streets of this beautiful city by herself, to soak it all in before she had to return to Whitehall.

She turned to the driver. He smiled and bowed, before extending his hand toward the elaborate staircase. "Miss Burgiss, I will see your belongings to your room. Mrs. Calhoun is awaiting your arrival." His English was perfect.

"Thank you, driver." She pushed open the gate and walked confidently toward the house. Ona followed her timidly. Stairs swept down grandly toward them from both sides of the wide front porch. She paused to consider which set to take.

"Miss Polly, is one set o' steps fo' white people and one set is fo' the slaves?" Ona wondered out loud. "I ain't about to take the wrong ones, no ma'am."

"Mrs. Calhoun told me that one side is for ladies and the other is for gentlemen, lest a man get a glimpse of ankle." Polly laughed.

"Then I 'spect that my door is in the back, so I just wait here with the bags," Ona said. Polly rolled her eyes and continued up the stairs, giddy with excitement. The huge brass knocker was in the form of a lion's head, with a thick circle in its ferocious mouth. Polly lifted the knocker and rapped firmly on the door.

A tall and elegantly dressed house slave answered the door. "Good evening, ma'am. You must be Miss Burgiss." He had a voice like melted butter. "Please come in. Mrs. Calhoun is expecting you."

Polly entered a large hall, which took her breath away. She looked around at the elegant wallpaper, the brightly colored carpets, and the cut-crystal chandelier with its winking candle lights overhead.

"Polly, dear," a voice called. "Welcome to Charleston!" Floride Calhoun came down the hall slowly. Nearly seventy years old, she walked haltingly with the help of an ebony cane. She still had the merry face and crinkled, laughing eyes that Polly loved. She reached toward Polly with her free hand.

"I am so happy that you decided to visit me. I trust your trip was a pleasant one," she said. The women embraced warmly.

"Very nice. This is the furthest I have ever been away from home," Polly exclaimed.

Floride grasped Polly's hand tightly. "My, you look more like your mother every day." She paused to study Polly's face. "It does me good to see you."

"Peter, have Nellie put the kettle on," Mrs. Calhoun instructed her servant. "We'll have tea now in the library and a late supper afterward."

The man bowed smoothly and said, "I will see to it right away, Madam."

At the mention of Floride's cook, Polly remembered that Ona was waiting outside in the gathering dark.

"Oh, gracious, Ona is still outside with my things." She looked first at her hostess and then to Peter.

The man nodded and said, "Yes, Miss Burgiss. The driver, David, will deliver your bags and show your woman to the servants' quarters. If you need her services before you retire, ring the silver bell in the parlor and I will send for her."

Floride locked arms with Polly and led her into the large and beautifully furnished parlor. It was warm and inviting, much like the smaller parlor in Floride's Pendleton home, lovingly christened Mi Casa. A cheery fire burned in the fireplace and elaborate tapestries lined the walls.

"Your Peter is quite an elegant house man," Polly quipped.

Quite serious, Floride nodded. "Oh, yes he is. I sent him to London to train as an under butler in the service of Lord Jones of Cheltenham. An old family friend." She smiled. "And my goodness, you still have your Ona. And she is traveling with you. Is that smart? The woman must be near my age . . . ," Floride said, sounding annoyed with her young friend. "Surely a younger maid would be more appropriate."

Before Polly could answer, Mrs. Calhoun had moved on.

"My dear, I am so glad you decided to visit me down here. I have much to show you!" The old woman sat across from Polly and settled her hands in her lap. "Tell me about the trip."

"We absolutely flew!" Polly said, wide-eyed. "The ticket agent said we would travel at forty miles an hour in some stretches. No wonder Father was so enamored. The entire time I wondered if he were watching me." Polly removed her gloves. "I was a bit teary. I know that he would be so proud of the railroad expansion, even though his tunnel hasn't materialized. It was an amazing journey. And this city—Floride, it is wonderful. The homes, the shop windows, the ships in the harbor; I can scarcely take it all in."

"Well, I am sorry about the tunnel's failure. I lost a lot of money there. We had high hopes once . . . high hopes indeed." Floride paused, remembering more prosperous times. "But my dear, I am glad that you have come. This trip will be a balm for your soul. Charleston is such an exciting city at Christmas time. I hope that we can fit in everything I would like you to see in just two weeks' time. It is a shame that my daughter will not arrive before you have turned around and gone home. You'd remember my Anna. Her daughter is about your age. We have so many people to visit and several parties. There is a gala at the Pinckneys' tomorrow night. The Governor will be there, I dare say." With a twinkle in her eye, she added, "And of course, you must meet Colonel Lee."

Polly cocked her head, "Who is he?"

"My dear, he is the most fascinating man! Colonel Robert Lee, from Virginia? And he is here now in our city visiting friends, after that most horrible standoff with that madman last year. He is a national hero. I am sure he will have stories to tell!" She nodded knowingly at Polly, her silver curls bobbing.

"Floride, I do not know what you mean. I confess that I do not keep up with current events. John is always chiding me about that. Who is this Colonel Lee?" At that moment, Nellie waddled in with a silver tea service and set it before the ladies.

"Thank you, Nellie. That will be all." Floride dismissed her slave and waited until she closed the parlor doors behind her before continuing. "So you are still keeping company with that John Stone? Hummpphh!" She snorted.

Polly decided to let her comment slide. "Tell me about this madman and Colonel Lee."

"That horrid man—John Brown, the northern abolitionist? He attacked a federal arsenal at Harper's Ferry in Virginia. He was the most violent man, a murderer, trying to rally slaves to kill innocent white people. The entire North glorified the fool." Mrs. Calhoun shook her head and began to pour out the tea. "Sugar? Cream?"

"Goodness," Polly said quietly, shaking her head to both. "I never heard of him. But then John and I rarely talk politics. I find it stressful. All he talks about is war, war, war. I just cannot bear it. I have had enough sorrow in my life. But—how does Colonel Lee come into the picture?"

"Well, Colonel Lee and his soldiers captured the vile thug and most of the other hooligans with him. The Colonel is a hero now. And that scoundrel, John Brown, was hanged for his crime!"

Floride used silver tongs to place a lump of sugar into her own teacup. "I wonder if Colonel Lee is here on war business. Since Lincoln was elected president, I fear the drums of war are ever increasing. We are all on edge here about secession. We expect to hear news any day from the Convention in Columbia. We will leave the Union."

"Floride, surely you exaggerate. South Carolina would never leave the United States. However, I would like to meet this Colonel Lee." Polly tried to sound interested, sipping her tea.

Floride chided her guest gently. "Polly Burgiss, you should be quite keen on meeting him. Colonel Lee has a great deal to say about the difficulties between the North and the South. I know that you are tucked away from the war talk nestled into the backcountry, but John Stone is correct. We in Charleston do fear war. I believe a mere spark will set it off.

Not three weeks ago, the General Assembly passed a resolution to call the election of Mr. Lincoln a hostile act."

"No wonder John was on edge," Polly said. "The train station was especially crowded with men heading to Columbia . . . Is Mr. Lincoln an abolitionist?"

Floride's eyes widened. "He supports equality and rights for slaves, Polly. Can you believe such a thing? As if blacks could fend for themselves without us."

Polly was tired from her long day of travel and only wanted to retire, but Floride was ready to hear all the news from home.

"So tell me about Mr. Stone. You are engaged to be married?" Mrs. Calhoun frowned.

"Yes, it is true." Polly held out her left hand and displayed her small ring. "I shall probably marry him next year after the cotton," she said defiantly. "He has been quite patient. And despite what you think, and despite what Mother thought about him, he is very good to me."

"Do you love him, my dear?"

The question surprised Polly. "His help was crucial in getting my cotton in after Mother died," Polly said defensively. "Twice now. I am fond of him, of course. And I cannot do this alone." Polly felt the need to defend her decision. "I am sure that he will manage Whitehall well. I plan to keep Mr. Roper as overseer. Mr. Wilkins shall stay at River Wood. I trust John will see the wisdom in keeping both men, one at Whitehall and one at River Wood." There was only silence.

"Will you give us your blessing?" Polly finally asked. Polly had heard the stories of how Floride Calhoun and her circle of Washington ladies had brought down poor Peggy Eaton, the former secretary of war's wife, accusing her of low morals. Polly needed Floride on her side if the match was to be accepted in the district.

Floride sighed and sipped her tea. "My dear, I love you like my own child. You remind me of my Anna, so far from me in Maryland. But I simply cannot give my blessing to the marriage. The man simply swooped in as soon as your mother died. Your reasons for wanting to proceed do not strike me as good ones. Do you love the wretched man?"

Polly blushed. "I suppose I do," she stammered. "He has been good to me."

"Yes, so you've said. Someone being good to you is not a valid reason for a marriage, my dear. Your mother, on her deathbed, asked me to keep you from him. While I realize I do not have that kind of power, I will offer my counsel. I believe him to be untrustworthy. A drunkard. You clearly have some affection for the man, but he is . . . he is no gentleman. Is he after your land? Of course, he is. Did he ever discuss his proposal with your mother? Of course, he did not. And as for getting rid of that nasty Mr. Wilkins, I fear the man will never leave River Wood."

Polly leaned forward. "If there is anything else you want to say to me, please say it now," she said sarcastically.

Floride Calhoun pursed her lips thoughtfully. As if reconsidering her words, she replied calmly, "I have nothing, save my woman's intuition. But it screams to me that you should not marry this man. I have only rumors to offer, and rumors will not persuade you. You are entitled to marry whomever you wish and I have said my piece. I was young once. I understand how you feel."

Floride regarded Polly for a moment. The older woman set her cup down and settled back in her seat. "I was just a girl nearly forty years ago when I married John Calhoun. Your age. Even as a very young man, he had such ambition, such passion. When he spoke, others listened. Of course, you know all of that. The world knows all of that. But to me, he was just my John. I loved him so. We settled at Fort Hill. It was my mother's land." She paused to let Polly digest this fact.

"When she died, I inherited the property fully. My plans were to raise children and grow cotton. But John's calling was politics. First, he served in the state legislature, then Congress, and well, you know the rest . . . He was an ambitious man with high moral standards."

A small smile played at Polly's lips. She thought of the infamous Peggy

Eaton affair. "And you were not uninterested in politics and high moral standards."

"Ah, you heard of my good intentions gone awry." Floride winked at Polly. "Those were different times, my dear . . ." Her voice trailed off and she dropped her head, toying with the sleeve of her dress for a moment. She looked up and continued, "Everyone assumed that John had managers and overseers attending to our affairs. What very few people knew was that John gave me charge of Fort Hill after our marriage. I had no idea how to run a plantation. But he was a politician, not a planter."

Polly sipped her tea. "Floride, you had a husband. He was the Vice President! You have over one hundred slaves. My entire family has passed away, and I have only nine slaves. Not to be crude—but I don't have your money," she said pointedly. She dabbed at her lips with her handkerchief.

Floride swatted the air with her hand. "Oh poo. Stop feeling sorry for yourself."

Polly blanched.

Floride continued, "In the first 18 years of our marriage, I bore ten children. I lost three as babies. Four more as adults."

Polly thought of her mother's own grief after the boys died.

"Having money is not a balm for loss and loneliness. However, I ran Fort Hill in my husband's absence and managed to put out a good cotton crop most years. I felt so alone during those years, but running the plantation gave me a purpose to my days. Even while in Washington, dealings here at home occupied my mind for the better. John was a man of strong convictions. His work kept him preoccupied with affairs of state his entire life. Looking back, I believe that his trusting me to run our estate was a great gift, not an obligation. Yes, life on a plantation can be quite hard for a woman." She leaned toward Polly and grasped her hands, "But Fort Hill saved me. If I had just stayed in a corner and sewed, I would have wasted away."

Polly nodded, remembering her own mother slumped over her needlepoint day after day, year after year.

"And Polly, Whitehall will save you. Give you something to fight for. You have good land and a prosperous farm. It is all yours. Keep an eye on your accounts. Just because you are a woman does not mean that you don't have a good head on your shoulders. I would hate to see you have to sell it for taxes after one bad year. There are unethical men moving south, just waiting for our places to fail, and waiting to take our land away from us. Speak with your overseer. Be sure he understands that you are watching him, that you are watching accounts. He seems a good man. Read the crop reports and keep up with current events. In short, do whatever you can to make Whitehall profitable . . . to make it strong. With or without John Stone." She braced herself with the cane and stood.

Polly nodded meekly, chastised.

"Now, dear, let us put this subject aside. We will have a bit of supper before you retire. Nellie has prepared the most delicious lobster bisque." She steered Polly into the dining room and kept the conversation light and easy for the remainder of the evening, for which Polly was thankful.

That night, Polly undressed quickly without calling for Ona. Wearing only her chemise, she slid between satin sheets, under a down comforter, and prepared herself for a night of fitful sleep. It seemed that there was something about John that everyone around her sensed and she did not. She resolved to have him clear the air with her before a wedding. Whatever skeletons were hiding in his closet would be out before she put a wedding date into her calendar.

She turned onto her back and stared at the moonlit ceiling. Ghostly shadows of swaying palms played over her head. Rumor had it that John had mismanaged his plantation, and his overseer was brutal with slaves. Was that the worry on everyone's minds? Or had he been with women? She would demand to know. He would only want complete openness and honesty. Polly tossed, trying to imagine her wedding. Strangely, she could not see the groom's face as she walked down the aisle to meet her husband at the altar.

Somewhere in the harbor, a ship's bell clanged. She supposed that a handsome man like John, without the benefit of good family upbringing, might have some sort of shady past, but she had not fully given it any thought.

For Floride to say that her intended husband was no gentleman was hurtful beyond words. The woman was old and had not been privy to all the good that John had done at Whitehall since her mother's death.

For a brief moment, Polly wondered what would happen if she asked him about his past. His anger would be kindled and then what? No, no, Floride was wrong. John was a good man, prone to a temper, yes, but a man who loved her and would help her save Whitehall. The thought of doing it alone was too much to bear. He, too, had lost both parents. They had relied on each other for comfort throughout the ordeal. When his blue eyes looked at her, it set her insides churning, and wasn't that love?

Polly finally slept, nestled deep in the sumptuous bedding. She awoke the next morning, still upset with her hostess, but filled with great anticipation.

— • —

A WARM BREEZE RUFFLED THE PALMETTOS ON the street outside her shuttered windows. Gulls cried in the harbor. Polly listened to the sounds of a city waking up, so different from the sounds of a morning at Whitehall. There was the continuous clip-clop, clip-clop of horses on cobblestones, the squeaky wheels of a carriage going past, and the clanging of the bells in church towers. She heard the muted voices of passersby and the lonely sound of a buoy bell in the harbor.

Floride had a lovely day of activities planned for Polly, designed to show off Charleston to her young friend. Polly stretched luxuriously and smiled. She sat up and looked around the room in the morning light. The room was decorated with fine fabrics and furnishings from Europe. The enormous mahogany four-poster bed felt like a ship to Polly. The plush Oriental rugs were of the highest quality. Wall coverings and draperies whispered of boundless wealth. She wished she could bring such finery back to Whitehall someday. Perhaps if the Stones and Burgisses were one family, they could afford small luxuries.

Over the next two weeks, Polly hoped to relax and enjoy the sights and sounds of the city. She would be careful not to mention issues at home. Floride planned to introduce new friends, show her the steepled churches and beautiful mansions of Charleston, and treat her to a picnic excursion near the coast. Polly looked forward to seeing the ocean for the first time, to marvel at its grandeur and power. It was wonderful to be young in this city, to release the worries of home and, finally, the sadness over losing her parents.

There was a timid knock on her door. "Come in," Polly said.

Ona entered, carrying a large silver serving tray loaded with dishes. She set the tray down and beamed at her mistress. "Miss Polly, I declare I ain't never seed such food come out of a kitchen before. I wasn't sure I could get it up to ya!"

She removed the cover from one dish after another to reveal a bounty of good things. There were several fresh-baked scones with clotted cream, and jams in small silver pots. Sliced fruits and cheeses were arranged just so on a small platter. Another held bacon, sausage, and thick slices of ham. A steaming pot of tea and one of coffee were also at hand.

Polly's eyes widened. "Ona, if I ate all of this, you would not be able to lace my corset." She laughed. "But, oh, does it all look wonderful! Have you eaten?" She picked up a bit of scone and began to butter it with a silver knife. When Ona did not answer, she glanced up from her plate.

Ona swallowed hard. "You ain't never asked me that before. No one ever asked me that. Yes'm, I ate. Nellie gave me as much as I could take in."

"Floride is quite the hostess." Polly reddened.

"I hear you has a real big party tonight. You gonna meet the gov'nor and some other important people, Nellie says. Miss Polly, wouldn't yo' parents be real proud of their little girl now!" Ona said.

She opened the massive mahogany wardrobe and began to air Polly's gowns for the day. Polly watched the woman work. Ona was getting older, she knew. She complained about her back, her hips, and her dimming eyes but continued to care for her charge as she had always done.

"Ona, how old are you?" Polly abruptly sat up in the large bed.

"'Scuse me, Miss Polly?" Ona continued to hang dresses and smooth them lovingly, taking great care with each one. "Goodness, I don't rightly know," she answered absentmindedly. "Mebbe forty-five, forty-six."

"Hmm. Floride thought you were about her age. You are much younger. Ona, when we get home, I want you to hand over the housekeeping to Cissie. When John and I marry, there will be two of us to feed again, and John eats like a horse. I prefer your cooking anyway. Focus on the cooking and the stores. Let Cissie clean the house. Maybe you will be able to rest a little bit more. How does that sound to you?" Polly awaited Ona's grateful response.

Ona finally answered, "Thank you, Miss Polly."

Polly was slightly peeved. "I thought that you would be relieved to turn over cleaning fireplaces and emptying chamber pots to someone younger. You know that I do not require much personal attention at home, and Cissie is young and can take over the laundry and the cleaning. After I am married, there will be twice the housework, with a husband, and one day, children. Let her handle it." She dribbled strawberry jam on another bit of scone.

Ona turned to look at the young woman. "Yes, Miss Polly. I rightly am relieved about that . . ." Her voice trailed off.

"But? Is something on your mind, Ona?" Polly popped the bite of scone into her mouth and licked her buttery fingers.

"So you intendin' to marry Mr. Stone soon?" Ona asked.

What's the matter with everyone? Polly wondered. Her defenses up once more, Polly swallowed and looked hard at her servant. "Yes, perhaps in the summer," she said coolly. "He has been good to me, and I am sure that he will be good to all of you. Do not listen to rumor, Ona. It will not serve you well. Unless you have something concrete to tell me about him, I do not want to hear any more." She dabbed at the corner of her mouth with a linen napkin. "You may lay out my clothing, and then you are dismissed."

"Ain't you needin' he'p with yo' corset and yo' hair?" Ona tried.

"No. Just go." Polly waved dismissively. She did not look at Ona as she left the room, chastened.

She pushed the breakfast tray away and lay back into the down pillows, her mind racing. First, her own mother, then Floride, Tom Roper, and now Ona.

Polly threw back her quilts and stood up. She took a long drink from the bone china coffee cup. She crossed the room to the wardrobe and yanked a simple day dress out of the cabinet roughly. She dressed herself, pinned her hair into a low chignon, laced her new boots tightly, and tied on a bonnet before slipping out of her room. Before she had gone ten paces, a dark young maid appeared in her path.

"May I help you, Miss Burgiss?" the woman asked earnestly. "My name is Victoria."

Her eyes were the most amazing yellow gold, Polly noticed. "Victoria, like the queen?"

"Yes ma'am." The woman's face lit up and she straightened proudly.

"I am going for a walk, Victoria. Please let Mrs. Calhoun know," Polly said briskly.

"The morning is chilly, ma'am. May I get your wrap?" the woman asked. Her diction was impeccable.

Polly relaxed slightly. "No, thank you. I have no need of a coat. I shall be back soon. I just want to clear my head."

"As you wish, Miss Burgiss. You will find the back stairs lead to the courtyard and the hothouse, and then to the street, ma'am." The maid pointed down the hall, bowed her head, and stepped aside to let Polly pass.

Polly descended the stairs quickly and pushed the heavy door open. She gasped as she gazed around at the lush beauty of the shaded Calhoun courtyard. She followed a winding brick path that led past a bubbling fountain. Polly had never seen such a wonder.

The door to the hothouse came into view and she turned the latch and entered. Warm and humid, the space felt alive. Delicate ferns and exotic red hibiscus nodded. A small still pond shimmered with goldfish. Polly stared at colorful bromeliads growing in low hanging branches of small trees. Curling silver moss hung from the boughs of a young live oak. She moved down the path silently, her senses delighted at every turn. She heard the *snip, snip* of pruning shears and followed the sound.

Crouched under a palmetto and blocking her path, an elderly white-haired slave trimmed brown tips from the spiky fronds. So as not to alarm the man, Polly cleared her throat. "Pardon me."

The man turned and tried to stand quickly, but Polly could see that his back was bent at an angle and he winced in pain before pasting a smile on his lips. "I so sorry, Miss. I didn't know anyone was usin' the garden this early. I come back later."

"Oh no, don't let me disturb your work. Victoria told me to use the courtyard door as a means to the street?" Polly said.

The old man nodded. "Yes ma'am. Follow the brick path around one more curve and you there."

Indeed, Polly could hear the muffled noises of the busy street ahead. "How wonderful!" she smiled. "This beautiful garden blocks the noise of the city"

Warmed by her admiration, the man grinned. "Ain't it the truth, ma'am? Mizz Calhoun don't come out here near enough, to my mind. It like heaven on earth."

"It is, indeed," Polly agreed. "Or the Garden of Eden. Tell me, are you the caretaker?"

"I am. My name's James. I know everythang about every plant out here. Why, some of them come from the island of Cuba!"

Polly's smile widened. "James. That was my father's name."

James nodded. "He got a good name."

"Tell me, James, when I return from my walk, might I come see you about taking some cuttings of these bright flowers for my place in the upstate?" she asked.

"No ma'am!" James frowned, limping toward a hibiscus with vivid pink flowers. Before Polly could take offense, he added, "Ya see, these here is tropical plants. They like it warm and wet. If they was outside, I'd have to cover them up some nights of a frost. They'd up and die if they was to be put out in the cold!" James touched the plant lovingly.

Polly's eyes widened. "Oh, I didn't know that. I know nothing about ornamental plants. I do love the pink flowers. Well, they are beautiful indeed, and I shall come back to your little kingdom again. I would love to at least learn the names of the plants."

James nodded. "I ain't never thought of this as my kingdom, but I sho' like the sound of it. Tell ya what, I do have a plant that you can take home, might last through the winter. I know it'll take a freeze. Oleander. Tall bush. Bright pink flowers. You can plant it outside in the spring. It'll remind you of Charleston. I'll pot some and send it to your maid. Jes' don't go eatin' it!" he cackled.

Polly warmed to the little man. "Thank you, James. And this is surely your little kingdom, so I shall call you King James. But now, I want to take a walk. Perhaps you can point me in an interesting direction?"

James looked at Polly strangely. "Hmmm. Well, Chalmers Street be real interestin'. Turn right out the gate, go past City Hall, and turn right on Chalmers. If ya keep makin' rights, you come back here eventually," he laughed.

"Thank you, King James." Polly smiled. She brushed past the little man and continued down the path. She left the greenhouse and was immediately assaulted by the cool salt-laden ocean breeze. She pushed open the wrought iron gate and stared at the goings-on up and down Meeting Street. She smiled as a gentleman in her path doffed his hat and then she turned right in the direction of Chalmers Street.

As Polly strolled, she admired one beautiful home after another along the cobblestoned street. Each courtyard was an enchanted garden hidden behind a unique piece of exquisite ironwork. She would have to tell Ben about the designs she saw. Her feet soon began to ache, and she realized that her choice of new boots was a poor one, but she was determined to finish her walk to Chalmers Street.

The signpost soon came into view and Polly turned the corner. Homes and businesses on both sides of the narrow street were tiny in comparison to the finer edifices on Meeting, but their quaint and colorful exteriors charmed Polly at once. Tiled roofs, cheerful facades, and shops of all kinds lined the street. Polly couldn't believe her eyes when she saw a house in a shade of pale pink with green shutters. *No wonder James recommended this interesting street*, she thought. Even in December, window boxes spilled over with delicate ferns and trailing ivy. The cobblestones beneath her boots were more bumpy and uneven than Meeting Street, and Polly marveled at the wagons passing by at a bone-jarring pace.

She scanned the lane and quickly noticed how different the crowd appeared than on Pendleton's Main Street. While some of the black people were dressed in uniform like Floride's slaves or in clothing that Polly would expect to see on an upstate farmer, sharply dressed freedmen and women conducted their business as well. They were at the small grocer's on the left, coming and going from the butcher's shop on the right and speaking in small groups with other freedmen. One elegantly dressed freedman was accompanied by a barefoot boy in rags who looked to be his own slave. Polly found it all strangely exhilarating.

A knot of bystanders had gathered further down the street and she squinted in the bright morning sunlight to see what might be going on. In front of her, a man handed out broadsheets and he thrust one in her hand as she approached.

"Sale today at Ryan's Mart!" he barked to the crowd. "Prime young field hands! Second men! Mr. Ryan has a light-skinned negress today, and two second-women starting at $800 apiece! Thirty pieces of chattel in all! Come on in! All are welcome!"

Polly stopped in her tracks. She looked behind her and was stunned to see business as usual going on in the street. Freedmen continued with their chatter, and white women of privilege stepped into and out of one small shop after another. Curious, she turned around, squared her shoulders, and headed toward the stone building with the word MART etched into the overhead stone arch.

Polly stepped through the double doors to find a row of benches lining either side of a large, but stuffy, lamplit room. There was a raised platform at the center of the room, devoid of activity at this point. Several gentlemen had already entered the room and were deep in conversation, notebooks, and pencils in hand. She took a seat on a bench and waited.

Slowly the room filled with people intent on purchasing slaves, and Polly watched as a young black boy handed out catalogs to anyone who raised a hand. She was surprised to see one of the freedmen from off the street enter the room and sit on a bench nearby. He raised his hand and the slave boy quickly brought him a catalog.

After a few minutes, a burly mulatto man entered the room through a side door, leading a group of manacled slaves to a platform. Men, women, and two children huddled together forlornly. A toddler clutched tightly to the hands of a tall dark man and a young woman. They must be his parents, Polly realized, with a pang of guilt. She thought of little Silas and her heart lurched. Two older women held hands tightly, their bodies shaking visibly. They were all directed to stand against the back wall, which they did obediently.

A nattily dressed auctioneer entered the room from the other side of the building and stepped up onto the platform. He held a copy of the catalog and reviewed it briefly before calling the room to attention.

"Ladies and gentlemen, welcome to Mr. Ryan's, where today we are selling off the last group of slaves from Widow Hotchkins' estate. As I said yesterday, it was Mrs. Hotchkins' desire that her slaves be sold together. However, this group was not purchased yesterday when Mr. Manigault completed his transaction."

"These fine specimens were available yesterday for inspection and have all been thoroughly cleaned and checked out. But, if you would like to have yourselves a closer look today, let me know and we can certainly let you inspect before you purchase. We will begin today with chattel number nineteen in your catalog."

The seated buyers murmured between themselves and consulted their catalogs.

There was the sound of pages turning and a general hum of conversation from the crowd as the mulatto man nodded at the first slave to be auctioned. The dark-skinned man who looked to be in his mid-thirties released the hand of the child and stepped forward and onto the platform. He looked back at the young woman, who had tears streaming down her face, but did not say a word. Polly shuddered and could not help but think of George and Cissie.

"Yes sir, yes sir, this here is chattel number nineteen, a strong and healthy field hand. This young buck is the last of Widow Hotchkins' field hands, a man in his prime. Number nineteen is used to being in the rice and in the cotton. He is a strong one with no injuries. He goes by the name of Jefferson." The auctioneer scanned the faces before him. "I know that both Mr. Spotts and Mr. Childress had a good look at him yesterday and liked what they saw. Let's start the bidding at $1000."

Immediately, hands began to raise as the bidding progressed. Polly felt the blood pounding in her temples and the slow creep of nausea in her gut as she watched the drama unfold. On the platform, Jefferson stood proudly, his eyes staring over the heads of the crowd.

Finally, the frantic bidding stopped and the auctioneer looked out over the crowd. "Chattel number nineteen going for fifteen hundred dollars, going once. Twice. Sold! Sold to Mr. Robert Childress." He banged his gavel and the slave stepped off the block. The mulatto led the way as the slave exited through a door in the back of the room. The woman continued to weep silently, and picked up the toddler, holding him to her chest tightly.

Polly's eyes were riveted to the platform as the mulatto pointed to the young woman and child. The woman slowly came forward, clutching the toddler tightly.

The auctioneer boomed, "This here is chattel numbers twenty and twenty-one. Got a fine negress here, as light-skinned as a young fawn, and her baby boy. Now, Widow Hotchkins' wish was to keep this young family together, so Mr. Childress, I am going to ask you first, sir. Any wish to take on a new house girl and her pickaninny? This here is Ginnie and her baby boy Wilson. She can cook and clean, she can operate a spinning wheel and mammy young children. Won't be long before young Wilson here can be put out to chores hisself! Sounds like a real sound purchase to me. What do you say, Mr. Childress? Can we start with you, sir, and the low bid of $700?"

Polly's eyes darted to the seated figure of Mr. Childress. She realized she was biting her lip so hard that she had drawn blood, and quickly wiped her mouth with her palm. The room was close and warm, and Polly felt the perspiration bead on her skin. *He just has to take them*, she thought. *He just has to.*

The gentleman puffed on his cigar and shook his head as if he couldn't be bothered to even consider the purchase.

The auctioneer pressed his case once more. "Come now, Mr. Childress. Have a heart! Don't separate this poor little family." His dramatic plea caused fat Mrs. Childress to elbow her husband in the ribs, but the man was resolute.

"I got no need for another nigger inside my house. I'll take the field hand and be done, thank you very much!" Childress barked.

From the platform, the young woman suddenly cried out, "Please suh! Please! I work real hard for ya missus! I c-cook and clean! I can spin and weave, suh. I's beggin' ya! Please take us!"

The mulatto was on the platform in an instant and slapped the woman across her mouth. He whispered angrily into her ear and she nodded, tears streaming down her wet cheeks. The baby began to cry, and the crowd murmured its discomfort.

The auctioneer barely blinked before continuing with his work. "Alrighty then folks, we got us a fine negress and a young boy here. Who will start the bidding? Can I get a $600 from an interested buyer? I'll split them up if I have to."

"Five fifty!" shouted someone in the crowd, and the bidding was off. Polly could hear the bidding continue at a pitch but she shut her eyes to avoid the sight of the woman's anguish.

Polly jumped up and walked quickly from the room, as a wave of nausea threatened to overtake her then and there. She emerged, squinting, into bright morning sunlight and leaned against the building to get her breath.

"May I help you, Miss? You look about to swoon," said a deep voice at Polly's elbow. She opened her eyes to find an older gentleman looking at her with concern. His amber eyes were kind and his suit bespoke wealth and status. Yet his skin was the color of strong tea. He tipped his expensive hat and exposed a thinning crown of snowy hair that matched his trimmed beard. "You look unwell. May I escort you somewhere to sit down? Perhaps call you a carriage?"

Polly touched her hand to her cheek and realized she had been crying. She reddened and shook her head vigorously. "Oh, no—sir. I am sorry. I suppose I was unprepared for the emotion of a slave auction. A family was just ripped apart. I am not from Charleston, and this was new to me. Though I am fine, really. Thank you for your concern. I will be on my way now." The words tumbled from her mouth before she could censor them.

The mulatto man smiled with a twinkle in his eye. "Auctions are not for the faint of heart, are they, Miss? They can be traumatic affairs. I have been to many. Are you sure I cannot give you a ride somewhere? My carriage is at the corner."

Polly glanced furtively at the crowd coming and going all around her. No one seemed to notice this strange interaction between an old Negro and a young white woman. She returned his kind smile. "No. Thank you. I am staying with a friend around the block. On Meeting Street. I should finish my walk. The fresh air will do me good."

The gentleman nodded. "Very well, Miss. Be careful not to turn an ankle. These stones can be the very devil." He tipped his silk hat again and stepped off the curb into the flow of the crowd.

She squared her shoulders and walked quickly toward the corner. Fifteen minutes later, Polly found herself standing in front of the iron gate to Floride's garden. Locked from the outside, she rattled the gate. "James? James, are you there?"

From deep within the courtyard, Polly heard the shuffle of feet and soon saw the figure of James, limping toward her. "I's comin', ma'am. I's comin'."

He flipped a latch on the gate and stood back as Polly entered. "How was yo' walk?"

Polly's eyes narrowed. "Interesting. I do not think I have ever seen such sights. Some of which I hope never to see again."

"Happy to he'p, Miss. Ol' James is always happy to he'p," James grinned up at Polly innocently. For a second, she could have sworn the old slave winked at her.

She regarded him a moment longer before turning and heading deeper into the courtyard and the door to the house.

Chapter Fourteen

BACK IN HER ROOM, POLLY SAT ON THE EDGE of the comfortable chaise and exhaled deeply. She arranged several pillows and leaned back, closing her eyes. The slave woman's pained expression haunted her. She wondered if the child had been separated from his mother. And the mulatto stranger who had been so kind? He seemed to take the auction of slaves in stride. It was all so confusing. Before long, Polly was asleep. In her dreams, she heard the clanging of church bells outside her open window. The longer she listened, the more bells began to chime in, clanging wildly.

She awoke and sat up, trying to get her bearings. She stood and opened the shutters for a better view. It was difficult to see anything from the narrow window, but it wasn't long before she heard shouts from the street and raised voices in the house.

"Polly! Polly! It has happened," she heard Floride cry from the hallway. She ran to the door and opened it to find an out of breath Floride clutching her dressing gown closed with one hand while holding a morning newspaper in the other. Her nightcap was askew, and her eyes were wide. "The Convention voted yesterday to secede. We have pulled out of the Union!"

Polly gasped. "What does this mean?"

"My dear, I do not know. The paper said that the vote was unanimous—169 aye votes! Do you hear the bells?" Floride continued to scan the paper. "President Buchanan says the whole thing is illegal, a sham." She closed the newspaper abruptly and said quietly, "Polly dear, we must not alarm the slaves."

"But the bells . . ." Polly began.

"'Tis a wedding celebration, if they ask! We must remain calm and continue with our day as planned. Tonight at the Pinckneys' party, I am sure that we will hear it all. Now, I must dress. I shall see you downstairs in one hour for our morning rounds."

The women spent the best part of the morning calling on several society matrons. Polly chatted and made small talk and heard lots of local gossip. Secession was the word on everyone's lips and the possibility of war was on every Charlestonian's mind.

Polly was quickly brought up to speed on the current events of the day. The ladies ended their morning with a luncheon at the home of Mrs. Augustus Smythe, of both Pendleton and Charleston. Polly had met the woman at her father's funeral and enjoyed getting to know her better. She was an ardent supporter of states' rights, like the Calhouns, and was quick to fill in the gaps in Polly's knowledge of the South's grievances with the North.

Polly spent the late afternoon resting in her room, preparing for the evening's gala at the home of Mr. and Mrs. Henry Pinckney. Mr. Pinckney was a former mayor of Charleston and a close friend of the Calhoun family. The Pinckneys had also owned a plantation in the upstate until recently. Although Polly had never met them, she remembered her mother and father referring to them with something akin to awe. Generations of Pinckneys had lived in South Carolina and their former summer estate in Pendleton was a fine place even now.

As the shadows lengthened outside Polly's window, she arose. She began to dread Ona coming to help her dress, as she didn't want to have to explain the pealing bells or get into another row over John. She was embarrassed to realize that she had not thought of the man the entire day. *Was this a normal reaction to being away from one's intended?* she wondered.

There was a timid knock on the door. "Come in, Ona." Polly steeled herself for Ona's sullen reaction to the morning's argument, but Ona was in no mood to continue the spat either.

"Good evening, Miss Polly. I brought you this drink from Mrs. Calhoun. S'pose to settle yo' nerves." Ona bore a silver tray with a single crystal glass. The deep ruby liquid within practically glowed.

Polly sniffed at the glass and coughed. "Goodness! It smells like one of Dr. Adger's elixirs. I believe my friend is trying to make me tipsy." Nevertheless, she took the small glass and sipped. "Mmm. I have never had a cordial before, but I believe I do like it."

Ona wrinkled her nose. "I wouldn't get used to it if I was you. A stomach full of that stuff and no food—how you gonna git through the evenin' without supper first?"

"I couldn't eat a thing anyway. My corset has never been so tight." Polly turned to regard her reflection in the narrow mirror.

Ona eyed her mistress with a frown. "How you gonna breathe? An' you want me to put yo' hair up with dem turtle and silver combs you bought in town?"

Her gaffe broke the tension. Polly laughed, "Sweet Ona, they are not turtle combs. Tortoiseshell, the word is tortoiseshell."

The slave woman sighed. "I knew they was somethin' strange. This whole town is somethin' strange, indeed . . . I heard those clangin' bells all mornin' and heard about the 'cession." Polly gave no reply.

Ona sighed. "Well, let me start. Yo' hair so thick, it gonna take a hour just to pin it up. Then we got that dress to git on."

Polly's dress was a work of art. Sewn in plum taffeta and satin, the beaded gown featured Brussels lace dyed to match at the scooped neckline and gathered off the shoulders. The color set off Polly's pale skin and chestnut hair. The hooped skirt was quite large, with ruffled flounces all the way from waist to floor. Tiny satin slippers completed the outfit.

"Miss Polly, I declare you be the belle o' the ball tonight! Mrs. Batson sho' did make a beautiful gown! Ain't no one gonna have a problem with you wearin' this color." She walked around Polly, gazing at her mistress proudly.

Polly studied her reflection in the mirror. "Ona, it is beautiful, isn't it? I hope I am not going to embarrass Mrs. Calhoun. It is quite the fashion and it does have bugle beading."

"Honey, I think you can wear whatever you want. It's been over a year . . . And you so pretty that every man there gonna be signin' yo' dance card. Ain't no chance of any man missin' a dance with you!" Ona suddenly remembered the morning's argument with her mistress and grew silent.

Polly clasped Ona's brown hand and said, "Ona, I am sorry. I should not have snapped at you earlier. Let's not have another word about goings-on at home while we are in this amazing city. Agreed?" She squeezed Ona's hand. "Do I really look beautiful?"

Ona smiled. "I wish Miss Mary could see how beautiful you is right now. She sho' be proud."

— • —

THE LIVERIED COACHMAN TOOK SPECIAL PAINS to take the ladies on the ten-minute detour through town on the least jarring streets, at Floride's instruction. Polly and Floride arrived at the Pinckney mansion at half-past eight, in a carriage drawn by two ebony horses. "My dear, these cobblestone streets make for a horrific ride, I assure you," she had confided. "You will thank me." Polly's sore feet could already attest to the horror of cobblestone paving.

The Pinckney estate was even more elaborate than the Calhoun mansion. Elegantly dressed footmen stood proudly outside of the open wrought iron gates, assisting guests as they alit, and directing coachmen with empty carriages toward the large stables at the back of the estate. Gaslights flickered everywhere, lending an air of magic to the night.

Polly followed Floride Calhoun into the home and was immediately caught in a swirl of elegant ladies who surrounded them. Mrs. Calhoun was clearly well-loved, and Polly was honored to be with her dear and famous friend. She was introduced to one lady of means after another, rich planters' wives, and of course the delightful Mrs. Harriet Pinckney, gracious hostess and the wife of the former mayor.

Most of the women were strangers to the upstate. But Polly was surprised to find that a few also owned plantations or summer estates inland, away from the heat and humidity of the low country. Mabel Gist invited Polly to visit her at Rosehill, the family's plantation in the heart of the state. Clara Laurens had a summer home in nearby Greenville County. The Pinckneys had only recently sold their estate to the Wells family, whom Polly knew of in passing. Their stories were similar and their love of the land was palpable. She was relieved to find that although they were rich and refined and important, they were gracious and kind and eager to make Polly their new friend. No one seemed affronted by her attempt at grand fashion. In fact, she received many compliments on her gown.

A well-dressed older gentleman approached the knot of ladies crowding around Polly and bent to kiss Floride's hand. "Mrs. Calhoun, it is always my great pleasure to see you." The man straightened. He had a balding pate and a clean-shaven chin. "I trust that we will see Anna and her family here for the holiday?"

Floride beamed at the mention of her daughter. "At the New Year. I am so looking forward to their visit. Mr. Pinckney, allow me to introduce to you, my dear young friend, Miss Polly Burgiss, daughter of the late James and Mary Burgiss of Whitehall, in the Pendleton District."

"Miss Burgiss, it is an honor to have you here this evening. You are a vision of loveliness." He bowed and kissed her extended hand. "I was sorry to learn of your mother's death. I recall that she was a lovely lady. We had a summer home near your place years ago. It was a good retreat from Lowcountry mosquitoes."

Polly smiled. "It is a pleasure to meet you, sir. Did you know my father?"

Mr. Pinckney nodded. "I remember a meeting at Whitehall with your father and John Calhoun and other planters, so many years ago, after—" He stopped and blushed crimson. "Well, no need to speak of it. My, that was more than ten years ago. My apologies." He cleared his throat. "I hope you have a lovely time tonight, Miss Burgiss. I am told that my wife spared not a penny on the food and drink. You ladies must eat, drink, and be merry, for tomorrow comes a war."

Polly warmed to the old gentleman. She longed to sit down with him and ask questions about her father. She had only recently begun to think of him the way that others saw him, an important man in the state, conducting business with other South Carolina leaders.

Floride turned to Pinckney. "May I prevail upon you to interrupt our dignitaries to introduce this young lady? I know that secession is on the minds of the gentlemen, but I dare say she should meet them since she has come all the way from the backwoods." Floride chuckled and winked slyly at Polly. "And it's not every day a lady gets to meet military heroes. Yet if we wait much longer, she will be too busy on the dance floor to be pulled away."

"Of course, Mrs. Calhoun. Miss Burgiss, allow me?" Mr. Pinckney extended his arm. Polly took it nervously and was led through the crowded ballroom into the smoke-filled library. A crowd of men clutching cigars and drinking brandy milled about the room. Polly's first glance was toward the extensive collection of books that lined the cherry-paneled space. Shelves of books spanned two walls from floor to ceiling. She gasped involuntarily.

Mr. Pinckney looked at Polly with amusement. "Don't let this group frighten you, Miss Burgiss. I promise that they have left their pistols and sabers at the door."

"Oh no, Mr. Pinckney! I am in awe of your library. Why, I believe that every book ever published must be on your shelves," Polly said. "I have read the books in my father's small collection at least twice, so forgive me if I look at your library like I am a hungry lion about to pounce!" A cluster of men turned and quieted as Polly approached on Pinckney's arm.

"Gentlemen, let me introduce Miss Polly Burgiss, houseguest of our own Floride Calhoun," Pinckney said. "Her father and I were neighbors in the Pendleton District years ago before I sold the summer estate. Sadly, James Burgiss and his dear wife Mary have passed on. Miss Burgiss is the sole mistress of Whitehall now." The men nodded solemnly. "I believe short-staple cotton is her crop," Pinckney offered. "Miss Burgiss's father was instrumental in beginning the railroad tunnel I mentioned to you all earlier," he added.

"Delighted to meet you, my dear," said one rotund gentleman, stepping forward. "Charles MacBeth, at your service."

"Mayor MacBeth." Polly curtsied deeply. "I am honored to meet you. I understand that your family once had a summer place near my home."

The mayor smiled broadly. "We did, indeed. My fondest memories are from my childhood summers there."

Polly opened her mouth to reply, when a trim mustachioed man stepped in front of her, bowing low.

"Such a beautiful creature—comrades, this is worth fighting for!" The man straightened and smiled. "G.T. Beauregard, milady. It is a pleasure to meet you. I am so sorry for your loss," Beauregard said. "Strong women gladden the heart of this soldier. It refreshes my soul to see such beauty and strength in these worrisome days. And there is no truer beauty than in the faces of the genteel young ladies of the South. Perhaps later I could hear more about your plantation."

The man had an accent that Polly could not place, and she wondered where he was from. His oiled hair and dark complexion seemed quite exotic and his half-lidded eyes, black mustache, and goatee captivated her immediately.

"Sir, I daresay you will frighten off this lovely thing." A man with a striking resemblance to her father clapped Beauregard on the back jovially.

"I think that the mud and muck of the Mississippi River have gone to your head, G.T."

The roomful of men chuckled.

"Miss Burgiss, this is our distinguished guest and man of the hour, Colonel Robert Lee, lately of Virginia and the victory at Harper's Ferry," Mr. Pinckney said. Hearty applause went around the room. "He will be instrumental in fighting for our rights in the coming days."

Polly curtsied politely. "I am honored to meet you, Colonel."

Colonel Lee bowed low. "Miss Burgiss, you are a vision. Don't mind my friend, Captain Beauregard. He's an old engineering colleague. He spends his days waist-deep in mud along the river in Louisiana, clearing debris and building new-fangled contraptions that confound every skipper to come down the river. I do not know when he last put eyes on such a beautiful young lady, but I fear by his aggressive manner it has been some time."

Polly smiled. "Colonel Lee, to hear my hostess, Floride Calhoun, tell it, you single-handedly saved the South from certain slave insurrection last year. For that, we 'genteel young ladies of the South' applaud you. Although, I must apologize for my limited knowledge of the event. News does not come quickly to my smallholding. I hope to change that in the future." Polly said a silent prayer of thanks for her friend's recent advisement of current events. "No doubt, the streets are safer for us all," she teased. Several men chuckled and nodded their heads approvingly.

Colonel Lee smiled again, and her heart skipped a beat. His eyes crinkled at the edges the way her father's had, clear and blue, warm, and kind. She missed her father terribly.

Pinckney raised his glass. "The fiend is hung and done, thanks to Colonel Lee here. And good riddance, I say. To the glorious days ahead, and to freedom." The men raised their glasses and returned the toast.

Lee leaned toward Polly conspiratorially and said, "Don't tell these old soldiers that it was a three-minute skirmish, or I may be demoted." He paused. "But a young lady like yourself must surely have more to think about than dealings with an irate abolitionist in Virginia. It is Christmas, after all."

Mr. Pinckney extended his arm. "Yes. Let me return this dear lady back to the safety of the women. My dear?"

Polly was about to nod an assent when a familiar face appeared before her.

"Miss, I trust that you have recovered from this morning's excitement?" The dark-skinned man from outside of the slave market stood in front of her. He was dressed in as fine a suit of evening clothes as Polly had ever seen. His amber eyes were warm.

Polly blushed. "Oh, yes. I am quite well now. Thank you again for coming to my aid," she stammered.

Mr. Pinckney looked perplexed. "So you've met Mr. Ellison?"

"This young lady and I met earlier today," Ellison said with a smile. "She was out taking a stroll. The momentous news of the secession had everyone in a state this morning, and the streets were quite crowded. It appeared she had been jostled in the chaos and I worried that she might have twisted her ankle on your uneven pavers. We did not exchange names, however."

Relief flooded Polly's mind. He had not mentioned her obvious distress at the slave auction.

Mr. Pinckney smiled. "Miss Burgiss, meet our friend and Confederate ally, William Ellison. He has a plantation over in Sumter County. His crop is also short-staple cotton. He is visiting Charleston as my guest as we plan for the future of the state."

The man bowed slightly. "Miss Burgiss. I did not know your father personally, but I was an early investor in his Blue Ridge tunnel project. His railroad tunnel would have saved me a fortune, had it been completed."

Polly's eyes widened, but she quickly regained her composure. "It is nice to meet you, Mr. Ellison," she stammered.

With that, other gentlemen in the room came forward to introduce themselves and Ellison turned to speak to someone else. Polly met several of the captains of industry and received her father's accolades. Her eyes darted toward Mr. Ellison frequently. She was intrigued.

Captain Beauregard approached again and leaned close to Polly's ear. "Miss Burgiss, may I ask for a dance later this evening? That is, if your *programme du bal* is not already full?" Beauregard ventured gallantly. His breath was warm against her cheek.

"I would be honored, Captain." Polly pulled her dance card from her silk bag with a gloved hand. "I believe I have a quadrille or two free this evening, as I have only met several gentlemen in all of Charleston."

"Allow me to take you around and make your introductions, perhaps?" Beauregard smoothed his dark mustache and grinned. His eyes were mischievous. "I would like to hear more about your father's mountain tunnel."

Mr. Ellison was immediately by her side. "Captain, I believe the young lady is in Mr. Pinckney's charge this evening. Leaving Miss Burgiss in your care is akin to leaving a lamb in a wolf's den." Ellison smiled easily, disarming the captain. Beauregard bowed curtly and turned away.

The man smiled down at Polly. "Miss Burgiss, I'd be careful of that one," Mr. Ellison said with a grin. "I would like to wish you a very pleasant stay here in the Holy City. Have you been to the opera yet? *The Barber of Seville* opens after Christmas."

"I'll be heading home right after Christmas. I hate to be gone away so long from my farm."

Ellison smiled. "I understand. I own a gin shop in addition to my cotton acreage. My son manages my businesses, and yet I still hate to be away."

Polly was surprised to find that she liked Mr. Ellison, despite the color of his skin. "Thank you again—for this morning," she said.

He sighed. "My dear girl, you are not the first person to react thus at an auction, and you will not be the last. They can be brutal affairs. I myself acquired several field hands in the very building, and it was dreadful, quite grim. I own sixty slaves now. But I still do not like the process."

Polly's mind reeled at the prospect of a Negro owning sixty slaves. Emboldened, she asked, "They grow your cotton, sir?"

Ellison nodded easily. "They do."

Polly wanted to ask the man so many questions. How much cotton did he produce per acre? How did he come to be free? How could he himself, a black man, own slaves?

Ellison paused and said, "May I give you a bit of advice on this, the eve of our secession? As a fellow cotton farmer?"

Polly smiled. "I would welcome your advice."

"Grow food crops, Miss Burgiss. That is what will see you through a civil war."

She opened her mouth to speak but Mr. Pinckney approached. "If you will excuse us, Mr. Ellison, I believe my wife would like to have the young lady safely back with the women and away from the menfolk."

Mr. Ellison bowed. "Good luck to you, Miss. Remember what I said. Grow food."

Mr. Pinckney extended his arm and Polly took it, with some regret. The pair left the library and strolled toward the ballroom, the strains of the orchestra just beginning.

They came to a circle of ladies, in which Harriet Pinckney was holding forth on some topic of great import.

"I hereby relinquish you to my wife, Miss Burgiss, whereupon you will be party to all the latest gossip Charleston has to offer." He bowed low and turned to leave the group. The ladies closed in to include Polly.

"Well, I just don't think they should be allowed." One plump woman shrugged. "Beef and pork are in short supply—and how do we know the meat isn't poisoned?" Her ample flesh suggested that she had never faced a shortage of meat.

Mrs. Pinckney turned to Polly and handed her a champagne flute from a liveried servant's silver tray. After introductions were made, Mrs. Pinckney announced, "Miss Burgiss, we are debating the merits of the new butcher, Lucas Bevere, who just opened a shop on King Street. It is near his home in Clifford's Alley. That is all well and good, but he is a freedman, doing business in the middle of the white district, up against Robinson's Meats, nearby. Tom Robinson is a white man. I have purchased Bevere's hams and beef cuts several times this season and simply think he has the best product. And at a lower price!"

An older lady wreathed in diamonds sniffed and murmured under her breath.

"How would he make a living, Lydia Stubbs, if he were poisoning his white customers?" Mrs. Pinckney asked, her eyes narrowed.

"Be that as it may, I will not patronize his shop," Mrs. Stubbs harrumphed. "As patrons of the Ladies Benevolent Society, how can we look the other way? This Negro man is taking business away from poor working whites. He should stay to the Negro side of town and sell his wares there. These free black people make me ever so nervous." She reached for a glass of champagne as a liveried slave appeared with another silver tray of crystal flutes. There were murmurs of agreement among the ladies. "We are positively outnumbered," she complained dramatically.

Polly glanced at the servant holding the tray, but the young man only studied the floor, his face unreadable.

"Some of these free blacks have slaves of their own. If there is slave trouble, whose side is a free black man on?" asked a young matron draped in emeralds. "My husband has hired two new overseers to control our slaves. One of them is a free black man, and goodness, I cannot tell you how he frightens me." She shook her head and her large emerald earrings jangled.

"What do you think, Miss Burgiss?" asked Mrs. Pinckney. The women turned curiously to hear from this backwoods planter's daughter.

Polly reddened and shook her head. "I regret that I do not have much experience with free blacks. I am woefully ignorant on the state of slavery in the Lowcountry. And just what is the Ladies Benevolent Society?" She sipped her champagne nervously, her mind on William Ellison.

"We are a charitable organization, my dear, primarily to aid white women who have fallen on hard times here in Charleston. Poor widows, lost seamen's wives, that sort of thing," Mrs. Pinckney said. "We try to keep white women and children out of the poorhouse."

"Exactly my point!" exclaimed Mrs. Stubbs, her neck wattle quivering. "These black men are taking work away from our poor, white women. Miss Burgiss, how is this problem addressed in your district?"

Polly thought of the white female mill workers who picked her cotton but wisely decided not to mention them. "We have slaves, black and mulatto, but no freedmen to speak of. I daresay that if a freedman tried to open a shop in Pendleton, he would be run out of town quickly." She took a long drink of the bubbly champagne and enjoyed the fizzy sensation on her tongue. She heard the orchestra strike up the first notes of a minuet.

"Of course he would," cried Mrs. Stubbs. "And Charleston is a powder keg. Slaves here outnumber whites. Why do we allow free blacks to settle here? My word! To work in competition with white merchants? It is too much. South Carolina's government, being rightly opposed to such measures, was compelled to secede."

Another woman spoke up. "Secession will lead to war any day now. I was completely against it. All this talk of war has my husband worried for our safety. What if our slaves rise up here, too? It could mean Denmark Vesey all over again."

"Why, Clarissa Deaton, didn't you hire a free negro washerwoman recently?" Mrs. Stubbs was practically apoplectic. "What were you thinking? She expects you to pay her to do your wash! The nerve . . . Keeping them under our control is the only answer. This new president-elect believes all slaves should be freed. And then what will they do? How will cotton be grown and harvested without slaves? We would be ruined."

"Enough war talk," exclaimed Mrs. Pinckney. "I for one want to enjoy the evening. Who knows what secession will bring?" She leaned into the group and asked conspiratorially, "And what do we think of Captain

Beauregard?" Several ladies tittered and the conversation continued on a lighter note.

Polly thought of Ona, Ben, and the other slaves at Whitehall. She wondered if they ever thought about their freedom. Probably not, she mused. Whitehall was their home. Why would they want to leave? Her mind wandered to the slave auction, and the anguish the young woman must have felt seeing her husband for the last time. She sipped her champagne politely and tried to shrink away toward the edge of the conversation. Clearly, she was out of her element here.

A striking young woman with golden hair, sapphire eyes, and a pale neck draped in pearls studied Polly appraisingly before announcing in a loud voice, "Miss Burgiss, I must ask—did you come out last season or this? I do not recall seeing news of your debut."

The ladies turned as one toward Polly. Polly felt her heart drop into the pit of her stomach. She sipped from her glass. Shame and humiliation swept over her and she felt the constraints of her corset only too well.

As she opened her mouth to answer, a sharp and familiar voice piped up behind her, "Of course she was a debutante, Eliza Lynne Cooper! What a silly question. Her debut last August was the event of the season in our district, despite all that the poor girl has been through." She gazed adoringly at Polly. "Why, Polly, I believe you had every young man from the state capital and northward in attendance. And the gown! Ladies, you have never seen a more beautiful dress—*haute couture* straight from Paris, it was! Her family spared no expense." The women nodded approvingly. "It was all the district could speak about for weeks. I believe the dress alone engendered several proposals!"

The first notes of a waltz began behind the group, and one by one, the ladies were escorted onto the dance floor by dashing partners. The rest of the evening was memorable, as Polly was able to dance until she could dance no more and make acquaintances with several important ladies. As the party ended, the two women finalized several social calls and engagements for later in Polly's visit and bid their hostess goodnight well

191

past midnight. As they collected their wraps and waited for the coachman to bring their carriage round, Mr. Pinckney stood by to see them off safely.

He bent to kiss Floride's gloved hand. "Always a pleasure, Mrs. Calhoun. Harriet and I are delighted that you could be here tonight. How long before you return to Mi Casa?"

"I shall be in Charleston through January unless politics intervenes. We will be seeing each other before I depart, I am sure. I expect I will see you and Mrs. Pinckney at the Hampton's gala on the thirty-first," Floride said, adjusting her cloak. "My children shall be here then, as well."

"And you, Miss Burgiss?" he asked kindly.

"I shall be here only through Christmas. I must go home immediately after the holiday. It is hard to be away when I am the sole owner. And I am to be married in the new year. There is so much to do," Polly said. Her words tumbled out of her mouth, and she made a mental note not to imbibe at the next Charleston soiree.

"Married? Congratulations, my dear! We had no idea that you were betrothed." He glanced at her gloved hand. "Floride, you have been keeping secrets. Either that or my wife is losing her ability to hold onto society gossip. Who is the lucky gentleman?"

Floride remained silent. Polly looked up at her host. "I am to marry John Stone, of River Wood, a farm near Pendleton . . . the late Sam Stone's son." She lifted her chin and forced herself to look Mr. Pinckney in the eye, sure of the chastisement to come.

The man looked from Polly to Floride, puzzled. "Sam Stone's boy? I knew the man. The New Yorker. Can't say I know his son . . ." He shook his head sadly. "Back in the day, Sam struggled. He bought land from some scalawag. The rotter promised him good bottom land and that's what he paid for, but Sam was cheated. And some folks just are not suited for farming. But Sam gave it a good try . . . God rest his soul. I wish better luck for the son. I had heard the place was to be sold for taxes."

He looked at Polly tenderly. "My dear, your young beau needs a good

192

overseer. Is that terrible man his father hired still working there? Whittaker? Wilkins? As I recall, the man was lazy and spent most of his time under the influence of drink. I might be able to recommend a few good men for that position. I could write to your young man."

"Thank you, Mr. Pinckney. I think Mr. Stone can handle his own affairs, without my meddling," Polly said stiffly. She noticed Floride's pained expression and softened. "But a word from you might be well received. Thank you for the kindness."

She opened her mouth to continue, but Floride cut in sharply. "Mr. Pinckney, Miss Burgiss knows all about her fiancé's business situation. At this point, all we can do is offer prayers and good wishes. Now we really must be going. The fog is beginning to roll in. Good night, sir," she said too brightly. "Merry Christmas!" She turned toward the carriage and allowed the footman to help her up and inside.

Polly looked at her host. "Mr. Pinckney, John Stone has been nothing but gracious and kind to me." She felt the sting of hot tears in her eyes. "I am not concerned about the fertility of his land or his overseer's faults, and I hardly think they are a fit reason to disqualify a husband," she said, the man's face beginning to spin.

Mr. Pinckney nodded solemnly. "Miss Burgiss, I apologize. I wish you only the best. Please accept my sincere good wishes for your marriage. I have no business judging a young man's reputation when I have only rumor to go on. And we all have our problems. Forgive me."

"You have been too kind to me and I will hold no grudge. Please thank Mrs. Pinckney again for her hospitality. I trust that I will see you again before I leave your beautiful city." Polly stepped dizzily into the carriage and the footman closed the door. She sighed heavily and closed her eyes. The carriage bumped across the cobblestones noisily and disappeared down the dark street.

— • —

A DENSE AND CHILL FOG HAD SETTLED OVER THE STREETS and alleys of Charleston. The women sat under thick lap blankets snuggly tucked around them as the carriage lurched across the uneven pavement. Polly watched the flickering gaslights and listened to the mesmerizing sound of horse hooves on cobblestones. Her stomach was queasy from nerves and from too much drink. Floride did not say a word, and finally, Polly could not bear her silence.

"Floride, thank you for a lovely evening. At first, I thought I would be eaten alive at any moment," Polly tried. "Those women glared at me like hungry wolves, especially the beautiful woman who asked if I had been a debutante."

Floride harrumphed in the darkness. "Yes, well, Eliza Lynne Cooper would have done just that if I hadn't been there, and she would have picked her teeth with your bones when she was finished with you." Floride's tone was clipped. "A little white lie told in the right circles can help you, not hurt you, my dear."

Polly's dread was palpable. It wasn't like Floride to be so short with her. She exhaled audibly, "I hope I did not behave badly, Floride. I know you are angry with me. I should never have mentioned marrying John. I may have had too much champagne, and I am terribly sorry."

In the darkness, Floride reached for Polly's hand and squeezed it tightly. "Polly, it is because I am a friend of yours that I tell you this. If I don't tell you what is on my mind, I daresay I could not call myself a friend."

"Go on," Polly said quietly.

"That family is nothing but trouble. Sam Stone hired that nasty Mr. Wilkins as overseer when John was a small boy, after Lena Stone died. Every time I saw that man in town, he was drunk and belligerent—or both, with that little boy tagging along behind him. You were too young to remember, but he led young John around by the nose. I mean, John had no mother and poor Sam Stone was off drinking at the tavern in town much of the time anyway. And there were rumors that Sam fathered several children by his slave women."

Polly gasped.

"Oh, it happens," Floride scowled. "Don't be naive. But the entire district has watched as River Wood has been subject of one scandal after another involving terrible treatment of slaves at Wilkins' hand. Why, any time there was talk of a runaway, the whole district assumed it was someone from River Wood—and wished them Godspeed!"

Floride dabbed at her nose with her handkerchief and continued, "John Stone has not been able to improve things at River Wood, either. He may have impressed you with his good looks, and by bringing in your cotton, but his own fields are in a terrible state. He has been the topic of much discussion at Pendleton Farmers' Society meetings. And yet he refuses to fire that horrible man. Fort Hill's overseer tells me that it is not simply a case of bad management. The man is foul."

Polly interrupted, "Floride, you can hardly condemn my marriage because John's land isn't producing the way it should or because his father was a scoundrel. I agree with you about Mr. Wilkins, but after we marry, I can discuss it with John."

"Why not discuss it beforehand, dear?" Floride asked.

"It is not my place," Polly replied. "It is a tender spot for John."

Floride snorted. "Well, he seems to think it is his place to tell you how to run your farm." Polly didn't reply, so Floride continued, "There is something else. You know that the word of a slave isn't worth a thing in public places. However, my Nellie, who has been with me since my husband was the Vice President, told me something I believe you should know. I do trust Nellie."

Polly stared out the window at the dense fog and ignored her friend.

"She told me years ago that your Ona was raped by Sam Stone while she was a slave at River Wood. Her son is a product of that wretched encounter. He wanted nothing more to do with her or the baby so he gave her to your family."

Polly felt the bile rise in her throat. It might explain her mother's animosity toward the whole Stone family. She leaned forward and dropped her head into her lap. "I think I am going to be sick," she said quietly, holding a handkerchief to her lips. "Please, stop the carriage."

"Goodness, Polly. I did not mean to upset you so." Floride rapped on the ceiling of the carriage with her ebony cane.

The driver called out, "Whoa, whoa, easy now," to the horses and the carriage creaked to a stop. The footman appeared at the door and inquired, "Is ev'rything alright, Mrs. Calhoun?"

"Miss Burgiss needs some air," Floride barked. "Please help her down right away." The footman ran around to Polly's door and opened it. He took her hand and helped her gently down. The night air was thick with fog and smelled of the outgoing tide. Polly's mind reeled at the images running through her mind, the things her mother had said about the Stones, and the way the slaves reacted when John or Wilkins came to Whitehall. The champagne made her dizzy and nauseous, as well.

"Did my mother know?" Polly asked, fanning herself with her dance card.

Floride Calhoun leaned forward from her seat in the dark carriage and said softly, "I don't think so, dear. But I remember that Sam's wife was eager to send Ona away. John may have been a boy then, but he is a man now. He may not have touched a hair on any slave's head yet, but the apple does not fall far from the tree. And it means that if you marry the man, his half-brother will also become his property."

Polly crouched on the ground in a cloud of voluminous skirts and vomited onto the cobblestones.

— • —

POLLY AWOKE TO THE SUNLIGHT STREAMING INTO HER windows and the sound of Floride calling through the door. She was in bed, without memory of having gotten there. She vaguely remembered someone carrying her to her bedroom and was mortified to realize that it was probably Floride's poor footman, or Peter, the houseman. She winced and closed her eyes. Her head pounded in rhythm with her heartbeat, and her throat felt dry and parched.

There was a frantic knock at the door. "Polly! Polly! May I come in?" Floride called before proceeding to open the door, her eyes wide.

"My dear, you must get up. There is a rider from Pendleton here to see you. From Dr. Adger. Something must have happened at home." Floride handed Polly her dressing gown as Ona stood quietly behind her, wringing her hands.

"A rider? From Dr. Adger? What . . . ?" Polly's mind was fuzzy both from lack of sleep and the champagne she had enjoyed the night before. She sat weakly and let Floride drape the gown around her shoulders. "What time is it?"

"After seven. Ona, help Miss Polly dress at once." Floride's voice was sharp. "Then get hot coffee from Nellie and bring it to your mistress quickly."

"Yes'm." Ona moved past Floride to the armoire to select a day dress. Floride turned and left the room abruptly.

"Ona, what's wrong? Do you know?" Polly stood and went behind the silk screen to use the chamber pot. She reappeared and allowed Ona to help her slip on a pale rose bodice and skirt.

"I ain't got no idea, Miss Polly. The man say he cain't talk to anyone befo' he sees you. I hope nothin' happened to Ben."

"What is this about?" Polly seemed more frustrated than worried. After all, John was in charge in her absence. Unless something had happened to John. Fear suddenly gripped her. *God no. Please no,* she thought. God wouldn't take away John too.

Ona tried to brush Polly's hair, but she waved her hands away. "Stop it, Ona," she snapped. "Let me go find out what happened." Polly hurried out of the room, coiling her nighttime braid into a messy chignon.

She swept down the stairs and into the parlor. Floride stood by wringing her hands as a young slave, hat in hand, looked in awe at his surroundings. She recognized the man. His name was Harlen, and he was one of Dr. Adger's most trusted slaves.

"Harlen! My God, what is it? Did you ride all this way on horseback?" Polly gasped.

"No ma'am," he began. "Doc Adger put me on a train to Charleston, all right. . . . I sho' nuf' almost got into some trouble along the way, ridin' alone without a white man for a whole day an' night. They ain't had no slave car, but Doc Adger sent letters with me to show to anyone who stopped me." He showed her a ream of wrinkled papers. "Miss Polly, I sho' was scared." The young man was still shaking, no doubt of that. "Doc tried to send a telegram, but when he didn't hear back, he sent me on."

Ona entered the parlor with a coffee tray. Floride scowled. "We received no telegram." Her mind flashed to the news of the secession. "Surely, the new telegraph office is overwhelmed."

"What is it, Harlen? What has happened?" Polly asked.

The slave handed her a sealed envelope, addressed to her in Dr. Adger's hand. She broke the seal and opened the letter with shaking hands.

Dear Polly,

I am compelled to send this letter to you by way of Harlen, whom you know. My telegram went without a response. While visiting town on Monday, I heard of fresh troubles at Whitehall. John Stone has seen fit to fire your Mr. Roper, and now Mr. Wilkins is in charge. Mr. Roper contacted me to say that Old Duke has died, he believes by Mr. Wilkins' own hand. I worry for your other slaves, Polly, and see it as my duty to notify you. If you are so disposed, Harlen has been instructed to accompany you and your woman back to Anderson by train as soon as possible. He has been given appropriate fare for his own return trip. My deepest condolences.

Sincerely,
Robert Adger

Polly sank to the sofa in disbelief. "Duke is dead." Ona cried out and then stifled her sobs with her apron. Polly did not want to disclose the rest of the letter while Harlen and Ona stood nearby.

"Ona, pack my things. I am afraid that we must return home right away. Harlen, Dr. Adger has instructed you to accompany me on the train home. Wait for me by the carriage house." Polly waited until the slaves had gone from the room before she turned to her friend in despair. She handed the letter to Floride and sat down, putting her throbbing head in her hands.

Floride read the contents of the letter and sighed. "Oh, my dear girl, I was afraid it would come to this. That Wilkins . . . The district should have run him out on a rail years ago." Seeing her young friend's anguish, she went and put her arms around her shoulders.

"Polly, Duke was very old . . . older than I am, for sure. It is possible that he simply collapsed after doing something that Wilkins asked him to do . . . Let's not assume the worst." She tried to put on a cheerful face for Polly. "Dr. Adger treats his slaves like his own family. It is possible that he is exaggerating the troubles at Whitehall," she offered. "Perhaps we can get a telegram out to him today. Please stay if you can."

Polly wiped a tear with the back of her hand. She stood shakily and looked at her friend. "Floride, I know what you are thinking. Thank you for not saying it. I am grateful for your friendship and I am sorry. I must leave right away. I couldn't possibly enjoy myself without knowing what is happening at home. Give my apologies to everyone. Let me pack and be off to the station, please."

"Very well. There is a late morning train. I will have a carriage readied and see that Nellie gets a basket together for you. You'll be hungry on the trip." Floride Calhoun hugged Polly tightly and said in a whisper, "I am coming back to you mid-January, dear. Please do not do anything rash."

Chapter Fifteen

THE TRIP HOME WAS LONG AND TEDIOUS, A FAR CRY from the exciting journey of just a few days earlier. A single blast from the steam engine's whistle announced the train's arrival in Anderson shortly after midnight. Exhausted, Polly stepped down onto the platform and felt the crisp, biting chill of winter on her face, so different from the balmy coast. The bracing cold acted as a tonic and revived her instantly. Dr. Adger appeared from the dimly lit station, hat in hand. He instructed Harlen to load Polly's baggage in his wagon, and then he pulled Polly aside gently.

"Miss Polly, I am so glad that you have come home. I did not want to confront John Stone on your behalf until I had spoken with you in person."

"Dr. Adger, I trust that you sent for me with good reason. What happened?"

"Harlen and Ona can follow behind in the wagon with your trunks. I will take you back to Whitehall in my carriage, so we can speak alone." He tilted his head back toward Ona, who was stepping down from a distant passenger car.

Once the baggage was loaded and Polly and Dr. Adger settled under thick lap blankets, the carriage and wagon began the forty-minute drive north toward Whitehall. Dr. Adger seemed hesitant to speak first, which concerned Polly.

"Dr. Adger, tell me everything," Polly implored. She could not make out his face in the darkness but knew that the man was troubled.

"Polly, Tom Roper showed up at my place yesterday. He told me that he had been fired from Whitehall—by John. Apparently, he had words with Clay Wilkins over Duke, and the two men came to blows. Mr. Wilkins chased him from your property with a shotgun. I am sorry to say, he came to me for doctoring, seeing as how his lip was split open. He would have stood his ground, but he thought that you were engaged to be married to John Stone? He was unsure of your position and did not get a response from a telegram he sent you."

Polly's mind reeled. "The Charleston telegraph offices must have been overwhelmed by secession communications traveling back and forth."

Adger continued, "Clay Wilkins had whipped Duke for something, and the old man collapsed dead. A nasty end for that sweet old man, I'm afraid."

"Oh, poor Duke. What could he have done to deserve a beating? He had been with my father since Virginia," Polly said.

"Ben and George were also punished harshly," Dr. Adger shook his head sadly.

Polly's thoughts leaped to Ben and to Floride's information about Sam Stone and Ona. It was too horrible to contemplate. She could not comprehend Ben standing for a beating from Clay Wilkins. She knew that Ona would never forgive her if Wilkins hurt Ben. She glanced back into the darkness toward the wagon following close behind.

"Mr. Wilkins beat my slaves in my absence." She said it as a statement of fact, and not as a question. Had she seen this coming? A new and righteous anger welled up inside her. How could John let this happen? Armed with the fresh revelations from Floride, she was aghast.

"Where is Tom Roper now?"

"He is staying in town. He got himself a room and is waiting for word from you. I wonder if we need to get the sheriff out there to straighten things out? No doubt you will wish to speak with John first," Adger said.

"No doubt." Polly's mind flashed back to the morning she had departed for Charleston. Guilt and confusion washed over her. Had she said anything to John about Wilkins before the trip? Had he? Up until that moment, it seemed as if John understood that Wilkins would not be invited back to Whitehall after the cotton harvest. He was crude and dirty and harsh. But in truth, she had been happy to leave Whitehall in John's hands and go traipsing off to Charleston with nary a care.

But now . . . She had so many questions. Did John know about his own father and Ona? Had Wilkins been lurking on her property the entire fall? John would terminate the man's employment. Surely, he had already taken steps to punish Wilkins and have Tom Roper reinstated, she told herself.

"Dr. Adger, do you know for what reason he beat my slaves?" Polly asked.

Dr. Adger seemed reluctant to say more. Polly pressed him. "Please tell me what you know. I must have all the facts."

"Miss Polly, a most grievous thing. I understand from Tom that Wilkins tried to go after Cissie, down by the springhouse. The slaves who were beaten were punished for trying to keep him away from her."

Polly gasped. She thought of Cissie and her strong but meek husband, George. She heard the blood rushing in her ears, even over the noise of the carriage wheels. Dr. Adger did not speak for a time, letting Polly deal with this horrible news. "Is Cissie alright?"

"I don't know, dear. This all happened on the day you left. I heard it from Tom. I would be happy to check on your slaves, but I needed your permission to go onto your property. Would you like me to get the sheriff out to Whitehall tonight? I don't think you should be there alone."

"I would like to hear the story from my own people first. I can deal with Mr. Wilkins tomorrow when I see John. The sheriff would only laugh when we tell him he was called out because a white overseer whipped some slaves. But please, will you get word to Mr. Roper? Tell him that his job at Whitehall is his own and no one else's. He has my full confidence."

"Miss Polly, I don't know if that is such a good idea, you riding into Whitehall late at night with that brute Clay Wilkins still on your property." Dr. Adger shook his head. "Let me at least get Mr. Roper over to your place before you go setting him off."

Polly looked at her neighbor, aghast. "Are you telling me that Wilkins is staying at my place?"

"Yes, Polly. He told Tom that he answered to John Stone, that Stone would soon be the new master at Whitehall." He peered at Polly's face in the dark. "I take it by your reaction that Tom was right. Then I apologize. I may have overstepped my bounds as your friend and neighbor in summoning you home. I did not know of your engagement." The man fumbled with his hat.

"No, Doctor. You did the right thing. It is true—we are engaged. I am sure that John is as disgusted as I am with Mr. Wilkins' behavior. When I get there, we will surely set this to rights. I appreciate you wanting the sheriff nearby, but I certainly don't think one crude overseer will be a problem, at least not tonight."

The carriage lumbered on, finally turning into the oak-lined drive to the house. Curiously, Polly saw that lights were aglow in several windows. Perhaps Cissie was there to open the house. She looked forward to seeing her hands and getting the entire story.

As the carriage came to a halt, with the wagon behind it, the front door opened and Polly saw John silhouetted there, Clay Wilkins behind him in a puddle of lamp light. Stone puffed on a cigar and the embers glowed orange in the darkness.

"Who's here at this ungodly hour?" John slurred into the night.

The carriage door opened. "John?" Polly's voice registered her surprise.

"Polly?" John came forward quickly, surprised to see his fiancé. He reached up and helped her down from the carriage.

"What is going on? Why are you at Whitehall?" She faced him, puzzled. Wilkins stepped from behind John without a word, hat in hand, and strode into the darkness toward Roper's cabin.

John pointed his cigar toward the carriage and wagon. "Who is that with you?" His breath condensed and appeared as a fog in the cold air. He reeked of too much whiskey.

"John, you have been drinking." Polly was angry. "Why are you in my house with your overseer this late at night? What happened to Mr. Roper and my slaves?"

John continued to stare at Dr. Adger, standing at the top step of his carriage.

"Hello, John." Dr. Adger tipped his hat. "Son, I think it is time for you to go on home now and let Miss Polly get some rest. She has had a long day of traveling."

Stone squared his shoulders. "Polly, tell me what is going on here. What has cut your trip short?" He peered into the darkness and saw Harlan and Ona waiting nearby in the wagon. "You were not due home for two weeks. Has something happened in Charleston? There were some business matters I needed to discuss with Wilkins. We were looking over the ledgers when we heard the carriage approach. Why have you come back so soon?"

For only a moment, Polly's courage faltered. "Where is Tom Roper?" she finally demanded; her hands clenched beside her. She saw John's body become rigid in the dark.

He lowered his voice and said, "Polly, I will discuss these things with you, of course, but not in front of slaves and not in front of your family doctor. Come inside please."

Dr. Adger spoke firmly. "John, Miss Polly needs her rest. Go on home now."

A shivering Polly turned to Dr. Adger. "Thank you, Doctor, for bringing me home from the station. Please go now. I will speak with John inside and then go straight to my bed. He will leave, I am quite sure, after our conversation. He wouldn't want to sully my reputation." She glared at John.

"Harlan, if you will unload my things, I would appreciate it," Polly called out. "Ona, you have had a long day. I can get myself to bed. I will speak with you in the morning." The slave woman climbed down from the wagon and shuffled off toward the slave quarters with her pack. Harlan began taking trunks and hat boxes off the wagon.

Dr. Adger shook his head. "I am warning you, John. Mark my word, you cause any trouble for Miss Polly and this whole town will be after you." He shook a bony finger at John and ducked inside the carriage. His driver clicked the reins, sending the horses lurching forward. The carriage and soon the wagon trundled down the dirt road into the night.

Polly stepped inside the warm house. John closed the door and followed a shaking Polly into the parlor. She sat down and began to remove her gloves.

"John, why are you here? Why was Mr. Wilkins in my house? You know how I feel about him," Polly said sharply.

John calmly picked up a cut crystal decanter and a glass and turned to Polly. "Let's have a drink. It will calm your nerves. I will explain everything," John said evenly. "Did Adger send for you or did one of the slaves get word to you somehow?" he asked. He poured the liquid slowly into the glass and placed it on the table in front of Polly.

Polly frowned and pushed it away. "I don't want a drink this late at night, John. I do not need my nerves calmed. I want you to answer my questions, please. How did Duke die? Did Wilkins strike him?"

John shrugged, sipping from the glass Polly refused. "Duke tried to interfere in a matter that wasn't his business. The overseer administered several lashes as a punishment . . . and he collapsed. I am sorry. The old man should have been sold years ago. Overseers must administer punishment. It is their job to control slaves," he stated firmly.

"It wasn't his job!" Polly cried. "He is not my overseer. You fired my overseer without my permission? How could you?"

John's face reddened and he sat heavily across from her, his breath foul with too much drink. Polly could see that she had overstepped some boundary that she had been unaware of until now.

"Your permission?" John growled, beads of perspiration dampening his forehead. "I managed your cotton harvest. Twice. As I am to be your husband, is it required that I ask your permission to attend to plantation business on what will soon become our land? Land that has not seen a strong profit in years? Am I to be your husband or yet another of your pampered slaves?"

Polly was afraid of this side of the man, but she continued, "Why did you fire Tom Roper?" She swallowed hard. "You had no right. He has been with my family for years. He knows how to run Whitehall," Polly said, her eyes stinging with tears.

"Damn it, Polly!" John snapped, his face contorted with anger. "I have managed River Wood, with the same overseer, by myself, for years. We brought in your cotton crop. This last time was one of your best harvests yet, allowing you to travel to Charleston to see that ridiculous Calhoun woman for the holidays—and you question which overseer is best suited to running Whitehall?" Polly winced at John's tone and turned away.

"Do you see that everything I do here I do for you?" He leaned back in the leather chair wearily and combed his hands through his blonde hair. "Your slaves are not used to working hard. They never have worked as hard for you as they should . . . Wilkins may have administered one too many lashes, but he was doing his job . . . for the good of Whitehall, Polly." John tried to calm himself. He reached for her hand, but she pulled away.

He slammed his fist down on the table and Polly flinched. She reached out a trembling hand and picked up the glass of whiskey. She tasted it and closed her eyes. She sipped a bit more and felt warmth spread down to her stomach. She could not lose him. What would she do without him, the only man who would have her? She had no dowry. She was ill-educated, without money to speak of, and little knowledge in the ways of running a small plantation. John was right. She had no idea how to manage Whitehall on her own. He was only doing what he thought best.

"John, you are frightening me."

John's look changed to one of forbearance. He leaned forward and took her hand in his. She resisted the temptation to pull away. "I am sorry. Forgive me. I didn't mean to lose my temper. I do become overwrought when I think of how this land has been mismanaged. For us, I must manage Whitehall on my terms. For us."

Polly took another sip of the whiskey and closed her eyes, gathering her courage. Her eyes blinked open. "Is it true that Mr. Wilkins tried to force himself on Cissie? Is that why he beat Duke?"

"Wilkins was wrong. I admit, he had been . . . fond of her at River Wood," John said.

"That is revolting," Polly snapped, pulling her hand away. "She is married to George. They have a child. I cannot have that man back here, John, not ever. I will not sanction that kind of behavior. If you want to marry me, you'll have to fire that man."

John glared at Polly. "Polly, a slave is a piece of property."

"Nevertheless, if you want to marry me, Mr. Wilkins must go. I don't ever want to see him again. Will you promise me?"

John sighed and shook his head. Polly opened her mouth to speak but John held up a hand to stop her. "I assure you, it will not happen again. Wilkins was acting without good sense. Of course, I will let him go. But you should know that your niggers set on him—on a white man, Polly."

"John, I hate that word," Polly hissed. "Please don't use it again."

John rolled his eyes. "That foreman of yours struck my overseer. That cannot be allowed to happen, or the next thing we know we will be dead in our beds, our throats slit, at the hands of damned slaves. It is happening all over the state now, Polly. Slave revolts are increasing."

Polly recalled Mrs. Calhoun's story about John Brown and his slave uprising and she shuddered.

John lowered his voice and continued, "It was that George. Ben and the old man went after Wilkins too, but thankfully, Zadoc came for me quickly. Wilkins was given permission to administer several lashes apiece for insolence. They were stripped and punished. A slave may not strike an overseer for any reason, Polly—that is the law. You will see a few bruises and welts, but the whippings were not harsh. In fact, I instructed Wilkins to give George no more than the other two received since he is the girl's husband."

Polly felt her resolve weakening. He was right. A slave was not allowed to hit a white man. For any reason.

"Now really, Polly, you should be off to sleep now. You have had a long day. We can discuss this in the morning. May I stay in the overseer's cabin tonight, as it is late and the ride home would be long? Will that be acceptable?"

Polly felt drained and utterly defeated. "Very well, John. I was taken by surprise. Duke has been with my family from the beginning. You understand. I will get up early and see to the others. Good night." She stood shakily and walked toward the front hall. She turned and asked tentatively, "And we shall retrieve Mr. Roper in the morning? I want him back here."

John cocked his head and looked at Polly reprovingly. "Let me tend to the business of the overseers. We can discuss Tom Roper tomorrow morning." He smiled and walked toward the front door. "Get some rest. This will all seem trivial after you have slept, and you will see that I was right." He put his hand to her cheek.

Polly relaxed a bit at John's change in demeanor. "John, did you hear the news of the secession? What will this mean for us?" Polly asked.

"I don't know what will happen here. It will mean war between the states. We will have to be prepared." John turned and opened the door. He quickly kissed Polly on her cheek, his breath foul. "Good night, Polly."

A chill wind blew into the hallway. Polly shivered and closed the door behind him. She watched John walk towards Tom's cabin in the pale moonlight and then silently turned the key in the lock. She dropped the key into the pocket of her skirt, gripped the newel post, and climbed the stairs wearily.

— • —

IN HER CABIN, ONA STIFLED HER CRIES AS SHE LIFTED the lantern and saw her son lying face down on his cot. Ben's back was furrowed with deep and bloody welts from the overseer's whip. He sat up and turned to face her. His lip was split and oozing still. She gasped once, then regained her composure and quickly filled a basin with water. She gathered some rags and approached Ben. She stood over him and began to hum an old spiritual that she had learned from her mother long ago and had sung to her boy as a baby. She tenderly dabbed a wet cloth on Ben's wounds. Tears rolled down her cheeks while she sang.

"Mama, what are you doing home?" Ben asked softly.

"Dr. Adger sent a man down to Charleston to let Miss Polly know what happened here. She came as quick as she could. What happened, son?" She sat down on the edge of the bed.

"I never said a word," Ben whispered, through gritted teeth. "I never said a word when Miss Mary died and John Stone came to Whitehall like he owned the place. The first day—when y'all left—Stone fired Mr. Roper for some reason, and Wilkins chased him off the place." He winced as Ona touched his torn lip with the cloth.

"Wilkins came around, telling us he was the new overseer, saying how things got to change around here. He went after Cissie. She was down at the spring house with Silas when he showed up. We all heard her scream, and the baby crying too." He paused while Ona dabbed cool water on his swollen brow. "It didn't take George a minute to get to his wife and boy from across the property."

Ona felt the nightmare of her time at River Wood rise from the depths of her mind. She remembered when Sam Stone had first come after her. She was a young girl, just arrived from Charlotte and had only had her woman's cycle for a few months when Stone found her alone in the chicken house and raped her right there on the ground. After, she curled into a ball and sobbed, her torn dress and legs caked in chicken excrement and her own blood. She shuddered at the recollection and pushed it back down into the depths. At least the pain of that terrifying incident had resulted in her precious son.

Ben continued, "George got there first, and I was right behind him. He pulled that son of a bitch off her. George hit him in the face, like to knock him out. He was screaming and yelling as to how he would kill Wilkins for going after his wife. Duke and I held George back until some other men showed up, and by then Wilkins was off to get his whip. Zadoc ran for Mr. Stone."

He continued, "Stone showed up and saw Wilkins bloodied, and he laughed. He laughed at Wilkins, said that he had cost him all the women at River Wood and now planned to start on Whitehall girls."

Ona closed her eyes. How such evil could ever come to find favor in Polly's sight, she had to wonder. She wrung the cloth out in the basin. The water ran crimson. She tried to touch his lip again with the cloth, but Ben gently pushed her hand away.

"Ma, someone's got to tell her," Ben said.

Ona looked at her son with alarm. "Now you know this ain't a time when Miss Polly gonna believe a slave," she snapped. "She got her man right here on-site runnin' things. He's gonna tell her one thing and she gonna believe it. Even if she don't, you think Mr. Stone and Wilkins gonna let this be?" Ona paused. "What happened with Duke?"

Ben shook his head sadly. "Twenty lashes each. Wilkins made us lean against the barn, our backs stripped bare. He took up his whip and came for us. He laughed when he saw not one of us had been striped before. We didn't have any scars. Stone told him he could give me and Duke twenty lashes apiece, but since it was George that hit him, he was to get thirty. Even though he is Cissie's husband, he was to get thirty. Wilkins wanted to string him up, Mama. They argued about that for a while, but Stone said he was the boss and Wilkins would do as he said."

Ben shook his head and continued, "Stone stood there and watched us get whipped and didn't say a word. Just smoked a cigar and watched. Old Duke was last. That old man didn't do anything wrong. Skinny old man, his ribs showing. He turned to try and talk to Wilkins, to stop the whip with his hands, and then he just collapsed. Wilkins hit him a few more times, but he didn't get up. He was gone. Stone didn't say a word. He started back to the big house, then turned and yelled for us to pick up Duke and get him to the cabin, but Duke was already dead. Must have been his heart had given out from the beating." Ben lay back on his side gingerly and closed his eyes. "We had to bury him that afternoon."

Ben watched as tears trickled down Ona's hollow cheeks. He continued "I can't stay here. If Miss Polly marries Stone . . . Knowing what I know? Mama, you're the only one she'll listen to anymore. She doesn't see me the same way as when we were children. You've got to tell her he was there. You got to tell her that they killed her brothers. That I am Stone's half-brother. She will believe you. I know she will."

Ona breathed deeply and said, "Ben if you try to run, they find you. They hang you fo' sure. You would have to git further than even Virginia before you'd be safe, and nowhere's safe enough. Mr. Burgiss got kin up north, remember? They'd be lookin' for his runaway slaves all over this country. We is surely stuck. From what I heard in Charleston, Miss Polly is dead set on marryin' that man. She even crossed Mrs. Calhoun on it, and that ain't a good omen." Ona wrung the cloth out a final time and carried the basin to the table. She sat down wearily. "Let's sleep on all this and I'll pray on it hard. Mebbe the Lawd still got his hand on us and can show us what to do."

Ben snorted and turned over, facing the wall of the cabin. "The Lord—when has the Lord ever shown any mercy on slaves?"

The night was long and Ben's wounds made it difficult to rest. He finally fell into a deep sleep at the rooster's crow. He was moving past the slave cabins towards the cotton fields. His eyes scanned the horizon, searching for the gap in the woods that meant the old path to the Kemp place. He saw her go through the gap and he quickened his pace. He saw her ahead, sprawled across the ground, Stone pinning her down. She was screaming, calling Ben's name. He came up behind John, threw the man off her, and knocked him to the ground. He sat on John's chest. His thick fingers closed around the white man's throat and he squeezed. Stone's eyes bulged and he squeezed harder. Stone kicked and writhed but it did no good. His color went from red to purple, and his mouth was flecked with foam. Then the man went limp. Ben couldn't relax his hands. His nails dug into Stone's flesh until crescent moons of blood appeared where ten fingers had gouged deep.

Ben gasped and sat up, his eyes wild with fear. In the dark, the flicker of firelight against the rough-hewn log walls of his mother's cabin cast eerie shadows. Outside, the first grey light of dawn began to tint the sky. He threw back the quilt, got up quickly, and headed for the quiet of the smithy shed.

Chapter Sixteen

POLLY WOKE EARLY TO FIND ONA CROUCHED at the hearth with a basket of kindling for her fireplace. The woman expertly laid the wood and set a light to the pile. Before long, the flickering fire warmed the cold room.

"I sorry to wake you, Miss Polly, it so early . . . But since we wasn't expected home yet, I knew your fireplace would be ice cold this mornin.' An' after all the fancy goin's on we seen at Mrs. Calhoun's, I figured you'd be angry if I didn't at least have yo' room picked up and yo' fire goin.' Cissie feelin' kinda puny today. She gonna stay downstairs, but I do the upstairs work. Soon you be nice and warm. You need anything before I git your breakfast?" Ona did not look at Polly as she chattered.

"Ona," Polly said tenderly. "Ona, I am so very sorry." Ona shuffled around collecting clothes to air, and then picked up the chamber pot.

"Ona, please stop it and look at me . . . please," Polly pleaded. Ona turned to look at Polly. Her red-rimmed eyes regarded her mistress warily.

"I didn't expect this to happen. How is Ben?" Polly asked.

"He pretty beat up, Miss Polly. Mr. Wilkins gave him twenty lashes with that bad whip—the one wit' the glass beads on the end." She shuddered, remembering her son's flayed back. "He were just tryin' to save

Cissie. They all was. Them men is good men, Miss Polly. Ain't a one ever beat by Mr. Roper or yo' daddy."

"I know. Is Cissie alright?"

"Cissie be alright. She been feelin' sick in the mornin's some. She been movin' slow anyway . . . She got some bruises, and she was scared, is all, but little Silas was real worried over her. That chile clingin' to her now like he gonna lose his mama if she goes out of his sight." She did not tell Polly that she suspected that Cissie was pregnant again.

"Ona, he won't touch them again, I promise."

"So Mr. Wilkins is the new overseer?" Ona asked.

Polly didn't dare look Ona in the eye. She twisted the edge of the bedsheet in her hands. "Wilkins is to be let go, thank God." She paused. "What about Duke? What had he done wrong?"

"What had Duke done wrong, Miss Polly?" Ona shrugged and stared at her mistress with sadness. "Lawd, but what has any of 'em done wrong, Miss Polly, 'sides bein' born slaves? Old Duke ain't never done any wrong thing in his life. An' that man was as proud of you as if you was his own kin."

Ona surprised herself with her brave talk. "Those men jes' tried to protect Cissie is all." She turned toward the door. "I have yo' breakfast ready soon, Miss Polly." Ona closed the door behind her softly.

— • —

POLLY SAT UP IN HER WARM BED, ashamed and embarrassed. Duke had come down the Wagon Road with her parents nearly thirty years ago. He had once whittled a whole menagerie of wooden animals for her brothers. She recalled how tenderly Duke had assisted her in preparations for her mother's funeral. She realized she hadn't even asked Ona about Duke's burial. For a brief moment, she wished that Floride were here to tell her what to do. But she realized that Floride would not offer the counsel she wanted to hear.

The images from the Charleston slave auction came to mind. A little family split apart. The young man's sorrow at leaving his wife and son was palpable. The woman's agony unbearable. Polly swallowed hard. The horror of the auction combined with seeing so many freedmen out and about in Charleston had set her mind to thinking.

Ona had been Whitehall's only house slave for so long that she seemed part of the family. And yet, she too had been ripped from her own family as a young girl in Charlotte. Polly had been taught that slaves were not the intellectual equals of their owners. But Ben and Martin read beautifully. She had been taught that they were incapable of making important decisions, holding political office, or supporting themselves with their skills. And yet, the freedmen and women of Charleston strolled about conducting business, had organized free Negro churches, and owned slaves.

She knew that many slaves were beaten occasionally and that as future master of Whitehall, John Stone was within his rights to have them punished. But it felt wrong. It was wrong.

Her slaves were human beings. Slave labor picked cotton across the South, but there had to be another way to earn a living on the land without enslaving an entire population. The white workers had opened her eyes to that.

It wasn't just the money, she thought. She knew that Tom Roper had never struck a Whitehall slave and that Dr. Adger had sent his own man to Charleston to give her news of Duke's death. She also knew that a Negro boy had taught her to read and shared his ideas about slavery with her. A Negro woman had raised her during her mother's long bout with depression. Polly tossed the quilts aside and put her feet on the cold floor. She would go to the slave cabins and check on her people. She dressed herself quickly and headed for the stairs. At the landing, she came face to face with a startled Cissie, who dropped a basket of laundry and let out a small yelp of surprise.

"Oh, Miss Polly!" Cissie cried. "Excuse me, ma'am." She fumbled to pick up the basket of spilled laundry. "I forgot you was home!"

Polly knelt and helped Cissie pick up several items. "Goodness, Cissie. These things don't need to be done today," Polly said, with some irritation. "Ona told me you were feeling puny, and I don't need you now. She is getting my breakfast. You go rest." Cissie nodded mutely.

Polly continued, "I am sorry about what happened to you . . . and to George. I promise that kind of thing will not happen again. I hope that little Silas is alright."

Both women stood up. Cissie hoisted the basket to her hip and said quietly, "Yes, Miss Polly." She absentmindedly smoothed the apron over her belly.

"How is George?" Polly asked nervously.

Cissie dropped her eyes and nodded. "Yes'm, we fine."

Polly sensed that she would not get anything more from the woman. "Very well. Again, I am sorry." Polly nodded and continued down the stairs. She grabbed her cloak from the coat rack and pulled open the front door. A blast of cold air hit her at once. She stood on the porch, hands on the railing, inhaling the crisp December morning. Christmas was just days away.

Two days earlier she had been miles away in Charleston, where warm ocean breezes blew through her windows and lush green gardens with tinkling fountains were the norm. But this, this wooded bottomland on the banks of a lazy upstate river was home, and it was the most beautiful place on earth. She had a mess on her hands, to be sure. *I will set things to rights, Father. I promise.*

"Now this is what I like to see," called a man's voice. Polly looked down from the porch and saw John striding up, hat in hand, from the overseer's cabin. His tousled sandy hair and piercing blue eyes made her stomach flip, even now. Her morning plans melted away.

"Good morning, fair lady," John grinned and bowed low, hat in hand. "Am I forgiven then?"

Polly smiled nervously. "Good morning. I haven't had a chance to see to my hair." She adjusted her combs self-consciously. "I forgot that you were staying here. What brings you out so early?"

John bounced up the steps and came close to Polly. "I do believe it is the chance to see my betrothed." He pulled Polly close and kissed her softly on the cheek. He tucked a loose tendril of hair behind her ear. "Are we better?"

"Goodness, John. Not in front of the world." She drew back, cheeks red. "I was just headed out to check on the slaves."

John rubbed his hands together briskly. "And yet I was hoping to be invited to breakfast. Your overseer had nothing to eat in his cabin. And there are things I want to talk about from last night." His easy smile disarmed her.

Polly looked past him toward the slave quarters. "Fine, then. I can check on them later. Come inside."

The pair walked into the dining room, where Ona had just set out a small tureen of steaming porridge, a pot of baked apples, and a platter of sliced ham.

"Mmm, Ona, it smells wonderful," John said as he sat down at the table.

Polly watched Ona's face. She knew Ona well enough to know her heartbreak at the sight of John at the breakfast table. The man had allowed her son's brutal beating. He had allowed Duke's murder.

Ona answered dutifully, "Thank you, suh. Some coffee?" John nodded, and she poured the strong black liquid into china cups for them both. She placed the coffee pot on the sideboard and quietly left the room.

Polly began to serve John a helping of porridge and apples, clearing her throat delicately as she did so. John speared a slice of ham and began to cut the meat eagerly. She served herself a portion of fruit before deciding to speak up.

"John, please don't be upset with me." Polly took a small bite of the apples and swallowed. "I need to know what you plan to do about Tom Roper. I do think that overseeing two plantations is too much for one man. Tom has been with my family since I was just a girl. I'm sure that he will do whatever you ask of him." She paused, waiting for him to jump in, but he did not.

She took a deep breath and continued, "I would like to reinstate him immediately. I have to consider what my late parents would have wanted."

John stiffened. He took a sip of coffee and looked at Polly. He put the cup back into the saucer and patted his lips with his napkin before saying, "I thought that after a good night's sleep, you would understand my position."

Polly looked down at her plate and tried to remain calm. "I do understand. You feel that Wilkins is the man to supervise Whitehall. But I disagree." She sighed. "I must stand by my request. I lost a good slave to your Mr. Wilkins. If you wish to marry me, he must go." She clenched her hands in her lap to keep them from trembling.

John was silent. He sipped his coffee and replaced the cup in the saucer. Finally, he spoke. "I don't like taking orders from a woman. Even you. However, I admit that I too have given some more thought to the matter overnight and I have decided that I overstepped. For that, I am sorry."

"He needs to go. If you want us to marry—"

"I will tell Clay Wilkins that he is no longer employed," John said sharply.

Polly leaped from her chair and hugged John's neck. "Oh, John, thank you! Thank you!" She planted a kiss on his cheek and then settled back in her chair happily.

"There will be changes," John added. "Mr. Roper let a lot of things fall apart around here after your father died. And since my field hands have picked your cotton twice now, you'll have no problem with your blacksmith working on some of the River Wood projects that have gone undone." John dabbed the corner of his mouth with his napkin and continued chewing.

Polly thought of Ben's reaction to this news. She leaned in and whispered, "You do know that our blacksmith is Ona's son, Ben." She waited for a reaction from John, some sign that he knew of his half-brother, but there was none. "He is one of the men who was beaten by Mr. Wilkins. I haven't seen him yet, but it may be difficult for him to run the forge for a few weeks."

John set his fork and knife down and said, "Ben. I've seen the wild in that one's eyes; he'd just as soon break my neck as act on my orders. That one bears watching. Has he been a problem in the past?"

Polly gasped. "John, none of our slaves have ever caused a moment's worry. Mother and Father were good to them and they have all served us well. Ben was almost a playmate to Caleb and Joshua growing up. He followed the boys everywhere."

John paled at the mention of Polly's brothers.

Polly continued, "Ben wouldn't hurt anyone. Father was never comfortable with having many slaves, as you know, but the ones we have are loyal to the family." She wanted to tell John that it was Ben who taught her to read, Ben who put her at ease the night of her eighteenth birthday party, Ben who was John's own half-brother. Instead, she said weakly, "Did I tell you that Duke came to South Carolina with my parents? He was a gift to them from my grandfather in Virginia. He was a good slave."

John ignored her comment and speared another slice of ham. "I am concerned with the war talk and secession and do not need slave problems, too." He pointed his fork at Polly. He paused and waited for Polly to look at him. "Going forth, I will expect Roper to be firm with the slaves. They are slaves, not paid labor, and we are not running a charity. If a slave tries to run or shirks his duty, he will be punished and then sold."

Polly nodded. "I understand, John." She stirred her porridge absentmindedly, uncomfortable with the turn their conversation had taken. She tried to change the subject. "You can't imagine the sound of the ringing church bells in Charleston when they announced the secession. It was incredible."

John looked at Polly sternly. "The news in town is not good. The talk of war now is at a fever pitch. With Lincoln elected president last month, things have turned ugly. He will be inaugurated in March and will take over our port in Charleston, I am sure of it. I don't see how South Carolina commerce can survive without that port. The federal government threatens a blockade of shipments of goods along the entire coast. Secession has only hastened the onset of a war. It is becoming more of a reality with each passing day. And if other states secede, it will mean a longer war."

Polly remembered the conversations she heard while in Charleston. She laid a hand near John's, tentatively. "What will we do? Surely, we will not have trouble so far away in the upstate. We are not anywhere near Columbia or the coast."

"I hope you are right, Polly." John nodded. "There may be goods that we can no longer purchase and I expect cotton prices to fall."

She remembered Floride's comments about the poor state of affairs at John's place. "Didn't River Wood have a better crop this year?"

"We'll get by." He nodded but did not look at Polly.

"Maybe there is another cash crop to consider?" she asked. "Something other than cotton?"

"So we shall set a wedding date?" John asked abruptly.

Polly had hoped for a more romantic discussion of their future together but realized she had already won a battle with the firing of Wilkins and the return of Tom Roper. "I was thinking of a late summer wedding."

"That is much too far away," John countered. "Since your holiday trip was cut short, we should plan to marry soon. Your mourning has ended. War is on the horizon."

Polly thought of her brief conversations with Captain Beauregard and Colonel Lee. They had seemed so calm, so at ease. She would never have known that war was imminent.

John took a bite of apples, swallowed, and said, "In the event that war is declared, I may be gone for quite a while. It is better to marry before that happens, don't you agree?"

"Of course," Polly said quietly.

John leaned forward, elbows on the table. "Go see a dressmaker. Have her make whatever you want—spare no expense, while good silks and velvets are still available. I shall even pay the bill. I want you to be the most beautiful bride in the state. Tell them to work quickly."

He stood and picked up his hat. "Let's plan on a winter wedding. How long does a dress take? A week or two?" He regarded Polly with a smile.

Polly laughed. "John, goodness no. A wedding gown and planning a wedding take months." Her thoughts raced. A wedding—there was so much to do. But she had already broached the subject with Mrs. Batson. "Maybe a March wedding?"

"March is so far away. Perhaps February," John countered. "Make up your list of guests and we can discuss it this evening. A small list, mind you. Have Ona begin preparations. I will send a girl over to help. Consider it my wedding present. It is settled then. Best to do this soon in case I am called up."

"John, you don't mean to go off and fight?" The thought of being left alone at Whitehall during a war frightened her.

John sighed. "Let's not borrow trouble just yet. The state may come to an agreement with the Union. I will ride into Pendleton this morning before heading home and get any news. I will try to visit with your Mr. Roper. If he is amenable to terms, we will have him back. If not, we should look elsewhere for an overseer."

Polly nodded mutely, afraid to say more on the subject. She recalled the talk of war at the Pinckney gala in Charleston, overhearing the men speak eagerly of their willingness to fight. *So much false bravado*, she thought. John, too, intended to leave her for the fighting. He sounded just like the men she overheard at the Pinckneys' party, for whom the thrill of defending South Carolina's honor was a noble calling. But what about the women and children left behind? The thought of Charleston made her glum. She would be there now, enjoying the festive city sights and meeting interesting people, if not for John.

"I despise this talk of war," Polly pouted.

John tipped Polly's chin up with his fingers until her brown eyes met his clear blue ones. His eyes. His eyes always caused her heart to skip a beat when he looked at her. He kissed Polly's cheek lightly and strode from the room before Polly could respond.

Polly leaned her chin in her right hand and glanced at the ring on her left hand. *Why did our breakfast conversation seem like a treaty negotiation?* she wondered. She sighed, remembering that Floride had said that she would not be home until after the holidays. She had also asked Polly to wait to make any decisions about marriage until she was back in Pendleton.

Polly shook her head. Nothing would convince Floride that John was good enough for her, but she knew the woman would be beside herself waiting to hear what happened at home to cause Polly to rush back to Whitehall.

She looked at the ticking clock on the mantle. First, she must write to Floride. Then, she needed to think about the details of the wedding and begin a guest list. Finally, she really should check in on Ben and the other slaves.

There was a knock on the front door, and Polly looked around for the women.

"Cissie? Ona?" There was no answer. Peeved, Polly went to see who was calling so early in the morning. She opened the heavy door and smiled with relief.

"Dr. Adger, come in." She extended her hand.

Dr. Adger grasped her hand with both of his and stepped inside. A blast of cold air followed them inside and Polly shivered. "What a cold morning. Winter is here for sure." She pulled her shawl around her shoulders and smiled at the man. "It is a bit strange to leave Charleston and warm weather and wake up to this."

"I am unannounced, I know, but I wanted to check on you and your people after last night, dear girl." The man smiled from under his silver beard.

"You have no idea how happy I am to see you, Dr. Adger. Do you care for some coffee? I was just finishing breakfast and could use another warm cup. Here, let me take your coat and hat. I have no idea where my girls have gone to . . ." She led him into the dining room and rang the silver bell on the sideboard.

Dr. Adger paused when he saw the dishes still at John's place. "I apologize. Am I interrupting?"

"Nonsense. John stopped in to have breakfast with me, but he had to attend to business at River Wood. And not to worry, we have cleared the air. It has all been a terrible misunderstanding. He is on his way into Pendleton right now to see Mr. Roper." She rang the bell again, with annoyance.

Ona appeared and said, "I'm sorry, Miss Polly. Oh, Dr. Adger, is you having some breakfast too?"

"No thank you, Ona. But a cup of coffee would warm an old man's bones."

Ona chuckled and set about collecting the dirty dishes. A fork clattered as it dropped to the table.

Polly felt oddly out of sorts with Ona and said sharply, "Not now, for goodness sake. Don't clear this mess while the doctor is waiting for his coffee."

"Yes ma'am," Ona said quietly and went to get a cup and saucer from the china cabinet.

"In fact, we will take our coffee in the parlor, Ona," Polly called after her. "I am sorry, Doctor. Follow me." Polly led the man into the parlor and sat down across from him in her favorite chair. She sighed. "It has been a tumultuous week."

"Polly, I have never heard you quite so sharp with Ona before," the man chided. "Are you alright?" Dr. Adger asked quietly. "Ona has had quite a night, too . . . her son was one of the men beaten."

"Yes. He was. And I am sorry if I seem harsh. Indeed, I think the long ride yesterday and the circumstances of our early return have frayed my nerves. And now the secession adds to my worries."

Ona appeared with a tray. She set it down on the low table and asked, "Anything else, Miss Polly?"

"No, Ona. Thank you. I am sorry I snapped at you. I am tired. Oh, but I will need to speak with you and Cissie later this morning. I have a list of things we need to do." She tried to make eye contact, but the old woman would not look at her. "I will have some extra help soon for you and Cissie though. Mr. Stone is sending a girl over."

"Yes, ma'am," she said. "I tell Cissie." Ona left the room and closed the parlor doors behind her quietly.

"Polly, may I ask what you meant when you said that everything was a misunderstanding?" Dr. Adger frowned.

Polly poured the steaming coffee into a cup and handed it to Dr. Adger. "Yes, John did fire Mr. Roper but he was wrong. He is on his way into town to see Mr. Roper and to ask him to come back. Mr. Roper will run Whitehall as always, and Mr. Wilkins will be told to leave. Wilkins overstepped his duties and he will be fired."

"Well, that is good news." Adger nodded as Polly poured cream. "You'll need a good overseer like Tom here should we go to war. Tom Roper is a good man." Dr. Adger continued, "And what of Duke?"

"I am so sorry that Duke died," Polly began. "But it is doubtful it was a beating that caused it. John said he collapsed as soon as the blows began. The slaves set on Mr. Wilkins because they found him attacking Cissie. Thank God, she wasn't hurt." She paused, waiting for a response from Adger.

When there was none, she continued, "John allowed Mr. Wilkins to punish the slaves for restraining him. He did administer beatings. He said that Duke dropped after one or two lashes . . . He was quite old." She leaned closer to him and whispered, "The slaves simply cannot set upon a white man, Dr. Adger. It can't be allowed. You know the laws."

Dr. Adger sat quietly and watched Polly as she nervously played with the fringe of her shawl. She felt a flush of shame creep up into her cheeks.

"I know that you think I have turned into a heartless and cruel mistress. I haven't. But hearing both sides of the story allowed me to see that I may have overreacted in coming home so quickly."

"And have you heard both sides, my dear?" he asked.

Polly felt a pang of guilt. But she sat up and looked squarely at the man. "I have heard your story and I have heard John's."

Dr. Adger sighed. "Have you talked to your people? Looked at their wounds? I heard that Mr. Wilkins owns a cat o'nine tails. That's a nasty whip. I would have been happy to tend to your slaves, to help with Duke's burial, but with you out of town, I was afraid to appear on your property."

"Of course I would appreciate your checking on the men while you are here. I haven't had time this morning to see to them myself."

Dr. Adger sipped his coffee. His silence hung heavily in the room.

Finally Polly said too brightly, "Dr. Adger, I want you to be the first to know. I am setting my wedding plans in place. It will be held in February. It may seem sudden, but John believes that war is imminent. I hope that you can be here. In fact, would you do me the honor of giving away the bride?" Polly beamed.

The old man set his cup into the saucer. "Polly, I think of you like a daughter. I am honored that you would ask me to give you away in marriage. However, I heard your mother beg you on her deathbed not to marry that man. In good conscience, I shouldn't give my support." He gazed at Polly's crestfallen face.

"But I ache for you in this situation. I really do. You're still wet behind the ears. You're an orphan with no kin to speak of and haven't had much training in the running of a household, let alone a farm the size of Whitehall. You haven't really had a proper courtship with John Stone either. Maybe getting married is not the best thing for you now."

Embarrassed, Polly looked down at her lap and toyed with her ring.

The man scratched his silver beard and leaned forward. "My dear, if you choose to break off this engagement, I will do everything in my power to assist you in running your place. I know your mother did not approve. I know that Mrs. Calhoun and friends of your parents would say the same. Tom Roper is a good overseer. If you feel that there are changes to be made, he will gladly discuss them with you and abide by your decisions. If you need a loan, why, I can assist you at the bank."

Polly blushed with embarrassment. She brushed a strand of hair from her cheek and said proudly, "I do not need a loan."

The doctor blotted his mouth with his napkin and nodded. "I did not mean to offend, Polly. I know that a young lady of your age should be looking for a husband, planning to begin a family . . . I just don't believe it is with this young man. The things that happened in your absence prove my point."

Chastened, Polly felt her stomach tighten in anger.

"I can see that I have hurt you. I am sorry. I have known you since the day you were born, and I feel I should look out for you. Please accept my sincere apology and best wishes for your happiness. Now, if you don't mind, I will check on your injured slaves and then I will be on my way. No need to see me out. I remember where the cabins are located." Dr. Adger stood. He patted Polly lightly on the shoulder and quietly left the room.

She watched through the window as her friend stepped off the porch steps and made his way toward the slave quarters. For both Floride and now Dr. Adger to refuse to celebrate her upcoming nuptials was a tremendous blow. She didn't know where to turn. At that moment, Polly realized how very alone she was. She ached for her mother and father, for her brothers. She went to the coat rack for her woolen cloak. Bundling herself against the cold, she stepped outside and headed for the slave cabins.

Ben stepped from the smithy just as Polly passed the wide-open door. Her head covered and low against the cold, she did not see him emerge until the two nearly collided.

"Ben!" She exclaimed, relieved to see him up and around. She had not really spoken to him since her mother's death. "I—I was just coming to see how everyone is this morning. Dr. Adger is just ahead of me. He is looking for you." She immediately saw the swollen eye and split lip, dried blood even now at the corners of his mouth.

"Are you alright?" Polly went pale at the sight of Ben's battered face. "Ben, what happened to your face? I thought Mr. Wilkins whipped you across your back."

Ben's eyes were empty and cool. "Yes ma'am. That too."

"I am so, so sorry about what happened," Polly tried. "I promise you, I did not give permission for him to punish anyone. He won't be back here.

And I am heartbroken about Duke. Is there anything I can, I mean, anything I should do? Was he buried properly?"

Ben nodded.

"Did Duke have words spoken over him?" She looked at him worriedly.

Ben nodded again. He sighed and put the back of his hand up to his mouth, dabbing at his wound tenderly as he tried to speak. "I expect Duke got the best we could do at the time." He looked around warily. "If you will excuse me, ma'am, I have repairs to see to this morning. Expecting it to snow later today and we have a lot to do." He looked up at the sky.

Polly managed a small nod. "Oh, of course. I didn't mean to keep you from work. Mr. Roper will be back. Hopefully soon. I will check on George . . . Let Dr. Adger have a look at your wounds. He is here somewhere." She turned to go and suddenly felt him grab her wrist gently. A surge of adrenaline went through her body as she looked at his brown fingers circling her wrist.

"Don't do it, Miss Polly. Please don't do it." Ben looked at her pleadingly. His eyes held a warning, but she didn't feel it to be malicious or threatening. Yet the shock of the black man touching her bare skin was plain to see in her eyes. Her face flushed. "Please, don't marry that man," he whispered. He released her arm quickly and headed toward the barn.

Polly stood still, heart pounding. She clutched her cloak tightly around her shoulders and watched Ben as he went. She put her cold fingers to her cheeks and felt the heat there. Embarrassed and surprised, she turned abruptly and went back towards the house.

Polly headed directly for the library. She sank into her father's favorite chair, unsure of what had just occurred. It was clear that her slaves were terrified of John and his overseer. It was also clear that her friends did not condone her relationship with him, either. For Ben, a quiet and private slave, to dare to reach out and touch his mistress was unheard of. He had never touched Polly, even in the weeks that he had tutored her in reading years before.

She gazed around her at shelves of books, hands on hips. In a methodical manner, she worked her way around the room, skimming the titles of every text, searching for the volume in mind. At last, she recognized the forgotten spine of *Uncle Tom's Cabin*. She pulled it from the shelf and settled back into her father's overstuffed chair. Why this book was becoming a touchstone for her she had no idea. Sharing it with any slave was now against the law in South Carolina, for it might serve to demoralize them and make them restless for change. But she was drawn to the banned novel and its moral courage.

Morning turned into late afternoon before Polly was interrupted by Ona's quiet knock on the library door. "Miss Polly, I got yo' supper set out for you, if you ready."

Polly abruptly closed the book, not bothering to mark her place and set it back on the shelf. Ona noticed and looked away.

"Yes, Ona, I am famished. Thank you for the early supper. I will be there in a moment." She quickly opened her father's desk drawer and pulled a single sheet of fine velum from a sheaf. Grabbing the pen and dipping it into the inkwell, she hastily wrote a few lines and blew on the ink to dry it quickly. She joined Ona in the dining room, where the woman had laid out a platter of pork chops, hot cornbread, and a dish of stewed okra with rice for her mistress.

Determined to try again with her servant, Polly said, "Ona, this looks delicious. I daresay I will sleep well tonight after several exhausting days." She sat down and placed her napkin in her lap, self-consciously. She was so tired, and the beginnings of a headache throbbed in her temples.

The long table was empty, except for the few dishes placed close to where Polly sat and a single lantern in the center. Its light cast harsh shadows in the gathering darkness. It depressed her. How Polly looked forward to having a family of her own, with children seated around the long table, and her husband at the far end, gazing at his abundant offspring in approval. She remembered the early days when she and her brothers, father, and mother ate their meals at this very table, boisterous occasions always, despite her mother's pleas for calm demeanor and good manners.

Ona began to serve Polly from the platter of meat when Polly stretched out her pale hand and laid it on Ona's brown one. "Ona," she said gently.

The old woman startled and pulled her hand away, the serving fork clattering to the table.

"Please sit down with me and have a meal. I need to speak with you."

— • —

LATER THAT EVENING, ONA GRINNED AS she made her way in the dark to her cabin. Firelight flickered through the cracks in windows shuttered against the cold. Sleet began to fall, making a crackling sound as it hit trees not yet shed of their leaves. She had stayed at the big house later than usual that evening. Although she no longer officially had to stoke the fires, ready the chamber pots, and turn down beds, Cissie's condition and the lengthy supper with Miss Polly had put her behind with her other work in the kitchen house. She opened the door and placed the covered plate she had carried in on the table. She shook the sleet from her headscarf and shawl and hurried to poke the fire back to life. As soon as the embers stirred and began to glow, she added a log and began to unpack the food she had toted from the house. The bitter cold seeped into her bones and made her back ache. It was too cold for so early in the winter, with Christmas more than a week away. Ona sighed. She had to admit, Miss Polly releasing her from house cleaning had been a Godsend.

And now this. The conversation that she had that evening with Miss Polly, seated with her at the white woman's own table, left her reeling. She had begun the morning angry and frightened at what would become of them in the days to come. She had been careful to avoid Polly when Dr. Adger stopped by but had eavesdropped on the conversation from the quiet of the library.

There was a sound at the cabin door and Ben appeared. "Hello, Mama," he said. He quickly shut the door behind him and blew on his hands to warm them.

Ona smiled and said, "Evenin,' son. Sit down. I have your dinner ready direc'ly. Law, this cold so early on 'bout to wear me down . . ." She bustled around, humming to herself, trying to decide how she would tell her son the news.

"What are you smiling for?" Ben asked. "Last time I saw you look like that, you told me you were going off to Charleston with Miss Polly. Don't tell me she's going back down there again?" he snorted.

Ona came forward with the plate for Ben. His eyes widened at the hot biscuits with gravy, fresh pork, and a heaping portion of okra and rice. "Looks like a feast!"

Ona sat down across from her son. Ben looked at her and frowned. "Where's yours?"

Ona smiled mischievously. "Son, I ain't hungry after the big meal I ate . . . Ask the blessin' now, afore you go digging in. I got some news." She could hardly contain her excitement.

The pair bowed their heads and Ben mumbled a short prayer. He began to take a spoonful of the rice before his mother had opened her eyes.

"This cold weather so early has to mean a bad winter," he grumbled. "George says we have to get up on that barn roof before a heavy snow comes. Every winter seems it loses half its shingles. The whole thing is about to fall in. Then we'd get beat for letting it happen." He paused to swallow a mouthful of pork. "It's gonna be hard up there with our backs torn up."

"I think Mr. Roper gonna come back real soon," Ona said. "They lettin' Mr. Wilkins go."

Ben looked at Ona hopefully. "That so? Miss Polly tell you that? Thank God."

Ona nodded. "But she still marryin' Mr. Stone."

"I don't plan to stay here if that happens." Ben poured water into his cup from a cracked pitcher. Ona hoped his threat was bluster, but she was no longer sure.

"Ma, this is real fine. How'd you get the fresh pork? This Miss Polly's way of setting things right after what Wilkins did?" he asked sarcastically.

"Miss Polly wasn't real hungry. I think she was 'spectin' Mr. Stone to join her fo' supper, but he never showed. Maybe I ate his share." Ona winked.

Ben stopped chewing and looked at his mother.

Ona leaned toward him. "Ben, I sat down at Miss Polly's fine polished dining room table and ate a meal with her tonight. Ate with her fancy silver forks and knives and crystal glasses, mmm-hmm, I did. I ain't never before set at the Burgiss table, not in all my years, but today I ate with the mistress of Whitehall." Ona smiled at her son.

Ben put his fork down and looked at his mother. "What is it, Ma?"

Ona grasped Ben's wrist firmly. "She gonna set me free, baby."

Ben swallowed a mouthful of pork and stared at his mother silently. The woman laughed and nodded her head. "It's true, son. She gonna set me free after the weddin' and I will be her paid cook." She pulled a folded piece of paper from her stained apron and placed it in front of Ben. "Read it to me, Ben."

He pulled the oil lamp close and read the handwritten words on the page out loud.

> I, Polly Caroline Burgiss, mistress of Whitehall, will hereby set my slave, Ona, free on March 1, 1861. She may keep her small cabin on the property as long as she wishes to live at Whitehall. I will employ her as a paid cook, salary to be determined.
>
> Polly C. Burgiss
> December 1860

"Ma, is this real?" Ben's eyes were wide. "Why is she doing this? Does Mr. Stone know?"

Ona nodded and said, "Can you believe it? She told me that since I was gettin' older, since I took care of her when she was a little girl, that she would give me my freedom. She wants me to stay here an' cook. She said after Christmas and the weddin',' when things is settled down, I will be a free woman. So I be free. Maybe I can save enough to buy yo' freedom. She says another girl from River Wood gonna be comin' here to help Cissie. They gonna keep both plantations. Law!" She took the paper from Ben, folded it carefully, and slid it into her apron pocket.

Ben shook his head, eyes downcast. "I'm happy about this, Ma. I am. For you. But I soon as wait for the end times as wait to see Mr. Stone honor this paper."

Ona shook her head. "I trust Miss Polly."

Ben shook his head and pointed his fork in her direction. "You deserve it, Ma. You've worked hard for this family all your grown life and raised Miss Polly after Miss Mary went crazy. And you should be free. But free far away from here. No one is safe here now."

Despite his harsh words, Ona beamed. The important paper would stay folded and tucked securely in the apron's worn pocket.

Ben put down his fork. "Ma, don't you want to go to a place where you don't have to serve white people all your days, whether or not you get paid? There's talk of war coming. The new president, he doesn't like slavery. If there's a war, I could run. I can go up north to New York and fight for the Union. Black people are free there. If you are free, we could be there together. I can't stand the thought of that man, my half-brother, becoming my owner."

Ona patted Ben's hand and said, "Don't go borrowin' trouble. Miss Polly say Mr. Wilkins won't be comin' back again. An' she don't know that Sam Stone is yo' daddy. She don't need to know that, just like she don't need to know about Mr. John and Mr. Wilkins and the way her brothers died. Mr. John was jes' a boy hisself then. She might not believe us. We might should have told her long ago . . . but Ben, it's too late now. Sure enough, there ain't no one else alive who would believe us." She paused.

"I am gonna stay here an' be free. Miss Polly'll pay me a real wage to cook fo' them. No more wiping out they pots and washing they underclothes."

Ben stabbed a bite of meat with his fork and put it in his mouth. He chewed slowly. After he swallowed the mouthful, he sat back in his chair. It groaned under his weight. "Ma, if you're a free woman, they can't punish you if I go missing."

Ona shook her head. "Ben, don't talk like that. You been tellin' me since you was a gnat of a boy that you gonna run. Martin always said this place couldn't hold you once you was grown. But think about it—if Mr. Stone and Miss Polly get married, and I get set free, maybe we can get you a wife. Please let me talk to her about it . . . Don't do anything stupid, son."

Ben shook his head. "There is no way in hell that Mr. Stone is going to let me marry, Ma. Ever. And any woman he brings here to help out is his plaything . . . You best forget about it," he said angrily.

Ona rose from the table and busied herself at the hearth, aware of the truth in Ben's words.

— • —

BEN FINISHED HIS MEAL IN SILENCE, his thoughts turning to Kate. He remembered her dragging her cotton sack behind her in the hot sun, Solomon slung across her back like so much baggage. She was pretty and strong and brave. Then he remembered what the old man had said to him. She was John Stone's woman. He shuddered.

Chapter Seventeen

December 24, 1860

TOM ROPER DECLINED TO MEET WITH JOHN INITIALLY. He asked for Polly to be in attendance at any meeting, and so the couple traveled into Pendleton to meet with Roper at the local inn on Christmas Eve morning. They sat at a table in the lobby, where Polly tried to smooth the relations between the men. Tom's busted lip had been cleanly stitched but was still bruised and swollen.

The animosity between the two men was palpable. Polly offered Tom a raise in his wages if he would return, to which he agreed. She wrote out a contract, of sorts, that placed him in charge as the Whitehall overseer. She signed it and slid the note across the table for Tom to sign as well.

"I am so relieved that you will come back, Mr. Roper. The entire episode was a terrible misunderstanding, one that we are anxious to put behind us." She glanced at John, who sat scowling through the entire process. "You have been with my family for years, and we value your experience."

"Yes ma'am," Tom replied, not bothering to look at Stone. "I don't mean to cause you problems, Miss Polly. I have always tried to do my best by your family. But I can't have another overseer interfering with how I run things. Wilkins cost us a good man in Duke. And he gave my mouth a pretty good shot as well." He touched his hand to his lip.

"We won't be troubled by that man, again," Polly said. "He has been let go."

"Is that so?" Tom asked.

John glowered at Tom but said nothing.

Tom shook his head and paused to light a pipe. He exhaled a plume of fragrant smoke and leaned back in his chair. Polly was surprised to see the man without his ubiquitous chewing tobacco. The pipe suited him.

"When are you two getting married?" Tom asked her pointedly.

John spoke up before Polly could answer. "February. With the secession vote, it might be best to get the affairs at both farms in order—in case there is war. I fear the bottom may fall out of the cotton market if the state continues down the path we are headed."

"Well, that is one point we can agree on," Tom said brusquely. "Futures are down." He turned back to Polly. "I plan to visit my mother in Greenville for Christmas before I come back to Whitehall. I haven't seen her in several months now, and with all the talk of secession and slave uprisings, she is nervous. I'll leave today, but I'll be back at the New Year. George knows what needs to be done until then." He paused. "How is George?"

"He is up and around, just more quiet than usual. Ona said that Duke was buried quickly, and I think they are reeling from that. They are understandably hurt, upset," Polly said quietly.

John held up his hand. "Wait. That George fellow—he was the slave who attacked my overseer?"

"Your ex-overseer attacked George's wife on Burgiss property," Tom said sharply, pointing the pipe stem at John. "He may be a slave, but he did what any husband would do, black or white." Several men at a nearby table glanced up at Tom's raised voice. "He has been their field boss since they came to Whitehall. He does a damn fine job."

Polly looked pleadingly at John and laid a hand on his arm.

Stone acquiesced. "You may keep him on as foreman for now, Polly." He turned to Tom and added, "After our wedding and his next misstep, this slave, George, will lose that position and he will be punished." He stood abruptly. "Our business is done here."

Tom stood and offered his hand. The men shook hands stiffly. After hasty goodbyes, John steered Polly toward the door and the pair left the inn, as the skies overhead grew low and threatened a winter storm.

Despite her success with Tom, Polly began to feel unusually tired and down. She was eager to get home, business concluded. The couple walked down Main Street, wishing a Merry Christmas to passersby as they strolled. Spotting Carolina Batson's shop, Polly stepped into the dressmaker's store to make an appointment for after the holidays.

The couple continued toward their carriage, noting signs in the mercantile window explaining shortages in many staple goods. John had been right. Tea and coffee were currently unavailable. The price of sugar had risen dramatically in the days since the vote to secede as Union blockades off the Carolina coast began to take effect.

They noticed a crowd gathering in the square near Exchange Street. Anxious to hear any news from Columbia, they joined the sizable throng. Town alderman Joseph Bingham stepped up on a platform decorated with patriotic bunting, cleared his throat, and began to read aloud.

"The Declaration of the Immediate Causes Which Induce and Justify the Secession of South Carolina from the Federal Union," he began. The crowd reacted with shouts and cries. When they quieted down, he continued to read. "The secession convention has met in Charleston at Institution Hall. All 169 voted for the state to secede." The meaning of the proclamation took hold when Bingham unfurled a copy of the *Charleston Mercury* newspaper, holding it high over his head. Its headline screamed, "The UNION is DISSOLVED!" Bingham rolled the paper up like a scroll and stood, awaiting the crowd's response.

A few snowflakes fell, and a man in the crowd stepped forward, asking solemnly, "Does this mean we are really going to war?"

Bingham nodded, red-faced. "Indeed it does. Ladies and gentlemen, listen to this from the *Keowee Courier*. It says that the aim of Lincoln's Republican Party is "to bring the Negro into equality, contact, and rivalry with the laboring white." If this is so, God be with us. Let us all be willing to die rather than free our slaves! Disunion is the only answer!"

"A militia is to be formed under Major McQueen this very day," shouted Bingham, speaking of the local congressman. "He has resigned from the Congress and is headed home to gather support. We should be prepared."

"Gentlemen, we do not need more vigilantes out and about," cried elderly Reverend Whitner. "Instead, we should all be in church this Christmas Eve praying for our state, that she may come to her senses and retract this abominable statement of secession." Some in the crowd murmured agreement. "It can only lead to our ruin," the minister shouted.

Bingham looked down at the minister. "Retract? Reverend, we should throw ourselves wholeheartedly into fighting against the Union. If not, every man's land will lie fallow for lack of labor to plant and harvest. Our slaves will turn against us. Our very livelihoods and what we hold most dear will be destroyed."

Voices were raised and there were shouts of agreement. Polly stood with John, her arm linked through his. Her hands were clasped tightly inside a fur muff. She felt lightheaded and so tired. Adding to her worries about the farm, this talk of war was surreal. John puffed on his cigar and watched the crowd.

"Mr. Bingham is correct." Alderman Davis moved to stand near Bingham. "Even for those of you who may not own slaves, if blacks are given the right to vote, to be free men, we are outnumbered in two-thirds of the state's thirty districts. Your worst nightmares would come true. Lawlessness would abound."

Several women in the crowd gasped audibly as thoughts of rampaging negros filled them with fear.

"Gentlemen!" cried Bingham, pointing to a man standing at the base of the platform. "Major McQueen's man, Lieutenant Marks, is here now. If you choose to enlist, we will have our militia in place should there be trouble. I urge you all to visit his table here and make your patriotism known."

Polly whispered in John's ear. John took Polly's elbow and the pair began to walk away from the demonstration.

"What say you, John Stone?" Bingham called out, seeing the couple moving away from the edge of the crowd. "Rumor has it that you are to marry next year and take over James Burgiss's place. Congratulations to you, sir, and to you, Miss Burgiss." He nodded toward Polly. "Surely you intend to defend your way of life. Won't you enlist, sir?"

Polly felt John stiffen. "Of course! I would defend to the death my right to own slaves," he shouted. There was scattered applause from the crowd. John released Polly's elbow and stepped forward. "Put an army of proud southern men up against Yankee scum and we will always come out ahead!"

Men shouted their agreement.

John continued, "I will take up arms and fight for River Wood and Whitehall in any skirmish to come our way. I imagine that each of you would do the same. Without slaves, our economy is destroyed." Several men in the crowd hollered their approval.

Bingham continued to goad Stone. "Then lead the way, sir! Be the first to sign your name here with Lieutenant Marks. Come on up, Mr. Stone. Show your southern pride!" There was a smattering of applause.

Polly's heart sank as she realized that John was moving through the crowd, toward Bingham. Other men followed him and soon there was a line at the lieutenant's table where men clapped John on the back and offered loud praise in the form of whoops and hollers.

She heard a familiar voice lean in and murmur, "Backwoods farmers and low country gentlemen do not an army make."

Polly turned to see Tom standing at her side, pipe clenched between his teeth. He kept his eyes on the raucous scene in front of them. "I do not see what South Carolina hopes to gain in seceding from the Union. And with federal blockades already in place, we are ill-equipped to supply an army we do not have." He puffed on his pipe and paused to blow out a cloud of fragrant smoke.

Polly looked up at Tom and felt a flood of relief, knowing he would come back to Whitehall. The thought surprised her, and she smiled. "Given up the nasty habit of chewing tobacco, I see. When did you decide to make the change?"

Tom looked down at Polly and smiled warmly. "The very day you told me it was a disgusting habit." He continued in a low voice, "This will not end well, Miss Polly." He pointed toward the platform. "This will certainly not end well."

She was tempted to ask him whether he meant the news of war or of her approaching marriage.

Polly looked at Tom and made to reply, but before she could speak, he tipped his hat and smiled, his blue eyes bright. "Merry Christmas, Miss Polly. I will see you in the new year." He winked and turned, quickly lost in the crowd.

Polly scanned the men in front of her, suddenly feeling quite ill. She spied John, talking excitedly with a soldier standing by the enlistment table.

"John!" she called, as the snow began in earnest. She moved through the crowd and approached him. "I want to go home."

John shook hands with the soldier and turned to Polly. He brushed snowflakes from her shoulder and smiled. "There. It is done." He steered her toward his cabriolet, helped her up, and then climbed in beside her. He appeared happy and excited, but Polly trembled in the cold. He clicked the reins, and the horse began for home.

"Polly, I think we should be married right away," he said, shaking the snow from his own coat and then brazenly draping a blanket across her lap.

"John, a dress will not be ready for weeks," she reminded him. "We had said sometime in February."

"January may see me elsewhere," John said, grinning like a schoolboy. "With pro-secession fever running so high, the entire state is celebrating independence already. We must be prepared for this powder keg to explode any day. If war is declared, who knows where I may be sent? And when? Lieutenant Marks said a militia will be called up to train any day."

Polly knew that John was not a romantic sort, but her spirits sagged at the thought of a rushed wedding. "So you have enlisted?" she asked weakly.

John nodded proudly. "It was an informal procedure, of course. I hope to be commissioned as an officer at some point. More pay. But Lieutenant Marks seems to think McQueen will call us up soon. He is going to the Convention. So a wedding now would make sense."

"What about a dress? And guests? Not to mention we have yet to decide where we would live . . ." Polly tried.

John only chuckled. "You have lovely dresses to choose from—gowns you did not get to wear on your trip to Charleston. You could wear a gunny sack, and I would still marry you." He continued, "We can have a simple wedding, maybe right after Christmas. Pastor Bynum can perform the ceremony with one or two witnesses. Wouldn't you rather be my wife now than wait until we are even closer to the uncertainty of war? Or do you relish the party more than the marriage?"

Polly felt hot tears in her eyes and turned away. She watched the faded brown landscape of the southern winter pass by her window. Bashful oaks, with their canopies of shriveled brown leaves, shivered in the icy wind. Their leaves would not choose to let go until the warming spring pushed new life into limbs and twigs. In the fields, wispy tufts of cotton clung to bolls quickly covered by falling snow. "That was a cruel thing to say, John," she said quietly.

Her entire body ached, and she only wanted to go to her bed. "I do not even know Pastor Bynum. My family is Presbyterian. Reverend Davis is our minister, and you know that he has been ill."

"Polly," John put his hands on Polly's shoulders and gently turned her to face him. "My intent is not to hurt you. But the world is not the same

241

today as it was last week. We must prepare for a fight. If I am to defend Whitehall, I prefer to do it as its legal owner. Your husband. We should be married as soon as possible."

The rhythm of the swaying carriage was the only sound they heard for a few moments. Weary and sad, Polly closed her eyes and leaned back against the seat. "Alright, John. That I can understand." She sighed.

— • —

THAT EVENING, POLLY FELT QUITE ILL AND excused herself from dinner with John and from Christmas Eve church services. She dismissed Ona and Cissie from the house. She was exhausted and fretful as she prepared herself for an early bedtime. A rushed wedding. And South Carolina hurtling toward a violent split with its northern neighbors. Polly was unsure of what she should do to secure her land, her living. She sighed and fumbled awkwardly with the tiny buttons on her bodice as she tried to undress alone in the chilly bedroom.

John had not pushed her further about the wedding, but he did not come by to check on her that evening either. Polly hoped it was due to the unexpected bad weather outside and not some unforeseen turn of events at River Wood. In any case, he would shortly be her husband and he would be with her every night. She would not be alone anymore. Unless there was war.

She remembered Tom Roper's strange comments about the futility of a civil war. Was he right?

She slid under heavy quilts and shivered. Closing her eyes, she tried to imagine her wedding night with John. The impossible, whispered acts that she giggled about with her brothers in her childhood came to mind. She had no married friend of her own age to discuss wedding night expectations with and did not dare ask a slave woman. The ache for her mother was a constant hurt, deep and unremitting.

The last few days had been overwhelming and Polly could no longer keep the tears from flowing. If her own mother, Floride, and Dr. Adger did not support her decision to marry John, who would? What if John turned out to be like his father? If her slaves were so fearful of her fiancé's overseer, what would they resort to in these strange times? She thought of Ben's hand on her arm, pleading with her not to marry the man.

And what would John say about giving Ona her freedom? Setting one slave free would do nothing for the others. She cried softly into her pillow, trying to muffle the sound. When she realized that she was alone in the house with no one to hear her or offer solace, her cries became sobs, and she did not try to stop them.

— • —

ON CHRISTMAS DAY, POLLY SLEPT THROUGH, too weak to leave her bed. With Ona steadfastly by her side, John only put his head in once before returning to River Wood. Boxing Day dawned with sleet peppering the windows of Whitehall and Polly shivering under a mound of quilts in her bed. She awoke and then slept again, spent, and exhausted. Despite wanting to get downstairs and see to household matters, her head throbbed each time she even tried to sit up.

There were things that had to be addressed. Before she could go forward with becoming John's wife, he needed to answer questions about his past, his treatment of her slaves, and whether the marriage itself was even a good idea. She wondered how to bring her concerns to John without angering him further. With a grimace, she heaved herself to a sitting position but did not see Ona anywhere. She rang the call bell at her bedside. Soon there was a timid rap on the door and Cissie appeared.

"Good morning, Cissie," Polly said, as the young woman entered her bedroom with a tray holding a pot wrapped in a tea cozy and a single china cup. "Merry Christmas . . ." Polly rasped.

"Mornin', Miss Polly. Merry Christmas to you, too. You slept through the whole day, you know, an' you don't sound good atall this mornin'

243

either." Cissie too appeared unwell even to Polly's untrained eye. The woman set the tray on the nightstand and gripped the mantle for support with one hand while she stirred Polly's fire to life with the other hand. "Ona gettin' yo' breakfast direc'ly, ma'am."

Despite feeling light-headed, Polly placed her feet into slippers. "I am not hungry, but I suppose I must eat something. I have a lot to do even though I don't feel well."

"Lawd, Miss Polly, ma'am, I is feelin' poorly myself these days." Cissie moved to open the drapes. Outside, heavy clouds hung low, with the promise of continued bad weather. The woman seemed nervous, as if there was more to her disposition than a possible bout with a virus. "I guess Ona didn't tell you? I's havin' a baby in the spring." She patted her abdomen. "The sickness of a mornin' bout to do me in."

"Cissie, that's wonderful news!" Polly said weakly. Her thoughts turned to Wilkins' attack on the woman. "Gracious, it's not . . . ?"

"Lawd, no!" Cissie exclaimed, reading her expression. "No ma'am, this here George's baby, sho' nuff. That man didn't git to me, thank God." Cissie's eyes darted toward the open bedroom door. She dropped her voice to a whisper and moved closer. "Miss Polly, I'm afraid. Is Mr. Stone gonna sell my babies like happens at River Wood? Silas is only two years old. We raise our babies to be good for you, Miss Polly. They be good field hands, like they father."

Polly stared, horrified. "For goodness sake. Mr. Stone would never allow slave children to be sold away. You must be mistaken. I cannot believe it. You have no need to fear. Anyway, that is not the way we run things at Whitehall. Your children are safe. Now you go on downstairs," she chided.

Cissie wiped her teary eyes with her apron. "Thank you, Miss Polly! Thank you, Jesus!" She scurried from the room.

Polly hoisted herself up and walked shakily to her vanity. She sat down, unsure of what to do next. She put her head in her hands and sighed. It was too much. Her emotions were raw and she ached everywhere. The room began to spin and she gripped the edge of the vanity.

She rose and took a deep breath. An illness now would be unacceptable, she thought. There was so much to do. Still, her body cried for sleep and her feet dragged as she fell back into her bed and succumbed to the influenza gripping the upstate.

— • —

DAYS LATER, THE WORLD OUTSIDE OF POLLY'S window continued to simmer in the heated rhetoric of secession, while the young woman alternately shivered uncontrollably and then burned with fever. Her breath rattled with each inhalation.

"Polly, Polly," John leaned over Polly's bedside. He shook her shoulder gently before turning to face Ona. "Ona, what is wrong with her?"

"She real sick, sir. I think she overtired, Mr. Stone, what with the trip to Charleston and all the hurry . . . I don't think she rightly over her Mama either. All her troubles settled in her lungs. She need to rest." Ona tucked a poultice in the neckline of Polly's nightdress and pulled a quilt snuggly around her chest. "Yessuh, grief like to settle in the lungs."

"Does she feel feverish to you, Ona?" John asked. The slave woman had not heard this level of concern from Stone before.

"She burnin' up." Ona nodded, dabbing Polly's brow with a cold cloth. "That poultice, it gonna draw out the sickness from her lungs. I got another one on her feet. She be alright," Ona said assuredly. "I tended to this baby's fevers since she were knee-high to a grasshopper, Mr. Stone."

John looked at Ona with a pained expression. "Thank you, Ona. I hoped we'd be married by now."

Shocked, Ona had the presence of mind not to react. She didn't say anything but smiled in return. Polly was young and would surely recover. When the time came for Mr. Stone to see Polly's written document tucked always in her apron pocket, she would need him on her side.

"Sir, if you want Dr. Adger, Ben could ride fo' him since Mr. Roper is gone."

She thought of the meal sitting untouched downstairs and said sweetly, "An' there is a platter of ham, eggs, and biscuits with gravy sittin' downstairs but Miss Polly ain't gonna eat it. You look like a bit of breakfast could do you good."

John's face was wary. "I could eat a little breakfast. Can I trust Ben to ride for Dr. Adger, after so recently setting himself against my overseer?"

Ona smiled. "Oh yes, Mr. Stone. Ben be real trustful. He can get word to Dr. Adger fo' ya. He in the barn right now."

"Very well," John said. "I will send Ben to town," he said. "I do expect Mr. Roper to return soon, Ona. I am giving him another chance here. Tell the others."

"Miss Polly must be glad about that, suh. Now I'll tend to Miss Polly, an' you go and eat." Ona wondered if she would ever really see the good-natured overseer Tom Roper again.

John nodded and left the room but not before he glanced worriedly towards Polly. When she was sure he was out of earshot, Ona shook her head and clucked her tongue. She would play a good game. She would simper and cook for Mr. Stone, staying in his good graces. But everything was falling apart. If Mr. Roper did not come back, if Polly married this man . . . Still, the hope of freedom, even if it meant living it out at Whitehall until the end of her days, was a promise that she would do anything to make happen.

Thinking about the others, though, and how they might fare under John Stone's authority made her shudder. He could sell Ben away at any time. She sighed and wondered how much money she could save as a paid cook for the new master and his bride. Would it be enough to buy her son's freedom one day? If not, would it at least buy him a wife? She pressed a cool cloth against Polly's flushed cheeks and wondered what the new year would hold.

— • —

BEN WAS IN THE BARN, LISTENING TO SLEET pound on the tin roof while he fed the stock and mucked out the stalls. Zadoc was also ill, and Ben had volunteered to take the man's chores while he rested. Ben heard the heavy door creak open and was surprised to see John Stone walking toward him. He stood and wiped straw bits from his face with one hand, his other hand tightly gripping the pitchfork.

"Ben. I need you to ride into town for Doc Adger. Miss Burgiss is very sick." John stared at Ben icily, silently daring him to refuse.

Ben slowly laid the pitchfork down. "Yes, sir." He had never been asked to leave Whitehall on Burgiss errands.

"Your mother said I can trust you. I need Dr. Adger here as soon as possible. My fiancé is burning up with fever. Follow the main road north. I know you cannot read, so when you get to Pendleton, ask someone for directions to the doctor's house. Here is a letter stating your purpose and a note for the doctor. Stick to the main road. I am not responsible if you are apprehended by a patrol."

Ben nodded, too stunned to say anything.

"Take the fastest horse Miss Burgiss owns. And if you are not back here by noon, I will send my overseer to fetch you home." He pointed a finger in Ben's face. His meaning was not lost on Ben. "Do not make a fool of me, boy. Your mother would not fare well otherwise," he threatened. "Do you understand?"

Ben nodded. "Yes, sir." Stone turned on his heels and stalked back toward the house. Ben cursed under his breath. He saddled Polly's thoroughbred, Delightful, and soothed the excited beast. He had only been on her twice before, after shoeing. He knew how "hot" she could be but needed a fast and sure-footed horse to run the errand quickly. He grabbed his hat and pulled the oilcloth coat that had once belonged to Martin from its peg. He tucked the papers into the coat pocket and stepped up into the stirrup to mount the quivering horse. "Easy, girl, easy. We got us a long ride in some bad weather, and I need you to make tracks." He nudged Delightful out into the icy downpour, and she trotted dutifully toward the road.

The road was muddy and treacherous, but the horse did not disappoint Ben. He held the reins with one numb hand and kept his felt hat on with the other, the brim drooping from the wet weather. Sleet stung his cheeks and made his eyes water.

As he approached Pendleton, he realized that a fast carriage was behind him and gaining, despite the sloppy road. He pulled Delightful over to the shoulder of the road and waited for the carriage to pass. Foam flecked her lips, and she chomped her bit. Ben knew he was liable to have a sick horse on top of everything else.

The carriage did not pass. Instead, it drew up near him and stopped. It was a beautiful ebony Clarence coach, with whale oil lamps burning brightly in the wet, grey morning. The coach looked vaguely familiar. Ben remembered the note penned by John Stone that gave him permission to be off Whitehall property and touched his inner pocket to be sure it was there.

The driver, a miserably wet man himself, said nothing to Ben. But the window nearest Ben opened slightly and a sharp female voice called out, "Ben from Whitehall? Where are you headed in this horrid weather? Is something wrong?" Ben was relieved to see the tiny, wrinkled face of Mrs. Calhoun peeking out from a fur-lined hood.

"Yes ma'am," Ben shouted over the pelting sleet. "I'm headed for Doctor Adger. Miss Polly got a high fever. Mr. Stone told me to go." He wiped his face with the collar of his coat.

"My goodness," cried the woman. "Make haste, then. The doctor's house is the white house on the left after the town hall. You'll see his shingle. Look for the brick building with a bell tower overhead. That is the town hall. His house is next door," she clucked. "Wait at Dr. Adger's, and I can have one of my boys bring you some dry clothing for your ride home."

"Thank you kindly, Mrs. Calhoun," Ben called out. "But I can't wait. Mr. Stone says I have to be back by noon. Don't rightly know what time it is now, but I know how long it has taken to come this far, and I am not sure I'm going to make it, ma'am."

"Good Lord," Mrs. Calhoun wailed. "I do not know what calamity called your mistress back home so urgently from Charleston, but things have clearly taken a turn for the worse." She reached inside her cloak and pulled out the gold watch pinned to her bodice. "There is no way that you can make that ride by noon."

Ben wanted to be on his way but the lady had not dismissed him.

"Ben," she called again from the narrowly opened window, "You ride on. I will turn around and go to Whitehall to check on your mistress. I will tell Mr. Stone that you are indeed doing what he asked. Now, tell my driver to turn for Whitehall immediately." The window slammed shut.

Ben cupped his hands and yelled Mrs. Calhoun's instructions to the miserable and shivering driver. The carriage began its three-point turn back toward the Burgiss farm, while Ben kicked Delightful with his heels and urged her to town.

It was not difficult to find Dr. Adger's house on Queen Street. His shingle was swinging in the icy downpour. Ben dismounted and leaped up the wooden steps. He knocked on the door and waited, dripping hat in hand. Trying not to shiver, he looked down at the puddles forming at his feet.

The door swung open, and Dr. Adger stood, pipe clenched between his teeth. "Can I help you, son?"

"Dr. Adger, I come from Whitehall. Miss Polly is real sick with fever. Mr. Stone sent me."

"Miss Polly is ill?" The man removed his pipe from his mouth. "You're Ben, Ona's boy. You'll catch your death out in this weather. Wait here, and I will find you a blanket to dry off." He disappeared and came back with an old woolen blanket.

Ben nodded his head and took the blanket gratefully. "Thank you, sir. Mrs. Calhoun is on her way out there now. I passed her on the road. She was going to tell Mr. Stone that I came directly to you. He said I have to be back to Whitehall by noon. Please come as fast as you can." His stomach tensed with the stress of wondering what Stone might do to Ona if he were late. He pulled the soggy letter from his coat pocket. "Mr. Stone said to give you this."

Ben saw the twinge of sympathy that passed over the kindly man as he took the proffered paper. He read the smeared words quickly. "Let me get my bag, and we will be on our way." He closed the door abruptly.

Ben wrapped the blanket around his shoulders and tried to warm himself. In a moment, the door opened and the doctor appeared, coat and hat in place, with his bag and several blankets in hand.

"Ride with me in my rig, Ben. We'll tie your horse behind." Ben started to object but Dr. Adger cut him off. "It is no good to Miss Polly to have a slave catch his death in this weather. Help me get the horse hitched, and we'll be off. Ride with me and I will vouch for your whereabouts with Mr. Stone. I doubt even Mrs. Calhoun has much sway with that man."

"I thank you, sir," Ben shivered. He followed the doctor to the stable behind the house and watched as he hitched one of the horses to a small cabriolet. Ben was grateful to get out of the weather but nervous about sitting next to the man in the small two-seater.

"Get in, boy," the doctor said. "My wife has the carriage at her mother's. This will have to do. We'll tie your horse on and head out." Ben shivered and stepped up onto the leather seat, aware of his own wet stench. The way the wind was blowing outside meant that both men would get wet, but it was better than riding horseback the entire way home to Whitehall. Ben was touched that Dr. Adger would allow him into the cabriolet for some relief from the icy weather. Ben's clothing was soaked through, and he realized his feet were numb from the cold.

They made good time and pulled into the Burgiss front lawn just after 1 o'clock. Ben hopped down and thanked Dr. Adger profusely, and the old man climbed the stairs to the house. Ben grabbed the reins and led the rig to the barn. He had not seen the Calhoun carriage in the driveway and wondered if the woman had changed her mind and ridden for home.

He dried both horses thoroughly and fed Dr. Adger's mare a ration of oats. Eventually, Ben could tell by the diminished noise on the tin roof that the sleet had eased up. He patted Delightful's flank. The horse snorted. He smoothed her with the currycomb and then poured an extra ration of oats into Delightful's feed bucket. The thoroughbred seemed none the worse for wear after the long, wet ride. Ben shivered and remembered that he was also soaking wet.

"Alright, hoss, you'll be fine." He stroked the horse one last time. He thought of Polly up in the big house, sick with influenza. His mind flashed back to his childhood, the sight of the girl curled in the fetal position under a clump of dog hobble, clutching her puppy, her eyes squeezed tightly shut. He remembered looking past her to the sight of the boys on the ground, to the flames in the window of the trading post. He saw John, standing amidst the carnage. He could still feel the slight weight of the little girl in his arms when he carried her to her father the following morning.

— • —

POLLY WAS ABED WITH PNEUMONIA FOR WEEKS. Influenza was rampant throughout the district. John asked Ona to make up a pallet for herself on the floor near Polly's bed so she could be available at any time. Ona could not refuse, and the hard floor stiffened her back so that she could hardly stand straight. Anyway, she didn't dare take influenza back to the slave quarters and sent word through Ben to tell everyone to stay clear of the big house.

Ona stayed by Polly's side, applying cool cloths and poultices to bring down the fever and feeding her broth and herbal teas. Dr. Adger visited Polly daily and supported Ona's treatments, which seemed to be working. After a week of house calls, he was relieved to see that Polly was responding to bed rest and Ona's ministrations. Polly's fever finally broke well into the new year.

On a crisp and bright morning in January, she sat up in bed weakly, propped up with fat down pillows, as Ona spoon-fed her from a bowl of bone broth. John sat near the window, winter sun streaming in.

"Listen, Polly," he said excitedly. He smoothed the Columbia newspaper out before him on the desk and read,

"We prefer, however, our system of industry, by which labor and capital are identified in interest, and capital, therefore, protects labor–by which our population doubles every twenty years–by which starvation is unknown, and abundance crowns the land–by which order is preserved by unpaid police, and the most fertile regions of the world, where the white man cannot labor, are brought into usefulness by the labor of the African, and the whole world is blessed by our own productions. . . . We ask you to join us, in forming a Confederacy of Slaveholding States. – Convention of South Carolina, Address of the people of South Carolina to the people of the Slaveholding States."

He smacked the paper with his hand. "I told you. Slavery, not states' rights, will be the cause of this war. This anti-slavery movement is a blow to commerce. Mark my words. We will not be alone in this fight though. Georgia and Alabama are poised to secede, as well."

Polly opened her mouth like a baby bird as Ona spooned warm broth between her pale lips. When she dribbled a bit of the dark liquid, the old woman was quick to dab her chin with a cloth. Ona did not say a word as John continued his rant. She preferred that he forget she was in the room, listening.

"Polly, there's more. On the day after Christmas, Major Anderson, a commander of the U.S. troops in Charleston, withdrew his men to Fort Sumter in Charleston Harbor. It says that our South Carolina militia swarmed over the mainland batteries they left empty and trained their guns on the island. Sumter is a key position for preventing a naval attack on Charleston, so the secessionists are determined not to allow U.S. forces to remain there indefinitely. It appears to be a standoff. War is surely upon us, for someone will fire sooner or later."

"John, you sound like a small boy playing at tin soldiers." Polly sighed, vaguely remembering her brothers at play in war games. She looked up at Ona. "Why is it that men never tire of battles and fighting?" Ona smiled and shrugged.

Polly glanced at John, still reading from the stack of newspapers at his elbow. "John, what is the date?"

"January 15."

Polly shook her head. "I missed the Christmas holidays."

"Yes, well, half the district has been down with illness," he said from behind his newspaper. "And with secession, the usual hosts didn't have much taste for festive holiday parties."

Polly leaned back into the pillows and sighed. "Ona, thank you for the broth. I have had enough. Can you take it away, please? I would like to talk to John alone."

"Yes, ma'am." Ona nodded and picked up the meal tray. She smiled at Polly. Her heart pounded as she realized that this might be the moment when her mistress would tell Mr. Stone of her decision to free Ona. January 15! The New Year had arrived, and with it, the promise of her freedom. She closed the bedroom door behind her and quietly said a prayer as she descended the stairs.

— • —

POLLY TOYED WITH THE RIBBONS ON HER BED JACKET. "John, I haven't forgotten what you said before I fell ill. About marrying soon."

John looked over his newspaper at her, blue eyes questioning. "And?"

He look like a hopeful little boy, she thought. And he was young and so handsome. "If there is war, I want you to be Whitehall's legal owner. I cannot do this alone," she said.

John folded his newspapers and stood. He brushed a hand against her cheek. "Polly, are you saying what I think you are saying? You will marry me right away? I hoped you would see that I have our interests at heart. We will be stronger together."

Polly nodded. "John, let's not make this sound so much like a business decision. If you . . ." She paused. "If you love me, that is what matters. A fancy gown and guests are not important, I suppose."

John knelt by Polly's bed and took her hand. "You are a romantic little thing," he said. "I will call on Pastor Bynum this afternoon. Perhaps he can marry us next week if you feel well enough?"

Polly smiled. "I am a bit shaky still, but whatever you think is best," she demurred. "I guess everything has changed with the idea of war coming."

John stood. "Exactly. And as a wedding gift, I will send my girl, Kate, right away. I held off while you were ill, but she should come now. It is high time that you have more help over here. You rest."

Polly flinched when John mentioned his "girl."

"John, can I tell you what I really want?" Polly began bravely. "Two things. First, I want Floride at the wedding. Is there any way we can wait until she is home from Charleston?"

John looked surprised. "Polly, you must have been out of your mind with fever. Mrs. Calhoun is back at Mi Casa. She left Charleston at Christmas and came to visit you on her way back into town. In fact, she gave me a real dressing down for sending that boy Ben out in the ice storm on horseback, for the doctor." He chuckled. "She acted as if I had committed a grave sin. Though, I am not sure whether it was the boy or the horse she was more worried about."

Polly's mind reeled. "Floride is home? John, I do want her here. As my guest at least, although I hoped she would stand as my matron. I will write her a note. Please send it to her?"

John stood. "Write your note. I will see that it gets to her, and then I will call on Pastor Bynum. Now, what is your second request?"

Polly took a deep breath. "I promised Ona her freedom. She has been like a second mother to me. You know she practically raised me. I would like her to stay on and be, well, be a paid cook."

John hooked his thumbs in the waist of his pants and shrugged. "Polly, you cannot free Ona. Manumission is illegal in South Carolina." When Polly looked confused, he added, "It is against the law to free a slave in this state. It cannot be done. And you treat that woman quite well. She should consider herself lucky to be your house woman. Now, rest easy while I see to our wedding affairs. Soon we shall become man and wife." He gathered his newspapers and kissed her forehead lightly. "And you, my dear, will become Mrs. John Stone."

Polly frowned as John strode from the room. She lay back and sighed. Then she shook her head and brightened. "Ben rode to Dr. Adger for me, in an ice storm."

Chapter Eighteen

A DENSE GREY FOG AND A COLD DRIZZLE HAD SETTLED AROUND Whitehall during the night. Kate arrived by wagon the next morning with her boy, Solomon, already one year old. She had Solomon wrapped tightly in a dirty blanket, but he shivered in the damp chill. She had no shawl or coat, only a thin dress and a bright blue scarf tied tightly around her head.

Kate peered through the fog at the large, well-kept home. Mr. Wilkins slowed the wagon near the front porch.

"Get out, girl," Wilkins barked.

A soaked Kate struggled to dismount with her infant on her hip and a small sack of belongings slung across her shoulder. As soon as she was clear of the step, Wilkins flicked the reins and drove away. The slave woman stared at the big house, wide-eyed. She noticed a movement at the window and saw John Stone staring down at her.

Kate adjusted Solomon on her hip and headed around to the back of the house. She knocked several times and was relieved to see Cissie and Ona at the door.

"Mornin'," Kate said without smiling. "Mr. Stone sent for me. I'm Kate." The woman shivered with the cold.

"Lawd, I remember you," Cissie said. "I thought you was the one that ran."

"Come in, now, outta' this cold." Ona pulled Kate inside quickly. "I ain't never been so glad to see someone as to see you comin'," Ona said. "Ain't you got no wrap? It's bitter cold out today." Ona shook her head when she saw the baby. "An' a baby? They's so much to do here, with a weddin' comin' up. Don't River Wood have any nigras without babies he can send over?"

Kate shrugged and stared at the floor, willing herself not to cry.

"Miss Polly was sick with the influenza. Now she plannin' a weddin'." Ona continued, "Cissie, here, is the house woman now but she got a baby boy Silas, and another one on the way . . . I'm s'pose to be cookin' but there ain't been no time fo' that. Law!" She put her hand to her brow. "Oh, never mind. We got to git yo' baby dry or he gonna catch his death." She held out her arms to take the child.

Kate glared at Ona and hugged Sol to her, "Ain't no one takin' my baby. Ain't no one touch my boy but me."

Ona was taken aback. "Well, I declare. S'pose you wantin' yo' baby to get sick, too?" She removed her own shawl from her shoulders and thrust it at Kate. "Take it." Kate took the warm shawl and dried Sol's face and arms. Ona noticed the baby's caramel-colored skin was in sharp contrast to Kate's ebony complexion.

"I was 'spectin' a woman without chi'dren. But you'll work harder if you haven't got a sick baby to tend. Can you cook? 'Cause you gonna hafta do all my chores in the kitchen while I tend to Miss Polly and this weddin'. I ain't gone let the meals in this house go undone," Ona grumbled.

"Don't know why y'all makin' such a fuss over a white woman's weddin'. But anything is better than pickin' cotton and doin' field work. And Sol ain't no trouble. I just sling him on my back an' he no trouble at all." Kate dried her own face and then wrapped the shawl around Solomon and held him even closer.

"Hush yo' sass," Ona snapped. "An' that baby's big enough to set with Silas in the playpen. Now come on in and dry off. I'll show you 'round the downstairs and the way Miss Polly likes things. I got to get back to her 'fore long. Then Cissie can show you the kitchen house."

"It ain't real bad work now, but Miss Polly fixin' to git married to Mr. Stone and that gone change everything," Cissie complained.

The women turned when they heard a noise in the doorway. John stood there, watching them. Kate stiffened at the sight of Stone, fear mixed with defiance.

"Hello Kate," John said.

"Mr. Stone." Kate dropped her eyes. Cissie stepped behind Ona.

"Kate, I trust that Ona and Cissie have been explaining the job you'll have in your new home?" John stared at the baby as he spoke.

Kate nodded. Sol wriggled and fussed at her breast.

Ona stood tall and said, "Mr. Stone, suh, we ain't about covered anything yet, but we sho' got enough to do with a weddin,' so we best get to work. Miss Polly called fo' us, so we gonna go." She grabbed Kate's arm and pulled the woman toward the back stairs. "Cissie, you work on that silver."

Cissie nodded, wide-eyed, turned, and hurried to the dining room.

Ona led Kate up the stairs and toward Polly's room. As they climbed the steps, she leaned close and hissed, "It ain't gone do you no good to glare at yo' master in this house, Kate. And when you meet Miss Polly, you best smile and be nice, or back you go to River Wood. You ain't doin' nothin' to spoil things fo' us. You here to he'p take care of Miss Polly and this house."

Ona knocked on Polly's bedroom door. The two women entered Polly's room and she sat up with a stretch and a yawn.

— • —

POLLY FIRST NOTICED THE WARM FIRE ALREADY blazing in the hearth, then a breakfast tray on the bedside table. "I have slept in, haven't I?"

Ona moved to open the heavy drapes at Polly's windows. The gray sky was dark and brooding. Ona approached the bed. "You look real good today, Miss Polly. You is on the mend, fo' sho.' Cissie got yo' fire goin' earlier." She glanced at the untouched breakfast tray on Polly's bedside table. "Now you must up and eat somethin', Miss Polly." She placed several pieces of correspondence on the table.

Polly shook her head. "I am not hungry, Ona, but a little coffee does appeal." She sipped from the china cup. She blotted her lips with a napkin and nodded toward Kate, standing quietly by the door. "Is this our new help? Kate?"

"Yes'm, this here Kate from River Wood. She gonna be a good housekeeper, and her baby boy, Solomon, he won't be in the way atall, Miss Polly."

Polly noticed Ona's defense of the infant and wondered if Cissie's stories of babies being sold away from River Wood were possibly true. Kate certainly had the baby wrapped protectively in her arms. Her mind flashed back to the horror of the Charleston slave auction and the way the young Negro mother had begged to keep her little family together.

"Hello Kate. Welcome to Whitehall. Is the baby's father still at River Wood? Perhaps we can have him join you here," Polly said anxiously. "Mr. Stone and I wouldn't want to split up families and I am sure we can use another field hand." Even as the words came out of her mouth, they sounded wrong. Ugly.

"His father is gone," Kate said with some finality.

Relieved, Polly decided not to probe further. She took another sip of the hot coffee and smiled. "Oh, that does taste good." Suddenly a coughing fit seized her, and she reached for a handkerchief. She was shocked at how much the gesture reminded her of her own mother's last days, the woman ill in bed with the consumption.

"Miss Polly, I declare you don't sound fit to get up and take a stroll, much less get married any time soon. I wish you'd wait a bit till you stronger." Ona crossed her arms and stared at Polly.

Polly gestured toward the wardrobe. "Ona, I am fine. Please take out the yellow silk I never got to wear in Charleston. It might do."

Ona frowned. "If half of it is cut away . . ." she grumbled.

"Then maybe the rose silk," Polly countered.

Ona opened the armoire and pulled out several dresses while Polly turned her attention back to Kate.

"Kate, do you sew?"

Kate started to say something when Ona interrupted. "Miss Polly, with the weddin' and all, we sure could use Kate in the kitchen house. I'll take in the dress. Let her cook, please. I hear she a good cook."

Polly frowned at Ona. "Cissie handles the housework, but she has a child. And she is expecting another baby. I want the house neat as a pin for the wedding."

"It will be. I promise, ma'am," said Ona.

Kate straightened and said proudly, "Miss Polly, I can cook 'most anything and it ain't no problem to have both chillun playing in the kitchen while I fix meals, ma'am. An' Mr. Stone likes my cookin'"

"Very well, then. I will discuss a wedding menu with you two later today." Polly's eye caught the tray of mail placed near the coffee pot and she brightened. She sorted through the correspondence and spent some moments reading, while the women stood quietly, Solomon's tiny mouth sucking on his mother's pinky finger.

Polly looked up at Ona. "Mr. Stone's minister, Pastor Bynum, can come out Thursday. It's settled, then," Polly said. "The wedding will be on Thursday. We have five days."

"Yo' people is with Reverend Davis. Why ain't you askin' him?" Ona was perplexed.

Before Polly could answer, she noticed a letter with a familiar return address. She slit the envelope eagerly with the silver letter opener and pulled the page free. After a few moments, she laughed and said, "Ona, a lovely bit of news. Mrs. Calhoun has offered to stand as my matron! I declare. With that bit of good cheer, I do feel better. The world isn't against me after all. I think I will go downstairs to sit. I want to see what has been going on while I was ill. I have been in this bed far too long, haven't I?" She placed her feet on the floor. Ona moved to help Polly, but Polly held up her hand to stop the woman.

"I can do this. I just need my dressing gown for now. You take Kate to your cabin. There are quilts in the mud room cabinet downstairs she can use. She'll have to stay with you, I'm afraid. Move Ben to the men's quarters. I know it will be crowded. One of the hands will have to build another bunk somewhere . . ."

Polly stood shakily and wrapped the dressing gown tight around her middle. "Kate, we are glad you are here. We can use your help. I expect you to be attentive and diligent in your work. I will have to meet with you and Cissie about long-term responsibilities as soon as I am back from our wedding trip. Mr. Stone is taking me to Charlotte. I can't very well expect a lavish trip right now, I suppose, when the whole state—" She stopped abruptly. "Oh never mind. You may both go." Polly waved her hand, effectively dismissing the slaves.

— • —

THE SLAVE WOMEN HURRIED WITH HEADS DOWN, through the icy drizzle toward the warm kitchen house. "Why she thinks she needs to marry that man is beyond me, an' I've known her since she was born," Ona muttered.

Cissie flung open the door to the kitchen. "Come in an' get outta da rain, gals." The women stepped inside the warm building. Silas sat playing in a makeshift pen built by George. The toddler looked up and smiled.

Kate set Sol down inside the pen and watched him as he reached out for Silas playfully. "This is Silas," Cissie said proudly. "He's two. And this here baby gonna be born this spring." She patted her rounded stomach. "How old is yo' boy?"

"About a year and some months. His name's Solomon," Kate said.

"George and me hopin' for another boy. Ain't it the baby girls that gets sold away at River Wood?" Cissie asked, wiping the table. "Miss Polly don't know what she gettin' into, marryin' Mr. Stone."

Ona nodded. "It ain't our job to tell her neither. We just do our work. An' she just tol' us the weddin' is Thursday."

Cissie ignored Ona and appraised Kate instead. "You he'ppin' me clean house?"

"I'm to cook fo' now," Kate muttered.

"Damn." Cissie slapped the rag down on the table. "I'm tired of doin' chamber pots and fires."

Kate turned to Ona. "Thank you fo' helpin' me to stay clear of Mr. Stone."

"We all know 'bout things at River Wood," Cissie clucked. "I'm still tryin' to stay outta Mr. Stone's way myse'f. And when Mr. Wilkins was here last month, he went after me. If he come to Whitehall, we gonna be in a world o' trouble."

"Stop it, Cissie!" Ona snapped. "Don't talk this way. Ain't good for the babies to hear such talk and ain't no idea who else listenin'. An' Mr. Wilkins is gone from there now. Miss Polly said so. Go tell Zee to get more firewood laid by in the big house. And then get back to work. Kate and me'll watch the babies while I show her what's what." Cissie, chastened, flounced from the kitchen house. The door slapped closed behind her.

Ona sighed. "Kate, I'll make up a pallet for you in my cabin fo' now. My son, Ben, he make you a bed frame soon enough."

Solomon began to fuss and Kate lifted him onto a hip. She glanced up at Ona, hot tears welling in her brown eyes. "Mr. Wilkins is still at River Wood. Miss Polly tol' you he wasn't?"

Ona stared at Kate, slack-jawed.

Kate shook her head sadly and lowered her voice. "He jes' dropped me here. An' I got to tell you something else. Mr. Stone, he got me pregnant, and he don't care. It don't matter none if they be boys or girls. You tell that to Cissie. If Mr. Stone want to sell her chile, he sell her chile. I had to be willin' to do his biddin' fo' the last year, else he threaten to sell my baby. His own son." Solomon started to fret, wriggling, and fussing from hunger. "But he ain't takin' my baby from me." Kate pulled down the neck of her bodice but said nothing more as she put the baby to nurse.

Ona put her hands on her hips, her mind flashing back to her own nightmare at River Wood. "Mr. Wilkins is still there? Miss Polly thinks he's gone. An' if she find out Mr. Stone has a baby by you, she go crazy. Do he still favor you? Ah . . . that's why he brought you here. You puttin' us all in a bad place," Ona said angrily.

"I didn't ask to come to Whitehall, old woman," Kate snapped. "That man brought me here. Solomon's his boy. He think he gonna use me here too, I know it." Solomon stopped nursing and began to fuss.

"Both of you, settle down now," Ona said. "You think you the onliest slave woman been used by a white man? Don't be a fool. Hush up. We think this through. We gonna do our work. Law, they's lot of things we can't do nothin' about, but we gonna work hard and give Miss Polly no reason to complain. If she likes you, he ain't gone send you away or come huntin' you. We keep you busy in the kitchen and with the chi'dren. He don't ever come to the kitchen house. No one else need to know this, certainly not Cissie. Her mouth get us all in trouble. Now, sit down and feed this baby right and then let's get to work."

Chapter Nineteen

January 20, 1861

THE MORNING OF THE WEDDING DAWNED CRISP AND CLEAR. Bright sunshine streamed through Polly's bedroom windows. She nervously sipped her coffee and twirled a lock of her hair around her finger as she stood admiring her bridal gown hanging from the armoire. The pale rose silk gown sewn for her trip to Charleston was simple but elegant. Ona had taken it in as best she could. The whalebone corset and hoop lay across the bed.

Polly ached for her own mother and was beyond grateful that Floride would be by her side at the ceremony. The older woman would also have the latest news from Charleston.

Dr. Adger had relented after Polly's illness. He felt somewhat responsible for the load he added to her young shoulders when he called her home suddenly from her low country trip. He decided it would be his duty to walk Polly down the aisle. He and his wife and the Baptist minister would arrive later in the afternoon. The ceremony would take place with the Adgers, Floride, and Tom Roper as witnesses.

She thought of all that had occurred since she was pulled home by Dr. Adger's urgent message. Ona had reported that Mr. Roper, on his return, had met with the field hands and expressed sorrow at the news of Duke's death. He reminded them that Whitehall was under new management. John Stone was the boss man now, and he would require each man or woman to work hard. He told them that there may be more slaves from River Wood as Mr. Stone planned to increase the Whitehall land dedicated to cotton in the coming spring. Whitehall soil was the better of the two properties for growing cotton.

Polly was relieved that Tom had come back, that Wilkins was no longer a threat, and that Kate had come as a new kitchen help. She knew that she should not press her luck and ask for any other concessions from her soon-to-be husband and master of Whitehall. She fretted about how much more would be required from her field hands and whether they would be subject to beatings if they did not produce what John expected. And how would the farm survive if they weren't able to sell cotton at market? She longed for her father's counsel but knew that Roper was a strong and fair overseer.

There was a knock on the door, and Ona entered. "I got your bath all ready, Miss Polly."

"Thank you, Ona." Polly brushed at her long dark hair vigorously. "I think I will sit awhile in that nice hot water and collect my thoughts. Land sakes, my nerves are going to get the better of me this day. Is everything ready in the kitchen? I know that you and Kate had a lot to do on very short notice. I am sorry that I couldn't give you more time to plan the wedding supper. At least we won't have a crowd."

"Yes, 'm," Ona said absentmindedly. When she didn't say more, Polly frowned.

"What is it, Ona?"

"I jes' wonderin' if you told Mr. Stone about the paper you give me before you got sick, my freedom paper," Ona said quietly. She twisted the edge of her apron in her hands.

Polly was caught off guard. "No, I have not. Not yet," she faltered. "I was so sick. And now, well, my wedding is today, and I have barely had time to think about anything else." She turned back to the mirror. "Be patient."

— • —

BY MID-AFTERNOON, THE THIN WINTER SUN CAST long shadows through the pines behind the kitchen house. Ona hurried along, her mind ticking off the things still to be done. The dining room table was set, the parlor clean and ready for the ceremony. The smell of roasting meat wafted from the kitchen chimney and made her mouth water. Her stomach rumbled as she pulled open the screen door.

Ona saw that Kate had the wedding supper well under way. A venison roast was on the spit, and side dishes were set by the fire to stay warm. Kate concentrated on the ginger cake that would not release from the pan. The baby and toddler played happily at Kate's feet, enjoying the warmth of the hearth.

"You gone have this ready in time, Kate?" Ona asked. "An' don't tear that cake, girl."

"You told me what you want me to do, Ona, and I done it," Kate said. "Sol ain't stoppin' me from anything you told me to do so far. I cook as good as you. Maybe better. Miss Polly like my food." The cake released from the pan in a perfect circle and Kate beamed. "An' she will love this cake."

Ona scowled.

Kate pointed the spoon toward the old woman. "I ain't bein' prideful, but it's a fact. An' why all this food for just a few folks?"

Ona pointed to several loaves of sliced bread. "Slice 'em thinner than that." She busied herself with her work and watched as Kate stirred the buttercream. Sol babbled from his makeshift playpen. Occasionally, Kate would extend the wooden spoon to her baby, and he would lick the sticky sweet icing and smile. Ona stiffened and stared at the child. She was irked by their constant presence already.

"Law, we got enough food here to feed everyone on the property," exclaimed Kate. "They ain't eatin' all this, is they? Can we stow some away? I sho' would like to give Sol a taste of that tomato jelly." She frowned and pushed at a bowl of tomato aspic, watching it tremor and shake.

Ona put her hands on her hips. "Mebbe less talkin' and more workin' is what we need right now. The both of us don't need to do nothin' to upset Miss Polly today." Ona shook a bony finger toward the young woman and added, "Put on yo' new white apron befo' you an' Cissie show up to serve. I don't want you to be there at all, but Miss Polly 'spects it."

— • —

POLLY SAT AT HER VANITY TABLE AND PEERED INTO the mirror hesitantly. Her skin was quite pale still, but her brown eyes were clear.

"My goodness, Ona," she sniffed. "I still look a fright, and that dress will not help my complexion at all." She pinched her cheeks.

Ona soothed her mistress, "You'd look pretty in a flour sack, Miss Polly."

"That's what John said, but I think I look sickly." She glanced at the dress, hanging from the armoire. "And a wedding dress it is not."

Ona began to coil Polly's thick braids at both sides of her head and then pinned them just so. "There ain't much that still fit you after that sickness."

"You and John are so good to me," Polly said.

Ona nodded. "Mr. Stone was right worried about you, I hafta admit. He was frettin' something awful over the holidays."

Polly smiled. "That's a comfort. He hasn't been in the house much since we decided on the wedding date. It seems he and Mr. Roper have been meeting a great deal. It is good to have Mr. Roper back. I do hope they get along."

"We all do, Miss Polly. And what's all them comin's and goin's on the big road this week? George say he ain't never seen so much wagon traffic and men on horseback hurryin' by."

Polly bit her lip. "I don't know." She, too, fretted about the comings and goings. She expected bad news of war at every turn. She remained quiet as Ona prattled on. She still had not found the words to tell Ona that she could not be free.

"Kate gonna be helpful, Miss Polly—a big help in the kitchen, 'specially with a new master here. She got that baby, an' kitchen work be easier fo' the baby, too. I come back into the big house and he'p Cissie fo' a while."

Polly picked up a diamond teardrop and clipped it to an ear. "You would rather keep Kate in the kitchen? I'll miss your cooking."

Ona nodded. She picked up the other earring and clipped it onto Polly's earlobe. "Kate is a better cook. Wait till you taste the cake she made." She smoothed a loose strand of hair behind Polly's ear.

Polly sighed, afraid to ask the question on her mind.

"You nervous about the weddin'? Ain't nothin' to be nervous about, Miss Polly. It will be a lovely weddin,' I'm sho' of it."

Polly turned to look at Ona. "No, I am not nervous about the wedding . . . I don't know what is expected of me—as a bride, I mean," she said quietly.

Confused, Ona looked at Polly.

"The wedding night," Polly said, her cheeks aflame.

Ona chuckled. "I remember you as a little girl cannin' apples with me ten years ago, askin' about yo' first lady's monthly. You jes' do what's natural and it all work out. I ain't sayin' the first time is anythin' special." She grinned. "Yo' mama would prob'ly have tol' you to close yo' eyes and do yo' duty." She chuckled when Polly reddened even more deeply.

"If you is askin' my advice, it's this. I loved my Martin till the day he died. It ain't never was hard to be with him. I loved him and he loved me. He was tender and good to me. That's how it should be, and then . . . Law! The fireworks!" She cackled loudly and Polly smiled.

— • —

ONA HELPED POLLY UP AND tied the bulky cage crinoline around her waist. She held up the soft rose silk bodice and slid it over Polly's outstretched arms. Since the conversation had turned so personal, Ona took a deep breath and decided to jump in with both feet. "Miss Polly, I was jes' wonderin' . . ."

"Hmmm? What were you wondering?" asked Polly, as she watched Ona work on the crinoline.

"I was jes' wonderin' about that freedom paper. I heard what you said about talking to Mr. Stone, and I know you been ill, but I was hopin' that I could start my freedom soon. Now that Kate's here, well, it might not be such a hardship for you."

Ona watched as Polly's face fell at the mention of the scrap of paper she had penned in a moment of tenderness. "Oh, Ona . . . ," she began. "Ona, please. As I said this morning, I must handle this delicately. Let's get through the wedding. Mr. Stone and I will be taking a wedding trip and we will discuss it then. Now, please don't fret. Be happy for me. I am getting married today." Polly turned away as Ona slid the full skirt over her head and fastened tiny pearl buttons.

Cissie appeared in the doorway. "Excuse me, Miss Polly. Mr. Stone need to see you. Is you coming downstairs? He say it's important."

"Gracious!" Polly exclaimed, grateful for the interruption. "Should he see me before the wedding?" The slaves stared at her blankly.

"Thank you, Cissie. I will come downstairs, although if you could see to it that I don't fall flat on my face, I would appreciate it. This dress will make it difficult to take stairs and I am still wobbly. Ona, we can continue our conversation another time," Polly said.

Ona was crestfallen. The mention of her freedom paper obviously did not elicit the response she had hoped for. Something must have changed. Ona watched Polly go, all of her plans for freedom crumbling into dust.

— • —

THE PAPER. POLLY HAD FORGOTTEN ALL about the piece of paper she had written out for Ona. How would she explain manumission? As Cissie helped Polly navigate the stairs in her oversized skirts, Polly wondered how long she could put Ona's questions aside. At the bottom of the staircase, she steadied herself and looked toward the drawing room.

John appeared in the doorway and smiled. "Now there is a sight to warm my heart." He reached for her hand and led her into the drawing room, closing the door behind him.

Polly twirled and said, "I hope you are not superstitious about the groom seeing the bride before the ceremony. This is not a wedding dress, so perhaps we aren't in trouble." She laughed. "Although I shall not sit, lest I ruin the skirt. I will change before we travel."

"You look wonderful. How do you feel?" John's nervous demeanor charmed Polly. He seemed more like his old self than the harsh man she had confronted upon her return from Charleston.

"I feel better than I must look right now," she said.

"Polly, I have something to tell you and I fear that it will impact our wedding plans greatly," John began. Polly felt her stomach flip, and she waited for him to continue.

"On the day you fell ill, the town received a dispatch from Columbia. It was read in the square in Pendleton. South Carolina seceded from the Union. Do you remember it?"

Polly nodded dully. "Of course, John. I was ill, but I remember that day. It is all you have spoken of since. War."

"While you were ill, shots were fired in Charleston. Federal troops took over the fort there at the harbor mouth—Sumter."

Polly remembered seeing the tiny island fort in the harbor.

"Recently, Citadel cadets from the Morris Island battery fired on a civilian merchant ship. The ship was attempting to bring supplies to resupply the federal soldiers at Fort Sumter."

"You mean to say schoolboys fired on federal sailors?" Polly asked. "How brave!" She thought back to the fiery conversations she had overheard about states' rights while at the Pinckneys' home in Charleston. "Gracious. No wonder Floride fled the city."

John continued, "School boys trained to fight courageously as soldiers. The ship was given a warning shot across the bow, and it turned about to leave the harbor mouth. She was hit three times. Her captain considered it too dangerous to continue and turned tail. The mission was abandoned, and the ship headed back to New York. We should consider it good news for our side, as the federal soldiers were not resupplied. But this effectively means we are at war, Polly." John pulled out a cigar and lit it, filling the room with the scent of fragrant tobacco. "Lincoln is inaugurated in six weeks. We will need to be prepared."

"What other states are with us?" Polly asked.

John nodded as he spoke. "Mississippi, Alabama, and Florida have joined South Carolina in secession. And rumor has it that Georgia has decided to join us as well." He puffed on his cigar and added, "But other states will come. I think that the entire slave-holding South will join in. Like dominos . . ." John paused and looked at Polly sheepishly. "In fact, there is a convention of seceded states taking place next month in Montgomery, Alabama. Major McQueen's company has been asked by state delegates to accompany them."

"It pains me to think of it." Polly shook her head. "Floride wrote such a brief note when she returned home—but she must be frantic with worry." She tried to picture the simple farmers and planters she knew going to war. "John, what does this have to do with the wedding?"

"Polly, I didn't want you to worry about this while you were ill. But we are about to declare ourselves free of the United States. We will be fighting to establish a new country."

"I understand that. It is terrible. I still do not understand what any of this news has to do with us. And the wedding." Polly's heart began to pound in her chest.

John stubbed out his cigar and blew out a thin column of smoke. "In an hour, your guests will be here. We will celebrate and eat our wedding supper—and enjoy the night. Unfortunately, I do not think that we can leave for our trip tomorrow as planned. We can travel when this skirmish is over. Perhaps even to Europe," he paused. "Remember that I added my name to the muster roll, Polly. I joined McQueen's company. A small entourage will be leaving soon for Columbia. He asked me to go along. I hope for a commission as an officer, remember? So I need to go." He chuckled. "Imagine—your husband an officer in the Confederate Army?"

"You're leaving?" Polly sank to the settee. "We won't take a wedding trip. And in fact, you go away next week?"

John continued excitedly. "The state delegation attends the Alabama convention in just weeks. South Carolina has six delegates, and Major McQueen counts it a great honor to have been asked to take his company along. He will be the aide-de-camp to James Chesnut. I hoped you would be proud of me."

Polly vaguely remembered being introduced to Chesnut's wife, Mary, in Charleston. The woman was intelligent and kind. Her mind reeled with the news. "John, how will I manage Whitehall and River Wood without you?"

John pointed toward the windows overlooking the broad front lawn and the fields beyond. "We are far away from any skirmishes this far inland. I will probably be lucky to gain a Captaincy and a few dollars from this whole thing, but it is an honor to attend."

Polly pressed her lips together.

"I think it wise to withhold this news from the slaves. Rebellions are afoot across the state. Mr. Roper is here. Overseers are easily exempted from any fighting. If a slave seems in the least likely to be a problem, he has my orders to punish the slave. There is finally a new ordinance. If a slave attempts to foment insurrection, the slave must be hanged."

Polly cried out involuntarily, "John, no!" She imagined Ben and gentle George swinging at the end of a rope.

"Shh, Polly," John said quietly. "This is serious. And we do not know who listens in." He looked past her toward the parlor doors. "Mr. Roper must always carry his weapon. We may not be in danger of military skirmishes here, but we do not know whether news of the conflict will mean more slave problems. I will not tolerate any breach in their conduct as our property. For they are just that, Polly, property. I am sure that it will all be over before cotton is planted this spring."

"John, my slaves would never do me harm," Polly scoffed. "And I have not even seen Mr. Roper since I fell ill. Have you two spoken about this?"

John crossed the room and picked up a decanter from the sideboard. He poured a generous whiskey and placed the crystal stopper firmly back into the decanter with a loud clink. He tossed back the shot and said sharply, "Do you honestly think that Ona and the others would not chase after freedom if it were so close? If we listen to those firebrands in town, our slaves would as soon murder us in our beds, torch our barns, take our valuables and thieve away to New York or Pennsylvania." His eyes burned. "If given half a chance, they'd murder you. The sooner we quench this civil war, maybe with a compromise reached at the convention, and get back to business, the safer we will all be."

Polly's mind raced as she considered what could happen at Whitehall if she was to be left alone with a dozen angry slaves who refused to work. What about River Wood? As the new mistress of River Wood, would those slaves rebel and come looking for vengeance? And Ona. Did she already know the news? Was that the reason she asked about her freedom paper?

"What about your slaves, John?" She knew that Cissie, Zadoc, and Kate had come from River Wood, and suddenly wondered who was left there. Were families split up, as Cissie had said? Polly remembered the auction in Charleston and the young man sold away from his wife and baby. She swallowed hard. "How will you find a new overseer so quickly?"

"I will have them in hand," John said simply. "Don't worry about River Wood."

Polly thought of the paper she had given Ona. What had she been thinking? She shook her head. Suddenly, she was very tired. "John, this is supposed to be a happy day."

"I know. It will be a happy day. We shall marry and begin our lives as husband and wife together before the world around us falls apart," John said.

Polly sighed. "Oh, John. I had so looked forward to going away. Even to Charlotte. No wedding gown. No party. And now no trip."

— • —

MOMENTS LATER, POLLY AND ONA WERE BACK in Polly's room to finish dressing. Polly stood and tried not to cry as Ona adjusted the illusion veil that fell the full length of her skirt.

She gazed at her reflection in the mirror and smirked at the illusion the veil could not hide, of this gown being a real wedding dress. Her mind flashed back to a day so long ago when she stood still for her mother as she pinned and tucked a little smocked dress that she was to wear for the great Senator Calhoun's first visit to Whitehall. The day her world crashed. Polly shuddered and drove the thought from her mind.

"You look beautiful, Miss Polly." Ona smiled.

There was a light knock on the door, and Floride appeared in the doorway. She wore a lovely, brocaded gown in emerald green. Her cheeks were ruddy from the cold, and she carried a small box in her gloved hand.

"Floride!" Polly exclaimed, throwing her arms around the woman's neck. "I am so glad that you are here."

The woman returned the hug and looked up into Polly's eyes tenderly. "My dear. I must say you look much better than the last time I saw you. I am glad you are well now. John Stone was quite worried about you. Forgive me, dear, for the things I said to you in Charleston. I had the best of intentions, but I know my words were cruel. I am sorry. Can you forgive me?"

Polly looked past her friend and said, "Ona, go now and see to the meal. Thank you." She noticed the tears in Ona's dark eyes as the woman closed the bedroom door behind her.

The women embraced again, and Polly invited Floride to sit. The woman laughed and said, "I cannot sit in this thing," pointing to her voluminous skirt. "You should have seen me in the carriage just now, dear. I was relieved to be riding alone as there was no room for a companion!"

Polly laughed, too, and felt the weight of the world lift from her shoulders. "Floride, you will stand with me then as my matron of honor?"

"I will do so with pleasure. Oh, I almost forgot. I have a wedding gift for you." She handed a small wooden box to Polly. "It belonged to my daughter, Martha. You may remember that she passed a few years ago. So I want you to have it now."

Polly opened the box to see a beautiful ruby necklace nestled in folds of black velvet. Tiny diamonds surrounded the oval ruby, the size of a wren's egg. She gasped. "Floride, this is lovely. But it is too much."

"Nonsense," clucked Floride. "It will make me happy to see it put to use."

Polly lifted it gently, and Floride moved to help her secure it around her neck. It lay in the hollow at the base of her throat and dazzled as it caught the room's candlelight.

"I don't know what to say. I will treasure it, Floride. Thank you."

Floride smiled. "It brings out the color in your cheeks, dear. I am delighted that you like it." She patted Polly's face tenderly and chuckled. "And if the new Confederacy falls, you may trade it for a few turnips from some Union officer."

"Floride, that isn't funny. John just told me that he plans to go with the McQueen delegation to the convention soon. To Alabama. So our wedding trip to Charlotte is canceled. What am I to do?"

Floride shook her head and said, "It is simple, Polly. You are to do what we all must do. Be the courageous and strong person I have always known you to be." She patted Polly's cheek affectionately. "We are entering strange times. A war will test us all. We will get through it. But we must celebrate while we can! So let's get you married."

— • —

DOWNSTAIRS, CISSIE WAS SETTING THE LAST of the beribboned swags of greenery into place in the large dining room where the ceremony was to be held. Ona appeared in the room, dabbing her eyes with the corner of her apron. Cissie turned and noticed Ona's tears. The older woman merely sniffed and said, "Ain't no need to stare at me, Cissie. Haven't I got a right to some cryin' this day?"

Cissie nodded as she stuffed pine boughs into a vase. "We all gonna be cryin' when this is over, and you know why!" she muttered.

Ona looked around at the beautiful room. The wooden table was polished to a high sheen. Crystal and silver sparkled in the light of the candle-heavy chandelier, and a bounteous repast would soon be laid out for Polly's small party.

Ona wiped her eyes and said, "You done good, Cissie. This room looks fine. Come back to the kitchen when you finished. Lawd knows we got to make this special for Miss Polly."

— • —

BEN STOOD WITH ZADOC OUTSIDE OF THE big house and looked up at the lights ablaze in the parlor windows. Inside, the wedding supper was in full swing, Cissie and Ona serving Polly's guests obediently. Ben took a puff from a discarded cigarette he had picked up in the driveway and exhaled deeply. "I don't know what to say, Zee," he began. "With her marrying Mr.

Stone, everything changes. And now we hear rumors of war, of South Carolina separating from the rest of the country . . ."

"Is that what all the commotion on the big road been since Christmas?" Zadoc asked. "Never seen so many white people headed back and forth." He shivered and blew into cupped hands. "Damn, it's cold."

Ben took another drag from the cigarette butt and handed it to Zadoc. "Secession. It means South Carolina has left the United States. They want to be their own country."

Zadoc's eyebrows went up in surprise. "How you know that?"

Ben shook his head and smiled. "Mr. Roper leaves his newspapers in the white privy."

Zadoc inhaled deeply and then coughed. "You can read? That how you learned to talk white?" Zadoc grinned at Ben. "You best hope Mr. Stone don't find out you can read. He'd tan yo' hide."

Ben lifted his chin proudly. "I even taught Miss Polly to read when she was a child."

"That a fact?" Zee's eyes grew wide. He handed the cigarette butt back to Ben.

Ben nodded. "My father taught me how to read when I was young. He spoke beautiful English. He told me that it'd be harder for a white man to treat me badly if I could speak well. It stuck with me." He puffed on the bit of cigarette.

"So what's all this 'session' mess got to do with us, anyway?" Zee asked, through a cloud of blue smoke.

Ben watched the movement of people inside the warm and brightly lit house. "Half of the country wants slavery outlawed. The new president believes no man should own another man. But South Carolina wants to keep its slaves . . . it's willing to go to war over it. Think about it, Zee. We're the ones who do all the work. Raise and pick white people's cotton. Tend white people's children. Grow and cook white people's food," Ben explained. "But the new president—a white man—knows it is wrong. Miss Polly will figure out it's wrong too—someday."

"That a fact?" Zee murmured again. "Law, jes' to know the president is willin' to fight fo' us is right hopeful. River Wood . . . you don't know how bad it is there."

Ben smirked. "And here you are about to fall back into the hands of its owner." He tossed the cigarette butt down and ground it into the dirt with his boot.

— • —

POLLY OPENED HER EYES TO FIND THE bedroom still dark and the fireplace cold. She realized that she had neglected to tell Ona her expectations of what to do the morning after the wedding. Now that she was a married woman with a husband in her bed, Ona would not dare walk in early to stoke the fire or bring breakfast unless asked the night before.

Floride had offered the couple a set of rooms at Mi Casa, but John had declined, so they had spent their wedding night at Whitehall. Polly shivered and turned over, pulling the quilts over her head. She reached her arm across the bed and found John, turned away from her and breathing quietly in his sleep. She inched over and laid her arm across his back, seeking warmth.

Married. Mrs. John Stone. Polly Burgiss Stone. She smiled to herself. She was happy. She thought back to the night before, and how nervous she was, a bride with little dowry except her land, little in the way of a beautiful trousseau, and no knowledge of the ways of men with women. John had been patient with her and tender, at first. She was surprised at the intensity that seemed to take over his body as he rolled on top of her, leaving him quickly spent and asleep beside Polly, and her own private places bruised and swollen.

Still, he seemed satisfied with the way the night had gone. She wondered if he would come to her again tonight, or retreat to his own room, separate, the way her father and mother had lived. She decided to have Cissie clean the adjoining room that had been her father's, in case that was expected. Her eyes grew heavy, and she drifted back to sleep.

Chapter Twenty

OUTSIDE, EARLY CLOUDS WERE GIVING WAY TO BLUE SKIES. Kate and Cissie had quietly dragged the woolen carpets from the formal rooms to the yard and hung them on the line. Kate used a broom to gently beat the dirt and mud from them. Although the day was cold, the crisp air and sunshine felt wonderful on her skin. Solomon sat on a quilt, bundled in his new clothes, courtesy of young Silas who had outgrown them. Kate couldn't help but feel like life had shifted for her. There was little chance of Wilkins appearing to torment her or her child now, and Mr. Stone had avoided her entirely after his initial greeting. Her new mistress seemed compassionate and easy to get along with. Kate prayed that as a newly married man, Mr. Stone would finally leave her alone.

Solomon gurgled and laughed from his place on the quilt. He was warm and safe. Kate smiled and began to sing to her son while she worked.

"I remember that voice," she heard from behind a hanging carpet. She startled. Ben peered around the carpet and chuckled.

"I'm sorry. I didn't mean to frighten you," he smiled broadly. He carried a ham in one arm and several small logs in the other. "If you could open the door to the kitchen house, I'd be obliged. Mama seems to think I'm her errand boy this morning."

Kate nodded and adjusted her headscarf nervously. "You didn't frighten me. I'm just not used to the comin's and goin's of men around here yet. At River Wood, y'ain't never see a black man near the kitchen or the big house. I thought you was the master."

Ben nodded. "I'm Ben. I worked in the cotton with you. I recognize your red dress."

Kate pulled her threadbare sweater tighter over the dress. John Stone had tossed the dress to her, after raping her on the floor of the River Wood kitchen house. He had ripped her old cotton dress badly, and as she lay quietly afterward, crying into the floorboards, she felt the new dress land on her back. The master cursed at her and growled, "Cover up." Who and where it had come from, she did not know.

Kate's face showed little emotion but she said, "I remember you—the chatty man like to git me in trouble in the field."

"I thought you were the chief cook now. Why are you out here beating rugs?" Ben inquired.

Kate's face clouded. "Folks tracked mud inside at the weddin'. Anyway, your mama thought Miss Polly would want her to bring up breakfast this mornin'. Don't want to run into Mr. Stone when I don't have to." She glanced at Sol and back to Ben. "Well, come on. I ain't got time to talk wit' you when there is carpets to beat the fool out of." She turned and walked toward the kitchen house, keeping her eye on Sol the whole time. The baby sat mesmerized by the carpets flapping in the breeze and did not fret.

"He's a fine boy," Ben said. Kate opened the screen door to the kitchen and held it while Ben entered and dropped the heavy ham on the wooden table with a groan. He put the kindling on the hearth and stood.

Kate's fiery eyes bored into his. "I'll do anything to keep Sol safe." The two looked at each other without saying anything further. Kate stepped outside quickly, back to her child and the carpets on the line. She had only to look at Ben to see that the Whitehall slaves knew that John Stone fathered her baby.

— • —

BEN QUICKLY FOLLOWED AFTER KATE. He wanted to tell her that he understood and that she would be safer here than at River Wood. He longed to share with her all he knew about the Stone family and their overseer and tell her that he would protect her and her son if she would let him.

"I'm happy that you came to Whitehall," Ben called after her. "What I mean is I am happy that you are here because it helps Mama out. She isn't as young as she used to be. And you can help us all stay out of trouble since you know Mr. Stone better." He regretted his words the moment he uttered them.

"Well, you go on now. I best be gettin' on back to work," Kate said icily. "I don't want Sol to be out here in the wind long." She turned and headed back toward the baby and the carpets on the line. Ben watched her go, admiring the curve of her hips under her thin red dress as she moved.

— • —

THAT AFTERNOON, POLLY MADE A BEELINE toward the kitchen clutching a list of items to discuss with the women. She planned to lay out her expectations as the newly married mistress of the house and was nervous at the prospect. There was something defiant about Kate. The young slave could stare a hole right through her, and she carried Solomon around as if guarding him from some fierce predator.

Nevertheless, it was the first time Polly had been outside in the fresh air since falling ill. She inhaled deeply, exhaling breath visible in the cold morning. She pulled open the kitchen door and found Ona and Kate already in the warm room, standing over the large table. Several hams, a side of bacon, and belly lay across the table. Kate and Ona worked a blend of salt, saltpeter, sugar, and pepper into each cut of meat.

Kate looked up briefly and wiped a bead of sweat from her forehead with the back of her hand. Ona smiled and said, "Looks like some good pork, Miss Polly." The women wiped their hands on their aprons and waited.

Silas and Solomon sat playing on the floor and Polly noticed that someone had woven tiny corn husk dolls for both boys. Solomon's cotton diaper appeared stained and threadbare, and Silas wore no pants at all, despite the cold outside. Polly's cheeks reddened. How had the child made do without any new clothing in the time since her mother had taken ill? She had not planned to discuss slave clothing, a grievous oversight, she now saw.

The door flew open and Cissie stepped inside, shivering. Seeing her mistress, she frowned. "I'm sorry, Miss Polly. I was puttin' away the last of yo' silver."

Silas stood and whimpered to be held. "Sshhh, baby," Cissie crooned and hoisted the toddler to her hip. The women waited expectantly for Polly to speak.

Polly smiled weakly and began. "Sit down, please." The women sat down obediently on the long wooden bench. "I called you here to discuss expectations going forward. Thank you for the fine job you did on the wedding supper, and in preparing the house. It was lovely." The women stared at her blankly, which unnerved Polly. She thought that at least Ona would offer her congratulations.

"I, uh . . . ," she stammered, referring to her list. "I must be sure everyone has warm clothing. Winter is far from over. I do not know how Mother handled the clothing allotments. Ona, when did Mother give you fabric?

Ona shifted on the hard bench and began, "Miss Mary usually give me cloth twice a year. She let me use her ol' sewin' machine and I sewed for ev'ry one of the men. We stopped gettin' cloth the spring before—before Miss Mary died."

Polly thought back to the trip into Pendleton for party clothes before her trip to Charleston and cringed inwardly.

"Kate and Cissie, how was it handled at River Wood?" The two women looked at each other. Cissie shrugged and said, "I had two dresses, long as I can remember. I ain't sure where dey come from."

Kate looked down at the worn calico dress that she was wearing. "Don't rightly know." She looked up at Polly with hard eyes. Polly felt a twinge of guilt. "Well, I want you to be clothed appropriately in the coming year." She pointed to Solomon. "Goodness, this baby is half-naked. He'll catch his death."

Kate quickly scooped up little Sol and said, "Ma'am, I can cut some of this dress off and make him a shirt. He ain't no bother, I swear it! Cissie done gave me some clothes from Silas, but he messed them. I gonna wash them out and he be dressed again real soon." The baby began to fuss and tears welled in Kate's eyes.

Polly put up her hands to calm the woman. "Kate, stop. Please stop. I just want to make sure that he is clothed, that is all. It is cold outside. I want you all to be clothed properly."

Cissie put her arm around Kate and the two leaned together on the bench, Sol protected between them. Ona looked at her hands in her lap and did not say a word. The meeting was not going the way Polly envisioned. A chill went through her as she thought about the reported slave insurrections happening as Negroes got wind of the coming war.

"I understand that you are uncomfortable here, Kate. I have known Ona all my life, and Cissie has been here a while now. I do not want to hurt you or your child. You came from my husband's farm, and I am sure that a household without a mistress meant that some things went . . . by the wayside. I am trying to make amends."

Ona reached out and took Kate's free hand and gave it a warm squeeze. Her liquid brown eyes beseeched Kate silently.

Polly pulled her shawl tightly around her shoulders, despite the heat in the room, unsure of what was happening with the three slave women. "After the pork is in the smokehouse, we can start on clothing. I will go into town and purchase cloth and notions. I would appreciate your help in my estimations for the cloth, Ona, as I have never had to buy for you all before. What do you remember?" Polly tried to put a bright smile on her face.

Ona began to count with her fingers and said, "What I remember from a long time ago with yo' mother was that men be given eight yards of cotton cloth each. I made three shirts for each man; five yards of Lowells or osnaburg for two pair of summer pants; and two or three yards of dungaree cloth for winter pants. She give me thirteen yards of shirting for three shifts and a gown; five yards of linsey for a winter gown. It took me all summer long!" She paused and added boldly, "I sho' would like it if we could get us some cloth for blanket coats, Miss Polly. I saw blanket cloth in Mrs. Batson's store." Her eyes began to light up at the thought of new clothing. "It been a long time since we had coats."

Polly smiled and began to hope that relations with her house help were not completely derailed. "Very well. Lowells or osnaburg for petticoats?"

At the mention of undergarments, Cissie brightened. "We gets a petticoat? Land sakes, I ain't never had no underclothes."

Polly blushed. "My word, everyone here should have undergarments. I can give you my cast-offs if need be. Cut them up for underclothing. Even the babies must have pants. I will draw the line at velvet or brocade underpants and diapers, mind you!" She attempted a joke. The women stared.

Polly continued, "Ona, please come to the house before tea and give me a complete accounting of the needs again, I will write them down and take the list into town. Kate, why don't you come with her and I can show you the house. Now that the wedding is over, you'll start cleaning the upstairs bedrooms."

Ona glanced at Cissie and Kate then spoke up. "Miss Polly? Maybe it best if Kate stay in the kitchen while she learn how we do things? The cookin' and stores an' all this pork to cure? I can serve the meals still, an' come up and he'p Cissie if she ain't movin' fast enough fo' you."

Cissie registered the fear in Ona's eyes and nodded eagerly. "Yes'm, I feelin' fine right now. Lemme keep to the upstairs since I know it best. Kate's cookin' is right tasty, ain't it?"

"Very well," Polly sighed, too tired to go up against their united front. "For now, Kate may stay in the kitchen. And Kate, Mr. Stone likes a hearty breakfast. Cissie, you stay with the bedrooms and laundry, and let Ona handle the downstairs. But I do not want to wake up to a cold room again," Polly chided. "Come in early. The door will be unlatched. Kate, please take over the chickens and the milking for Zadoc. Zee has other things to attend to now. And I would like to know what is left in the cellar, please."

The women nodded mutely.

Polly thought for a moment. "And Kate, just a simple supper tonight. No fuss. Mr. Stone has gone to River Wood." Polly's mind tumbled with ideas and plans.

"Cissie, if you will clean and prepare the bedroom adjacent to my own, Mr. Stone may like to use it of an occasion." The women nodded in unison.

Polly looked at each of the women in turn. "I want to be a fair mistress. If you all work hard, we will have a well-run home and you will be well treated. What questions do you have?" Polly folded her arms in front of her. The women shook their heads meekly.

An idea popped into Polly's head. "One more thing . . . As a thank you for a job well done, I would like you girls to take the leftover fare from our wedding supper and distribute it amongst yourselves and the men. Consider it a gift from Mr. Stone and me."

Cissie spoke up, eyes wide. "Mizz Stone, you mean that turkey an' venison and the bread?"

"All of it," Polly said firmly. "Be sure the children eat well." She stood, satisfied.

"Mizz Stone, thank you kindly. Bless you." Cissie grinned. "You a fine Christian woman."

"You are welcome. And call me Miss Polly. That will not change." Polly smiled and left the kitchen house. Not a bad first meeting as a newly married mistress of two plantations. Squeals of delight echoed in her ears from the kitchen as she made her way back to the house.

— • —

POLLY'S FIRST FULL DAY OF MARRIED LIFE CONTINUED much as life had before the wedding. She had hoped the newlyweds could spend the day together, but John had quickly apprised her of his own plans. He had been up and out early to River Wood and was not expected back until late evening. He had agreed to live at Whitehall but insisted that his days would be primarily spent on affairs elsewhere. He assured Polly that he would take her on a guided tour of River Wood before setting off for Alabama and the convention.

She tried hard to stay busy, even though their dashed plans for a wedding trip seemed to nag at her. With an afternoon to fill, she wandered to the barn where Zadoc stood running a currying comb over Delightful. He nodded and continued his work silently while Polly paused to feed the mare a turnip.

She found George and Cyrus hanging pork cuts in the smokehouse. The smithy shed was open and Ben stooped over the forge. The hammer rang loudly and Polly knew it wouldn't do to stop and chat. She longed to go in and visit but it was unseemly. She was the mistress.

There was no sign of Mr. Roper anywhere. Polly hesitated to call for him as there was really nothing she needed. She shook her head and turned back toward the house. *I'm lonely*, she realized.

By late afternoon, as Cissie set about lighting the lamps against the early dark, Polly found herself pacing at the library windows, waiting for John's return. In the distance, she heard the baying of hounds and wondered who was hunting so near her land.

She peered out of the library window and noticed a rider trotting down the long drive. The black man dismounted and hurried up the front steps. She met the man at the door and was greeted by one of Floride Calhoun's slaves.

He doffed his hat quickly. "Mizz Stone? Mrs. Calhoun tol' me to deliver this invitation fo' tomorrow night. I'm to wait fo' yo' answer." He stared at Polly.

Polly quickly opened the envelope and read the contents. She looked up and said, "Please tell Mrs. Calhoun that we would be delighted to attend." The slave nodded and hurried down the steps, mounted his horse, and trotted away.

Polly shook her head at the strangeness of the encounter, closed the door, and returned to the library. She picked up a thin newspaper that John had left behind and sat down to read. On the front page, there were two editorials concerning the secession, which Polly scanned quickly. It seemed that the country was truly headed to war. There was an advertisement for an upcoming slave auction and notices of local meetings in the community.

One particular notice caught Polly's eye. The Pendleton Farmers' Society would hold their monthly meeting the following Thursday afternoon. The name nagged at Polly's memory—The Pendleton Farmers' Society. She tapped her fingers absentmindedly on the arm of the chair as she thought. Finally, she smiled and stood. She crossed the room and pulled a large drawer open in her father's desk. Polly rifled through papers and clippings left behind.

Her memory sharpened. She remembered herself as a little girl, snooping in her father's desk while he was away, searching for penny candies and lozenges sometimes secreted there. She slowly pulled the drawer free and set it on the desk. Kneeling down, Polly reached her arm into the back of the desk and groped for what she was looking for – a small latch. She flipped the latch and released a hidden compartment at the back of the desk. She gently pulled the box free and sat back in her father's worn leather chair, the box in her lap.

Polly removed the lid and a small cry escaped her lips. There, nestled in its velvet-lined case, was the pewter medallion she remembered.

To Mr. James Burgiss, President
Given in grateful recognition for service to the community
And the improvement of agriculture
On this day, September 28, 1847

The Pendleton Farmers' Society

Polly smiled and held the forgotten keepsake to her chest for a moment. It brought back warm memories of her father from a time before her world fell apart. She remembered peeking through the closed dining room doors during the dinner hosted by her mother, where the Farmers' Society had awarded her father their highest commendation in recognition of his initial work on the tunnel project.

Polly laid the medal aside and picked up the next item in the box, a lock of her mother's hair, tied with pink ribbon. She inhaled the scent of Mary Burgiss as she did so.

There was an 1844 letter from her mother addressed to her father while he was away in Charleston. It told of the day-to-day happenings at Whitehall in a time when Polly and her brothers were small children. Polly wiped tears from her eyes with the back of her hand and set the letter aside.

Next was a folded sheet of faded newspaper. Polly opened it carefully and saw that it was the obituary for her brothers. A knot began to form in the pit of her stomach. She quickly folded the page back into a square and placed it aside, emotions still raw. There was a gold watch chain and a small volume of poems by Victor Hugo. She opened the cover to find a loving inscription from her mother to her young beau, James. She admired her father's small diamond cufflinks and a few English shillings.

The last item in the box was a large parchment, folded many times, blotted, and water stained. She opened it carefully and read, eyes wide with surprise.

The sound of footsteps on the front porch made Polly jump. She folded the parchment and tucked it in the box quickly. She replaced the contents of the box and fitted it back into its hidden location. The drawer was replaced with a shove. Polly retrieved the small key from the vase and fitted it into the lock. She turned the lock and quickly pocketed the key in time before the parlor doors swung open with a rush of cold air.

"There you are, Polly," said John. He crossed the room and bent to kiss his new bride lightly on the lips. Polly registered the taste of whiskey but threw her arms around him and also inhaled the scent of winter pine and wood smoke on his coat. "Your cheek is so fresh!" she exclaimed.

He moved to the sideboard under the window as Polly came to stand near him. He pulled a decanter from the cabinet and poured a whiskey into a cut crystal glass. "Anything for you?"

Polly smiled and shook her head. "No, thank you. I am so glad that you are home. I missed you today. Ona should have supper ready soon. How are things at River Wood?" she asked nervously. "Have you found a new overseer?"

John tossed back the shot of whiskey in a single swig and sat down in James Burgiss's chair, propping his dirty boots on the man's desk carelessly.

"Winter chores, preparations before I go—that sort of thing," he said absentmindedly, pulling out a cigar.

Polly sat down across from John. "I would like to ride over there with you soon, John. I should see the house before you go away. I am the new mistress."

She noticed John's eyes were red and wondered how much drinking he had done while at River Wood.

John continued, "No need. I may close my house temporarily to save money. Or sell it. It is lunacy to keep fires lit and food stores there, when really, it is just the land and outbuildings that we want. With my thirteen slaves and your ten, we might be able to rotate the labor around to where we need it. Still, I am going to Anderson for the auction Friday if I am still here." He picked up the paper Polly had been reading.

Polly thought of the sad auction in Charleston and shook her head. "Hopefully, we won't need more slaves, John." She studied her fingernails, waiting for a reply. There was none. "I heard dogs baying. Did you see anyone out hunting? The dogs sounded so close," she said. "Somewhere near the river."

"Hmm? Oh, maybe someone hunting deer," John murmured, absorbed in the newspaper.

"I'm going into Pendleton tomorrow. The women will be starting the soap soon and they'll need warmer clothing. That's cold work outside," Polly said. John did not look up from the paper.

She tried again. "Shouldn't you hire a new overseer before leaving for Alabama with Mr. McQueen? I imagine that it would be good to have someone in place before you leave."

John continued to scan the paper. "Do not worry about my affairs, Polly," he said evenly.

Stung, Polly stood and said, "I'll check on our supper. Kate should have it prepared by now."

"Did you read this article on the front page? Georgia leaving the Union means we will finally begin to see the 'seeds' of a new country." John smacked the paper with his hand. "Mark my words. The entire south will join us."

"A new country?" Polly asked. "That won't come easily. Maybe this skirmish can be settled in court in Washington. How can we possibly become a new country?" Polly played with the hem of her shawl nervously. "I don't think this new President Lincoln will give us up easily, and an all-out war would be devastating." She thought of what Mr. Roper had said back in December in the town square. "We don't have an army, John. We're just cotton farmers and merchants."

John lowered the paper and frowned at his wife. "The federal government will not recognize us as a separate country, so it will mean a civil war. I hope that fighting will be limited to the port cities and maybe border states, but we must prepare as if for an onslaught. The North threatens our very livelihood. I expect to hear from McQueen tomorrow. I certainly will not tell him that his fighting men are just cotton farmers and merchants."

He struck a match on the heel of his boot and looked at his new wife critically. "So where is Kate? I brought her here to help you out and I haven't seen her around," John said as he puffed on a cigar. He inhaled deeply and exhaled a plume of pale smoke overhead. "You're still recovering."

Happy to have her husband's full attention, Polly perked up. "I told you. Ona asked if Kate could work in the kitchen, and I said yes. Ona isn't as young as she used to be," Polly said defensively, "and I don't really know Kate yet. It is hard to have someone I barely know in the house after so many years with just Ona. Besides, the food was delicious yesterday, was it not?"

"Ona has no business deciding how to assign slave labor. That woman is getting too uppity for my taste," John said. Polly's face fell.

"Very well," he grumbled. "As long as the food coming out of the kitchen is tasty and hot, you may have your two kitchen slaves. Although it seems to me that Kate should be helping inside with the housework."

— • —

AFTER SUPPER, CISSIE STOKED THE FIRE IN POLLY'S bedroom and then moved into the adjoining room and began to build a fire in the cold fireplace. John stayed downstairs, absorbed in his newspapers. Polly appeared in the room and watched the woman as she worked. "Thank you, Cissie," Polly said softly. "I don't know whether Mr. Stone will use this space, but I wanted it to be available."

"You welcome, ma'am," Cissie replied, as she arranged small oak logs on top of the kindling. Polly noticed that the usually chatty woman had little to say.

"Cissie, how is Silas?" she asked. "I am sure that Kate's baby boy might be a playmate for him. And soon his own little brother or sister."

"He fine, ma'am," Cissie put a candle to the kindling and the fire leapt into being. "He don't get in the way of my work. He almost old enough to start he'pin' me in the house," she smiled. Both women were startled when the baying hounds began again outside in the darkness.

"Gracious!" gasped Polly. She quickly crossed the room to close the drapes. "Who would be out hunting this late?" She wondered if the sound was evidence of something more sinister than a deer hunt. The howling seemed to be coming from the direction of River Wood.

Cissie shivered and said quietly, "Ma'am, if they ain't nothin' else you need from me tonight, can I go on back?"

"Yes, Cissie, you may go. Please tell Ona that she may go as well. I will see you both in the morning." Polly tried to smile cheerfully. She closed her bedroom door gently and turned to the doorway between her bedroom and the adjoining one. The fire crackled merrily and Cissie had turned down the quilts on both her own four-poster bed and the bed next door. Unsure of what to do next, she sat at her vanity and began to unwind her hair. After combing it out, she braided the dark tresses for sleep and quickly got into her flannel nightgown. Cissie had placed several hot stones underneath Polly's quilts and she gratefully jumped under the covers to warm her feet.

The minutes ticked by and Polly's eyes became heavy with fatigue. She sighed deeply, rolled over, and went to sleep.

In the middle of the night, Polly awoke with a start. She lay still in the dark, listening to embers crackle in the fireplace. She reached out her hand to feel for John. With relief, she touched his shoulder and could tell that he was asleep with his bare back to her. The steady rise and fall of his breathing comforted her. She untangled her legs inside her flannel nightgown and inched closer to feel his warmth.

Why had he not come up to bed with her? Why hadn't he at least woken her when he finally did come to bed? This new married life was strange to Polly. The tender affection she expected from a husband seemed somehow lacking. The war and a failing farm were heavy on his mind, she knew. Perhaps that explained his lackluster warmth toward his new bride. Or maybe she had disappointed him? Her knowledge of the ways of men and women was limited at best. She wanted to be a good wife and silently vowed to do whatever was necessary to satisfy him.

Polly inched closer until she was snuggled against John's back. He stirred slightly but did not wake. She remembered the daring French undergarments she had read about in *Godey's*—silk knickers embellished with Brussels lace. Perhaps some new frills and a new hairstyle would captivate her husband. Moisture came to Polly's eyes and she wiped away a tear before succumbing to sleep once again.

Chapter Twenty-One

POLLY RAN HER HANDS ACROSS THE BEIGE BLANKET CLOTH in Caroline Batson's store and nodded. "Mrs. Batson, this will do nicely. Do you think you have enough in stock?"

Mrs. Batson smiled. "Yes, Mrs. Stone. We are fortunate that the blockades have not completely closed us off to good, sturdy cloth. Thanks to a few southern mills, we should get by. It's the pretty fabrics, the silks, and velvets, which are difficult for me to get." She sighed and added, "I would be happy to send all of this out to Whitehall if you have other shopping to do in town."

Polly took a breath and looked at the seamstress. "In fact, I have another item or two I would like to ask you about, Mrs. Batson. I wanted to order some of the new knickers I have seen in *Godey's*—the silk ones with lace at the hem. And possibly corsets to match? But maybe the blockades have ended that already . . ."

Without batting an eye, Mrs. Batson nodded and bustled to a table of magazines and patterns. She laid a hand on Polly's arm. "My dear, you have discriminating taste. For you, I can order from a seamstress friend in Charlotte. It will be a pretty steep price. I would not do this for just anyone, but you are a newlywed."

Polly blushed.

Mrs. Batson stabbed her finger on an advertisement in the latest *Godey's* and smiled. "Aren't they indeed beautiful? So delicate and lovely. If Mr. Batson were a younger man, I myself might order a pair!" She smiled at Polly over the tops of her spectacles. Polly felt herself go crimson all over again.

"And if her silk is no longer available, I can stitch them myself from a beautiful sea island cotton with a soft hand. I have your measurements and could begin at once. What price point are we looking to meet?"

Polly, relieved and warming to the woman, said, "Mrs. Batson, I did not get to have a wedding gown, nor a trip away. I do not care how much this costs. Write to your friend in Charlotte. Bill me when they are ready, and I will gladly pay." She laughed, and the women embraced lightly before Polly's departure.

— • —

OUTSIDE OF THE STORE, ZADOC WAITED FOR his mistress to conclude her errands. The day was warm for January. A brilliant blue sky warmed the man's upturned face. Polly emerged from the general store, frowning. She had been unsuccessful in finding coffee or sugar. The Mercantile owner, Mr. Jones, would only agree to put Polly's name on a waiting list for the next shipment.

"I'm sorry, Miss Burgiss, we had a run on sugar and coffee after the secession. And with Christmas just past . . . hopefully, we will get some through here soon, and I can send it out on credit."

Polly didn't have the energy to apprise the man of her newly wedded status and simply nodded. She was frustrated by the delays and shortages. Since she had been sick for weeks and then hosted the wedding supper, there was no sugar nor coffee left at Whitehall—and how John loved sugar in his coffee.

As she approached the carriage, she had an idea. "Zadoc, can you drive me by River Wood on my way home? It's such a lovely afternoon. Maybe they have sugar." She imagined how pleased John would also be if she brought him sugar and coffee from forgotten River Wood stores. "Mr. Stone does have a cook, or at least a house woman, correct?"

"Yes ma'am, her name's Jane!" Zadoc grinned so enthusiastically, that Polly wondered if he was sweet on the River Wood cook.

The man helped his mistress into the carriage.

Once she was settled, Zadoc clicked the reins and the horse trotted slowly down Pendleton's Main Street. The warmth of the sun soon had Polly in good spirits. Polly inhaled the sweet air, crisp but with the promise of spring.

The phaeton rounded a bend in the main road and turned down a packed red dirt drive. Polly saw the ornate wrought iron gates of River Wood plantation for the first time. Whitehall did not boast iron gates at the road, and Polly expected to see a stately home soon coming into view. Zadoc slowed the horse and drove the carriage through the open gates.

"An' Mr. Wilkins is gone, ma'am?" Zadoc asked.

She glanced toward Zadoc and saw him scanning the area nervously.

"Yes, he is. My husband will be looking for a new overseer."

Seeing no one, Zadoc appeared to relax a bit as he eased the horse into the carriage circle. "Whoa there, hoss," he said softly, and the mare obliged.

Polly found herself staring up at a tall and once-elegant brick home, nearly twice the size of Whitehall. Soaring columns were now bare of whitewash, but the porch ceilings were still clinging to their traditional pale blue paint. Overgrown shrubbery and English ivy spreading across the face of the house gave Polly the sense that the house was abandoned. Windows were shuttered and the front door warped and stained.

"My goodness," Polly said under her breath. "How grand this must have been in its day."

Zadoc helped Polly down and stood near the horse's head, smoothing her dark mane.

Polly wondered whether to just walk inside the front door, as the new mistress, or wait to be let inside. Maybe there was no one even available to answer the door. Yet, she remembered John mentioning a pair of house slaves still there, and she wanted to make a good first impression. Patting her bonnet in place, she ascended the stairs and knocked tentatively on the front door. Although there was always the chance that Wilkins now resided inside, she was River Wood's new mistress, and he would treat her accordingly.

There was no sound from the other side of the door. Polly knocked again, a little louder. Hearing nothing, she turned to ask Zadoc what she should do, when suddenly the door opened a crack. The tiniest woman that Polly had ever seen peeked through the narrow opening. The slave wore the most threadbare of homespun and an even thinner apron tied around her waist. She wore no kerchief or turban, and her hair was a mass of dirty grey cornrows.

The woman appeared quite old, and she had not a tooth left in her head. She looked up at Polly and said softly, "He'p you, ma'am?"

Polly was taken aback. Compared to this woman, her girls were attired like African queens. "Y-yes, I am Polly Burgiss. Polly Burgiss Stone? John Stone is my new husband. I believe that my husband is here on the property but did not expect me. I wanted to ask about some staples."

The old woman's eyes grew wide. "Yes, ma'am." She shuffled aside and opened the door widely. She self-consciously patted her hair and said, "Come in, Mizz Stone. I sorry. We didn't rightly know you was comin' but we heard tell Mr. Stone had married and is gone to live at Whitehall." The woman smoothed her thin dress and Polly blushed to see that she had on no undergarments of any kind. Her sagging breasts were only cinched in place by the tattered apron she wore high at her rib cage. She peered past Polly toward the phaeton and grinned broadly when she saw Polly's driver.

"I am the one who should apologize, coming unannounced." She turned to follow the woman's gaze. Zadoc was smiling with equal joy toward the old woman. "Do you know my driver, Zadoc? Of course you do."

Tears welled in the old woman's eyes. "Zadoc's my boy." She beamed. "My son."

"Gracious! Zee, come here," Polly called. "This is a surprise."

Zadoc took the stairs two at a time and ran toward the woman. He wrapped her in a warm embrace. "Mama," he said and rocked her in his arms. The pair began to weep softly together.

Embarrassed at witnessing such a tender moment between slaves, Polly backed up and waited. The woman soon noticed and let go of her son. She wiped tears from her eyes with the back of her hands and said, "Zee, let Mizz Stone come in now. It her house."

Zadoc backed away from his mother.

"Zee, why didn't you tell me your mother was here? Of course, you must visit her often," Polly announced. "We'll see to it."

Zadoc nodded gratefully. "This here is my mama, Jane. She and my daddy is house help for Mr. Stone. They been here since before Mizz Lena died some thirty years ago."

Polly smiled. "Oh, this is Jane. It is lovely to meet you. I hope that you'll be happy with me as the new mistress, although I won't be living here."

Jane looked from Polly to Zadoc. "You already made me the happiest old woman alive cuz' you brought my boy to see me, ma'am." She reached up and patted Zadoc's cheek. Tears shone in Jane's tired eyes. "Come in, ma'am, and I get you a cup of tea. We ain't got much here, but what is here is yours, Mizz Stone."

Jane led Polly inside. Polly turned back to Zadoc. "I supposed you should wait by the carriage, Zee? I won't be long." Zadoc nodded and backed down the steps. "I will let you two say your goodbyes after Jane shows me around," Polly added kindly.

"Yes, Mizz Polly," Zadoc murmured. He looked past Polly to Jane. "Mama, how is Daddy?"

Jane's lips trembled and she swallowed hard. "He fine, boy. We both fine. Now go and do what Mizz Stone asked." She nodded at her boy, a man of at least twenty years himself.

297

Zadoc smiled tenderly at his mother. "Yes'm."

Polly followed Jane into the dark main hall. In the rooms on both sides of the hall, upholstered furniture was covered in drapes. Wooden shutters were closed tightly over floor-to-ceiling windows. The fireplaces were empty and cold. Jane wrung her hands nervously. The house was dark and quiet, the air heavy and still. It felt to Polly as if death itself lived here.

"Mr. Stone, he don't like too much fuss in the house. Said it was easiest to shut ev'rythang up after his daddy died. He keeps to his upstairs rooms when he here. I can open dem shutters so you can see the place," Jane offered. "Or start a fire."

"No . . . no . . . don't bother," Polly said. "If that's the way my husband left things, for now they should stay that way. I do wonder you don't catch a cold." She did notice that the wooden tables and knickknacks were polished to a high shine. Jane was trying to do her job.

"Mizz Stone, I can git word to Mr. Stone that you is here. I'll ask my husband to see about findin' him?" Jane's face betrayed her nervous fear of doing something to displease her master. "He don't like it when I don't tell him someone's paid a call."

"Thank you. Please, call me Miss Polly." Polly suddenly felt as if she were trespassing. "Jane, never mind. I have other calls to make. I will come back another time. I am sure that you have work to do." She paused and said, "But I was hoping that you had sugar or coffee?" Polly wished she had never set foot on the property and wanted to be as far as possible from River Wood. She did not belong here.

"No ma'am, we ain't got sugar nor coffee," Jane apologized. "We don't barely have nothin' to eat at all, ma'am." She leaned closer and looked up at Polly. "My husband and I try to keep up the garden though. The men make do on that and some rabbit and squirrel trappin' and such, but we ain't had more than one or two meals set by for a real long time now. The stores is low in the cellar. The dirt jes' stopped growing anythang here, 'ceptin' some sweet taters and corn. My husband and I like to go hungry half the time." She looked at Polly expectantly.

Polly frowned and tugged at her gloves nervously. "That seems like a matter for an overseer. Nevertheless, I . . . I can speak to Mr. Stone." She turned to leave, but not before seeing a small dark face duck behind the sofa in the dim parlor.

Jane followed Polly's eyes, and a fresh wave of fear caused Jane to cry out. "Oh, Mizz Polly. I so sorry, ma'am! She ain't no trouble. Lydia's a real good help to me and she gonna be trained to be a fine house slave, yes ma'am. I git her back outside if you want in the spring, but her mama ain't here and all, and it real cold this winter." The old woman looked at her new mistress with what Polly could only describe as pure terror.

Polly looked quizzically at Jane. "Jane, what on earth is the matter? Tell this child to stop hiding and show herself."

Jane reluctantly crossed the room and hauled the tiny girl out of her hiding place. She hoisted the child onto her bony hip and presented the girl to her new mistress. "Mizz Stone, this here is Lydia. She only three years old," Jane began bravely. She hugged the little girl to her chest. "Her mama gone away, so I'm watchin' her now," she added.

The girl leaned her curly head on Jane's shoulder. Large dark eyes and skin like milk chocolate showed Lydia to be a beautiful child. Despite the cold, she was barefoot and dressed only in thin homespun. Polly felt a twinge of guilt when she realized she hadn't given any thought to new clothing for River Wood slaves.

"Hello, Lydia." Polly reached out her gloved hand to pat Lydia's arm and the child flinched and squeezed her eyes tight.

"Lydia, Mizz Polly ain't gone hurt you none. She our new mistress," Jane soothed. "We gonna work fo' her now."

"Where is her mother?" asked Polly, suddenly quite ill at ease.

Jane looked at Polly solemnly. "Ma'am, her mama ain't here."

Polly remembered the baying hounds she'd heard in the night. She let the horrible thought go. "What did you mean—get her back outside? What was this little thing doing outside?"

Jane looked at Polly sadly. "Ma'am, Lydia was in the fields this past summer. She picked cotton fo' Mr. Stone."

Polly felt as if she had been punched in the stomach. "What? This child was out in the heat, picking cotton? Why, we have slave children at Whitehall. Two little boys. Silas and now Solomon. They stay with their mothers as house help. They don't go into the fields so young." She shook her head in disbelief. "And what of her father?"

Jane dropped her head and said quietly, "Yes'm, well. . . . She ain't got one."

Polly sighed. *If the slaves would stop behaving like rabbits. . . . First Kate and now this child's mother. . . .* Polly immediately regretted the thought. It was so like something her mother would have said.

Jane stared at Polly, emboldened to speak. "Mizz Polly, how is Kate? I hope she workin' well fo' ya. I miss her. I miss Sol. You know, they was in the fields last summer too. I think they came and picked at yo' place." She whispered into little Lydia's ear and lowered the girl to the floor, where she tiptoed off into the back of the house.

When she was sure that the child was out of earshot, Jane straightened and said, "Please let me keep Lydia inside with me. I teach her kitchen work."

Polly's mind reeled at the thought of Kate toiling in her own steamy cotton fields. Surely John would not have sent a woman with a baby to pick.

Jane continued, "Lydia's mama, Eva, she couldn't handle things here. Things were bad fo' her . . . and so she ran. Even with a sweet baby girl like Lydia, she ran."

Polly shook her head, afraid to ask what Jane meant.

Jane twisted the corner of her apron into a knot and lowered her voice to a whisper. "I think she dead. I'm sure you heard them dogs. Half the county musta heard them dogs a few nights ago. Mr. Wilkins was trackin' her. . . . And I's afraid for Lydia. She be the only girl left here, and Mr. Wilkins . . ." Jane's voice trailed off.

"What about Mr. Wilkins?" Polly asked, with a feeling of dread.

"Never mind, Mizz Polly. I'm an old woman speakin' out of turn. Thank you so much for lettin' me see my boy. Thank you very much." Tears came to her eyes. "Please, I beg you. Please don't hold anything against Lydia. She jes' a baby. It was me brought her into the house. We work real hard fo' ya."

Polly was overcome with emotion. She detested Wilkins and could only imagine the fear he had struck into the hearts of River Wood slaves. "Jane, what made Eva run away? For a mother to leave her child . . ."

Jane's eyes grew wide. "Oh, ma'am, I'm not even sho' they's true. Forgive me. Y-You know how slaves talk," she stammered, backing away.

Polly took a deep breath and said, "I knew Mr. Wilkins. He did not hold any favor with me. But he is gone now. Isn't he?"

Jane shook her head. "No ma'am! He here. Law, Mizz Polly, I done said too much already. That man gonna beat me if he hears I even talked to you."

"I won't allow that, Jane," Polly said quietly. A horrible feeling arose in the pit of her stomach. She adjusted her hat with shaking fingers. "Where is Mr. Wilkins now?" she asked innocently enough.

"I don't know, ma'am. He ain't come to the house today. Mebbe in his cabin." Jane pointed out the windows with a gnarled finger.

Polly let out a long breath. "So tell me what he did to Eva."

Jane crossed her thin arms. "She first come to River Wood as the cook . . . after Cissie left here . . . tol' us she been sold away from her husband over Greenville way. She was real sad, missin' her husband and knowing she ain't never gone see him again. And she was eight months along. She had baby Lydia pretty soon after she come here. As soon as the chile was born . . ." Jane put her hand to her heart and leaned in. ". . . Mr. Wilkins took to Eva."

301

Jane looked at Polly wide-eyed to be sure she understood her meaning. "You a married woman. You know what I mean. Mr. Wilkins started callin' Eva into his cabin most nights. She ain't even had her time to heal up, Mizz Polly. She would come out cryin' and all beat up so many times. . . . It was all I could do to tend her after such nights, and he'd call her back again the next. I thought she'd die from the bleedin'. I started takin' care of her and Lydia."

Polly's heart pounded in her chest. She wanted to turn and walk away from such horrific news but knew there was more.

"Then Eva got a baby in her belly. Twice. And both times, ma'am. . . . Both times, he . . ." Jane paused and looked around. "Both times he called her into his cabin and . . . got rid of her babies." Jane's brown eyes reddened with tears as she gestured with her hands. "Made her drink somethin'. 'Bout killed her."

Polly felt faint with the horror of Jane's tale. She knew in her gut that what Jane said was probably true. Wilkins was an evil man, a monster capable of aborting his own babies. But John had promised to get rid of him.

Jane continued her story in a whisper. "It was Eva's idea to git Lydia away from the slave cabins. She was afraid he might hurt the baby on her account. . . . An' I was worried, too, about what Mr. Wilkins might do to the chile, 'specially after Eva ran away. She only three, but I seen him lookin' at her." The woman's eyes were frantic with fear.

Polly took a deep breath and audibly exhaled. "Does Mr. Stone know?"

Jane looked at Polly strangely. "That ain't a slave's place to say nothin', and well . . ." Jane shook her head. "Please don't tell Mr. Stone I said anything. Please? I'll get the tar beat outta me."

"Jane, do not fret about Lydia. She will stay with you in the house, as your little helper." Polly smiled. "This house is enormous. You have my permission to light a fire in here. It's horribly cold for the child. You could use some food so I will see about having some meat and some preserves sent over. Zadoc can bring them."

"Thank you, ma'am," Jane said, wiping tears from her eyes with the back of her hand. "We don't want to cause no trouble. Please don't say nothin' 'bout Mr. Wilkins. Ol' Jane don't want no trouble, now."

"I will take care of things. I am sure that when my husband's father died, it was hard on him to run such a large estate. My parents have also both passed, and I have felt like a lost little girl half the time. I know Mr. Stone did not mean to let things get so bad for you all." At a loss for words, she said, "Now, I must go. Please come outside and say goodbye to your son. I promise—you will see him again soon."

The women walked outside and Zadoc held his mother in an extended embrace, as Polly sat stiffly in the carriage, looking toward the road home.

Chapter Twenty-Two

THAT EVENING, AS POLLY DRESSED FOR DINNER, she thought about the strange trip to River Wood. She had wandered the Whitehall hedgerows all afternoon, as she wanted space to process the events of the afternoon and to plan how to discuss Wilkins with John. He had lied to her, that much was evident.

Her complexion was pink from the exercise, and she felt stronger than she had in months. Donning one of her never-worn gowns, a deep green silk taffeta made for her journey to Charleston; she adjusted the bodice and admired her tiny waistline. She placed her mother's pearl earrings in her ears and pinched her cheeks slightly. A dinner at Floride's was something to look forward to, but for some reason, Polly sensed the couple had been summoned, not just invited. John had only grudgingly agreed to go to Mi Casa, having just seen the lady Calhoun so recently.

Polly looked at herself in the vanity mirror. The dress was divine. The gown's décolletage was decidedly lower than Polly would usually wear for a dinner, but it was not in bad taste. Quite to the contrary, she looked as if she had stepped out of the finest of Charleston salons. John would be home soon, and this was the wife he would see. The wife who would confront him.

Polly rose from her dressing table and rang the silver bell on her nightstand. Ona appeared quickly. "Miss Polly, you look beautiful!" she exclaimed. "Lordy, you look like one of them fancy ladies in yo' woman's magazine." She laughed.

Polly tried to sound cheerful. She did not want to let on that Mr. Wilkins might still be at River Wood—and might still be a threat. "I was sick for so long. I want my husband to see me looking pretty and in something elegant. Especially since John does not want to go."

"You gonna be the prettiest one there," Ona said, as she tidied her way around the room. Polly watched the woman as she worked and thought of Jane.

"Ona, would you be honest with me and tell me if you'd heard— negative, I should say, bad—things about River Wood?" Polly watched as Ona poked at the fire.

Ona did not look up. "Miss Polly, I don't know what you mean."

"You do know. If a slave ran away or if someone there was in trouble, would you tell me? I know that you hear things. Would you tell me if I needed to know something?" The fire leapt and crackled as Ona prodded the logs with a poker.

Ona straightened up to stand, but she did not turn to face her mistress. Instead, the slave woman used a corner of her apron to dust around several framed daguerreotypes of Mary and James on Polly's mantle. Ona clucked her tongue and said finally, "Miss Polly, you know I don't know anything about anyone 'round here. I jus' try to do my work and get by."

— • —

JOHN WAS WAITING FOR POLLY IN THE FOYER. He looked up at her as she descended the staircase, and he whistled when she appeared. "Polly, you look lovely. You take my breath away," he said, catching her in his arms. He tipped her chin up to meet his gaze and kissed her hungrily.

Polly felt her stomach flip. He was so handsome. So charming. How could he have lied? There must have been a good reason. "Thank you for agreeing to go to Floride's dinner. I know you don't want to go." Her face betrayed no emotion.

"I wanted us to have a romantic supper together," he said lightly. "I do not have the affection for the Calhoun family that you do, and we just saw the woman at our wedding. But I take it that you had a good day. The trip into town was a good one and your new undergarments are on order?"

Polly gasped. "John! How did you know?"

John smiled. "You left your shopping list on the parlor table. It made me wholly agreeable to your trip into town, and will make for a most-welcome night, post-party." He extended his arm and the couple walked out to the waiting carriage.

— • —

"POLLY, MY DEAR! AND JOHN, PLEASE COME IN," Floride swept toward the young couple in the large foyer of her home, Mi Casa. The older woman wore a chocolate silk gown trimmed in black fox and had forgone her large hoop skirts for a more decorous silhouette. The butler stepped aside after taking their wraps, and Floride embraced Polly.

"You look like a queen, my girl, simply beautiful," Floride said. She glanced at Polly's low décolletage, leaned closer, and whispered playfully, "A wolf has come to our little dinner. He had better be on his best behavior when he sees this dress." Polly pulled back and looked at her friend in confusion.

Floride led the pair into her cheery parlor, sumptuous in every detail. Rich fabrics covered the walls and plush carpets were underfoot. Pale marble busts of ancient philosophers lined the bookshelves, and crystal chandeliers winked overhead. A liveried servant offered them flutes of champagne, which they accepted readily.

Floride steered her guests to three men standing nearby. "Governor

Pickens, I would like to introduce Mr. John Stone of River Wood and Whitehall. You remember Mrs. Stone."

Polly smiled and curtsied politely. "So nice to see you, sir. I had the honor of meeting you in a receiving line at the Pinckney gala before Christmas." Her heart raced as she recognized the familiar face standing next to the governor.

John glanced at Polly strangely before bowing and then extending his hand. "It is an honor to meet you, Governor."

"Good to meet you, my boy," the governor said jovially. He clapped John on the shoulder as if the men were old friends. "Congratulations on your very recent marriage."

Floride continued, "And soon to be Brigadier General G.T. Beauregard. Polly, you remember then Captain Beauregard, also from the Pinckneys' Christmas party. And this is his aide, Lieutenant Bright."

Polly's face could not hide her admiration as she looked into the face of the infamous officer from Louisiana. The dashing Creole smiled and glanced quickly at her décolletage before bowing over her extended hand. He then turned to shake hands with her husband, who merely nodded.

"Yes, of course. Brigadier General? Congratulations on your promotion, sir," Polly said. The man is incredibly handsome, she thought.

He leaned toward Polly. "Thank you. My dear Mrs. Stone, congratulations on your recent nuptials. When we met, I had no idea you were betrothed. You were the belle of the ball that night and my dance with you was the highlight of the evening. However, I must be gallant and wish you both the greatest happiness." He lifted his glass and offered a toast. "To wedded bliss."

The small group lifted their glasses. Governor Pickens turned to John and explained, "Beauregard is soon to be named a Brigadier General in our Provisional Army of the Confederate States. He will begin his duties next month in Charleston."

"Ah, I see," John said stiffly. He tipped his champagne flute and drained the contents, much to Polly's horror. "We all must do our part."

The governor continued, "As you may know, Major Anderson has taken control of Fort Sumter, which was deemed a hostile act. But Beauregard here was a pupil of his at West Point. We hope that G.T. can help us with that . . . situation. We do not think President Buchanan will act further, but soon after the inauguration, we expect Lincoln to make a move. And we hope to be ready."

Beauregard smiled. "We will be."

The houseboy, Henry, quickly moved to refill John's champagne flute. John turned to Pickens. "Governor, my wife and I are honored to be in your company tonight. Truly. But we seem an odd group. What is the reason we are here? Surely this isn't a social invitation."

Polly flushed with embarrassment. Floride scowled at John, then glanced at the two slaves standing ready to serve and said, "That will be all for now, Henry and Clara. Wait for us in the dining room. We will have supper shortly." The slaves nodded obediently and left the parlor, closing the heavy oak doors behind them.

"Mr. Stone, I needn't remind you that you are speaking to our new governor," Floride chided. Before John could overreact, Polly put a hand on her husband's arm and squeezed.

"My apologies, Governor Pickens. I meant no disrespect. But my question remains," John said.

"You're correct. The abandoned train tunnel is the reason," Beauregard said sharply. "Three tunnels, actually. The project that James Burgiss labored over for so long." He crooked a finger toward Polly and added, "Come, my dear."

He moved across the room to a large table, where a few large maps were laid out. The others followed. He leaned over a map of the mountains and stabbed his finger at a circled site.

"Stumphouse Mountain, Middle, and Saddle tunnels were to run through this ridge. One was completed—the shortest—Middle. It was dynamited, cut through granite right through the heart of Rabun Gap, a low place in the mountain range. We sent Lt. Bright up that way yesterday evening. The tunnel is clear but quite narrow. Maybe a small wagon's-width. Abandoned and filled with rusting mining equipment, but open through the mountain, correct?"

The Lieutenant nodded in the affirmative. "We think so, sir, based on airflow at the entrance. It is quite full up with debris, sir, but appeared dry and cool."

"My father's tunnels," Polly murmured.

Floride cut in quickly. "Whiskey for us all?" She bustled across the room to personally retrieve a decanter and glasses.

Beauregard accepted a whiskey from Floride, glanced at Polly, and continued, "We had hoped to use the larger one, Stumphouse, to run munitions and other supplies through to northeast Georgia. That will not be possible. But it could still be used as a place to store Confederate supplies. The confederate army could use the new rail lines running into the Upstate to move equipment toward Georgia and East Tennessee, and store anything covertly that needed our protection. However, without a survey, we dare not bring this idea to the Confederate leadership."

"A survey?" John asked.

Beauregard traced the topography of the mountains with his finger. "We need to find the engineering surveys that show the structure, the safety, and accessibility of the tunnels. The Saddle was never blasted beyond a few hundred feet. Stumphouse is reputed to be 1,600 feet long and wide enough for wagons to pass each other. That would be the equipment storehouse."

Polly and John exchanged surprised looks. Polly had no idea a tunnel had gone so deeply into the heart of the mountain. "The tunnels could help in the war?" Polly asked.

"Not without surveys," Beauregard said. "Too dangerous."

"Can't you send an engineer into them to make a new assessment?" John ventured.

Beauregard frowned. "We can spare no engineers. All of our personnel are involved at the coast, with other aspects of state infrastructure. After all, that is where the trouble is—for now."

Beauregard's eyes narrowed as he looked at John. "The most recent survey was done just months before Polly's father passed. But nothing could be found in the construction company's Columbia office, nor in Walhalla. A survey would have everything we need to show proof at the upcoming Convention that our plan could work."

Polly reddened at the man's use of her Christian name. "It seems strange to me that the construction company does not have a copy of the survey," she said evenly. The memory of the parchment document in her father's desk crept into her mind.

"It is quite strange. When the project failed, any surveys were possibly destroyed," Pickens shrugged. The governor and Beauregard exchanged glances before Pickens continued, "We took everything we could find from the Walhalla offices. Those documents are in the hands of the state now. Of course, a disgruntled employee could have taken the survey to give to the Union, but as best we can tell, no one had a reason to expect incomplete tunnels might be used in a war."

Beauregard smiled at Polly. "A survey would be quite valuable. Perhaps it is with your father's private papers?"

Polly thought of the desk drawer contents. "I wish I could help you, but my mother disposed of so much after his death," she lied, her heart hammering in her chest.

"Your family attorney, perhaps?" Governor Pickens asked.

"Ah." Polly nodded. "You want to consult Father's attorney, Mr. Legarre. In fact, you already have, haven't you? I am guessing that you went to him first, before you decided to have Mrs. Calhoun invite us to dinner."

"Polly, please," began Floride.

Beauregard held up a hand. "In the interest of the State, we had no choice."

"This is an invasion of our privacy," John said, his voice trembling.

Beauregard sniffed. "Nonsense. The young man claimed attorney-client privilege. We need Mrs. Stone's permission to access her father's papers there. He may have left a survey in the attorney's care and the man doesn't know what he has."

Polly sensed there was a good reason that her father hid the survey away in a desk drawer away from prying eyes. "Gentlemen, I have not been privy to my father's legal papers, but by all means, you go first," Polly said icily. "Is that why we are here this evening?"

"If you would be so kind as to give us permission to see what the attorney has in his care?" Beauregard nodded toward Lt. Bright, and the man quickly produced a document and slid it across the table toward Polly along with a fountain pen.

She quickly signed her name and slid the page across the table angrily. Lieutenant Bright grabbed the paper and exited the room quickly.

"Gentlemen," John shook his head. "If my wife's father had his name on any of the plans, and they have fallen into enemy hands, don't you think that this places her in danger? Her father was the principal contact for the tunnel project." He downed his whiskey in a gulp.

Beauregard's face grew red and he looked at John, considering his words. "The tunnels are a valuable resource and South Carolina must be prepared to use them, whatever the cost."

Governor Pickens spoke up. "The chances of Union soldiers even sending scouts this far inland is small. The ports and military garrisons of value to them are all along the coast. Those are the areas to defend."

Beauregard stroked his moustache thoughtfully and challenged, "Your trepidation, Mr. Stone, hints at a lack of patriotism."

Polly squeezed John's arm, silently urging him not to react.

John glared at Beauregard and growled, "How dare—"

"Easy, Beauregard. And calm yourself, Mr. Stone," the governor said sharply, stepping between the two men. "Mr. Stone, I am sure that G.T. did not mean to offend," the governor said. "We assure you that your wife will be safe."

Beauregard fixed his eyes on John. "The convention in Montgomery is in just a few weeks. At that point, we shall have a new government in place and Union sympathizers will become traitors to the confederacy. They will be dealt with harshly, even up here in these backwoods."

John looked past the man and said, "Governor Pickens, I deeply resent his insinuation. I am a born and raised son of this state, which he is not. I have already added my name to the district's muster roll under Major McQueen and will accompany the state delegation to the very same convention. However, I stand by what I said. Confederate soldiers scouting about up that way will only serve to draw the enemy into the upstate." He paused and added defiantly, "If we find a survey, we may choose to keep it."

Beauregard swirled the whiskey in his glass. "Is that a threat, sir? Secession strategists are anxiously awaiting the maps and documents that can help finalize plans for our war effort. So if you are indeed a soldier, then I must warn you of the folly of going against a superior officer's directives." His blue eyes were hard. "If you withhold information—"

The governor, ever the politician, intervened. "Gentlemen, lower your weapons," he chuckled, hands raised. "Mr. Stone, even though you may disagree with the strategies of our military, of which you are now a part, I am sure that we have your word that the state's interest in the tunnels will remain top-secret—even if you believe them to be in error. And you understand the penalty for withholding documents pertaining to them— should you find anything."

Polly had never seen John so angry. Her husband nodded, red-faced.

Beauregard turned to Polly and turned on the charm. "My dear, I need the lady's assurance that if she finds a survey in her father's personal effects, she will forward it to us with all haste."

"Of course." She tried to smile sweetly while her pulse raced.

Floride stepped between the men and raised her glass. "Gentlemen! Let us all take deep breaths. We are on the same side, here in this room. We may have differing opinions on how to achieve the same ends but we are all loyal to the State. And Captain Beauregard, I have known the Burgiss family since my husband was in the White House. You can count on these young people to do as you have asked," she said with an air of finality. "Now, a toast to the Confederacy."

The group raised their glasses and drank. Polly wished she had declined the invitation to dinner and prayed nothing would be found with the attorney that would lead Beauregard to Whitehall.

"Now, if I may, dinner is ready," Floride said. " I do not wish to ruin good guinea fowl. Let us go in and enjoy our meal. No more of this war talk tonight. I will end up with an ulcer."

Beauregard turned to Floride as if to counter, but she cut him off. "A delicious vichyssoise will be our first course."

— • —

THE REST OF THE DINNER PARTY WAS UNEVENTFUL, but the continued tension between John and Beauregard was palpable. Governor Pickens and Floride made polite conversation about goings-on in Charleston, to which Polly wasn't able to contribute. A seething John was noticeably quiet. Lieutenant Bright had been dispatched with Polly's signed consent, in a leather satchel bearing the seal of the great state of South Carolina.

The couple said their good-byes immediately after dinner. Polly watched as John's mood continued to deteriorate on the ride home, due in part to champagne followed by four whiskeys.

"John, please tell me what has you in such bad humor tonight. You seemed excessively put out by the General," Polly said. The creak and groan of the carriage wheels were her only answer.

She sighed. "I understand you're angry about this scheme to move men and equipment through the tunnels, but I daresay it has nothing to do with us, really." John did not respond. She thought of the document locked away in her father's desk. "Without a survey, it will come to nothing."

Polly grew impatient when John only stared straight ahead.

"Please John. We have been married just forty-eight hours and so far, I am not enjoying this . . . this honeymoon!" she sputtered. "I wish we had taken our wedding trip. None of this would have happened if we had gone away after our wedding."

John finally turned to his wife and looked at her with a cool expression. "Just how much socializing did you do with that Beauregard fellow in Charleston, Polly? You made no mention of him when you returned from the coast. He seemed quite pleased to see you again—and you, him. With his pomaded hair and trimmed goatee. He's nothing but a greasy Louisiana libertine, a roué. . . . Is that why you wore this revealing dress?"

Polly refused to rise to the bait. "That is hurtful, John. And as you'll recall, I returned rather quickly after the news of my slave, Duke." She paused. "Why did you antagonize those important men? Best to nod and leave it—"

John grabbed Polly's arm. He jerked her body close to his own and hissed through gritted teeth, "Do not tell me what to do." Even in the dark, his eyes burned into hers.

"John, you're hurting me!" Polly cried. His hand was tight on her upper arm. "Is this how we will begin our marriage?"

John released his grip. "You provoke me. I do not like that Beauregard fellow," he said. "I do not care a wit for how important the man may be. He has no business here, and he appeared to be overly fond of you and your decolletage. I suppose your choice of a low-cut gown had more to do with him than your own husband? Stay away from him."

Polly moved away from John and rubbed her sore arm. "I haven't done anything to encourage him, and I had no idea he would be there! I do not appreciate your behaving like a little boy whose toy might be snatched away. I am your wife." She turned to look out the window. "You have had too much to drink."

John shook his head. "Polly, I know a cad when I see one. And I will

314

be leaving for the convention shortly. What if war is declared soon after? War secrets are incredibly dangerous knowledge. I do not want to leave you with more problems than you will already have to deal with on your own as the mistress of two holdings."

Polly took a deep breath, appreciative for the opening John had unwittingly given her. "Their plans are out of our hands. And we have a more important thing to discuss." She turned toward her husband. "I had Zadoc take me by River Wood this afternoon," she said.

"Did you?" John asked coolly. "I asked you to leave River Wood alone."

Polly shrugged, the fight rising in her. "You yourself just said I am the mistress of two holdings. So I went to the house, where I met your sweet little house woman, Jane. She was most kind," Polly said simply. "I wanted to introduce myself. In fact, I was going to ask about sugar and coffee, neither of which is available in town. But Jane said there was none to be had at River Wood either."

"Jane is not aware of what we have or do not have in stores," John growled.

"Isn't Jane also your cook?" Polly asked. She suddenly wondered whether her line of questioning would get Jane beaten or worse.

"Jane is the housekeeper, the cook, and the kitchen gardener," John said impatiently. "She should see me if she needs something. I am quite disturbed that she felt compelled to whine about anything to you. And seeing as I will be living at Whitehall now, she will cook only on occasion." John shrugged and looked out the window at the moonlit fields rolling by. "I may just sell the old hag away."

"Do not punish her for answering my questions," Polly said. She enjoyed watching John shift uneasily in his seat. "Jane told me that food stores were low. Perhaps we can have Zadoc deliver some provisions to them—just to carry them through to spring? You told me that the soil at River Wood isn't as productive as it used to be."

"I was referring to the cotton crop," John muttered.

Polly ignored John's tone and pushed forward. "I would like to get some wool and muslin to her. For new dresses. I could see through the bodice of her dress, it was so thin. I want to be a good mistress. And there was no fire burning. The house was like ice."

"Very well, Polly. Gather some jars from the cellar, some venison from the smokehouse, if it pleases you. Make Jane a present of a new dress. Zadoc will take your gifts over there. But that old woman had no business laying out a list of laments. She should be glad that she is allowed to bumble around my home polishing the odd fork and dusting the chifforobes," he grumbled. "I should sell that damned house."

Polly smiled to herself, suddenly enjoying the game. "I found her delightful. I had no idea that Zadoc was her son. She misses him. Are there other slave families at River Wood?"

At that, John's demeanor plunged further. "Dammit Polly, your interest in my slaves, however well-intentioned, is unnerving. Send the food if you must, but leave the running of River Wood to me, do you understand? You have no cause to return there. None. Stay away. If you start to mollycoddle my slaves, they will become soft and lazy, like your own."

Polly bristled. "My slaves are not mollycoddled, but they are fed and clothed." The carriage creaked to a stop in front of Whitehall. "Kate and her baby came to us with the most threadbare of clothing, and little else. Aren't we legally bound to—"

"Enough, dammit!" John snapped. "Your incessant nagging tonight is like a fly buzzing in my ears. Do as I say, Polly! This entire evening has been exasperating." John opened the carriage door and stepped out quickly. He helped Polly down but released her hand abruptly.

"Exasperating? You lied to me. You kept Wilkins on as overseer," she cried. "The man is hideous!"

John spat on the ground. "That's what this is about? You had no right to dictate the terms of my overseer's employment. The man will not return to Whitehall. That's as much as I will give you. I'm keeping him at River Wood."

Polly felt her pulse throb in her temples. She climbed the front steps angrily and waited while John opened the front door, where the warm glow of candlelight greeted the couple. Home. She watched as Ona came forward from the shadows to collect their coats.

Ona could see that Polly was upset, that John was angry. She nodded at her mistress and asked quietly, "Miss Polly, would you like me to he'p you undress tonight? The fires is all stoked against this cold."

"No, Ona, thank you. You may go," she answered numbly. "Good night." Ona nodded and backed into the shadows.

"I am going to read the papers and have a drink. Do not wait up." John crossed into James Burgiss's library and slammed the doors behind him. Polly climbed the stairs, the sting of unshed tears burning her eyes.

— • —

OVER THE NEXT FEW DAYS, POLLY THREW HER attention to the mistress's business of managing Whitehall. McQueen's trip was pushed back repeatedly as convention dates slipped. During that time, John was noticeably absent, but she was determined not to let the sting of his lie take over. Instead, she dutifully attended to women's work. She did not ask Mr. Roper about the hog butchering or about the outlook for the coming cotton season. She did not bother to look at the household account ledgers although she wanted to desperately. Instead, she directed Cissie and Kate to finish the messy job of soap making, and she oversaw the sewing that Ona undertook for the slaves. New garments were made for every man, and evenings found Polly stitching several of the blanket coats herself by a warm fire when it became clear that Ona's hands were in pain from rheumatism.

She decided on vegetables for the winter gardens and began to sow seeds in the sunny kitchen house windows. Seedlings would be transplanted into the ground at first thaw. She started extra seedlings for Zee to take to Jane.

She directed Zee to take canned vegetables and a pork shoulder over to River Wood. She knew that John was there and sent a note along with him that gave written consent to stay the entire afternoon to help his elderly parents.

Keeping busy buoyed her sagging spirits. John had not come into her room nights to be with his bride. Polly sometimes saw a thin flicker of light from under the door of his adjoining bedroom, but by morning the room was empty. He had only made the most casual of contact with her during the day. She knew that he was still angry about her trip to River Wood and about their confrontation over Wilkins. But something else had to be wrong. These dark moods, heavy drinking, frightening swings in emotion, they were new to her. The coming convention trip must weigh on him, she reasoned. His departure date with McQueen's company was unknown to her and seemed to be pushed back daily.

One brisk morning in early February, Polly busied herself by tidying up in the house. Cigar stubs littered the ashtray and newspapers lay strewn around the library, which told Polly three things. John was still around. Ona was not. And the convention of the seceded states was approaching. From everything Polly read, it seemed that commissioners to the convention had finally been named. Major McQueen was prominently listed as an aide de camp to the convention delegates and John Stone was listed as a member of the former senator's entourage soon to depart. The group would be traveling by train and would leave the following morning. Major McQueen would give a speech at the train station before departure.

Polly dropped the *Keowee Courier* onto her father's desk with a sigh. She was determined to set things right with her husband before his departure, even though he owed her an apology. She glanced at the completed slave coats she had stitched over the past few days. She pulled on her cloak and picked up the stack of coats to take to the slave quarters. She stepped outside and shivered as she made her way toward Ona's cabin. The crisp morning chill and the aroma of wood smoke were invigorating.

She inhaled deeply, letting the sharp bite of icy air fill her lungs. Her exhalation was both a deep sigh and a frosty cloud around her face.

She knocked on the door of Ona's cabin and waited. The door opened and Polly stepped back, confused. "Oh!" she said, as Ben filled the doorway.

"Mama's sick," Ben said, as he glanced over his shoulder. "She woke up in the night with a fever. Kate and Sol moved over to Cissie and George's cabin."

Polly wondered who had come to tend the fires that morning, burning so brightly when Polly woke. She stepped back, puzzled. "I see." She held the stack of woolen coats out toward Ben. "I finished these coats. This should be the last of them. One for everyone. Your mother sewed the rest," she noted self-consciously.

"Alright," Ben said. He took the bundle from his mistress. Polly tried to see past Ben but could not make out anything in the dim and smoky interior. "I will pass them out," he said.

Polly nodded again and turned to go. "I will ask Kate and Cissie to take up her chores while she's ill, so she can rest. Perhaps Cissie can make a poultice—"

"I did that already. Mustard plaster. But Ma could use a good bone broth if Kate can make it, and you'll allow," Ben said stiffly.

Polly found herself exasperated yet again with Ben's demeanor. She nodded silently and turned to leave.

Ben cleared his throat. "Martin died of the influenza, remember? And Mama, she never left your side when you were sick, Miss Polly," Ben said accusingly.

Polly shifted from one cold foot to the other. "Yes, Ben, I know. I am so sorry that Ona is ill." She had a sudden thought. "Ben, ride out for Dr. Adger. He was so good to come when Duke died. He said he would treat anyone, slave or free. You rode for me. Now ride for your mother," she said. "You know the way. Let me write a note for you to carry. I will sit with her until you return. I have already had this illness this season."

Ben's brown eyes met Polly's briefly. "Thank you." He stood aside while Polly stepped into the cabin.

— • —

BEN FOLLOWED THE SAME ROUTE HE HAD taken only weeks earlier, but now there were many more signs of activity on the way to Pendleton. Riders on horseback and dusty carriages raced along the rutted road, as if on urgent business. Several white farmers drove heavily laden wagons slowly toward town, and Ben knew enough to follow behind unless encouraged to pass. In the bright sunshine, Ben could clearly see the fields and woods along the main road; tidy farmsteads and fine manor homes tucked back behind gated pillars. Polly's horse, Delightful, took to Ben's hand immediately and obeyed his every command.

As Ben turned onto Queen Street, he realized that he was the only Negro around. Two white men stopped across the street to watch Ben dismount in front of the doctor's house. Again Ben was relieved to have a note inside his coat that gave him permission to be in town alone.

He knocked timidly on Dr. Adger's front door. A spindly dark girl of twelve or thirteen answered the door. "Yessuh?"

Ben pulled out the note from Polly. "Is Dr. Adger home, girl?"

The girl shook her head. "Naw, he out tendin' to sick folk. Mrs. Adger be inside. You want her?"

Ben nodded. The girl closed the door and Ben waited, nervously scanning the boardwalk behind him. The two white men across the street were still staring.

The door opened again and a plump white woman appeared, wearily wiping her hands on her apron. Her spectacles were dusted with flour. "What is it you need? I am in the middle of baking, and my husband isn't home." She sighed.

Ben nodded slightly and removed his hat. He handed the woman

Polly's note. Mrs. Adger took the paper and unfolded it. She read it and refolded the paper, handing it back to Ben daintily with forefinger and thumb. Peering over her glasses, she said, "I'm sorry. My husband is out attending to families who are sick with the very thing as your mistress's slave woman. The whole district has been ill with the fevers." She shrugged. "All I can do is tell you that the doctor cannot come out today. I will give him the message, though. But Mrs. Stone will have to handle this without my husband. I don't even have a tincture to sell. I'm sorry. Now goodbye." She closed the door firmly and Ben heard the deadbolt slide into place.

Ben's shoulders sagged. He pocketed the note and turned to leave. As he did so, the two men crossed the street quickly and came toward him. Ben concentrated on tightening Delightful's saddle and prepared to mount.

"Well, looka here, Jacob," said a familiar voice behind Ben. Ben turned slowly to find Clay Wilkins and another man, standing behind the horse. Wilkins grinned up at Ben, tobacco-stained teeth twisted into a malevolent smile. Wilkins' breath was foul with liquor. Ben dropped his head and stood, hat in hand.

"This here's one uppity nigger, Jacob," Wilkins spat onto the toe of Ben's shoe. "This here nigger boy, why, he used to think he didn't have to listen to ol' Wilkins none." He cackled. "This nigger boy tried to hit me. So I whipped him. I stripped the hide off his back real good." He laughed.

"That so?" asked Jacob, who appeared to be cut from the same cloth, with his angry grimace, greasy hat, and tobacco-stained beard. "Ain't niggers s'pose to listen and do what they's told? He's lucky you didn't hang him from a tree."

Wilkins continued, "Yessiree, Jacob, but times have changed. This nigger's purty mistress done married John Stone. You know what that means. That means that now he Mr. Stone's property. We gone have us a real good time, eh?" He guffawed and spat a stream of tobacco juice toward Ben's face. Jacob laughed and slapped his knee with his hat.

"It's too bad I got to head home, Jacob. We could stand here and mess with this boy all day. Why you in town alone, nigger? You best answer me now."

Ben pulled a handkerchief from his pocket and wiped the spittle from his face before reaching for the folded paper in his pocket. He handed it to Wilkins, his pulse pounding in anger.

Wilkins noticed a small crowd forming near the men and lowered his voice. "Lessee here. . . . Oh, yer mama's sick. Now that's a damn shame. That old nigger woman must be about a hunnerd years old. Right nice of Miss Polly to help you out." He turned back to Jacob. "Damn, Jacob, you should see that Polly Burgiss. She is one fine woman."

He handed the note back to Ben and said loudly for the crowd to hear, "Go on home now, boy. I'd hate to have to report you as a runaway!"

Ben quickly mounted Delightful and the crowd began to disperse. Ben kicked the horse's sides with his heels and lit out of Pendleton as quickly as he could, Wilkins' cackling laughter trailing him down the road.

— • —

THE DAY OF JOHN'S SEND-OFF DAWNED MILD AND CLEAR. The weather was perfect for a parade and farewell celebration. The entire district, it seemed, was waiting at the train station in Anderson to see the brave delegation of new soldiers off to the Convention.

Polly, alone in her room, dressed herself for the trip to Anderson. She wore a navy blue gown with ivory trim. She had braided her own hair and wound the braids at the back by herself. She held a new blue rabbit-trimmed bonnet in her hands. Without Ona's help, she was at a loss as to how to place the bonnet atop her head at a stylish slant.

When Ben had returned without Dr. Adger, Polly could see the rage in his face and she assumed it was because Adger was unable to tend Ona. He refused to talk about it. She asked George to wait on several pieces from the smithy while Ben cared for his mother. Luckily, Ben's mustard plasters seemed to pull the illness from Ona's lungs. Neither Kate nor Cissie volunteered to nurse Ona, because of their little boys. Polly could not blame them. Ben was strong and well able to tend his mother, she reasoned. Better to contain the sickness than risk more slaves becoming ill.

There was a knock on Polly's bedroom door. "Come in, Cissie," she called. "I am struggling with this hat and could use your help."

Instead, John opened the bedroom door timidly. He was dressed in a new black wool frock coat and trousers, a fine outfit in which to travel. He held a glossy new silk stovepipe hat in his hands. With a lump in her throat, she remembered that it was the expensive hat she had ordered for him for their wedding trip.

"Good morning, Polly," he said hesitantly. "May I come in?"

"Of course," Polly said coolly. She continued her toilette without looking at him.

John shifted nervously from one foot to the other and ran a trembling hand through his blonde hair. "I must apologize. I behaved badly at Floride's dinner—and afterward. My behavior in front of the governor was inexcusable. I was anxious about many things—our wedding, leaving for Alabama, how to handle two plantations, a war which may begin in earnest at any time . . . and . . . I was jealous of Beauregard's attentions." He turned his hat over in his hands nervously. "I have a terrible temper, Polly. I shall try to control it. But it would have been difficult to find someone to replace Wilkins on such short notice. You understand. It was a business decision. I would not dare leave you without an overseer to manage River Wood while I am away. Forgive me?"

Polly looked at John's reflection in her mirror. His blonde curls and broad shoulders made her heart leap every time. She propped her head in her hands. "John, we have wasted precious time since we became man and wife. I have barely seen you, and with so much to discuss—and learn about one another. You lied to me. And that man is still at River Wood. I do not want him ever to show his face here. But I do forgive you." She wanted to be brave, a wife sending her soldier off with a smile, but her face remained stern.

John looked down at his young wife. "I will be away just a few weeks. I have spoken to Mr. Roper and to Mr. Wilkins. They have chores well in hand. Since they are exempt from enlisting, you shouldn't worry. They will be here and are armed. You do not have to go back to River Wood again. Leave it to Mr. Wilkins while I am away. We can discuss my slaves and their . . . needs . . . when I return," he conceded. "You should not have to lift a finger. Attend that sewing circle you spoke of last summer or spend some time with Floride. Her son, Andrew Calhoun, from Fort Hill, is also in McQueen's entourage. Goodness knows, your affection for that old hawk puzzles me . . ." John's words were strong but his tone was gentle. "Zadoc has my bags loaded. Let's be on our way to the station."

— • —

KATE KNOCKED ON THE DOOR OF ONA'S CABIN. When Ben answered, she held out a kettle of fragrant broth. "Miss Polly asked me to bring this fo' yo' mama."

Ben took the steaming kettle and nodded. "Thank you, Kate. This'll set her up real good, I'm sure," he said. "She's sleeping now. Her fever is down. Dr. Adger isn't coming out for a slave woman, I guess, so anything y'all know to do for her is appreciated." Ben set the pot on the wooden steps and closed the door behind him to keep out the cold.

Kate smiled. "I'll have to think more kindly of Miss Polly. She did send you to get the doctor. That's more than anyone ever did fo' a slave at River Wood."

At the mention of River Wood, Ben's expression darkened. "I think we're all breathing a little easier with Mr. Stone going away for a while," he said. "One of these days, Kate. . . ." He stopped in mid-sentence and looked at her. "I don't know how much longer. . . ."

"I know, Ben. I know what you thinkin'," she said. "I got Sol, so I ain't gone do nothin' to make Miss Polly or Mr. Stone angry. When George married Cissie, I thought she was the luckiest woman alive—to get away from River Wood. You heard Mr. Wilkins sold children away from their mamas— as a punishment? Law, he did that to a poor girl named Sara before I came. He up and sold her baby boy away after he caught her stealin' extra bread. She hung herself from a oak tree near the slave cabins. I woulda done the same."

Ben rubbed the stubble on his chin and looked at Kate. "Wilkins is straight from the devil. At least here, he can't hurt you."

Kate shivered and hugged her new coat around her shoulders more tightly. "I heard somethin' from Zadoc, just las' week. His mama tol' him that her kitchen help, Eva, finally ran away after Wilkins attacked her again. She was all tore up inside from things he done. He beat her up real bad, so she ran. She has a little girl, but she ran anyway. She just couldn't take it no mo'. Maybe it was fo' the best."

"That a fact?" Ben sighed. "She got away?" he asked hopefully.

"Wilkins and his pack o' dogs went after her. The way Jane tol' it, he prob'ly set the dogs on her scent and then strung her up from a tree somewhere. No one seen her. Jane's hidin' the little girl in the house so's Wilkins won't get to her. Said Miss Polly knows! And she sent cloth over to Jane for some dresses for the chile."

Ben shook his head slowly. "Kate, Miss Polly is a kind white woman, but we are in new territory—now that she's married. I ran into that Wilkins yesterday in town. That man is the most evil I have known in one person. He's been dogging me since I was a boy. . . ." Ben's voice trailed off as he remembered Polly's murdered brothers. He had managed to keep those memories down for years, but he could clearly picture Caleb and Joshua Burgiss lying dead behind Kemp's trading post.

He could not burden her with this. "Mr. Roper is in charge here. Wilkins isn't coming to Whitehall. You've got nothing to worry about. Sol is safe."

"Wilkins ain't the only one to be afraid of. I ain't sayin' no more but take my word." Kate looked up at Ben with tears in her eyes. Ben saw so much fear and sorrow there, and he was tempted to tell her he knew what she meant. Instead, he glanced over his shoulder at the sound of Ona calling and let the moment pass.

Kate sighed. "I best get back to work. I got washin' to tend to. . . . I hope Ona feels better soon."

Ben smiled at her. "Thank you for the soup, Kate. You were good to go to the trouble."

Kate waved him off. "T'aint me that made it. Miss Polly made it herse'f. She real worried about yo' mama." She smiled and walked back toward the kitchen house, humming to herself.

— • —

February 8, 1861

POLLY STOOD IN THE WARM KITCHEN, admiring tiny green seedlings emerging from trays of rich soil. Broccoli, spinach, lettuces, and carrots were up, emerald heralds of the spring soon to come.

"Land sakes, Miss Polly." Kate shook her head as she kneaded dough for bread. Sol played quietly with a cornhusk doll in the corner of the room. "We ain't never planted seeds inside at River Wood. Look at how they is comin' up even though it's so cold out."

"Ona taught me to start them indoors early. They are hardier than starting from seed in the cold ground. We'll have some wonderful spring vegetables in weeks. Did you and Cissie plant the peas?"

"Yes'm. Well, we let Silas lay some down. I s'pose some of the rows ain't gone be too even." She smiled. "But we did it just like you tol' us otherwise."

Polly laughed. "Crooked rows will taste just as good as straight ones," she said. "Kate, after you finish the bread, take several loaves to Zadoc. I want him to take some to River Wood for his parents."

At the mention of River Wood, Kate's smile faded. She slapped the dough onto the table and kneaded it roughly. "Yes ma'am."

Polly noticed the change in Kate's demeanor. She leaned against the table and looked at Kate. "I know that River Wood was not a good place for you. I am aware of some of the horrible things that have happened there." Kate slapped the dough again and remained silent.

"You don't have to fret. I think one of the reasons my husband brought you here was to get you away from . . . from Mr. Wilkins," Polly offered. "I had noticed, in the last few days, that you seemed less fearful than when you first came."

Kate looked at her mistress guardedly. "Miss Polly, I don't want no trouble with anyone. I always do what I'm told. Anything to keep Sol safe."

"I know. And I will tell you again—no matter what, I would never take Sol from you. Ever. That kind of vile thing does not happen here."

Kate nodded silently as she continued to work the dough.

— • —

POLLY HAD COLLECTED A FEW EGGS FROM THE hen house and stopped to wash her hands at the pump. She leaned in to get a drink of the icy water. As she sipped from the dipper, she glanced toward Ona's cabin and saw the old woman sitting, wrapped in a blanket, sunning herself on the front stoop. Squaring her shoulders, Polly waved and walked toward her.

"Ona, you look so much better than when I saw you last," Polly exclaimed. The woman looked thinner and her eyes were bloodshot and tired, but she smiled and pointed toward a bare dogwood tree. "Yes, Miss Polly. I thought I would get up and see what that there bluebird was singin' about. He must be thinkin' it near spring. I hope he right." The little bird with iridescent blue wings chirped merrily from his branch.

Polly squinted toward the bird and playfully shook her finger at him.

"As long as he doesn't alert his cousins, the crows, to the pea patch. I should get Silas onto making us a scarecrow."

Ona smiled at her mistress. "Thank you for tryin' to get Doc Adger out here fo' me. Ben tol' me you let him ride into town after him. I sho' thank you."

"I am sorry that he didn't come. So many people are sick with the same thing apparently. Ben nursed you well, I see. He must have learned how to make your potions." Polly looked down at her feet. "I just made soup."

"You look like you is feelin' better yo'se'f, Miss Girl. I ain't seen you lookin' so well in a long time. Marriage must agree with you." Ona squinted in the sunlight.

"We had a big fight right before he left. He has gone to Alabama with Major McQueen." Polly wondered if she had said too much.

"Uh huh. . . . Maybe it's good fo' Mr. Stone and you to be separated for a while. What's that sayin? 'Absent makes'—what now? 'Makes the heart more fonder?' You got married right after you was sick. Maybe when he come back, y'all can start over." Polly was silent. She lowered the egg basket to the ground gently.

"You got somethin' else to say, don't you, Miss Girl?" Ona asked gently.

Polly took a deep breath and tucked a loose strand of hair behind her ear. "Ona, I have to tell you. When I wrote that paper, the one granting you your freedom, I had every intention of keeping my word," she began.

Ona dropped her head and closed her eyes. "But you cain't?"

"I didn't know. It is against the law in South Carolina to give a slave his—or her—freedom. I didn't know . . ." Her voice trailed off.

Ona rocked back and forth, with her hands clasped between her knees, for minutes. Polly stood looking down at the woman who had helped birth her into the world over twenty years earlier, who had stayed by her side when her own mother succumbed to illness and death.

Finally, Ona looked up at Polly, her brown eyes shining with tears. "Well then. That's the end o' that."

Polly exhaled sadly. "I am so sorry. But Ona, I don't want you to get up and go to work again until you are completely well. Rest. I thought that maybe, when you're better, you would like to mind Silas and Sol while Cissie and Kate tend to the kitchen and housework? You love those little boys, am I right? And they are much too young to work."

Ona regarded Polly with dark eyes touched with grief. "Yes'm. They sho' is."

Chapter Twenty-Three

February 28, 1861

TOM ROPER KNOCKED ON THE FRONT DOOR OF THE HOUSE, a newspaper tucked under his arm. Cissie opened the door and showed him into the library, where Polly sat expectantly behind her father's desk.

"Good morning, Miss Polly," Tom said cheerfully, removing his hat. "You wanted to see me?" Tom's face was lined and tanned from the sun, but it was open and friendly, and if Polly had to be honest, handsome for a man of his age.

Polly smiled and held up her copy of the *Keowee Courier*. "I see we are both caught up in the news of the day." She waved her hand toward the chair opposite the desk. "Come and sit. We have much to chat about. I haven't seen you since Christmas."

"My boots, ma'am. They're caked in red clay."

Polly remembered John repeatedly propping his filthy boots on her father's mahogany desk and smiled. "This room has seen worse."

Tom sat down and let out a long sigh. He ran a hand through his hair.

"How is your mother?" Polly asked. She noticed the man's dark hair had thinned, but his frame was still lean and strong.

"Very well, now. She was near to apoplexy over this secession. But I calmed her down." Tom shifted in his seat. "Yes ma'am, it looks like we have ourselves a new government. With a new president—Jefferson Davis."

"Hmm, yes." Polly cleared her throat and tried to focus on the news. "But it looks like South Carolina isn't getting much in the way of leadership positions in the Cabinet. Maybe the Secretary of State if Mr. Barnwell accepts," Polly said. "Then they will still have to ratify this new constitution."

Tom's blue eyes crinkled. "I'm glad to see you following the events in Montgomery. I guess we're all following the news more closely," he said with a playful grin.

"Don't act so surprised." Polly folded her paper and set it aside. "It seems this convention may drag on for a long while. I have heard nothing from my husband about his return as of yet but the needs of this farm go on. Tell me how he left things with you."

Tom leaned forward in his chair. "He knows I've been doing my job here a long time. After our run-in while you were away, we are taking things slowly. Hopefully, when he returns, he'll let me be." He began to tick off a list of completed projects. "Ben spent a fair amount of time with Ona while she was sick, and that slowed him down on finishing nails. Hogs were processed. Had the boys repair the bridge over the creek. I have some men frost seeding clover in the pastures. We can't do much else till the other grounds thaw fully. The hay is still plentiful. Cows will be calving soon, and Zee is watching them."

Polly picked up a pen. "What do you need from town? I am going this afternoon. I need to settle accounts at the Mercantile."

"I guess we haven't got a chance of getting sugar and coffee for a while? Lord, I miss my coffee." Tom grinned.

Polly laughed. "I do, too. I hope that coffee and sugar are the only things we go without while this government seems bent on splitting the country apart. Should I be worried about the slaves, with talk of war?"

Tom's face became serious. "They likely know war is afoot, but I haven't seen any signs they're riled up about it. I run a fair place. We are not like River Wood. His slaves are as likely to slit Clay Wilkins' throat in the nighttime as obey that man, should war come."

Polly shuddered. "Mr. Roper, don't entertain such thoughts. I mean to speak with my husband again about replacing Mr. Wilkins." She leaned forward. "I mean for him to leave. Did you hear?" She paused. "Did you hear about the slave girl, Eva?"

"The one who recently ran? Wilkins and his dogs never found her, best I know. I have heard other things in town. Someone told me he bragged about stringing her up near the river. Wilkins talks a big story, though. . . . Can't say if the rumors are true."

Polly gripped the arms of her father's chair to stay calm. "I have it on good authority that he repeatedly set himself on the poor girl—and then killed two of her unborn infants before she ran."

She stared at the overseer, gaining confidence as she spoke. Tom didn't say anything, so she continued, "I'll assume she was killed. So Mr. Wilkins' behavior has cost us $500." Polly hoped that adding a dollar value to the slaves would aid her case. "I don't understand why my husband won't discharge the man."

Tom stared at the woman, emboldened by Polly's willingness to speak of such things. He spoke up. "You don't have to convince me that Wilkins is a bad seed. Your father and I avoided the man as best we could. He is cruel and violent, and he abuses the slaves, especially women. Always has. He murdered Duke. If that man ever steps foot on Whitehall property again, I might shoot him myself. But unless he does, he isn't any of my affair," Tom said evenly.

"No, I supposed he isn't any of my affair, either." Polly sighed.

— • —

POLLY SAT WITH THE NEWSPAPER IN HER LAP, sipping the last of her weak coffee. The girls had taken to reusing the grounds to boil morning coffee for their mistress. The grounds had been reused so many times that Polly only vaguely tasted the original flavor of the beans. Mostly, she tasted the iron-rich well water used in the brewing. She looked at the bottom of the china cup and used her finger to wipe up the bits of coffee sludge left behind.

The news was grim. Militias in Georgia, Alabama, and South Carolina had seized federal arsenals. Troops were being organized in Washington, D.C. Even the Choctaw were choosing sides—fortunately taking up with the Confederates.

Cabin fever. *Ennui.* Nerves. She sat and stared out the window. She had not had a letter from John since his departure. The convention continued in Alabama, where the delegates hammered out a new constitution.

Polly folded the newspaper and reached for the silver bell on the table. She shook it a few times and waited. Cissie appeared, her swollen belly a testament to the new life growing inside. Polly felt a twinge of jealousy. If she had a baby to tend to, maybe she wouldn't feel so bored and lonely. There was little chance of her being pregnant, however. She had been with John only once before he had gone away, and her time of the month had come and gone as usual.

"Yes'm?" Cissie asked.

"I've decided to go into Pendleton and check for mail, maybe see if the Mercantile has any chicory at all. Tell George to drive me in about an hour." Polly dabbed her mouth with her napkin and rose from the table.

"Ma'am," Cissie began, "George fixin' the hay mow floor in the barn with Mr. Roper and Meenie. He tol' me they be there most of the day. You want me to git him down from there?"

Polly felt irritable and snapped at the girl. "No. Just—get Zadoc or Ben. Get someone. I don't care who. I just don't want to drive a gig today." Polly was frustrated with herself. She was not comfortable with the other hands she owned, men who had served her family at Whitehall for years. George, Zadoc, and Ben were the men she trusted, that she counted on to come to the house, to tend her horse, run errands and do her personal bidding. Cissie nodded and waddled out of the room.

An hour later, Polly stood waiting in front of the house, cloak and bonnet in place. The sun shone brightly and warmed her back. Carolina wrens flitted above her in the trees, as they gathered materials for their tiny nests. She closed her eyes and enjoyed the sun's warmth for a moment. The peace that pervaded Whitehall was a fragile thing, she knew.

Just down the road, slaves toiled at River Wood—men she did not know, but who ultimately depended on her while John was away. And the looming threat of war hung heavy on everyone, with its insistent drumbeat that only grew louder.

Polly heard the approach of the creaky old phaeton and opened her eyes. Good. She wanted to ride in the open air and her parents' old phaeton always made her smile. With its oversized back wheels and daringly high seat, how the Burgisses ever made it down to South Carolina from Virginia in the thing was a wonder in itself.

Ben slowed the horses and the phaeton creaked to a stop. "Thank you," Polly said. "I hope that Mr. Roper wasn't too put out. I need some things in town and did not want to drive myself."

"You saved me from the forge for a few hours." Ben hopped down easily. "Help you up?"

Polly shook her head and deftly maneuvered her skirts as she climbed into the high carriage. She adjusted her bonnet and folded her hands in her lap. "We'll stop first for the mail. Don't go too fast. I don't want to muss my new bonnet." She stared straight ahead.

"No. We can't have that." Ben smiled and muttered under his breath before climbing up beside his mistress. He flicked the reins and the little gig began to move down the drive.

Once out on the main road, Ben urged the horse only a little, as to obey his mistress's instructions. Polly quickly became uncomfortable with the silence between them.

"I am glad to see your mother so much improved," she ventured.

"Yes'm. I am, too. Thank you for the soup." Ben stared at the road ahead.

"You never told me what happened in town when you went to get Dr. Adger. But when you returned that day, well, you looked . . . you looked so angry. I am sure that he would have come if there weren't so many others sick."

Ben shrugged. "I was angry. But not because Dr. Adger couldn't see Ma. Ma's potions and poultices usually do the trick. And I knew as soon as Mrs. Adger opened that door and saw I was a slave, she wasn't going to tell her husband anything." He glanced at Polly. "But I appreciate you letting me try."

Polly cocked her head to one side and looked at Ben. "Ah, that's why you were so angry."

Ben stared straight ahead and sighed deeply. "Actually, your Mr. Wilkins was in town that day," he said. "He decided I needed another lesson on who is the boss man. I'm going to leave it at that. I don't want to do anything to cause that man to threaten Mama, on my account."

Polly saw how tightly he gripped the reins. Her cheeks flushed in anger. "My Mr. Wilkins?" She reconsidered Ben's words. "I suppose he is, at that. . . . I thought that man was out of our lives, but I was mistaken. He will not show his face at Whitehall again. How dare he speak to one of my slaves, on my errand, no less!" Polly scowled and bit her lip, thinking.

"Ben, take me to River Wood."

"No ma'am, you and I both know that isn't a good idea." Ben shook his head. "Mr. Wilkins is your husband's overseer. There is nothing good to come from confronting him when your husband is out of town. He'll know I said something to you. That isn't good for me and it isn't good for Mama." He shook his head and added "You should know—"

Polly held up a hand. "Ben, I have a lot to say to that man and it has nothing to do with you," Polly lied. "This is strictly about River Wood. In a way, he works for me now. I will not mention anything about your trip to town or about anyone at Whitehall. Do as I say before I lose my nerve." Polly looked at Ben. "I have let that horrible man interfere in my life long enough." She straightened her back and frowned. "You heard me."

Ben could not help the slow grin that crept across his own face. "Yes ma'am, Miss Polly." He flicked the reins again and urged the horse on toward the narrow road to River Wood.

When they arrived at the rusted iron gates, Ben tugged on the reins. "Whoa there, horse." He turned to Polly. "You sure you got the spine for this?"

Polly silently weighed her options. She felt fairly sure that nothing good would come of it but was determined to have her say or burst. She nodded. "Drive on in."

Ben clicked the reins and they moved down the tree-lined drive. The phaeton slowed as it reached the old brick house. Polly's heart pounded in her chest and she looked at Ben. "Wait here. I may be a while." She turned to dismount and felt Ben's hand on her arm. Polly looked down at his fingers, surprised.

"Miss Polly. Be careful. He is a dangerous man. He's been causing problems for your family since we were both little children. I think you should wait and do this with Mr. Roper."

Polly smiled weakly. "If I wait, I will lose my nerve. Now help me down, please."

Ben released her arm and climbed off the phaeton seat. He hurried to her side of the gig and extended his hand. Polly grabbed his hand and climbed down carefully, holding her skirts in the other gloved hand.

She straightened her bonnet and inhaled deeply. She blew out a steady breath. "Who knows? Maybe he isn't near the house today and this is all for naught."

Ben watched as Polly climbed the broad front steps. He stroked the horse's nose and thought of Wilkins. The putrid spittle running down his own face after the man spat at him. The pain of the still-healing stripes across his back.

Polly lifted the tarnished brass ring and knocked loudly. After a few moments, the door opened and Jane stood in front of her. The old woman's face broke into a broad and toothless smile.

"Mizz Polly, come in. It's so good to see ya." She shuffled aside and led her mistress into the main hall. Polly was gratified to see the old woman wearing one of the new dresses her girls had sewn, and a new blanket coat over it.

"I got to thank you ma'am," Jane gushed, as she led Polly into the parlor. The house was still dark and very cold. "I got to thank you for this here coat and new dress. I said to my husband, I said, 'They's Jesus in that woman, they sho' is!'"

Polly blushed at Jane's effusive praise.

"And fo' lettin' my Zadoc bring some extry food! Lawd, Mizz Polly, you done us a world of good."

"I was glad to do it, Jane. And now I would like to know where I can find Mr. Wilkins." Polly began removing her gloves nervously.

At the mention of Wilkins, Jane's face fell. "He be out in the back. His cabin is by the slave quarters. You want him in here? In da big house?"

Polly remembered Lydia, hidden away in the house, and shook her head. "No, Jane, I suppose not. Is little Lydia safe?"

"Yes'm, I keep her by my side all da time. I tucked her away when you knocked, jes' in case."

Polly relaxed a bit. "I think I shall go find Mr. Wilkins. Just tell me where to look for him. Or send someone to take me to the man."

"Wait here, ma'am. I git my husband. Ezra take you to 'im." She bustled toward the back of the house and returned with a wizened old man not much taller than Jane. His right arm dragged uselessly by his side and there was a broad scar across his neck, the likes of which Polly had never seen. He wore no coat despite the chill.

"Mizz Polly, this is Ezra, my husband. An' Zadoc's daddy." She smiled lovingly at the man.

"How do you do, Ezra?" It is nice to meet you. I hope that you received one of the coats your son delivered. We made enough for everyone."

Ezra nodded but did not answer her. Jane piped up and said, "Mizz

337

Polly, he cain't talk real good. With his throat an' all. . . . But he got a coat, yes'm."

Polly wanted to ask how Ezra had sustained his injuries but decided against it.

"That's fine. Ezra, could you please take me out to Mr. Wilkins?" Polly looked at the old man and then at Jane.

Jane shook her head. "Ezra, is he in the cabin?" Her husband nodded. "Best you should follow Ezra to Mr. Wilkins' cabin."

"Alright then. Let's go," Polly said. As she followed Ezra through the house, she steeled herself for the encounter. She was the new mistress of the home. Wilkins worked for her husband, and in his absence, for her. His treatment of the slaves was untenable, bad management. She would state her case and leave quickly. Doubts flooded her mind and her heart pounded in her chest.

As Ezra led Polly out the back door, she took in the sights at the rear of the house. They came first to the kitchen yard. Polly saw little in the way of prepared seedbeds or transplants. A few scraggly beanpoles still bore the shriveled remnants of last summer's crop.

"Ezra, wait. Can you show me the kitchen first?" Polly asked. The old man took the steps to a small nearby building slowly and opened the door to the cookhouse with his good arm. Inside, no fire smoldered in the cold hearth. There was not much in the way of food stores that Polly could see. Jane had not exaggerated in her tale of deprivation. Polly was surprised to see a pantry off to the side, with a small unmade cot taking up space instead of food stores. Polly wondered who used the room, as there was no longer a cook at River Wood. Maybe Jane let Lydia nap there. "Is there another pantry?"

Ezra pointed to the little room. He croaked hoarsely, "Empty." Polly could tell that it hurt the man to attempt speech.

Ezra then led her past several outbuildings, similar to those at Whitehall. The large barn and chicken house looked to be in good repair, at least. Several scrawny chickens pecked about in the dirt outside. The milk house looked empty. The wash building stood nearby, where a rusty mangle sat outside exposed to the elements. There were no slaves anywhere around the yard. At Whitehall, slaves would be about the business of the day, making repairs, doing laundry, hoeing gardens, and feeding livestock. The laughter of the young boys, Solomon and Silas, was also now a welcome sound at home. River Wood was eerily silent and empty.

Ezra led Polly past a cluster of dilapidated cabins. A lone black man sat on the stoop of one of the cabins. He stared at Polly and Ezra as they passed. Polly suspected that Eva, the runaway, must have been the last young woman at River Wood. She wanted to ask Ezra where the other men were but did not want him to try to speak on her account. They neared a larger, well-maintained cabin set far back from the others. Smoke billowed from a brick chimney. Ezra pointed at the place and nodded. Wilkins' cabin.

Polly motioned for him to knock on the door. Ezra rapped on the door lightly.

After a moment, a slurred voice called out. "Whaddya want?" Polly recognized Wilkins' voice at once.

Ezra looked at his mistress helplessly. The door suddenly flew open and Wilkins appeared, dazed, looking down at the pair. He had obviously been napping and pulled up suspenders over a stained undershirt. He scratched his head in confusion, looking first from Ezra to Polly. A slow smile of recognition spread across his face.

"Mizz Polly. What can I do fer you?" His yellow teeth and tobacco-streaked beard made her slightly nauseous.

She straightened her shoulders and pointed to a wooden table set up near the cabin. "My name is Mrs. Stone. Perhaps we can conduct our business in a more seemly fashion from over there." She nodded toward the table.

"Ma'am," Wilkins drawled. "I ain't sure what business we have." He scratched his stomach and yawned. Polly was appalled by the man's rude behavior. He reeked of stale alcohol. "Best I remember, John said you was to stay away from here."

"Mr. Wilkins, I am the mistress of River Wood. In my husband's absence, I have a few questions to ask the overseer. Would that still be you, sir?" she asked icily. "If so, please join me across this table, as I will not discuss business with someone standing half-dressed in a doorway in the middle of the day." Polly turned and walked to the table, knees trembling. She sat down facing away from the cabin and waited. She heard grumbling and cursing. The cabin door slammed.

"Ezra, git the hell outta here!" Wilkins barked.

"No, Ezra. Stay here," Polly called sharply. "I won't be long and I want you to show me the other outbuildings." Ezra stood under a tree and waited, wringing his hat in his hands nervously.

In a moment, Wilkins stood across from her.

"Sit down please, Mr. Wilkins." The man sat down, a fresh plug of tobacco in his cheek. He glared at her with small, blue eyes. Polly thought he resembled a wild hog, complete with red bristles, foul odor, and an angry glare. The humorous thought relaxed her somewhat.

"I heard that you had words with one of my slaves in town recently," Polly began.

Wilkins smirked and slouched across the table. "Is yer boy tattlin' now?"

"You will not have anything to do with any of my slaves ever again. My husband should have made that completely clear. You confine yourself to overseeing River Wood, do you understand?" Polly said boldly.

Wilkins turned and spat a stream of juice onto the ground.

Polly continued, her heart pounding in her chest. "Mr. Wilkins, I sent provisions over by Zadoc several times in the past weeks. Seeds, young plants, some preserved vegetables, and a haunch of meat. This was meant to help the slaves here get through the last weeks of winter while your own gardens and fields were being prepared. And yet I have seen no winter gardens, no canned fruits or vegetables, an empty pantry, and an unheated manor house, just to name a few things. I saw no horses turned out to pasture on such a fine day. As the mistress, I find this unacceptable. I assume you now have a full smokehouse, as the hogs were recently butchered."

"We had meat." The man leaned back in his chair and regarded Polly defensively. He turned his head again and spat. "John had me sell it all in town."

"How are the hands provisioned?"

"Not that it's yer concern, but they git a cornmeal allotment. A share of the root vegetables they dig. I let 'em trap squirrels an' rabbits. Ain't no need for a winter garden. Damn niggers ain't worth feedin' fresh food in the wintertime."

Polly blanched. "They are our property and our responsibility. They still must eat. Where are the men?" She looked around. The lone slave she passed had disappeared.

"I make 'em stay in their cabins when there ain't no chores."

Silently, Polly began to enumerate chores undone. "There are always chores. The buildings can use some attention. Mend the fences. The front gate is broken. And the men can start seeds for vegetables. Churn some butter. You have chickens, albeit scrawny ones. Are there eggs? When spring comes, cover crops can be plowed, if you planted any cover crops."

Wilkins leaned forward and put his hands on the table, inches from Polly's. She noticed that his fingernails were caked with filth. She drew hers back into her lap. "How dare you tell me how to do my job? I think I know best how to run this place. I been workin' for the Stones for the last twenty years. If there is a problem, I 'spect John will tell me. Now 'zactly what is it you really here for today—Mizzus Stone?" His tiny eyes bored into hers.

The disgust and anger Polly felt toward this man made it difficult for her to sit so near him. Polly stood abruptly. "What I need, Mr. Wilkins, is an overseer who will do his job properly. One who will treat the slaves appropriately in the owner's absence and who will not misuse property. Is that clear?"

Wilkins spat on the ground again and wiped his mouth on his sleeve.

Polly ignored the appalling gesture. "My husband is due home shortly. We will return together and meet with you about the spring chores. If you are not amenable to doing as I say until then, then we can part ways at this moment." She slowly pulled on her gloves as she thought about what she would say next.

Wilkins stood. "I ain't about to start takin' orders from a woman," he barked. "If John has any objection to what I'm doin,' he'll tell me. I work for him. Not you," he growled.

Polly was stung by his words, but she kept a brave face. She stood and adjusted her bonnet. "Mr. Wilkins, if I see or hear of one more slave being mistreated, your employment will be terminated immediately." Polly grew emboldened as she spoke. "Make no mistake. Your abuse of our slaves is costing us money. Money we can ill afford to lose. Think about that. Because if there is one thing about a looming war that I am sure of, it is that an unemployed overseer with no references will be quickly drafted into the army."

Wilkins stepped forward, red-faced and trembling with rage. "Is that a threat, bitch? Does yer husband know you came out here messin' in his business? 'Cuz he and I go way back. Way back. Somehow I don't rightly think he'd take too kindly to you ridin' out here and tellin' me how to run his property. Ain't no woman's place." He spat onto the ground and glared at her.

Although the color had drained from her face, Polly screwed up her courage. "Indeed you are wrong, Mr. Wilkins, and calling me foul names does not change a thing." She looked around her and waved her hand. "In my husband's absence, this is literally my place. I can certainly visit my lawyer and provide you with an eviction notice to prove my point. Good day." She turned and angrily flounced toward the main house, Ezra limping along behind her.

As they reached the back porch of the house, she thanked Ezra and hurried around the corner toward the carriage, where Ben stood huddled in conversation with Jane. At the sight of their mistress, the pair looked at Polly nervously.

Polly's face was pale and her hands shook. It took everything she had not to collapse into the carriage after Wilkins' harsh words.

"Jane. I wanted to see you," Polly said hurriedly. "Get Lydia. I want her to come to Whitehall where she will be safe from that monster."

"Mizz Polly—" Jane interrupted.

"Do as I say," Polly snapped. "I will wait here." Tears filled Jane's eyes as she turned to go.

"Lydia?" Ben asked.

"She is the little girl whose mother was chased down recently and . . . probably killed by Wilkins. After unspeakable things were done to her mother, I am worried for the child. She can stay with Ona for now." Polly had no idea where this idea came from, but she was sure of her decision. "I cannot in good conscience allow that man to abuse anyone else," she said. "Certainly not a child."

Ben opened his mouth to speak, but then stopped himself.

Minutes later, Jane emerged, carrying Lydia on her hip. The child clung to Jane desperately and whimpered into her neck. The old woman whispered soothing words, but her own face streamed with tears.

Polly tried to peel Lydia off Jane with little success. "Ben, help me," she called. Ben gently unwound the little girl from Jane's arms and held her tightly while she cried.

"Jane, I am sorry, but I am sure this may save her life," Polly said. "I cannot leave her here— after seeing that man."

Jane wiped her face with her hands and smiled through her tears. "Mizz Polly, I know you is right. She gonna be fine. I just gonna miss her real bad, but she ain't safe here. No one is," Jane sniffed.

"Where are her things?" Polly asked.

Jane shrugged. "She ain't got nothin' else."

Ben smoothed the child's braids while Jane whispered tenderly into her little ear. "I told her Auntie Kate and Sol was there. An' that you had warm clothes and food and prob'ly some play purties for her at yo' house. I pray I ain't lied to the chile." Jane stifled a sob and turned away.

Polly patted Jane's shoulder. "Jane, I promise we will take care of her." She looked up at Ben and said, "You'd better hold her and I will drive." Ben nodded and swung up into the seat of the old phaeton with one arm, holding Lydia tightly in the other.

Polly straightened and looked at Jane sternly. "Jane, if Mr. Wilkins asks you, I came in and took the child away forcefully. There was nothing you could do to stop me, do you hear? Neither you nor Ezra could stop me. Tell anyone who may ask that I took her for a kitchen slave. I will write to my husband immediately and let him know what I have done."

Jane nodded and smiled through her tears. "Thank you, Mizz Polly. Thank you fo' savin' this baby girl."

Polly nodded and quickly hoisted herself into the driver's seat. She clicked the reins once and the phaeton moved rapidly down the long drive.

Chapter Twenty-Four

March 1, 1861

IN THE SMALL AND OVERHEATED ROOM, POLLY FIDGETED nervously. She glanced at the framed legal documents on the wall of the office and sighed. Presently, the door opened and a tall, bearded young man entered. Handsome in a scholarly way, Polly noticed he wore no coat, and his shirtsleeves were rolled up to the forearms. He carried a thick stack of papers in his arms and smiled at her over wire-rimmed spectacles too large for his thin face.

"Mrs. Stone, I apologize for keeping you waiting. We seem to have a great deal more business lately, and I am trying to see to everyone as quickly as I can." He dropped the papers on his desk with a thump and sat down wearily across from Polly. "I have taken the liberty of quickly reading over your late father's papers before coming in, in case this is in regard to his will. How may I help you this morning?"

She sighed. His face reminded her of sketches of the new president, Abraham Lincoln, who would soon be inaugurated and probably would hurl the country into full-fledged war. "I don't wish to be rude, Mr. Legarre, but I was expecting someone . . . older. I thought I had seen my family's lawyer at my home a time or two, years ago." Polly peered at the man curiously.

The man grinned. "Ah, you were expecting my father. I am sorry, but with this looming apocalypse of a war, it seems that every one of his clients has decided to get his affairs in order at the same time." He chuckled. "If you want to see him, you really will need to make an appointment," Mr. Legarre apologized. "But you may have to wait several days."

"I see. I apologize for coming into the office unannounced. Are you an attorney? You do not appear any older than I am," Polly said.

"I am, indeed. A new one, but a real attorney-at-law, nonetheless." He pointed to a framed diploma on the wall. "Harrison Legarre, Junior, Esquire, at your service. I just returned from law school in Virginia about a month ago. I am happy to be home and working in my father's legal practice." He paused and asked, "Did you know that state government men were here recently to inquire into your holdings? They did have your signature."

"Yes, Mr. Legarre," Polly said. "The governor himself apprised me of the fact. I understand they were looking for a tunnel survey. I have no knowledge of one. Was there such a document in my father's papers?"

The young man shook his head. "I saw nothing of the sort."

Polly felt a wave of relief. "Did they take anything, then?"

Legarre shook his head sheepishly. "They perused the will, looked over bank statements, and then left. There was nothing from the Blue Ridge Railway in his personal papers."

Polly relaxed, loosening the grip of her gloved hands on her bag. "I would like to engage your services in a small matter of property rights. I am in a unique situation."

Harrison Legarre's brown eyes grew wide with interest. "Ah, well let me take some notes as we speak. This is a copy of your late father's will, which you may not have seen," he said, nodding to the slim portfolio on the desk.

"Oh no, I have no questions about my father's will right now. I was told I inherited fully, at my mother's death. Isn't that correct?"

"Well yes ma'am, but—"

"I know there was no money." She continued, "But I recently married John Stone and became mistress of River Wood, as well. My questions involve my rights there."

A strange expression passed quickly across the man's face before he regained his professional demeanor. "I believe that the Samuel Stone family were also clients of my father's at one time, but I was away at school and never met the son. Congratulations on your recent marriage."

Polly nodded. "Mr. Legarre, I wish to terminate the employment of River Wood's overseer, in John's absence. You see, my husband is with Major McQueen in Montgomery. At the Convention," she added proudly. "And the overseer of his property—of our property—has behaved most abominably in his absence." She paused. "I had to take one of the slaves from River Wood home with me to Whitehall, to keep her safe from the horrible man. He abuses the women and possibly the children."

Mr. Legarre placed the pen into the inkwell and leaned back in his chair. He regarded Polly sympathetically. "Mrs. Stone, I know that with many men away, and with a war about to begin, we will have new and, until now, unknown legal challenges to address but this is not one of them."

"What do you mean?" Polly asked, her heart pounding in her chest.

"Mrs. Stone, I will put this as gently as possible. You do not have the right to terminate anyone's employment at River Wood in your husband's absence. As a woman . . . I am terribly sorry, but the law clearly would not find favor with you on this." Mr. Legarre looked genuinely sorry to deliver this news to Polly. "Now, if you have some document, some piece of paper stating that Mr. Stone has given you broad authority at River Wood in his absence, well, that is an entirely different matter."

Polly paled and shook her head. "I do not."

"I am sorry, ma'am. The law is clear," Mr. Legarre said. "As I said, with so many men preparing to leave home for war, perhaps the legislature will address property rights issues at some point."

Polly stood abruptly. "Thank you for your time, sir. I am sorry to have bothered you. I am utterly astounded at this news. What is mine is now my husband's. What is his should also be mine." She paused and said curtly, "I trust you will bill me for your time."

Mr. Legarre stood too. "Mrs. Stone, please sit down. I think I should discuss your father's will with you while you are here. I don't believe you have been made aware of its contents." He motioned for Polly to sit.

Polly was wary of talk of her father's will. "He died well before my mother. Whitehall passed to her. When she lay on her deathbed, she told me that Whitehall passed to me. My brothers both died when they were boys. I am the last member of my family," she said defiantly. "Because I bear the grave sin of being female, have I lost all rights to my own land, now that I am married?"

"On the contrary, Mrs. Stone." He pulled a bookmarked page from the portfolio and turned it to face Polly. "Your father directed that Whitehall would remain yours, solely, after both of your parents passed. His will stated that you would always retain full ownership and control over the property, even if you married, until the day of your own death. Any heirs, children or others appointed, must be named in writing by you, in order to inherit."

Polly put her hand to her mouth. She was dumbfounded. "So it is mine alone? Not even John's?"

Legarre smiled conspiratorially. "It is yours alone. Not even your husband can touch it." He leaned forward and continued in a low voice. "And as far as the slave you took away from River Wood, I do not think there is a judge around here who would find fault with your decision as wife of River Wood's owner, to relocate a slave to where the need is greater."

Polly warmed to the man. "Thank you, Mr. Legarre. I appreciate your advice. Is there anything else I need to know? I was obviously not privy to any of the particulars."

Legarre flipped through several summary pages of the document. "Yes! There was a sum set aside by your father for upkeep of the property . . ." He glanced at a paper clipped bank note. "I do not know why it was never given to you. I do apologize." He detached the check and handed it to Polly. She took the proffered check and gasped. It was for more money than she had ever seen in the ledgers at Whitehall. "Five thousand dollars? My goodness! What a surprise!"

Legarre smiled. "A happy surprise, correct? I do not know why you weren't given it at the time of your mother's death." He turned several pages and then pulled a piece of correspondence from the stack. "Our office has been so busy. Again, I apologize for the oversight.

"My mother was in ill health after his death. She died not all together in her right mind," she said. "If she knew about it, she said nothing."

"Here is something else, though. This is a letter from your grandfather's attorney in Virginia. Again, I am so sorry . . ." Mr. Legarre looked at Polly over the top of his spectacles. "Mrs. Stone, did you know that both of your mother's parents passed away in the last year?"

Polly shook her head. "Both of them? Gracious, no. Other than a few letters over the years, I did not know them. We never traveled back to Virginia. I know that my mother missed them very much. She was too ill to travel herself when she got word that my grandfather was on his deathbed."

Mr. Legarre nodded and continued reading. "It seems that your mother wrote to your grandmother early last summer, advising her of her own worsening ill health. Your grandmother then wrote a letter, to you, in care of my father." He handed the letter to Polly. "Please accept my apologies again. My father should have seen that you received this letter when it arrived in October of last year."

Polly took the letter and began to read.

September 26, 1860

My dear granddaughter Polly,

I write to you with a heavy heart, having just received the news of my daughter Mary's untimely death. Losing both my

husband and my daughter in such a short time is almost more
than I can bear. And now you have lost your mother. My own
health is not good. Mary's last letter to me was brief, but her
entire concern was that you be taken care of as her only
surviving heir. Your mother's sister, your Aunt Phoebe, will
inherit our family home and properties here in Richmond at my
death, but upon wiring instructions from your solicitor to my
mine, Phillip Pound, Esq., I have a sum of money set aside to
send to you as Mary's inheritance. It is my fond wish to meet
you in person one day, if the Lord wills it, but if we do not meet
here on Earth, we shall surely meet in heaven.

Your loving grandmother,

Elizabeth Davis Kent

Polly leaned back in her chair, brown eyes filling with tears. Harrison Legarre quickly offered his handkerchief. She dabbed her eyes and smiled through the tears. "You must think me a weak and frail woman to be crying over someone I have never met," she said.

"On the contrary, ma'am." The man shook his head kindly. "I do not think there is a body in town who does not marvel at your strength in the face of so much adversity."

Polly looked at the man. "Thank you. I am frustrated that this correspondence wasn't given to me when it arrived in the fall. I would hate to think that it was deliberately kept from me."

Legarre shook his head vehemently. "I am sure that it must have been an oversight, as my father has been so busy in the last several months and lost a clerk or two. In good conscience, I cannot charge you anything for your visit today. In fact, it would be my pleasure to act as your attorney pro bono in this matter, without charge, in order to restore my family's good name. Would you like me to write to Mr. Pound about your inheritance?"

"I would indeed, Mr. Legarre. It may be a pittance, but with the blockades and war ahead of us, any extra funds may be crucial. I trust that when the inheritance comes through, you will be prompt in contacting me?" Polly stood and extended her hand.

Legarre shook her hand and replied, "Yes, Mrs. Stone, I will see to this right away. I will notify you as soon as I hear from Mr. Pound."

Polly thanked the young man and stepped outside of the small office. She breathed in deeply and even smiled when she saw Zadoc dozing in the driver's seat of her carriage. She squared her shoulders and walked down the block to the small branch of the Bank of the State of South Carolina.

— • —

KATE STOOD IN THE KITCHEN, WATCHING SOL play on the floor while she tended a pork loin on the spit. The boy was crawling now and difficult to watch as she worked. He was occupied with a cornhusk doll and several spoons. Nearby, Ona rhythmically rocked Lydia in a chair borrowed from the big house. Lydia's eyes were closed, but she clung desperately to the old woman, even in sleep.

"Did Ben tell you what happened?" Kate whispered. "At River Wood?"

Ona nodded. "Zadoc's daddy, Ezra, heard it all. Mr. Wilkins called Miss Polly a horrible name to her face. Lawd Jesus . . ." Ona continued, "Ben said Miss Polly had words with that man, and then she came out all flustered and tol' Jane to bring Lydia out to the carriage. Ben had to 'bout peel this gal off Jane, and he held her tight the whole way here. Said Miss Polly didn't say a word the whole drive home. I do think it he'ped her to see you, Kate, when she got here yesterday. She remembered you." Ona smoothed the little girl's hair lovingly. "I guess we gone keep her here."

Kate turned the spit a few revolutions and then stood, stretching her back. "Cain't see as how this is gone go well when Mr. Stone git home, though. He got a real temper and don't like to be crossed."

"I know, but Miss Polly is stronger than you give her credit fo'," Ona said softly. "I know her longer than anyone here. She do the right thing when she know what it is."

— • —

March 4, 1861

POLLY WAS ELATED WHEN SHE RECEIVED a note from Harrison Legarre asking her to come to his office. As the late winter day was a mild one, she decided to ride Delightful into town. The dogwood trees along the way were heavy with buds about to open into snowy white flowers. Purple redbuds bloomed. Buttercups dotted the fence lines and hedgerows leading into Pendleton. The road was clear of traffic, and she made good time. Pendleton was busy with folks out on their errands, conducting business cheerfully on a mild and blue-sky day, after such a long winter. She stopped first at the post office, her mood buoyed by the lovely weather.

The postmaster greeted her warmly. "Mrs. Stone, there is a letter for you today! Postmarked Montgomery, Alabama, I do believe. I know you've been waiting," he smiled. He reached under the counter and produced an envelope addressed to her in John's strong hand.

Polly clasped her hands in delight. "Oh Mr. Phillips, how wonderful!" She took the letter and held it to her chest. "I cannot believe the delegation has been gone so long. What is the latest word from Montgomery?" she asked jovially.

The postmaster scratched his beard and considered Polly's question seriously. "Well, it takes a long time to create a whole new government, I suppose. The newspaper said they drafted a new constitution which has to be ratified—and now they're going to elect a new president. Imagine that!"

Polly smiled. This was old news to her. Clearly, the local postmaster did not have his ear to the ground as Polly had hoped. "These things do take time, I am sure. I am comforted to know that you are keeping us all informed. Thank you for the letter, Mr. Philips."

She turned to leave, but Mr. Phillips continued, "So I hear tell that there were some government folks up looking at the old tunnel your daddy and his group started."

Polly flinched, then turned around casually. "Oh, really?"

"Yes ma'am. They was wantin' information. Seein' if anyone who worked on it was still around." Phillips tugged on his suspenders and watched for Polly's reaction. "Of course, the tunnel won't do for anything, not bein' finished. Heard tell a chunk of rock fell on one of the government men. About killed him. They took off after that." He chuckled.

"I am sorry that the property can't be put to use. Good day, Mr. Phillips."

The postmaster was not finished yet. His eyes narrowed. "It's a shame. Your daddy worked hard. But rumor has it that the men condemned it as unsafe and now the whole area is blocked off."

"Well, it is too bad that the project was never completed." Polly shrugged.

The postmaster's tone softened. "These are strange times. Mark my word, Mrs. Stone, it won't be long before the mail is going to be disrupted. The Union doesn't want the post office to send mail down here now that we've seceded. Anything coming out of or going into Montgomery, Alabama, by U.S. mail is suspect. How are we going to function without the mail, I ask?"

Polly shrugged, anxious to be going. "I am sure that better minds than mine are working on that very thing as we speak, perhaps in Montgomery? You should write the new government a letter." She smiled and nodded at the man before stepping outside, clutching the envelope. She wanted to savor its contents but was too excited to wait. She stood on the wooden boardwalk, gently peeled back the seal, and opened the envelope. She pulled out a single sheet of paper and unfolded it with trembling fingers.

February 14, 1861

Dear Polly,

I apologize for not writing sooner to let you know of the goings-on at the Convention. We have been very busy attending to Major McQueen and indirectly, to Mr. Chesnut. The delegates are at work from dawn until after midnight most days and therefore we stay busy as well. Crafting a new constitution and building President Jefferson Davis's cabinet have been exciting events to watch firsthand. I count myself fortunate to be here as it all unfolds. Your friend, Mr. Beauregard, seems in the middle of it. I have had no occasion to be in conversation with him, for which I am thankful.

I trust that Mr. Roper keeps you apprised of the needs on the farm. I hope to be home with you before the Lincoln inauguration next month. It seems that the Confederacy will pause in its business and then hold a second session in the late spring.

My thoughts are on you constantly.

John

Polly refolded the letter and tucked it into the envelope. As best she could remember from the newspaper, Lincoln was to be inaugurated in early March. Several weeks from now. Her spirits sagged. It wasn't a very comforting or newsy letter, she mused. He was busy. The letter had been written two weeks earlier. A response might not even get to him before he left to return home. Polly stuffed the letter into her bag, adjusted her bonnet, and headed for Legarre's office.

— • —

"MRS. STONE, THANK YOU FOR COMING IN TODAY," Mr. Legarre said kindly as he welcomed Polly into the tiny, cramped office once more. He motioned her to a chair that he was simultaneously clearing of books. "May I offer you a glass of water?"

Polly nodded. "Goodness, Mr. Legarre, it seems that you have managed to fill this tiny room with even more books and papers than when I was here before. Perhaps a good cleaning session is in order."

Legarre laughed. "I begin to see why my father's own spacious office is overflowing. We are busier than I could have imagined, Mrs. Stone." He poured water from a carafe into a glass and handed it to Polly with a slight bow.

"Because of the war?" Polly asked. "It disrupts everything although it is an event that has yet to really begin. A letter from my husband in Montgomery took two weeks to arrive. The U.S. mail is soon to suspend its services, according to Mr. Jones."

Legarre grew solemn. "Ah, he is right about that. But a new Confederate mail service will commence next month, I am told. Mail between the confederate states will continue, but mail between the Union and seceded states will be . . . a struggle."

"Well, then I am all the more relieved that you were able to contact my grandmother's solicitor so quickly," Polly said. "Virginia has not left the Union."

"I deemed it necessary to use the telegraph, ma'am. Our office had delayed one piece of correspondence intended for you. I was determined to handle this affair correctly. So I have here a telegram from Mr. Pound, your grandparents' solicitor." He slid the telegram across the cluttered desk.

"Thank you, Mr. Legarre." Polly slowly removed her gloves as she looked at the slip of paper. "Goodness, I have never received a telegram before. I feel like a queen," she said with a grin. She briefly read the slip of paper and looked up at Legarre, wide-eyed. "It is not easy to understand, with the 'stops' and abbreviations. I see an incredibly large figure here. That cannot be my inheritance, can it?"

"Yes ma'am," Legarre said slowly.

"How would I receive this money? Gold coins heaped in a treasure chest? For it does seem a treasure to me!" She laughed. Polly could hardly wait to see John's face when she told him of their good fortune. "Have Mr. Pound send it here right away, Mr. Legarre. I can hardly believe our good fortune."

Legarre sighed and removed his spectacles slowly. "Mrs. Stone, I have to tell you something that you will not like."

Polly's heart sank.

"Mr. Pound wrote that ordinarily the money would be sent to you in bank notes. The notes would be redeemed here for gold coin if you wish. With a war, interstate banking may soon not be available, so I took the liberty of contacting officers from our local branch." Legarre's face clouded. "Mrs. Stone, there is the matter of two mortgages on your husband's property."

"I don't understand." Polly lifted the glass of water to her lips and drank deeply, hoping to steady her nerves.

"In my discussions with the bank officers, I was made aware of first and second mortgages on your husband's place. Your husband has not made payments in quite some time, so the bank has called the mortgages."

Polly shook her head dully. "I know nothing about this. What does it have to do with me?"

"I am sorry. The bank will seize the inheritance to pay your husband's debt. He is quite behind on the payments." Mr. Legarre looked at Polly with concern. "Legally, you must surrender the money to pay the debt."

"All of it?" Polly gasped. "Do you mean that I will not see a penny of my $20,000?" A wave of nausea threatened to make Polly ill.

"The debt with interest is at $22,000, ma'am." Mr. Legarre shook his head. "And he owes back taxes. About $800. When we last spoke, of course, I had no idea about this. But when I went to clear the way for your inheritance, they told me of their intent, should money become available. It is the law."

Polly fanned herself with the telegram. "This is ridiculous. I have only been married a few weeks. Surely the mortgage was taken out well before that time."

"Yes, but his debts became yours at the time of your marriage. I am sorry. It is the law," he said once more. "You can be doubly thankful that your father put Whitehall solely in your name. Because of equity law, it cannot be touched for any of your husband's debts or liens."

"Oh yes, Mr. Legarre. So very thankful," Polly snapped. "Can I assume that the five thousand dollars I deposited several days ago has also found its way to my husband's debts?"

Legarre looked down sheepishly.

Polly stood abruptly. "Then our business is completed." She pulled on her gloves. "Let the bank take my inheritance to satisfy John's debt. When the debt is cleared, notify me immediately."

Legarre rose. "Of course, Mrs. Stone. And I do apologize. I know this is not the news you came for today."

"No, it is not, Mr. Legarre." Polly was indignant. "And the irony here . . . ," she stammered. "The irony is that while I am paying off my husband's debt with my own money, I imagine that I still am not allowed to terminate Mr. Wilkins as an employee of ours, am I?"

Legarre sighed and looked at Polly with some compassion. He did not speak.

"I thought not," she said and flounced angrily out of the tiny office.

Chapter Twenty-Five

March 5, 1861

POLLY PACED THE LENGTH OF HER FRONT PORCH, eyes scanning the road and ears alert for the sound of hoofbeats. She pulled her shawl around her shoulders and fidgeted with the tassels as she paced. There had been no further mail from John. She had no idea if he would be home that week or not. The horrible notion that John had married Polly for what he could get out of Whitehall began to nag at her unceasingly. It made sense. His huge debt. Her parents both deceased. How he rushed marriage while she was still ill. Her infatuation with him made it so easy.

Polly longed for a word from Floride Calhoun. She knew that her friend had gone back to Charleston shortly after the embarrassing confrontation between John and Beauregard at Mi Casa. Perhaps a trip to Charleston would be in order if John was to be gone much longer, she thought. Then again, war was soon to come calling in South Carolina, and Charleston was assuredly the front door.

Lincoln had been inaugurated the day before, according to Roper. She had dispatched her overseer into town for news of the new northern president's inauguration. He had been gone for several hours now.

A warm breeze rustled tiny new leaves on the white oaks near the porch. Birds twittered high in the same trees. Polly thought proudly of the kitchen garden with its emerald carpet of baby vegetables, just out the back door. Broccoli, greens, English peas, onions, and carrots were coming in strong and healthy. A soft rain in the night had only sharpened the colors of early spring.

She gazed into the far distance at the hazy line of mountains that ran west to east, and looked to her like some magical dragon's spine, undulating and mysterious.

"You know what the Cherokee call those mountains?" she heard a voice call out.

Polly turned abruptly. Tom sauntered toward the house, coming from the barn. He jumped nimbly up the steps, carrying several newspapers under one arm.

"You surprised me. I was looking toward the road," she said.

"Sorry about the delay. I hurried back as fast as the horse would take me. I did get the *Courier* and the Columbia papers, though." He thrust the folded newspapers toward her. "The train from Montgomery arrives tomorrow."

Polly gasped. "Are you serious?" She grabbed the papers and looked at the front page of the *Keowee Courier*. The headline indeed declared that the train carrying the local delegate's entourage would arrive the following day. In an uncharacteristic display of relief, Polly reached up and hugged Roper's neck.

The man grinned and said, "I thought that bit of news would make you happy."

"It has been a month." She shook her head and sat down in a rocking chair. She motioned for her overseer to sit and together they began to scan the newspapers for other news of the day. Polly read the official announcement of Brigadier General G.T. Beauregard's appointment to command the state troops in Charleston. She warmed to think of how this important man had flirted with her at the Pinckney gala. Below the fold on the front page, there was a reporter's firsthand account of the inaugural festivities in Washington, and of the new Union president's promise that he would not disrupt the business of slavery in southern states. She reread the excerpt from Lincoln's inaugural address.

"In your hand, my fellow countrymen, and not in mine, is the momentous issue of civil war. The government will not assail you. You can have no conflict without being yourselves the aggressors. You have no oath in Heaven to destroy the government, while I shall have the most solemn one to preserve, protect, and defend it. . . . We are not enemies, but friends. We must not be enemies. Though passion may have strained, it must not break our bonds of affection. The mystic chords of memory, stretching from every battlefield and patriot grave to every living heart and hearthstone, all over this broad land, will yet swell the chorus of the Union, when again touched, as surely they will be, by the better angels of our nature."

She leaned forward in her chair. "Mr. Roper, this President Lincoln seems hopeful that we can avoid a civil war. He said it is in our own hands now. Whereas the confederate President Davis gave a fiery address that clearly threatens the last bit of peace. Is there any chance for a reconciliation now?"

Tom gazed at Polly over the top of his bit of newspaper. "Wishful thinking if you ask me. Has the South changed its stance on slavery? So many southern militias have already seized federal arsenals and forts all over the place. They aren't giving them up. The whole thing is a tinderbox, about to go up in flames."

Polly looked at him, worry painted across her face. "I had a large inheritance from my grandmother. It would have helped Whitehall tremendously. All of it went to pay River Wood debts."

Tom put down his newspaper and said gently, "That doesn't seem at all fair. But we're going to be fine here. Planting cotton and harvesting cotton, like we've done for the last twenty-five years. I am not going anywhere. Your husband comes home tomorrow, looks like. You're safe."

Polly folded her newspaper. "Mr. Roper, you have been with my family since before I was born. I cannot express how relieved I am that you came back after Christmas. I remember when I was a little girl and you'd chastise me for bothering the mules while the men plowed."

Tom laughed. "As I recall, you'd sit on the fence and throw peach pits at them at the turns. If I didn't feel elderly before, I do now."

"I didn't mean to offend." Polly smiled. "Going forward, you have my full assurance that your job here, your decisions on how to manage the crops and the slaves, they will not be challenged again. My father's will left Whitehall to me. I have it in writing. To me alone. I won't lose it too," Polly said.

Tom's eyebrows went up and he nodded. "Thank you, Miss Polly. I was fond of your mama and daddy. I just hope that Mr. Stone and I can come to a good understanding. Are you going to tell your husband about the little girl you took from River Wood? He's sure to see her running around. Not that I blame you. I don't want to see Whitehall's slave quarters turned into a nursery, but children of any color are not safe with Clay Wilkins."

"Yes, I have much to tell him, in fact, in regard to River Wood." She stood and handed her newspaper to Tom. "But first, I have a 'welcome home dinner' to plan with the girls and I need to get myself in better order." She touched her sloppy bun and laughed. "Will you drive me into Anderson tomorrow to meet the train?"

"I would be delighted."

Polly stopped and regarded Tom curiously. "So what do they call those mountains? The Cherokee?"

Tom gazed toward the ancient ridge of mountains to the north. "That there is the Blue Wall, Miss Polly. Na Sakonige Atsoyv."

"Again?" Polly tilted her head, confused.

"Nah sa-ko-ne-gey ah-cho-yun." He pronounced the words slowly. "The Blue Wall. It stopped your father's tunnels—it might also stop a war from coming to your doorstep."

— • —

AN EXCITED CROWD HAD GATHERED NEAR THE Anderson Depot to await the return of Mr. Chesnut's party. Blue skies and puffy white clouds drew the locals out in droves, Polly noted. Children danced in the street while a farmer strummed a Stephen Foster song on his out-of-tune banjo. Women traded gossip in small groups and craned their necks down the train tracks. The festive atmosphere was contagious.

Several men dressed in uniform carried wooden flagpoles with hastily stitched replicas of the new flag of the confederacy: a large red bar across the top and another at the bottom, with a broad white bar between. In the upper left corner was a blue square containing seven stars, for the seven states of the Confederacy.

Polly scanned the crowd for familiar faces while Tom Roper chatted with a friend from town. She hoped to see the Adgers or one of the Calhouns but did not. She made another mental note to join one of the ladies' sewing circles in Pendleton, in an effort to meet other women.

She nervously straightened the bodice of her brown silk day dress and clasped her parasol tightly. At a loss for what she would do or say upon seeing her husband for the first time in a month, she instead concentrated on the gaiety of the crowd. Their exuberance was in support of the returning men, of course, but it was primarily a celebration of the new and independent country, being birthed at that very moment in towns and villages across the South. She moved toward the outskirts of the throng and lowered her parasol to see further down the track.

"Good afternoon, Mizz Stone." The raspy drawl instantly sent a shock wave of recognition through Polly. Adrenalin coursed through her system, but she turned calmly toward Mr. Wilkins.

"I will not wish you the same, Mr. Wilkins," she replied icily.

"Guess we're both here for the same thing." He smiled. "I know you'll be happy to see John." His small blue eyes leered at her.

She returned his stare and said crisply, "Yes, it will be good to have my husband home." She turned back toward the crowd but added, "I am surprised that you are able to be here today, being such a busy man. I know my husband is looking forward to seeing all that has been accomplished at River Wood in his absence. I remember a list of improvements that he expected on his return." Her heart was in her throat. "I doubt they were accomplished."

Wilkins' face reddened and he leaned forward to spit tobacco juice. He wiped his rusty beard with the back of his hand. "Mizz Stone, me and John go way back. Way back. You might even say we was like brothers. You want to keep that in mind—ma'am." He tipped his hat and glared at Polly, before turning and getting lost in the crowd.

Polly watched him go, her knees weak. She glanced around to locate Tom. He was still engaged in conversation, his back to her.

She hoped that she held the ace card as John's wife. There was something in his relationship with Wilkins that kept John tied to the man. His threats seemed genuine. It made no sense to Polly. She prayed that her plan to oust Wilkins from his post at River Wood had a chance. Surely, once John saw his wife for the first time in a month. . . . She would surprise him with his favorite meal, and with the news that his mortgage was paid in full. She would tell him of the confrontation at River Wood. Then she could ask that Wilkins be let go—as a favor to her. She thought of the never-worn, lacy undergarments tucked in her bureau at home. She would even offer to write the small advertisement for the *Keowee Courier*; "Wanted: experienced overseer for a small plantation."

A shrill blast by the steam locomotive whipped the crowd into a frenzy. Folks craned their necks to see the first sight of the train as it rounded the bend coming into Anderson. Polly's heart skipped a beat at the sight of the ebony engine, roaring into the depot. Confederate flags were in the hands of the passengers, leaning out of the windows, waving, and shouting.

Tom worked his way through the throng to stand near Polly. "Quite a sight, ma'am. Quite a sight!" He waved his hat in the air joyfully.

Brakes squealed as the train ground to a halt. The first passenger car opened and Major McQueen stepped into the sunlit doorway. The crowd erupted in loud applause and a little brass band struck up their musically sharp version of Dixie. The former U.S. Senator wore a pale grey coat that Polly vaguely recognized. He waved his hat in the air and smiled at the crowd but did not speak. When he stepped down he was engulfed in a sea of well-wishers. Polly soon lost sight of him. She looked back up at the car and saw John emerge. Behind him, two other men from the upstate waited to disembark. Dressed in the same grey coats, she realized with shock that the men were wearing the uniforms of the state militia, a sight she had only seen previously during the annual Independence Day parade.

John seemed to scan the crowd. In her excitement, Polly called out, "John! Here I am!" John's eyes darted over the crowd and locked onto Polly's face. He jumped down from the platform, hat in hand, and made his way through the crowd. He reached for her. All of Polly's worries faded away as the young couple stood in an extended embrace.

Tom Roper clapped John on the back jovially. "Welcome home, Mr. Stone." John let go of Polly and turned to the overseer.

"I must say, it is good to see even you, Mr. Roper." John extended his hand, and the men shook hands cordially.

Roper nodded. "Let me get your bags." He tipped his hat and strode toward the train.

John turned back to his wife and sighed. His face was haggard, despite his fresh shave and haircut. "You are a sight for my sore eyes. What a month it has been." He touched Polly's face with his fingers.

"It has been quite a month here, too. I am so relieved that you are back safely. May we go home now?" Polly asked.

"Yes, let me say a word to Major McQueen. And I believe I saw Wilkins. I will speak to him briefly, and then we can take our leave, hmm?"

He moved past her into the milling crowd.

A woman sidled up to Polly and smiled. "You must be glad to have your husband home. Even if it's just for a few days."

— • —

POLLY GRIPPED JOHN'S HAND TIGHTLY AS THE carriage bumped across the deep ruts in the dirt road, relics of the long winter. John was quiet and his eyes closed once or twice before the rhythmic swaying of the buggy lulled him into a nap. Polly could not imagine the sights and sounds her husband must have experienced in Montgomery but stayed quiet as he dozed. She leaned her head on his shoulder and smiled.

Maybe everything will be better now, she thought. They could begin their marriage in earnest and prepare Whitehall for an unstable few months while the conflagration simmered on the coast.

— • —

FROM THE WASH HOUSE YARD, KATE HEARD the approaching carriage. She stood still and listened as it came to a halt. Mr. Roper's laugh carried on the breeze. As she pegged one of Polly's damp petticoats onto the clothesline, she heard John Stone's voice and closed her eyes in a silent prayer. She was so thankful that Miss Polly had given charge of the children to Ona. The petticoat flapped in the gentle breeze. Kate bent to pick up another piece of damp laundry.

"You dropped this."

Kate whirled around to find Ben standing behind her, a child's shirt in his hand.

"Oh, Sol's shirt." Kate took the piece of clothing and smiled up at Ben. "You scared me."

Ben heard the voices and his face fell. "He's back."

Kate continued to peg the wash onto the line. "Yep, and I wonder what he gonna say when he sees Miss Polly came back from River Wood with one of his slaves."

"Miss Polly will smooth things over with him. She's braver than you give her credit for. Anyway, that child won't be seen. I like to see Mama watching the kids all day. She says it's hard work, but I know she likes it."

"Your mama is a good woman, Ben," Kate said.

Ben smiled. "You remind me a lot of her. You are strong and proud. When she was young, she had some real tough times. She helped me through some mighty bad things, too. She just keeps going, like it's all going to be alright one day."

Kate stretched to hang the little shirt on the line and felt Ben's eyes following her shape as she moved.

"Well, we all got to keep goin', else we jus' gone lay down and die from worry." Kate sensed Ben's lingering gaze and she paused, looking over her shoulder playfully. "Boy, ain't you got work to do?"

Ben broke his gaze and shook his head. "Yes'm, yes, I do." He smiled and tipped his hat, turned, and walked toward the barn. Kate watched him move away, his shoulders broad and strong underneath the faded homespun shirt. He glanced backwards, caught her stare, and burst out laughing.

— • —

JOHN SAT DOWN WEARILY IN HIS FAVORITE CHAIR, as Polly rang the little bell for Cissie. He pulled out a cigar, struck a match, and lit it slowly, then puffed several times, with eyes closed. He picked up the newspaper and began to scan the local news as Polly stood nervously at the door.

Cissie entered the room timidly. "Yes ma'am?"

"Some tea please, Cissie?" Polly said.

"Make it coffee," John said, without looking up from his paper. "With cream."

Before Polly could speak, Cissie shrugged and said, "Suh, we ain't got no coffee. It all run out."

Polly nodded. "It's true, John. We've been without coffee for a few weeks. The whole district is out of coffee and cane sugar . . . the blockades, you know."

John sighed. "I see. We were able to get good coffee in Montgomery. With chicory . . . still, I shouldn't be surprised." He looked at Cissie's bulging abdomen crossly. "Good God, woman. You're with child again?"

Cissie's eyes grew wide. Polly touched the trembling woman on the shoulder. "Cissie, please. The tea? And some of that lemon cake Kate baked for Mr. Stone's return. Thank you," she said softly. Cissie hurried from the parlor.

John puffed on his cigar and regarded his wife. Polly sat down quietly next to him. This was not going according to her plan. "Tell me about Montgomery. How exciting to be involved with forming a new government."

"I sat in the gallery most of the time, awaiting instructions," he said wryly. "Not exactly in the middle of the debates, but it was interesting. President Davis expects war at any time. He wants your friend Mr. Beauregard to go after Fort Sumter, in the middle of the Charleston harbor."

Polly frowned but thought better than to remark on John's use of the word "friend." She sat down across from him. "What do you mean?"

"The federal troops there need supplies, too. While they blockade our shipments into the harbor, we are also keeping them from being resupplied. Eventually, this will come to a head." He paused. "Major McQueen had been informed about the tunnels, by the way. He has had men up that way surveying the area."

"Yes, the postmaster told me about men wandering around up there. He said that a gentleman from the Lowcountry was buying the property for a summer home. Imagine that!" Polly said, trying to lighten John's dull mood.

"Let's hope that story holds. Beauregard and his officers left Montgomery the day before our group. I expect that he is down in

Charleston now." John puffed on his pipe, lost in thought. "I don't want him sniffing around you again looking for a damned survey."

She pictured the handsome Brigadier General, so dashing and brave, but caustic when introduced to her husband. She wondered if he was even now visiting with Floride or the Pinckneys in some planter's lively salon.

"Polly, I have other news." John leaned forward and tapped his cigar over the ashtray.

She felt a knot in her belly, anticipating what would come next. John began quietly. "We leave next week for Columbia. The local militia, our company, rather, is joining up with several other militias under Colonel Rutledge. A regiment will be formed."

Polly's heart sank. "You just got here. So that is why you all were wearing uniforms on the train." Rubbing her temples with her fingers, she said, "John, there is so much I need to discuss with you. There are decisions to be made. A war coming. And we have spent only a little time together as husband and wife."

John leaned back in the chair and closed his eyes wearily. "No more talk of conventions and decisions and war tonight. I hardly want to think about any of it at the moment."

Polly stood up and faced John, her arms crossed. "I don't understand why you felt the need to participate in this whole debacle anyway. You could have waited until war was declared and enlisted only then."

There was a soft knock on the door and Cissie entered with a tea tray. No one spoke as she began to lay out the cups and saucers, the teapot, and a plate of lemon cake, on the sideboard.

Suddenly Polly barked, "Leave it, Cissie. Go, please. I'll ring if you're needed." Cissie scurried out of the room and closed the parlor doors softly.

Polly whirled around. "John, besides the fact that we have yet to get our marriage off on the right foot, there are issues at River Wood that cannot wait until you return. How long will you be away this time?" She looked at her husband, exasperation straining her young face.

John regarded his wife for a moment and shrugged. "I don't know.

None of this is going the way I expected either." He stood and walked toward the sideboard. "Polly, you have handled your affairs without me for so long. You have your Mr. Roper here, the overseer you begged me to keep. You don't need to fret." He pushed the teapot aside and reached for the whiskey decanter. He poured a shot of whiskey and downed it quickly.

Polly felt anger well up, despite her plan to stay calm. "I do not know whether to scream or cry. Please listen to me because I have some things to tell you as well. I will fairly burst if I do not speak of them."

She told him of her trip to River Wood and her unpleasant confrontations with Clay Wilkins. She spoke of the empty pantry, the fallow kitchen garden. Growing angrier as she spoke, she explained why she had taken the slave child, Lydia, away from River Wood.

"John, it is just horrible—the things he has done. You cannot possibly condone Wilkins' behavior. He cost you at least one slave. And remember, he was responsible for Duke's death."

Finally, she looked John in the eyes and said firmly, "I cannot abide that man any longer. The whole town seems to know how awful he is. When we were courting, you spoke as if you welcomed a new mistress at River Wood. You promised to send him away! In view of your extended absence, I would like to let this man go. Please. I know that with Mr. Roper's help, we can find another overseer, someone with whom I can work to keep River Wood prosperous for you, for us. Please do this for me."

John poured himself a second whiskey and downed it immediately. He poured another and returned to his chair, slumped and silent. She was prepared to argue over this for some time. The words fairly wanted to explode from her lips.

"John, you drink too much," she said.

He sipped the third drink and looked at his wife blankly. "Polly, I cannot ask Clay Wilkins to resign. Please don't ask me again."

Polly exploded with a cry, "What is this hold that he has on you? I am your wife! He is just a hired hand. He abuses your slaves. He threatens me.

369

He's a drunkard. And yet, he tells me that you are like brothers. Help me understand!" Tears welled in her eyes but she did not bother to wipe them away. "Is it money? Did he loan you money?"

John's face darkened. "Polly, stop this. I already told the man to keep away from Whitehall. He has done that. You disobeyed me and went to River Wood, where you saw things that you did not like. Do you have any idea how difficult it has been for me to run a place that my father let fall apart? He was drowning in debt. The soil is so poor it no longer grows cotton."

"I showed Jane how to start a kitchen garden," Polly began. "She told me—"

"I don't care what tales old Jane has been telling you!" He slammed the glass down. "I am not angry about the slave child you took, nor am I too upset that you allow Zadoc to visit his parents repeatedly—as if he is able to come and go as he pleases. But I do not want you going back over there again. You only make trouble. Do you hear me?" He pointed his finger at Polly. "Stay away from River Wood. If you avoid Wilkins, he cannot vex you. You have no business there."

Polly smoothed her dress with shaking hands. Her rage had nowhere to go. "Very well. The place can rot, as far as I am concerned. But there is something else you must know." She looked at John. Indeed, his face was haggard and tired from a long trip. She knew now wasn't the time to tell him of the mortgage, but she persisted.

"I paid off your mortgage, John. I paid off your mortgage—and back taxes—with money that was my inheritance. Mine. From the recent deaths of my grandparents. And I was not even allowed to intervene. Because I am your wife, that money went directly from my grandmother's estate in Virginia into your debts." Her eyes bored into his and she did not blink or turn away. "Debts I had no knowledge of, John." Her pulse pounded in her temples. "Does that give me any say in our overseer there?"

John's eyes narrowed to slits and he shook his head, "Polly, I didn't ask you to do this. The mortgages were incurred on my watch and on my watch I would have paid them off. Eventually. You cannot fault me."

Polly continued defiantly. "That is why I am so upset! All of that money spent on your debt and yet I do not have a say in how the farm is managed." She thought of what $20,000 could have done to improve Whitehall and secure their futures and felt physically ill. "If you had a strong overseer, you might not have gone into such debt. The River Wood house is shabby, the slaves are ill-treated, the topsoil has blown away, and the man called me foul words to my face!" Polly began to pace in front of John. He sat silently during her tirade, but his silence only made her angrier.

"My hands are tied. I am not the true mistress of River Wood." She paused, bitter emotions rising in her chest, while he stared blankly at the floor. She only wanted to hurt him. "And in case you thought that Whitehall would be your next conquest, you should know that it is solely mine. Legally mine. No one can inherit without my written permission." As soon as the words were out of her mouth, she regretted them. In her anger, she knew she had gone too far.

Color drained from John's face. He leaped from his chair and grabbed the back of Polly's head with one hand. The other hand he clamped over her nose and mouth. He squeezed his palm over her lips, bruising the tender flesh with his nails.

"Shut up," he said icily. "Shut up!" Polly's eyes grew wide with terror. "I am tired after a long journey and only wanted a bit of peace and quiet— which I am not finding here. The carping of an angry wife was not what I came home for. Have you become such a shrew already?" He let go of her and pushed her back onto the sofa harshly.

Polly rubbed her lips and tasted the tang of blood against her teeth. John picked up his hat. "Have Zadoc take my things to River Wood."

Polly panicked, wiping tears from her cheeks. "John, I am sorry." She touched John's sleeve tentatively. "What can possibly have gotten into me? I was just so upset by Wilkins' threat at the train station, so angry about this war taking you away from home again. Please, don't go. Don't go," she begged. "I am sorry. I so wanted us to have a happy reunion after our month apart. Forgive me."

John stared at Polly, her face now red and blotchy from crying. She sniffed, "Stay. Let me call Cissie to draw you a hot bath. I will freshen up and then we can try again over supper. Kate has cooked a roast." She smiled through tears.

Polly glimpsed the shadow that passed across John's face at the mention of Kate and for a moment, her thoughts went down a dark path.

"Very well. A hot bath would be nice," he said.

Polly quickly rang the tiny bell and Cissie reappeared, nervously rubbing her belly. Her eyes darted from Polly's bloody lip to John and back again. "Yes ma'am?"

"Draw a hot bath for Mr. Stone, please. And tell Kate that we will have supper in one hour."

"Yes, Miss Polly. Right away, ma'am." She nodded.

"No, Cissie," John Stone said smoothly.

— • —

CISSIE LOOKED AT HER MASTER WORRIEDLY. "SUH?"

"In your condition? I don't want you to carry buckets of hot water. That wouldn't be right," John said coolly.

Cissie was flustered. She wrung her hands nervously and glanced at Polly.

"Send Kate to do it," he said. "You serve my dinner and Kate can draw my bath." His face showed no emotion.

Polly knew that Cissie wanted to say something, but she shook her head to stop the woman from speaking. "Cissie, how thoughtful of Mr. Stone. Go on now. Call Kate to fix the bath right away."

"Yes ma'am," Cissie said. She closed the door to the parlor and waddled down the hall and out the back door. She moved quickly through the gathering darkness toward the kitchen house. The aroma of roasting meat scented the night air but Cissie had no appetite.

She threw open the door, hissing, "Kate! Kate!" Kate stood at the table, slicing a loaf of bread. Ona and the three children sat on the floor together playing with corn husk dolls. All of them turned to look up at Cissie expectantly.

Cissie rushed to Kate and hugged the woman, who was still holding the knife in her hand. Her words tumbled out of her mouth. "I so sorry. I so sorry," she whispered. "Mr. Stone done called fo' you to draw him a bath. I don't know what happened. He and Miss Polly done had a terrible fight and she asked me to fix him a bath. She look somethin' awful, like he hit her—she been cryin.' But he looked right at me and said fo' you to fix it. Not me."

Kate slowly put the knife down. She glanced at the children, untied her apron, and laid it on the table.

"No, no, Lawd, no. . . ." Ona stood and came over to the two women. She put her arms around both and spoke in a low voice. "Now listen to me, girls. Don't say nothin' loud enough to upset these chi'dren. Ain't gonna he'p to have squallin' babies on top of whatever else be goin' on in the big house. Kate, you finish up this meal. Take yo' time but don't bring it up to the big house until I come back, you hear?" She nodded toward the children. "Cissie, take these young'uns to yo' cabin. If you see George, don't you go tellin' him they's anything wrong. I'm just he'pin' Miss Polly out. Have him tote water. That's all. You hear me?" Both women nodded.

Kate patted Ona's face and said, "No, Ona. I have to go. He asked fo' me. I know how to handle him. If you go in there, he is one to have a fit. Just keep Solomon safe, all's I ask." Kate moved toward the door, but Ona blocked her way.

"No," Ona hissed sharply. "I know what needs to be done. It gonna take a ol' haggity woman to settle him down. Else this whole thing ain't gone go right. You'll just rile him up and cause problems for Miss Polly. Now do as I say. Start the water boiling and I'll take it upstairs with

George's he'p." She pushed up her sleeves and smiled shakily. "This ain't River Wood. We done with all that." She picked up the teakettle and said sharply, "Tell George to hurry."

— • —

ONA ENTERED THE BIG HOUSE AND CLIMBED THE STAIRS. From behind Mr. Stone's bedroom door, she heard him rustling about. She crossed into the bathroom and faced the cold porcelain tub. How had she ever lugged all that water into this room for so many years? Feeling her age, she sighed. She lit the candles placed around the room and pulled out a clean sheet of toweling. She plugged up the tub and poured the kettle of steaming water around the inner edges to warm the porcelain surface. She rummaged through Polly's collection of bath salts and potions and found one tinged with soothing lavender. She picked it up and sprinkled some of the aromatic salts into the tub.

George soon appeared behind Ona, carrying two five-gallon buckets of hot water. Ona put her finger to her lips to stop George from speaking. The man dumped the heavy pails, one after the other, into the tub. The salts released their soothing fragrance into the steamy air.

"They got more comin'?" she whispered. George nodded and quietly left the room. Ona swirled the water with her hands and imagined what a hot bath must feel like. In all her born days, the best she'd ever been able to do was wash herself with a lukewarm bath in a leaky trough or a splash in the river.

George returned with more water, sweat trickling down his face. She smiled as he poured the hot water into the tub. He patted Ona on her bony shoulder and left the room.

Ona padded softly across the hall and tapped on the bedroom door. John's voice was calm. "Come in, Kate."

Ona took a deep breath, put a huge smile on her face and turned the doorknob. "Land sakes, Massa Stone! It's me, ol' Ona. We glad to have you home, suh," she simpered. John stared, shirtless, surprised to see the old woman instead of Kate.

"Law, I drawn you a hot bath, suh, with some of good-smellin' bath salts to ease yo' muscles and soothe yo' worries after that long, important trip. It all ready fo' you, Massa Stone. And I git you some fresh clothes all laid out while you bathe." She did not give him time to answer. "Yessuh, we's cookin' up a real feast fo' you and Mrs. Stone, a welcome-home meal the likes of which no one in Pendleton be eatin' tonight." Ona fussed about the room picking up John's discarded clothing but did not make eye contact. John grabbed his shirt from the bed and put it on, without buttoning it.

"I expected Kate to draw my bath," John began angrily. "Did Cissie not understand me?" His eyes were red from drink and fatigue.

"Oh, please forgive us, suh. We all in such a happy frenzy to have you back, suh, that I asked her to keep workin' on yo' delicious supper while I git the bath ready. She made roast beef with a savory gravy, some new potatoes dug from Miss Polly's garden, greens, and some of them new baby peas just up. Miss Polly wanted you to eat like a king tonight!"

She prattled on nervously, sensing a softening in Stone's demeanor. "Yessuh, and fresh yeast rolls, suh. Miss Polly was so excited to have you home that she asked us to find some sugar. She say, 'Ona, you best find me some sugar fo' my husband's tea, and fo' a cake.' They ain't no cane sugar in all of Carolina, but she wanted to be sho' you had sugar fo' yo' tea and cake, Mr. Stone." Ona laughed as if her life depended on it.

John eyed the old woman suspiciously but Ona just smiled at him. "Now, that hot water is waitin' on you. Is there anything else I can do before I go . . . Massa?" Ona had never, ever used that word when speaking to James Burgiss, but she looked Stone in the eye and grinned when she said it.

John relaxed his scowl and sighed. "Thank you, Ona. That will be fine." He pointed his finger at the old woman and said, "But I want a huge slice of that lemon cake after dinner. A huge slice."

Ona nodded and closed the door behind her. She listened for the sound of Stone sliding into the water and then lifted her hands to the ceiling. "Thank you, Jesus!" she mouthed silently.

She quickly crossed the hall and knocked softly on Polly's bedroom door. "Who is it?" Polly asked.

Ona opened the door without a word. When Polly saw the woman, she got up from her vanity and ran to her. Ona opened her arms and Polly fell into Ona's hug. Stifling a good cry, Polly whispered, "Ona, it's all going wrong . . . terribly wrong." She clung to the woman as tears streamed down her face.

Ona held a finger against her own lips to quiet her mistress. "Sshhh now, it ain't as bad as that. What happened, Miss Girl?" Ona stroked Polly's dark head and held her as she had done years ago many times after Polly's brothers were murdered, and after Polly's father and mother died.

Ona led Polly to the edge of the four-poster bed and they sat down, Ona's arm protectively around her mistress.

"We had a big fight," she whispered. "He is going away to train for the war. Then I told him I wanted his overseer gone. I told him that he could never have Whitehall . . ." Her voice trailed off. "I was just so hurt."

Ona studied Polly's swollen lip. "I see he didn't take it none too well." She thought of the man in the bath, now her master. What a tangled-up mess. She knew enough to know that her fate, and Ben's, and Polly's, were tied up in the emotions and decisions made by John Stone. As much as she mistrusted this new side of Polly's husband, she knew he held the reins now.

Ona smoothed the hair from Polly's face and chuckled. "Oh, girl, you think you the onliest young woman ever had a fight with her new husband? Naw, it happen to everyone. Well, maybe not the hittin' part. He been away since right after you got married. You both nervous and scared and don't know each other well as of yet. It ain't so bad. I can tell you what to do to fix it up, though." She rubbed Polly's back like she did when Polly was a little girl.

Polly wiped her eyes with her hands and looked at Ona expectantly.

Ona leaned closer and whispered, "Take yo' husband a glass of whiskey while he in the tub."

Polly's eyes widened. "He's had enough. He should apologize to me!"

Ona nodded. "But men want to be treated like kings. Take him a whiskey. Then come back in here and fix yo'self up real pretty. Kate's got that good dinner 'bout ready. Y'all can set down and have a nice meal, only talk about happy things. Build him up, girl. Make him feel important. He gonna be a soldier now." Ona sat up tall and mimicked a solemn soldier in full salute.

Polly smiled. "I suppose you're right. I yelled at him. And then he threatened to leave me and go back to River Wood!"

"Well, that ain't gonna happen. But men are prideful creatures." Ona stood and patted Polly's cheek. "And Miss Girl, one more thing . . ." She grinned mischievously.

Polly looked up at the slave woman. "Yes? What else?"

Ona whispered, "Them lacey new underclothes? From Mrs. Batson's shop? I think it time to put 'em on, hmm?" Ona patted Polly's cheek. She put her finger to her lips. "Shhh . . ." She chuckled and left the bedroom quietly.

Ona scurried back to the kitchen house and found Kate setting the roast and side dishes on the table, to be carried into the house. She closed the kitchen door behind her and leaned against it heavily. "I am too old fo' this," she said wearily.

Kate looked at Ona fearfully. "Tell me what to do."

"You fine fo' now. I settled the man down some, and I think Miss Polly's gone have him under control tonight. Best not to flaunt yo'se'f by goin' into the big house tonight. I git Cissie to he'p me serve. You stay here. Polly said he's goin' away again soon. If we can just git him gone without another fight, an' without him seein' you, we be alright."

— • —

OVER THE NEXT SEVERAL DAYS, Ona left the cooking and the care of the three children to Kate, while she and Cissie took over the many spring chores in the big house. Warm weather meant hauling all the carpets and drapes to the clothesline to beat out the dust and dirt. It was hard on Ona's back, but the reward was spending more time in the breezy outdoors underneath flowering dogwood trees.

From the clotheslines, Ona could watch the comings and goings between the big house and the outbuildings. She directed Kate to stay away from the paths to the barn and smokehouse where John Stone might see her on his way to the pastures. When John was headed to Tom Roper's cabin, Kate was sent across the property to the washhouse with Cissie and the children. Ona did her best to keep Kate out of view, and to bow and scrape whenever she spoke to her new master as he passed.

She noticed that Polly and John spoke to each other more civilly and was relieved to see evidence that he was sharing Polly's bed once more. Ona believed that Whitehall might be on an even keel again. Once John left to train for battle in a few days, she prayed that life might return to some semblance of normal. With Miss Polly healthy and happy, three growing children to tend and Cissie's baby on the way, Ona believed she would be able to put the dream of freedom behind her and focus on life for herself and her son. She watched Ben follow Kate's every move, and she knew deep in her heart that he favored the woman.

George's clanging bell rang earlier each morning as sunrise backed itself up. At Tom Roper's direction, the slave gardens were turned and summer seeds sown. New calves frolicked near anxious mothers in the pasture and Polly's beds of lettuces, chard, peas, and spinach flourished in the sunshine. From her cabin, Ona spotted John and Polly on several warm mornings, out walking the fields, hand in hand. She prayed that all was right with the young marriage, so fragile, so much at stake.

The hands knew that backbreaking fieldwork would begin again in earnest as the weather warmed. Any day, the truly backbreaking work would commence, as King Cotton would be planted, followed by corn. Then, harvest season would begin when the winter wheat was gathered. The cycles of seedtime and harvest on a plantation meant a never-ending list of chores at Whitehall.

Each morning, at Polly's request, Ben checked on Delightful, who was due to foal any day. Although Zadoc oversaw the other livestock, Delightful received Ben's attention. Finally, early on a rainy Friday shortly before John Stone was due to leave, Ben and Zadoc found themselves tending to the mare in her labor. Delightful was struggling to birth her first foal and was near exhaustion. She lay still in the straw of her stall, heaving and whinnying. Foam flecked her lips and her body was wet with sweat from her efforts.

— • —

THUNDER RUMBLED AND SPRING RAIN PATTERED on the barn roof. Tom Roper leaned over the top of the stall. "Dammit, you're going to need that winch, Ben."

"Should we tell Miss Polly?" Ben asked.

Tom nodded. "Zee, go to the big house and let Mrs. Stone know that Delightful is foaling."

Zadoc nodded and ran from the barn quickly.

In a wooden toolbox near the back of the stall, Ben found the equipment that he would need to pull the foal free from its mother. In the smithy, he had designed a sort of winch that had been quite helpful in birthing stubborn calves, using leather straps wrapped around the stuck calves' legs. Ben knelt by the horse's flank. The men conferred quietly as they watched the mare struggle with pain.

A soaking wet Zadoc returned quickly. "Miss Polly comin'. Mr. Stone's comin' too," he gasped. "What we gonna do?"

Tom crossed his arms. "Ben has done this before, Zee. You follow his lead. That horse doesn't like me anyway."

Ben stood. "We're going to try to turn this foal. If that doesn't work, I have to use these straps and the winch to pull it. She's tired. She can't push this baby out." Ben pointed at Zadoc. "You have to keep her still if she tries to stand."

"What's wrong with her?" cried Polly, running from the entrance to the barn. She had thrown on an old oilcloth slicker over her clothes, and her hair was matted to her head. Water dripped in puddles at her feet. Ben put his finger to his lips to quiet his mistress. John arrived behind his wife, and stood still, taking in the scene.

"Foal's breech," Tom said quietly. "I'm sorry, Miss Polly. Ben's going to try to turn it. He's done it with calves."

They watched as Ben crouched in the straw and stroked Delightful's ebony flank, soothing the mare with his whisper. He turned to Zadoc. "You hold her bridle, Zee. She's more easy with you than Mr. Roper."

"Put me to work," Polly said quietly. "I can do something here."

Ben looked up at Polly. "You want to help, you can stroke her flank and talk to her while Zee holds her head and I pull. She would probably be calmer with you than anyone else."

"Now just a minute here," John said sharply. "I don't want my wife in this cramped stall. That horse is liable to kick and hurt someone."

"Of course, I will help. She's my horse." Polly moved into the crowded stall and knelt by Delightful's side. She leaned over and put her cheek on Delightful's flank.

"Sweet girl," she murmured soothingly. "It's alright. We're going to get your baby out for you." The horse snorted in a contraction but stayed still as Polly ran her hand down her swollen side.

Ben nodded at Polly and Zadoc before gently pushing his hand and forearm into the mare's swollen birth canal. His face was lost in concentration as he felt for the foal's head and legs. Polly continued to stroke the horse and whisper to her. Roper and Stone watched from the stall entrance.

"All I get is legs and sharp hooves," Ben sighed. "The foal's head is thrown backwards and his legs are splayed. I can try to turn the baby, but it doesn't look good, Miss Polly."

Polly sat up. "Please, Ben. Please." She looked at Ben with desperation. "Please."

Ben shook his head. "I'm trying. Alright, let's go. Zadoc, hold tight. Miss Polly, if she decides to get up, just back away real fast. No sense in you getting hurt trying to hold her down. I'll try to turn the baby by its back legs first. Then I'll put the straps around whatever I get and pull."

Polly nodded obediently. Zadoc tightened his grip on the bridle. Ben reached back inside the mare. He broke the bag of waters and steaming liquid gushed out of the birth canal, soaking his pants. He felt with one hand until he found the foal's back legs. He pushed on the baby's legs, rotating the little body in the confines of its mother's womb. He pushed and twisted again. Polly whispered in Delightful's ear and scratched her withers as the horse became increasingly uncomfortable.

Sweat poured down Ben's face as he worked. After long minutes, he realized he had been holding his breath and he gasped for air and leaned back against the wall of the stall. He looked at Polly. "I think I turned him some. But I'm going to have to try to pull him out—his back legs first."

Ben wound the ends of the leather strap around his upper arm and inserted the strap into the birth canal. He probed again for the spindly legs and looped a section of the strap over the baby's sharp hooves. He cinched the back legs together tightly in a noose and then wrapped the ends of the straps into the winch. When they were secure, he nodded at Zadoc. A contraction tightened the mare's belly and she whinnied. "Alright, here we go." Zadoc nodded and pressed the mare's head and strong neck toward the ground.

"What's he doing?" John barked at Roper.

"The horse isn't as likely to struggle when her head and neck are weighed down. It doesn't hurt her. And it'll keep her from jumping up and hurting your wife," Tom said quietly.

Ben began to turn the winch, tugging at the strap gently at first. Nothing. "Wait for the next contraction," he said calmly. He sat with his spine braced against the back wall of the stall, and his boots planted firmly on either side of the horse's rear end. Sensing another contraction, he pulled as the horse's body spasmed. When the contraction ended, he wound another length of the strap around the winch. With each contraction, Ben was able to pull a bit more of the strap out and wind it up. He was pulling so hard that the straps cut into his flesh, but he did not loosen his hold.

"Again," he said and pulled with all his strength as Zee held the horse's head still. Ben's temples dripped with his sweat, and his breathing was labored. "Again."

After twenty minutes of pulling, Ben leaned back and gasped. "Zee, at the next contraction, I need you to pull her head forward as hard as you can. Alright, one more time." He took a deep breath and tugged with a groan. Delightful struggled to rise, but Polly threw herself across the horse's neck as Zadoc pulled the mare's head forward.

"Polly, get out of there!" John yelled. He tried to move into the stall but Tom blocked his way.

"She can do this, Mr. Stone. Nobody on this farm knows that horse better than Polly. Delightful was a gift from her father. She knows that horse," Tom said reassuringly.

Ben's arms shook and the muscles in his neck bulged as he strained to birth the foal. Feces covered his arms and smeared his face. Polly wiped sweat from her brow with her muddy hand. "Ben, please. Keep trying."

The horse strained with a contraction and Ben tightened his grip and pulled, groaning as he did so. Suddenly, tiny hooves poked out from under Delightful's tail. Ben pulled again and the hind legs emerged, cinched so tightly that the cord was cutting into the baby's flesh. Ben worked quickly to free the matchstick legs and then rubbed them briskly. On Delightful's next contraction, he pulled with his hands as the rear end of the foal emerged. He knew he needed to get the head out quickly before the baby tried to inhale. Polly stroked the mare tenderly.

Ben struggled to grasp the slick foal with his hands. After the midsection was birthed, Delightful heaved and groaned once more and the foal's head slid out limply. The tiny body lay still on the straw. Ben opened the baby's mouth. Its gums and tongue were deathly white. He used his finger to clear mucus from its throat and began to rub the baby briskly from head to toe.

"See if she'll get up now." Ben nodded toward the mare. Zadoc and Polly let go of their holds on the horse. Delightful lay panting, as another wave overtook her body in a spasm. In one final contraction, the steaming afterbirth emerged. Ben grabbed a pocket knife from the wooden box and sliced the umbilical cord. The mare stumbled to her feet and turned to regard the slimy creature that had come out of her body. After a few sniffs at its head and behind, she began to clean the baby with rhythmic strokes of her long dark tongue.

Polly said a silent prayer as she watched Delightful clean her baby. The foal appeared lifeless. "Is he dead?" she whispered.

"If the mama can't bring it back, none of us can," Ben said softly. "Let's just wait a minute and see."

Slowly, as the mare bathed the foal, Polly noticed the faintest flutter of eyelashes. Moments later, the baby sneezed and opened its brown eyes. It struggled to lift its wobbly head and Delightful slathered the baby's face with her tongue.

"I knew Delightful was a strong horse. Looks like this new one will be, too." Ben grinned at Polly.

"Well, I'll be darned." Tom chuckled. "I think he's going to make it alright."

"Thank you, Ben. Thank you for saving my girl and her baby." Polly smiled.

"Yes, that was wonderfully handled," added John. "You certainly have a way with horses, boy. Tom, remind me to send him to River Wood with that contraption the next time a foal is due." He clapped Tom on the back, turned, and walked out of the barn.

Ben looked at Polly, crouched in the straw, stroking her new foal.

Chapter Twenty-Six

March 13, 1861

"ONA!" JOHN BARKED. HE DESCENDED THE STAIRS QUICKLY, hat in hand. His grey uniform was starched and pressed. Brass buttons were polished. His black leather boots had been buffed to a glossy sheen. Polly met him at the bottom of the stairs and beamed at her handsome husband. She hoped they had indeed repaired the breach in their young marriage. Still, he seemed eager to be off again.

Ona scurried to meet her master. "Yessuh?" she asked meekly.

John placed his hat squarely on his head and admired himself in the hall mirror before remarking, "Thank you for your attention these past weeks. You have been very good to me. And I hope I don't outdo Colonel Rutledge this morning. I look rather sharp, thanks to your care of my uniform."

Ona smiled, her heart pounding in her chest. "Thank you, suh."

His gaiety the morning of his departure frustrated Polly, but she was determined to keep a sweet spirit this day of all days. John wasn't sure when he would return. His orders told him where and when he would depart for Columbia, but not if and when he would be able to come home. He did not expect that his regiment would see any action and hoped that any skirmish would be over by summertime. Polly's only comfort was that John was leaving on good terms, and that other southern wives were in the same predicament.

She had done everything in her power to restore herself as a loving, obedient, and desirable young wife. She blushed at the thought of their nights together. I'm truly a married woman now, she mused. She prayed that her monthly time would not arrive as usual.

"My husband will be the best-dressed man at the station. Why, Rutledge himself may promote Mr. Stone to a general—just at the sight of him." Polly laughed and patted his lapel playfully. She readjusted his hat and placed it jauntily atop his blonde curls. "Perfect," she proclaimed proudly.

The pair locked arms and continued out the front door toward the carriage where Zadoc and Tom Roper stood waiting. John had met with both overseers the day before, and he seemed confident that both farms would be in good hands until his return. Without that debt hanging over his head, Polly hoped that River Wood could manage with Wilkins at the helm until John's return. She absolutely had no plans to visit that wretched place again.

"Mr. Stone, the best of luck to you, sir," Roper said, extending his hand. He shook hands with his new boss cordially.

"Thank you, Tom. Remember what I said about any trouble." Stone eyed Tom steadily and the overseer nodded.

"We'll be fine. Everything is under control."

Polly wondered to what trouble John was referring but decided to stay silent. She hoped she would be spared the knowing. John helped her into the carriage, where she arranged her skirts and waited. John climbed in beside her. Zadoc clicked the reins and the carriage lurched down the drive.

— • —

FROM BEHIND THE PARLOR DRAPES ONA watched the carriage leave. As soon as it turned onto the main road, she felt a physical release of the tension she had carried for days. She heaved a great sigh and sat down wearily on the plush parlor settee.

Grateful for this brief reprieve, she was determined not to think about what lay ahead when John would return for good. That's weeks away, she reasoned, and there was finally space to breathe for a while.

— • —

BEN DIPPED THE LAST NAILS INTO THE TROUGH and watched the water hiss with a release of steam. He looked up when he heard the bump and rattle of the carriage as it made its way down the drive. He smiled and put down his tongs. A set of nails for Delightful's shoes was finished and Stone was gone. He left the building and made his way to the barn to speak with Zadoc.

Zee was in the process of mucking out stalls when Ben called to him. "Zee! He's gone!" Ben grinned broadly.

Zadoc paused and looked up toward the haymow. "You can come down now," he said. From behind a hay bale, Lydia peeked down at Ben and Zadoc with wide eyes.

Ben chuckled. "It's alright. He's gone for a while. Come on out and help Uncle Zee with these stalls. He has let you play up there with your corn dollies long enough," he winked at Zee.

Zee laughed. "I'm done here. I'm going to the pasture to check on the foal." He leaned the shovel against the wall and turned to go.

Ben heard Lydia's feet run across the floorboards overhead, and then watched as she appeared, coming down the ladder in her bare feet. She clutched two of the dolls Ona had made for her, and her plaited hair was full of wheat straw.

She looked up at Ben and grinned as he plucked the straw from her hair. "Lawd, girl, you a mess. You spread the fresh straw in each of these stalls that Zee cleaned out. Do that for him. You have to earn your keep around here," he said. He grabbed the pitchfork and shoved it at Lydia.

"Ben, that chile is too little fo' a pitchfork. An' she ain't supposed to be out here, not without her shoes," Ona clucked from the barn entrance. She crossed the floor, hands on hips. "Lydia, where yo' shoes Miss Polly gave you? Ain't every little girl gits new shoes."

The girl shrugged but stayed mute. In fact, Lydia had not spoken since she came to Whitehall. Her appetite and demeanor told Ona that she was healing from the grief of losing her mother, but whether she could speak remained in question. She worried that the child had seen terrible things at River Wood and was traumatized.

"Go on, now," Ben said. "Do as Ona says." Lydia skipped out of the barn and toward the slave cabins.

"Lawd, that chile sho' has taken a shine to you, Ben," Ona clucked.

"She still hasn't said a word. You think she can talk?" Ben asked as he leaned against a stall.

Ona shook her head and said quietly, "Kate worried about her, too. Ain't never heard her say a word at River Wood. But you remember how long it took Miss Polly to talk after what happened when she saw her brothers killed? And you, Ben, you wasn't the same after that day yose'f," she said. "If Lydia saw any of the things Wilkins did to her mama, I'm surprised she can even act a chile . . ."

"Well, she doesn't like being around Mr. Stone either," Ben said.

"Who does, son? Who does?" Ona chuckled. "But he gone again. Thank the good Lord. He gone. So we can all breathe a sigh of relief for a few mo' weeks. I may dance a jig."

Ben looked at his mother tenderly. "Ma, what do you think about Kate?"

Ona's eyes grew wide and she smiled, hands on hips. "What you think about Kate, son?"

"I think she's mighty nice, and easy on the eye," Ben grinned. "I am sweet on her. Her baby, Sol, could use a daddy. . . . You think I have a chance with her? Should I ask to court her?"

Ona's smile faded and she reached up to pat her boy's whiskered cheek.

Ben squeezed his mother's hand. "Aw, Mama. You know you'll always be my first gal."

Ona sighed. "Oh, my little boy. I jes' can't help wonder about what Mr. Stone will do if he finds out."

Chapter Twenty-Seven

April 14, 1861

POLLY SAT ASTRIDE DELIGHTFUL AND WATCHED AS THE hands began to plow the last section of acreage designated for cotton. The day was warm and Polly enjoyed the feel of sunshine on her face, her bonnet stuffed in her saddle bag. The smell of freshly turned earth and a gentle breeze conspired to elevate her mood. She had not had a letter from John since his departure, but carefully read the weekly papers, which supposedly followed the regiment's training schedule in Columbia and brought the news of the day to Whitehall.

The city of Charleston was reportedly enraged at the Union's siege of Fort Sumter. Scathing editorials from Unionists and Confederates denounced their opponents in the vilest terms. Polly marveled that Brigadier General Beauregard was truly at the helm of the armed forces stationed there. Newspaper accounts wrote of a city at fever pitch. Civilians stood on rooftops watching the goings-on in the harbor. All business was practically shut down. It seemed to be a great chess match, and checkmate was imminent.

But Charleston was a world away from Whitehall. The most excitement Polly had seen was getting cotton in the ground. In the distance, three mule teams worked at a pace to plow the last red dirt field allocated to King Cotton. The plows kicked up clouds of red dust. Near the tree line, Polly could see George cracking his whip harmlessly over the heads of her field hands at the turn.

Polly heard the sound of hooves and turned toward the road. She squinted in the bright sunshine and watched as Tom approached at a gallop, cutting across the lawns. She squinted and noticed that the overseer was indeed wearing a pistol and had his rifle stashed in its saddle scabbard. She wondered if this was at John's insistence. She had never seen Tom armed before.

She reassured herself that her men were neither lazy nor prone to violence. Polly doubted they knew there was trouble on the coast. She refused to worry and was doubly thankful that because of their early start this season and good weather. There was no need to enlist the help of River Wood slaves with planting. She had no plans to visit River Wood ever again.

Polly felt good, she realized. Happy. Spring alone seldom did that for her. But this year, even though her husband was away playing at war, and she had no other family to speak of, watching the rhythmic activity and new life of the spring season at Whitehall brought her joy. Whitehall was hers. The cotton was going in ahead of schedule. There were three new lambs, two calves, and Delightful's foal in the pastures. The soil was fertile and the crops thrived.

Polly was surprised at how the bright laughter of the three slave children made her smile. Cissie's baby would arrive later in the summer and there would be four slave children at Whitehall. Still too young to work in the fields, Polly was glad to get the children involved in some small chores early on, and so Silas and Lydia were responsible for collecting eggs and cutting grass for the chickens each morning.

She thought of the other reason for her good mood. Her time of the month was late. She dared not ask Dr. Adger about such things. She wished

Floride was at Mi Casa so she could share her news. She placed a hand on her belly and smiled.

She scanned the field again and flicked the reins, ready to head back to the house. She was satisfied that George had things well in hand. There would be an extra ration of meat and flour for him and his little family that night.

Tom was still riding toward her at a breakneck pace, so she urged Delightful toward him. "What is it, Mr. Roper? You are riding like you have the devil himself on your tail!" she called.

"It's war! War!" he shouted. "The Confederacy finally attacked Fort Sumter and the Union army surrendered. General Beauregard sent 'em packing. The Union had relief ships waiting outside the harbor to collect their troops."

Polly was too shocked to respond. Tom pulled up next to her and shoved a newspaper toward his young employer.

Polly shook her head and said slowly, "Are you sure?"

"Look and see. I rode into town to see the farrier. When I came out, the newspapers had just been delivered." He thrust the paper toward Polly. "They are asking for volunteers down at the post office and selling out of everything at the Mercantile. They did not let me have anything on credit. Graybacks only. Confederate dollars, Mr. Jones said. So I couldn't get the leather we needed for new reins—unless you have Confederate money to spend."

As the full realization of what Roper said dawned on Polly, she took the proffered newspaper with a shaky hand.

"You had a letter at the post office, too. From your husband. But don't you go worrying about him. His regiment appears to be far away from Charleston," Roper offered, noticing Polly's frown. He pulled a crumpled envelope from his vest.

"Mr. Roper, don't you understand? What will happen to the cotton market?"

— • —

THE NEXT MORNING, POLLY SENT TOM back to town early for any updates out of Charleston. While she waited for him, she rocked furiously back and forth on the porch, in the same rocking chair her mother had brought down the old Wagon Road. The fingers of one hand gripped the arm of the chair. In her other hand, she held the letter from John.

Written over a week before the conflagration on the coast, it contained little in the way of news. John had written of how bored his unit was with drills and marching, how weary already of barracks and mess tent meals. Many of the men had taken ill from the terrible food, and that was before they had even left Columbia. He had closed his letter with "Yours, John."

Polly didn't know whether to laugh or cry. She knew from his time in Alabama that John wasn't much of a letter writer but had hoped for more affectionate posts after their recent time together. She laid the letter aside and ticked through a list of items to discuss with Roper on his return from Pendleton, absentmindedly chewing her lower lip as she rocked.

The morning was cool with the promising scent of rain. Thunder rumbled in the distance. Polly hoped the rain would be a gentle shower, just enough to dampen the earth. Now was not the time for a deluge, she fretted. Oh, how they needed this cotton crop. Cotton kept the farm running. It was the lifeblood of Whitehall and so many upstate Carolina farms. War would surely disrupt the economics of producing and marketing this all-important crop. She looked down at the newspaper in her lap. The dateline was April 14. A great deal could have happened in 24 hours.

Polly tipped her head back and looked at the pale blue porch ceiling. She lay her hands on her belly and sighed. It was so hard to sit and wait. *What on earth is taking Roper so long in town?* she wondered.

"Looks like we're in for some rain," said a familiar deep voice coming from around the corner of the house. Ben appeared, leading Delightful by the bridle. Her young colt followed closely behind on spindly legs. Polly jumped up from her seat.

"Miss Polly, what has you so on edge this morning? You about jumped out of your skin." Ben looked up at Polly and pointed toward her face. "You hurt your mouth." He stared at her unpinned hair in a jumble around her shoulders. "What's wrong?"

She blotted her lips with her handkerchief. "Gracious. I am bleeding. I bit my lip, I guess. I'm waiting on Mr. Roper," she began. "We are at war, Ben. Against the Union itself. I sent him to town for news."

Ben looked up at Polly with sad eyes. "Over what?" he asked.

She looked at him quizzically. "What do you mean, over what?"

Ben stroked Delightful's nose and watched Polly as she considered her answer.

"I–I don't really know," she said, avoiding his gaze. "I suppose over slavery. The Union wants to limit our ability to own slaves and South Carolina believes it is an issue of concern." She looked past him, scanning the main road.

Ben nodded. "Oh, it's an issue of concern. You're right about that. Is South Carolina going to fight the whole Union army?"

Polly couldn't tell whether Ben was being sarcastic. She began to pace the length of the porch, her heels clicking on the wooden slats. "Ben, I do not wish to debate the Confederacy's stance on slavery with you. I do my best to treat you fairly. It's all I can do," she snapped. "I cannot let you go." There was no answer.

"Where are you headed with my horses?" Polly asked, changing the subject.

Ben calmly answered, "Just put new shoes on Delightful. We had a good canter. Moving them to the front pasture now. Found the baby wandering toward a patch of something new along the fence line in the back pasture. Think he just had a nibble. But Mama said it's deadly. She said you brought it back from Charleston."

Polly's attention switched to the horses. "My Oleander? I didn't know it was poisonous. Floride's gardener gave it to me. I asked Zee to plant it somewhere sunny. How on earth did it end up in our horse pastures?" she said, hands on hips.

"You told Zee to plant it somewhere sunny. I guess he did," Ben said wryly.

Polly remembered the pretty plants that James had wrapped up and delivered to Ona on her behalf. "I didn't know that oleander was poisonous. It was such a pretty plant. Why would her gardener have been so careless?"

Ben smirked. "Hard to say. But I'm glad I found it, or this little boy here would be in a heap of hurt. Zee's pulling it out now. Can't burn it. It's deadly even to burn, Ma said." He nodded toward the colt. "I'll dose this boy some charcoal. That's the remedy. The most he'll have is some sloppy manure." Ben turned to go.

"I am sorry. I should have asked more about the plants before taking them from Mrs. Calhoun's garden." She wondered if James had known of oleander's toxicity. Of course he did, she realized.

Ben nodded and began to lead the horses away.

"Ben—wait!" Polly said. She came down the steps quickly and faced him. She patted Delightful's withers and leaned her head onto the mare's broad side. "Thank you. Thank you for taking care of my girl. And the foal. I do appreciate it."

"I know you do," Ben said. "You got a name picked out for him yet?"

Polly ignored Ben's question. "I need you to know something," she began. Ben looked down at her. For a brief moment, she felt just like the little girl who begged him to teach her to read his family Bible. The moment passed. Time had certainly changed her. No longer a lanky slip of a girl with ringlets and pinafores, she was beautiful, grown and married, and his mistress.

"What is it, Miss Polly?" he asked.

"Your mother has always been so good to me and I wanted to give her freedom. I truly did. I wrote a note stating that she was to be freed. She may have shown you. I didn't know that it is against the law to free a slave. I just want you to know that. I really hope that she can forgive me." Polly nervously tucked a loose strand of hair behind her ears and waited for Ben's response.

"Shouldn't you tell her?" Ben asked sharply.

Polly blanched. "I did tell her. But I wanted you to know, too. We grew up together. I value your work here. I know that you work hard. I will never be able to apologize enough for Wilkins beating you while I was away. It won't happen again. But thank you for working hard on my behalf." She fidgeted with her newspaper.

Ben remained silent, so Polly continued nervously, "The cotton went in quickly this year. Thank you for helping get it in. I know it meant your work in the smithy piled up." The effort of thanking a slave was difficult. "I don't know what will come of this fight with the Union. I hope and pray it doesn't spread into the upstate. I worry about the cotton."

"The cotton?" Ben scowled at Polly, leaned to the side, and spit forcefully. Polly stepped back, alarmed.

He shook his head angrily. "I have been a slave all my life. If, like you said, the Union is fighting against your right to own people, I hope and pray that fighting does spread into the upstate, to Fort Hill and River Wood—and Whitehall. To free me and Mama and the others here. Because once war starts, it can't stop until one side or the other wins outright. You can't imagine how all of us long for that day. Not one of us would lay a hand on you. We aren't monsters, but you can't honestly believe that if offered a chance to get away from here, any of us would want to stay. So a war that means I could be free? Like you or Mr. Wilkins? That's what I pray for then. War." Ben turned and led Delightful and her colt away.

Polly stood stunned and chastened. She hadn't realized that Ben thought about his freedom. All her life she had known him to be a person unafraid to say what was on his mind, but the clarity of what he said hit her hard. "Free. Like you." She watched him walk the horses toward the front pasture before she turned and climbed the front steps.

It was close to noon before Polly heard Tom Roper knocking loudly on the front door. Before Cissie could get to the hall, Polly had yanked open the heavy oak doors and beckoned her overseer inside.

"Come in, Mr. Roper. What on earth kept you?" she asked, more irritated than curious.

Tom stepped inside. "President Lincoln has ordered 75,000 troops to fight the southern rebellion." He removed his hat and continued, "In the district, they've mustered everyone that can fight. The sheriff has a deputy down on the square—signing up a local militia made up of overseers and those too old to fight, but the Confederacy itself is asking for all able-bodied men to enlist."

Polly's hand flew to her mouth and she gasped.

Tom nodded as if he could read her mind. "Yes, Miss Polly. This is really war. I guess Mr. Stone's in the thick of it soon enough. But don't fret about Whitehall. Although overseers and farm managers are asked to enlist, we are to stay where we are for the time being." He smacked the newspaper and added, "In case there is slave trouble, we are the bona fide local militia." She thought of Clay Wilkins as a member of a militia and shuddered. Polly crossed the room and closed the parlor doors quietly.

"What will you do?" Polly asked.

"It's planting season, ma'am. And I am apparently not going anywhere." He fanned himself with his hat. "I'm thirty-six. An older man like me isn't likely to be called up right away anyway. And I doubt we're going to see any action up here, so no need to worry. All the fighting is down on the coast."

Polly thought of General Beauregard and the tunnels and shook her head. "I hope you're right."

Tom handed her the folded newspaper and added, "It says your husband's regiment is still in Columbia but is heading to Charleston soon."

Polly sat down on the settee and motioned for Roper to take a seat as well. She scanned the newspaper for a few minutes and then slapped it down on the table. "Blockades! We're as far away from the coast as one can get in South Carolina. Yet these blockades threaten to do us in."

"It's mighty bad news," Tom remarked. "There wasn't much left in town. Certainly, no tea. No tobacco or sugar. Only a few cans of beans. I'm going to take to chewing birch bark before this is over." He chuckled.

Polly tapped her fingers on the table, deep in thought. "Mr. Roper, tobacco and tea may be the least of our worries. We shall have to be completely self-sufficient until this blows over. You can hunt, and we have meat in the smokehouse. We have seed corn, and vegetables . . . milk cows and laying hens. . . . Be sure the hands tend their garden. But cotton? Let's not hang our fortunes on selling cotton through the markets in Charleston and Savannah this year. This might end before cotton harvest, but what if it doesn't?"

Tom shook his head. "This is purely politics, and we don't have the resources down south to run this out for long." He scratched his beard thoughtfully. "Once men are getting killed, one side or the other's going to give way," he said hopefully. He glanced at Polly's worried expression and added, "Your husband didn't seem too worried when he left." He shrugged. "He should be well away from harm."

Polly stood up and crossed her arms in resignation. She wondered who would make the next move in this giant chess match. If troops were being sent to the coast, it might mean that the Confederacy planned to fight the blockades. She pushed the thought from her mind.

"This is going to test us," she said. "There won't be an easy way to get cotton to market if the Union has the ports blocked. We could try to get it as far as Columbia and see if the market will come to us there . . ."

Tom stood. "I am sure that every upstate planter is thinking the same thing. Everyone in Charleston will be sending their valuables there too, for safekeeping. I'm sure of it."

He began to pace the room, lost in thought. "And then Columbia becomes more of a target. It is the capital city. There is a large population, a state college, a great deal of commerce and banking. The Union will want it destroyed."

"How do you know so much of Columbia?" Polly asked.

Tom chuckled. "This might surprise you, but I am a city boy from Columbia. I even went to South Carolina College there. But life stepped in and things changed when my father died. I was nineteen. I was six months shy of a degree in the classics. But I had to find work to support my mother. And here I am."

"The classics?" Polly's eyes were wide with surprise. "Really, Mr. Roper. You may be the most overqualified overseer in the state," she said with admiration.

She had many questions, but Tom continued, "If summer comes and we're still fighting, we've got to sell the cotton somewhere else. Columbia will be flooded with it." He brightened. "Oh, I almost forgot. I saw Mrs. Calhoun in town. She's just back from Charleston with her son. Half the town was crowded around to hear what Andrew Calhoun had to say about the goings-on in Charleston."

"What did Mr. Calhoun say?"

Tom shook his head. "Mr. Calhoun seemed as proud of the Confederacy as if he had birthed it himself. To hear him talk, we're going to whip the Yankees in no time and raise up a New South. Mrs. Calhoun looked a ways more worried than her son, but she asked that you pay her a call soon." Tom twisted his hat in his hands. "I've got to get back out and see how the hands are doing with that new field for corn. George was to have them plow the field by the river today. I must admit I'm a little worried that this war news is going to have the men in a temper. I haven't said anything, but I know that word travels."

Polly reddened and thought of her conversation with Ben. "Word does travel. I saw you with your rifle and a pistol," Polly said.

Tom patted his hip. "I carry my guns. Your husband was worried that war talk might rile up the slaves."

"Do we need to be worried? I ran into Ben and mentioned the possibility of war. He was so angry, and all for it. I have never seen him like that."

"Did he threaten you?" Tom asked.

"No, nothing like that. He did say he'd leave if he had a chance."

Tom shrugged. "No surprise there. Everyone wants to be free. And while we treat your slaves well, they are still your property. Of course, they would leave Whitehall if they could. At the drop of a hat."

Polly stared at Tom for a minute and pondered his words. "I suppose they would," she murmured.

Tom continued as if he hadn't just dropped a bombshell. "Your husband wanted the smithy shut down. He had visions of Ben forging knives and pikes late at night," he smirked. "Ben is a hothead, but he is not violent. And George is a good man with a family to think of. The hands will continue to work hard for you as long as we treat them fairly. It's a powder keg, Miss Polly. We have to do our best to keep it from exploding." He shook his head. "Anyway, the weather looks nice and warm for planting corn as soon as we can, so let me get to work."

"We'll need all the corn we can grow, I suppose." Polly walked with Tom to the front door. "Mr. Roper," she said, "I have a thought. What about that back acreage? The area that abuts the old Kemp place? I don't think anything has been done with that land in years."

"The old orchard? That hasn't been touched since your brothers . . ." He paused and looked at Polly with surprise. "It'd take a few weeks at least to get it cleared out. It's at least ten acres of neglected or dead fruit trees. You want to grow something else in that area?"

She remembered the mulatto planter William Ellison's advice. "I believe that we need to focus on feeding ourselves, Mr. Roper. All of this cotton we just planted might not have a way to market. But if we have a producing orchard, enough staples on hand, and our cash crops are in good shape, we will not go hungry. We can barter for things we do not have. Go ahead and have the men clear the orchard of brush and call me out to inspect it before taking down any trees there."

Tom smiled. "That's not a bad idea. Maybe you don't need an overseer."

"You are the most highly educated overseer in the state, Mr. Roper. I wouldn't dare let you go." She paused and considered the man. "You have many secrets."

"Yes, I do." Tom plopped his faded hat on his head at a jaunty angle, and walked out the door, whistling as if he hadn't a care.

Chapter Twenty-Eight

April 19, 1861

BEN CLICKED THE REINS AND THE HORSE LURCHED FORWARD. The wagon bed carried the myriad tools and the two other men who would be clearing the old orchard under George's supervision. Tom trusted George to manage the small group dispatched to the far corner of Burgiss property, while he stayed nearer the hands working in the fields and outbuildings. Zadoc and Cyrus rode silently in the wagon, loaded with hoes and small hand axes. Clearing the overgrown orchard would be tough, but the men were used to hard work. George would work right beside them, despite his title of foreman. He rode ahead of the wagon, following the overgrown wheel ruts toward the orchard.

Ben's heart sank as they paralleled the river. The water moved south slowly, and Ben wondered what was happening in Savannah, where the fresh water from these hills emptied into the ocean. He remembered as a boy how Martin would carefully spread out a pilfered map of the United States and expound on the wonders of the country. He traced the Savannah River all the way to the sea and pointed out the route that

Whitehall cotton took to markets on the coast. He showed him the coastline, and traced it up to the state of Virginia, where he had been born, and told him just how long such a trip by horseback and heavy-laden wagon had taken. He pointed to North Carolina, where Ona and her family once lived. He spoke of the magical western territories, filled with cutthroat Indians and strange land formations. There were tales of steaming pools of water so hot a man could boil just by falling in, and vast, red-walled canyons nearly a mile deep. How Martin was aware of these things Ben would never know.

He recalled the faded pamphlet tucked in Martin's Bible, the printed evidence of a great Independence Day speech by the abolitionist Frederick Douglass. Martin had told Ben that Douglass was a free black man, someone who had escaped slavery and made himself a great statesman for his people. Ben had read the precious pamphlet whenever allowed, which was rare. To possess such a forbidden document would have meant death if it had been found, and in fact, Ona had buried it with Martin.

Most curiously, Ben remembered the tiny, barely discernible dots on the map, linked like a necklace of penciled beads. The necklace stretched from Georgia all the way up to the farthest reaches of the country, across lakes, into a place called Canada. Ben had asked once what the dots meant, but Martin carefully folded the tattered map and told Ben it was nothing.

"Ben, the orchard's up ahead, right?" asked Zadoc. "Near the border with the ol' Kemp place?"

Ben nodded. His attention was brought back to the task at hand. As they neared the woods so close to the abandoned Kemp property, he shuddered. Many times he had revisited that horrific day, and he still most plainly saw Clay Wilkins' face after the man had dashed little Caleb Burgiss's brains out with the butt of his rifle.

— • —

POLLY FINGERED THE RUBY NECKLACE AT her throat as her carriage bumped down the muddy road toward Mi Casa. She had decided to wear the gift from Floride on her visit, as a peace offering of sorts. The last time she had seen her friend was at the uncomfortable dinner with the governor and General Beauregard. Polly could hardly believe how the world had changed since that night. To think that now those very men were involved directly in a war against the rest of the nation.

The carriage splashed through one wagon rut after another. Polly fretted about the newly planted cotton, and the sodden fields surrounding Whitehall. Several inches of hard rain had fallen in the past few days, carrying rivers of precious cotton seed away from her land toward the river. The deluge was not over. The western sky hung heavy with the threat of more rain. It felt to Polly as if the skies wept tears over the events taking place on the coast. Nevertheless, she was excited about the outing and had much to tell her friend.

The carriage came to a halt in front of Floride's home. Mi Casa was a cottage compared to Fort Hill, but it suited the old woman perfectly. Purple irises edged the front walkway and flowering dogwoods formed a living canopy over the porch. Zadoc came around to Polly's door and helped her from the carriage.

"Polly, my dear!" called Floride from the front entrance. Polly looked down to see her friend, leaning heavily on her cane but waiting patiently for her guest. Floride appeared tired, despite her obvious joy at seeing Polly. "Do come in. I am so looking forward to a nice chat." She called out to Zadoc as well. "Boy, go around back and you'll find my stable. Wait for your mistress there."

Polly embraced Floride. "I have missed you, Floride. I am so happy that you're back home." The women walked arm in arm into Mi Casa's spacious front hall, where Nellie took Polly's wrap and hustled quietly away.

"Let's enjoy the parlor," Floride said, squeezing Polly's arm. The ladies sat down in front of a crackling fire. The room was a little too warm for Polly on this bright day. She removed her gloves and hat quickly. The woman noticed Polly's discomfort and chuckled. "A blazing fire keeps my bones warm. I hope you can bear it. I know the day is fair out."

Polly patted Floride's hand. "I think it is just fine. Cozy, actually." Polly noted the silver tea service set before them. Scones, shortbreads, and pots of jam were arranged artfully on a platter. Rich clotted cream was heaped into a cut crystal bowl.

Floride sighed. "I confess that I stayed too long in Charleston. To see the fever of war there, was almost more than I could bear. I fret for the house and my things, but I trust that this shall blow over soon and we will be back to soirees and salons by Christmas time," she said hopefully. "And I have it on good authority that the Brigadier General will defend my place if it comes to it."

Polly cocked her head in confusion.

"Brigadier General Beauregard is using my house as a base," she said conspiratorially. She poured a cup of tea for Polly. "One lump or two?"

Polly smiled at the little bowl of sugar cubes. Of course, Floride would have sugar when no one else could find it in all the upstate. "Two, please. So tell me what you know of the war. John's regiment has been dispatched to Charleston. Is there much fighting going on or is it all showmanship?"

"The bombardment was real, and a few volleys have been fired since then, of course. I believe that we will see more action when our soldiers must defend some of the other forts in the area. The blockades are real too, however. No imports coming into the harbor, and nothing going out. The stores are scarce of goods. No silk to be had. . . . Why, calico was five dollars a yard!" she exclaimed. "Beauregard has Sumter secured for now, but the Union will attempt to halt railroad traffic further north as well, I fear. Trade will come to a halt, everywhere, at least temporarily."

Floride offered Polly the platter of buttery shortbreads. "And yes, this is the last of Mi Casa's cane sugar." She laughed and her eyes crinkled merrily. "I cannot think of anyone else I would rather share it with!"

Polly took a cookie eagerly. The first bite of the lightly sweetened treat melted on her tongue. "Oh, how I have missed sugar." She sighed. "I am thinking of growing sorghum, if I can find the seeds or plants. Not just for our needs. But to barter or sell if need be. I am not sure that cotton will make it to market this year and I want to have crops to trade if necessary."

Floride looked skeptical. "Goodness, my girl. I will not tell Andrew of your dire forecast. He has Fort Hill planted in more cotton than ever before. The North will still need it." She sipped her tea. "What else have you been thinking while I was away? I had hoped that you would take up with some of the women your own age in town. Join a sewing circle or a reading group perhaps. Something to occupy your time." She picked up a sampler and began to stitch.

Polly chided her friend gently. "Floride, you of all people? You used to tell me to pay more attention to managing Whitehall, not less. I am a grown woman, and Whitehall is my own. I have enough to keep me busy with John away. My finances are not . . . not as sound as I had hoped. Besides, you know that I have always preferred my own company to the company of most other women. The ladies of my mother's acquaintance were hardly sympathetic in the years following my brothers' deaths. I could see them lean in to gossip when Mother and I passed by in town. So I doubt their daughters would be much company to me. I appear to be damaged goods. Bad luck. But now you are home." She squeezed Floride's hand tenderly.

Floride shook her head. "But my girl, I am here only briefly. I have decided to go to my daughter Anna's home in Maryland. I may stay for the duration of this political mess. While South Carolina sorts itself out, I can be with my daughter's family and see my grandchildren." At Polly's downcast expression, Floride patted the young woman's hand. "But we have time to catch up before I leave. Tell me your news, dear."

Polly began to relate the events of the past few months as Floride picked up a bit of needlework. She stitched while Polly unburdened herself. She told of the meetings with Mr. Legarre and the confrontations at River Wood. She exclaimed about being compelled to take the slave child back to Whitehall.

Floride's eyes brightened when she heard about Lydia. "Oh, I might be interested in purchasing the girl from you. She could help Nellie in the kitchen, or I could give her to my granddaughter. How old did you say she was?"

Polly was uncomfortable with Floride's interest in the child. "I believe she is too young to be sold right now, Floride. She is three years old, and after such a traumatic start, I will not sell her away." Her mind flashed back to the Charleston slave auction from which she had fled.

Floride snorted. "She's a slave, Polly, not your kinfolk." She stabbed the needle into the sampler, but then looked at Polly tenderly. "However, I am sorry to hear of your lost inheritance. The legalities of marriage can be tricky," Floride offered. "One hopes that the love and affection found in a good marriage offset some of the legal unpleasantries. I was fortunate. My John allowed me plenty of freedom to run things as I chose."

Polly found Floride's words of little comfort. "I hardly feel like I have spent any time at all with my husband. It is as if we were married and then this war has conspired to keep us apart. And the few days he was home, I picked fights with him. His temper is, well, it is short," she confessed. "And he does not like me meddling in affairs at River Wood. The last thing he wants to come home to is a nagging wife. In three months I have only seen him for a fortnight, and when he was home, all we did was argue."

Polly put her hands on her belly and gazed at Floride. She wanted to share her happy news but wondered briefly if the idea of a pregnancy would upset Floride. The woman had borne the sorrow of losing eight of her ten children. But she knew she would simply burst if she couldn't tell someone.

"Floride, I saved the most important news for last. I may be expecting a child," she exclaimed.

Floride laid her needlework frame aside. "My love, that is exciting news. Have you called for Dr. Adger?"

"No, I wanted to see you first. You are like a mother to me. I hardly knew who else to tell." She blushed.

"My dear, you must take care of yourself. Bed rest, if possible. Your corsets mustn't be too tight," Floride admonished. "And are you ill in the mornings? Oh, with mine I was always abed, months into confinement. I couldn't abide a morsel of food until I was three or four months along." She sighed. "You'll want Dr. Adger to be informed."

Polly frowned. "I haven't noticed any problem with my corsets. I did not think of that. And I do not seem to have a problem with nausea, either. My appetite is hardy."

Floride patted Polly's hand. "All women go through these things differently. Perhaps you will be one of the lucky ones who avoid the unpleasantness."

Polly was crestfallen. "Perhaps." She looked at Floride with alarm. "I have been so excited about the thought of a pregnancy. I never thought that maybe I was just . . . late. I have had my hopes up."

Floride reached for the teapot. "Wait and see. The good Lord's timing is not our own. You may be in the family way, indeed. But if not, it could be a blessing for now. Caring for a child on your own can be difficult, and with the threat of war? Goodness. And if I may be so bold, I have to say . . ." Floride paused and stared into Polly's eyes. ". . . that if you have the slightest idea that this marriage might be a mistake, if Mr. Stone has deceived you as to who he truly is, why, it is not too late to have it annulled."

Polly gasped in exasperation. "Why won't you believe that we can make this work? He would be here, if not for this war. It changes everything."

"I am an old woman." She shrugged, as if that were reason enough for her words. "You know that I have trouble keeping my mouth closed. I am so fond of you and I do not want to see you hurt further," she said, patting Polly's cheek. "Please forgive me. I just don't believe that he has done anything to help this marriage get off on the right foot. He rushed into this and then abandoned you. . . . But I have an idea! Let me organize a tea before I leave Mi Casa and reacquaint you with some of the young ladies in the area. I will even show you the guest list and you can have first right of refusal on anyone." Her face was so mischievous that Polly couldn't help but smile. "You can announce your good news there."

Polly sighed. "Oh alright, Floride. Host your tea party. I will come and I promise to be polite—but in return, you must promise me not to say unkind things about my husband again. Then we shall have a deal." Polly sipped her tea and tried to ignore the truth in her friend's words.

— • —

LATE THAT EVENING AS POLLY PREPARED FOR BED, Cissie knocked on the door timidly.

"Yes, Cissie, come in. I don't think I need a fire up here tonight. Just hang my skirts and take my tea things. Be sure to bank the fires downstairs. I'll be up early, so tea and an egg for breakfast."

Cissie nodded obediently. Polly watched the slave woman move around the room, her belly round and straining the seams of the shift she wore. Her thoughts drifted into a quick prayer that she was indeed pregnant and would soon get to experience motherhood for herself. With a jolt, she realized that she was a bit jealous of her slave.

"Gracious, Cissie, do you have another skirt? You're fairly bursting out of that one," she remarked.

Cissie patted her belly. "Yes ma'am. I have one I set aside from when Silas was born. Your mama was kind. She gave me extry calico that year so's I could make a second skirt. I ain't wantin' to put it on yet. Savin' it for a few weeks from now when this one won't button up." She stretched to hang Polly's skirt in the tall armoire.

Polly felt a prick of conviction. "You have how much longer? I have some old petticoats that you can remake as skirts. Mr. Roper said that there was no cloth to be had in town."

"Thank you, ma'am," Cissie said, picking up Polly's empty cup and saucer. "I got about three weeks, I think." Polly found herself irked that the woman wasn't more effusive in her thanks.

"Anything else you want tonight, Miss Polly?"

"You may go."

Cissie nodded and left Polly's room, closing the door softly behind her. Outside, a barn owl called from the woods. Moments later, Polly heard another owl answer from somewhere near the house. Polly yawned. She reached to turn down her lamp and wondered if more kerosene was even available in town. Best to conserve oil and rely on candles. She leaned back on her pillows and closed her eyes, as worry after worry invaded her mind. She tried to relax and picture herself with a belly as round as Cissie's. Would John be excited or angry? They had not talked about children. Where indeed would she find clothes for her expanding waistline? Who would help her when her time of confinement arrived? Which of the slave women would she trust as her child's nursemaid? Polly finally let go and drifted off to sleep.

— • —

AT DAWN, POLLY STIRRED AND LISTENED to the cacophony of birdsong outside her window. The faintest thread of pink sky showed through heavy grey clouds. More rain. She sat up and felt a familiar rush of warmth between her legs. With a sinking feeling, she rushed for the chamber pot. The telltale red stain on her underclothes confirmed her fears and she dropped her head between her knees and cried.

Chapter Twenty-Nine

April 30, 1861

TOM ROPER SCRATCHED HIS BEARD AND CHUCKLED. "I'll be damned," he said under his breath. "I'll be dog-damned."

"Suh?" George asked.

"George, I'm just surprised to find these trees alive. You boys did a fine job getting this orchard cleared out for Mrs. Stone. I just didn't think we'd find peach trees still alive. And with buds, no less. It's been ten years since we have been back here."

George grinned. "It's a nice break from cotton and corn, suh. We's hoping to set by some peach preserves ourselves if Miss Polly—Mizzus Stone gits extry, suh."

Tom nodded. "We'll wait and see what Mrs. Stone decides to do with it. Well, y'all get on back to the fieldwork now. There's weeding to be done in the corn rows. We'll replant that flooded acre of cotton by the barn, too. Go ahead and get the boys out there, hmm?"

George nodded and turned to leave. As he did, Tom called out, "George, when Cissie's baby due?"

At the mention of his wife and child, George smiled. "'Bout a month or so, Mr. Tom."

Tom grinned. "That Silas is a fine boy. You're a lucky man."

George's smile dimmed only slightly as he nodded. "Yessuh, Mr. Tom. Yessuh."

— • —

EARLY THE NEXT DAY, POLLY OPENED THE front door and found Tom clutching a letter in one hand and the latest newspaper in the other. Her daily meetings with Tom were pleasant diversions, and she knew that he would have news of the abandoned orchard.

"Come in, Mr. Roper. I have just a few minutes this morning. I am expected at a tea at Mi Casa." Polly's hair was swept up and pinned with tortoiseshell combs and she wore a mauve silk gown tiered in ruffles.

Tom removed his hat politely and followed Polly into the parlor. "You look real nice, Miss Polly." A small pot and two china cups were laid out on a tray and Tom gulped. "Do I smell coffee?"

Polly clapped her hands in delight. "Yes, Mr. Roper. Isn't it wonderful! Floride gifted me just a little from her stores. The aroma alone is sending me into a swoon," she said, laughing lightly. "I thought that we should have a cup, together. One can hardly drink good coffee alone."

"Oh, you've made this simple man very happy. Very happy, indeed." Tom sat down eagerly and Polly poured out two small cups of the steaming brew. Both of them sat with their cups pressed to their noses, inhaling the heady scent. Finally, Tom sipped his coffee and sighed. "It's right sad to think that this is what is floating offshore behind those blockades." He laughed.

Polly smiled and leaned forward. "I am sure that President Davis will hold onto any coffee the soldiers come across. We'll have to reuse these grounds until they're dust." She sipped heartily and set her cup in its saucer. "So tell me the news of that old orchard. Shall we clear it for corn?"

"I liked to dance a jig when I saw for myself. The boys cleared out all the underbrush and found living trees. Healthy peach and apple trees your father planted, and they are budding right now. You have ten acres of trees. I think they must have liked the sandy river soil there. It's a miracle. They're wild and leggy—just need proper pruning."

Polly sat up abruptly. "Oh! Mr. Roper, I remember my father had a notebook he kept on the orchard. I believe it contained sketches on the way he liked to keep them trimmed. I will look for it and be sure that you get it. We may have peaches and apples this summer, and that is exciting news!"

"I wasn't sure you'd want to have anything to do with that orchard. Seems your mother and father let it go after what happened so near there— to your brothers." Tom sipped his coffee and set the cup in the saucer.

Polly shrugged. "It is land we must utilize," she said simply.

"Oh, I brought a letter from your husband," Tom offered. "I went to town this morning and the postmaster had it set aside. I had one from him, as well. It was concerning a slave matter he wanted me to be aware of. No news of the fighting at all." He handed her a worn envelope.

Polly studied Tom's expression. He couldn't hide the look of uneasiness on his tanned face. "I brought you the latest newspaper, too. Seems little skirmishes are breaking out, but for the most part, everything is calm on the coast."

"Hmm, the calm before the storm?" she said as she pocketed the letter. "Anything in the paper about my husband's regiment?" She scanned the headlines.

Tom shrugged. "I didn't see anything. All we know is they are headed to Charleston. Maybe the newsmen figure the Union is reading Southern newspapers so they stopped reporting troop movements. Mr. Stone's letter to you may have news."

Polly did not offer to read the letter in front of her overseer.

"This might not be a good time, but I need to ask a favor, Miss Polly."

Polly set down the newspaper. "I thought you had something on your mind. What kind of favor, Mr. Roper?"

"I need to go to Greenville, ma'am, to check on my mother. I had word that she was doing poorly, and what with not having Mr. Stone here, I was afraid to ask you. But now she's taken a bad spill and is laid up at her cousin's." He looked at Polly apologetically. "I trust George to handle everything while I am away. He is a good man."

Despite her reticence, Polly nodded. "Of course, you must go. How long will you be away?"

"I think two weeks at most, ma'am. But with the cotton and corn in the ground and the summer storms not yet in view, it should be a quiet time here. Except for that pruning in the orchard, we're ahead of things right now. George can be trusted to keep the men in line, and I have an extra pistol. I can give it to you. Just in case." Roper tilted his head toward the parlor doors.

Polly nodded and quickly crossed the room to close the heavy oak doors. "That seems strange," Polly said. "You were the one assuring me we are safe here. Was there anything that my husband wrote to you that would lead you to believe that I would need a weapon?"

Tom's face gave away his worry. "He wrote that Wilkins wants one of the female slaves to go back to River Wood. I guess Jane isn't doing so well, so he asked your husband for permission to collect Kate or Cissie back over there. As a cook and house slave." Tom nodded toward Polly's pocketed correspondence. "Mr. Stone said he would tell you himself in a letter."

Polly stood up abruptly and snapped, "Absolutely not!" Her hand flew to her pocket and she pulled the envelope out hastily and ripped it open.

Dear Polly,

I am writing from the depot in Columbia. Our train leaves shortly. I know that you have been waiting on some small news from me. By now you have heard what happened at Fort Sumter. Our regiment is traveling to the coast. Beyond that, I cannot tell you where we will take up our stations. Do not worry. The Confederacy sent Major Anderson and his company of Yankee cowards scurrying back to New York straight away. We will be in good company wherever we disembark and will probably guard some remote fort and feast like kings on oysters and clams.

There is a matter I must make you aware of. Wilkins has been left without a cook and house girl, as Jane has taken ill and you removed Lydia from the premises. It will not do to leave River Wood with neither a house slave nor a cook. Wilkins requested having the child returned to be trained as a cook and house girl, but I remembered how adamant you were about keeping and training the child yourself. Therefore, I have given Mr. Wilkins permission to take Kate or Cissie back to River Wood for the time being. Perhaps when this conflagration is over, we can make arrangements for another female slave if needed at Whitehall. Please forgive me, as I know that Kate was a wedding present of sorts to you, and Cissie is married to your foreman, but these are tough times, and you must be prepared to make sacrifices.

I wrote to Mr. Roper about this matter, and instructed him to handle the slave transfer, so that Mr. Wilkins does not visit Whitehall, as you requested.

The train whistles as I write this note, so I must close. I will write again when I can.

John

Polly folded the letter and shoved it in her pocket angrily. "Mr. Roper, you know of the horrors inflicted by that awful man on female slaves. He is inhuman. This is a ruse designed to get a woman back there for his own purposes. John didn't even remember Lydia. She is a small child," she cried. "She could not be a house slave. . . . Wilkins knows I will not release Cissie, so he expects I will send Kate. He has no need of a cook!" She spit the words. "I will not release her. I simply will not!"

— • —

TOM LOOKED AT POLLY SYMPATHETICALLY. "My hands are tied, as much as I hate this. She is Mr. Stone's property. She isn't yours legally, like Ona or Ben or even Cissie, who married one of your father's men. You haven't got papers on her—do you?"

Polly ignored his question. "Surely Jane will be well enough to resume her duties soon," Polly pleaded. "This is unacceptable. Kate was a wedding present to me. I would call on Mr. Legarre, but he would tell me that the law is on my husband's side."

"I don't like it any better than you do," Tom said softly. "But these are your husband's written instructions. We both detest Clay Wilkins, and the best I can offer you is that I'll let Mr. Wilkins know that we will keep a watch on her. Who knows? Maybe Jane will recover. Send Zadoc over to help his mama for a few days. He can watch out for Kate, too. Be happy that he did not demand to have the child back."

Polly was nearly frantic. She stood and wrung her hands together. "Please, Mr. Roper. Tom. I'm pleading for your help. What can we do to stop this? What about Kate's baby, little Solomon? Will the sheriff listen?"

"I have never seen you so distraught over a slave issue, Miss Polly. But as ugly as it may be to think about, Kate is your husband's property. She will have to go back to River Wood if he desires it. We both have written directions from your husband as to this matter."

Polly shook her head. "No! Tell Mr. Wilkins that this was a surprise and will upset the workings of my household. Make him wait until your return. Take her there in three weeks' time." She clasped her hands tightly against her chest, knuckles white.

Tom hesitated. "I think we both know that she needs to return right away. You don't want to take a chance that he'll ride over here and try to take her. I know that Mr. Stone wrote to him, too. I should leave tomorrow for my mother's. I will take Kate and Zadoc to River Wood on my way out of town, but I'll be back as soon as I can." He lifted the cup and drained the remaining contents in one gulp.

Polly was beside herself with fury. "I thought you would be on my side! We must tell Kate that this is temporary. How could she bear it otherwise?"

Tom sighed. "Tomorrow morning, we can tell her together. I would like to leave by mid-morning on the train for Greenville if I may."

Polly fumed. "Very well. Take Ben along. He can drive the wagon back home from the station. I will let Zadoc know of his mother's illness and that he will be going to River Wood to care for her," she said, her anger having nowhere to go.

Tom turned his hat brim in his hands as he spoke. "Thank you for the coffee. I'm so sorry about all this. But George has got the farm chores under control, and the boys'll be busy enough with the livestock and pruning those trees. Kate will be fine. Your husband surely wouldn't send a valuable slave back there if he thought she was in danger."

— • —

POLLY PULLED ON HER GLOVES ANGRILY and glanced at her reflection in the carriage mirror. She pinched her cheeks and adjusted her straw bonnet. The last thing she felt like doing was attending a silly tea, but she had promised Floride. The old woman planned to leave for Maryland in two days, and Polly knew that she might not hear from her friend until the political upheaval ended. The postmaster had been right. Mail runs between the South and states north of Virginia had been severed, and many families were separated by the lack of communication.

Her thoughts tumbled over the problem of Kate and the move to River

Wood. She wondered if she should plan to visit the place every few days and check on the slaves herself. But she remembered John's words, warning her to stay away from River Wood if she wanted to avoid Wilkins. Zadoc would watch out for her, she knew, and Jane, too. There was no sense in troubling Floride with the news. Floride was not sympathetic to the plight of slaves. She believed that they were only property, something that her late husband had proclaimed his entire political life.

Polly looked out the window as the fields and woods moved slowly past. At one time, Dr. Adger had seemed interested in her slaves' wellbeing. Maybe she could appeal to Dr. Adger.

The carriage creaked to a halt in front of Mi Casa. Zadoc appeared at Polly's door to help her down. Polly sighed heavily at the dreadful thought of idle chatter and the silent sizing up she would be subject to yet again. There was a time when I longed for such frippery, she thought, as a young girl alone with my mother.

But every social call had been fraught with gossip and backhanded compliments.

"Oh, Mary, how well you look—for having gone through such a trauma."

"I heard that slave boys at Whitehall did the deed. My niggers would never!"

"Mary, I wouldn't be able to show my face after such a blow."

"I know you haven't had the strength, dear, but someone should help you with Polly. Her dresses are too small, and her hair is atrocious."

"He'p you down, Miss Polly?" Zadoc's voice snapped Polly back to the present.

"Thank you, Zee," she said. She stepped onto the gravel drive and paused before going up the walkway. "Zee, I had word from Mr. Roper that your mother is ill. We would like you to spend a few days with her at River Wood—help her get back on her feet."

Zadoc's eyes grew wide with alarm. "Mama's sick?"

"Now don't go making a mountain from a molehill. I'm sure it's just a little thing, but Mr. Wilkins did want us to know. Mr. Roper will take you out that way first thing tomorrow morning. Be thankful that you get to spend some time with your parents," she said too sharply. "Wait for me in the stable."

Zadoc nodded silently as Polly climbed the steps to Floride's front door. She lifted the heavy brass knocker and rapped sharply on the door.

Floride's man, Henry, answered the door with a smile. "Good afternoon, Mrs. Stone." He bowed slightly. "Come in. The ladies are in the parlor. Please follow me." His buttery-smooth voice soothed Polly's nerves.

"Thank you, Henry," Polly said. The man led her into Floride's cheerful parlor. Sunlight streamed in through the tall windows and bounced off the polished silver tea service. Plates of petit fours, small sandwiches, and heaping bowls of cream were laid out beautifully. A tall Limoges vase of pink and white hothouse flowers and delicate ferns anchored the lovely display. Women stood around the room in small knots, lost in genteel chit-chat.

"Mrs. John Stone," Peter announced to the room. Floride smiled broadly and came quickly to greet her friend. "My dear, I am so glad that you could come. We were just discussing the situation in Charleston." She led Polly to the bounteous table and turned to her cook. "Nellie, pour for Mrs. Stone."

Nellie nodded obediently and poured a steaming cup of tea into a beautiful porcelain teacup. "Cream and sugar, ma'am?"

Polly's face registered surprise at the mention of sugar and she caught Floride's eye. The old woman shrugged and held a finger to her lips.

"Two lumps, Nellie," Polly answered. "Thank you."

Nellie handed the cup and saucer to Polly with a gloved hand and a nod. Polly turned to Floride and said wryly, "Gracious, when you leave for Maryland, dear friend, I will gladly take any sugar left at Mi Casa in exchange for all my worldly goods."

Floride chuckled. "This is the end, my dear. I promise. We celebrate this afternoon, for I leave tomorrow. Now, come and speak with my other guests."

She steered Polly toward two women deep in conversation. Polly's pulse raced in her veins and she became weak in the knees. The younger woman Polly recognized from ill-fated encounters in town.

"Mrs. Davis and Lucinda, you remember my dear friend, Polly Stone, nee Burgiss," Floride said. "Mrs. Davis' husband, Captain Oliver Davis, is with Brigadier General Beauregard right now. And Lucinda is newly married to Dr. Adger's son, Ward."

Polly smiled at Lucinda. "Congratulations, Mrs. Adger," she offered. "I do not know Ward well, but I think so highly of his father. In fact, he gave me away at my own wedding. I believe Ward, too, is training to be a doctor?"

"Ward has finished his training and is assigned as Major McQueen's personal physician," Mrs. Davis harrumphed. "He is an integral part of his staff."

Lucinda's green eyes appraised Polly quickly from head to toe before coolly adding, "Thank you, Mrs. Stone."

Polly tried again, valiantly. "Mrs. Adger, were you able to find fabric for a wedding gown? These times are so difficult. Mrs. Batson said that fine fabrics are so hard to come by now."

Mrs. Davis rolled her eyes and spoke up before her daughter could open her mouth. "This ridiculous war! We had planned a wedding in England next summer, at the home of Lady Elizabeth Campbell, one of Queen Victoria's ladies-in-waiting. Lucinda had a design from London for her gown, but with the war . . . they decided to marry right away."

Lucinda interjected, "So Mother's wedding gown was remade for me."

Polly smiled. "My gown was a day dress Mrs. Batson had made for an earlier trip to Charleston. We just married in January."

Mrs. Davis piped up, "Still, Lucinda and I sail next month for Europe. We plan to wait out this conflagration abroad."

"Possibly, Mother. We shall see." Lucinda looked around the room uncomfortably.

Mrs. Davis sniffed. "If you'll excuse us, Mrs. Stone. I want to chat with my daughter's godmother, Mrs. Pinckney, before we depart." She smiled sweetly, but the ice in her veins made Polly cringe.

"Yes, of course, ladies," Polly demurred. "And Mrs. Davis, do please give my regards to General Beauregard through your husband. I haven't spoken to the dear man since we had dinner with him right here in January." Mrs. Davis's eyes grew big as saucers.

Polly continued merrily. "I was also able to dance with him at the Pinckneys' Christmas gala. He was the most wonderful dancing partner. Why, he is as light of foot as a French danseur. Oh, what fun we had . . ."

Floride smiled into her teacup at Polly's antics.

Polly continued, "I must speak with Mrs. Pinckney later. Christmas was a delight, and we enjoyed ourselves immensely, didn't we, Floride?"

Mrs. Calhoun's face crinkled in mirth. "Yes, and as I recall, you danced with Beauregard most of the evening. So much dancing that I fear you later fainted," she added wryly. "You must indeed speak to Mrs. Pinckney. She may have an update on your friend, General Lee."

At the mention of another important military hero, Mrs. Davis became almost apoplectic. "General Robert E. Lee?" She coughed delicately. "Of Virginia?"

Polly nodded and leaned in conspiratorially. "The very man. Although he was just a Colonel the last I saw him, but to hear his story of Harper's Ferry, my, it made my blood run cold," she said with a shudder, then smiled. "A wonderful man, indeed."

"Come, Lucinda," Mrs. Davis snapped. She turned to Polly. "It was lovely to meet you again." Her voice dripped with honey as she added, "We simply must try to call on you some time before we depart. But Lucinda's calendar is quite full. You are . . . where? Whitehead? White Thorn?" She shook her head and small diamond earrings twinkled in the sunlight.

"Whitehall." Polly smiled sweetly. Lucinda grabbed her mother's hand and pulled her away.

Floride chided her young friend quietly. "Oh alright, she deserved that. But you do need to make a friend here. This may be a long war, and your husbands will be gone a while. You'll need another young woman to keep company with."

"What makes them so high and mighty? Hasn't Lucinda married a country doctor's son?" Polly frowned.

"Oh, let it go, my dear. Lucinda is actually quite a delight away from her social-climbing mother; her mother—who was not invited today—by the way." Floride winked at Polly.

"Floride, I told you that these women consider me a pariah. I have no need of their false charm and silly ways. I have a farm to run." Polly sipped her tea and felt her strength return.

Chapter Thirty

May 2, 1861

TOM KNOCKED ON THE FRONT DOOR EARLY THE NEXT MORNING, a leather bag slung over his shoulder and his hat in his hands.

Polly opened the door and sighed. "I asked Cissie to bring Kate and Solomon. Best to tell her here, away from the others," she muttered.

Tom nodded solemnly. "Miss Polly, if there was another way . . . but you know our hands are tied until your husband gets back or writes again."

Polly glared at her overseer. "Her blood may be on our hands," she whispered. "Can you live with that? Because I am not sure I can!"

They heard footsteps and Polly turned to find Kate coming down the dark hall, with Sol hoisted on her hips. He grinned when he saw Polly and gurgled a greeting. Kate smiled at him proudly and then looked expectantly at her mistress. "You wanted to see us, Mizz Polly?"

Polly crossed her arms over her chest and frowned. "Kate, I have some news. I expect you to bear this bravely, as it is only temporary. It will not be permanent. You're needed back at River Wood. Today. Jane is ill and there is no one to cook or clean."

Kate's mouth opened and a small gasp escaped before she regained her composure and looked Polly in the eyes steadily. "Who I cookin' fo'?"

Polly looked at the threadbare carpet at her feet. "Mr. Wilkins requires a cook and house girl, until Jane recovers. Now, Zadoc is going with you. He will tend to his mother and get her back on her feet. And I am hopeful that you can return to us quickly. Please get your things and meet us by the wagon out front. Zadoc will get some milk and butter from the springhouse for Solomon, and a bag of cornmeal from the kitchen. I don't know what is in store at River Wood. Last time I was there, the pantry was empty."

Kate's lips began to tremble. "Mizz Polly, I have to beg you—"

Tom cut the woman off abruptly. "Kate, don't go causing trouble. You heard Miss Polly. It isn't permanent, but you have to go. She has no choice in the matter."

"I know that, Mr. Roper," Kate began softly. "Mizz Polly, please let Sol stay here with Ona. Please, ma'am, I'm beggin' you." Tears welled in her eyes and Polly's gut wrenched in response. "Please don't make me take Sol back there."

"Kate," Mr. Roper began. "You heard Miss Polly. Get your things and—"

"No, Tom," Polly interrupted. "Kate, we will be happy to take care of Sol while you're away. He will be safe with us here." She looked into Kate's wide eyes and nodded. "You won't have to worry about your little boy."

Kate wiped her eyes and nodded. "Thank you, ma'am." She hugged Sol, who babbled and grabbed at his mother's nose playfully. "Solomon, my sweet baby boy," she whispered.

Polly gently reached out for the baby. Kate dutifully handed him over, whispering sweet words to him the whole time, bestowing a blessing on her young son. Sol laughed and grabbed at Polly's earrings in momentary distraction. Polly smiled at him through her own tears. "Go now, Kate, while he is occupied. My prayers are going with you, and we'll get you back here in no time."

Without another word, Kate slipped back down the hallway and out the door.

Polly looked up at Tom. "This is the hardest thing I have ever done."

— • —

POLLY SAT ON THE FRONT PORCH, enjoying the breeze and the scent of the climbing roses that tumbled over the railings. She rocked absentmindedly, watching the road for signs of the wagon returning from River Wood. Solomon played at her feet with an old coffee can filled with pebbles. He would fill and shake the can, dump it out and start to fill it again, babbling all the while. Once he looked up at Polly and asked, "Mama?"

Polly smiled. "She'll be back soon." She heard the rattle of the farm wagon coming loudly down the hard-packed road. She lifted Sol to her hip and started toward the wagon as it pulled into the drive.

Ben slowed the horse and stopped the wagon in front of Polly. Sweat glistened on his forearms and he wiped his dusty face with his kerchief. He looked down at her and shook his head.

"Miss Polly, you know you sent that woman straight into hell again." He yanked off his hat and slapped his thigh with it.

Polly startled. She straightened and nodded toward the baby. "Ben, watch yourself. Do you think I don't know that? Do you think that I had any recourse? But Zadoc is there. He will keep an eye on her. When Jane is better, Kate will come back." She bounced Sol on her hip, but he fidgeted to get down.

"That man is a bad seed, Miss Polly," Ben said. "Do you know what he—"

"That's enough, Ben!" shouted Ona from the front porch. The woman hurried down the steps and held out her arms to take Solomon. "I take him, Miss Polly. He about ready fo' his milk and lunch anyway. You come on inside, too, and I'll fetch you a cool drink of water, ma'am."

"I'll feed him, Ona." Polly said, bouncing the baby on her hip. "I need the distraction."

Ben opened his mouth to speak but Ona held up a hand and glared angrily at her son. "Ben, watch yo'se'f!"

Polly squinted up at Ben, shielding her eyes from the sun, with her hand. "I know the things he is capable of. More than you know. And I remember what he did to Duke, and to you. My hands are legally tied. Kate belonged to my husband and he wrote to me and to Mr. Roper of his instructions. There is nothing else to be done except pray. If I had not sent her, Wilkins might have come here with patrollers. At least Zadoc is there with her. She'll be fine." Solomon began to whimper. She wheeled and marched up the wooden steps, skirts clutched in one hand and the baby on her hip.

— • —

ONA APPROACHED THE WAGON. "Don't you do it, son," Ona warned. "It ain't gonna do us any good to tell tales on that man. It'll just get you killed is all."

"Ma, Kate hasn't got a chance. Jane is sick. She's old. You think Zee is going to be able to heal her? Nah. . . . And Zee told me that his daddy has been beaten so many times that he has a bum arm and can't talk for the scars around his neck. He's even older than Jane. Now with Kate goin' back? She's the only young woman on the place. You know what will happen!"

"Kate ain't your concern!" snapped Ona. "Now you got chores to git to. Enough said. We is slaves, not freedmen. Remember that." She turned and left Ben fuming atop the wagon bench.

Ben sighed and closed his eyes, letting the bright sun warm his face. He heard the sharp metallic sound of an ax against wood and he opened his eyes. He scanned the neatly furrowed fields where tiny cotton plants emerged in straight rows, like emerald soldiers given their marching orders. His eyes swept across the drive to the far horse pasture where the tiny figure of a slave busily hacked out spreading oleander seedlings from the fence line.

— • —

May 28, 1861

ZADOC STAYED LONGER AT RIVER WOOD than expected. After weeks of agonizing pain in her gut, Jane finally died in her son's arms, Ezra by her side. Zadoc buried his mother in the small, fenced cemetery out past the slave quarters, under a spreading beech tree.

He comforted Ezra and spent some time repairing the tiny shack that was his elderly parents' home. Ezra was no longer a field hand, but his chores were difficult with just one good arm. He smoked and salted meats, tended the livestock, and worked the meager kitchen garden by himself. Wilkins had the other hands in the fields from sunup until sundown six and a half days a week.

Now that Jane was gone, Kate was the only woman on the property. In the weeks that Zadoc was there, he watched as she kept to the kitchen house and used the pantry as a place to sleep. While Jane was alive, Kate had helped Zadoc nurse his mama, but she had chores to attend to and did not want to make Wilkins angry. So afraid was she of the overseer, that she frequently asked Zadoc or Ezra to bring her vegetables from the gardens or eggs, milk, and meat from the far outbuildings. She rinsed out her dress at the kitchen pump and splashed herself with water from a pail, rather than venture to the washhouse. Zadoc had not seen the overseer anywhere near the slave cabins and relied on Ezra to guess the man's whereabouts during the day. Evenings, Ezra reported, the man usually drank himself to sleep after Kate's suppers and was unconscious into the night.

Zadoc did his best to avoid Wilkins, who said nothing to the man of his mother's passing. His parents' shack was tucked up under an ancient white oak tree, farthest from the overseer's cabin. During her illness, Zadoc was able to use a low-hanging branch out of sight of Wilkins' place to hang Jane's rinsed bedding and dresses after she had vomited or bled on them. The morning after her burial, he pulled the ragged quilt and a stained petticoat off the branch, planning to toss all her ruined things into the fire before he left for Whitehall. They'd be of little use to Kate. Ezra stood by, lost in his own sadness.

Zadoc hugged his father tightly, whispered in his ear, and then carried the quilt and ragged clothing toward the kitchen house. A steady wisp of grey smoke snaked from the chimney. He pulled open the screen door and saw Kate stooped over the hearth, stoking the fire. Her eyes were puffy from crying, and her lip was split and crusted with blood. She had tried to use her blue turban to blot her lip and had rewrapped the bloodstained cloth around her head haphazardly.

Zadoc gasped. "Aw, Kate." He dropped the soiled laundry. "What happened, girl?" He came to the young woman and she crumpled in his arms. "I didn't think he was botherin' you none."

"I tried to stay outta his way, Zee. But he moved into the big house. I was leavin' his meals in the dinin' room and Ezra would get him. It wasn't till last night—when I jes' stepped outside the kitchen to refill the kindling box. Even in the dark, I knew it was him out walkin' around. I thought he'd be drinkin' and passed out again upstairs, that's why I chanced it. I tried to be quiet, but when he saw me in the shadow of the kitchen, he pulled me inside. Lawd he'p me, Zee. . . . I'm so thankful that Mizz Polly kept my boy, but Mr. Wilkins threatened to take Sol if I screamed out. He say Sol rightfully belongs to River Wood. Zee, I'll do anything to keep my boy safe. Please tell Mizz Polly. Let her know to keep Sol safe."

Kate gripped Zee tightly. Zadoc had never seen Kate so cowed and afraid. He sat her down in the rocker near the hearth. He tossed Jane's dresses and tattered underthings into the fire, and the flames leapt to consume the old cloth hungrily. He gently unwound the blue turban from Kate's head and swished it in the pail of water, scrubbing the fabric against itself until it had rinsed clean. He laid it out on the hearthstone to dry and set about tidying the little room.

Kate fingered her frizzy, knotted hair and whispered. "Zee, I'm so afraid. How we ever come to this? Ain't there a God in heaven fo' us?"

Zadoc crouched by the rocker. "I know . . . I sho' won't miss this place. An' I got to go today. I'm gonna talk to Miss Polly 'bout getting you and Daddy back on to Whitehall. I tell her what Wilkins did to you. She's a good white woman."

Kate's eyes grew frantic. "No! Zee, if you say somethin' to her, she gone say somethin' to Mr. Stone and make it worse." She winced and blotted her oozing lip with her apron. "What if he goes askin' for Solomon? All Mr. Wilkins got to do is ask Mr. Stone for Sol, and he'll give him up. Please don't say anything."

She leaned forward and wiped the tears from her cheeks with dirty hands. "And Zee, please don't say nothin' to Ben. 'Bout what happened to me last night. I don't want him knowin'. Promise me."

Zadoc sighed heavily. "Ben," he said finally. "I see." He stood up. "Kate, ain't nothin' that's happened to you your fault. Nothin.' But I promise I won't say nothin' to Ben about this."

Kate smiled gratefully. "Don't say nothin' to no one. But give my boy a hug and a kiss from his mama. I love him so." She covered her face with her dirty apron and began to weep. Zadoc patted her shoulder and kissed her tenderly on the top of her head. He turned and walked out of the kitchen house and headed quickly for the barn, where a driver waited for him in the wagon bound for Whitehall.

— • —

May 27, 1861

Dear Mrs. Stone,

I must apologize for my long absence. I had unexpected business to attend to but have now got Mother settled into her sister's house in Belton. She is much improved and seems right spry for seventy years. I am sorry that I have been away longer

*than anticipated. I trust all is well in my absence. Please have
Zadoc collect me on June 5 morning train from Greenville into
Anderson.*

Sincerely,
Tom Roper

Polly angrily slammed the letter down onto her father's desk and sank
back wearily into James Burgiss's leather chair. She missed Tom. Since he
left, she had realized how terribly alone she was out at Whitehall. With
Floride off to Maryland, and John who knows where, her only companions
were Ona and Cissie and the children. Since Kate had been sent away, they
were quiet and sullen. She peered out the tall window overlooking the
front lawn. The sky was overcast and threatened a storm.

She pulled open the long drawer in the polished maple desk and began
to rifle through her father's papers and old crop reports. She found his
notes on correct pruning of fruit trees and laid them on the desktop.
Chiding herself for not checking the orchard earlier, she knew that the
trees would have set fruit by now. Proper pruning kept the trees strong and
healthy. She would have to have it done as soon as possible.

Polly reached into the back of the desk and felt for the concealed latch.
She flipped the latch and removed the hidden drawer once more. She
removed the large, folded document and opened it, smoothing it, and
laying it on the wide desk.

The topographical survey was notarized and dated just months
before her father's death. Nearly three years had passed. It showed the
progress or lack of progress in each of the three tunnels, much of which
Polly did not understand. She could see that Stumphouse was the
longest, widest, and straightest tunnel under the mountain, as
Beauregard had said. It would have been the tunnel that steam engines
would have been able to navigate, had it been finished. But it was far

from complete. She sighed. Her father's dream had been a tunnel a mile long through blue granite.

She could see that Saddle Tunnel had barely begun excavation, but that Middle Tunnel, about a quarter mile further north, was complete. It was quite narrow, with twists and turns unsuitable for trains or wagon caravans, but indeed cleared in the months before James' Burgiss's death. The survey must have been done at the completion of Middle Tunnel. So why wasn't it publicized? Her father had not mentioned it. There had been no notice of its completion in the newspapers. Other than the governor's scouts and a few high-ranking soldiers, did anyone know or care?

But this information was not the most important detail on the survey. For written on the back of the survey, Polly had seen a scribbled note in her father's hand.

> *Dearest Mary, in the event of my death, please give this survey to TR or RA. Please do not share it with anyone else. It is the only one left. The tunnels will not be utilized for trains, as the State has ceased funding. Therefore, this survey map is useless to the government. It is not useless to these men. Forgive me.*
> *Love, James*

Forgive him for what? Had her mother even seen the survey? Had Polly not seen the note, this survey would have gone straight to the governor at his request.

She screwed up her face, perplexed. What did it mean? And Tom was still away, so she couldn't ask him. Was he TR? She folded the survey and replaced it in the secret drawer, then fitted the drawer in its niche behind the larger drawer.

Polly shook her head and muttered, "'Tis a mystery for another day." She pulled out her father's agricultural notes and studied charts and diagrams of proper pruning for several hours, making her own notes as she did so. As the day rounded toward noon, Polly grew restless and hungry. She leaned over and rang the little silver bell, waiting for Cissie or Ona to appear. The house had seemed eerily quiet since Ona brought breakfast at dawn. Polly listened for approaching footsteps, but there were none. She stood and headed down the hall, curious.

"Cissie? Ona?" There was no answer. Polly wrenched open the service porch door and headed out toward the kitchen house. "Cissie? Ona?" she called.

Suddenly, Polly saw George come at a run from the slave cabins. Sweat poured down his face and he gasped for breath.

"Miss Polly! Miss Polly!" he cried. "Somethin's wrong with the baby. It ain't comin' out. Cissie's bag of waters broke this mornin' but the baby stuck. It ain't comin' out right. Please he'p us, please!"

Polly gasped. "Oh my God!" She followed George to the cabin. Lydia sat in the hard-packed yard with Sol in her lap, while Silas drew in the dirt with a stick.

George stopped abruptly and motioned for Polly to go in through the open door. In the dark room, Polly could barely make out Cissie squatting on the floor, groaning in pain. Her dress was hiked up around her waist and Polly involuntarily grimaced at the sight. The room was thick with the smell of birth. Ona knelt on the floor next to Cissie, her arm around the laboring woman.

"What is happening, Ona?" Polly asked, stooping next to the women. Her eyes avoided Cissie's naked legs. The guttural cries coming from the distraught woman terrified Polly.

"This baby too big, Miss Polly," Ona said over her shoulder. "It ain't comin' out, and she stop pushin'. She been laborin' long. I felt up in there and all I feel is legs folded all cockaninnny. I cain't find the head. I don't think it's movin' either. . . . What we gone do? This baby ain't like Silas. He slid right on out."

Polly's eyes widened. "We have to get Ben. He delivered Delightful's foal when its legs were presenting first. He can do it."

Ona shook her head vehemently. "Lawd, no ma'am. Cain't have him in here lookin' at Cissie like that. He ain't never seen no woman parts. Cissie'd be ashamed if she weren't hurtin' so bad. This is women's work."

"Ona, we do not have time to debate. I have no idea what to do. I could send for Dr. Adger but he may not come. Ben has delivered difficult livestock. He will have to try." Polly stood and stepped around the women to the open door. She leaned out of the shack. "George, get Ben right away! Cissie's life depends on it. He knows how to get the baby free."

George opened his mouth as if to protest but Polly shouted, "Now, George! Unless you want to help!"

The foreman nodded and jogged off to the barn. In just moments, Ben and George were running across the dusty yard. Polly stepped aside as Ben bounded up the rickety steps into the cabin. He shrank back when he saw Cissie.

Ona had helped Cissie recline, knees bent, onto a blanket spread on the floor, a quilt draped across her lap. Cissie groaned and writhed, her eyes rolled back in her head in agony.

"Ben, Miss Polly says you can get this baby out?" Ona asked.

Polly gripped Ben's arm. "Ben, please help her. The baby is stuck. You can pull this baby out."

Ben leaned over the woman and shook his head. "I might hurt her. This isn't a calf or foal. I can't deliver a breech baby."

Ona reached up and put a hand on her son's face. "Ben," she said calmly, "I tried. I ain't strong enough to pull that baby out. If you cain't do it, Cissie will die. The baby might already be dead, so do what you hafta do to get it out. Miss Polly says you can do this. She seen you do it."

"I will help if you tell me what to do," Polly added.

Ben shook his head and dropped down to one knee beside Cissie. He smoothed the hair away from her damp brow and said calmly, "Cissie, I'm going to try to get this baby out. I know you're tired. I know it hurts something fierce, but you have to help me. Don't push until I tell you to. You hear me? It will be alright if you do what I tell you."

Cissie looked at Ben with wild eyes. A guttural groan escaped her throat and Ben sprang into action. "Miss Polly, you come up here by her head and keep her focused on you. Talk her into little breaths, no pushing yet." He switched places with Polly and sat near Cissie's legs. "Cissie, I need to press on your belly pretty hard. I may have to reach in and turn your baby around if I can. It will hurt, but it's for the best. You breathe with Miss Polly now." His eyes locked on Polly's and she nodded.

"Cissie, little breaths like you're blowing out a candle, perhaps," Polly offered. "Look at me. Think of getting your baby out. Help it out, Cissie. Little breaths." The slave woman looked up at Polly skeptically and began to pant softly.

"That's right, Cissie. You do what Miss Polly tells ya now," Ona said. Outside, thunder rumbled in the distance. The little cabin grew darker as the sky threatened rain. The pitter-patter of a few raindrops began on the roof.

Ben spread his fingers wide and placed them on Cissie's stomach. He pressed and prodded, causing Cissie to groan. His face was lost in concentration, and beads of sweat appeared on his forehead. "It won't move," he murmured.

"Cissie," he said quietly, "I have to reach inside for its head or legs. I'm so sorry." Cissie nodded furiously, tears welling in her brown eyes. She lay back and closed her eyes.

"Ma, push on her stomach at the next contraction?" Ben said quietly, as he reached gingerly inside Cissie's birth canal.

"Ben, I done that," Ona said. "That baby don't move none. I ain't strong enough to push any harder." Outside, thunder rumbled again.

"I know, but someone has to push the baby's head when I pull the legs," Ben said.

"I can do that," Polly said. "Ona, you tell her how to breathe. I haven't had a baby. I don't know what I'm saying."

"You did alright." Ben smiled. Ona and Polly switched places. "Miss Polly, lean across her with all your weight when I say." Ben continued, "I know you aren't used to this, but you'll have to trust me. It won't hurt her more than she's already being hurt. And if you feel the head, something hard and round pushing up, push it down toward the floor, not toward me, understand?"

Polly nodded. Cissie groaned and arched her back in another contraction. "Alright, Miss Polly, now," Ben ordered.

Polly draped herself across the slave woman's abdomen with all her weight. Cissie moaned and gasped for breath. Polly felt the rolling heft of a tiny skull under her rib cage and cried out, "Ben, I feel the head."

"Push down hard, harder than you think she can bear," Ben said. He had his hand around the baby's chubby leg and reached between Cissie's spread legs for the other. "I may have to break the other leg," he murmured. The patter overhead of raindrops on tin quickly became a deafening drumroll, as small pellets of hail pelted the roof and bounced to the ground.

Ona nodded. "We know, son. We know. You got to save Cissie." She wiped the sweat from Cissie's face.

"My baby!" cried Cissie, sobbing into Ona's shoulder.

The stink and close air of the tiny shack made Polly want to wretch, but she pressed the little skull down hard toward his mother's spine. She felt the sting of hot tears running down her own face.

She watched Ben, who was lost in concentration.

"I found the second leg," he said. He pulled it slowly from the birth canal. The baby's torso spilled out onto the bloody blanket. "Let go now, Miss Polly!" Ben shouted, and then wiped his brow on his forearm.

Polly sat up and saw that the infant was a boy. An exceptionally large boy. The baby's head and one arm were still wedged inside Cissie's body.

"Cissie, this boy wants nothing more than to come on out and meet his mama. You got to help me get him here, you hear me?" Ben barked. He quickly wrapped the torso in a piece of dirty quilt. "Do not push until I say so." He looked at her tenderly. "Little breaths, Cissie."

Cissie moaned but focused on Ben's face.

"Miss Polly, run get the straps. You remember the foaling box in the barn?"

Polly nodded.

"Run quick," Ben whispered. "If this baby tries to take a breath, he'll die."

Polly hiked up her skirts and ran out into the deluge. Her boots splashed through muddy puddles. She threw open the barn doors and ran the length of the building. She remembered exactly where the box was stored and grabbed it roughly. The tin box slid out of her hands, and she grabbed at it harshly, slicing her left palm. She winced and dropped it into the hay.

She crouched and replaced the contents with her shaking right hand and raced back into the storm. The children were nowhere in sight as she heaved the door open. The stench and smoke from the damp fire nearly drove her outside, but she stepped in and handed Ben the box.

Ben quickly cinched one leather strap tightly under the baby's rib cage and looked up at Polly. If this worked, Polly knew that Cissie's life might be spared, but the infant could suffocate if it weren't already dead.

"Ma, you have to stand her up when I say so," Ben barked. He turned to Polly.

"Help my Ma. But on the next contraction, you need to pull on the legs. Just lay down on the floor and pull. If that doesn't move it, I'm gonna have to reach in to find the arm and you pull around his stomach."

Polly nodded. Cissie's belly began to tighten up and a low moan escaped her throat. "Now, Ma," Ben snapped.

Together, Ona and Polly hoisted Cissie up to a crouching position, and then Polly quickly slipped to the floor. She grabbed the baby's dangling feet and gasped at their cold and slippery feel. Ben grimaced as he pulled on the baby's rib cage. Nothing. Cissie moaned.

Ben closed his eyes and reached between Cissie's legs, feeling for an arm. When he found it over the baby's head, he repositioned it before pulling it through the birth canal. The arm slid out easily. Cissie screamed in pain, and then collapsed in a faint on top of Ben and Polly.

Ben scrambled out from under Cissie's weight and pulled Polly to her knees. Polly barely had the strength to get up. The baby's gray body lay limply between its mother's legs, all of it delivered except the head.

"God he'p us," declared Ona. "What we gonna do now?"

"If it doesn't come the next pain, Cissie's likely to die," Ben murmured wearily.

Polly gasped. "Ben! Help her!" She wiped a bloodstained hand across her forehead.

"It isn't moving," he whispered. "It's too big. I think it's dead."

"Save Cissie's life, Ben," Polly cried. "If the baby's dead, do what you have to."

Ben thought for a moment. "I'll wrap the strap around the neck. You pull the hips. While she's in a faint, maybe we can pull this child out whole. Ma, hold under her arms to keep her from sliding toward me." Ben watched as Cissie's abdomen hardened again. "Quick. Pull as hard as you can, Polly!" Ben tightened the strap around the child's neck, tears streaming down his dark cheeks.

Polly's lips quivered as she realized that any last chance for the baby's life was literally crushed in the very act of saving his mother. She wrapped a strap around the baby's hips and strained to pull as Ben directed. Slowly, Polly felt the body begin to move. As the two of them pulled, the baby's head began to emerge above the tightened strap. The tiny, pointed chin thrown back, open mouth next, button nose, and then the crown slipped out easy and smooth. The baby lay grey and lifeless, while Ben and Polly gasped for breath on the floor. A slow-spreading ring of purple encircled the baby's neck like a noose. Ben gently loosened the leather strap and arranged the baby's head at a proper angle.

Polly quickly knelt and scooped up the infant tenderly. She rubbed him briskly with her skirt, silently mouthing prayers to God as she did so.

She slapped his feet. She scooped a finger into his mouth and out again. Nothing. His head fell limp in Polly's lap.

"Polly, his neck's broken," Ben whispered, stifling a cry. "He's gone. Let's tend to Cissie."

Polly sat back in a heap with the baby in her arms, crying in huge shaking sobs. Ben rolled Cissie onto her back and placed a balled-up quilt under her head for a cushion. Ona took a rag and a basin and began to clean Cissie's legs and abdomen. In minutes, a gush of blood and afterbirth poured from between Cissie's spread legs, and Ona quickly cut the umbilical cord, mopped up the mess, and placed it in the basin. "It all there."

Ben scooped up an unconscious Cissie and placed her on the bed tenderly. Ona covered Cissie's legs with a threadbare blanket and sighed heavily. "She breathin' alright. An' she didn't lose too much blood, thanks to you, Ben. I'm gone let her sleep a bit." Ona stood and stretched before picking up the basin. Outside, the sudden rainstorm began to ebb as quickly as it had started. "I take this mess out. George'll bury it later. I come clean up and tend Cissie tonight if that's fine with you, Miss Polly. George can watch the chi'dren."

Polly nodded. Ben squatted next to her and reached for the baby. "Here, let me take him to his daddy. I got some explaining to do to George," Ben said sadly. He took the baby tenderly, wrapped him in an old blanket, and cradled the body in one strong arm. He noticed Polly's bloody hand and pointed at the nasty gash across her palm.

Polly shook her head. "It's nothing. And you did not do anything wrong. You saved Cissie's life. If you hadn't done what you knew to do, they both would have died." Ben gazed at Polly and finally smiled. She knew her brown hair was wet and matted to her forehead. Blood was smeared across her cheek and bodice. Her skirt was mud-stained and dripping onto the wooden floor. "Miss Polly." He smiled and continued playfully, "You are one ugly mess."

Polly put a hand to her face and smiled weakly. "If only Floride Calhoun could see me now."

— • —

POLLY STAYED AWAY FROM THE SLAVE quarters for several days while Cissie and George mourned the death of their baby boy. The hands held a small ceremony and laid the infant to rest behind the cabins, in the makeshift slave cemetery. The tiny grave was dwarfed by the plots belonging to Ezekiel, Martin, and Duke, whose final resting places were no longer mounded and fresh, but sunken places in the ground marked by rough wooden crosses.

From inside the house, Polly could still hear Cissie keening for her baby boy, as the field hands sang of God's mercy, in their rich tenor and bass voices. The older children stood by obediently, but George carried Sol in his arms. Ona stood at the grave with Cissie, supporting the bereft mother. Ben sulked and stayed busy on the forge.

Polly decided to wait before asking George to begin the pruning. It didn't feel right to intrude on their mourning time. Tom would soon be home soon enough and he could take over in earnest. She had excused Ona from house chores and had put a kettle on for her own morning tea. She regretted letting Kate go. I really need her now, she thought.

The weather was clear and cooler after the storm, and the cloudless blue sky promised no more rain that day. Polly decided to ride Delightful into the fields and check the young cotton plants after the hail. She slipped on the bridle and saddled the mare by herself. She put one boot into the stirrup and began to hoist herself up, before the sharp sting of pain in her hand shot right up her arm.

"Ow," she cried, hopping back to the ground. She quickly removed her glove and winced at the long crimson slash in her palm. Blood slowly seeped out of the wound. The gash would heal badly, she thought, if she didn't get it tended. She pulled out her handkerchief and used it to staunch the blood, then pulled the leather glove on delicately. "Well, my girl, a change of plans.

We are going into town," she said under her breath, patting Delightful's mane. A visit to the doctor was in order, and a welcome change of scenery after the gut-wrenching experience with the birth. She took a deep breath and pulled herself into the tall saddle with just her right arm. She knew that her position atop her horse was precarious enough with one hand, so she lifted her leg and swung it across the horse's back, to ride astride. Sidesaddle was out of the question. After adjusting her skirts, she pressed her heels into Delightful's flanks and cantered down the long drive.

— • —

DR. ADGER BENT INTENTLY OVER POLLY'S PALM, carefully stitching the wound closed with a small, curved needle. Mrs. Adger had given her a full shot of whiskey to ease the pain, and Polly marveled at its sedating powers as the doctor stitched. Her eyes were squeezed shut, but she related the traumatic events of Cissie's labor and delivery as the doctor tended the gash.

"It's deep, Miss Polly. I am quite impressed that you can bear this so well." Dr. Adger chuckled. "I could give you a stick to bite on, but you seem fine."

Polly winced. "It does sting, but I am using my new and hard-won fortitude. I am going to have to come up with more pleasant ways to spend my time than assisting at slave births. I've never been near a labor and delivery, much less a slave's delivery. It was quite horrific and very personal. The baby was breech and wedged tightly. Ben did a masterful job of saving Cissie. I think that it will be difficult to treat them quite the same way after that experience."

"Babies all come out the same way, slave or free. It was good of you to help Cissie out. She could have died. I know many mistresses would have let the slave mother and baby die, for want of a helping hand," the doctor muttered.

"You have a tender heart for all men, Dr. Adger. And women. I am beginning to appreciate how rare that is around here," Polly said.

The doctor looked into Polly's face for a moment before resuming his stitches.

"There you are, my dear. All finished. Now, are you sure I can't have my man drive you home in the carriage? You must refrain from using that hand for a while," Dr. Adger admonished.

"Nonsense, Dr. Adger. I am fine. These will stay tight, I am sure, and Delightful knows what to do," Polly said as she admired the tiny row of stitches down her palm.

"Besides, I thought I would check in at the Post Office and the Mercantile first." Polly gingerly pulled on her glove.

Dr. Adger sighed. "No need to visit the Mercantile. Did you see how empty it is? Neither a bag of salt nor a pound of nails to be had, my dear."

"On the contrary." Polly smiled mischievously. "I am going in response to the sign in the store window."

"Did they get in a shipment of dry goods?" Dr. Adger asked eagerly.

Polly shook her head and grinned. "Puppies!"

Chapter Thirty-One

June 3, 1861

COME ON THEN, COME ON!" POLLY LAUGHED and patted her thigh as the mongrel pup tumbled head over heels in his haste to follow her. The day was pleasant and breezy, and Polly had decided to take her new puppy on a long walk to the orchard. She wanted to see the trees for herself before they were pruned. Her wide-brimmed bonnet shaded her from the bright sunshine, and she carried a straw basket in one hand. A small water jug, a wrapped ham biscuit, a spade, and shears weighed down the basket.

The black and white puppy stopped at every fence post, sniffing at hidden scents, and chasing grasshoppers as they buzzed and shot up out of the hedges. *It's a glorious day for gardening*, she mused. Polly was pleased to see the cotton and corn coming up nicely. Several of her field hands stooped low to their work, using hoes to hack at weeds between the emerald rows. She could not make out exactly who they were from such a distance. They lifted their hands to her in greeting and she waved back, pleased that her assistance with Cissie's delivery had, in a way, canceled out the slaves' displeasure at her sending Kate back to River Wood.

Kate. After Jane died, Zadoc had come home sad and worn down, as Polly expected. Of course, he had lost his mother and his poor father was still miles away and in ill health, himself. Polly made a mental note to have Zee take some staples to River Wood so that he could visit his father and provide extra fatback and venison for Kate to prepare for the hands. Feeling benevolent, she would send assurance through Zee, that Sol was doing well under Ona and Cissie's care.

Her thoughts drifted like the swaying milkweed and she realized that she had not named the pup yet. Combing through a list of names in her mind, she remembered her childhood pet fondly, a short-haired mutt named Jack. This new pup was so similar in personality, she thought, as she watched him chase a butterfly along the property line. *Why not?* she mused.

"Alright, my little one. You shall be my Jack Two." She laughed. "Come on, Jack!" She whistled the way her brother Caleb had taught her years earlier, and Jack turned on a dime to follow his young mistress.

They approached the orchard, with its gnarled old fruit trees still standing in neat rows. Polly could see that George and the boys had worked a miracle, clearing out the underbrush that threatened to consume the place. Nearby, several piles of debris stood way over her head. Blossoms still clung to some of the trees, but most had shed their pink and white petals and tiny green leaves fluttered in the breeze. Small hard fruits, the size of marbles, replaced the tiny flowers.

Polly smiled with pleasure at the serenity of the place. Peaches and apples. Her father had planted the trees before Polly was born, on the beautiful hillside at the edge of the property. She noticed that many trees had split and cracked where branches were too heavy or at odd angles. Some were indeed dead, but most were just in need of a correct pruning to begin bearing again.

Jack pranced around the orchard, yipping and chasing scents, and digging into abandoned groundhog burrows. Polly trimmed small branches and pulled weeds, all the while admiring the orderly precision the rows of trees exemplified. Carolina wrens flitted around her and a nuthatch chided her for being so near its nest. She felt happy and close to her father out here, and wiped beads of sweat from her face joyfully. As far from the house as she could get and still be on her own property, she breathed in deeply and thought, *This is mine.* One of the slaves had left a shovel behind, and Polly used it to dig up a few grapevines that had reemerged and would strangle the less healthy trees if left alone.

Several hours passed quickly and afternoon shadows lengthened under the trees. Polly removed her bonnet and wiped her forehead with her sleeve. Her wounded left hand throbbed under its bandage.

She saw Jack head into the woods at the far end of the orchard. She whistled. "Jack, come now. Come on!" she called firmly. The pup ignored her and continued his romp along an old deer trail. Exasperated, Polly put down her basket of tools and headed in his direction.

"Jack! Come, pup!" she called again, and climbed over the split rail fence that marked her property line. She ducked under low-hanging branches, batted at spider webs, and sidestepped poison ivy. Pushing aside the branches of a beech sapling, she soon came to the charred, barely visible remains of the old Kemp trading post, now swallowed in Virginia creeper and poison oak. Jack nosed through the old boards, searching for the mouse or chipmunk he had been chasing.

Polly inhaled sharply and stopped in her tracks, her feet afraid to cross an invisible boundary. Her quickening heartbeat was the only sound that she heard. *Even the birds do not sing in this God-forsaken place,* she thought. She exhaled slowly. In a daze, Polly began to walk slowly around the perimeter of the collapsed structure, now little more than a debris pile.

I remember this place, she thought. At the far edge of her mind drifted vague images of her big brothers. At first, Polly tried to shut them out. She kicked at the charred timbers with her boot and they disintegrated into ash. She knelt in the dirt and drew with her fingers.

From that low vantage point, she instantly remembered the little girl looking up at Joshua, with his gap-toothed grin, splashing through the creek. There was tall Caleb, laughing while he thrust the spider-like crawdad toward his little sister.

She remembered trying to keep up with her brothers that day, on their way to tell Mr. Kemp about an Indian man. But Jack had dawdled and there were so many daisies along the path. Daisy chains and a licorice twist and peaches from the orchard. She remembered.

Polly shivered even though the day was warm. She sat down on a charred stump at the edge of the blackened pile and reached her shaking hand toward the decaying remains of a wooden beam.

Remember? she heard Caleb whisper in her mind.

I owe my brothers this, she thought.

Polly closed her eyes. Suddenly, the graphic images came unbidden. She saw the events unfold again, but this time, instead of watching in a child's trance, a grown Polly made herself look.

The small cabin was on fire and Mr. Kemp was dead. She knew it from the way his head lay cockeyed in the dust, like Cissie's baby after Ben broke its tiny neck. His scalp was bloody and hairless. Still, Polly watched and listened. Old Nancy Kemp burst from the store, yelling for help, pushing Caleb and Joshua ahead of her. Polly saw her brave brothers, just children, kicking and pummeling their attackers, to no avail. Nancy was pushed back inside the burning building. Polly heard her screams of rage turn to agony.

Remember. Polly knew that there was more. She understood that she had to keep watching, that there was so much to see. With a deep breath, she looked into the past and saw sweet, towheaded Joshua launch himself at one of the thieves, hanging around his neck for dear life. The man heaved and tossed the boy down hard, his spine hitting the sharp edge of the porch steps. Joshua lay still. Caleb cried out angrily and threw himself at the man, but the rifle butt came down hard and Polly winced.

Remember. She wiped her eyes with trembling fingers. The little store was ablaze. Timbers snapped and fell inward as the dry roof burned. Polly stared at her brothers and Mr. Kemp, all lying dead in the dirt. *Remember what? What am I looking for?*

As if in answer, the two thieves came into focus, one red-bearded and rough. He lifted his kerchief from his face. He laughed and spat a stream of fetid tobacco juice on Mr. Kemp's bloody shirt. The other man, younger and trim, ran a hand through his blond curls before pulling a bottle from his back pocket. Polly gasped in disbelief and felt the bile rise in her throat. He uncapped the bottle and drank deeply of the amber contents, before replacing his handkerchief and crouching in front of the black cast-iron safe.

It was too much. Too much for a little girl. No wonder Polly had pushed it down all those years ago. The child shut her eyes tightly.

"Miss Polly! Miss Polly! We have to go!" The familiar voice quieted her mind only a bit.

Polly opened her eyes and saw the skinny brown boy tugging her arm, eyes as big as saucers. Ben. She shook her head and yanked her arm from his grasp. She curled into the fetal position and her mind went blank.

Polly was jolted back to the present by the cicadas buzzing rhythmically in the heat. Jack had retreated to the shade, tongue lolling, to wait for his mistress. Her dress was stained with sweat and her throat was parched.

She slowly lifted herself to stand and shook the dirt from her skirts. She began to walk unsteadily away from the burned-out cabin and hoisted herself over the split rail fence, snagging her petticoat on the rough wood. She dragged back into the orchard and collapsed under the apple tree where her basket and tools lay.

Polly whipped off her hat and reached inside the basket for the jar of water. She uncapped it quickly and drank the cool contents in one long gulp. Then she leaned back against the tree trunk and closed her eyes and slept the sleep of the righteous.

She startled awake to Jack's pink tongue lapping at her cheeks and chin. "No, Jack. Stop it!" she snapped, wiping her face with her apron.

The sun was low behind the orchard and the far river. She scrambled to her feet and stretched. Looking down at her stained skirt and dragging piece of petticoat, she wondered at how she must look. She imagined what John would say and then damned the very thought of the man.

Polly reached up to find that her hair had tumbled to her shoulders and her combs were missing. She angrily stashed her tools and bonnet in the basket and headed for home, Jack trailing obediently behind her.

— • —

EARLY EVENING FOUND BEN AND ZADOC in the barn finishing chores. Standing in the loft, Ben pitched several bales of hay to the floor below down below to Zee. The oppressive heat of the day had accumulated in the rafters and left him sweat-soaked and thirsty. He climbed down the ladder and watched Zee toss the sweet-smelling hay into the cows' stalls. "You almost done? It's about quitting time."

"Yeah. 'Bout done. I'm happy to see Lydia obeyed me and cleaned out the manure and watered the horses earlier," Zadoc began. "She's little, but she's startin' to he'p out." He propped the pitchfork against a stall and turned to go. "I see you later, Ben."

A cool breeze blew through the open barn doors and Ben paused and wiped his face with his handkerchief. The smell of roasting meat made his stomach rumble and he wondered what his mother would have for his supper.

Delightful whinnied, and Ben stopped and spoke softly to the horse, stroking her silky nose. He reached in his pocket and produced a single turnip, which she took from him gently. The foal appeared from behind his mother and nudged Ben's hand. He shrugged. "Haven't got another one. Your mama can share."

He stopped at the trough in front of the barn and splashed cool water onto his face and neck. He took off his sweat-soaked shirt and tied it around his waist, sighing with relief. The last shadows of the day stretched long across the yard.

"Ben," a sharp voice said from behind him. He wheeled around to see a bedraggled Polly, hair down and unkempt, the hem of her dress torn and stained. Her new pup danced at Ben's feet, eager for affection.

"What happened to you, Miss Polly?" Ben asked, taking in her appearance and basket of tools. "Ma said you went to the orchard. Looks like you brought some of it home with you." He smiled and crouched low to scratch the pup's ears. "Bet you'll be glad when Mr. Roper comes back."

Polly came closer and leaned over Ben, stabbing her finger toward his face. "How dare you. You were there," she hissed. "You were there and you didn't say anything." Polly glared at him, her face pale as chalk. "All those years. . . . You knew what happened to my brothers. How could you?" she wailed. She turned and began to walk to the house, her head bent low.

In an instant, Ben made the connection between the orchard and the proximity to the Kemp place. He stood and jogged after her. "Miss Polly! Polly, let me talk to you!"

He caught up to her and walked quickly to keep pace. He reached for her arm and she jerked it away harshly. "Don't touch me! Don't you ever lay a hand on me! I hate you!" She ran her hands through her hair. "Do you understand?" she spat. "My poor mother languished for years after they died. My father's heart probably gave out from the stress of those years. Do you know what you have done?" She put a shaking hand to her chest. "You let me marry that man!" In the gathering dark, Polly could hardly make out Ben's face. "You let them get away with murder for years!" she cried, balling up her fists.

Ben lifted his hands in defense and said gently, "Please, Miss Polly! Listen to me. We were children. I was twelve! You were in shock. Yes, I followed you and your brothers that day, which was wrong. I could have been whipped for that alone. I came up behind you at the Kemps and saw what happened. You were curled up in a ball on the ground. I tried to drag you away. You wouldn't move." Ben shook his head at the memory. "They left after they killed everyone—after they took whatever was in the safe—I knew you'd be alright for a while. I had to go back."

He swallowed hard and searched her face. "If I had tried to call out or stop them, they would have come after us too. It looked like a robbery gone wrong and the boys got in the way. So I ran home. Your daddy had everyone out looking for you all that night and I knew right where to go. And Mama said that those white men who came to meet with your daddy would never believe me, so she told me to keep quiet. To wait until you could speak of it. We thought surely you'd remember. But as time went by, you didn't seem to be able to tell any of it . . ."

"Oh my God," Polly groaned.

"You never spoke of it. They'd as soon string me up as to believe what I said. A slave boy's word against white men. And every time I wanted to talk to you, Mama would remind me of what a man like Wilkins would do to me—and to her. I couldn't let anything happen to her." The words tumbled out.

Polly poked her finger in Ben's chest. "Ben, you stood aside and let me marry that man. I don't care how afraid you were. You allowed me to marry the man who was there and watched Clay Wilkins kill my brothers." she put her hands to her face. "God in heaven. I saw John barricade an old woman in a burning building. Oh, I'm going to be sick," she wailed, putting a hand to her mouth.

"I'm a slave. How could I stand a chance accusing white men?" Ben cried. "But now that you remember, what can you do?"

Polly shook her head sorrowfully. "I don't know. . . . But this must be the hold that Wilkins has on John. John was there that day with him."

Ben extended his hand. "Miss Polly, it's getting dark. Come into the kitchen house. We can talk there. Mama will be wondering what to do with your supper."

"I'm not hungry. I must think about this. About what to do." She wiped at her dirt-streaked face.

Ben spoke softly. "There's more you should know. But I think Mama should be there, too. Come with me." He turned and started for the kitchen, Polly reluctantly trailing behind him.

Ben stepped up to the screened door and yanked it open. Polly stepped inside and Ben followed. Ona stood at the table, slicing a loaf of bread. She put the knife down. "Miss Girl!" she said. "What on earth happened to you? I wondered why you didn't call fo' yo' supper! You a mess!"

"I was in the orchard," Polly said softly.

Ona looked at Ben expectantly. "What y'all up to? You both look like you seen a ghost."

"She finally remembers, Mama," Ben said. "About Caleb and Joshua."

"Sweet Jesus!" cried Ona. She rushed around the table and gently steered Polly to the chair. She poured a cup of water and handed it to Polly, who gratefully took the cup with shaking hands. She drank and then sat quietly. Ona tenderly tucked loose strands of hair behind her ears.

"Babies, how did this happen?" Ona looked from Polly up to Ben.

Polly sat up straight and looked at Ona. "I went past the orchard, looking for my puppy. When I came to the burned-out Kemp place, it came back to me in a flood. As if Caleb and Joshua needed me to know. I can hardly take it in even now. But I remember everything."

Ona knelt by Polly's chair. "You know I couldn't let my boy go to yo' daddy with the truth. He was off Whitehall property, followin' you chi'dren. No one woulda believed him. They woulda taken Ben away and strung him up or whipped him to death. He was just a boy hisself." Ona stroked Polly's hand. "All we could do was take care of you and yo' mama, and hope that the truth would come out. That you would remember soon."

Polly jerked her hand away but then softened. "It's true. If the law didn't take Ben away, Wilkins and his cronies would have done the deed themselves."

"What do you think John was doing there?" Polly whispered.

"He weren't raised right. I think he was a young man caught up in Wilkins' drinkin' and carousin'. Stealin' from ol' Kemp musta sounded excitin' to yo' husband. Ev'ryone knew Mr. Kemp had that safe on his property. Yo' husband's mama had died years befo' and his daddy wasn't no great thing. Old Sam had his way with the slave women, and even some little girls. Never paid no mind to John . . ." She paused. "I think John

Stone got mixed up in somethin' he couldn't get out of, an' if he tried to get rid of Wilkins, Wilkins woulda turned him in to the law."

"How sick. How twisted," Polly muttered.

"Remember, Miss Girl, I lived there at River Wood. I was a present to yo' parents from Sam Stone. I know lots of bad things."

Polly shifted in her seat and looked at Ona directly. "Tell me," she whispered. "I have to know everything."

— • —

IT WAS AFTER MIDNIGHT WHEN POLLY left the kitchen house. She held the lantern high and walked slowly up the steps to the back door of the house. Ona had offered to come and help her prepare for bed but Polly had declined. She wanted to be alone, to think about what would come next.

She moved through the dark house in shadows, ascending the stairs as if climbing a great mountain. Too tired even to take a wet cloth to her face, she stripped her dirty clothing off in a heap on the floor and climbed into bed naked. Jack leaped up onto the quilt beside his mistress. Polly was sound asleep before Jack snuggled into the space vacated by her husband.

Chapter Thirty-Two

June 4, 1861

POLLY OPENED SLEEPY EYES TO FIND ONA BUSTLING quietly about in her room. A tea tray lay next to her bed, and the aroma of hot biscuits wafted into her nostrils. Polly stretched out her hand and smoothed her puppy's silky fur. Jack's tail thumped the mattress in subdued greeting.

"Ona, can you ask someone to get hot water for a bath?" Polly sipped the hot tea gratefully. "I think I got into chiggers yesterday," she sighed, scratching her thigh.

"Yes, Miss Polly," Ona said. "An' I git some pine salve fo' them chiggers."

Polly watched Ona move about the room, opening drawers and getting Polly's clothing ready for the day. Things were different now. The women shared a powerful knowledge. John had murdered a woman. Wilkins had killed Polly's brothers as John watched. John had raped Kate and fathered Solomon. Polly shuddered. It all reminded her of her mother's penny dreadful novels, still lining the parlor shelves. "How is Cissie?"

"She fine. She knows Ben had to do what he done. I think havin' Sol and Lydia around takes the sting out. She back on her feet and in the kitchen this mornin'. I'm gone get the chi'dren and take 'em out to pick them early beans after I get you in the tub."

Polly shook her head. "Did Mother know about Sam Stone—and you?"

"Gracious, no!" Ona frowned. "Leastwise I don't think so. She jes' knew you could do better than marry the likes of John Stone, is all."

"Ona, what should I do?"

Ona picked up Polly's torn petticoat from the floor and gazed at her young mistress. "I 'spect you gone hafta figure that out by yo'se'f. Nothin' changed for me or for Ben, but everything's changed fo' you. Jes' please don't tell Mr. Stone nothing about Ben bein' there. Please."

"I won't mention Ben. Ona, I don't think there is much I can do about this."

"Why not, Miss Girl? You is white! You can go to the law and tell 'em what you remember. How it happened," Ona said. "Yo' husband he'ped murder four white people, he did. Your kin!"

Polly thought of her meetings with Mr. Legarre. "I am a white woman. Just a woman. My word means nothing against my husband, and no one would believe my story after all this time. I went to see a lawyer about getting rid of Mr. Wilkins as overseer and was told I have no power . . . and in fact, they took the inheritance money from my grandparents and paid off John's mortgage with it. They would see this as an attempt to get an annulment. No, my word means nothing because I am a married woman."

Later that morning, Polly stepped outside and headed for the barn. As she passed through the weathered doors into the cool dark space, she heard Lydia and Silas laughing from overhead. She looked up into the dim loft in time to see the children tossing handfuls of straw down onto Ben below. Straw drifted down like confetti in shafts of sunlight. It stuck out at odd angles in his black hair, and down his collar. When the children saw Polly, they ducked behind bales of hay and were quiet.

"Goodness, you look like a scarecrow." Polly chuckled.

Ben shook his head and pulled handfuls of straw from his faded shirt. "I feel like one, too." He looked up toward the loft and said loudly, "These children best get to work now. Didn't I tell you both to go slop the hogs?" Polly heard the tiny footfalls of the children scampering down the ladder and watched them shoot out of the barn's open doors without a word.

Polly turned to watch the children run by. "They're afraid of me," she said. "And I don't blame them one bit." Delightful whinnied softly and Polly walked over and stroked the mare's mane. The foal nudged Polly's hand expectantly and Polly laughed, pulling several carrots from her apron pocket. "Where is Zee?"

Ben leaned on a pitchfork. "George sent him to hoe corn with the others. Delightful threw a shoe. I just put a new one on and I'll get your horses out to pasture now."

Polly nodded. "I can take Delightful and . . ." She paused. "Courage." She looked at Ben and then the foal.

"Courage, huh? Sounds like a good name for a horse. Need some more courage around here." He chuckled.

Polly offered a wan smile. "I need your help."

Ben shook his head. "I am not going to the law with my story. Don't ask me to. You know what could happen to Mama and me." Ben paused. "Even if I am your husband's half-brother and you are my sister-in-law."

Polly grimaced and shook her head. "I have no recourse with the law, either. Not in this. But I want to get Kate back," she said resolutely. "I want Ezra here, too. I'm going to River Wood this afternoon. I plan to walk into the house and take them. I am the mistress. If that man dares come onto this property to get them back, he'll find himself at the other end of a gun."

Hope leaped in Ben's chest but he tempered his reaction. "That's big talk. Isn't Mr. Roper coming back tomorrow? Wait for him and see what he says," urged Ben.

"No. He will talk me out of it. John wrote letters to both of us. It said that Kate was to go to River Wood. Mr. Roper won't go against John, not on this. He doesn't know the details, and I am not sure I want to tell him." She reached into her skirt's deep pocket and pulled out a silver pistol.

"Whoa now, Miss Polly!" Ben said sharply. "That's a lot more courage than you need right now." He raised his palms and backed away. "Have you ever used the thing?"

Polly ignored his question. "Ben, drive me over to River Wood this afternoon in the wagon. If anyone asks, we're taking supplies to Kate. You'll wait by the wagon. I will go inside the house to get Kate and Ezra. You help Ezra up into the wagon. I hardly think the man is in any shape to climb aboard himself, and we may need to move quickly. I don't want you to come to any more trouble with Wilkins than you have to, though. We can hide them under tarps in case Wilkins makes an appearance. But I will come home with Kate and Ezra," she said firmly. "If we plan it right, Wilkins won't be around the house in the middle of the afternoon. He'll be in the fields. Or passed out drunk. If he dares show up here later, I have this. Daddy's pistol is a just-in-case."

She looked up at Ben. "I have to do something. You understand." She shoved the pistol down into her skirt pocket and added, "They took my entire family from me."

Polly didn't wait for an answer. She opened Delightful's stall and led her out by the bridle. The colt followed willingly. "Meet me in the front of the house with the wagon when George rings the lunch bell. Bring tarps and some jugs of water. And Ben," she paused. "Do not mention this to anyone else. Not even Ona." She clicked her tongue and Delightful began to walk slowly out of the barn into the bright sunshine, Courage trotting close behind.

— • —

POLLY ROCKED IMPATIENTLY ON THE FRONT PORCH, Jack asleep at her feet in the heat of the midday sun. Her ears alert for the sound of the slaves' lunch bell, she watched a wasp as it constructed a nest in the corner of the ceiling and thought of all that had changed in twenty-four hours. Her straw bonnet lay in her lap, the cold heft of her father's pistol nestled inside. A Colt Walker revolver, it weighed in at well over four pounds unloaded. But now it was loaded.

She walked through the plan in her mind, unsure of exactly how it might unfold. The gun is only for show, she told herself, if there happens to be a confrontation. Polly tried to remember the specifics of the few times she had gone out to target shoot with her father. She had been ten or twelve years old, maybe. It hadn't held much interest at the time, but she was a good shot.

Kate was sure to be in the house or in the kitchen when they arrived. Ezra was another story. Zadoc had told her of his failing health, but without knowing where his cabin was or what his chores were, she was unsure of how to locate the old slave. Anger welled up again in her chest. What could be done? If she went to the sheriff or to Mr. Legarre, they would both think her story a lie in response to a rushed marriage gone bad, soured by John's debt and the bank seizure of her large inheritance. Her brothers had died over twelve years ago. Why would she come forward now?

Briefly, she considered the idea of asking Ben to corroborate her story, but that could mean that Ben or even Ona could come to harm. No, she thought, but I will do what I can to take back what is mine. Even Mr. Legarre had given the nod to her moving a slave from one holding to another. She would take Kate and Ezra and be done with River Wood for good. Only after securing their safety and having Mr. Roper back on the property would she then go see Harrison Legarre about an annulment of her sham marriage.

The loud clanging of the lunch bell caused Polly to nearly jump from her seat. Her hands shook as she stood and tied her bonnet under her chin. She carefully placed the gun in her brocaded bag. I will do what I can to take back what is mine. Jack sat up and watched his mistress as she began to pace the length of the porch.

The rattle of the old wagon made Jack perk up his ears in anticipation. He barked and then trotted down the steps, tail wagging, as Ben slowed the horse to a stop. It whinnied and danced nervously, the little dog yapping at its hooves.

"Whoa there, Jack. This ol' boy is likely to squash you flat if you aren't careful," Ben warned. He turned to see Polly gathering her things and he called out, "You sure this is the day for this? Tomorrow afternoon with Mr. Roper back—might make things easier." Polly hurried to scoop up the puppy. She climbed up the steps, opened the door, and closed him inside the house.

"Mr. Roper will not need to be involved in this," Polly answered firmly. "I must get Kate and Ezra today, while I have the resolve. Did you get water jugs? Tarps?"

Ben nodded toward the supplies in the back of the wagon. "I threw in some sacks of cornmeal, in case we needed proof we're bringing supplies."

Polly climbed up into the wagon and sat down next to Ben. She looked at him defiantly, her dark eyes flashing. "Good thinking. Let's go."

He eyed Polly's drawstring bag as she laid it carefully at her feet. "Looks like you're toting more than usual. I sure hope that thing isn't going to blow off my foot if we hit a pothole," he said wryly.

"I said let's go, Ben." Polly leaned over and grabbed the reins and flicked them lightly, urging the horse down the driveway.

— • —

THE WAGON BUMPED DOWN THE rutted road to River Wood, clouds of red dust swirling behind them. "We aren't exactly coming in unannounced," Ben said.

"No matter," Polly answered. "If Wilkins is not about, we can take Ezra and Kate and leave quickly. If Ezra answers the door, I will tell him we have cornmeal to give to Kate. I will ask to see her. When she comes to the door, we'll get them both quickly into the wagon and you'll drive us home as fast as possible."

Ben frowned. "That'll take care of two possibilities, Miss Polly . . . but I can think of a whole passel of ways this could go. And not any of them turn out well."

"Ben, you stay with the wagon. You're just my driver today, and you'll unload the cornmeal if it comes to that, while I locate them. I have a right to visit my slave and see how she is faring, especially since her child is at Whitehall and not with her." Polly's fingers were clenched tightly in her lap but she tried to force a smile. "It's a hot day and lunch time at that. Maybe Wilkins is napping away his morning whiskey under a tree somewhere far from the house."

As the wagon approached the house, Polly noted that the exterior was even more dilapidated than her last visit. A wooden shutter hung cock-eyed from a front window and the daylilies once lovingly sown near the front porches were overgrown and struggling in the dry heat.

"I am ashamed to be associated with this place. The sooner this is over with, the better," she muttered. "Ben, wait here. I do not want to get you any more involved in this than you already are. Only if Ezra needs to be carried will I call on you."

Polly gathered her skirts in one hand and held onto the wagon frame as she climbed down from the buckboard. "Hand me my bag, please," she directed.

Ben made to argue but she cut him off. "Ben, my bag." She reached up for the brocaded purse. She looked at him directly and he briefly glimpsed the anger in her eyes before her mask of calm descended again.

Ben shook his head. "No. This is going to go a whole lot better without your bag. Go ahead and knock on the door. You're just taking a slave back to Whitehall and you told me that a lawyer said you have the right. Wasn't Kate a wedding present?"

She sighed and turned toward the house. She climbed the front steps and lifted the tarnished brass knocker. She knocked loudly and waited. She was about to knock again when the door flew open and an astonished Kate confronted Polly.

"Miss Polly!" she whispered. "What you doin' here?" She looked past Polly and saw Ben. Her face broke into a huge smile, and tears came to her eyes. Polly turned to see Ben smiling back, hand outstretched in a wave. She looked at Kate again and noticed a front tooth missing, a dark hole where there had just weeks ago been a beautiful grin.

"Ah, I see," Polly said. "You're fond of Ben. I had no idea."

"Please, Miss Polly," Kate admonished. "Please come in but I beg you to be quiet. Mr. Wilkins upstairs asleep and I sho' don't want to wake him up."

Polly's anger flared. She motioned Kate outside. "That man is sleeping inside the house?" she hissed.

Kate nodded. "He livin' upstairs in Mr. Stone's room. On the back side of the house."

"Did he knock out your front tooth?" Polly whispered.

Kate nodded.

"He forced himself on you, didn't he? Like Mr. Stone did?"

Kate's face clouded with fear and she looked past Polly to Ben. Ben nodded and said quietly, "Kate, she knows. Miss Polly knows it all. Mama told her. She's here to help."

Kate put her hands to her face and shook her head. "Miss Polly, I ain't never done nothin' to make Mr. Stone favor me!" she whispered sadly. "He ain't bothered me since you all got married and I swear I tried to be a good worker from the time I set foot at Whitehall."

Polly reached for the woman's arm. "Shhh. I believe you, Kate. It wasn't your fault. I need you to quickly get into the wagon bed and cover yourself with a tarp. It will be terribly hot but you must be quiet and very still. I'm taking you away from this God-awful place. But I need to get Ezra, too. Where is he?" she asked. Kate looked past Polly to Ben.

He nodded and said softly, "Come on, Kate. We haven't got much time."

Kate's confusion was obvious but Polly had little time to explain further. She pushed Kate gently toward the steps. "Go quickly. Just tell me where to find Ezra."

Kate shrugged. "I don't know. He was still in his own cabin when Zee was here, but I ain't hardly seen him since. He don't do field work, and ain't allowed in the house no mo.' I ain't seen him, Miss Polly. You want me to go look fo' him, ma'am?"

"No! Get in the wagon. I will try the slave cabins. If I can't find him, we'll go home. I will have to worry about him another time."

Polly followed Kate down the steps. She looked up at Ben. "Get her covered up. It must look like I am just here to check on Ezra and Kate. If Wilkins shows up, that's what you tell him. Tell him I knocked on the door and no one answered so I went to the kitchen to find them."

Ben nodded and hopped down from the wagon seat.

As Polly made her way around the side of the house, she looked back to see Ben take a frightened Kate in his arms. A knot in her stomach tightened and she pulled her eyes away and headed for the slave cabins.

Polly lifted her skirts to move through the tall grass. A few scrawny chickens clucked and flapped their wings to get out of her way as she passed. At the back of the house, she paused and looked up to scan the back windows. Only one window was open, and curtains fluttered at the sill. Polly assumed it must be the window where Wilkins slept. It would be too hot to sleep upstairs without a breeze. She would have to be very quiet.

She turned to see the slave cabins in the distance. As with her last visit, there was no sign of life. Either the hands were in the fields, or they were inside their cabins. It was nothing like Whitehall, where slaves bustled about at chores around the farm during the day. Lunchtime on a warm summer day usually found them sitting amiably under the shade trees eating their lunches of salt pork or beans and biscuits.

A thin line of smoke swirled up from the kitchen house chimney and Polly quietly stepped up and opened the screened door. It screeched loudly and Polly winced. There was no sign of anyone. She thought to check the tiny pantry, since the last time it looked to be used for someone's bed. She peered inside the dark space and gagged as the odor of stale feces and urine hit her in the face. In the dim light, she saw the wizened shape of Ezra curled up on the filthy cot. She quickly covered her nose and mouth with her handkerchief and knelt by the cot.

"Ezra. Ezra, it's Miss Polly. You are ill." In the dark room, Polly could barely make out Ezra's face, but when he opened his rheumy eyes, her heart sank. The whites of his eyes were a deep yellow, a color that Polly remembered from her mother's final days. "Oh, Ezra, I'm going to the wagon to get Ben. He can carry you. I am taking you back home with me to rest and get well." The old man closed his eyes and Polly stood and left the room quickly. She stepped outside and grimaced, as the bile rose in her throat. She forced it back down and closed her eyes, inhaling fresh air in big gulps.

"What the hell are you doin' here?" the now-familiar voice rasped. "John said you was to stay away."

Polly opened her eyes and squinted in the sunlight to see Wilkins coming toward her. As before, he was only half-dressed, and his beard was streaked with tobacco juice stains. He reeked of alcohol despite the time of day. She stood taller and wiped her mouth with the handkerchief. "How dare you speak to me that way? Ezra is sick and needs a doctor's care. I am taking him to Dr. Adger," she said firmly.

"Dr. Adger ain't gone waste his time on no old nigger." Wilkins sneered.

"Nevertheless, I am taking him. I will not stand by and watch another slave die under your watch." In her mind, Polly was only a step ahead of the man. Would he know to check Kate's whereabouts, too?

Quickly formulating a plan, she added, "We had word from Zadoc after his mother passed, that his father was also ill. I have come to collect him. I'm going to have my man, Ben, carry Ezra to the wagon. When he is well, I will return him to River Wood." Polly turned and began to walk toward the front of the house, carefully measuring her steps to give Ben and Kate more time. Horrified, she realized that Wilkins was following her.

She sent up a silent prayer that Kate would be tucked under the tarp as she rounded the corner of the house. Ben was sitting slumped in the driver's seat, hat in his hands. There was no sign of Kate. Ben looked up slowly.

"Ben," called Polly, her voice wavering only a little. "I need you to go get Ezra from the kitchen. He's quite ill and cannot walk. We will take him to see Dr. Adger at once. Zadoc was right to ask me to check on him." She looked at Ben beseechingly.

"Yes, Miss Polly, right away," Ben said obediently. His tone told her that Kate was well hidden under the heavy tarp. He replaced his hat, nodded, and climbed out of the wagon.

"The kitchen is right behind the house. You'll see the chimney smoke," Polly said lightly. "Mr. Wilkins, perhaps you would be so good as to show my slave where the kitchen is?" Polly asked.

Wilkins looked suspiciously from Polly to Ben and back again. "I think Kate should be around here. She can show your nigger where the old man is sleepin', while we chat a spell." He leaned to one side and spat a stream of tobacco juice. The image of the man spitting on Mr. Kemp as he lay dying in the dust sickened her.

"Kate!" he yelled toward the open front door. "Goddammitt, Kate! Get out here!" He looked at Polly suspiciously. "Why is the front door open?"

Ben spoke up. "I can find it, Miss Polly. No need to bother anyone else."

Polly nodded. "Then go along quickly and get Ezra. Dr. Adger is waiting." Ben looked at Polly with concern but said nothing. "Ben, hurry now. Dr. Adger is expecting us town soon," she said. Ben turned and jogged around the side of the house.

Wilkins watched Ben leave and then turned back to Polly, leering with icy blue eyes. She looked away and said too casually, "I saw Kate walking back toward the slave cabins when I was looking for Ezra."

Wilkins spit again and wiped his mouth with the back of his hand. He chuckled and said, "Mizz Stone, fer some reason, I don't believe you." He nodded toward the bed of the wagon. "Fer some reason, I feel like I should check on what you got covered up back 'ere."

Polly's heart dropped into her stomach. "Cornmeal," she faltered. "To sell in town."

The man advanced toward the wagon slowly. Polly stepped forward.

"Mr. Wilkins, you have no right," she stammered, trying to keep the panic from her voice. "As the mistress of this God-forsaken place, I can do what I think best with the slaves and the rest of the property. And you, sir, are terminated as an employee of my husband's. I will have my attorney, Mr. Legarre, draw up the termination papers at once."

Wilkins looked down at her with hatred. "You ain't got any authority over me. I only take direction from yer husband, and he ain't gonna do nothin' to get rid of me." Wilkins quickly sidestepped Polly and moved to the back of the wagon. He reached over the sideboard for the edge of the tarp.

Polly felt as if something inside broke open and a flood of rage overwhelmed her.

"I know what you did, you piece of scum," she said slowly. "You killed my brothers at the Kemps' store. I will see you jailed and hanged for murder before the summer is over," she threatened. "Now get away from my wagon."

Wilkins let go of the corner of the canvas and wheeled around. The color had drained from his face and he actually looked afraid. He grabbed Polly with his strong hands and squeezed her arms tightly. He leaned down, his face inches from her own. The hot stench of stale whiskey was on his breath.

"I'm about fed up with your sass, bitch. An' you ain't got no proof." He shook her, and then pitched her hard into the side of the wagon. Polly felt a rib crack as she hit the iron wheel felloe. She groaned and stood, clutching her side.

Trying to get her breath, she wheezed, "You'll hang for murder. I'll see to it. You and John can both go to hell, as far as I am concerned." She glanced toward the house but there was no sign of Ben.

Wilkins spewed a string of curse words and reached again for the tarp. Polly watched in slow motion as he leaned over the side of the wagon to pull the tarp free.

Suddenly, a shot rang out. The percussive blast smacked Polly's eardrums and she reflexively covered her ears with her hands. She looked up to see Wilkins clutch his stomach and reel back from the wagon in dazed confusion. A crimson stain began to spread across his undershirt. He dropped to his knees, mouth open in surprise. Polly followed his gaze up to the wagon, where Kate sat, drenched in sweat, holding James Burgiss's pistol in her shaking hands.

"Kate! Oh my God, Kate!" Polly screamed.

Kate dropped the gun and began to sob. "I thought he was goin' to kill us! Oh, Jesus, help us, Jesus!" she cried.

Polly watched as Wilkins struggled to get to his feet. "You bitches," he gurgled, trying to stand. The man grimaced and clutched his gut.

Polly quickly hoisted herself up and toppled backward into the wagon bed on top of Kate, crying out in pain as she did so. Grasping her side with one hand, she fumbled for the pistol. In the distance, she heard a voice shout, "Polly! No!"

As Wilkins appeared over the top of the sideboard, Polly raised the pistol and pointed it at the man's face. He lunged toward her and she instinctively pulled the trigger. Wilkins convulsed backward and dropped to the ground.

Polly and Kate clutched one another and slumped to the wagon bed, their tears mingling as they fell.

Ben's voice was sharp. "In God's name, what did you do?" He carefully lifted Ezra into the wagon bed, where the man curled on his side, breathing hard, eyes closed. Ben looked from Kate to Polly in horror. "Polly, what did you do?"

"Is—is he dead?" Polly asked.

Ben leaned to look at the man and grimaced. "I'd say so. His face is half blown away and he has a hole in his gut."

Polly gasped for breath. "Ben, he was reaching for the tarp. And when I challenged him, he threw me into the wagon wheel. I knew he would find Kate. I didn't know she had the pistol. He would have killed us both."

Polly winced when she tried to inhale deeply. "I can't get my breath." She paused to exhale slowly, trying to calm herself. "What do we do? Someone is bound to have seen us or heard the gunshot!"

"I don't know. Let me think . . ." Ben looked around but there was no sign of anyone. "Kate, where are the field hands this time of day?"

"The men get thirty minutes to eat in the fields. That time's long past so's maybe they all back at work. The cotton and cornfields is way behind the slave cabins and no one tends the stock in mid-day. The only slave man I knowed to be around the house was Ezra." Kate leaned over and wiped the man's feverish brow with the corner of her apron. "He burnin' up." Kate lifted a water jug to Ezra's lips and the sick man drank gratefully.

"Got to go," Ezra moved his lips and tried to speak. "The men be lookin'."

Ben looked at Ezra. "Old man, can you speak up? What did you say?"

Kate looked at Ezra tenderly and said, "He cain't speak well on account of his neck, Ben." She gently pulled his dirty collar aside and Ben saw the angry scar encircling the old man's throat. "Wilkins did that to him years ago."

Ezra reached out a gnarled hand and touched Ben's sleeve. In a rasping whisper, he said, "Won't take five minutes fo' some of de men to come lookin' for the gunshot. They'll tell. They tell what happened if the law comes lookin'—'specially if they's a reward. We got to go!" He lay back, exhausted from the effort of speech.

Ben spoke up. "Kate, lie down with Ezra. Get under the tarps. Polly, we have to take Wilkins with us. We can't leave a body laying here." He unbuttoned his shirt quickly and took it off. He bent to the ground, picking up fragments of flesh and bone, wrapping them in the folds of the shirt. He used his boot to scuff the bloodstained dirt.

Polly screwed up her face in disgust.

465

Ben stood and took Polly's hand. He squeezed it. "Polly, you can do this. After all that man took from you, don't let him win now." He tucked the shirt under the buckboard.

"Alright, Ben," Polly said. "If you can haul him into the wagon, we can put him under the tarp, I suppose." Her stomach threatened to revolt and send her breakfast back into her throat at the thought of the dead man's mortal wound. "Hurry." She moved up to the box seat and gritted her teeth as stabbing pain gripped her side.

Ben paused. "We have to bury the body somewhere at Whitehall."

"Just get him in here and let's head for home," Polly said, scanning the yard for signs that someone heard the commotion. She closed her eyes and tried to breathe. The ache in her side throbbed in time with her pulse.

She heard Ben struggling to get the fat man's dead weight into his arms. Eventually, Ben stumbled up to the low back of the wagon, cradling Wilkins against his chest. He managed to roll the body into the bed of the wagon with a grunt. Polly turned to watch but averted her eyes to avoid looking at where the man's face used to be.

Ben looked at Kate tenderly. "I'll drive as fast as I can."

Kate nodded. She quickly covered the body lying next to her and recovered herself and Ezra. Ben jumped down and scuffled in the dirt, trying to cover any remaining bloodstains with his boot. Satisfied with his efforts, he hopped up on the box seat.

Polly looked at him and shook her head. "I am so sorry, Ben. I should not have gotten you involved in this."

Ben made a final cursory glance around but saw no one. He clicked the reins. "We're all in it, now," he said. As the wagon bumped down the drive toward home, he took a deep breath and exhaled loudly. "What'll we do with him?"

— • —

THE WAGON LURCHED TOWARD WHITEHALL, and every sudden jolt made Polly cry out in pain. Ben knew that the heat under the tarps had to be unbearable for Ezra and Kate, but they could not risk the chance of running into travelers on the road, with two River Wood slaves sitting in the bed. There would be questions.

Suddenly Polly spoke up, "Ben, I know what to do with him. We cannot bring him onto Whitehall property. No one there can know what happened. We'll cut through the orchard and get close to the Kemp place. It's accessible a half-mile before the turn and no one will be in the orchard until Mr. Roper is back."

Ben nodded. "That might work. The old road to the trading post is overgrown anyway. But we have nothing to bury him with."

Polly brightened. "There was a shovel left behind, when I was there the other day! And I remember exactly where I laid it down. It's near the head of the first row of peach trees."

"Well, it seems the good Lord's looking out for you today," Ben said wryly. The wagon approached the Whitehall property line. Ben slowed the horse and jumped out of the wagon. While Polly scanned the road in both directions, Ben lifted the weathered timbers of a section of split rail fence, one by one. He laid them aside carefully. When a wide section was disassembled, Polly slowly guided the horse and wagon through the gap. Ben picked up each timber and placed it back where it belonged, until the fence looked completely untouched. He hopped back onto the seat and the wagon moved slowly into the covered arbor of fruit trees.

When the wagon was deep into Whitehall's orchard, Ben stopped. He hopped off the seat quickly and hurried to the wagon bed. He whipped off the heavy tarp. Kate lay still, drenched in sweat, her arm protectively around Ezra. On the other side of the wagon lay Wilkins' body, wedged into the corner.

Polly eased herself down from the seat, wincing with every movement. She joined Ben at the back of the wagon and surveyed the scene. Ezra appeared out of his head with fever, his teeth chattering and eyes half-closed.

"We have to get him to Ona. She'll know what to do . . . ," she began. "Ben, do you think you can bury the body without any help? We can take the wagon only a bit closer, and you'll have to drag him. The site is abandoned. No one has gone there in years. It is completely overgrown."

Ben's eyes registered his displeasure. "You want me to drag this fat old man through the woods to the burned trading post."

Polly frowned. "I don't want that man's body on my property. I know it won't be easy. I will drive Kate and Ezra back home. Our story must be this—I went to check on Ezra and Kate. When I saw Ezra's condition, I decided to bring them to Whitehall. We saw no sign of Wilkins. In fact—" She shrugged. "Kate, if anyone asks, you two must say you have not seen him in days. It could be that he abandoned his post for a more lucrative offer somewhere in the Lowcountry. And Ben was never with us. He stayed at Whitehall all day."

Kate nodded mutely.

Ben looked at the women and then nodded in agreement. "I'll go get the shovel. We'll be real lucky if that's the end of this mess. But when Mr. Roper comes back, Miss Polly, what then?"

Polly sighed. "With a little luck, our story may hold. Mr. Roper never liked that man, either." She looked up at the angle of the sun. "Get started, Ben. I'm going to take Ezra home."

— • —

BEN DRAGGED THE CANVAS TARP THROUGH the rows of peach trees. Wilkins' body was wrapped inside it, ready enough for a grave in the remains of the trading post. When he approached the clearing, he dropped the heavy load and crouched to catch his breath.

The abandoned site unnerved him, and he knew Ona would say it was cursed ground. The air was eerily still. No songbirds or squirrels dared to make noise in this place. No wildflowers grew. The clearing held only memories of death. No wonder Polly remembered, after her visit here.

Ben finally stood. He hacked away the Virginia creeper and ivy that had smothered much of the collapsed structure. Small saplings grew through rotted timbers. He pushed aside some of the debris, charred and crumbling, to dig out a space for the body. Truly, no one had been to this God-forsaken spot in years. The air was heavy with an oppressive feeling, without birdsong or sunshine.

Ben's mind turned over the horror of what had happened, and what could happen if Wilkins' body was found. He bent to his task with sweat burning in his eyes. Kate was back, but for how long? And what would happen to all of them if some River Wood slave had seen Polly and Kate?

As much as Ben hated Wilkins, he hated John Stone more. And John was still very much in charge of his life. He dug deep into the charred layer until he reached the red Carolina clay. His shoulders quivered with fatigue and sweat soaked his hat. Still, he dug. He hacked through roots as thick as his arm and jarred his aching back when he struck granite chunks. Both hands blistered and bled.

The hole needed to be deep enough that an animal wouldn't dig it up, that the smell of decay wouldn't waft over the orchard. When Ben stood chest-deep in the earth and the sun was low in the west, he sighed. Using the last of his strength, he climbed from the hole. Only four feet wide, it would have to do. He dragged the dirty tarp up to the grave and then heaved the body headfirst into the hole. It hit the bottom with a sickening thud and the crunch of breaking bone.

As the first star appeared in the deep blue moonrise, Ben began the laborious task of filling the hole. When the dirt was replaced, he dragged branches and charred beams back over the top. As best he could tell in the gathering dark, the place looked like it did before. He wiped his brow with his stained bandana and headed for home, dragging the shovel behind him as if it were the weight of the world.

Chapter Thirty-Three

June 5, 1861

POLLY LIFTED HER SKIRTS AS SHE WALKED THROUGH THE dew-soaked grass toward the slave cabins. The morning humidity was already steamy and oppressive. Gray clouds threatened thunderstorms later in the day. She had decided to ride with Zadoc to the Anderson train depot but wanted to check on Ezra first.

As she neared the cabins, she noticed that two of them were missing the chinking that kept the elements at bay. The tin roof on another cabin, a luxury her father had been proud of, was rusted out in places. Ona's cabin was well taken care of, but then Ona had Ben to keep it in shape. She would have to talk to Mr. Roper about repairing the little cabins before autumn. Perhaps even adding one or two more. It seemed that Ben and Kate had a fondness for one another. And there were the children to consider. A new cabin for a new family.

She had not spoken to Ben since he trudged off to bury Wilkins' body. Polly had driven Kate and Ezra to the cabins, then stabled the horse and cleaned up the bed of the wagon by lantern light, her rib cage burning in pain. Many rags and buckets of water later, she had cleaned most of the rusty red stains from the wagon bed. In a pinch, she had taken a bottle of castor oil and splashed it over the remaining stain, scrubbing the liquid in until the oil hid the evidence. She had dragged herself back to the house way past dark. Adrenaline and pain kept her awake most of the night.

Birds called and Polly winced as she climbed up the rickety steps and knocked on George and Cissie's cabin. The chatter of children from inside reached her ears and she smiled. The door opened and Cissie leaned out. Surprised to see her mistress, she gasped. "Miss Polly!" Silas and Lydia stood at her hip. "I'm comin' back into the big house with the wash as soon as it's dry," she offered. "And Kate and I will be dividing up the chores like befo'. Did she get breakfast fo' you?"

"Yes. That's fine, Cissie. I'm here about Ezra actually. Whose cabin is he staying in?"

Cissie pointed to the kitchen. "He in there fo' now. Ona givin' him broth and tea and her herb medicines. We's kinda crowdin' in here of late and thought mebbe to keep him away from the chillun"

Polly nodded. "Yes, I'll need to speak with Mr. Roper now that he's coming home. We may need a new cabin or two. Where are Kate and Solomon staying?"

"They's with Ona again. Ben bunkin' with the men." Cissie looked at Polly blankly.

Polly shifted from one foot to the other. "Cissie, how are you? Do you feel strong enough to be at work again?"

"Yes'm. I'm a little tired but I'm alright. Gotta keep up with these two and keep the food comin'." She smiled weakly. "Miss Polly, I never said thank you for he'pin' with my labor time. Ona said it took you and her and Ben to deliver my baby. She said I'da died if y'all hadn't got him out." There was no sense of shame coming from Cissie at having her mistress see her in such a state, just a sincere gratitude. "I don't think I'll be havin' no more babies," she added sadly.

"I am sorry that we could not save the baby, but I am very glad that you are well." Polly backed down the steps and turned to go. She paused and turned to Cissie once more. "Kate and Ben." It was meant to be a question, but it came out as a statement.

Cissie's eyebrows went up and she laughed. "Yes'm, I guess it easy to see. Ben so happy you brought her back. Sol too. We all is. You a kind woman, Miss Polly. And she he'ps ease the cookin' and cleanin' work between us."

"I'm glad she is back, too. Now let me see to Ezra." Polly smiled and walked down the path back to the kitchen. When she stepped through the door, the usual aroma of baking bread and roasting meat was replaced with the odor of sickness and disease. Polly held her handkerchief over her nose briefly, before stepping into the small pantry. Her side throbbed with pain and she yearned to lie down somewhere and close her eyes.

Ona sat in a rocker knitting while Ezra slept on a makeshift cot nearby. Zadoc sat on the floor near his father's head. The space was tight and close, jars of canned goods lining the shelves above Ezra's head and sacks of meal under his cot. Ona smiled at Polly.

"How is he this morning?" Polly asked quietly. She looked from Ona to Zadoc.

"Ezra dreamin' of seein' Jane real soon. He ain't in this world no more. He talkin' with the angels." Ona put down her mending and gazed at Zadoc. "Zee was able to say his goodbyes while Ezra was awake. All I can do now is keep him comfortable till he ready to go home. Thank you fo' givin' him a peaceful place to rest."

Zadoc stood. "I'm ready to drive you, Miss Polly. I said my goodbyes, ma'am. I cain't jes' sit here. I want him to go on now. I thank you for bringin' him here. I didn't want him to die alone at River Wood. I git the carriage ready."

"Thank you, Zee. But I've hurt myself and don't think a wagon ride would be a good idea. Can you go without me? Take the wagon. I will write a note."

Zadoc nodded and glanced at his father before heading out the door.

472

Ona tilted her head and looked at Polly with concern. "What's wrong with you, Miss Girl?"

"What do you mean?" Polly asked haltingly. She smiled and tried to stand up straight. "Just a bit bruised."

"Is you bad hurt? Seems to me you is standin' all catty-whompus," Ona remarked.

Polly's smile vanished. "I bumped into the wagon hard yesterday, helping Ezra up," she said. "It is a nice excuse not to wear a corset for a few days."

Ona looked down at the yarn in her lap and rocked. "Mmm hmm. I see. Couldn't have nothing to do with puttin' up a fight agin' Mr. Wilkins?"

Polly's eyes narrowed and she shook her head. "I don't know what you mean, Ona. Mr. Wilkins was nowhere to be seen yesterday. Ben and I had to lift Ezra into the wagon. I must have strained a muscle as we handled Ezra."

"Miss Polly, I ain't one to pay no mind to an old man's rantin's so close to his passin' . . . but I'm prayin' you didn't do nothin' to bring down trouble on yo'se'f."

Polly stared at Ona defiantly but said nothing.

"Best to keep Ezra an' me here alone till he passes. I wouldn't want no one else to hear some of the things Zee and I heard from him last night." She eyed Polly sternly and then softened. "It won't be long now." Ezra's breath came in rasps and wheezes.

Polly nodded. "Should I ask Zee to look for anything in town that may help him?

"Naw, I make better medicines than you got in town, an' he on his way to Jesus soon enough." Ona smiled and resumed her sewing. "He got Jane waitin' on him."

"Thank you for taking care of him," Polly murmured. "When Mr. Roper is settled, I will ask him about adding a cabin or two. With Kate back, maybe it's time. I mean, with Ben . . ." Her words trailed off.

Ona looked up, surprised. "Well, well, he asked you? Ben was wantin' to jump the broom with Kate. We didn't think Mr. Stone would allow it."

"Ben didn't say anything to me, but I saw how they looked at each other. I'm—I'm happy for them both. I will talk to Ben." Polly rubbed her side tenderly and tried to exhale deeply. "Mr. Stone will no longer have a say in how I run Whitehall. I plan to have the marriage annulled just as soon as I can. He was an accomplice to my brothers' murders. Whether or not the law will recognize that, I certainly will."

"Miss Girl, he ain't gonna take that news well at all. If you tell him that you know what he's done, how you think he gonna handle it? He gots a temper on him."

Polly sighed heavily and then winced. "I know. But I have Whitehall. He never will. I will figure out something." She closed the pantry door quietly behind her and made her way toward the house.

— • —

BEN'S SHOULDERS ACHED FROM DIGGING the grave the day before and sweat soaked his thin shirt even though it was well before noon. He hacked at the thorny nettles and muttered under his breath. The summer season was certainly upon them and his work at the forge interrupted. Verdant rows of corn marched across hillsides previously devoted to cotton. The new sorghum was up in the bottomland and would be a welcome source of sugar and a good money crop for Whitehall should the war drag on. Wheat was high and waved in the breeze, in motion like waves on the sea. The roadsides were dotted with yellow goldenrod and dandelions.

George had pulled Ben from the smithy into the fields as soon as the corn was up. With only eight hands at Whitehall, every man was needed come summertime. Zadoc was at his father's deathbed, instead of the barn, and would soon be headed to pick up Mr. Roper from the depot. The loss of one hand to outside chores was tough. The men worked sunup to nearly sundown. George scrambled to put the men hoeing where weeds were sprouting, but spurge, crabgrass, and chickweed ran rampant.

Tending the smithy, acting as farrier, and helping Zee with livestock were Ben's primary chores, but come summer, he was a field hand, too. Ben stooped low as he hoed nettles from between cornrows. The "three sisters," a triumvirate of corn, beans, and squash, kept most of the weeds at bay, but George wanted the fields to look especially good for Roper's return. Besides, Ona wanted the nettles to boil into a soothing tea for Ezra.

His thoughts were on Kate. He retraced his steps the previous day, trying to remember if there had been any sign that he was being watched as he carried Ezra to the wagon. The cabins and yards seemed deserted. There was no one near the barn or kitchen as he'd passed by. The hands must have been in the fields, he reasoned.

If someone had seen the Burgiss wagon and heard the shots at River Wood, Ben and Kate were in danger. He thought of the rushed attempt to roll the body into a tarp and stash it in the wagon bed. Would anyone have come running from the cabins or the fields? Or waited and watched quietly from a hidden spot? Ben suddenly stood up. His shirt. He had stashed his bloody shirt under the wagon bench and forgotten about it in the rush to bury Wilkins' body and get home unseen. Surely Polly would have found it, he hoped.

He looked around for any sign of George, and seeing no one, dropped his hoe and ran for the barn. It took nearly five minutes for him to reach the barn, and he swung the doors wide. He jogged past the few animals not turned out to pasture and stopped in front of the bay where the wagon was kept. It was gone. Ben realized that Zee and Polly would have taken it to Anderson to pick up Mr. Roper. He groaned and pounded a wooden post with his fist. How stupid of him. What if Mr. Roper spotted the bloody shirt? Would he recognize it as Ben's? He owned only two. What if someone in town remembered seeing the wagon on the road to River Wood yesterday and could describe the piece of clothing? Ben realized that his thoughts were running away from him, and he took a deep breath to calm himself.

"Ben?"

Ben wheeled around and saw Polly standing in the barn doorway, a shawl tightly wrapped around her shoulders. She looked pale and tired.

"Miss Polly, I thought that you went into town to get Mr. Roper? Where is the wagon?" Ben exclaimed.

"I don't feel well—my ribs. I sent Zadoc to fetch Mr. Roper home," Polly said quietly. "I may have to call on Dr. Adger for this." She paused and asked, "Did—did everything go well last night? In the orchard?"

Ben looked past Polly before answering. "It's done. But . . . I left my shirt under the wagon seat. If Zee or Mr. Roper find it, they will know it's mine. And it's covered in the man's blood."

Polly closed her eyes. "Oh my God."

Ben spoke. "What happened yesterday was a lot to take in . . . but you did the right thing. That man is never going to bother you or any of us ever again." Ben hoped his words soothed her troubled spirit. "He was the devil himself. He killed your brothers. He hurt Kate. Justice was done. We're all safer for it." He paused. "I've never killed a man, but I imagine it takes time to recover from it—even when done for good reason. And as far as your ribs, ask Mama to fix a poultice. She can bind you up tight and you'll heal if you stay still. I've seen her do it on some of the men. Don't know what she uses, but her potions heal quicker than Dr. Adger could even get on a horse and come out here. No need to call on him. He'd ask too many questions anyway."

Polly nodded sadly. "You're right. I should not have involved you. If someone finds out . . ."

"If Mr. Roper finds the shirt, you have to say I got hurt. A horse kicked me while I was shoeing," Ben said. "Can we agree on that story?"

Polly nodded sadly.

— • —

POLLY LOOKED PAST BEN TO MOVEMENT in the rafters near the back of the barn. A barred owl flapped his wings, perched high overhead on a long beam. He settled and closed his eyes. She stared at the bird for some time. She envied his peaceful sleep, something that had eluded her for months.

She looked down at the ground in embarrassment and nervously continued, "I am not sorry that I killed the man. And your cool head afterward probably saved me. Kate and me."

Ben waited for Polly to continue. She finally looked up at him. "You have permission to marry Kate. If you want to be with her, I will agree to it. And none of this "jumping the broom." I will call for the slave parson at Fort Hill to perform a real wedding. It's the way your mother and Martin were married, I understand."

Ben's eyes widened and he grinned. "Thank you, Miss Polly. I don't know if she'll have me, but I would like to ask. I think we'd make a good match."

Polly smiled weakly. "She'll have you. I saw the way she looked at you when you showed up at River Wood yesterday. And you'll keep her safe from—from my husband."

Ben's face turned serious. "I wonder, can we take in Lydia and raise her up? She was real attached to Kate and Solomon before they came here. Cissie isn't herself since the baby died and I think she's too tired to do right by Lydia."

Polly looked at Ben fondly. "I think you and Kate taking Lydia sounds lovely." For a moment, she felt a pang of jealousy at the happy family unit she was helping Ben create. "Ben, I have no more family on this earth, and I don't know what will happen when John comes back, but I want you to know that, in some way, you and Ona are the closest I have to kin."

Ben nodded stiffly. "Thank you, Miss Polly."

She registered the change in his demeanor and regretted her words immediately. "I did not mean to make you feel uncomfortable. I'm sorry. And we will take what happened yesterday to our graves. I killed the man, defending myself and Kate. Kate will be safe. You and Ona have stood by me and I will do everything I can to stand by you. I cannot free you, as you know. But I will try to make your life here a safe one. It's the least I can do. How many times have I put your life in danger?" She tried to muster a smile.

Ben bowed his head in thought. "Let's see. That day at the trading post. Yesterday I buried a white man that you killed. And let's not forget teaching you to read, which is a hanging offense . . ." He looked down at Polly. "We've traveled down a strange path. You have always had my life in your hands. Even now, you could lie and turn me in for killing Wilkins and I would hang."

Polly took a step back. "Ben, I would never—I have tried to be good to you all. Maybe one day when this war is over, we can make some changes. Somehow . . ."

Ben looked into Polly's dark eyes. "I'm still a slave. I best get back out to finish hoeing that cornfield or George will have my head. Thank you for permission to talk to Kate." He tipped his hat and walked past Polly out into the sunshine. She had never felt so alone. Hot tears made small rivulets down both cheeks.

— • —

TOM ROPER STEPPED DOWN FROM the passenger car platform and waved at Zadoc sitting in the driver's seat of the wagon.

"Howdy, Zee," Tom said amiably. "You alone?"

"Yessuh," Zadoc answered tentatively. "Mizz Polly tol' me to pick you up, suh. She feelin' poorly."

"Well now, I'm sorry to hear that." Tom flung his canvas satchel under the bench seat of the wagon and then hopped up next to the slave. "What's wrong with her? Is Mr. Stone home?"

"No suh, I ain't know nothin' 'bout when he comin' home. But Mizz Polly and Ben went over to River Wood yesterday and brought my daddy and Kate back. My daddy's on his death bed an' Ona's tendin' him. Mama died right after you left. I 'spect he ain't got long either." Zadoc snapped the reins and the horse trotted away from the station. "Mizz Polly hurt herse'f somehow," he added with a shrug. "She walkin' around holdin' her side."

"What?" Tom barked. "They went to River Wood?" He slapped his knee angrily with his hat.

Zadoc reflexively clamped a hand over his own mouth.

Stunned, Tom was not sure which point to address first. "Well, I'm sorry about your mama, Zee. I really am. Sorry about your daddy, too. . . . It was kind of Miss Polly to bring him to Whitehall so you could spend time with him." He watched the familiar countryside move by the wagon on both sides. "And Kate is back? Huh, I was away longer than I expected. But I hope Miss Polly didn't hurt herself doing something one of you should have been doing?" he asked sternly.

"No suh!" Zadoc exclaimed. "She went off to River Wood with Ben to get Kate and my daddy. She came back hurt." Zadoc realized he'd said too much and fixed his eyes on the road ahead.

Tom read the fear in Zadoc's expression. "I'll see what happened. You just check on your daddy when we get back and then tell Ben to come see me after I visit Miss Polly. Did Cissie have a boy or a girl?"

Zadoc nodded obediently. "Yessuh, well, she's well enough now but the baby died when she tried to birth it. Mizz Polly and Ben he'ped but the baby was stuck. Ben had to use those straps he uses when birthin' foals and calves. Else Cissie woulda died."

Tom leaned back against the bench seat and sighed heavily. Between the latest news of the war, his extended time away and the distressing events at Whitehall in his absence, he was tired. At thirty-six, he was no spring chicken. Overseeing Whitehall wasn't an easy job even as a smallholding. And now cotton prices were near rock bottom and the war was spreading like a disease across the southland. Hopefully, John Stone wouldn't be home any time soon. Maybe Stone had directed Polly to retrieve Kate. Maybe not. Polly Burgiss Stone was a stubborn female.

Zee slowed the wagon and turned into the long driveway in front of

Whitehall. Tom was relieved to be back after his trip away. Whitehall had been the only home Tom had really known for the past twenty years. He smiled as the horse picked up its pace, sniffing the familiar smells of the farm. He squinted in the bright sunshine and saw Polly waiting for him on the front porch, her shawl wrapped around her tightly despite the heat.

His heart lurched. *I'm growing fond of Polly*, he thought. *Too fond.* She was married, fifteen years younger, and surely thought of him as an old uncle at best. But he had known her long enough to see she was troubled about something. How many times had he approached the front porch and seen her mother, Mary, standing the same way, her own mind troubled and moving a mile a minute?

He sighed and raised a hand in greeting as the wagon stopped. He turned to Zadoc. "Zee, go and check on your daddy. I'll put the wagon up after I speak to Miss Polly."

"Thank you, suh." Zadoc nodded.

"Let Zee take the wagon now, Mr. Roper," Polly called quickly. "Ben needs it," she lied. "Come and chat. I'm glad you made it back to us safely."

"I'm right sorry it took me so long to get back. Zee started to fill me in on all the goings-on." Tom reached under the seat and felt for the strap of his canvas tote. As he dragged the satchel out, he saw the bloodstained piece of fabric and pulled it out as well. He lifted the wadded shirt and cocked his head. "What the—"

Polly froze as Tom pulled Ben's shirt from underneath the wagon bench. He turned to look at her and knew instantly that things were not right. Her face was pale and her hands trembled as she clutched the shawl around her.

She was caught in some lie, but he watched her recover. "Gracious, Mr. Roper, I was going to tell you. Delightful kicked poor Ben hard the other day. You know how that horse can be." She smiled weakly. "Leave it folded. It's a nasty mess. I'll have Ona scrub it."

Tom frowned and heaved his satchel to the dusty ground. He hopped down with the shirt in hand. "Judging by this shirt, Ben took quite a hit. He must be hurting something fierce." He eyed Polly warily.

"He's remarkably better today," she said. "Now enough of that." She extended her hand. "I'll have Ona wash it out. It'll be good as new."

Tom shook his head and reluctantly relinquished the shirt. "Whatever you say, Miss Polly." Polly grabbed it and winced as she did so.

Polly looked hard at Zadoc. "Go on now, Zee," she snapped. The slave clicked the reins and the horse plodded toward the barn.

"Looks like you got kicked too," Tom said. "You alright?"

Polly was evasive. "It has been a tough time here, Mr. Roper. I won't lie to you. But I was able to retrieve Kate—and Zee's ailing father. Kate will be of great help here. I was wrong to have ever let her go. She is missing a few teeth, courtesy of Mr. Wilkins. And I know he abused her in other ways, but that is over now. That man should be in jail. Kate is back where she belongs." She stared at Tom with defiance.

He removed his hat and looked at her pained face. She looked so much like her mother, only with more fight in her eyes. *I just want to take her in my arms and make her safe*, he thought. He finally threw up his hands in mock defense. "Yes ma'am. Remember, whatever happened, I'm on your side."

Polly appeared to relax slightly. "As a matter of fact, Mr. Roper," she began the lie, "Mr. Wilkins has apparently run off. Gone away. Kate said she hadn't seen him in days. We heard from another hand that he took a better job somewhere in the Lowcountry and hightailed it down there without so much as a by-your-leave. I say good riddance."

Tom nodded slowly but said nothing.

"Come and sit, Mr. Roper," Polly said. She led him to the walnut rockers and Tom sat wearily. He noticed that Polly winced as she sat down, but she did not cry out. She still clutched the balled-up shirt tightly in her hand.

"What news of the war?" she asked. "I have not had a moment to even get to town and collect the mail or get a newspaper." Polly closed her eyes and rocked gently.

"Well, there have been some skirmishes on the coast and up the Virginia way. It looks like your husband's company and a few others from around here are headed to Richmond. Under Beauregard. He is getting them ready for something big. Have you gotten a letter?"

"I told you. I have not had time to get to town. If a letter is waiting for me, I wouldn't know it. Frankly, I do not care."

Tom leaned forward, his hat in hand between his knees. "Miss Polly, I apologize for being gone so long. Much longer than I'd planned. Take the time out of my pay, of course. I know this must be hard having to run your place without your husband here, and it isn't my business, but if there is something I should know, I wish you'd tell me. You're clearly injured. Ben's shirt is a bloody mess. And Zee was as skittish as a colt. Did someone hurt you?"

Polly waved away his question with a flip of her hand. "I am fine. But indeed, Mr. Roper, there are some things you should know." Polly leaned forward with some effort and placed the shirt under the hem of her skirt.

Tom waited for the bad news.

She braced herself with her hands on the rocker arms and let out a long slow breath. "I would like you to see to two new cabins for the slaves. Ben and Kate are to be married. They will keep Lydia and Solomon with them. And I want Ona in a bigger place. She is getting up in years and has been a good friend to me. We can use her current cabin to spread the men out a bit."

She paused. "Let's see . . . the orchard looks good. George can tell you more. And the sorghum is coming in nicely, so let's plan to give each slave a share when we harvest. What a chore that will be. Boiling syrup. Ten gallons of sorghum juice only makes one gallon of syrup, but we've all been without sugar for so long. I'd like to sell it in town." Polly stared at Tom, her face ashen, but her tone firm. "That is all."

A slow smile crept across Tom's face as he stood. "I understand. I think we have a busy summer ahead of us, Miss Polly. I'd better get to work."

— • —

LATE THAT EVENING, POLLY STOOD in front of the crackling fire in the parlor. She prodded the logs with the poker, sending a hiss of sparks up the chimney. She gazed at length toward the flickering orange flames, lost in memories, as the remains of the tattered shirt blackened, curled, and burned away.

Chapter Thirty-Four

July 1, 1861

THE SUNRISE CREPT OVER THE TREE LINE EAST OF WHITEHALL, and early birdsong woke Polly. She opened her eyes and watched the play of light across her bedroom floor. There was a knock at the door.

"Come in, Cissie," Polly called out. But Kate's familiar blue turban peeped through the open door.

"Gracious, Kate!" said Polly. "I thought that Cissie would do breakfast this morning. It's your wedding day. Your day off."

Kate shrugged and smiled. "Law, Miss Polly. I cain't set still I'm so nervous. Sol and Lydia had me up at the crack a' dawn anyway, they's so excited." She set the silver breakfast tray on Polly's bedside table. The sight of hot biscuits, fresh strawberry jam and herb tea made Polly's stomach rumble.

Polly noticed an extra touch. A crystal bud vase held a single perfect pink rose, no doubt plucked that morning, the dew still clinging to the petals. "And what is this for?" Polly asked, sipping the spiced tea.

Kate clasped her hands together and smiled, the gap in her teeth a jarring reminder of Wilkins. "It's to thank you, Miss Polly. When I think back to the last few weeks. Law. . . . Thank you fo' bringin' me here and fo' letting me and Ben marry. And for all you did for Ezra. He died here in peace." She paused and smoothed her new calico skirt, tiny pink and green flowers dancing across a cream-colored field. "Thank you fo' my new dress and our cabin an' fo' well . . . for what you done at River Wood. You saved my life an' I won't never forget it.

"No more of that talk. We will not mention that God-awful place anymore. I am glad that you are happy here. Now, you scoot on and let me be. The parson will be here in a few hours. I am sure that you have other things to attend to besides bringing me breakfast on your wedding day." Polly's tone was firm but affectionate.

Kate nodded and slipped out of the room quietly. Polly leaned back against her pillows and smiled. She was happy. Truly happy. Tom Roper had taken her directions and worked over and above anything she could have hoped for in so short a time. The orchard was filled with ripening freestone peaches and the tiny green fruits that would soon become crisp, sweet apples. The sorghum crop thrived. Corn and wheat also flourished. Squash and beans overran their beds. The fallow fields where cotton had grown only last season would be turned into more corn, wheat, and tobacco next year if cotton did not rebound.

She took a bite of the flaky biscuit and chewed slowly. There had only been one letter from John in the last month. As Roper had reported, John wrote that his division would take the train up to Richmond and make camp there. It seemed that a battle near the very capital of the Confederate nation would soon commence. John asked for news of Whitehall and River Wood and expressed how much he missed his young wife. Polly had immediately torn up the letter and tossed it into the fireplace. In her prayers, she had frequently come so close to asking God to kill John in combat, for the thought of him coming back to Whitehall was repulsive to her.

Polly finished her breakfast, blotted her lips with her napkin, and rose to wash and dress, without calling for Cissie or Ona. Lately, it seemed a silly custom. After all, she was quite capable of attending to her toilette and selecting her own clothing without someone's assistance, especially now that her ribs had healed up. She actually liked the early quiet time to think and to pray. It was the closest she had gotten to church since her mother's funeral eulogy.

She splashed cool water on her face and neck, marveling at the heat already building upstairs so early in the day. June had been blistering, with temperatures much higher than usual. But so far, intervals of rainfall kept the crops from drying out. The creeks were running. The grasshoppers had not shown up yet, thank God.

Right now, her focus was on the peaches. One more good rain and they would swell overnight to their peak of sweet and juicy flavor. Too much rain and they would quickly turn flavorless and mushy. Tom had spoken to Mr. Jones at the Mercantile and he was excited to offer peaches in a store that was sparse of goods. He had offered Polly a good price, paid out in Confederate coin. No one else in the district had an entire peach orchard. Polly was grateful for that. She silently prayed for a bountiful harvest that would put some money into depleted Whitehall accounts.

Polly dressed quickly and brushed out her hair. She twisted it up and stabbed a pin in the coil, chignon-style. She peered at her reflection in the mirror. There was color in her cheeks and a sparkle in her brown eyes. Did it even matter that she no longer read *Godey's* and hadn't thought of a new dress for herself in ages? There was her farm to run and prosperity to be had, if only she worked hard and treated her slaves fairly. This war would be over soon enough and John would come back. She knew she would have to face the idea of annulment or divorce but put the thought out of her mind once more. For now, she would enjoy the fact that Wilkins would never be a threat to her and her workers again and had no hold on her husband. She rose from her dressing table, picked up the chamber pot, and headed downstairs, humming a tune as she went.

— • —

THE SLAVE QUARTERS BUZZED WITH EXCITEMENT, as Ben and Kate's wedding was less than an hour away. The slave parson from Fort Hill, a Methodist man like his father before him, showed up early and was given a stool under the shade of a hickory tree, along with a large glass of sweet tea.

Ona and Cissie had baked a whole ham with Polly's permission. The tables fairly groaned under the weight of the repast. Beans and squash, cornbread, and rhubarb pies rounded out the post-wedding meal and the men quickly completed their Sunday chores and waited anxiously for the festivities to begin. They milled around under shady oak trees, shirts and trousers freshly washed, the mouth-watering aroma wafting their way.

Tom knocked on the front door of the house, hat in hand. He and Polly would walk together to the wedding site and would watch the ceremony quietly, before slipping away to allow the slaves to celebrate.

Jack barked and jumped at the sound of the brass knocker. Polly pulled the front door open and smiled broadly at her overseer. "My goodness, Mr. Roper, you clean up well," she said. Tom wore a clean white shirt and had even trimmed his unruly beard. Jack growled at the man.

Tom smiled good-naturedly, showing even white teeth. "It's a wedding, by God. I may as well bathe and wear clean clothes for a slave wedding. I don't get out much for any other kind of social gathering," he mumbled. "Stop it, dog! It's just me, Tom," he commanded, pointing a finger at Jack.

Polly stifled a laugh. "We do live a sheltered life out here. And to be honest, we both probably wouldn't have it any other way, would we?" Her brown eyes danced. She closed the door behind her and the two stepped off the porch and began to make their way to the slave cabins.

"You seem in a particularly good mood," Tom said.

"I am in a good mood." Polly smiled.

"Any word from Mr. Wilkins or your husband?" Tom ventured.

At the mention of both men, Polly scowled. "No, and I'll thank you not to bring up their names again today." She laughed.

"Alright, Miss Polly." Tom shrugged. He wondered what could have happened while he was gone. Something had soured Polly completely on her ill-chosen husband. He continued, "It's just that I have no idea what's going on at River Wood. Are the slaves working? Did they all run off? I know it isn't my place, but I sure don't want Mr. Stone to come back and wonder why I didn't go over there to have a look-see. Maybe Wilkins ran off. Maybe not. Should I check? Write to your husband?"

Polly wheeled around and confronted Tom, arms crossed. "Mr. Roper, while you were away, I received notice of a large inheritance from my grandmother after she passed."

Tom's eyes widened. "I am sorry, Miss Polly. So sorry for your loss."

"Thank you," she said more gently. "I appreciate the condolences instead of congratulations. Anyway, the money was seized to pay John's debts. My one chance to invest in Whitehall is gone. We could have done so much with that money. But because I married, his debts became mine. I paid his mortgage and back taxes on River Wood. No wonder Mr. Wilkins abandoned his post. He probably was not being paid. My one consolation? Father left Whitehall solely to me. No one can take it away and my heir must be named by me to inherit. Between that and some other . . . issues, I plan to ask for a divorce when John returns. I was misled by him."

Tom sighed. "I am sorry. I can't imagine how hard that must have been for you, on top of everything else you've dealt with." *No wonder she's soured on her husband*, he thought. "No more talk of River Wood. I promise."

Polly smiled. "I truly think we'll have a good peach crop this summer, followed by the apples."

Tom took up the thread. "Our sorghum and corn are in good shape, and if the cotton market rebounds, well, you can sell it at a profit. I think things are looking up for you."

Polly relaxed. "As do I, Mr. Roper, as do I. Leave River Wood to its owner, and Wilkins, if and when he should return. I want nothing more to do with the place. We need to focus on Whitehall."

And when you decide to tell me the truth, I'll be happy to listen, Tom wanted to say. Instead, he nodded and moved toward the crowd gathered under the oak trees.

— • —

POLLY GREETED THE PARSON CORDIALLY and thanked the man for coming. He was to be paid in food stores, and Tom handed him a sack of cornmeal and a small package of fatback, which he took gratefully, nodding and smiling the entire time. Polly had wanted to say a word to Ben but hadn't found a good time to speak to him. Their awkward conversation about the bloodstained shirt had been the last time they had spoken. She looked around the grounds for him, but he was with his mother, deep in conversation.

Polly and Tom took their places near the back of the gathering, seated on wooden benches perched precariously on the rocky ground. Jack sat obediently at Polly's feet, tail thumping. The parson stood and extended his hands, asking Kate and Ben to step forward. Kate looked pretty in her new frock. A new rose-colored turban covered her dark hair. Ben wore a new shirt of blue-dyed muslin, and Polly was again relieved to have an excuse to give the man fabric for a new shirt.

The children had each received a good scrubbing and sat quietly on the front row. Lydia's hair had been carefully braided into neat cornrows. Solomon sat next to her, swinging his chubby legs over the edge of the bench. Silas, almost three years old, sat with Cissie and George, drawing in the dirt below his feet with a long stick.

The parson began the service and Polly watched the couple while he spoke. Ben and Kate gazed at each other, reciting their solemn vows as instructed by the minister. He announced that the pair were henceforth man and wife and called for a broom. Ona sidled up and handed the man a broom, her grin as wide as Polly had ever seen. Polly was surprised to see Kate and Ben link arms and stepped across the broom together, laughing. Only then did the slaves erupt with whoops and clapping, before glancing back to see their mistress's reaction. Polly smiled and the slaves turned back around. The parson produced a fiddle and began to play a toe-tapping tune. The others began to sing and dance with wild gyrations that made Polly and Tom uncomfortable.

"I think that this is our cue to leave them alone," Polly whispered behind her hand.

Tom nodded and the two stood to leave. As they stepped away from the bench, Polly glanced in Ben's direction once more. Ben's eyes were watching her go. Polly smiled warmly and Ben mouthed the words, "Thank you, Polly." He nodded his head. Polly nodded back and turned toward the house.

"That was right nice," Tom quipped. "I had never attended a slave wedding."

Polly looked at Tom. "I thought you'd seen Ona and Martin marry."

"No. Your daddy allowed the marriage and we heard them shout and holler back here, but we didn't come out to watch. They were different times, back then."

"Different times . . ." Polly mused. "Tom, come inside. I need to ask you a question. I found something in my father's desk and I think it is important. About the railroad tunnels."

Tom stopped in his tracks, eyes wide. "What is it?"

Polly was about to say more, when they both saw the rider on horseback coming quickly up the driveway, a cloud of red dust trailing him. Her heart dropped when she recognized Pendleton District's sheriff's deputy, Tanner McBee. Polly had never liked the coarse man and had actually seen him with Wilkins in town once or twice. She tried to steady her hands and took a deep breath to calm herself.

"Now what do you think he's doing out here?" Tom asked Polly innocently, as they waited for the horse to slow and then stop in front of them in the carriage circle.

"Afternoon, Mr. McBee," Tom called amiably. "What brings you out this way?"

"Afternoon, Tom. Mrs. Stone." McBee dismounted and removed his hat before approaching the pair. "You got some kinda soiree goin' on today?" McBee smirked and pointed toward the noise from the slave quarters.

"Yes, Mr. McBee. We had some slaves who were just married. If you're here about Parson Jacob, we have him visiting with permission from Mr. Calhoun at Fort Hill." Polly tried to smile, despite her nerves. "We will send him back shortly."

"Hmmm, I ain't never cottoned to the idea of slaves bein' allowed to marry," the man said with disdain. "Seems like a waste of time to me."

"Won't you come up and have some tea?" Polly asked sweetly, ignoring his remarks.

McBee's face relaxed only slightly. "Yes, ma'am, I can't turn that down." He followed Tom and Polly up the front steps and into the cool and darkened parlor. Polly quickly opened the drapes and said, "Let me get that tea. My house girl is out back, but I will only be a moment."

Polly ducked out of the room, grateful for a chance to collect her thoughts. She made her way to the butler's pantry. A fresh pitcher of tea sat on the sideboard. Polly was thankful that Kate had made the tea as usual before the festivities began. She poured a tall glass for both McBee and Roper with shaking hands and carried the glasses back into the parlor. Both men stood and accepted the cool glasses.

Polly sat down and tried to ask casually, "Now what brings you out to Whitehall on a Sunday, Mr. McBee?"

McBee took a long drink from his glass and wiped his mouth with the back of his hand. "Well, Mrs. Stone, it's like this. I understand that Mr. Stone is off fightin' in the war . . ." He paused. ". . . and for that, I'm appreciative." He leaned forward. "He has two overseers, Mr. Roper here at Whitehall, and Mr. Wilkins over at River Wood." He held up two fingers. "Am I correct?" Polly wanted desperately to disabuse McBee of the notion that Whitehall belonged to John, but she held her tongue.

"Yes, Mr. McBee. And what is your point?" Polly asked.

"Well, it seems that Mr. Wilkins disappeared a while back. He usually came into town every week or so for supplies and whatnot. We'd meet up, you know, to have a whiskey at the hotel on occasion." He looked from Tom to Polly. "He hasn't been seen in town since the end of May."

Polly interrupted. "Yes, I am well aware of Mr. Wilkins' proclivity for drink. But clearly I am not the man's keeper."

"Yes ma'am. Well, I went out to River Wood the other day to see if he was there, laid up or somethin.' I know that with Mr. Stone away, if he was sick or if he fell into slave troubles, there'd be no one to know. Unless you'd been out there." McBee eyed Polly suspiciously.

Polly picked up her needlepoint to give her hands something to do besides quiver. She picked at an errant stitch and said, "I did go out there. Mr. Roper knows. I went out to check on a slave who was ill. You know my man Zadoc. His elderly parents were slaves at River Wood. I sent Zadoc there to nurse his mother before she died. He stayed maybe a week or ten days. And Mr. Wilkins knew that he was there. After she died, I heard of the condition his father was in. I brought the sick man back here, where he died peacefully a few weeks ago."

She looked up and added, "The place was in a deplorable condition, and I know my husband will be furious with his overseer. I did not see any sign of Mr. Wilkins at that time. I assumed he was either out in the fields or passed out drunk somewhere. A slave mentioned that Wilkins had taken off for parts unknown." She bent to her needlepoint once more.

Red-faced, McBee looked at Tom. "Mr. Roper, I know that you have been away, but did you know that Wilkins had disappeared?"

Tom looked to Polly and then to McBee. "When I returned to Whitehall, Mrs. Stone told me what happened with Zadoc's parents. She did mention that she did not find Mr. Wilkins while she was there. I believe a slave told her he had gone to the Lowcountry. As I am not paid to oversee both properties, you will understand why I have only a passing interest in goings-on over that way. If it helps, I can produce a letter from Mr. Stone that says I am to keep to Whitehall. River Wood is not my job."

McBee held up a hand. "No need. You're not the one I need to question."

Polly put down her needlepoint. "Mr. McBee, are you accusing me of something?" Color rose in her cheeks.

"I'm not accusing you of anything, Mrs. Stone." McBee shrugged. "I apologize." He paused. "But, I do have a few questions, because I had someone come forward when I was out to River Wood. Little nigger boy name of Reginald. Didn't say nothin' about Wilkins high-tailin' it to the Lowcountry. Said he seen a Whitehall slave totin' Ezra to the front drive. Zadoc's daddy? His name is Ezra, right?"

Polly nodded weakly. "That's the man I brought home." *They know Ben was there.*

"Well, now, Reginald is just a nigger boy. I don't usually take the word of a slave. But he says after he saw that, a few moments later he heard shots in the vicinity of the big house. By the time he got to the house, he said all he saw was a wagon headed out the front gate. But by the way he described who he saw totin' Ezra, I had to come over and speak with you. Reginald said he recognized the slave. Said he worked with the man in your fields last summer. A big fellow. Name of Ben?"

Polly swallowed hard and forced herself to maintain eye contact with McBee.

He continued, "Reginald said he saw a white woman drivin' the wagon, settin' next to the slave man on the bench seat. She was wearin' a blue dress. Does that sound like it could be you, Mrs. Stone?"

— • —

TOM STOOD ABRUPTLY. "I think that is quite enough, Mr. McBee. Mrs. Stone and I already told you that she went and got Ezra. A slave boy thinks he hears a gunshot and you tie that to Mrs. Stone caring for a slave? The boy could have heard hunters."

Polly jumped in. "Not just one slave, Mr. McBee. I also removed my former house girl, Kate, from the premises. She had been severely mistreated by Mr. Wilkins, and I will not stand idly by while someone mistreats my husband's property. I had a legal right to remove her. We did not see Mr. Wilkins."

"No, Mrs. Stone. I am not accusing anyone of standing idly by," McBee said wryly. "I am wonderin' if your slave, Ben, had a hand in the overseer's disappearance. Maybe you didn't see it. Maybe you were off locatin' the girl. Maybe you were distracted by something else, but it seems like it all fits. The slave'd just need access to a gun." He shrugged and lifted his hand to chew a ragged fingernail.

"McBee, you know I'm in charge of Mrs. Stone's slaves—" Roper began.

"Ah, but you didn't come back to town until the next day, isn't that right, Mr. Roper?" McBee cut him off. "You came in on the train from Greenville the day after Mrs. Stone went to River Wood."

McBee turned to Polly. "Now, a slave scufflin' with a white man? Well—" He chuckled. "That's something we just don't put up with around here."

The deputy stood. "And if a slave killed a white man outright, he'll get his just reward. Probably before there can be any kind of trial, a slave's likely to get taken out by a patrol and punished—appropriately enough. The patrol might have its own set of rules in these times. And the patrol don't take kindly to coddlin' slaves."

Polly stood abruptly. "Mr. McBee, your veiled threats do not become your office. I'll ask you to leave the premises immediately. This reeks of cronyism and you're preying on a weak woman while her husband is away fighting Union soldiers to protect your rights. I am appalled. And I cannot believe that you would take the word of a slave boy over mine. I have never run afoul of the law, which is more than I can say for Mr. Wilkins. For all we know, he abandoned River Wood and enlisted. He'd get better pay," she huffed. "I will speak to my lawyer and write to my husband about this." Polly stood and walked quickly toward the front door. "I do not expect to see you on my property again in regard to this matter. Good day, sir."

McBee looked down at the floor. "Ma'am, I apologize if I came off a little harsh. Clay Wilkins is a friend of mine. And I do plan to find out what happened to him."

"You'd better go, Mr. McBee. You have upset Mrs. Stone enough for one day." Tom led the deputy out onto the front porch. "If you come back, you'll need a warrant."

McBee glared at Tom before he strode to his horse and hoisted himself into the saddle. "I'm fairly sure that one of Mrs. Stone's slaves had a hand in Clay Wilkins' disappearance. There will be a reward for any information . . . so it is best if she knows anything, to come forward soon. Protecting a slave from the law is a hangin' offense. Even for a woman." He tipped his hat and wheeled the horse around and galloped down the long drive.

Tom watched until the man was out of sight and then quickly climbed the porch steps. He let himself inside and found Polly seated on the divan, busily attending to her needlework.

"Miss Polly, I think we need to talk."

"Oh yes, Mr. Roper. We do indeed."

— • —

POLLY POURED WHISKEY FOR HERSELF and for Tom with a shaking hand. As afternoon shadows lengthened outside, she started at the beginning. She told Tom of her trip through the orchard to chase after Jack, and what she remembered about the day her brothers died. With her head in her hands, she described how each boy was killed. She told him about Ben's corroboration of her story and how Ona had denied Ben the chance to divulge what he knew all those years ago.

She spoke of John's relations with Kate, and Wilkins' disgusting behavior with every female slave John had owned, including Lydia's mother, Eva, who ran away and was likely killed at Wilkins' hand. She described the scars on Ezra's neck, signs of a near lynching. She told him about John's hot temper with her. Finally, with tears in her eyes, she related Floride's revelation, that John and Ben were half-brothers—and how Ona corroborated the story.

Tom sat quietly, taking it all in. He was transported back in time thirteen years. He remembered how young Ben used to follow Caleb and Joshua Burgiss everywhere, usually when he was supposed to be doing chores. He recalled the horror of the day the boys were found. He himself had carried one of James Burgiss's sons to the waiting wagon, although which boy he cradled he could not tell. The wounds were so brutal, so violent. He had burned the blood-stained shirt he wore that day.

He recalled Mary Burgiss's screams of agony, her very soul ripped from her. She was lost after that day. James Burgiss wanted to believe that a rogue band of Indians had attacked the trading post in a raid. Tom knew it was highly unlikely. Even the idea of runaway slaves attacking the store seemed improbable. Yet no one would entertain other ideas. When a young Cherokee man was intercepted while hunting, he was shot and strung up near the post, and the hysteria died down. People needed to believe that the perpetrator was caught and punished.

Polly's story made sense. It made sense in every way.

"Do you believe me, Tom?" Polly asked hesitantly. "That's the complete truth about what happened."

"I don't want to, but yes, I do." He looked at Polly tenderly. "My God, girl. How have you been able to handle this?"

"I am not sure that I am. I cannot go to the sheriff. Who would believe me? The deputy suspects Ben. And to be married to the man who—" She closed her eyes.

Tom drank the liquor in one gulp and set the glass down. "I am willing to back you up, Polly, but no court will believe you without another white person at the scene to corroborate it. It's been thirteen years. The sad truth is that some would see it as a way to get a divorce after the man wiped out your inheritance. Knowing this and knowing that you were forced to pay his debts on River Wood, which McGee can find out easily enough, it does look a little suspicious . . . you and Ben going to River Wood."

He leaned forward. "Ah. Ben's shirt. If he killed Clay Wilkins and you want my help, you have to level with me. I wouldn't blame him. Be honest with me, Polly."

"I killed him," Polly said softly. "I made Ben drive me there. I took Father's pistol with me. Ben told me not to take it. In fact, he wouldn't let me take it to the front door of the house when I was after Kate. He was just there to carry Ezra out, which he did. Kate was hidden under the tarp. Wilkins appeared out of nowhere. He wanted to know why I was there. I got angry and told him I knew that he killed my brothers. He called me names. He threw me against the wagon wheel. That's how I hurt my ribs. Then he went looking for Kate in the wagon bed. But Kate had taken the pistol from under the wagon bench. She shot him first. In the stomach. She didn't kill him. He didn't go down for long. When he lunged toward us both, I grabbed the gun and shot him. In the face."

"Oh, my God, Polly. Oh, my God . . ." Tom put his head in his hands. "Do you know what you've done?" He ran his fingers through his hair.

"I would do it again. That man took everyone who was dear to me," Polly said defiantly. "He murdered my brothers, abused slaves, and raped women, Tom. Ben didn't even see the shooting. He was carrying Ezra all the way from the kitchen house. The boy Reginald was right about that."

"They'll come after Ben. McBee will find a way to get to him." Tom stood and paced the room.

"Ben didn't do it. I will swear to it."

"Polly, think!" Tom said in exasperation. "Even if you were to confess, they will take this out on your slaves. McBee and his ilk. He may be a deputy, but they were all friends with Clay Wilkins. They're in the patrols. They'll say you're protecting Ben." He stopped pacing and turned to her. "Where is the body?"

Polly put her hand to her mouth. "Oh my God. I have set him up for a murder charge. I had Ben bury the body in the ruins of the Kemp place." She looked at Tom beseechingly. "I made him bury the body. What have I done?"

Tom looked past Polly toward the open parlor doors. "It's suppertime. Will someone be coming in?"

"No, I gave everyone the entire day off for the wedding. I have some cheese and bread set by. Are you hungry?" Polly asked.

"Not at all. We do not need anyone coming in the house while we talk," Tom said. "Polly, we may need to . . . get Ben and Kate away."

Polly cocked her head. "I don't understand. Get them away? Where?"

Tom frowned. "You're not the only one with secrets."

Chapter Thirty-Five

July 2, 1861

THE COOL NIGHT SAT HARD ON THE GROUND HEATED by yesterday's sun, and a dense and creeping fog had settled in the hollows and low places around Whitehall. It moved, ghostlike, along the ground, in swirls and ribbons. Polly, up before dawn, used the fog like a cover. She moved quietly toward the slave cabins, happy to have the mist as a hiding place.

She knocked softly on the door of Ben and Kate's cabin. She heard sleepy murmurs from inside. Ona had kept Lydia and Sol on the couple's first night as husband and wife and Polly blushed at the thought. The door opened and a surprised Ben stood shirtless in the doorway.

"Miss Polly, is everything alright?" Ben pulled suspenders over his shoulders. Soon Kate joined him at the door, her hair a wild thing yet to be tamed by the ubiquitous turban.

"May I come in? I am sorry, but this is very important," Polly said quietly, glancing around toward the other cabins. George would have all the hands up within the hour. She ran a hand through her damp hair.

Ben and Kate stepped aside and Polly entered the newly erected cabin. It smelled of fresh-cut lumber, piney cool and inviting. She turned to the couple and said, "I won't mince words. Deputy McBee, from town, was here yesterday after the wedding. It seems that one of the River Wood slaves saw Ben carrying Ezra . . . and heard the shots. He didn't see our skirmish with Wilkins, but he saw us driving away. He knows your name, Ben. He recognized you from working in our fields last summer. And he correctly assumed it was me with you that day once he remembered where you were from."

Kate gasped and Ben sank to the unmade bed. "What does this mean?" he asked. He looked at Polly with angry eyes.

"It means that despite what I could say to clear your name, Ben, I have put you in a terrible position. I am so sorry. I should never have asked you to drive me that day. I shouldn't have asked you to bury the body. I don't think anyone could tie Kate to it, but I think that you're both in trouble."

Ben looked down, his hands clenched together. "What does this mean?" he asked again.

"You and Kate need to go away. Now. I know someone who can get you out of Whitehall safely and on the road to another life," Polly said.

"No!" Kate cried out in surprise.

Ben stood up and shook his head in disbelief. "I'm leaving Whitehall? You are sending me away to another farm?" His expression betrayed his hurt.

Polly shook her head. "No, Ben. I would never do that! You misunderstand. I'm sending you both to your freedom—far away from here."

Kate reached for Ben's hand.

"It's the only way to keep you safe. Tom, Mr. Roper, that is, agrees with me. He knows everything, Ben. Everything." She paused. "But there is something we did not know about him. He's what some people call a conductor. He conducts slaves out of the South from one safe house to the next. On what the abolitionists call the Underground Railroad. All the way up through the North and even into Canada, to freedom. All this time, we thought he was visiting his sick mother, or taking trips for business, when he was actually leading runaway slaves to the next safe house. He has been doing it for years, he says. He is an abolitionist."

Ben's mind reeled. "To freedom. With Kate."

Kate spoke softly. "I ain't leavin' the chillun." She eyed Polly warily.

"Of course not, Kate. You all must go together. You and I both shot Mr. Wilkins. I am responsible for his death, and I could go to jail. But you would be hanged if someone found out. You'll have to trust Mr. Roper."

Ben nodded. "Martin had a map. It showed something like what you said."

"He did?" Polly exclaimed. "Martin helped Tom on occasion. Martin knew of some of the worst cases in the area. As Father's blacksmith, he was frequently sent into town on errands. He heard things. Martin was a contact for slaves trying to run. Slaves who were being abused badly. Tom said he himself grew weary of slavery soon after he saw the conditions of so many slaves in this district."

Ben's eyes widened. "But he is an overseer."

Polly grinned. "And so who would suspect him? Near the end of his life, my father had begun to help runaways, too. My own father—a slaveholder—helped runaways by giving Tom money. And when the tunnel project closed down, one of the tunnels was open all the way through. It is just wide enough for a small wagon to scrape through. Father wondered if they could use it as a faster way to move runaways toward Tennessee and the Ohio Valley. His most recent survey showed the way, marked several hazards, and proved that the rock is stable enough to try. It showed the tunnel width, its length, its twists and turns, that sort of thing. The government men don't know that one is safe to use. Father hid the survey away. I found it. I've given it to Tom."

Ben looked skeptical. "So we just walk through a tunnel and we're free?"

Polly continued. "Not exactly. They've been closed. But Tom has used one of them already. The survey will help him move through more quickly."

Polly sensed Ben's trepidation and added, "Tom knows what he is doing. If you get close and he sees signs that it is occupied or dangerous, you'll have to come back. Ben, trust me. If you get there and it won't work, Tom will bring you all home. It's the only way. McBee will have patrols at the train stations and on the roads."

"What about between here and Walhalla?" Ben asked.

"Tom will drive the large wagon. He built wagon benches that could conceal a person, secret panels in crates, that sort of thing. You may have to stay hidden for hours, but you will be on your way to freedom."

Tears welled in Kate's eyes. "I believe you. You been good to me. I have to believe you." She looked at Ben, who appeared dazed and confused. "Ben, we have no choice." She wiped tears from her face with the back of her hand.

Ben looked at Polly sadly. "And Ma?"

"Tom doesn't think it would be good for her to try the trip. Five people is too large a group. And you have the children. Ben, I promise you. I will take good care of her here. You knew I wanted to free her. She will be safe. You can write, once you're far away and safe." Polly looked toward the window, where the gray light of the new morning was beginning to brighten to gold. "Tom thinks it best if you go tonight. Before Deputy McGee decides to come question my slaves."

"Tonight?" Ben snapped. "Tonight?"

"He has it all planned out. He will get you to a safe house somewhere in North Carolina or Tennessee. After that? I can't know. It would be dangerous. Go about your chores as usual today. Be happy. You were just married! I will come back for you all after dark. Please don't tell Ona just yet, Ben. Wait until it is time to leave. I don't want her to break down and tell Cissie or the men until after you're well away. Tom will come for you after dark tonight."

Ben crossed his arms defensively. "Do you trust Mr. Roper?"

Polly looked at Ben tenderly. "Ben, I do trust him. And you'll have to trust him, too. This will be a dangerous trip, I am sure, but Mr. Roper said he has taken twelve slaves to safe houses without mishap. Twelve! And what other choice do we have? Do what he says and you will all be fine. It's the only way."

Kate grabbed Ben's arm and held it tightly. "Miss Polly, we be ready at dark tonight. I'll have Lydia and Sol ready, and we do whatever Mr. Roper says." Her brown eyes were fearful and sad, but brave, too.

Polly smiled at the newlyweds. "Congratulations on your marriage," she said. "Now let's get you on your wedding trip."

— • —

BEN JABBED THE PITCHFORK INTO THE HAY and tossed the sweet-smelling fodder down onto the barn floor. How quickly the pleasure of his first night as a husband evaporated. Last night, the warm touch of his wife in the dark was a sensation he had dreamt about, an exquisite joy. Yet today he wondered how long this happiness would last.

Could he really trust Mr. Roper to get all four of them safely away? If they were caught, his most hellish nightmares would come true. If they weren't killed, they would surely be separated, children from parents, husband from wife. And what of his own mother? Ona was so happy to have a daughter in Kate, and the children to care for as her own grands. Would she survive this blow?

He remembered the notations in Martin's Bible all those years ago. The penciled string of dots connected one small town to another, all the way up the Eastern United States into Canada. A route to freedom.

Ben climbed down the haymow steps and dropped onto the barn floor. Delightful whinnied as he neared. He reached into his pocket for a turnip. The horse nuzzled his palm and delicately took the proffered morsel with a snort.

He could be framed for a murder he had tried to prevent, a murder committed by his mistress. Yet, his new wife had pulled the trigger first. If

Polly hadn't killed Wilkins, Wilkins would have surely killed Kate. They would have to go away.

"Ben. What you doin' here?" Zadoc appeared behind him, confused. "Ain't Mizz Polly gave you a whole day off? A new married man an' all?" he smiled. "Why you doin' my chores? No one ever gets a whole day off."

Ben lifted forkfuls of hay and dropped them into the two cow stalls. "I got a lot on my mind, is all. I need to work. Already sharpened the shovels and fixed a sickle handle in the smithy."

Zadoc opened Delightful's stall. "Damn. Well, thank you. . . . I'll take Delightful and the colt out to pasture, an' come back an' do the milkin'."

Ben grabbed the milking stool silently and set to work under the Guernsey, her teats firm and warm. His anger bloomed. His happiness with Kate was jeopardized because of Polly. And yet, happiness with Kate was because of Polly's willingness to fight for the woman.

Zadoc shrugged and held up his hands. "Alright, suit yo'se'f. If you ain't gonna take a day off, take my work. Mizz Polly wouldn't do that fo' no one else. I'll go hide an' take a nap." He chuckled and led the horses past Ben and out into the cool morning.

Ben watched him go. Polly had always favored Ben, it was true. He had seen how the other hands snickered when Ben left the work of the forge and joined them in the fields only for the summer's hardest weeks. Ben was the one sent to town for errands. Ben was called to the big house when something needed to be repaired. Several of the men had crossed Ben early on with raunchy jokes and innuendo, but Ben's strong arms and ready fists had shut them up quickly. He knew that any favor he had with Miss Polly was because of his own mama's place as her "mammy."

The cow stamped her foot and nearly upset the pail. Ben cursed at her and leaned again into the animal's broad flank.

"I knew you'd be working. You must be furious with me," a voice said softly behind him.

Ben closed his eyes and tried to ignore Polly's presence.

"This is a mess and I'm sorry," she tried again. "The only way I can see out of this is for you to go. I trust that Mr. Roper will deliver you safely. But I have something for you. Can you stop for a moment?"

Ben sat up and turned around to look at Polly. She looked miserable, for which he was grateful. He sighed heavily.

"I have wanted to run away to freedom all my life. And now that I have that chance, all I can do is worry about Kate, the children, and Ma," he muttered.

Polly nodded. She clutched a brown leather pouch in her hand and suddenly extended it toward Ben. "I want you to have this." Ben did not move. "Go on. Take it," she urged.

Ben reached for the pouch. He felt the heft and jingle of the contents and cocked his head. He slowly opened the bag to reveal eight gold coins, more money than he had ever seen in his young life. "What—what is this?"

Polly finally smiled. "My eighteenth birthday gift from Mother," she said. "Use it to get you and Kate started on your new life. Up north."

Ben looked at Polly and shook his head. "I can't take this. A runaway slave carrying money?" He closed the pouch and tried to return it to Polly.

She closed Ben's fingers over the pouch and pushed it back. "Ben, take the money. Let Tom hold it until you're safely away. Use it to get a place, to buy food for your family, to keep going until you have an income. I cannot send you off without knowing you have something to live off for a while. The kindness of strangers only goes so far. Please. You won't be able to write to us for a while. It would be dangerous. But your mother and I would be worried sick if we thought you were destitute."

Ben nodded. "I don't rightly know what I can do to earn a living, so this will give me some time to get settled into a trade. Thank you."

"Nonsense. You are a wonderful blacksmith, like your father—Martin," Polly clarified with a grin. "You're a farrier. And a good horse trainer. I can send a letter with you, a recommendation of sorts," Polly offered.

"I don't think that would be a good idea. If someone finds it, you'll be in more trouble. Just . . . take good care of Ma. It will about kill her that we're leaving." Tears welled in his eyes. "I don't know if she'll survive it."

"She is strong," Polly said. "She will be fine." She turned quickly and hurried from the barn.

Ben prayed that her words were true.

— • —

THE DAY SEEMED TO MOVE AT A SNAIL'S pace but finally, Kate and Ben looked out the tiny window of the cabin and acknowledged to each other that the day was done. Lydia asked over and over why she and Sol were going to bed in their clothes, but Kate shushed them and tucked each child into their shared cot. "You'll see." She smiled. "You is going to have a wonderful dream tonight, but you gotta have your clothes and shoes on to see the magic."

A soft breeze moved through the cabin, taking the day's heat with it. Ben stood by the open door, a sentinel. He stood there for an hour, watching the night settle. In the darkness, he finally saw approaching shapes. The hairs at the base of his neck rose, but soon he recognized Tom and Polly coming quickly along the dark path. He stepped back to let them in.

"Ben. Kate." Roper removed his hat and looked somberly at the young couple. He inclined his head toward the bed. "The children ready?"

"They're dressed, yessir," Kate answered softly.

Tom turned to face Ben. "Ben, this won't be easy. Not with your family along. But I have done this for a long time. I have a safe house in mind. I will take you as far as that house, and then another conductor will take you along to the next house. That's how it works. A long, long string of stops. You may be at a house for hours. Or days. Hell, I had one man who stayed in North Carolina a month before moving along. That one about aged me twenty years." The overseer chuckled, scratching his beard.

Ben pictured Martin's map. "Where is the first stop?"

"Through the tunnel and across the Chattooga, which is a pretty mean river if the water's high. I got someone to get you on to Cherokee County and into the mountains." Tom looked from Ben to Kate.

Kate's eyes grew wide. "How will we take these chillun into a dark tunnel, across mountains, and through a wild river?" she whispered. She glanced at the pair snuggled together in their cot, sound asleep. "None of us can swim!"

Polly refused to entertain the thought that the tunnel might already be in use by the Confederates. She looked at Kate's worried face. "You'll go under the mountain and across the river in the wagon. You'll be safe with Mr. Roper," Polly reassured.

Tom put a hand on Ben's shoulder. "Ben, if we can get going, we'll have plenty of time before first light to get through."

Ben looked at Tom skeptically. "But what if we get stopped?"

"You'll all be hiding in the wagon compartment this side of the tunnel. Hopefully, the children and Kate can ride in the open after we leave the county. If we're questioned, I'm selling four slaves for Mrs. Stone. She has written a letter to that effect."

Ben and Kate exchanged glances before Ben nodded. "We are ready."

"I will wake Ona and bring her here. You'll say your goodbyes and be off," Polly said. She turned and quickly disappeared into the dark.

Tom sprang into action. "Alright then. We've got a wagonload of peaches all crated up. You'll go into the cutouts under the wagon. It won't be pleasant. Kate, you'll have some room to lie still and turn over but you'll have to keep the children quiet. Ben, ordinarily you could ride with me on the bench, but if McGee's men are waiting to see something happen, well, you'd be a sitting duck. You'll have to hide, too. I'm sorry. Once we're through the tunnel, you're slaves to be sold, if someone stops us."

Ben nodded slowly and Tom continued, "It's near a thirty-mile ride up that way. That's going to take us most of the night at a clip. We will be right near Clayton Georgia when we're through. Maybe you'll be back into the crates for a few miles, but I think you can do it." He looked at the young couple and added, "But I won't even try unless you tell me you're fine with this. It might take several months to get to a final location, and if we're caught, I can't promise I can help you. If McGee catches up to us, things could fall apart."

Kate looked up at Ben and then across the room to the sleeping children. Her brown eyes brimmed with tears. "What choice do we got?" she said softly.

"We're ready to go, Mr. Roper. I just need to say goodbye to Ma. Then, we're in your hands." Ben extended his palm and the two men shook hands.

Minutes passed while the couple sat nervously and waited hand in hand on the worn and sagging mattress. Polly finally tapped on the door and quietly entered with Ona, the older woman's eyes wild and fearful. She looked with surprise at the overseer standing in the shadows, his hat in hand. Polly handed a sheaf of papers over to Tom and then put a comforting arm around Ona. The old woman shrugged it off and stepped toward her son.

Ona started to speak but Ben hushed her with a finger to his lips. "Shhh, Ma. Don't wake the children."

"Ben!" Ona whispered. "What's goin' on? Miss Polly wouldn't say. It's the middle of the night."

Ben reached out his arms and enfolded his mother in his embrace. "I have to go, Mama. Kate and I are taking the children and leaving Whitehall. We have to go. Now."

Ona backed up to look up into her son's face. "What do you mean you have to go? Where? Why?"

"It's a long story," he swallowed hard. "When we went to River Wood to get Ezra and Kate, Mr. Wilkins showed up. He threw Miss Polly into the wagon wheel. That's how she hurt her ribs."

Ona nodded sternly at Polly. "I knew you hadn't jes' pulled a muscle, Miss Girl."

"Mama, Miss Polly killed him. She told him she knew about her brothers. She shot him dead with her daddy's pistol. I buried the body near the old Kemp place. But now, the deputy in Pendleton knows I was there that day. One of the River Wood men heard shots and recognized me from last summer's fieldwork."

Ona looked confused. "But you didn't do nothin'."

"They'll come after me, Mama. For murder. I am a slave. So Mr. Roper is taking us away. Far away. I won't be able to write to you, least not any time soon. Maybe one day I can send for you." Ben's eyes filled with tears that trickled down his brown cheeks. He wiped his nose on the back of his sleeve.

Ona dropped to the bed and put her gray head between her knees. She moaned softly, rocking back and forth.

Ben sat down beside her and whispered, "Mama, I love you so much. Thank you for everything you have done for me. I'm a grown man now and we have the children to think of, too. You will be in my heart all the days of my life. One day, we may be together again. Up north in one of those places on Pa's old map. Maybe New York, or even Canada. I'll send for you, I promise." He wrapped the old woman in his arms tenderly and they wept together.

Polly felt as if her own heart would break. She crept back into the shadows and waited, the realization that she was the cause of this pain almost too much to bear.

Ona finally lifted her head and placed her gnarled hands on either side of Ben's dark face. Her face was puffy and wet with tears. "My baby boy. My sweet boy, I love you. You've always been such a good boy. Now you is a man—a fine man with a family. I will pray to Jesus for all of you on this journey. I will pray that you get all the way to a safe place where you can be free. Maybe that Canada place Martin always talked about. Then you'll write your mama and tell me all about it. What it's like to be free! Oh, praise Jesus! My baby's gonna be free! And one day, when you send for me, I will come to you all. Like you said. One day."

She unwrapped Ben's arms and said softly but sternly, "Now you got to go. Do what Mr. Roper say and keep Kate and them chillun safe." She dried her eyes with the corner of her apron and stood. "God bless you, my sweet boy," she said, her voice steady.

Kate rushed into her new mother-in-law's arms and hugged the woman tightly. Ona pushed her back gently and patted Kate's cheek. "I got a sleepin' draft to give the babies, so they sleep all night and not cry out. I run git it now while y'all load up."

— • —

NOW WELL PAST TEN, BY THE LIGHT of a waxing moon, Polly and Ona watched uneasily as Kate and the two groggy children climbed up into the wagon and were hidden away in the coffin-like cabinet under the wagon bed. The children were silent, given the late hour and the strong sleeping draft. Kate soothed them with a quiet lullaby as they lay down. Ben leaned over to kiss his new bride, then replaced crates of peaches, and soon there was no evidence that three people were hiding under the load.

Ben would join his small family in hiding under a second compartment, smaller than the one his bride and the children shared. Once inside, he wouldn't be able to stretch his long legs out or even turn over. If stopped in the night, Tom had the ruse of a letter written by Polly, directing him to sell her peaches in Walhalla or Clayton, wherever the market was better. Tom prayed it wouldn't come to that. If they had to unload the fruit, the game was over.

Ben came around from the back of the wagon and hugged Ona tightly. Ona sighed wearily. "I best git on back to bed. It's late." She smiled at him with trembling lips and stepped back. "I love you, son, but I cain't watch you drive away." Her tiny frame was quickly swallowed by the night.

Ben looked down at Polly, who was biting her lip to keep from crying. "We'll be fine. Just take care of my mama."

Polly shook her head sadly. "There could never be so brave a soldier as Ona. I promise I will try to make her life an easier one. When you get settled, you can write to her. Give yourself an alias, a false name, and write in care of Whitehall, to me. Who knows? It may get through," Polly tried. "I'm sorry, Ben. I'm terribly sorry."

Ben considered this young white woman, big brown eyes hiding so much of her own pain and sadness. He actually felt sorry for her. She had no one. She had seen the deaths of everyone she loved, one by one, and finally discovered the source of so much pain was her own newlywed husband. He was lucky in comparison.

Ben reached out to touch Polly's cheek and realized that she was crying. "Goodbye, Polly. I'll remember you as a friend."

Polly reached up and clasped his hand against her cheek. Ben squeezed her hand and then let it drop. He turned and quickly mounted the step to the wagon seat.

"Alright young man, we got a long way to go and we're late. Let's head out," Tom said.

Ben lifted a hidden latch on the wagon bench and raised the seat. He lowered himself inside and Tom closed the lid, before replacing a cushion and sitting on the bench.

Tom looked down at an anxious Polly. "They'll be fine in there. There's plenty of air. I should be back here in two-or-three days' time. If McGee and his cronies come around again, just tell 'em I took Ben with me to sell your peaches. Send 'em south toward Anderson, if they want to catch up to me," he winked. "If you have any troubles with him, you need to go see that lawyer fellow in town. McGee hasn't got any right to mess with you, Polly."

Tom clicked the reins and the horses began their slow plod down the long drive, as cicadas and crickets sang their hymn to the night.

— • —

ONA DARED NOT LOOK BACK AS the wagon rolled away. It took every fiber of her being to take steps away from her son, and toward her cabin. Each footfall was a desperate plea to God to go ahead and take her soul. Surely the crushing pain of her loss was too much to bear. Death must come for her quickly. *Please, Lord. Ben is leaving.* It hurt too much. And she knew deep inside that she would never see her boy again.

Chapter Thirty-Six

July 9, 1861

A WEEK PASSED AND POLLY SOON BECAME FRANTIC WITH WORRY. Tom said he would be home in a few days, and it had been a week. She dreaded the worst. She ran scenarios through her mind and all of the outcomes were bad ones. Were they intercepted at the tunnels? Had McGee's men followed them? She tried to keep herself busy but nearly jumped out of her skin whenever Jack barked at something outside.

She went out to survey the cotton with George. Polly sat astride Delightful, while George rode the old mule, Betsy. Delightful pawed the ground and appeared agitated, stretching to urinate. Polly wished Ben were here. He knew her horse well.

The fields were in bloom once again and Polly took courage from the very sight. Soft white flowers blushed to pink as they matured. "George, the cotton does look good."

George nodded. "Yes'm. The aphids ain't a problem right now, but we keep watchin'." He shifted in the saddle uncomfortably. "Come to find the harrow's broke. Is someone gonna be your new blacksmith to fix it?"

Polly avoided making eye contact with George. "We'll see," she murmured. Polly had instructed Ona to let slip that Ben and Kate had been sold away, and the drop in morale was palpable. As for Tom's disappearance, Polly tried to stick to the script that she and Tom had concocted. Tom had gone to sell peaches and tend his ailing mother in Greenville again. "Consumption, I think." Polly did not want the slaves to think badly of Tom, as the man who had taken Ben to a new master on her behalf.

She tugged on the reins and trotted toward the orchard. George followed, cursing the recalcitrant mule, who only wanted to stop and eat at every patch of stray timothy.

Jack tagged along behind them, sniffing at the breeze, and yapping at squirrels in the trees. The orchard was a thing of beauty and symmetry, rows of trees marching in neat lines down toward the river, clingstone peach on the sandy side nearer the water, and Red June apples further up the ridge in the loamy soil there. The newly pruned trees appeared healthy and strong.

"Mr. Stone doesn't think we can grow apples and peaches both. I'd sure like to prove him wrong," she said, attempting to lighten the mood.

"Yes'm," George said. "When he back?"

"I don't know, George," she said. "Let's check on the sorghum now."

The foreman nodded his head slowly, worry shadowing his weathered face.

For the first time, a creeping fear began to lodge in Polly's mind. She was alone with her slaves, who were angry and upset at her for abruptly selling Ben and his new family away. Ona had sold the lie. If one of the field hands wanted to run, or hurt her, it would not be difficult. Her husband and white overseer were both gone. She tried to shake off the thought.

She slowed the horse to a walk, waiting for George to catch up. Delightful seemed eager to move but took a moment to relieve her bladder a second time while Polly scanned the field. The flowering sorghum looked good, too. Rain showers had been plentiful and it seemed to like the soil.

Polly glanced at her foreman as he rode up. "George, you and the men are doing such a fine job that I'm not sure we'll need Mr. Roper once his mother recovers her health," she said. "Look at this beautiful crop." She paused and added, "In fact, tell the boys that, in recognition of a job well done with the orchard and sorghum, they may come in from the fields at five o'clock in the afternoon instead of seven, until harvest." She smiled. "As long as the grasshoppers and the blights stay away, that is."

George grinned happily and tipped his hat. "Thank you, Miss Polly! Thank you. "It's the head worms and stink bugs everywhere that got me worried," he muttered as he swatted a stink bug in mid-flight. They dismounted and walked through the flowering sorghum, now waist high. George had a wooden bucket with him, and Polly watched as he used the "beat bucket" method of shaking the seed heads over the bucket to look for stink bugs.

"Yes ma'am, it's all lookin' good so far," he said cautiously. "We keep checkin' though. Is you gonna sell it all?"

"I think we will keep a good portion for our use here on the farm. We may trade the surplus. We'll see what we can get," she said absentmindedly. Her thoughts kept running back to Tom and Ben and Kate.

Polly tugged on Delightful's bridle and the horse balked. "Delightful seems a little unwell today. Colicky. Did Zee say anything to you?" she asked, wondering what Ben would think. Was Ben even alive?

George frowned. "No ma'am. He didn't say nothin' to me. . . . He ain't the horseman that Ben is. I doubt he even noticed." George paused to see if Polly was angered by his words. "You want me to dose her with somethin'? Maybe best to jes' keep her on forage a few days. She probably eatin' a lot of grain. I tell Zee."

"George, what would I do without you?" Polly felt an inclination to extend her benevolence. "I think you deserve a flask of my father's whiskey."

George's eyes widened and he laughed. "Miss Polly, thank ya kindly, ma'am. I do 'preciate that. I try to work hard fo' ya."

"I know you do, George. I'll send it by way of Cissie after supper tonight. How is she?" She put a foot in the stirrup and mounted her horse.

"Well, she stronger every day, ma'am. It's a right hard thing to her that Ben and Kate was sold off. It leave her and Ona to do the house and cookin.' Ona ain't takin' it too good, is she? We sho' wasn't expectin' it," George said, eyes never leaving Polly. He shook his head. "But we take care of everything fo' you, yes ma'am. We get it all done."

Polly nodded and tucked a wisp of dark hair behind her ear. She thought her foreman seemed to be taking the news surprisingly well.

"George, it's just me in that big house now. I don't need three house girls. Sometimes I just want to build myself a little cottage and be rid of the big house—and its memories." She sighed heavily.

George blinked and stared at his mistress. He wasn't Ben, always ready with a smart remark about her being a white woman of privilege. She missed his angry retorts and was surprised by the fact. The silence was uncomfortable.

"Yes, well, I know you have work to do. I might ride into town and see if there is any mail. Please have Zee hitch up the phaeton for me, hmm?" She smiled at George and called for Jack. The pup followed obediently as Polly turned her horse toward home.

— • —

THE TRIP INTO TOWN SEEMED TO calm Polly's nerves. It was good to get out of the house and away from Whitehall. The drive was a pleasant one, the hedgerows brimming with wildflowers. Polly noticed much more traffic than usual. Drivers raised hands in greeting, but Polly did not know many of them.

She drove the rickety old phaeton, and perched high upon her seat, the wind blew cool and refreshing. Polly wished she had the wagon, in case there were goods to purchase, but it was away with Tom somewhere.

She remembered her last trip into Pendleton. Maybe there would be goods available at the Mercantile this time. She planned to speak to the proprietor about her fruit. Her fruit. It had sickened her to think of the ripened peaches loaded onto the wagon, as a ruse to disguise the slaves. By now it would have rotted, all that produce slowly fermenting into a sour mess.

The boardwalks were crowded with people, and the streets bustled. Polly stopped first at the post office. She dismounted and tied up to the crowded horse rings, adjusted her bonnet, and stepped inside. As Polly's eyes adjusted to the dark interior, she was surprised at the line of customers waiting to speak to the postmaster. She stepped to the back of the line behind a young woman wearing an elaborate bonnet, rolled pleats of ivory silk bedecked with dyed ostrich plumes and satin ribbon. Polly's eyes went wide at such finery in downtown Pendleton.

"Mrs. Stone?" Polly heard a man's gentle voice. She turned and was happy to see Harrison Legarre take his place in line behind her.

"Mr. Legarre! How nice to see you." She smiled, putting a hand nervously to her simple straw bonnet. *Here is my chance*, she thought. But the idea was fleeting. Who would believe her story now? And it would only draw Deputy Mcgee's attention once more.

"And you." The young man bowed slightly, his grin warm and kind. "What brings you into town?"

"I'm hoping for a letter from Mrs. Calhoun. She has gone to Maryland to wait out the war." Polly looked around the small room and whispered, "Tell me, who are all these people? I have never seen so many strangers in town before."

Legarre nodded and adjusted his spectacles. "I believe that the Blue Ridge Inn advertised our fair town as a safe alternative to summer up north for wealthy Charlestonians and Columbians. It currently has no vacancies and I hear they are going to add more rooms. We will be inundated while there is war," Legarre said softly, as two elegant women entered and stood in line behind him.

"We're safe enough from any conflict here, I would hope. What news of the war?" Polly smiled at the two women and returned her gaze to Mr. Legarre.

"Troops are amassing near Richmond. I think McQueen's company is there."

Polly nodded. "That much I do know although I have not had a letter in some time. Has there been a skirmish up that way?"

"Not as yet," Legarre said. He shook his head. "I feel that I am not doing my duty by continuing with my father's legal practice right now, but he begs me not to enlist. He is overwhelmed with business, as you can imagine, with all of the new clients in town."

Polly nodded and moved forward in the queue. "So many of our local men have enlisted, it's true." She paused and inhaled. "Did you know that my husband's overseer, Mr. Wilkins, may have run off and done the same? Without so much as a by-your-leave!" Polly looked into Legarre's eyes with an air of exasperation. "I certainly didn't like the man, but I ask you, couldn't he have given me notice?" She exhaled calmly, surprised at the ease of her lie.

Legarre looked confused. "This is most unsettling, Mrs. Stone," he said. "Deputy McGee came in last week and asked about your relationship with the overseer, Clay Wilkins. I know you despise the man, but I did not divulge that. He did not tell me he was looking for a missing overseer."

Polly feigned surprise. "Really? My word. As if I have any say in that man's whereabouts! As we both know, a married woman has no say in her husband's affairs."

She was not surprised that McGee had gone to her attorney. The deputy was sneaky. "You could have told him the truth. I do hate the man." She tried to remain calm but her pulse raced. How would she ever bring up the murders and an annulment now? It would surely seem linked to his disappearance.

Legarre shrugged. "He had no call to ask me for client information. I wouldn't divulge anything. I simply told him that your affairs were none of his business, and that your husband oversaw all decisions at River Wood."

Polly lowered her voice. "I am not sorry that Mr. Wilkins has run off. After my inheritance went to pay my husband's debt, you remember that I washed my hands of River Wood."

Legarre returned her smile. "Yes, of course."

"Next!" called Mr. Phillips loudly.

"It was a pleasure to see you again, Mrs. Stone. I hope you receive only good news from your husband." Mr. Legarre tipped his hat.

Polly nodded and stepped up to the window. "How are you, Mr. Phillips?"

The usually talkative postmaster looked haggard and in low spirits. "All these summer folks are overwhelming the post office," he griped. "I have mail and packages coming in from down south at a record pace. I can't get it all sorted." He sighed. "And every single Charlestonian who comes in here acts as if he or she is the only person expecting mail in this town!" He glared at the long line that had formed behind Polly.

"I am truly sorry, Mr. Phillips. I will conduct my own business quickly. Do I have anything?" Polly asked.

"I think you do, Mrs. Stone." He rummaged under the counter and produced a worn and stained letter. "It's from your husband." He slapped it on the counter with uncharacteristic haste.

Polly stashed the letter in her bag and nodded to the man. "Have a lovely afternoon." She turned and stifled her laughter as she passed Legarre. "Good day, Mr. Legarre."

Outside, Polly looked for a quiet place to read her letter, but the crush of humanity on the boardwalk was overwhelming. She decided to wait to read it at home and headed for the Mercantile. She doubted that there would be anything on the shelves with all the Lowcountry people coming into town but decided to have a look anyway.

She pushed the door open and heard the little bell overhead announce her arrival. Mr. Jones looked up from his ledgers eagerly and said, "There is my fruit lady! Did you bring me peaches, Mrs. Stone? Boy, can we sell them. I've had so many folks asking about fruit."

Polly shook her head and said, "Not today, Mr. Jones. I know that we have a deal, but the first peaches off the trees were horribly mealy. I couldn't sell those to you," she lied. "I'll have another type ready in a week or so. If you can wait, I know they'll be good ones."

The storekeeper looked unhappy. "If you say so, Mrs. Stone. You're the only producer willing to sell to me this season. We did have a deal."

"Of course we did. And I'll not disappoint you with low-quality fruit. I will have your peaches in ten or twelve days. I need to barter the price because I want baskets from you now."

"Baskets? I thought you had all those wooden crates Tom came in for last month."

Polly thought quickly. "We have decided to use baskets. The peaches can breathe easier and are lighter to transport."

"Yes ma'am. I have baskets. But—"

Polly cut the man off abruptly. "Now, what can you give me for my sorghum? I will have a good crop ready this fall."

Mr. Jones smiled. "If you cook it down and sell me the syrup, the sky's the limit."

"Coffee, Mr. Jones." Polly smiled. "I want real coffee. I'll not drink another brew made from bark and beans."

The storekeeper laughed and nodded in agreement. "Yes ma'am, I'm tired of that Confederate Coffee myself. Although I've heard tell that cottonseed makes a good cup. I can't get you any real coffee." He waited for another customer to exit the store, and the tiny bell over the door tinkled a goodbye.

The storekeeper leaned over the counter. "Mrs. Stone, these Lowcountry folks have a lot of money and a lot of connections up north. I did have one woman come in, a right fancy older lady. Well, she wants Madeira. The coastal blockades mean she cannot get her Spanish wine. She told me she can get me coffee if I can get her wine."

"Hmm. I can try my hand at a peach cordial."

Mr. Jones brightened. "If you can make a high-quality cordial, and in quantity, we may just have a deal."

Polly smiled and extended a gloved hand. "We do have a deal, Mr. Jones.

I will return in a few weeks' time with your peaches. Some peach cordial . . . and possibly some hard cider. I do have apples."

Mr. Jones grinned. "Thank you, Mrs. Stone. I will let the lady know." The man shook Polly's hand and his face turned serious. "Say, I heard that your husband's overseer disappeared. Is Mr. Roper working both places?"

Polly was beginning to enjoy the tale she spun. She leaned in conspiratorially. "It's true! Mr. Wilkins up and ran off to enlist. Or possibly took a job on the coast. Of all the nerve. Leaving us without a River Wood overseer . . ." The clerk's eyes grew wide.

Polly continued, "I cannot concern myself with my husband's business, of course. It isn't a woman's place. But Mr. Wilkins did mention to me once that he would make a better living as a soldier than working for my husband. He made good on his threat to leave. He wasn't doing a good job at River Wood. Between you and me, he was a man prone to drink in the daytime."

Polly could see that Mr. Jones was eager to collect all the gossip he could pass along. "Now, I really must go. I have much to accomplish while I am in town. Oh, and please don't repeat anything I said. I wouldn't want to tarnish Mr. Wilkins' good name. Poor man. . . . Goodbye, Mr. Jones." She smiled and exited the store quickly.

Polly kept her head low as she made her way down the boardwalk toward her horse and the phaeton. It was easy for her to blend in with the milling crowd near the post office. Men and women on their errands passed in both directions. She quickly loosened the horse's reins and hoisted herself into the high leather seat.

"Good afternoon, Mrs. Stone!" called a loud and familiar voice from across the street. Polly's blood ran cold at the sound of Deputy McGee's greeting. She looked down to see the man approaching the phaeton.

"Hello, Deputy. I must be on my way," she said, flicking the reins lightly.

"Whoa, now hold on a minute." McGee reached out and grabbed the horse's bridle. He looked up at Polly and grinned. "What's yer hurry? I wanted to let you know that I'm still tryin' to find yer overseer. Mr. Wilkins, remember him?"

"Mr. Wilkins is not my overseer. Tom Roper is my overseer. If you have business dealings with River Wood in Mr. Wilkins' absence, you should write to my husband. Now let go of my horse, sir." Polly's voice shook in anger.

"Please do as the lady says, Deputy McGee." Harrison Legarre appeared at McGee's side. He stared down at the smaller man, eyes calm but firm. "You have no cause to harass this good woman. You're a man of the law. You'll soon attract a crowd, and who will appear the bully here? Is that what the Sheriff needs before an important election?"

Bristling, McGee let go of the horse's bridle. He looked up at Legarre and said, "I know this woman is behind Wilkins' disappearance." He turned to glare up at Polly before stomping off down the street.

Polly inhaled and exhaled to calm her nerves. "Mr. Legarre, I cannot thank you enough. The man knows that I detest Clay Wilkins and has it in for me." Polly's voice wavered. "But I'm sure that when Mr. Wilkins posts a letter or turns up again in the saloon, the whole thing will be forgotten. In the meantime, he does seem bent on bothering me. Can you help?"

Legarre pushed his spectacles up the bridge of his nose. "Unless he secures a warrant, he cannot come onto your property to execute a search. Without probable cause, even a deputy cannot roam where he wills."

Polly frowned. Without probable cause. Polly remembered what McGee had heard from the River Wood slave boy. Had Mr. Legarre also heard?

"I can see about a restraining order, if you would like. My father is a friend of Judge Williamson," Legarre offered.

Polly smiled sweetly. She wove the threads of her lie more intricately. "No, Mr. Legarre. That shouldn't be necessary. I have nothing to hide. Deputy McGee is a friend of Mr. Wilkins. He knows that I dislike Wilkins, and so I am sure that is what drives his emotional outbursts when he sees me. When Mr. Wilkins turns up again, and he will, like a bad penny—all will be set straight. Now, I must get home. We have peaches to harvest."

She flicked the reins and moved down Main Street slowly, merging into the flow of traffic.

— • —

POLLY ROCKED SLOWLY ON THE FRONT PORCH, the letter from John in her hand. In the deepening shadows of the late summer afternoon, she watched the play of light across the front lawn. The air fairly hummed with the heat of the day. Jack drowsed at her feet. In the distance, Delightful whinnied from the far side of the pasture. Her baby answered in his own time, from across the field, a voice growing stronger each day. Soon he would be a young stallion, and Polly wondered whether to sell him or geld him and keep him at Whitehall. Ben would have known what to do. Ben. She missed him.

Ona would not speak to her. The old woman would not even look at Polly. She carried out her chores obediently but had not said a word to her mistress. After the happiest day of Ona's life, her newly enlarged family was ripped away. Despite Polly's promise to Ben, how could she hope to soothe the old woman's pain? This was how she repaid Ona for her years of care. She had involved her son in a terrible thing. Where was he now?

Something must have gone wrong. Tom should have been home by now. Her imagination planted terrible scenarios in her mind. Tom had lied and had taken her slaves away to be sold. Or they had been discovered by military men as they approached the Walhalla tunnels. Or the children and Kate had suffocated, buried alive under the heavy load of fruit.

Polly dabbed her damp brow with her handkerchief, sighed, and looked down again at the letter from John.

Dear Polly,

I do not know if my letters even reach you. I have heard nothing from you or from the overseers. I trust that everything is

well at home, and the summer chores keep everyone busy. Please
write to me. Urge the overseers to keep me informed as well. We
are encamped outside Richmond, near Manassas Junction. Many
of the volunteers are without uniforms. We do not look like any
army I have imagined. Truth told—we are a sorry lot. Some of the
men have never been away from their farms before and cannot
even line up for drill, much less march and follow orders. The
crowded encampment takes its toll as well. It is stifling and our
camp has quickly taken on the stench of filth and disease. There
is order to our days, though. We drill. We sleep. We drill once
more. Your General Beauregard seems to be waiting on the North
to send soldiers our way. So, we wait for something to happen. I
rue the day that I enlisted. Even now, as an officer, yes! Your
husband commissioned a captain! But I find that I am homesick
for you, for River Wood, and for Whitehall.

Yours,
John

It was difficult for Polly to reconcile this man with the monster who stood by and watched her brothers die as children. And yet, he had. She crumpled the letter and stood to go inside. Cissie would have an early supper laid out for her. Polly patted her leg, beckoning Jack to come in. Jack opened his eyes but did not follow her. She scowled, tossed the wad of paper at the dog, and went in for supper.

Later that evening, Polly sat reading in the library, the oil lamp burning brightly on the table next to her. She yawned and struggled to stay awake, Walt Whitman's *Leaves of Grass* not stimulating enough to hold her attention.

"Cissie said you needed to see me?" Ona appeared in the doorway, deep in shadows the lantern did not reach.

Polly closed the book and rubbed her eyes. "Come in, Ona. Close the door behind you. Please sit down." She extended her hand toward the settee and Ona crossed the room quietly. She sat down on the velvet settee across from Polly and stroked the luxe upholstery with her hand.

"It reminds me of peach fuzz," Polly said.

Ona looked at Polly, confused.

"The velvet," she said, pointing to the settee. "It is soft, like the skin of a ripe peach."

"Hmm, I suppose it is," marveled Ona. She looked up at Polly expectantly.

Polly began. "Ona, I cannot stand this rift between us. I sent them away to save their lives. That deputy might show up here one day soon with the slave from River Wood, the one who recognized Ben. Don't you understand? My word will not matter—especially if John is back. John never liked Ben. And Ben would likely say that he shot Wilkins, to save Kate. It was a horrible tragedy, one that I regret every day."

She stood and moved to sit closer to Ona. The slave woman smelled of kitchen fires and lye soap. Ona turned her tiny head and looked away proudly.

Polly continued, "I know that you are angry with me, Ona. But I trust Mr. Roper to get them far away from here. They will be safe—and free. I cannot imagine your pain. Especially for that, I am sorry."

A single tear traced a path down Ona's brown cheek. "It is hard to bear, girl. And it didn't have to be." She swallowed hard. "Still, I ain't the only one with pain and loss. You lost everyone you had. I pray for strength each day and each day I git enough. Jes' enough."

"Can you forgive me then?" Polly asked.

"I try, Miss Polly. Lawd knows, I try."

Chapter Thirty-Seven

July 18, 1861

"GEORGE, THEY'RE BEAUTIFUL!" POLLY CRIED, HER PALM HELD up against the bright sunshine in the orchard. Her straw hat cast only a small bit of shade on her cheeks and the heat shimmered in waves in the distance.

Fuzzy golden orbs hung low in the trees. Polly reached up and twisted a peach free from the tree. Uniformly yellow with a faint red blush, Polly held the smooth fruit in her hand. She lifted it to her nose and inhaled the heady aroma.

"Are they ready?" She smiled up at her foreman eagerly.

George laughed and said, "You tell me, Miss Polly." He wiped the sweat from his face with the sleeve of his already damp shirt.

Polly took a bite of the tender flesh. Sweet and soft, without any bitterness. The crop was ready. This variety looked even better than the load of peaches that Tom had taken off with two weeks beforehand. Sweet juice dribbled down her chin and she laughed like a child.

"It's delicious!" She picked another peach and handed it to George. "Taste for yourself," she urged. The man took the proffered fruit and took a large bite.

"Mmm hmm!" George murmured. "They is good eatin', Miss Polly. Like the ones yo' daddy used to grow. You gonna sell 'em all?"

"Well . . ." Polly frowned. "I have promised the Mercantile in town about 300 pounds of fruit. We can take supplies in trade. Supplies we desperately need. We'll preserve the rest and eat as many fresh as we have left. Mark the best trees. We'll take those pits and dry them over the summer. At the end of the season, we plant them. Maybe in October. Isn't that when Father started new trees? We can't very well buy saplings anymore." Polly was striding down the row of trees as she spoke. "Pits will have to do."

George followed her, nodding. "Yes'm, Miss Polly. We save them pits and we start new trees." The foreman grinned. "You wantin' to grow lots more peach trees?"

"Yes, George. We need to expand our orchard. This is what Whitehall was meant to produce! Not cotton. We're close by the river, and the soil is sandy here. It drains well, too. Peaches love it. That must be the difference between here and River Wood. They have a heavier, clay soil. Nothing is growing there anymore."

George nodded knowingly. "They's a evil spell sittin' on River Wood, Miss Polly."

Polly stopped and regarded George. "That very well may be, George. Anyway, I don't know when Mr. Roper is returning from seeing to his mother, but in the meantime, we must all pull together to harvest this peach crop." She put both hands on her hips, lost in thought.

"I have an idea. You and the men shall get five percent of the crop by weight if picked correctly. It's what is called incentive. I offer something to you as an extra, a bonus, to help get the work done quickly. If we get this crop picked before the fruit is overripe, we can sell it for a higher price and get supplies we need. Cloth. A load of bricks for that chimney repair. More baskets. Maybe coffee—for us all."

At the mention of coffee, George's face erupted into an astonished grin. "Yes ma'am! We do 'most anythin' for coffee!"

"Well then, after the men have finished in the cotton today, start them picking. Peaches are delicate. The men must be gentle when they place the peaches into these baskets. One layer only. No tossing or throwing. That's why I am offering an incentive. It must be done correctly, or they will bruise. Bruised fruit will not sell for as much."

George nodded and made to reply when he stopped and looked over Polly's shoulder. "There he come, Miss Polly. There's Mr. Roper!"

Polly wheeled around and scanned the horizon. In the shimmering heat, she saw Tom riding toward the pair. George raised his hand in greeting and Tom returned the wave. He urged his horse more quickly and pulled up near Polly and George and dismounted.

"Howdy Mr. Roper!" George called. "Welcome back! What you think about these peaches?" He spread his arms wide and grinned at the overseer.

"Mighty fine crop, George. Mighty fine. Looks like you've taken good care of these trees for Miss Polly. I'm back just in time for the peach harvest." Tom scanned the row they stood in and finally looked at Polly, his blue eyes calm.

Polly stared up at Tom, speechless. She wanted nothing more than to jump up and hug the man tightly. He grinned and removed his hat. "Yessiree, it's good to be back. Miss Polly, may I borrow you for a while? I am sure there is a lot I need to catch up on." He waited expectantly.

"Oh yes, of course," stammered Polly. She had never been so happy to see the man as now. "George, as I said, have the men start the peaches. Tell them about my incentive. I want to limit bruised fruit. Store today's fruit in the barn in the shallow baskets. The men must finish tomorrow. I'd like it to go into town tomorrow evening."

"Yes'm. We's glad you back, Mr. Roper. Hope yo' mama is feelin' fine now." George turned back toward the fields.

Polly watched him go and then wheeled around to face Tom. "My God. Where have you been?" she asked.

Tom smiled casually, his eyes crinkling in merriment. "Miss Polly, you must be so proud of this orchard. I had no idea it would produce like this after years of neglect. You're a born peach farmer."

"Tom! Please. Tell me everything." Polly untied her hat and removed it, fanning herself with the wide brim. Tendrils of damp hair clung to her neck and forehead. "You told me you would be gone only a few days! How are Ben and Kate? Why were you away so long?"

Tom wiped the sweat from his forehead with his handkerchief. "Everything is all right now. I got them to a safe house, and they were to be on their way to Tennessee the next day. Of course, they have to get through the mountains, and then on into Kentucky and Indiana, but I have faith they'll get where they're going. There are good people on that route."

Polly was elated. "Thank God! Did you use the tunnel?"

He chuckled and continued, "We got to Walhalla before dawn the morning after we left here and sure enough, there was one lone Confederate officer stationed on the spur road heading to the tunnel. I'd never seen that before. He was part of a new detachment out of Clayton. He refused to let me pass."

Polly gasped. "What happened?"

"I had to think fast. I told the young corporal that I needed to get your peaches to Franklin, to a regiment there, that had commissioned fruit for the army. The poor boy said he had no orders about any fruit going up that road." Tom smiled. "We got to talking, and he claimed to be some distant kin to the Calhouns, so I used Floride's name. Told him that she had recommended that route to save time."

Polly marveled at Tom's quick thinking.

"I told him that Mrs. Calhoun said even though the tunnels would never be used for Confederate trains, the shortcut into Georgia certainly wasn't to be wasted if it would bring food to hungry troops. We didn't want to show up with spoiled fruit for our soldiers. I offered to show him the whole load, and luckily he backed down. He thought about it long enough before letting me through. If the children had cried out, we would have been done."

Polly shook her head in wonderment. "My word . . ."

Tom nodded. "I did give him a crate of fruit. Hell, the poor boy was stationed out there all by himself, without much to occupy him. He was mighty obliged. But it wasn't easy at all. He followed us for a good ways, nearly to the tunnel entrance itself."

"What happened then?" Polly asked.

"It is a right small entrance, and this was the largest rig I have taken through. The survey showed it could be done though. I had to clear debris, and then after I got the wagon in, I put it all back. It had to look deserted in case someone tried to follow me. There were a few places where I thought we'd get stuck. I am not one for tight spaces anyhow. About spooked the horse. But I'd shift the load and it all worked. Halfway through, I was able to let them out to stretch their legs and what have you. The children took it better than I thought they would. But once we got to the other side of Middle Tunnel, danged if there wasn't a guard there, too. Don't know how he didn't hear the wagon coming."

Polly shook her head. "So the Confederacy must have plans to use the tunnel, even though they found no survey."

"This will be my last trip that way. Luckily, I had scouted ahead before taking the wagon the whole way through. Early, the soldier was asleep. Finally, he left his post to take care of . . . personal business." Polly watched in amusement as Tom's cheeks reddened. "He was gone a while, thank goodness. It was full daylight when we got out and on down the main road maybe a mile or two. About ten minutes after that, he came riding down the main road toward us and I could tell he was wondering where the hell I came from." Tom laughed, easy and calm.

Polly smiled because Tom seemed so at ease. He continued, "I wasn't sure what unit he might be connected to and didn't want him to offer to take us to his superiors, so I changed my story and said that the peaches were to be sold in Franklin. He let me pass. He was still wet behind the ears, so I was lucky." Tom shrugged. "I have to commend the good Lord. The children didn't make a sound."

Polly smiled. "And where did you actually end up?"

"I shouldn't say much more. You sent me to sell peaches and I sold them." He leaned in and added, "No time for goodbyes, mind you. I delivered them to someone I trust, then turned right around and headed for the town. I wanted townsfolk to see me there and to see I had fruit to sell. And sure enough, I was able to sell it all. The owner of the general store was quite happy to have it." He turned his hat over in his hands and smiled broadly. "I have Confederate money to hand over, in fact."

Polly was overwhelmed. She placed her bonnet back on her head and tied the ribbon slowly, with shaking hands. "So they are safe."

"I am expecting a letter any day now from a friend, a man named Lucas Johnson. Lucas will write and tell me how—how his cotton is doing." He winked. "If he says his cotton crop is looking strong this year, it'll mean they made it to the next stop along the route. I'll hopefully get letters like that as they move along. Hard to say with the mail disrupted. And I should not even be telling you this."

"I understand." Polly nodded. "But why did it take you so long to come home after you left?"

"I didn't want to go through the tunnel again and risk questions. I went through the mountains and back down to Greenville. I saw Mama. If anyone asks, she'll say I was visiting and it won't be a lie." He kicked the ground with the toe of his boot. "We'll have to have a story ready, though. About what happened to Ben and Kate. If not for your husband, then in case someone else comes looking."

"The only slave who knows the truth is Ona. She told George and Cissie that they were sold away."

"Hmm. Might have been easier to say they ran."

"The patrols would have chased after them if I said they were runaways. Mr. McGee did accost me in town about Mr. Wilkins. Luckily, my attorney was right there and told him to leave me alone. Mr. Legarre said McGee will need a warrant to come back," Polly offered.

"Easy enough to get a warrant, Miss Polly." Tom shook his head.

"If it comes to that, I will say that I sold them," Polly said defiantly.

"Do you have a bill of sale?"

"I do not," she said curtly. Her shoulders sagged. "Perhaps I should have?"

Tom nodded. "I'm only trying to protect the good thing you did. I'll see what I can do."

"Thank you. You're a good man, Tom Roper," Polly said. "And I am very glad that you are back with us on the farm."

Tom reddened and looked down at his hat. "Oh, Ben asked me to give you this." He pulled a folded square of linen from his waist pocket and handed it to Polly.

She took the fabric quizzically and unfolded the small, embroidered square. Frayed, smeared with inky black stains, and stitched with a delicate edge and an embroidered "P," Polly recognized the childhood handkerchief immediately. Her eyes welled with tears. She held the handkerchief to her nose and inhaled the faintest scent of licorice.

— • —

July 22, 1861

POLLY SAT ERECT NEXT TO TOM on the bench seat as the wagon rocked down the dusty road. Zadoc dozed in the wagon bed, surrounded by baskets of peaches. This was the final load of fruit heading to the Mercantile.

"It's a good crop, Miss Polly. You should make a profit for sure." Tom grinned at his boss. "You're a born orchardist."

"Tom, we were lucky," Polly said guardedly. "How those trees survived so much neglect for so long is beyond me."

"Enjoy the moment, is all I'm saying. You done good." He grinned. Tom knew that it was difficult for Polly to acknowledge a good thing. The world had taken every good thing she had known.

Polly nodded, a small smile on her lips. "Very well. The sale of this crop will indeed keep us in a good place for a while. Even Cissie's dried peaches are selling for twelve cents a pound. We'll be able to get calico and shirting, more kerosene, the bricks we needed, and the coffee!"

Tom nodded. "You were smart about that orchard, Miss Polly. Seems it was less labor intensive, too. Compared to cotton." He leaned in and added softly, "I don't think your incentive idea was a bad one, either. The boys seemed right happy about their share."

"Yes, I believe that my days of being the ignorant slave owner have ended," Polly said under her breath. "But I will never have Ona's trust again."

Tom squinted from under the brim of his hat, as two horses came galloping down the road toward the wagon. Clouds of dust billowed around them. Their riders whooped and hollered as they approached. Tom recognized the two, a local farmer and his teenaged son. He raised his hand in a wave. They slowed their horses and pulled up alongside the wagon.

"Afternoon, folks!" The man tipped his hat towards Polly. "Have you heard the news?" He was out of breath. Sweat stained his blue shirtfront.

"What's the news, Jim?" Tom asked. "Someone finally find Old Man Jenkins' still?" he joked.

"The Confederacy whupped the northerners in Virginia. Right outside Richmond!" said Jim. "Little town called Manassas Junction. We killed three thousand soldiers. Sent those yellow-bellied Yankees back home with their damn tails tucked a'tween their legs, if you'll pardon my language, ma'am." He tipped his hat toward Polly.

"Well, I'll be. . . . So where are you headed in such an all-fired hurry?" Tom asked.

"It means my brother Cree'll prob'ly be comin' home soon!" shouted the boy. "We're goin' home to tell Ma! I only wish I was old enough to have gone to fight. Looks like it's all over before I could turn sixteen." The young man's eyes were animated with the excitement of battle. "I wish't I coulda shot me a Yankee." He sat up tall in his saddle and let out a blood-curdling scream. Polly flinched and shut her eyes.

"Is that a fact?" Tom marveled.

"Prob'ly means the fightin' is over soon," Jim avowed. "My boy'll be comin' home."

Tom nodded his head and watched solemnly as the two riders wheeled and turned their mounts, continuing their gallop down the road toward their farm. Clouds of red dust swirled in their wake.

"Could it all be over then?" Polly asked.

Tom flicked the reins and the wagon continued its slow trek toward town. "Not likely. Winning one battle isn't likely to end this thing."

Polly turned to Tom. "John is posted outside of Richmond," she said.

"It sounds like he was on the winning side of the skirmish, so I am sure that he is safe. He is probably in jolly revelry somewhere with his unit, as we speak," Tom said hopefully. "You have nothing to fret about."

"You mistake my feelings, Tom," Polly said curtly.

Chapter Thirty-Eight

August 18, 1861

THE NEWS OF THE CONFEDERACY'S SUCCESS AT MANASSAS JUNCTION initially gave hope to everyone in Pendleton District that the war would soon be over. With a Confederate battle victory so easily achieved, people reasoned that the Union would back down and allow the South its autonomy. Hope quickly faded when southern newspapers gave lie to stories of Confederate superiority. Detailed accounts of the carnage, mayhem and stunning disorganization on both sides hinted at a lengthy conflagration. Political finger-pointing led to the dismissal of some generals and the promotion of others.

As the summer wore on, there was the grim realization that the war would be longer and bloodier than anyone imagined. President Lincoln had even issued a call for Northern volunteers to enlist for three-year terms.

In Polly's mind, the one bright point to the escalation of war tensions was that Deputy McGee had seemingly abandoned his search for Clay Wilkins. She devoured the newspapers that appeared twice a week courtesy of Tom's trips into town, hoping for word of John's whereabouts. According to news accounts, Stone's regiment had regrouped and moved further south after the Manassas victory, but the soldiers' new location was not given.

Even meager supplies disappeared from the Mercantile's sparsely stocked shelves and scarcity became the norm. The naval blockades off the coast were chock full of holes, but most pilfered supplies were consumed in the Lowcountry.

Her successful peach harvest meant that she was luckier than some. Polly received the long-awaited coffee as promised in trade for her peach liquor. She was able to buy two badly needed wagon wheels, a bolt of linsey, a new mirror, and two brand new leather-bound ledgers. After the last of the peaches were sold, there was even some money set by, but there was not much else on which to spend it. And with the apples and sorghum looking healthy and strong, the cotton crop did not have to go to market for Polly to survive.

Over coffee, she spent contented hours on the veranda in conversation with Tom, discussing cotton prices, tree pruning techniques, and news of the war. Some days she worked with Zee tending the horses. Other days were spent in the orchard, explaining pruning techniques she'd read about to George. She preferred to be busy and found joy in making Whitehall into what she dreamed. After all, it was her land.

As late summer crops began to ripen, Polly and Ona worked together to preserve the harvest while Cissie and Silas cleaned and minded the big house. The vegetable gardens would feed Polly and her slaves into the winter and there was nothing to be wasted. Squash, beans, sweet corn, and okra simmered in kitchen pots. They put up pickles and chutneys, too, and preserved the last of the peaches. Over the course of weeks, neat rows of preserves lined up on the cellar shelves, their jeweled tones a beautiful sight to see.

One morning, as the women labored yet again over the boiling jars in the kitchen, Tom pulled open the screen door with a slap and stood to face Polly and Ona. A red-faced Polly wiped the matted hair from her cheek and looked at Tom worriedly. "You look like you've seen a ghost," she remarked. "What is it?"

Tom quickly glanced behind his shoulder. "Deputy McGee is here. With a search warrant."

Polly felt as if the breath had been knocked out of her. But she nodded toward Ona and said calmly, "Ona, you stay inside. Please keep up with the jars while I see what's what." She untied her stained apron and patted her hair back into place as best she could before she took a deep breath and stepped outside after her overseer. The screen door slammed shut behind her. Ona stepped into the pantry and waited in the shadows.

"Deputy McGee, what on earth are you doing here? Surely you have a million more important things to do, than harassing a woman alone while her husband fights for the cause," Polly said sharply. She stayed on the top step, hands on hips, so as to look down at the deputy.

McGee removed his hat and thrust forth a piece of paper. "I got a warrant to search your property. I'm lookin' for your nigger, Ben. And I want to talk to John Stone's girl Kate, who you removed from River Wood without permission from her owner."

"Now see here—" Tom interrupted.

"No, you listen to me, Mr. Roper," McGee snapped. "This warrant took me a month to get, and while I am here, I will uphold the law by conducting a thorough search for the belongings or body of Clay Wilkins. I aim to speak to your slaves, too. I have the boy who says he saw Mrs. Stone with the slave, Ben, at River Wood the day Clay Wilkins disappeared." He turned and shouted to several men standing at a distance. "Robert! Clyde! Bring that nigger boy over here!"

Polly watched as a lanky white man stepped forward, pushing a young slave boy in front of him. The boy looked to be no more than eleven years old, bone-thin and scared stiff. His brown eyes were as big as saucers. Polly's heart lurched. She hadn't known there was a child left at River Wood.

McGee pointed to the white man. "This here's Deputy Miller. Deputy Miller is helpin' me in this case. Boy, what's yer name?"

The child whispered inaudibly.

"Speak up, nigger!" Deputy Miller shoved the boy forward.

"That's quite enough, Deputy. I detest the use of that word. And do not touch this boy again," Polly snapped. "If he is from River Wood, he is my property. I don't want to have to get my lawyer involved." She looked down at the frightened boy and asked, "Is your name Reginald?"

"Yes ma'am," he answered, trembling with fear. Polly noticed that his voice had not yet changed. He was all knees and elbows.

"Reginald, I am Mrs. Stone. We haven't met. Do you have any family at River Wood? A father or an uncle?"

The boy shook his head. "No ma'am." His cheekbones were sharp and angular, and his thin arms and legs too long for his outgrown and patched clothing.

"See that pump over there? Get yourself a dipper of cool water and wait there for my instructions." The boy nodded and walked away quickly.

Polly turned to Tom. "Mr. Roper, gather all the field hands, and George and Zee. Have them sit under the big oak by your cabin so Mr. McGee can see them." Tom looked at Polly with narrowed eyes. She nodded imperceptibly and he hurried off toward the fields.

For some reason she could not name, seeing Reginald gave Polly strength to speak up. She descended the steps slowly and looked up at McGee. "Mr. McGee, I do not appreciate the manner in which you apparently went to my farm at River Wood and took a slave child off the premises without my permission. Unless I am mistaken? Maybe the warrant you procured gave you authority there, too, hmm?"

She looked from McGee to Miller expectantly. She extended her hand and McGee silently laid the warrant in her palm. She read it slowly and then handed it back to McGee. "Ah, I thought not. I will have to take this up with the sheriff and with my lawyer. You did read the warrant, didn't you?" she asked icily.

Deputy McGee and Deputy Miller exchanged glances. McGee spat on the ground and said, "That don't change the fact that we need to see Ben. And the girl, Kate."

Polly dismissed McGee's demand with a wave of her hand. "I gave those two away to an Alabama planter. An old friend of my father's from his military days has a daughter, Margaret, my age and just married. We were girlhood friends and her father was so good to me after my brothers and my parents died. I so wanted to attend the wedding . . ." She paused. "But I am too busy running my farm alone."

McGee looked fit to burst.

"I wanted to give Margaret a special wedding gift. I no longer needed Ben here, and Kate is his wife." She shrugged. "Now Margaret and her husband have a young slave family to help them start on their own land. She was most appreciative."

Tom reappeared behind her. "The men are waiting, Miss Polly."

McGee's eyes narrowed into slits. "You have proof of sale?"

"I did not sell them, Deputy. I gifted them." She knit her brows together in thought. "The only proof I have is a lovely letter from Margaret thanking me for my generous gift. I would be happy to show it to you. Now, is there any other reason that you want to see my slaves? If not, I would like Mr. Roper to put them back to work."

"Yes, Mrs. Stone. I want to see your letter. And your slaves. I'll take the boy and we'll see who all he recognizes. Miller here can search the house and the buildings." He pointed his finger in Polly's face. "You had no right to get rid of a slave when you knew he was implicated in a white man's murder."

Polly ignored McGee's threat and continued, "Implicated by a slave boy?" She gasped. "You would take a slave's word over the word of the mistress? And my attorney, Mr. Legarre, assured me that River Wood slaves are my property to move where I will, while my husband fights for the Confederacy."

McGee fumbled for words but Polly held up her hand. "Now, I shall accompany Mr. Miller into my home if he would like to look around. We must do this quickly. I have work to do. We're in the middle of preserves," she said.

She turned to Tom. "Mr. Roper, will you accompany Mr. McGee to see our men? Bring Reginald to me after Mr. McGee is finished with him. These gentlemen will have no further reason to trespass onto River Wood property."

Tom smiled. "Yes ma'am. We won't be long, I'm sure." He waved for the boy, who followed the men toward the overseer's cabin in the distance.

Polly regarded Deputy Miller as they walked toward the house. "Are you a friend of Clay Wilkins, too?" She smiled warmly, disarming the young man.

Miller shuffled uncomfortably. "Yes ma'am. We was drinkin' buddies." His face clouded when he realized what he had said.

Polly appeared unfazed. "I understand, Mr. Miller. A friend has gone missing and you want to help find him. Of course! But between you and me, I cannot tell you the number of times that Clay Wilkins threatened to leave River Wood."

She leaned close and said, "When he found out how much the Army was offering enlisted men, why, he flat out told me that my husband couldn't hold him down on the farm any longer. His wages were poor, I admit. . . . Just think of it, Mr. Miller. Clay Wilkins might have been one of the heroes at Manassas! When he comes back, won't he have stories to tell!" Polly clapped her hands together, caught up in the moment. Miller seemed to consider her words.

"However, his leaving did put me in a predicament," Polly added, her lips in a pretty pout. "I'm alone while my husband fights for the cause and my River Wood overseer has gone away."

"I am sorry, Mrs. Stone, I really am," Miller mumbled, red-faced. "McGee has this idea Clay's been murdered. I was deputized to help find him . . . if I can just take a quick look-see in your house, and maybe a check of your outbuildings, that should be fine," Miller said. "I do apologize."

"Mr. McGee bases his suspicions on a little slave boy's vague recollection. And yet, I am white, born here and raised here, a property owner. You are an intelligent man. You understand. It is my word against a slave child's story." She sighed and shook her head angrily. "Alright, Mr. Miller, where would you like to begin?"

— • —

MCGEE PACED BACK AND FORTH IN front of the slave men while Tom stood by impatiently. The deputy stopped in front of each slave and turned to get the boy's reaction. So far, the boy had shaken his head after looking into each man's eyes.

"How long must you keep these men from their work?" Tom asked. "Mrs. Stone already told you that she gave Ben and Kate away to a family friend in Alabama." He looked directly at George when he spoke, and George nodded.

Exasperated, McGee slapped his hat against his leg and turned to Reginald. "Boy, you ain't seen no one else you recognize from River Wood? Don't lie to me now."

Reginald glanced at Zadoc and swallowed hard. "No suh."

McGee cursed under his breath and shouted, "You boys know what happened to Ben?" The men stared blankly. McGee switched tactics and pointed at George. "You're the field boss? Stand up."

George scrambled to his feet obediently. He was inches taller than the white deputy. McGee came close to the man and narrowed his eyes. "How long you been at Whitehall?"

George answered proudly. "I came down the Wagon Road with Master Burgiss in 1835, suh."

"Is that a fact?" McGee scratched his beard. "You the big boss man. So you must know everything that goes on with slaves here. With Mr. Roper away so much lately, you pretty much run things. You'd know what Ben was up to the day Mrs. Stone showed up with the slave girl, Kate."

George looked over McGee's head. "Suh, I do what I's told. Miss Polly has me in the fields and the orchard. Ben ain't a field hand, suh. He ran the smithy, tended Miss Polly's horses. I see to the field hands."

The men turned to watch Deputy Miller and Polly appear in the distance. Tom stepped up and said, "Mr. McGee, you'll find no better foreman in the entire district. George is a hard worker, a man of his word. Now, if you've heard nothing interesting, I strongly suggest you let me get these men back to work." He glanced at the darkening sky and added, "They've got fields to hoe before it rains."

"What'd you find, Miller?" asked McGee sharply. "You search the house?"

Miller shrugged and said, "I didn't see nothin' suspicious anywhere. Mrs. Stone did have the letter from her Alabama friend." He passed the folded correspondence to McGee.

"What did it say?" McGee scowled, grabbing the letter roughly.

"Aw, hell, McGee. You know I cain't read good." Miller shook his head, coughed nervously, and looked at Polly. "Pardon my language, Mrs. Stone."

McGee mumbled his curses and scanned the letter quickly. He thrust it back toward Polly. She took the paper and refolded it neatly.

"Are you satisfied, Deputy? Please leave us in peace now. Mr. Wilkins has moved on. He had no love for my husband or me. John paid a meager wage. Clay Wilkins either enlisted, as has half the town, or had better offers to oversee in the Lowcountry."

Thunder rumbled in the distance and a breeze stirred the leaves of the white oak overhead. McGee looked at the leaden skies and then at his deputy. "I guess we're good to leave here." He crossed his arms defensively. "But first, Mrs. Stone, I have to ask you something. Does your husband know his place is fallin' apart?"

A trace of a smile played across Polly's lips as raindrops began to fall. "Not that it is any of your business, Mr. McGee, but I'll tell you. All my money and my efforts remain here. At Whitehall. When I married John Stone, I married River Wood. But when he decided to enlist, and his overseer abandoned the place, I had no choice but to let it be. And he gave written instructions to my overseer to stay away."

She continued, "I saw the state the River Wood slaves are in." She glanced at Reginald's thin frame. "I may send some food their way. It is my Christian duty. Beyond that, I cannot help." She shrugged. "If you know of a good overseer, please let me know." Raindrops fell on her dark blue dress and made a splotchy pattern of polka dots on the fabric. "If you'll excuse us now, we all have work to do." She turned around and walked quickly toward the kitchen house. Halfway there she stopped and turned. "Reginald, come with me."

The boy jogged after Polly, as thunder rolled. She heard Tom dismiss the men with a shout just as a heavy downpour engulfed the group.

The screen door slapped shut loudly behind Polly. Ona emerged from her hiding place, drying her hands on her apron. The roar of the heavy rain on the tin roof made it difficult to hear, so Ona came close to Polly and the boy. She looked from Polly to the scared youngster and back to Polly. "Is everything alright?"

"It is now." Polly put her hands on Reginald's shoulders. "Ona, this is Reginald. He will be staying here. For now, may he stay with you? Until we get things figured out? He has no kin at River Wood."

Ona smiled down at the boy. "You remind me of my own son when he was your age. I bet you is a might hungry. If you go into that pantry, there is a jar of sweet corn and one of peaches settin' on the table. Why don't you go eat and let Miss Polly and me talk a spell, hmm?"

Reginald swallowed hard and looked at Polly, eyes still fearful.

"It's alright, Reginald. I don't know what you think you saw at River Wood, but no one did anything wrong. You will stay here now. You won't be hungry." She smiled and the boy eagerly headed for the pantry.

Polly took Ona's hand and patted it gently. The tiny bones felt birdlike in Polly's palm. "Thank you, Ona. I don't think Deputy McGee will be back to bother us or go after Ben. I told them what happened."

Ona opened her mouth to speak but Polly put her finger to her lips and pointed to the open pantry door. "I told Deputy McGee the truth," she said clearly. "I gave Ben and Kate to a family friend in Alabama. As a wedding gift."

543

Ona's eyes widened and then narrowed suspiciously. "They believe you?" she mouthed in astonishment.

"Why, of course! I have a letter from the family, thanking me for the gift." Polly winked and added slyly, "I'm just glad that I saved it."

Chapter Thirty-Nine

August 20, 1861

POLLY SCOWLED, ARMS CROSSED, AS GEORGE AND TOM led her through the orchard. Reginald followed the group closely, skipping across the row with Jack barking at his heels. His task was to collect damaged fruit. A hailstorm had followed heavy rain the day before and had left bruised fruit on the trees and fallen apples scattered across the wet ground. Broken branches hung limply, clusters of still ripening fruit doomed to die.

"Is the entire apple orchard like this?" she asked.

"Yes ma'am, but I got two men pickin' up as much of the fruit that fell as they can. Have to wait an' see what happens to the bruised ones still hangin' on." George leaned over to pick up a few apples in his path, and he cradled them protectively in his arms.

Tom palmed a large apple hanging low and noticed the brown oozing blemish spreading across the yellow-green flesh. "These Nickajacks took the brunt of it. They were the closest to harvest. I'm not sure you'll have enough early apples to sell to Mr. Jones."

"Damn," Polly murmured under her breath.

Tom chuckled.

Polly frowned. "Tom, if I was ever going to use a curse word, now's as good a time as any. We needed this apple crop. We can't rely on cotton making it to market anymore. How will I pay the farrier and buy the parts for the wagon, much less cover the tax bill this winter?"

"Barter. You have the sorghum coming in soon enough." He picked up an apple from the ground and observed the hail damage. "You said the Mercantile will take it."

"Tom, everyone in the district will have hail-damaged crops to unload. The farrier won't want twenty gallons of sorghum syrup or jars of preserves," Polly said crossly. "I'm just glad that we did most of our vegetables already. The gardens are a disaster." She watched as a few yellow jackets hovered and then landed on a rotting apple, their taste for sugar driving them to swarm over the rancid fruit in number.

"We can press cider!" Polly brightened and began to walk down the row. "That's what we will do. George, have the men bring all the windfall and the damaged apples still on the trees to the kitchen. Especially the green ones. They make the best hard cider. We'll make hard cider and sell it or barter it. We'll have to work fast. Let's just pray we have yeast enough on hand to make this work. Let me think . . ." Polly quickened her pace. "It will take two weeks to ferment, if I remember correctly. No one in the district has as many trees as we do. If we make a quality hard cider, we can sell it for top dollar. After all, there's a war going on. Liquor is hard to come by."

Tom smiled. "It is, at that, unless you want 'shine. George, get Meenie out of the cotton and have him help Zee collect this fruit. Reginald, you help them get it all, and fast."

The boy smiled and nodded. He had settled in quickly, appreciative of a kind mistress, hot meals, and a clean cot to sleep on.

"That settles it, then. I will let Cissie and Ona know that we'll be pressing apples for a few days. I will take the wagon into town. We'll need jars, and I know we do not have enough of those here." Polly smiled and looked at Tom. "We might just make it through this war, Tom. Cotton will rebound eventually. But until then, I think we will be alright."

— • —

MR. JONES STROKED HIS BEARD and looked at Polly shrewdly. "Mrs. Stone, I am amazed by your ingenuity. I truly am. Your peaches sold like lightning. If you have good quality hard cider coming in soon, I will advance you the glass jars, sure enough. No need to pay me now. Promise me you'll sell cider to me and not the Inn. Seventy-five cents a gallon."

Polly nodded and said, "One dollar ten a gallon and we have a deal."

Mr. Jones sighed. "You drive a hard bargain. One dollar a gallon and we're done bickering? I'll throw in the jars no charge. And I'll have my boy load the jars into your wagon."

Polly smiled. "We have a deal." She extended her hand and shook the merchant's hand firmly. "Three weeks or so, and you'll have your cider. Thank you, Mr. Jones."

Polly stepped outside of the Mercantile and exhaled audibly. She was doing it. Making her own way on her own land. She felt a pang of regret that her father was not here to see what she was capable of, sustaining Whitehall in a time of war.

She ambled down the boardwalk and stopped to peer into Caroline Batson's storefront window. The shop, formerly filled with displays of silks and satins, beribboned bonnets, and feathered hats, was now empty of fine goods. Bolts of faded calicos, cotton flannel, and sheeting were all that remained. Polly thought of the beautiful Charleston-bound dresses she had purchased from the shop so recently, dresses that hung abandoned in the back of Polly's armoire.

I could at least attend a town dance, she thought, but put the idea quickly out of her head. Her years of voluntary solitude had put Polly in a lonely situation. After Floride left for Maryland to wait out the war, all other social invitations ceased.

Polly sighed and continued toward the post office, still hoping for a letter from her friend. She pushed open the post office door and stepped to the back of a short line to wait her turn. Several Lowcountry society matrons turned to look at her, but quickly looked away when they did not recognize Polly as one of their own. She self-consciously smoothed her skirt and waited her turn.

Finally, the gentleman ahead of Polly collected his mail and turned to leave. The postmaster greeted Polly warmly. "Hello Mrs. Stone," he said. "I haven't seen you for a good while. How are things at Whitehall?"

Polly returned the smile. "Very well, thank you, Mr. Phillips. I'm hoping I have a letter from my husband or from Mrs. Calhoun?"

The man frowned. "I'm sorry. I don't think I have anything for you from your husband. I know you must be anxious about Mr. Stone. His unit was at Manassas? Our men came out just fine, the papers said. But I know the women folk are waiting for word directly from their husbands. That young Ward Adger's wife was distraught over the whole thing, about having a baby and all, but he wrote her that he and Major McQueen were fine, not many men in their company killed. I think a few out of Anderson were, 'tis a pity . . ."

Polly's face darkened and Mr. Phillips scrambled to apologize. "Oh, Mrs. Stone, that was unkind of me. I am so sorry. I am sure that your husband is fine. He was not on the roll—the list of those killed in action. But I am sorry." The man prattled on and reached under the counter. "There is a letter here for your overseer. Can I give that to you? Again, my apologies. And don't you worry about Mr. Stone."

Polly took the letter. "These are strange times, Mr. Phillips. Do not apologize. I'm not worried about my husband, not in the least."

She smiled and left the post office quickly. Polly felt a surge of determination. She was determined to rejoin the living. She had just marked the passing of her twenty-first birthday. Long life stretched ahead of her and she would have to make use of it. Maybe she would attend the next dance after all.

Outside, she watched the traffic move back and forth down the dusty street. Pendleton was growing and changing. All around her, life moved at a quickening pace. She recognized several young women moving down the sidewalk, children now in tow. Two of her late father's friends doffed their hats in passing, their hair now silver instead of dark.

Polly hoisted herself into the wagon as Mr. Jones's boy put the last of the crates in the wagon bed. "Anythang else, Mizz Stone?" the young slave asked meekly, his brown skin glistening with sweat. He reminded her of a young Ben.

Her heart leaped. Ben was gone. The thought of him made her chest ache. It still surprised her every time she thought of the man. He had been so loyal to her. To her family. And now, he might be dead. Kate and the children dead, too. All because of her.

No further word had come of their escape.

Polly shook her head. "No, Timothy. Thank Mr. Jones for me." She grabbed the reins in one hand and moved to place the letter in her bag when she happened to glance at the return address. Lucas Johnson, Sevierville Tennessee. With trembling fingers, she tore open the letter addressed to Tom and scanned quickly.

Dear Tom,

Thank you for the peaches you brought us. My wife and I have enjoyed the fruit immensely. We will be happy to sell Whitehall peaches again next year. Please tell Mrs. Stone that her fruit was the best we've had in these parts for some time. Cotton is looking real good this summer. I plan to sell to a merchant in Kentucky. He has buyers above the big lake expecting all that I have. I was happy about that, and know you are too.

Polly stopped reading and held the letter to her chest. *Cotton is looking real good this summer. I am selling to a merchant in Kentucky. He has buyers above the big lake expecting all that I have.*

Were they safe? Had Ben and Kate and the children made it safely to Kentucky? She slowly read the rest of the letter, but it was all about goings-on with the man's farm and their shared acquaintances.

Polly folded the letter and tucked it back into the envelope. She clicked the reins and the wagon moved down Main Street.

— • —

IN THE SUNLIT LIBRARY, TOM NODDED as he read the letter silently. Polly waited expectantly for his reaction, her brown eyes dancing in anticipation. The heavy oak doors were closed.

"Yes ma'am," he said finally. "That is the good news we have been waiting for. They made it to the Tennessee safe house, all right. Headed for Kentucky. Sounds like their final destination is Canada."

Polly wrung her hands nervously and asked quietly, "How do you know?"

He shrugged. "That's what *above the big lake* means. Lake Michigan. It's a Union state, so they should be fine there. You can rest easy. It means he got someone big to take them there. A rich Tennessee planter, whose name I will not mention, moves folks by train sometimes. Whole families. Escapees posing as his own slaves until they get out of Tennessee and Kentucky. I assume that's who Lucas has lined up." He grinned at Polly and said, "Not sure how I feel about you opening my mail, though."

"I'm sorry. But when I saw the return address, I knew it had to be news of Ben and Kate. I can't wait to tell Ona that they are on their way to Michigan," Polly said.

"If I may, can I offer a bit of advice?" Tom asked gently.

Polly cocked her head. "What advice?"

"The fewer people with all of the details, the better for everyone involved. I understand your wanting to let Ona know he is safe, but maybe leave it at that." Tom looked at Polly sternly. "If McGee decides to come back and interrogate your slaves, or if Mr. Stone comes back angry that they're gone, you wouldn't want Ona to be in danger, right? Or if Stone decides to use the Fugitive Slave Laws to go after Ben?"

Polly shuddered. "I hadn't thought that far ahead. Of course, you are right, Tom. After all you have done to get them away, I would be putting you in danger, too. I am sorry. I will just let her know that they are safe. That is all," Polly said.

Tom nodded. "The boys collected the windfall and the damaged fruit still on the trees. A dozen bushel baskets are in the kitchen already since you left for town. That boy, Reginald, he can sure pick. I can't wait to see what he does with cotton."

Polly looked at Tom. "Do you ever feel bad about the slaves here at Whitehall? I mean, since you are in the side business of helping slaves to their freedom, does it bother you that we run Whitehall with slave labor?"

Tom's blue eyes narrowed. "Slavery is all I'd ever known." He shrugged and looked down at his worn boots. "But then when my father died I had to drop out of college. I moved here and took on the job of your father's overseer. I was so young. We'd had a few slaves growing up; it was expected. We were good to them, I thought. Your father—he saw slavery as a necessary evil if we were to grow cotton. Not a license to abuse them. He treated his slaves well and even let me try those Irishmen. I admired that. But you can't grow cotton without slaves. You just can't right now." He shrugged. "White folks won't take the work. Not in the numbers needed. Maybe someday. Mr. Burgiss was fair. When he saw abuse, he helped out. That tunnel was a Godsend for a few folks. Maybe not anymore, now that there is a war, but it did save some lives." He sighed, lost in thought. "One day, though, I hope that cotton farmers will pay a fair wage to all pickers."

"How did you start helping runaways?" Polly asked.

Tom leaned forward in his chair. "There is someone in Pendleton who has Underground connections. I won't say who it is because his life would be in danger. He and I both happened to see the same altercation in town years ago. . . . A gal named Jenny overstepped and was beaten with a cane within an inch of her life, right there in the street. I'd never seen such a thing. People just walked on by. I knew then that I couldn't abide owning someone. I said something that gave the fellow to know that I was sympathetic. When he later offered me money to help her get away, I made the trip up into Tennessee with the girl. I knew I had to try."

"Dr. Adger," Polly said simply.

Tom's eyes widened. "You assume," he said firmly.

Polly shrugged. "The note my father penciled on the back of the survey referred to TR and RA. Robert Adger. It wasn't a difficult assumption to make. You didn't see it because it was erased completely before I showed it to you. No one will know."

Tom shook his head. "And the survey is safely hidden away?"

Polly nodded. "Was it Wilkins who beat her?"

"Sam Stone. . . . Old Sam wasn't right in the head. He abused many girls. But Jenny got to her freedom."

Polly considered his words. "I went to a slave auction in Charleston. It was horrific. I watched a slave family split apart. I think that was when I realized what it meant to own people. I wish I could let everyone go free. It is hard to justify, and it cannot be right . . . and yet our way of life would fall apart without them."

Tom sighed heavily. "Our way of life will fall apart anyway."

Polly knew there was truth in what he said. "Reginald said there are eight men still at River Wood. I don't know what to do for them. Should we bring them here?"

"No. I can check on them if you'd like. I'm sure they are getting by. I'll take some stores. Without Wilkins there to beat them and terrorize them, it must be better. He was an evil man. . . . I watched you take those poor souls away from River Wood, and I knew that you felt the same way about it as . . . as I do. No one deserves to be treated so badly." Tom smoothed his hair and looked at Polly solemnly. "I worry about what will happen when your husband comes home."

Polly shook her head. "I won't let him hurt the slaves. And he can't get at Kate."

"I don't worry about them. It's you I am worried about." Tom's eyes met Polly's briefly before she looked away.

Polly tugged her shawl around her shoulders. "With all of the fighting in Virginia, I doubt he will be home any time soon."

Tom played with the edge of his hat. "This war does seem to be dragging on, doesn't it? We seem to be putting up more of a fight than I anticipated. If the South wins, this Underground, of sorts, will never go away."

"I guess we're walking along a fence line. Is 'benevolent slavery' a thing?" Polly ventured.

Tom laughed and it eased the tension somewhat. "It will have to be. We have hard cider to make!" He put his hat back on his head firmly. "And cotton, and sorghum, and hell, I better get back to work." He smiled broadly, his blue eyes bright. He stood, tipped his hat, and walked out of the library.

— • —

POLLY STEPPED INTO THE THICK, humid air of the kitchen and found Cissie, Silas, Ona, and Reginald hard at work. The pungent aroma of rotting apples filled Polly's nostrils. The three manual presses were small, which meant that the work was long and laborious. The boys turned the cranks, using pieces of lumber for leverage, while the women cleaned the apples before they went into the presses, poured the juice into pots to heat it to a simmer, poured it into jugs, and added starter to begin fermentation. The slaves' happy chatter stopped when Polly opened the screen door.

Polly smiled. "It smells good in here." She looked at Ona. "Ona, may I have a word with you outside, please?"

Ona put down a full jug of cider and wiped her brow with her apron. "Yes, Miss Polly." She followed Polly outside and held up a hand to shield her eyes from the strong sun. "What you need, Miss Girl?" Although her words were affectionate, her tone was cool.

"I have some news. Good news. Ben and Kate and the children are safe. And headed to a good place," Polly said.

Ona gasped. "Where are they?"

"I cannot say. They would be in danger if too many people know where they are. Trust me. They are safe."

Ona's lower lip trembled but she remained calm. "Thank you. I miss him so much. Ev'ry day I say a prayer for his safety and happiness."

Tears welled in Polly's own eyes. "One day, I hope that you'll be able to join him. Just know that." She paused. "One day."

Chapter Forty

September 10, 1861

A COOL BREEZE FRESHENED THE AIR AND THE FIRST TINGES of red and yellow touched sourwoods and dogwoods, as autumn tiptoed into the upstate. The early morning sun sent bright rays into the oak tree near the veranda, where a flock of starlings chattered like children. With the cotton ready to be picked and baled, and the cider ready to take into town, Polly's mind was full. She found herself in the fields early, fingering the open bolls of fluffy white cotton that covered the field like snow. She had a pick sack bunched in one arm and a large canvas tote in the other. She looked into the contents of the tote she carried and counted each item off carefully.

George and Tom stood in the distance, discussing where to begin the picking, as the hands waited nearby. They leaned against fence posts, picking sacks slung over their slumped shoulders. A twinge of guilt pricked Polly's conscience. These eight field hands, virtually strangers to her, were men like Ben, after all. They would be spending yet another day doing her bidding. Thank God they were usually out of her sight, she thought. It was uncomfortable to look at them, to watch them from under the wide brim of her straw bonnet.

Reginald stood with them, just a boy, Jack yapping playfully near his legs. Reg had filled out a bit and grown taller in the weeks he had eaten Ona's good cooking. He wore newly stitched pants that covered knobby knees and thin calves. Sturdy shoes that had belonged to Ben were now on his long feet. He bent to scratch Jack's ears. At least Polly had done right by Reg. Or had she? Here he was about to begin the backbreaking work of picking her cotton.

Polly sighed heavily and tried to shake off her guilt. "Mr. Roper!" she called sharply. The overseer left George and headed toward Polly.

Tom pointed out at the field, "We're about ready to start, Miss Polly. George thinks the north fields can wait a day or two, so we will start the men here. Is there anything else?"

Polly thrust the sack forward. "Yes, give these to the men."

Tom took the bag and peered inside, before looking up with a grin. "What the—?" A dozen pairs of new leather gloves lay nestled in the sack. "What have you done, woman?"

Polly said, "They were part of what I got for the peaches. Give a pair to every man and to Reg. They are theirs to keep, so they mustn't lose them. They're kid leather, thin enough to feel the bolls. But that doesn't mean they can pick shoddily."

Tom whistled as he pulled a glove from the sack. "That was kind of you."

Polly shifted from one foot to another uncomfortably. "There are enough for all of us."

"Us?" Tom's eyebrows went up.

"I'm going to try my hand at picking my cotton, Tom. You've done it." She pulled a smaller pair of gloves from her apron pocket. "I'm going soft in the head or something. But I want to try." Polly squinted up at Tom in the bright morning sunshine.

"Miss Polly, picking cotton is not easy. These gloves will be appreciated, for sure. But you shouldn't be out here picking." Tom glanced over at the field hands, waiting in a huddle for their orders. "I've picked a lot of cotton in my years. I don't recommend it. It may be cool now but by mid-day, that hot sun will bake your skin."

"I may quit by midday," Polly laughed, "but I want to see for myself what it is like. Kate was out in my fields and picked cotton with Solomon on her back. The mill girls picked. I aim to pick two hundred pounds today. Maybe a whole bale."

Tom snorted good-naturedly and reached in the bag. "You realize the average slave can pick two hundred fifty to three hundred fifty pounds a day? And that a bale weighs nearly five hundred pounds? I'd be surprised if you could get one hundred."

"The other small pair in there is for Reg," Polly directed, ignoring Tom's jibe. "And Tom, I don't want him out here all day. Send him over to help Zee with the livestock after lunch."

Tom looked at Polly with admiration. "Yes ma'am." He tipped his hat and turned to go when she called out.

"Wait! Before you leave me, how does this contraption work?" Polly held the pick sack limply in her arms.

Tom chuckled and took the sack from Polly. He placed it over her head and shoulder and pulled the length of it out behind her. "Polly Burgiss Stone, you are the most confounded woman I have ever known." He handed her his full canteen and added, "Drink water at the end of every row, or you'll soon be dehydrated. You hear me?"

"Yes sir," Polly said, mock-saluting her overseer with a smile. She watched Tom's broad back, as he strode across the field toward the hands. *What a good man*, she thought. *And not at all bad on the eyes.*

George and Tom dispersed the men to different areas of the south fields, as she pulled on the new leather gloves. The sun was already warm on Polly's back. She made her way to a row of cotton. She bent and plucked a fluffy head from a hard boll and thrust it into the long sack. Continuing down the row, Polly pulled the fibers free of the bolls and added to her pick sack. At the end of the first row, she wiped her brow with her hand and adjusted her bonnet. She was surprised that her bag was so light, perhaps the weight of one down pillow. Maybe. She paused to take a swig of cool water from Tom's leather canteen, inhaling the smell of the man as she did so. She turned to the next row and began again.

The pick sack dragged behind her, snagging on rocks and twigs. By the eighth row, Polly took it off and decided to pull it with her left hand. The sack still snagged on low branches and the occasional briar and Polly had to yank it free to continue. The warming September sun beat down on her arms and back and sweat soon stained her bodice. Tom's canteen ran dry. Despite her pale skin and her modesty, she rolled up her sleeves.

Soon she had discarded the gloves, as they made it difficult to pull the fiber from the prickly bolls. But her fingers were soon bloodied and sore.

At the end of the twelfth row, Polly was able to dump her cotton into a large basket with some effort. Her back throbbed and sweat trickled down between her breasts and under her arms. Her heart pounded in her chest. The nearest water was from the pump way back by Tom's cabin, and Polly was too tired to go all the way back for it.

In the distance, she watched as Tom rode through fields shimmering in the heat, checking on the hands' progress. She could hear George's deep voice singing, a rhythm to pick by. She removed her bonnet and let her scalp catch a bit of the cooling breeze, before placing it securely on her head again.

The incessant drone of insects lulled her into a trance and she stumbled forward, fingers automatically reaching for the fluff in each open boll. The light was so bright it was hard to see, and the ringing in Polly's ears became so loud that she hardly heard George ring the noon bell, the signal for the men to come in and eat their lunch and rest in the shade for thirty minutes.

How did they do it? Some years the men had been out in her fields picking cotton in late August, on days reaching well upwards of ninety degrees. Sunrise to nearly sunset. Kate had picked with Sol strapped to her back. Polly felt rising blisters on her palms and blood oozing from cuts on her fingertips. Hunger gnawed at her stomach. She paused to pull a ham biscuit from her pocket but decided against the salty ham when her throat was so parched.

She heard a rustle behind her and Reg appeared, lugging a wooden bucket. His full pick sack was slung over his shoulder. Jack followed the boy, happy to have a new companion. "Miss Polly, I brung you some water, ma'am. I'm sorry. Some of it sloshed out." He extended the bucket toward Polly sheepishly.

Polly gasped. "Reg, dear boy! How did you know I had run out?"

"I saw you with a little canteen and I knowed it wouldn't last long. An' you wasn't dippin' into the barrels at the row ends." He frowned. "They's nigger barrels anyway. You ain't supposed to drink from dem."

"I didn't even notice water barrels, Reg. Thank you for telling me." Polly crouched shakily to fill the canteen, lifted it to her lips, and drank deeply. "You're a good boy." She smiled and drank again.

"I got this water at Mr. Tom's pump. I didn't touch it either, I swear." Reg paused and then asked, "Why you out here? You the mistress. Mr. George tol' me I can go in at the noon bell. But why you still here?" He looked at Polly with innocent brown eyes.

Polly gazed at him with affection. "I suppose I wanted to find out what it feels like to pick cotton all day. I am already finding that I do not like it much." She drank again and refilled her canteen. She handed the empty bucket to the boy. "Thank you."

Reg nodded. "I'm real glad you let me stay here, Miss Polly. This real good compared to River Wood. I'll work hard for you. But I don't like pickin' cotton either." He frowned and pointed toward the river. "An' ma'am, watch out. They's a snappin' turtle laid out by the end of the rows that way. He wasn't in no hurry to get on back to his pond."

"Thank you, Reg. You be careful, yourself. Let George know to get rid of it."

"I'd eat it!" The boy laughed. "Can I gig it and take it back?"

"Please don't." Polly grimaced. "I saw no food crops in the fields at Riverwood. What did you all eat?"

Reg's expression clouded and he looked down. "After Miss Jane died, I guess we jes' ate what we find. Chickens gone. Mr. Wilkins sold all da' hogs. We made snares for squirrels and rabbits. The garden wasn't real good, especially after Ezra was gone."

He paused. "Some of the men ran away after Mr. Wilkins left. I promise—I wouldn't a said nuthin' to Mr. McGee 'cept I was real hungry. There was just eight of us left by then. We found some bags of seed corn in Mr. Wilkins' cabin an' made hoe cakes. I chewed on seed corn a lot."

He looked at Polly with wide eyes. "So a snapper don't seem like such a bad thing to try. One of the men, Jefferson, kilt the ol' nag with a board to the head so's to have meat. Tol' the foreman that it stepped in a hole an' broke its leg, so he kilt it, but it weren't true. It tasted awful, but least we had meat. I wanted to let the other horses go, Miss Polly, so's they didn't get ate up too. I let 'em out to pasture the morning I came here. I been worryin' about them."

Polly spoke reassuringly. "I will send Zee to check the horses. Did Mr. Wilkins treat you badly?"

"Sometimes he hit me." He shrugged. His brown eyes looked up at Polly. "Miss Polly, I heard a shot, but it coulda been someone huntin'. I jes' saw a slave man I remembered from yo' place. He was carryin' Ezra. By the time I got to the front yard, I saw the wagon rollin' away, an' I was afraid. I was real hungry when that deputy showed up. He said I could have some food if I tol' him where Mr. Wilkins went."

Polly sighed and considered what the boy said. "Thank you for the water, Reginald. Go and eat some lunch. Then see Zee in the barn. He will be expecting you."

"Yes ma'am," the boy said, relief on his face. He called to Jack and the pair raced down the row and out of sight.

— • —

LATER THAT EVENING, TOM AND POLLY sat together in the dining room. Polly had invited Tom to eat with her, ostensibly to catch up on the day's harvest. Cissie placed a simple supper in front of them. A platter of roast chicken and vegetables smelled divine to Tom after a day in the cotton fields. The aroma of hot biscuits made his mouth water.

"I have quite the appetite tonight. I'm sure you do, too. We worked hard," Tom said, shaking his head.

Polly waited until Cissie left the room and said, "Imagine my surprise when you said I had only picked sixty pounds." She stabbed a piece of chicken and laid it on Tom's plate. He gazed at her burned wrists and scabbed and swollen fingers which attested to her time in the fields. She quickly put her hands in her lap when she noticed Tom staring at her wounds.

"I assure you, I will not be out there tomorrow. I have a new appreciation for the work the men do. You, too," she said. "You're a good overseer, Tom."

— • —

"THANK YOU." TOM SMILED AND SIPPED his glass of whiskey, uneasy with the compliment. He was scrubbed and dressed in his good white shirt, his hair slicked back with pomade. A tie encircled his throat and gave him the feeling of being strangled. Dressing up always made him nervous.

To make matters worse, Polly's cheeks were flushed from the sun. Her chestnut hair was swept up loosely and away from her small face the way he liked. Her eyes sparkled in the candlelight and the scarlet silk dress flattered her curves. She was beautiful. Tom felt a flush of heat to his own face and looked down at his plate, embarrassed at his reaction.

Polly looked at Tom. "I'm sending Zee to River Wood tomorrow. Reg mentioned good horses left in the pasture." She chewed a forkful of vegetables and swallowed.

"Is the chicken to your liking?"

Tom studied his plate and didn't answer.

"You have been very quiet tonight. Is something wrong?" she asked, putting down her fork.

Tom quickly regained his composure and shook his head. "No, no. I'm sorry if I was lost in thought. I'm always going through crop yields and harvest dates in my head, I suppose. Thinking about buyers for the crops and whatnot. We'll get that cider to town soon enough for you, though." He knew he was making for terrible company but couldn't help his nerves. She was lovely.

Polly nodded and continued eating her meal silently.

Tom finally put down his fork and knife and looked at Polly. "It's none of my business, but have you heard anything from your husband since Manassas?"

Polly was clearly taken aback. "Why bring up that unsavory topic, when Cissie has prepared such a nice meal for us?" she asked curtly. "Had I known the way this conversation was going to go, I might have taken a tray in the parlor in front of the fire, as I do most nights."

Tom reached out his hand and laid it near Polly's. "I am sorry. I certainly didn't mean to offend you. Remember that I do work for him, legally, and it's just that, any day now, I half expect him to come riding down the drive, and everything that you have worked for, have done to make Whitehall a good place, it'll be in jeopardy."

Tom blotted his mouth with his napkin and added, "You must know that I am fond of you. I don't want to see you hurt."

— • —

POLLY SIPPED HER WATER, SELF-CONSCIOUS now of the low décolletage of the dress she had foolishly worn. She felt her already pink cheeks flush beet red. She looked down at her plate, afraid to look at Tom.

Tom's hand was so near her own. "If he comes back and lays a hand on you, I don't know whether I'll be able to keep from killing the man with my bare hands. I know that you don't think of me the way I have come to think of you. I'm an old man to you." He chuckled. "I'm thirty-six years old. But I have watched the hell that man has put you and your family through. There must be a way to hold him accountable, even now."

Polly twisted her napkin in her lap, unsure of how to respond.

"Will you confront him about your brothers?" Tom asked.

"I don't want to talk about that," Polly murmured. "It's none of your business anyway. You are my overseer." The tangle of emotions running through her mind were too much. *I should not have asked him to dinner. This isn't right.*

"I apologize," Tom said coolly. "I won't say anything more on the subject. Just know that if John comes home and threatens you in any way, I am here to help. If you confront him with the truth of what he did to your brothers, I will stand by your side. He deserves to be in hell. Or at least jail."

"You're not helping, Tom!" Polly wailed. She tossed her napkin on the table.

Tom pushed his chair back abruptly and rose from the table. "Thank you for the dinner, Miss Polly, but I remember that I have some evening chores I need to attend to. If you'll excuse me?"

Polly watched Tom cross the room and let himself out quietly. Tears welled in her eyes and she pounded the table with her fist. She grabbed Tom's whiskey and downed it before slinging the glass toward the wall. It shattered in pieces and caused Cissie to come running from the butler's pantry.

"Gracious sakes, Miss Polly! What happened?" She knelt and began to pick up shards of glass in her apron front.

"Leave it, Cissie!" Polly cried out. "Just leave it and go." She pushed back from the table abruptly and hurried up the stairs.

— • —

September 20, 1861

IN THE DOORWAY OF THE WHITEHALL BARN, three hundred bales of un-ginned cotton were stacked high like a child's blocks.

"What do you mean, that President Davis wants it?" Polly asked as she stood with Tom and the local cotton factor, Bart Hammond.

Hammond peeled off a roll of bills from a stack of Confederate currency. "Mrs. Stone, as I said, I can offer you eight cents a pound. You'll not have to gin it, nor ship it, you only need to sell it to me and I'll get it over to the Exchange. Those are my instructions. What the new President intends to do with it is not your concern. Nor is it mine."

Tom folded his arms over his chest and said, "Mr. Hammond, last year, Mrs. Stone got eleven cents the pound. Even with the offshore blockades, we'd hoped to sell for fifteen this year."

Hammond guffawed. "Well, you won't. President Davis is buying up the cotton. There is an embargo, you know. So if you want to sell it, you'll sell to me and to the Confederate government. Not a shred of Southern cotton is going up north or to England this year." The factor huffed impatiently. "Now, I have other customers. Take it or leave it, but I have to be going. My instructions—"

Polly interrupted. "Alright, I will take it. We need the money."

Hammond nodded. "It's the right decision, ma'am. If you dilly-dally, it may end up rotting in your barn. Be thankful that President Davis wants it. Maybe he's outfitting the entire army with new uniforms and such. I hear the Union soldiers have identical navy blue wool coats with brass buttons, new boots for every man, and new guns, while our boys have mismatched pants, threadbare jackets, and rusted rifles." He laughed.

He counted out the correct number of bills and handed the money to

Polly. "Rumor has it that the Confederacy might even ban cotton sales next year. Anyway, my boys'll load it up and we'll be out of your way, Mrs. Stone." He doffed his hat and turned away.

Polly and Tom walked slowly toward the house. Both had ignored the awkward dinner of weeks before. The work of picking and baling cotton and harvesting apples kept them busy enough.

Polly tucked a loose strand of hair behind her ear. "An embargo? Tom, this is ridiculous. If England does not get cotton from us, they will get it from elsewhere. Does President Davis really think that an embargo will move England to our side?"

"South Carolina sold a record amount of cotton to England over the past four years. They won't be in a hurry to get involved. They'll wait this out . . . and when it runs out, they'll find other sellers. They aren't likely to get involved in this mess."

Polly chewed on her lip and then turned to Tom. "I hate this war. Cotton is all we know. Now what?"

"Not true. You were smart to diversify. The orchards and sorghum will be profitable, and your corn is fine this year." Tom scuffed his boot in the dirt. "Any chance you want me to see what happened at River Wood? With the corn they started in the spring?"

"No. I have washed my hands of that place, Tom. You know that. Reginald told me that there was nothing left by the time . . . by the time Mr. Wilkins died. If there is corn there, let it go to seed. His slaves can have it." She shook her head vigorously. "We have the animals here now. I don't care about the rest."

"Reg told me your husband's slaves quit the fields long ago," Tom muttered. "What will he say when he comes back and finds his cotton fields abandoned?"

"We'll not do cotton here again." Polly ignored Tom's question. "I will have to find another crop suitable for the poor soil in those fields. The land cannot lie fallow." A mosquito landed on Polly's cheek and Tom absentmindedly reached out his hand to brush it away. Polly stepped back in surprise.

"Mosquito," Tom said softly, palms up. "You don't have to worry about me."

"I'm sorry," Polly murmured. "You understand."

"Yes, I do." Tom sighed and looked out past the barn toward the bedraggled cotton fields. Wisps of white fiber hung from acres of spent plants, dotting the landscape like shredded paper tossed in the wind. "Peaches as your cash crop," he said. "Think about more peaches."

— • —

DARK SETTLED EARLY THAT EVENING, clouds low and brooding. Polly sat in the parlor with a lapful of clothing to be mended. Torn skirts and snagged stockings gave evidence of the briars and thorns that caught her unawares in the fields. The first cold front of the season had moved into the upstate, and she was happy to have a cozy fire going in the fireplace. Squinting in the low light, she reached to turn up the kerosene lantern, its glow a comfort in the big, empty house.

As she stitched, she ran numbers in her mind. The cotton was a disappointment, but Polly reminded herself that she had put fewer acres under cultivation this year because of the uncertainty of the war. Her premonition paid off. Some area planters had planted more cotton and surely lost money. She wondered about Andrew Calhoun, up at Fort Hill.

Despite the low cotton price, the other cash crops had done well. The hard cider and peaches were a huge success, and meant needed supplies were on hand and a little money was in the bank. The Pendleton Inn had already placed a peach order for the following year, which pleased Polly immensely. The remaining apple crop was lackluster, but after putting up gallons of applesauce, apple chutney, apple jelly, and stewed apples, Polly had been able to sell the remainder in town for a fair price.

There was a knock on the front door and Polly put down her sewing. Cissie was at the door before Polly could rise, and she heard Tom's voice in the hallway. Cissie peeked into the parlor. "Miss Polly, Mr. Roper to see you. Is there anything else you need me to do tonight? I lit a fire in yo' bedroom fireplace and left some stones fo' yo' feet. It's right chilly."

"Thank you, Cissie. That will be it tonight. I will see you in the morning. We can cut out that osnaburg for the boys' new pants." The slave woman smiled and left the room.

Tom entered the room, hat in hand. Polly chided herself for being nervous around her overseer. "Goodness, Tom. What brings you up to the house so late?" She pointed to a chair and Tom crossed the room and sat down. She looked back down at the pile in her lap. "I'm catching up on my mending. I seem to have ripped every garment I had on, the one day I picked cotton."

Tom cleared his throat. "I found out what President Davis is doing with the cotton." His face was difficult for Polly to read in the lamplight.

"Was Mr. Hammond correct? Are the soldiers wearing fancy new uniforms?" Polly chuckled and resumed her stitching.

"They burned it." Tom's voice was steady but Polly detected the anger in his tone.

Polly set the sewing aside and looked at Tom. "What do you mean, they burned it?"

"Governor Pickens' factors bought up most of the crop in the state. Hammond was ordered to dump all he bought around here over near the Exchange. Hammond and his boys set it all on fire. Several thousand bales, I heard. It seems that Davis didn't want it to get into Lincoln's hands, and the embargo meant it wasn't going overseas . . . so they were authorized to burn it." Tom struck a match on his boot and lit his pipe.

Polly gasped. "What a waste. What an incredible waste. It almost makes me ill."

Tom puffed on his pipe and nodded his head slowly. "Sheer political stupidity. When this war ends, the cotton prices will go through the roof.

We are talking about two very large egos, if you ask me. Lincoln and Davis will not sit down and work this thing out. Too much is at stake."

"How long can this go on?" Polly asked. For a moment, she wondered where John might be in all of this. She liked to think that he might never come home, but the likelihood was that he would. She shivered and tried to push his face out of her mind.

Tom shrugged. "The sorghum is ready to pick. We had so many deer in it yesterday morning, I was able to add some venison to the smokehouse for you," he smiled and stood, still puffing on his pipe. "Anyway, I wanted you to know about the cotton."

"Thank you, Tom. Can you stay and visit a while?" she asked.

"No. I best get back to my cabin."

Polly stood and followed Tom into the hallway.

Tom turned and took the pipe from his mouth. He stared down at his feet while he spoke. "I'm thinking I might go into town Saturday evening for the square dance. I'm not usually one for those town shindigs, but it is the Harvest Dance, and, well . . . I heard the fiddler is right good." His voice trailed off and he looked apprehensively at Polly.

Polly smiled. "May I catch a ride in the wagon with you? It would be good to go, to get out and catch up with the neighbors and hear the latest news of the war. Mind if I tag along?"

"I'd be delighted to have the company." Tom smiled and stepped out into the dark.

Chapter Forty-One

September 23, 1861

IN A STEADY STREAM OF HORSE AND WAGON TRAFFIC, the phaeton bumped along Main Street, following the sound of music in the distance. The Harvest Dance was the biggest social event in the district each year, and even with the war, attendance was expected to be high. Wealthy planters, local merchants, and farmers were excited to mingle and exchange gossip. Because so many Lowcountry families had fled Charleston for the Upstate, there would be many new faces and stories of the skirmishes on the coast.

Polly scanned the large crowd milling about outside the enormous cotton exchange building, as Tom pulled the phaeton to a stop. He tied up the horse and hurried around to assist Polly out of the carriage. He offered his hand and she accepted it nervously.

This is ridiculous, she thought, remembering the many other times that Tom Roper had helped her out of a wagon. She stepped to the ground and adjusted the skirts of her green taffeta. With its puffed sleeves and cape of lace, it was an elegant dress, one Polly had not worn in years. Her dark hair was held in place with a matching wreath.

"You're as pretty as a picture," Tom said, smiling easily. "This is the first time I have seen you in a dancing dress since your eighteenth birthday. It is good for you to get out. You're young." He offered his arm, and the pair joined the throng of folks headed into the Exchange.

"It is good to get out. Thank you for suggesting it." Polly smiled up at Tom. They entered through the double doors into the great hall, decorated with colorful lanterns and silk swags in blue and gold. From their raised platform at one end of the hall, the musicians began a Stephen Foster tune and dancers filled the floor. A good-sized crowd milled around, and Polly was surprised to see so many familiar faces. There were a good number of boys in what passed for Confederate uniform, some with bandages and supported by crutches.

The music swelled and Polly couldn't help it when her foot started tapping in time to the music. Tom leaned in. "Can I get you a glass of punch?"

"Thank you." Polly nodded. She watched as Tom made his way through the crowd toward the refreshments table and then turned back to watch the dancers. Many of the women she watched reel and dip were partnered with other women, their husbands off fighting somewhere.

"Why hello, Mrs. Stone," said a feminine voice from behind Polly. She turned to find Ward Adger's young wife, visibly with child. The bodice of her dress formed a tent over her expanding abdomen. "I haven't seen you since Mrs. Calhoun's tea party. Lucinda Adger."

Polly smiled at the young woman, relieved to have someone to speak to at last, even Lucinda. "Yes, I remember you, Mrs. Adger. I thought you and your mother had sailed for England. And please call me Polly." Polly recalled that Ward Adger was now Major McQueen's personal physician.

"Please call me Lucinda. No, our plans changed when I told Mother I was expecting a baby. I thought about calling on you but could not get up the courage. Mother treated you so badly. And I was quite nauseous at the time," she said, pointing to her belly. "How is it that I am drawn to you now simply because our husbands fight in the same company?" Lucinda's green eyes flashed but there was honesty behind her gaze.

Polly smiled. "We have a war in common now. In the past, we did not run in the same social circles. Your mother made that clear."

"Yes, and I'm—I am sorry for that," Lucinda stammered. "Mother has always been a bit of a social climber. She embarrassed me at Floride's tea party. I apologize if she offended you. You have been through so much."

Polly softened and said, "Thank you, Lucinda. Floride tried to pull me into Pendleton society, but I had no desire to play the woe-is-me card. And I suppose I do prefer my solitude now."

"Well, I admire you. You are quite brave. Running your own place alone. . . . I am practically bereft without Ward and a festive party. Yet here we both are without our husbands, like so many women these days." Lucinda paused. She nodded toward a couple of young men leaning on crutches. "Poor boys. The war will leave many widows and orphans in its wake." She patted her stomach and added, "I am about to enter my confinement—in the home of my in-laws. But I believe my husband will be granted a short leave when I have the baby."

Polly felt a pang of jealousy, but said, "Congratulations, Lucinda. I am very happy for you. You are in good hands with Dr. and Mrs. Adger."

Lucinda put a gloved hand over her lips and said, "I would prefer a midwife. And my mother-in-law may be the death of me." Her green eyes twinkled with humor and Polly thought she might have found a friend.

The band began to play *Turkey in the Straw*. "I saw you come in with that man over there." Lucinda nodded toward Tom. "Who is he? He is quite handsome. Perhaps an uncle?"

Polly blushed. "He is just my overseer, Tom Roper. I think he felt sorry for me." She realized the truth in this and made a silent promise to herself to get out more. "I tend to be too much of a homebody. Even now I am anxious for my own hearth and home."

"Rumor has it that you drove away one overseer already. Or maybe sent him to enlist? That Mr. Wilkins was a horrible man. I am glad that he isn't roaming around town anymore." Lucinda looked at Polly playfully

571

and added, "Don't lose this one." She chuckled. "He's easy on the eyes."

Polly reddened and changed the subject. "Tell me, what has your husband written of the war? Is Major McQueen's unit still in Virginia celebrating Manassas? John does not write much."

"Land sakes, Polly!" Lucinda gasped. "You really are out of touch. McQueen is Colonel McQueen now. Has been for some time. There have been several Union victories since they took Manassas Junction. There were heavy casualties among the men from our district." Lucinda eyed Polly soberly.

Lucinda pointed toward a cluster of women across the hall. Two of the women wore black from head to toe. "The second son of the milliner, Mrs. Drake over there, died at Manassas, and Fred Stills, a farmer out on the Belton road, took a bullet at Cheat Mountain. There is his widow, Cassie Stills, and his mother. Certainly, no one faults them for coming out tonight, even in mourning. We all know that our men could be next. That red-headed Jim Boyle who worked in the back of the post office, he lost a leg at Manassas." She sighed. "Ward wrote that it is a grisly business indeed."

Polly felt a knot growing in her stomach. *He might not come back*, she thought.

"You have not heard from your husband since Manassas? You must be worried sick." Lucinda gave Polly a look of real concern.

Polly shrugged. "He is not a writer."

Lucinda continued, "You'd have received word if he were mortally wounded. Ward would have written something. He wrote that hundreds were wounded. That includes everything from a sprained ankle to missing limbs. It sounded horrific. He said that it was difficult to treat that many wounded. Minor injuries got pushed to the end of the line. The field hospital was overwhelmed, and Ward had to tend to the men as best he could."

Polly wondered whether John had been injured. Would he be less amenable to a divorce if he needed someone to care for him?

"Oh Polly, I am sure that you will hear from your husband soon enough. And I am sure that Ward would have said something if John was injured. Their unit is on its way south. The men who were too ill to go on were to be discharged and sent home by train. That was two months ago. So he must be safe." She stroked her abdomen absentmindedly. "Well, I should go now. I see by her scowl that Mother Adger is ready to leave."

Polly tried to muster a smile. "Yes, well, I am so glad that you spoke to me. If there is anything I can do while you are confined, please let me know."

Lucinda smiled warmly. "I am glad, too, Polly. You know, some of the women at Mrs. Calhoun's tea party were quite offended by your . . . aloofness. If that is a word." She chuckled. "But I admire you. And I would like to get to know you better. You seem a mysterious creature and I am bored stiff. Will you call on me? I have another month before I have the baby."

Polly nodded. "I would love to call on you."

The women hugged affectionately and Lucinda turned away. Tom appeared with two tiny punch glasses and said, "I see that you met Lucinda Adger. Did she have any news to tell?"

"Enough to remind me that I must read the obituaries now that we are at war." Polly took the small glass and sipped delicately. "Cider." She laughed. "Too bad it isn't ours!"

The band struck up a reel and Polly watched as dancers partnered up and surged onto the dance floor in a long line.

"May I have this dance?" Tom asked hesitantly.

Polly shrugged. "Why not, Mr. Roper? Why not?" They set down their glasses and stepped onto the dance floor, joining in the merriment.

Polly and Tom danced through several popular songs, both waltzes and reels. In fact, they moved well together. Finally, laughing, she begged to sit, her feet pinched in her shoes. She plopped down in a chair while Tom went for more cider. As she leaned over to adjust the strap on her shoe, a pair of scuffed men's boots appeared in her vision.

"That was quick, Tom!" She laughed and sat up. Her smile faded. Standing before her was a stranger, a young man dressed in a faded Confederate jacket, right arm in a sling. He was barely a man, his chin covered in fine peach fuzz.

Over his right eye, he wore a black patch. "Are you Mrs. John Stone?"

Polly stood. "I am," she said, as Tom reappeared by her side with a glass of cider. "And this is my overseer."

Tom nodded cordially.

The man brightened. "You are the other person I was supposed to find, then. You Clay Wilkins?"

"My name is Roper. Tom Roper," Tom said gruffly.

"May I speak to you privately, then, ma'am?" the man asked, over the noise of the crowd.

"I will ask Mr. Roper to stay here. Anything you have to say to me you can say in front of my overseer."

The man stared at Tom for a moment before turning to speak to Polly. "I'm Will Stevens. Private Will Stevens," he said. "From Anderson. I served under Captain Stone. I stopped by Whitehall but your woman told me you were here."

Polly had forgotten that John wrote of being commissioned an officer. A captain. "How can I help you?"

"I'm sent by your husband. He was hurt at Manassas Junction. Not bad." He added quickly, "Which is why he ain't home. I lost my eye there, and the use of my arm. Captain Stone took a ball in the leg. Healin' up in the hospital."

Polly stared at the man, her face blank.

"Thank you for your service, son," Tom said quietly. "I heard that Manassas was hard-fought. You must be very brave. How old are you?"

The young man looked at Tom with sadness and softened. "I'm eighteen, sir. I appreciate your kind words." He shifted from one leg to the other and said, "When we was gettin' ready to be shipped home, Captain Stone asked me to get a message to his wife. He thought you must not be gettin' his letters. Mr. Wilkins either. He asked me to check on you both. To make sure you were alright. And to be sure to give you a message." Behind him, the dancers waltzed in rhythm to the music.

Polly bristled. "Mr. Stone's overseer, Clay Wilkins, abandoned River Wood. He has been gone for a while—probably down to the Lowcountry, where overseers are getting paid top dollar to stand their ground and keep slaves in line while the planters run off to hide," Polly snapped. "As you can see, I am fine. Now, what message have you from my husband?"

Polly was surprised to see Private Stevens pull a crumpled and stained envelope from his vest pocket. "Well, it is a letter. He wanted to be sure you got it. I kept it on me all the way home on the train."

Polly took the letter from the soldier. "Thank you," she said. "I'm sorry if I did not sound appreciative of what you have done."

Private Stevens nodded. "I better be headin' back to Anderson. You sure I can't find Mr. Wilkins out at River Wood? It was my next stop."

Tom reached out and patted the young man's shoulder. "Don't trouble yourself. He is long gone. You've done as Captain Stone asked. Go on home now."

The soldier nodded and said, "May I leave his letter with you, in case he returns?"

"By all means," Polly said quickly. "I can hold it for him should he come back."

The young man handed Polly another crumpled envelope.

"Do you have kin in Anderson, son?" Tom asked gently.

"I got my Mama. I need to find work. But no one wants to hire a half-blind and lame man, do they?" he asked. He tipped his hat, turned away, and disappeared into the crowd.

Polly turned to Tom and murmured, "Please take me home." Tom steered Polly through the happy people deep in conversation at the edge of the dance floor. He asked no questions and said nothing as he helped her into the phaeton. They rode silently through the cool night, the creak of wagon wheels and the rhythmic cadence of the horse's hooves the only sounds.

Polly leaned back against the high backrest and sighed. She was weary to the bone. She looked up at the sliver of moon overhead and the stars twinkling in the deep blue night. After some time, she finally turned to Tom in the dark. "Will you help me, Tom? I don't know what this letter will say, but please . . . don't leave me. I don't think I could bear it. Pray for me."

Tom leaned over and planted a small kiss on Polly's forehead. "I always do."

— • —

AUTUMN AT WHITEHALL HAD ALWAYS BEEN Polly's favorite time of year. She woke at sunrise, a chilly breeze ruffling the curtains at her window. She shivered and hurried to close it, before turning to stir up the embers of the night's fire. She added a log and poked and prodded. Soon the fire was warm and crackling. She quickly jumped back into the bed and covered her legs with quilts. Jack thumped his tail against the mattress, stretched, and laid his head back down.

There was a knock on the door and Cissie entered with a tea tray. "Good mornin' Miss Polly," she said cheerfully. "George says the sorghum harvest starts today. We all so thankful you gone give us a share!" She placed the tray on Polly's bedside table and waited.

Polly felt a pang of sadness. She missed Ona's morning visits but the woman had not been into Polly's bedroom since Ben and Kate left. She inhaled the aroma of biscuits and hot tea. "You all work hard. A share of the syrup boiled is a fair reward."

"Yes'm. It's easier to work hard when you get rewarded fo' yo' work," Cissie said.

Polly cocked her head and looked up at Cissie uneasily.

"An' I hear George say that all them seed heads have to be cut while it's dry out," Cissie continued.

Polly shifted uneasily against her pillows. "Yes. We need to get it all in while we're in a dry spell. Hopefully, we get it all done today."

"You puttin' everyone in the fields then?" Cissie blinked, her eyes easy to read.

Ah, there it is, Polly thought. "The weather is cool. I think Reg can work with the men. He tries to behave like a man. Silas is much too young for field work. Let him stay with you."

Cissie broke into a grin. "Thank you, Miss Polly. He cain't cut no canes, no ma'am. But he can help me bile up the syrup. He's a big help in the kitchen house. He's in there now shellin' peas with Ona. He is jes' a baby still."

Polly sighed wearily. "He is three." Her mind flashed back to the night of Silas's birth—the night her father died.

Cissie nodded. "Yes'm." She frowned and continued, "He surely misses Ben and Kate and the chillun."

Polly ignored Cissie's comment. She thought a moment and said, "I have some bolts of flannel that you can take to make shirts for Silas and Reg. If you can also assess the needs of everyone else as far as winter clothing, we can start on that soon. Best to have that out of the way, come real cold weather. Set up the sewing machine in the dining room. You will have more room there."

Cissie blinked, surprised. The machine sewing usually took place in the cramped kitchen house at the big pine table. "The dinin' room? Yes'm. Thank you. I'll do that." She smiled and left the room quickly, leaving Polly feeling glad for the little things she could do to make her slaves' lives easier but well aware that their work was involuntary.

Below her windows, Polly heard Tom and George laughing together in the front yard as they planned for their day in the sorghum. She wanted to leap out of bed and call out to him from the window. Instead, she listened to Tom's laugh, deep and hearty. He had laughed last night while they danced. So had she. Tom was a good dancer and had steered Polly across the floor adeptly, one hand firmly on the small of her back, the other holding hers. It had been ages since she had laughed and danced like that, and it felt as if the cobwebs were finally cleared from her head.

She blushed to think of Tom's tender kiss on her forehead last night. The two of them had not spoken after that but the ride home was warm and comfortable. His gentle gesture had stirred something in her chest, but it was a good sensation, something new, like being safe or protected. Loved even.

She glanced over to her vanity table, where the unopened letter from John sat propped up against the mirror. She flipped the quilts back once again and crossed the floor in bare feet. She picked up the letter and ran her fingers over the handwriting. She remembered how John's writing used to make her feel—as giddy as a schoolgirl. She had been just a schoolgirl when she had fallen for him. She should have listened to her mother and Ona, Floride, and Ben.

Whatever message the letter held for her, it would not be welcome news, she was sure. They had parted badly after the fight concerning her inheritance, complicated by his desire to send Kate back to Wilkins.

She broke the wax seal on the envelope and lifted the folded letter from inside. A few Confederate twenty dollar bills fell from the envelope. With trembling hands, she opened it and began to read.

Dear Polly,

> *I asked Private Stevens to give this letter to you in person. I am not sure whether you received my earlier letters. Maybe the mails are disrupted by this war. Stevens is also carrying a letter for Mr. Wilkins. Since he has not responded to my letters either, I am compelled to think that there truly is a problem with the mail delivery.*

> *Stevens lost his eye at Manassas and heads home with a group of injured men who are now unfit to serve. It was a bloody battle, one not likely to be repeated in scope or size. I myself took a ball to my thigh, but my leg is on the mend. Colonel McQueen has been kind enough to allow his own surgeon, Ward Adger, to attend to me, so I know that I am getting the best of care.*

> *I am afflicted with fevers that come and go, as are many of*

the men after months of poor conditions in the field and in camp. So many of the soldiers have fallen ill with maladies unrelated to combat—more than have fallen in battle.

By now, the cotton has been picked, baled, and sold. I am sure that Mr. Wilkins did what he felt best for the crop, as he was instructed at my leave. Please be sure that he deposits the proceeds from the sale into my bank account in town. In my letter to him, I gave these same instructions. Last year, my cotton brought in $1,200. I hope for a similar amount this year, because I have good news, in two parts.

First, I know that you were angry about the use of your inheritance to pay off debts, but since we are in the clear now, the cotton money will have an exciting purpose. I was fortunate to find out that Colonel McQueen has owned the piece of land between River Wood and Whitehall, near your old orchard. It is about thirty acres in size. Too far from his own holdings, he agreed to let me buy it at a fair price. On a handshake, the deal was done. Now our two properties will become one. Ask Mr. Roper to work with Mr. Wilkins and the slaves to clear this property of debris and prepare it for winter wheat. I believe it was once the location of Kemp's general store.

Colonel McQueen has given me leave of absence to coincide with Ward Adger's own leave home. His wife is soon to enter her confinement. I will be home for a fortnight. We plan to leave for South Carolina by train at the end of October. It will be good to come home and see the progress on our farm and begin to get the new acreage under control.

I look forward to the day when there will be a ceasefire and I can be home permanently. Enclosed is some money to help out until my return. Until then, I remain,

Yours,
John

A wave of nausea swept over her. The man had gone off on a handshake and purchased the old Kemp place? The very place where her brothers' blood had been spilled into the earth. Polly quickly tore open the envelope addressed to Wilkins and found a similar letter. Seething with rage, she dressed quickly. She pinned up her hair sloppily and sat down to lace her boots. After downing the lukewarm tea, Polly stormed down the stairs and out the front door.

— • —

TOM WATCHED FROM THE END OF A ROW as the hands began to strip the valuable seed heads from the sorghum plants. The seeds would be saved for grinding into flour and only then would the canes be cut down for syrup. The weather was clear and beautiful, a perfect fall day. The work would not take long. Fluffy white clouds sailed overhead, and the sourwoods and dogwoods were already a brilliant red in the distance. George rode through the rows on horseback, checking the progress of the pickers. Because the hands had been promised a share of the syrup, and because the day was fine, several of the men began to sing the old songs, and one by one the others joined in.

Don't be weary traveler,
Come on home to Jesus . . ..

Reg worked with the men, happy to be treated like a grown man who would earn his own share of cane syrup. He joined in the singing, his alto voice a contrast to the deeper voices of the men.

My head get wet with the midnight dew,
Come along home to Jesus.
Angels bear me witness too,
Come along home to Jesus.

Tom smiled and turned from the field to see Polly walking quickly toward him, her skirts raised high to avoid the heavy dew. In her hand, she clutched a sheet of paper.

"Tom!" she called. "Tom, I must show you this!" She was out of breath from the long walk to the fields. She clutched at a stitch in her side.

Roper smiled and reached for the letter. "Is this the letter that Private Stevens brought?"

Polly nodded and held her ribs, trying to catch her breath. "It is not too personal. Nor is it good news."

Tom frowned and began to read. "You're right. This is not good news. What on earth can he be thinking?"

"Tom, he will be home in less than a month! I must tell him that I know what happened with my brothers. Then I have to ask for a divorce. I cannot live with him as his wife any longer. And now he has put himself into another debt. Will I be forced to cover that one too? We just cleared enough to put something into the bank," Polly cried.

Tom glanced at Reg, who was close to them at the end of a row and clearly listening to Polly's rant. "Calm down. Let's take this conversation away from the men." He steered her away from the field, his hand on her elbow.

As they walked back toward the house, Polly shook with rage. "Of all the nerve. . . . I will have to see Mr. Legarre. I cannot be responsible for any more of his debt."

"I can go with you to see Legarre, if you wish. I will vouch for your handling of Whitehall, and attest to Mr. Wilkins' disappearance."

Polly didn't seem to hear him. "How can John expect this deal to go through without knowing the value of his cotton crop?" Polly asked. "I shall go to the bank first, withdraw my money and keep it here. I will not have my income garnished again."

She quickened her stride and Tom hurried to keep up. They reached the front porch, where Polly wheeled around to face Tom. Her eyes blazed with fury. "I will not let this man ruin me!"

— • —

POLLY FIDGETED NERVOUSLY AS SHE and Tom waited in Harrison Legarre's tiny office. Eventually, the door opened and Legarre entered, glasses askew and shirtsleeves pushed up, despite the autumn chill. The law office was incredibly busy that day and Polly was thankful that the young attorney was able to fit her in on short notice.

"Mrs. Stone. Mr. Roper. Good news," he said, waving the letter from John Stone. "It is as I thought. Without Mr. Wilkins on-site to handle River Wood affairs, this deal is null and void. My father agrees with me." He smiled and handed the letter back to Polly. "I admit that this is the first case we have seen like this, but it will not be the last. With so many men away fighting, legal matters at home are sure to fall into disarray. Because the River Wood overseer has apparently abandoned his post, the contract is invalid."

Tom leaned back in his chair and blew out a long breath.

Polly frowned. "While that is very good news, Mr. Legarre, what can I do to protect Whitehall in the future, should my husband decide to use income from my crop sales to revisit this deal? You remember that my grandmother's entire inheritance was taken to pay off his debts. I cannot let John Stone continue to take what isn't rightfully his."

Legarre looked uneasily from Polly to Tom and back to Polly. "Mrs. Stone, are you sure that you want to continue this conversation now? Perhaps we can make arrangements for another time."

"Nonsense. Mr. Roper has been with my family for years. He has seen what John Stone did to his own place, and knows I want Whitehall to avoid the same fate. He also is aware that I married Mr. Stone under false pretenses."

Behind his smudged spectacles, Legarre's eyebrows went up.

Polly leaned in. "I now have information about him that I was not privy to at the time of our marriage last winter." Polly stared at Legarre and added, "Because of this, I would like to have the marriage annulled."

Legarre shifted uncomfortably in his seat. "Mrs. Stone, I can understand how frustrating it must have been to have your grandmother's money garnished to pay debts that Mr. Stone incurred before you married. Unfortunately, marital law in most places would have done the same thing. In a typical marriage—"

"This is not a typical marriage," Polly interrupted. "I only recently found out about something criminal that he did to my family a long time ago. When I was a child."

Legarre leaned forward. "Please go on."

Polly sat up and cleared her throat. "In 1848 . . . you may remember that my brothers were murdered in an apparent robbery attempt at the Kemps' store?"

Polly waited for Legarre to nod before she continued, "I was just a little girl, eight years old. After the murders, my mother was practically catatonic. She lost two sons and struggled to cope. Everyone knew her state of mind. Few people knew mine." Polly glanced at Tom, who nodded for her to continue.

"I . . . I was a witness to the crime. I had followed my brothers through the orchard to the Kemps' store. I lagged behind but got to the Kemps' moments after my brothers interrupted a possible robbery. I hid in the brush. When I saw them killed, I blacked out, fainted. That is where I was found the next morning by our slave, Ben."

Legarre's face clouded. "I do remember. I was maybe ten. The entire town was horrified. Nothing like that had ever happened in the district. We heard that you had been found at the scene, but no one really knew what happened to you. So you know who killed your brothers?" Confusion written across his young face, Legarre looked to Roper and then back to Polly. "I don't understand. Why is this just now coming to light?"

Tom said, "That morning Mr. Burgiss had us all out looking for the children. Ben alerted the search party. I remember him yelling out for Mr. Burgiss. After Polly was found, she was unable to speak for a long time. But I saw the safe, laying there busted open. It did look like a robbery gone awry. Mr. Burgiss tried to find the murderers. The town blamed Indians, runaway slaves . . ." His voice trailed off.

Tom appeared lost in thought, but then continued, "Your father will remember. Kemp always did like to trade with those poor Cherokee stragglers that came out of the bush. Some folks didn't like that. And there were rumors that he had stashed Revolutionary War gold taken off dead Brits when he fought at Cowpens. The man was a damned old fool and got himself into a bad situation. A lot of folks wondered about that gold."

He shook his head. "But after a Cherokee man was shot in the woods nearby the whole thing died down, as if the crime was solved. Mr. Burgiss could not get the sheriff to continue to investigate. At the time, the sheriff was Sam Stone's brother-in-law. It was case closed." Tom folded his arms and sat back in his chair.

Polly continued the story. "I did not remember anything. I was so young. An entire segment of my life was blank. It was nearly a year before I spoke again and three years before I felt like myself, but I still had no memory of that day. My father never spoke of it. My mother certainly was never the same. The orchard on the property line was abandoned. It was only recently, when I went through the orchard again for the first time since then, and continued into the woods after my dog, that it all came back to me."

Legarre removed his spectacles and asked again. "Who killed your brothers?"

Polly clasped her hands in her lap tightly. "I came upon the ruins of the store, and suddenly it was clear as day. I remembered it all. There were two men. A young blonde man, really still a boy, pushed Mrs. Kemp inside the store while it was on fire. I can still hear her screams. He secured the door with a leather strap. She must have burned alive." Polly's eyes welled with tears. "Mr. Kemp was bashed in the head and practically scalped by a second man, a red-headed man, big and rough."

Tom handed her a handkerchief but she waved it away impatiently. "Joshua jumped on the second man's back. The man threw him to the ground so hard that he must have broken his neck. And Caleb—Caleb was hit in the head with a rifle butt or a hatchet. It . . . it killed him instantly."

"Mrs. Stone, who murdered your brothers?" Legarre asked impatiently, poised with pen in hand.

Polly inhaled and exhaled a dozen years of pain and sadness. She smoothed the folds of her skirt with trembling hands and said, "They were drinking. I remember that. They wore bandanas over their faces, but they removed them before I blacked out. After everyone was . . . dead."

She paused and looked at Tom for reassurance, before turning back to her attorney. "Mr. Kemp was dead when I got there. But I saw Clay Wilkins murder Caleb and Joshua. John Stone locked Nancy Kemp in the burning building. I will swear to it."

Legarre stared at Polly for a moment and then wrote a few lines. He put down his pen slowly and exhaled a long breath. "Could this have been your imagination? Hysteria due to the trauma?"

Polly huffed indignantly. "I have a slave woman who will corroborate my story and she is trustworthy. I want nothing to do with John Stone. Clearly I cannot remain married to the man any longer."

Legarre looked at Polly sympathetically. "Was the slave woman there at the scene?"

Polly's shoulders sagged. "No."

Legarre rubbed his temples. "Anyway, her testimony would count for nothing in court. It would be an expensive undertaking to prove your accusations. The statute of limitations has expired for fraud, which would support annulment. Our best hope would be a murder charge, but you would have to endure a trial, and we would need—other corroboration."

Polly thought of Ben but quickly remembered he was gone. "You mean from white men, don't you?" She looked to Tom, and finally back to the young attorney. "A slave's word is not valid, and a jury won't believe a woman."

"I'm sorry. It is a tough story to swallow, Mrs. Stone. And in this political climate especially, no judge would listen to a case for annulment against your husband without other witnesses who could attest to what you say you saw—

and forgot— until now. I can't summon Clay Wilkins—who has left town for God knows where. And there is a war." The young man shook his head. "Let me be honest. Because your inheritance was garnished to pay your husband's past debts, a judge might think it the real reason for your wanting to dissolve the marriage. That is what I would assume. Pointing a finger at him with a murder charge twelve years later only makes you look desperate."

Polly gasped and turned helplessly to Tom.

Tom ran his hand through his hair and thought a minute before he spoke. "I believe her. When I heard her story, it all made sense. She really was unable to speak for over a year. I thought it was strange that the sheriff didn't pursue the case further. It was odd that Sam Stone was almighty sure it was Indians. In 1848?"

Polly shook her head sadly. "What recourse do I have to save Whitehall? He is clearly after my land. He will bankrupt me." Polly stated her claim with a shaky voice.

Mr. Legarre nodded. "Mrs. Stone, he cannot legally do anything to your property. He cannot sell it, add to it, or divide it in any way without your express consent. Your father made sure of that."

Polly thought for a moment and then swallowed hard. "What if I die? Who would get my land then?"

Legarre rubbed his weary eyes and put his spectacles back on. "As it is set up, it would go into probate court. And eventually, the court would decide to pass it to your husband. Unless you make up a will and name other beneficiaries. But even then, a husband could contest the will—with good reason."

Legarre jotted a few more notes. "You are in a unique situation. First things are first. If your husband comes home and wants to continue with the purchase of Colonel McQueen's adjacent property, he may do so to add onto River Wood. The parcel may not be considered a part of Whitehall without your consent. However, I must warn you that he will be able to use any funds you have on hand to make the purchase. He is your husband. Do you have funds available?"

Polly shifted in her seat and looked at Tom.

Legarre nodded and said softly, "Mrs. Stone, as your attorney, I should advise you that if you have funds in the bank and do not want the money used without your consent, you may need to . . . make a withdrawal."

Polly raised her chin and said, "I have no money in the bank, Mr. Legarre."

"Ah, good for you," Legarre said solemnly. "And now to address the other situation. It may take time for our office to know how best to proceed in the matter, time that I do not have. Whether to file for an annulment—"

Polly interrupted, "But you must make time. John is due home on leave soon. I will not live with the man as his wife."

Legarre removed his spectacles and laid them on the desk blotter. "You realize that the state of South Carolina does not recognize divorce?"

Polly leaned forward, exasperated. "How can I continue as his wife? He is a murderer."

Mr. Legarre leaned back in his chair. "I want to believe you, Mrs. Stone. I really do. Without a witness, however, it would be your word against his. I would consider taking the case and working on an annulment for you at least, but I am sorry. I will not be in the office after the end of the month. I have accepted a commission in the Confederate Army, under General Kershaw. I leave the practice to train in Virginia on October 3. It seems that this war will not be ending any time soon."

Polly and Tom exchanged worried looks.

Polly stood and extended her gloved hand. "Then that is that. It seems I have no legal recourse. Thank you and good luck to you, Mr. Legarre. I will keep you in my prayers. Please do the same for me."

Tom shook Legarre's hand and added, "Thank you for your advice. Godspeed, son."

Legarre stood. "I wish I could do more. I will discuss the situation with my father. If Mr. Stone has any questions about the McQueen property, direct him to my father. He is Colonel McQueen's own attorney. But without question, the handshake deal is off the table because the overseer is missing. And there are no funds with which to purchase. You should have nothing to worry about. Good luck to you, Mrs. Stone."

— • —

POLLY LIFTED THE BRASS KNOCKER AND rapped lightly on the Adgers' front door. A wisp of a girl answered the door, skin as dark as ebony. Polly's first thought was of Ona's Martin, whose blue-black skin enchanted her as a child.

"Yes'm?" the girl asked while staring at the floor.

"I have come to call on Mrs. Adger. Lucinda Adger," Polly said with a smile. She handed the girl her calling card.

"Who is it, Seeta?" shouted Lucinda's mother-in-law as she waddled down the hall. She primped her hair as she advanced toward the door. When she saw Polly, her face fell. "Oh, Polly Burgiss. Stone. What can I do for you, Mrs. Stone?" she asked.

Polly reddened. How was it that someone as kind as Dr. Adger had married such a sour woman? "I have come to call on Lucinda."

"I'm sorry. Lucinda is confined to bed. You'll have to come after she delivers the baby."

A voice from down the hallway called, "Mother Adger! I'm expecting Mrs. Stone. Please send her in!"

Mrs. Adger harrumphed and opened the door to allow Polly inside.

"Take your coat, ma'am?" Seeta asked softly.

"Why yes, thank you," Polly said, removing her coat quickly.

"Please do not stay long, Polly," chided Mrs. Adger. "Lucinda needs her rest."

"Yes ma'am," Polly said, as the older woman led her down the hall to a small bedroom turned into a nursery of sorts. Lucinda Adger sat propped up in bed, amid a nest of downy pillows, with a copy of *Godey's Lady's Book* in her lap.

At the sight of Polly, Lucinda's face brightened. "I am so happy to see you, Polly. Come in and sit down." She motioned to a chair slipcovered in a rose print. A matching rose print covered the walls and the duvet at the foot of the bed was the same design.

Mrs. Adger leaned against the doorframe. "Lucinda, you mustn't have too many guests. You'll tire easily in these last few weeks."

Lucinda smiled sweetly. "Yes, Mother Adger. Will you be a dear and make us some tea?" The sour woman frowned but left the room.

Lucinda shook her head and whispered, "I know she means well, but I am going insane. It is so nice to have a visit. I have read this old *Godey's* from cover to cover—twice!" The young ladies chuckled, and Lucinda continued, "Have you had any word from your husband?"

"Yes, I have. He will be coming home on leave while your own husband is here." Polly tried to sound excited but knew her voice was insincere.

"Wonderful!" Lucinda clapped her hands together. "We will have to get together while they are home. You must be elated."

Polly demurred, "Goodness, Lucinda, I know how precious the time will be with your husband home and a new baby. The last thing you need is another couple taking up your family time." She picked a speck of lint from her glove absentmindedly.

Lucinda's green eyes narrowed. "Polly Stone. You are practically a newlywed, am I right? I get the feeling that there is something wrong in paradise. Do tell!"

Polly laughed, warming to Lucinda's spicy personality. "My, you have a nose for gossip. It's nothing, really. Let's just say that we don't know each other as well as we thought. Do you know the date they're expected back?"

"No, I suppose they are at the mercy of the trains." Lucinda toyed with a ringlet of her blonde hair. "I do love a good gossip session, I won't lie. When you feel like talking about it, I am here. My other girlfriends have practically abandoned me since I entered my confinement. They have their children and their homes. The last tea I attended was the one where I met you at Mi Casa. Perhaps that is why Mrs. Calhoun wanted me to know you. You needed a friend. She knew I did too."

Lucinda saw the hurt in Polly's face and changed the subject quickly. "What an interesting woman she is. So strong and so self-sufficient. Kind of like you, Polly. I, on the other hand, have been living with my in-laws since Ward went off to war. Papa Adger is a dear man, of course. It is Mother Adger who just might be the end of me! I only hope that she will leave us to chat when she brings the tea."

Polly's mind briefly lingered on the thought of Floride. Oh, how Floride and her mother had tried to dissuade her from marrying John. *If only I had my friend's wise counsel now*, she thought.

Mrs. Adger entered the room with a rattling tea tray in her hands. A rose-patterned teapot and three teacups did not go without Polly's notice. Lucinda rolled her eyes as her mother-in-law bent to set the tray down. Polly smiled.

"Here we are, then, settled in for a nice chat," Mrs. Adger said, sitting down across from Polly in an overstuffed rose-print chair. "Girls, I will pour out. Now, will you both take cream?"

Chapter Forty-Two

October 20, 1861

A THIN COLUMN OF WOOD-SMOKE CURLED FROM THE kitchen house as autumn leaves drifted around the yard and crunched under feet. Polly turned the heavy crank a quarter turn and watched the sticky liquid drip into the wooden bucket. She paused to rub her aching lower back and then said, "Reg, this is the last of it." She wiped her hands on her stained apron. "Try not to spill."

The boy quickly took the full pail and lugged it toward the cast iron cooking pot that Ona tended across the small yard. He hoisted the heavy container and watched the juice pour into the already simmering mixture. "I cain't wait fo' syrup!" he exclaimed, his brown eyes wide with excitement. He wiped the rim of the pail with his finger and licked it. "Mmm, mmm." He dipped his finger into the bucket and then held it up to young Silas's lips. The boys grinned and rubbed their stomachs. Reg told the younger boy, "That there is just the juice! Wait till you taste the syrup! Miss Polly say it'll taste like heaven!"

Ona playfully smacked Reg's hand. "Boy, don't get your dirty fingers in the syrup. You'll ruin the whole batch." She used a long paddle to skim foam off the steaming brew. Silas watched Ona work with eager eyes.

"It's a good thing that this cider press lasted the whole season since the other one gave up halfway through the apples." Polly sighed, approaching the group. "I have three on order from Mr. Jones for next year. Good sturdy ones."

Ona smiled and continued to skim off foam. She scooped it into a large crock and would use it later to fertilize the garden.

Silas looked at the contents of the pot and asked, "Why's it green?"

Polly pulled her sleeves back down over her wrists and said, "It will turn as brown as your skin in a bit. You just wait and see!"

Silas beamed.

Ona frowned at the boys and said, "You boys best go now. Git all them clean jars into the wheelbarrow and bring 'em out here. Don't you go breakin' a one of them or that one will be the jar that was to be yours, y'all hear me?"

The boys nodded and raced off to get the wheelbarrow from the barn. Polly was happy to see that they wore the new shirts Cissie had stitched. Polly watched them go, hands on hips, and laughed. "Ona, what are the chances that those two won't break a single jar?"

Ona grumbled and continued her work quietly.

Polly tucked a loose tendril of hair back behind her ear and wiped her brow with her apron. She sighed heavily. Her back throbbed and she was bone tired. She finally crouched and began to disassemble the cider press for cleaning. She regarded Ona silently for a few minutes before speaking. "Ona, you are noticeably quiet these days. Are you well?"

Ona did not look up from her work. She slowly stirred the thickening syrup and finally answered, "I'm well enough. Jes' missin' my boy."

"I know. I wish I could change things. But with John coming back any time now, and with me ready to confront him about what happened with my brothers, maybe it's best that Ben is . . . away and safe," Polly said. "John may lash out."

"Well, at least I got these chi'dren to tend to. Them boys keep me on my toes. That Reg reminds me of Ben at the same age. He got the same build, the same kinda laugh. It jes' reminds me of Ben. But he safe up north, I got to remember that. He and Kate and Sol and Lydia. Ain't nothin' Mr. Stone can do to them."

Polly said a silent prayer that it was true. She thought of the Fugitive Slave Laws and shuddered.

Ona smiled. "It's good to imagine them happy and free, wherever they are."

"And when this war ends, you can exchange letters," Polly added hopefully.

"Maybe you right, Miss Girl. Maybe you right," Ona said.

Polly laughed.

"What you laughin' about?" Ona looked up, confused.

"That's the first time that you have called me Miss Girl in a long time. I had forgotten how much I liked it," she said playfully. She saw Zee run past the boys quickly as he came from the barn, where he had just stabled an excited, whinnying Delightful. He headed across the yard toward Polly at a trot, his face pinched with fear. Polly stood and walked briskly to meet him. "What happened, Zee?"

"It's Courage," he said, breaking into a pitiful whine. "Miss Polly, I don't know what happened. We thought we got it all—that oleander—but he musta' found a patch. He had the colic, ma'am, it's what I thought, but was feelin' a little better, so I turned him out with Delightful in the north pasture. When I went to get him, I found him laid out by the fence line. There was that oleander growin' there and he had eat up some bits o' leaves." Zee held out a handful of the noxious plant. "I'm sorry, Miss Polly. We thought we got it all a while back."

"Take me to him," Polly snapped. She hurried along after Zadoc, her heart pounding. Ben would never have let this happen. *My beautiful and neglected colt,* she thought. Polly berated herself for not checking the pasture herself or spending more time with the young colt or for riding the mare. Both horses were turned out each morning and placed back in their stalls each night. Polly had not even attempted to train Courage to the bit or saddle and Delightful had not been taken out to gallop in months. And Delightful had been so colicky herself recently. *I should have known.*

Polly followed Zadoc into the north pasture, green and lovely in the autumn sunshine. But sure enough, along the fence line, there were small clumps of leggy oleander here and there. Zee climbed over the split rail fence and then turned to look at Polly sheepishly, having forgotten she wore heavy, long skirts.

"Good Lord, Zee, the gate is too far away. Help me over," she said, extending her hand. Polly bundled her skirts in one hand, exposing her stockings and petticoats. Zadoc grabbed Polly's hand and helped his mistress over the fence. She hopped onto the ground and headed toward the colt, lying on his side, and breathing heavily. The animal shivered and spasmed, blowing out bits of oleander in the froth around his pale lips.

Polly bent and laid her head on the colt's heaving flank. He was cold to the touch and nearly gone. "Zadoc, get Ona. Tell her to get my pistol. She knows where I keep it." The young man turned and ran for the kitchen house.

Polly stroked the colt's withers and whispered into his soft ear. "You are a beautiful boy. You deserved better than this. I had no idea it was this poisonous." Tears welled in her eyes and she began to cry in choking sobs. Her tears dampened the horse's bristly black mane and ran down his neck. He breathed hard, shuddered, and then lay still. Polly wailed and fell across the colt's body. She covered her face with her hands and cried into his withers.

Polly felt the weight of a woolen blanket draped across her spent body and soon someone had lifted her up. She instinctively threw her arms around his neck and leaned into Tom's chest. The soothing scent of wood smoke and tobacco emanated from his clothing. "I can't do this," she whispered. "I can't."

"Sshhh, now. Yes, you can. It will be alright. Everything will be alright," Tom murmured softly as he carried her across the field toward the house.

— • —

TOM ORDERED GEORGE TO TAKE SEVERAL MEN and scour the pastures for any remaining oleander. With leather gloves, the men pulled it up by the roots and burned the noxious plants down by the river, well away from anyone. The cows never pastured in the same fields as the horses, but Tom had the men check every last inch of the fields and livestock pens for the poisonous plant.

Polly grieved the colt's passing and blamed herself for her inattention. She threw herself into caring for her horse and curried the mare until her coat shone. She fed Delightful extra mash and turnips and took her out for gallops along the property line.

— • —

ZADOC'S REMORSE WAS ALSO DEEP. He enjoyed caring for the workhorses and took pride in his precarious position as Ben's replacement with Delightful. Tending stock was highly preferable to working in the fields. The death of the colt was a huge hit financially for Whitehall, and emotionally for his mistress. He knew he would face consequences for missing the deadly oleander in the pastures. Zee wondered if losing both his job and share of sorghum were soon to be his fate. Or worse. At River Wood, men had been stripped and flogged for lesser offenses.

Polly had called a meeting of all the hands for early evening after chores were complete. Zee busied himself at his work, watching as the autumn sun slanted further across the floor of the barn. He mucked out stalls and salved a milk cow's sore udders. He checked on a sow about to farrow. He examined the workhorses' hooves for cracks and short shoes.

His attention strayed from his chores as he worried about why his mistress would do such a new thing. A meeting. When Tom had announced the meeting, the hands began to gossip among themselves immediately. Even the women were not privy to the reason for the meeting, according to George. Tom had just directed the slaves to gather near his cabin in the early dusk, before they went in for their suppers. Were more to be sold or given away? Was Zee to be beaten publicly for his mistake?

Zee heard George ring the quitting time bell and he quickly checked Delightful's stall for any fresh manure. Seeing the mare contentedly resting her head on the stall door, he stroked her mane and reached in his pocket for an apple. The mare's soft lips nibbled at the fruit before taking the whole thing in her mouth. Zee whispered, "I'm so sorry about yo' baby. Wish me luck, girl."

Zee closed and secured the heavy barn doors and headed quickly for Mr. Roper's cabin. In the gathering dark, he saw the hands milling around under the large bashful oak, its brown leaves quivering in the chilly evening breeze. Somewhere, a barn owl hooted. Silas and Reg stood near the porch, scratching in the dirt with sticks. The women were the last to arrive, from the direction of the kitchen house. Cissie and Ona pulled a small wagon behind them, and Polly followed with a large box in her hands.

— • —

TOM ROPER STOOD ON HIS NARROW FRONT PORCH, lantern held high, as Polly climbed the steps and stood beside him. The men looked up at their mistress and waited.

Polly cleared her throat and spoke. "Thank you for being here promptly. I know you are all hungry for your suppers, so I will be quick." The slaves stared at Polly, blank-faced.

"Whitehall had a successful year. We all worked hard. George, thanks to you and the men for tending the old orchard. We were able to sell peaches, apples, and cider in town. The cotton work was hard as always, but we had a good crop." Polly did not dare mention the fate of the cotton, lest it remind them that there was a war on, a battle against their freedom.

She marveled at the field hands, standing stone-faced with their hats in hands. Some of the men had been with her father as long as she could remember. Others had been purchased near the time of her father's death. These men did the hard work at Whitehall. They wore whatever clothing she gave them, ate what food she offered, and slept when given permission. *How did they not rise up and attack, slit my throat as I slept?* she wondered.

Polly took a deep breath and continued, "When Mr. Roper calls your name, come forward and collect your share of the sorghum syrup." She pointed to the wagon holding gallon jugs of the sweet elixir. The men turned and began to smile and mumble to one another. A gallon! They were hopeful for a pint jar apiece. A gallon of syrup would last all winter. Syrup on biscuits, cornbread, and in grits. Syrup with ham. Syrup in watered-down tea.

Tom stepped forward and pointed to George, who stood near Cissie. "George, you did as fine a job for Mrs. Stone as I have ever seen. And Cissie and Ona, not a man here would be able to work without your good cooking. Come up and take your syrup."

Ona and Cissie lifted their jugs proudly, and George handed his to wide-eyed Silas, who struggled to hold it. As Silas accepted the prize, Polly saw Reg frown with an apparent twinge of jealousy.

Tom then pointed to a tall man in the back of the group. "Cyrus. Come on up." The lanky man pushed through the others and went up to the wagon, where George handed him his jug. The man whooped and hollered, which broke the ice. He held the jug high and whooped again. The men clapped him on the back as he reentered the group, laughing and smiling.

Polly grinned and called out, "Thank you for your work, Cyrus." The man turned, surprised, and tipped his hat. "You welcome, ma'am."

Tom called the eight field hands one by one. Polly sheepishly tried to remember their names as they came forward. After Cyrus' example, Meenie, Jake, Sam, Reevus, Job, Robert, and James all tipped their hats and thanked Polly for the treasure. Zadoc moved back into the shadows and leaned against the oak tree.

Tom stepped to the porch railing and called for Reg. The boy's shoulders relaxed and he came forward eagerly. George slapped him on the back and handed him a jug. "You work hard, boy. Keep it up, you hear?" George said gruffly. Reg grinned and nodded enthusiastically.

There was one jug of syrup left in the wagon. Tom glanced at a forlorn Zee, cleared his throat, and said, "This last jug is for Zadoc. Zee, come on up." Zee ambled forward and lifted the lone jug out of the wagon. He turned to go when Tom called out. "Just a minute, Zee. Mrs. Stone would like to say something."

Polly gazed at the scared young man. "Zee, in addition to caring for the stock, I would like you to take your permanent place as my new blacksmith. You'll have to go to Fort Hill for a spell to learn the trade. Do you think you can handle the responsibility? The blacksmith there has been with Mrs. Calhoun for years. Reg will help with the horses and other stock, to free up your time while you learn."

A small smile played at the corners of Polly's mouth, and Zee broke out into a relieved grin. "Oh yes, ma'am. Yes, indeed." Zee tipped his hat and mouthed a "thank you" to her in the flickering lamplight.

Reg sat down in the dirt, cradling his jug in his lap. The men began to talk and several turned to go, when Tom put two fingers in his mouth and blew a piercing whistle. The group quieted. "Mrs. Stone has one more thing to say."

Polly had not rehearsed what she was about to say and do but felt the need of it before John Stone came back.

"I value the work all of you do for me. Evidence of that is your share of the sorghum tonight. But there will be further evidence. From now on, if the farm is successful, you will profit. We will move to make the orchards and the sorghum our primary crops for the duration of the . . . conflict up north. The success of these crops will hinge on your hard work. If the crops fail, you'll get nothing. But if they succeed, you will benefit."

The men looked at each other in confusion. Finally, Cyrus raised his hand shyly. "What you mean?"

"I mean, Cyrus, that you will get a share of the peaches, the apples, the cider, and the sorghum at the end of next season. Your share will be in proportion to how well we do at market. It is my way of recognizing your work on the farm."

The men looked at one another in amazement. Cissie turned and hugged her husband tightly.

"And since this was an especially important year for me and the crops have already been sold, I have a special reward at hand for you. An eagle penny for each of you. Wages earned." The slaves gasped and murmured among themselves. Polly removed her coin purse from her dress pocket and stepped off the porch. She went up to each man and called him by name, as she handed each his penny. When the field hands had received their pennies, Tom dismissed them all and the men whooped and hollered and rejoiced on their way back to their cabins.

George and Cissie stepped up to face Polly. George shook his head and said, "Miss Polly, I ain't never thought I would see the day. Thank you, ma'am. Thank you so much. We in high cotton now. I's proud to work for ya."

Polly reached into her purse and then handed George and Cissie two pennies each. Their eyes grew wide.

Polly shrugged and said, "Heaven knows where you will be allowed to spend it, but we can work something out. Cissie, you'd better go now. I know those men are hungry and want something to put that syrup on."

Cissie nodded and wiped her eyes with her apron and hurried away with George and Silas, into the darkness.

Polly said quietly, "I think that went well."

Tom asked, "Can I walk you back to the house, Miss Polly?"

"No thank you, Tom," Polly said. "I would like to speak with Ona privately on our walk back." Tom handed Polly the lantern, tipped his hat, and went into his cabin. The door closed softly and Polly and Ona stood together in the circle of lamplight. "Will you walk with me, Ona?" The old woman murmured a soft assent and the women set off.

The pair walked in silence down the dark footpath both women knew by heart. Polly felt the distance that hung heavy between them. Ona still blamed Polly for Ben's absence.

Finally, Polly broke the quiet. "I haven't given you your wages."

"I don't need wages. Like you say, where is a slave gonna spend money?" Ona asked. Polly had never heard Ona so bitter.

"Come eat with me, Ona. I am lonely for your company and I have something for you, in the house."

Ona mumbled under her breath, but followed Polly, tears in her eyes.

Polly led the way quietly. She remembered the last time that she had asked Ona to sit in the big house dining room and share a meal. It was the evening when she promised Ona her freedom. It had seemed like the happiest moment of Ona's life. And now, her world was torn apart.

Ona followed Polly up the back steps and into the warm house. The dining room was set for two, with a covered platter set in the center of the polished table. The aroma of roasted meat filled the room. Ona gazed at Polly in confusion. "Who cooked yo' meal?"

Polly laughed and lifted the lid. "I did. And it may be obvious when you taste it. Please sit down."

Ona sat in the upholstered chair and fingered the polished silverware as if it were a priceless artifact. "My. This is fancy," she said softly. She watched as Polly placed her own napkin in her lap and then did the same. "I ain't ate in the big house since the time you gave me my freedom paper."

Polly smiled and reached for a decanter. "Would you join me in a glass of whiskey?"

Ona's eyes widened. "I ain't never had a taste. I seed how it worked on Martin back in the day." She chuckled, then pushed her glass forward and added, "I try a taste."

Polly smiled and poured the amber liquid into Ona's glass. She poured one for herself and lifted it up. "We will have a toast. Lift your glass, Ona," she directed. "To Ben and Kate. May they fare well." Her eyes glinted but Ona's face fell, as she touched her glass to Polly's.

Ona sipped the whiskey and swirled it around on her tongue and swallowed. "Hmm. I don't see the attraction." She harrumphed.

Polly sipped her drink and felt its warming sensation in her chest. "You will." She laughed and began to butter a biscuit. "I think it's wonderful."

Finally, Ona picked up her fork and nibbled at the green beans. "I 'spect you got somethin' to say that I ain't gonna like. But I 'preciate the chance to eat in the big house," she said grudgingly.

Polly reached into her pocket and pulled out two pennies. She slid them across the table. "Your wages."

Ona picked up the coins and dropped them into her apron pocket. "Thank you, Miss Polly," she said. She picked up her glass and drank another swallow of whiskey.

"My goodness, Ona, you are hard to please. Oh, alright, here . . ." She reached back into her pocket and pulled out a folded sheet of paper and slid it across the table mischievously. "Your surprise."

"What's that?" Ona regarded the paper cautiously.

"Read it. I know that Ben taught you how to read last year. Then I can explain it. For your own safety and theirs, we will burn it afterwards." Polly watched as Ona picked up the page and began to read it.

Dear Friend,

> Words cannot describe how desperate I was to get word to you all sooner, but the journey was long and hard. I am happy to tell you that we made it and our small packages fared well. We traveled further than planned. We have set up a smithy shop in a small village far north of the big lake and cherry orchards, where I am kept busy with orders for grates, fence gates, and household items. I am able to provide for my family.

My wife is well, and she expects a child next month. I miss my
kinfolk more than words can say. Please tell them I love them.
I know the mail is unreliable, and war continues, but I am
hopeful that you will get this letter.

Your friend

Ona put down the letter and looked at Polly. "Is this from Ben? I ain't never seen what his writin' might look like," she whispered, a hand to her chest.

"It is from Ben. It arrived the other day. It was addressed to me, but in a different hand. How it got through, we can only wonder. There is no mail between the Union and the Confederacy. I asked Mr. Roper to explain it." The women leaned over the letter.

Polly continued, "He thinks one of the Underground conductors was kind enough to get it into the Confederacy and then post it."

Ona nodded, pressing the letter to her chest. "From Ben!" She grinned. Ona read it and looked up expectantly. "What do it mean?"

Polly smiled. "This is what it means. Mr. Roper said that the packages are the children. They are safe. They made it north of the big lake. That means to the north of Michigan!" Polly searched Ona's face for a sign of recognition. "That means they are safe in Canada." Ona shook her head in confusion.

Polly stood and left the room, her heels clicking quickly down the hall. She returned with an atlas and laid the heavy book on the table. She thumbed through it until she found a map of the United States.

"See, we are here." She stabbed her finger at South Carolina. "You were born in Charlotte, North Carolina. That is right here. But Canada is way up past the top of our country. See it?" she asked excitedly. "Canada is an entirely different country. It is quite cold, I am sure. But they are safe there. And free! No one can go get them and bring them back!"

"Why, that looks like a mitten." Ona laughed, poking her brown finger at Michigan. "And it is so far away! But they is safe? Oh, praise Jesus!" Ona's eyes glistened. "And Kate is expectin' a baby?" She laughed and clutched her hands to her chest. "A grandbaby!"

Polly's heart swelled for the woman steeped in grief for so long. Her face grew serious and she reached for Ona's hand in an uncharacteristic display of affection. Ona's eyes grew wide as Polly squeezed her hand.

"I gave you that freedom paper long ago. If you want to try to join them, Mr. Roper says that the same people who helped Ben and Kate have a trip leaving in a month or so," Polly said softly. "If you are up for the journey . . . we think you should go. Hopefully, you would not have to ride under crates of peaches." She squeezed Ona's hand again and let it go.

Ona cocked her head and regarded Polly skeptically. "What you mean? You mean I could go live with my boy? And be free?"

"If you want to join them, we have a plan. I would write a bill of sale and Mr. Roper could conduct you to a buyer. From there, I am not allowed to know what happens. And it isn't without danger. Many people do not make it."

Ona sat back in her chair, her eyes wide. "You mean I could leave Whitehall and be with them? In Canada?"

Polly looked at the woman who had practically raised her. "Ona, you are like family to me. I hope you know that. But Ben is your son. And I promised you your freedom."

Ona placed both of her brown hands around Polly's hand and squeezed. "I want to be with them with all my heart. But Miss Girl, who gonna take care of you? He will hurt you," she said.

Polly knew who Ona meant but dismissed the woman's worry with a toss of her head. "He has no say in the concerns of Whitehall. No reason to stay around here. And this time it is just a two-week leave . . . I hope for an annulment. I have an attorney friend in Pendleton aware of the entire story. And I have Mr. Roper here."

"Then I would like to try. To be with my family," Ona said eagerly. "Oh, land sakes! I cain't believe it! But what do I tell the others?"

"Nothing," Polly said quickly. "You cannot mention it to anyone. For their safety and yours. After you are gone, I will say that I sold you away. The others already think I sold away Ben and Kate. I know what they must think of me." Polly frowned. "But if you leave in a month's time, it should be well after John has come and gone on his leave."

Ona grinned. "Thank you, Miss Girl. God bless you."

Polly blinked her eyes and looked heavenward. "Yes. I wish he would."

— • —

THE NEXT AFTERNOON, POLLY WATCHED as the men loaded the wooden crates packed with sorghum syrup into the wagon. The day was fine and breezy. She decided to ride Delightful into town, following the wagonload of sorghum syrup. Tom drove the wagon, while Reg and Zee sat in the back to steady the precious cargo when the wagon hit ruts and potholes in the road. They watched dutifully, eyeing the wooden crates of syrup, the jars gleaming deep gold in the sunlight. Several times a dark hand shot out to steady a crate or save one from a pothole taken too hard. When the wagon finally stopped in front of the Mercantile, Polly climbed down from the saddle while the men waited in the wagon.

The dim and smoky interior of the store could not hide the bare shelves. Besides the barrel of pickles, a row of tinctures, a display of tinned food, and a few bolts of flannel and calico, there was little to be purchased. Boxes of ammunition and a few of Mrs. Wright's home-canned preserves rounded out the inventory.

"Good afternoon, Mrs. Stone." Mr. Jones looked up from his newspaper and pipe. "Your new press came in."

"Wonderful," Polly said. "Although I ordered three. Mr. Jones, will your man help my boys unload the syrup and load the presses?"

Mr. Jones nodded and called for his boy. A skinny teenager emerged from the stockroom and headed outside. Mr. Jones puffed on his pipe and said, "I'm glad you have the syrup. We've had several folks this week looking for it after that sign you put in the window."

"It is important to advertise, Mr. Jones. Now, what about my other presses?"

Mr. Jones exhaled a plume of pipe smoke. "These days, I am surprised you got any of them. The maker is just over in Toccoa, Georgia, and deliveries weren't always this slow. But with the war . . ."

"Don't remind me," Polly said good-naturedly. "Now, how will you take payment for this press? May I give you Confederate notes?" Polly reached into her bag for a small leather wallet with bills her husband sent.

"Yes ma'am. Didn't know you had money to spend. Thought you were just bartering lately. Let's work out the math after I see how much syrup you have." Mr. Jones laid down his pipe as Tom entered with the first crate of syrup. He placed the crate on the floor gently.

"Just wait until you taste it." Polly smiled. She lifted a jar of the deep brown syrup out of the box and held it out to the proprietor. "Have a bit," she said. "You'll not find a better syrup in the district."

The man pried off the lid and stuck his index finger into the jar. He placed his dripping finger into his mouth and rolled the sweet substance around on his tongue. "Mrs. Stone, it is deeee-licious! I know that it will sell in no time. It might bring me some new customers. I believe we agreed on sixty cents a gallon. How much you got?"

"We shook hands on one dollar a gallon, Mr. Jones," Polly corrected. "I have fifty gallons, in quart jars." Zadoc and Reg reentered and placed several more crates on the floor. Soon the crates were stacked like blocks around the perimeter of the store.

The merchant scowled but began to add up figures in his head.

Polly interrupted his computation. "It comes to $50, Mr. Jones. I have done the math. We must also account for the presses. And I need some kerosene and a new lamp."

The man grumbled and went toward the stockroom.

Tom appeared behind Polly. "Do we unload the beer?"

Polly shook her head and whispered, "I think we will get a better price from the Inn. We'll go there next."

Tom looked at Polly admiringly. "You have quite a head for business, Miss Polly."

Polly smiled. "Why, thank you, Mr. Roper."

Mr. Jones came from the stockroom and placed a lamp and a jug of kerosene on the counter. He dropped a receipt on the counter, too. "With the kerosene, the lamp, and the press, I still owe you $35." He turned to his boy and shouted, "Billy, the press is in the back. Get it." He peeled several notes from a roll and handed them to Polly. Polly took the bills and placed them in her wallet while Billy carried the new press to the wagon.

Polly waited expectantly by the store counter, purse in hand while Billy loaded her purchases.

"Is there something else I can do for you, Mrs. Stone?" Mr. Jones asked.

"I will need my crates back, sir. Can Billy also unload the syrup?" she asked sweetly.

— • —

THE DRIVE BACK TO WHITEHALL WAS A MERRY ONE. Polly had managed to get top price for her sorghum beer at the Pendleton Inn, and her small wallet was stuffed with bills. To celebrate, Tom and Polly had shared a meal at the Inn. On the drive home, Polly had uncorked two bottles of the cool beer and she and Tom sipped the fizzy drink. Zee was ecstatic, riding Delightful as she trotted behind the wagon where Reg slept to the rocking motion. The sun was close to setting on the late fall day and the western sky swirled in shades of pink and orange.

Polly felt warm and relaxed after a few sips of the brew. She had done it. Sold her sorghum for a good price. She closed her eyes and removed her straw bonnet, to enjoy the autumn breeze in her hair. There was no conversation, which was fine with Polly. Tom was a man of few words anyway. They sat together quietly, the rhythm of the horses' hooves lulling Polly to doze.

When they got home, she would take the money from the sorghum and add it to the hidden stash from her bank withdrawal. Frustrated that it would not earn her any interest, she knew that at least it would be safe from John, should he return and try to secure funds for his deal with McQueen.

Polly tilted the beer to her lips and finished it. She stretched her arms and yawned, then turned slightly to watch Tom as he drove. His stained hat was low over his head and his scraggly beard was in need of a good trim. He could do with a new shirt or two, she thought. He would clean up fine. She smiled and drifted into sleep.

Polly was still drowsing in the moving wagon when she felt it pull to a stop. Home.

"Whoa, horse," she heard Tom mutter too quietly. She opened her eyes and saw a stately brougham parked in front of the Whitehall veranda in the fading light. A Confederate flag hung limply from a small rod. The lone black driver sat hunched in the seat, his livery fine and new. Her heart sank as they neared the carriage.

Jack saw his mistress and barked a welcome from the veranda.

Polly called out to the driver. "Are you Colonel's McQueen's man?"

The slave nodded. "Yes'm, I'm deliverin' soldiers home on leave from his unit."

Polly's hands trembled as she patted her hair into place and covered her head with the bonnet. She tied the bow with shaking fingers.

Tom leaped off the wagon seat and came around to help her down. She only vaguely heard him give instructions to Reg and Zadoc, who quickly began to lead Delightful to the barn. She clutched her purse tightly in one hand and gripped Tom's hand in her other one, afraid to let go.

"Do you want me to come inside?" he asked, worried.

"No . . . no, I'll be fine," Polly said. "We knew he would be coming back."

Tom frowned at the fear behind her courageous tone. "I'll be right here, steps away."

"But . . . Tom, will you hold onto this while John is home?" She handed Tom the brocaded bag, its contents the proceeds from the day's success in town. He took the bag and tucked it inside his jacket. Polly inhaled and then exhaled audibly. "Go on now. But pray for me." She smiled nervously.

Tom tipped his hat. "I always do."

Chapter Forty-Three

POLLY PUSHED OPEN THE FRONT DOOR AND THE TANG OF cigar smoke hit her at once. Jack pranced into the hallway, yapping at the strangers in his home. John was back. Immediately, Cissie trundled out of the back hall and met Polly with wide eyes.

Polly and Cissie exchanged glances as Cissie helped her out of her coat. Polly untied her bonnet and handed it to Cissie. "He's in the library with someone. He asked where you was an' I tol' him you and Mr. Tom went to town, is all," the woman whispered.

"Thank you, Cissie," Polly said too brightly. "You may go. Wait in the kitchen house. I'll come for you if he decides to eat later." She removed her gloves and laid them on the hall table, patted her hair, and smoothed her gown before crossing the hall and throwing open the library doors.

"John. And Mr. Adger! Or Dr. Adger, I should say!" Both men stood. Polly kissed John quickly on the cheek without making eye contact. She extended her hand to the young surgeon and clasped his in her shaking palm. "Dr. Adger, congratulations on the impending arrival! I was just out to call on Lucinda last week. My, she looks wonderful. I know that your parents are taking excellent care of her."

The young doctor beamed at the mention of his wife. "That is good news. I regret that I cannot stay. I am anxious to get on home to her. I am sure you understand."

Adger ran his hand through his dark hair. "It was good of you to have me in for a drink, Captain."

John downed the contents of his glass and shook hands with his friend. Polly noticed he leaned hard on a cane. "Good luck to you, Ward. Fourteen days. Let's make the most of it." He winked at Ward. Polly felt her stomach convulse.

Adger turned to Polly. "It was nice to see you, Mrs. Stone. I know that you will enjoy having your husband home for a time. Now if you'll excuse me, I better let the Colonel's boy get me to town." He smiled and firmly shoved his hat onto his head before striding from the room.

Polly turned to John. "So, you're home." She tried to smile politely as John came toward her.

"I am." John kissed Polly firmly and wrapped one arm tightly around her waist as Jack gave a low growl. "I see you got yourself a damned dog."

Polly pulled back and said, "It seemed the thing to do. There is a lot we must talk about, John. A great deal has happened in nine months. Can I get you some dinner?"

"And maybe we can make a great deal more happen in another nine months," John said, reaching to loosen the pins in Polly's hair.

"John, I've only just come in." She pulled back forcefully and patted her hair. "Are you quite well? You wrote of fevers. And how is your leg?"

John frowned and dropped his hand. "The best medicine for me was to leave the camp and come back home. I have had neither chills nor fever since we left Virginia. There was so much sickness and filth . . . the lack of sanitation in the camps, even for officers' quarters, is hard to comprehend." He looked at Polly and added, "This is hardly a topic I want to discuss with my wife at the very moment I return home. And it is not the greeting I expected."

"I—I am sorry. You caught me unawares. We are just back from Pendleton," Polly stammered. She pointed to the cane. "It was thoughtful of Colonel McQueen to send you home by his carriage."

"Why were you in Pendleton?" John asked, turning to pour another whiskey.

"We sold sorghum. We turned it into syrup and we just sold it," she said nervously.

"We?" John asked.

"Zadoc, Tom, and I took the sorghum syrup into town. We traded it for cider presses and kerosene. Things like that . . ." Her voice trailed away. She despised how John made her feel small. "You wouldn't recognize the Mercantile now. There is nothing to buy. Everything must be bartered."

"This damn war," John muttered, swallowing his drink.

Grateful for the change of subject, Polly sat down on the sofa. "Was the fighting awful?"

John lit a fresh cigar and nodded. "Words cannot describe the things I have seen. The ways that men can die." He limped toward the sofa and sat down next to Polly. Exhaling a plume smoke, he leaned forward on his knees. "It isn't something I want to discuss while home on leave." His eyes narrowed. "What do you think about my deal with Colonel McQueen? You did get my letter. From Private Stevens? I asked him to hand-deliver it."

Polly sat up. She realized that as many times as she had rehearsed how she would begin her story, it had not helped. There was so much to tell and the words began to tumble out without order. "Yes, I did. Your soldier brought it to me. But John, no cotton was picked at River Wood. Without Wilkins, I don't know what happened. And the cotton factors burned what they could buy in the state. . . . Didn't you know? I wrote to you," Polly lied. "I didn't plant as much cotton this year. Smart growers didn't."

John put down his cigar and leaned back, throwing his arms across the back of the sofa. "Slow down. What do you mean without Wilkins?"

"Well, he took off soon after you went away. He just disappeared.

The slaves there were left on their own. So I took Kate back. Wilkins had abused her. Zee's mother, Jane, died and his father has since died." Polly attempted to remain calm but realized her nerves were getting the best of her as she stammered.

"Clay Wilkins is gone? Who the hell is running my place?" he growled. Polly had forgotten how quickly John's temper could escalate.

Polly shrugged and held up her hands. "That's all I know, John. So there isn't any money for your deal with McQueen. We can ride over tomorrow and visit Mr. Legarre, if you don't believe me," she said. "Unless you have money somewhere. He assured me the deal was null and void because of Wilkins' absence."

"So as my wife, you didn't think it prudent to send Roper over there to manage my affairs?"

"I wrote to you," she said softly.

"You should have done a damn sight more than that!"

Polly bristled. "As I recall, you told me to stay away, and you instructed each overseer to stay to his own place of employment."

"Then how did you know about Zadoc's parents? Or find it necessary to retrieve Kate?" John asked.

"My goodness." Polly thought quickly. "You gave Kate to me as a wedding present, and then snatched her back to Wilkins when he whined about house help. An overseer—a man you promised me would be let go. Of course, I went to check on her. I found that Kate had been attacked by that horrible man. I had to get her away. And when I saw Zee's parents so ill, I left him to tend his mother for a time. After Jane died, I brought his father here to die in peace."

"Wilkins hurt Kate?" John asked, frowning.

Polly realized that she had not planned what to say to John about Kate and Ben. She felt the room grow warm and groped for the right words.

"Kate is . . . fine." She touched a shaking hand to her throat. She needed time. His anger over Wilkins simmered too close to the surface and threatened to explode.

"Goodness, it is warm in here. The exertion of the day in town has left me parched. I need a drink. May I bring you another whiskey?" she asked.

John stood with some effort. "I can get it." He limped to the cabinet where the liquors were kept. "I had hoped we could get past our falling out from the winter, and try again," he said, his back to Polly. The image of him barricading Mrs. Kemp in the burning store flashed through her mind in an instant. *He will hurt you*, Ona had warned.

Polly watched as he poured a small shot for her and a larger one for himself. She regretted not tossing out all of the remaining alcohol at Whitehall before he came home. But sensing his anger, she exhaled and tried to smile. "Pour yourself a double. You deserve it. Your trip has been a long one. Come sit and relax. We will have supper soon. Then you can sleep. Tomorrow will be a new day and we can talk and make plans." *Maybe getting drunk will calm him down*, she hoped.

John downed his own glass, turned, and crossed the room, drink in hand. "That sounds fine," he said, wearily. "It has been a long trip." He leaned over and slid the whiskey across the table toward Polly before taking a seat next to her. He eyed her guardedly and pointed a finger at her. "Something is different. You are different."

Polly picked up the glass and downed the whiskey in a single shot. It seared her throat, but then warmed her belly and gave her courage. "I am different, John. It has been a long year for me, too." She leaned back on the settee, her eyes closed. "A very long year, indeed."

"How so?" John asked, placing his hand on her thigh.

Polly instinctively flinched. "John, be patient with me. We haven't been together in quite a long time."

John wiped his mouth with the back of his hand. "I'm not a patient man."

"Be that as it may—" she began.

John leaned over and grabbed Polly at the nape of her neck and pulled her to him. His mouth was rough on her own, his tongue thick in her throat. He pushed her back on the couch, despite her protestations.

"Cissie is in the house." She gasped, pushing on his chest. "Not here. Not like this. You're hurting me."

"Damn Cissie," he murmured, pulling her hair hard. His breath reeked of alcohol. He fumbled with the buttons of his pants. His other hand bunched Polly's skirts above her waist. His weight kept her pinned to the sofa.

"John, no!" she said sharply. She pulled at his hair, to no effect. He kissed her harshly, crushing her mouth, bruising her lips. He pulled hard on the bodice of her gown and Polly heard the fabric rip. She felt the sharp sensation of him entering her and she cried out, but to no one.

After a minute, he shuddered and rolled off her, spent. She sat up, eyes spilling with hot tears, and covered her legs with her skirts. Her lip was bleeding and her dress badly torn.

She sat up and looked at the man, lying drunk on the settee, limp, pants splayed open.

"That's right, Polly. You just keep on looking at me with that holier-than-thou face of yours," he slurred.

"You disgust me," she hissed, holding her torn bodice together with one hand. "That is not the way you should treat your wife. You are a piece of human trash. I want an annulment and—"

She did not see the punch coming until John's fist connected with her cheekbone. The searing pain sent shock waves through her body and her head snapped back and hit the table edge behind her. She slid, unconscious, to the floor of her father's library.

— • —

THE GRANDFATHER CLOCK IN THE HALLWAY tolled nine times and stirred Polly from her faint. The room was dark, except for the glow of embers in the fireplace. Her head throbbed. She opened her eyes and instinctively touched the swollen side of her face. She winced and tasted the iron in her blood. Her nose was sticky with it. Her lower lip was split and oozing.

Polly wanted to call out to Ona or to Cissie but remembered she had sent them away. In the darkness, she felt along the wall to get her bearings before she tried to stand. As she did, the pounding in her head increased and she gasped in pain. She slowly made her way to the hall and began to ascend the stairs. Each step was a task, but she gripped the rail and went slowly.

At the top of the stairs, she saw that the door to John's adjoining bedroom was ajar. She eased closer and peered into the inky blackness. The fire was smoldering in the fireplace and she heard a rhythmic snore coming from the four-poster bed.

Polly passed the doorway quietly and entered her own room. She closed and locked the door softly and pocketed the key. She removed her shoes and padded across the floor to the doorway between the bedrooms. She closed the door without a sound and quietly turned the deadbolt.

Moonlight cast shadows across the floor of dark limbs, bare of leaves. She sat down on the bed and dropped her head in her hands. Her entire body ached. Suddenly she stood and crossed to her bureau. She opened the top drawer and removed her father's pistol from under a stack of linens. She checked to be sure it was loaded and then placed it on her bedside table. Only then did she strip off her torn and soiled clothing and drop into bed.

— • —

THE MORNING LIGHT STREAMED THROUGH Polly's window. Jack scratched on the other side of her door and whined to come in, but she lay still in the bed. Someone tapped on the door and called softly, "Miss Polly. I got yo' breakfast."

Polly eased herself out of bed and crouched down to rummage for the key in the pile of dirty clothing. She wore only her underclothes but crossed to the bedroom door and unlocked and opened it.

Jack shot into the room, eager to lick and jump on his mistress but Polly waved him off and gingerly moved back to the bed.

Ona entered the room with the tray and gasped loudly. "Miss Girl! What happened?" She hurriedly placed the tray on Polly's bedside table, and her eyes widened when she saw the pistol there too. "Never mind. I think I can puzzle it out myse'f." She grabbed the pitcher and poured cool water into a basin. She dampened a cloth and began to clean Polly's split lip.

Polly cried out and pulled away, but then nodded and let Ona tend to her. The area around Polly's left eye was badly bruised, and her face was swollen. Ona dabbed at the crusted blood around Polly's nose and soon the water in the basin was tinged pink with blood.

"Oh, Miss Girl. I'm so sorry he did this to you," Ona whispered.

Polly looked toward the open door. "Is he still in there?" It hurt her mouth to speak.

Ona shook her head. "No ma'am. He up and rode out to River Wood early. Took Mr. Roper with him. He was angry so I thought it was best to wait till he was gone to bring up yo' breakfast." She shook her head.

Polly leaned back into her pillows and sighed deeply. "The last thing I should do is drag Mr. Roper into this mess, right? John will only be home for two weeks. I can survive two weeks if I can manage to stay away from him," she muttered.

"Don't bring Mr. Roper into your bedroom problems is what I say." Ona hesitated before adding, "But I got a tincture for your mouth. Did he hurt yo' privates?"

Polly blushed shamefully and nodded.

"Then we need to get you into a tub. I got a salve fo' your nether places if you tore. Poor girl . . ." Ona reached out and smoothed Polly's hair.

"Thank you, Ona. A hot bath, and then I will be ready to face this mess."

"Yes, Miss Girl," Ona said. "I git right on it. Will he be wantin' meals with you while he home?"

"I certainly hope not but ask Cissie to serve meals for him while he is here. I don't want him taking out his anger on you. He knows how fond I am of you. Stay in the kitchen. I will eat with him, if only to placate him."

— • —

POLLY EMERGED FROM HER BATH feeling markedly better. She dressed and sat at her vanity table and began to powder her face. The bruised cheek diminished some with each application. The black eye and split lip were not so easily concealed. Polly was grateful that she had no reason to go into town that morning. She opened a small jar and dabbed a bit of Ona's healing balm on her tender cheek and lip.

Polly selected a simple calico gown, dressed herself, as was her custom, and descended the stairs. Cissie gasped when she saw Polly's face but said nothing. Polly made for the barn, Jack at her heels. A thick fog had rolled in off the river that morning, and Polly was grateful for the cover. She passed two field hands about twenty-five yards away but the mist concealed her face.

"Mornin' Mizz Polly," one of the men called.

"Good morning, Cyrus, Meenie," Polly called out into the gray air. She entered the open barn and found Zadoc preparing to let the draft horses out into the pasture. His eyes widened and he looked at Polly with surprise. "Mizz Polly, you alright?"

"Yes, Zee. I am fine. I tripped and fell. Did Mr. Stone take my horse?" she asked worriedly.

"Yes, ma'am," Zee said, head down. "He came in here 'bout the time Reg finished milkin,' and took her. He asked me where was her tack. I'm sorry but I didn't know what else to do." The man shrugged.

"There was nothing you could have done. I am sure that Delightful will be fine." Polly strummed her fingers nervously on the edge of a stall. "Did he say anything else?"

"Jes' that he wanted to see Mr. Roper before he rode out to River Wood. He left and headed that way."

Zadoc hesitated for a moment and finally asked, "Mizz Polly, can I tell ya' somethin' else?"

"Of course, Zee," Polly said. Polly's heart began to pound in her temples and her swollen cheek throbbed.

"When Mr. Stone came in, Reg was in the cow's stall. He was so nervous that he knocked over the milk pail. He was scared stiff. That boy couldn't wait to get outta here and he hightailed it back to Ona's cabin." Zee shook his head. "I don't want to get no one in trouble," he mumbled. "You been good to me. I have to tell ya' what I know." Zadoc frowned at the wounds on Polly's face.

Polly touched her cheek self-consciously. "Go on, Zee," she said.

Zadoc shook his head. "Reg's mama was one of the girls that got sold away a long time ago at River Wood. Mr. John an' Mr. Sam beat on her a lot. They whipped Reg too, to git her do what they wanted. I never seen a girl used so bad." He looked down at the ground, embarrassed. Polly knew what Zee meant, and blushed.

"But one day, she went after Mr. John for beatin' on Reg. Mr. John beat the daylights outta her, then sold her away. 'Bout broke everyone's heart for Reg. We all was made to watch her git in the wagon and Mr. Wilkins' drove her away, while Reg looked on, jes' screamin' for his mama. He was maybe four years old. It 'bout broke my own mama's heart. . . . Mr. Stone tol' Mama to look out fo' him . . . an' after a while, he was jes' one of the field hands, and knew to stay outta sight. An' then sho nuff . . . I saw Reg's face when Mr. Stone walked in here, well, I never seen someone so afraid."

Polly closed her eyes and tried to think. No wonder the boy had jumped at Deputy McGee's visit to River Wood as a chance to escape John. She shook her head. "You said he ran to Ona's cabin?"

Zee nodded. "I guess he didn't know that Mr. Stone is here now . . ."

Polly opened her eyes and looked at Zee for a long moment. "Thank you for telling me. I will go talk to Reg. Help me do what we can to keep him out of sight until Mr. Stone leaves again. I will have a word with George and Mr. Roper, too. I will not let Mr. Stone find him. I promise."

Zadoc looked at Polly doubtfully.

Polly pursed her lips and looked away. "Thank you for your help, Zee." She turned and quickly left the barn. She hurried toward the slave cabins. How everything had changed since the pleasant evening a few nights ago, handing out jugs of syrup with Tom and celebrating a good harvest.

When she reached Ona's cabin, emotions threatened to overwhelm her. She wiped her moist eyes and knocked on the thin door, before pulling it open and peering inside. The fireplace was cold and it took a moment for Polly's eyes to adjust to the dim interior. She saw a shape huddled under quilts on the sagging bed frame in the corner.

"Reg." Polly sighed. She crossed the floor and crouched in front of the dark fireplace. She struck flint and steel until she had a small flame and held it to tinder. A gentle breath and the flame grew. Finally, she added some small pieces of wood and a bigger log before sitting back in Ona's rocking chair. She looked around the cabin and noticed Ona's small touches: a vase of mums, patchwork quilts, and rag rugs she had stitched from cast-offs over the years, a sampler Polly had embroidered for her as a teenager. There was a small movement from under the quilts.

"Reg, you are safe here," Polly said softly. Reg did not respond.

Polly sighed. "Zee told me what happened in the barn. I am not angry at you. I had no idea that Mr. Stone had hit you before."

The boy rolled over, sat up, and wiped his nose on his sleeve. His face registered shock at her appearance, and he frowned. "Did he do that to you?"

Polly almost asked to whom he referred, but they both knew the answer. She self-consciously touched her eye and said, "Mr. Stone won't hurt you. I won't let him."

"He hurt Mama real bad. Then he sold her away. Is he gonna sell me away too?"

"No. I will not let him sell you away. What happened?"

Reg sighed and looked down, absentmindedly picking at loose stitches on the threadbare quilt. "When he sold my mama away, Miss Jane watched over me some. She would bring me food and see I had clothes. Fo' a while I got to stay with her in the daytime, but as soon as I was five years old, Mr. Wilkins put me to cotton. I wasn't good at it an' Mr. Wilkins hit me a lot. Sometimes I thought Mr. Stone was beatin' on me jes' because I made Mr. Wilkins so mad in the fields. Even when I got bigger an' pick my share, even when I did everything asked of me. Mr. Stone jes' get a look in his eyes and go to whipping me with his belt. The other hands didn't like me around 'cause I made Mr. Stone so mad, so Miss Jane let me sleep in the kitchen house." He turned away and raised his shirt. Long scars crisscrossed his back and brought tears to Polly's eyes. He turned to face her again.

"Oh, Reg, I am so sorry."

Reg lowered his shirt and nodded at Polly knowingly. "When I saw him come in the barn this mornin', that's when I knew I was done for. I didn't know he would come back lookin' fo' me, but here he is."

"Oh Reg." Polly sighed sadly. "He didn't come looking for you," she explained. "He lives here now. He is my husband, home on leave from the war."

"Well, he's my pa," Reg murmured.

— • —

POLLY HURRIED TOWARD TOM'S CABIN, her heart pounding in her chest. She banged on the door with an open palm. There was no answer. She turned and headed for the kitchen house, taking the wooden steps two at a time. She threw open the screen door and went in, breathing hard.

Ona stood at the table, cutting up vegetables. She looked at Polly with concern. "Is he back already?" she asked softly.

"Not yet. But I must tell you something. Reg just told me that John is his father."

Ona put down her knife and wiped her hands on her apron. "Lawd . . . I thought that boy favored Ben. Now I know why." Ona shook her head sadly.

Polly continued breathlessly, "Reg saw John this morning in the barn. Zee said he panicked and ran. Thank God, John must not have seen him." Polly paused as a wave of nausea washed over her. "Ona, think about it. Reg is all of eleven years old. If John is his father, then John raped the boy's mother when he was fifteen or so. He is truly a monster."

Ona stood with both hands gripping the edge of the table, her head down.

"I need you to keep him in your cabin during the day while John is home on leave," Polly said sternly. "John cannot find him here when he returns from River Wood."

Ona put a hand on her hip and asked, "Miss Girl, you best think this thing through. . . . Mr. Stone's at River Wood right now. He's countin' up who is left and who done run off. Hearin' all kinda stories. . . . Ain't no cotton planted or picked, you said. And he might hear from the men that Reg up and left with Deputy McGee to come here. And what about Kate? Does he know about Ben and Kate?"

Polly stared blankly at the floor. Ona smacked the table with her hand, and Polly jumped back in surprise.

"This ain't gone go well, not for that boy or for you," Ona warned. "He like to kill you already and the law ain't no help, you said!"

Polly pulled her shawl around her shoulders. "I'm going to come up with a plan."

"Lawdy, girl, you ain't got much time for a plan. He be back sometime today."

Polly frowned at Ona. "I have to tell him that I gave away Ben and Kate. It's the story I told Deputy McGee. I'll do it with Tom here."

Ona snorted and said, "Mr. Roper be at River Wood today."

Polly felt her knees weaken. "I have one of John's sons hiding here and sent another son away . . ."

Ona folded her arms over her chest defiantly. "Don't give the man no more reasons to beat on you. If you go confrontin' him with all this and then tell him you know what he did to your brothers, I think he would kill you. In fact, I know it."

Polly felt the blood pounding in her temples and steadied herself against the table. "I must tell Tom," she whispered. "He will know what to do . . ." Her voice trailed off. "God knows what is happening at River Wood today."

"No!" Ona hissed. "Leave Mr. Tom outta this. It'll only make Mr. Stone more angry. The one weapon you got left is you is the man's wife. You gonna have to play to that. I hate to say it, but it all you got. He gone be mad as a hornet when he gets back here." Polly recognized some truth in Ona's words and nodded solemnly.

She stayed inside for the remainder of the day. She changed out of her day dress and put on a lavender gown she knew that John admired. She put her mother's amethyst earrings in her ears and had Ona style her hair in an elaborate braid. She reapplied power to her face, but the blue swelling on her cheek and eye socket showed through the makeup.

As the early evening came on, Polly found herself sitting tensely in the parlor, a glass of sherry by her side. Liquid courage was what Tom called alcohol, and so he rarely drank the stuff. Polly had downed one already and was ready to quaff the second when she heard John's steps on the front porch.

Cissie appeared in the doorway and asked softly, "Supper soon, ma'am? I got a pork roast about ready."

Polly nodded. "Yes, thank you. I hear him now." Cissie retreated quickly. Polly heard the front door open and the scrape of boots in the entry hall. She stood and said a silent prayer. She could only imagine his anger after a day at what was left of River Wood.

John entered the room, surprised to see Polly standing there. His face registered shock at the bruises on her face but he quickly recovered. He frowned and crossed to the liquor cabinet. In the well-lit room, Polly could see that John was sick. His red-rimmed eyes and pallor were evidence of some undiagnosed illness.

He grabbed the whiskey bottle and a glass and poured a shot, his back to Polly.

"Polly, I apologize for last night. I was drunk and overwhelmed with worries and anger. I should not have struck you." He tipped his head back and drank the whiskey before turning around again. "But you vex me. And now, the fever has returned and it makes me ill-tempered." He growled.

Polly wanted to lie and tell him that he was forgiven, but she could not make the words come forth. Images of her brothers, of Kate and Sol, Reg and his mother, of her own beating, clouded her mind. Instead, she held her tongue and nodded.

"Supper is ready," she murmured. She turned and headed into the dining room, where the savory aroma of roast pork and potatoes greeted them. John grabbed the bottle and followed his wife.

They sat and ate in silence. Cissie brought a plate of hot biscuits and gravy, refilled water glasses, and then sat quietly in the butler's pantry, awaiting instructions.

John tilted his head toward the pantry and mumbled through a mouthful of potatoes, "That one had her baby, I suppose."

Polly glanced toward the pantry and said quietly, "Stillborn, I'm afraid."

John nodded and took a sip of water. "Nigger children are a drain on a farm anyway." Beads of perspiration formed on his forehead despite the cool room.

Polly looked at her husband and felt a fresh wave of disgust. Had the war changed him further or was his true nature coming to the surface? Polly suspected the latter. "Don't be cruel, John," she said.

John glared at Polly. He touched the sore on his lip and winced.

"Is everything alright?" Polly asked coolly.

"I'm ill," John snapped. He sipped his water, winced again, and set the glass down hard.

Polly sipped her sherry and decided to tumble headfirst into the fray. "How did you find River Wood today?"

"I found it." He glared at her. "I found it run to shit, Polly. What'd you expect?"

Polly clenched her napkin under the table and replied softly, "I'm sorry."

"There was no sign of Clay Wilkins anywhere and no one knew where he'd gone. His cabin looked like he had just stepped out, except the slaves had taken any food left. The house was a mess and there was no food to be had there. When I left for training last winter, I had an overseer, two house slaves, and fifteen hands. I had fields ready for tilling and seed to be sown. Today I counted eight hands. Seven slaves had run, including a boy. The rest were living on squirrels, rabbits, and turnips, best I could tell. My foreman told me they made a start on the fields but gave up after Clay ran off. I'll send the patrol after them. Every single runaway will hang."

He swallowed a forkful of beans, before adding, "I'm going to town tomorrow for the patrol. Damn niggers are a thorn in my ass, but I will do what I can to retrieve them. Then I'll personally whip the snot out of each one."

"Clay Wilkins let you down, not your hands," Polly said. "How were the slaves to function without him?" She dabbed her lips with her napkin and stared at her plate.

"My foreman should have taken over. I beat the tar out of him for stealing food out of my house and overseer's cabin," John mumbled.

"Oh John. You can't punish the ones who stayed," Polly argued. "They had no overseer." She silently rejoiced that apparently no one had divulged Reg's whereabouts.

"I took Roper with me and left him there. You and George'll have to do without him for a while," he said, pointing his fork in Polly's direction. "He has his work cut out for him. Seems you have things well in hand here. Roper will need to salvage what he can of the seed for me and get the men back onto chores. I don't have time to attend a slave auction while I am home, but I have instructed him to get to the one next month in Greenville. I'll need more hands before next spring. Two field hands at least. And a girl."

Polly tried to remain calm. After all, she reasoned, if he's focused on rebuilding River Wood while home, maybe he will not be a threat here. And Tom away meant he wouldn't see her face, proof of John's violent streak. She would have time to gather other evidence for the annulment request.

"I need money," John stated abruptly, putting down his fork. Polly offered a silent prayer that her earnings were somewhere safe with Tom. "Officer pay isn't going to cover what I need." He licked his lips and grimaced in pain. "I went into town and the bank told me that you had withdrawn all funds and closed your Whitehall account recently. About eighteen hundred dollars." He continued, "I need some of that for at least two field hands. And property taxes are due next month."

Polly immediately shook her head. "That money went to pay for wooden crates for the sorghum syrup, the presses, seed, supplies, and such." She focused on cutting a morsel of meat and did not look at John. "Repairs around the farm . . . you understand. The cotton brought us just a pittance and was burned in town by the factor. Ask any other grower. It is true. I had to spend cash on what was needed here."

John sighed heavily and leaned back in his seat. He didn't feel well, Polly could tell. The chair groaned as he tipped it back on two legs, one of Polly's pet peeves. "Is that a fact?"

Polly felt the hair on the nape of her neck stand up. "John, please. I gave up everything I had for the mortgage debt and the back taxes you owed. I had to have something to cover Whitehall's taxes. I worked hard this year. Any money made went right back into the farm."

"Hmmm. Mr. Jones at the Mercantile told me how much he paid you— in cash—for your syrup. The bank told me how much you withdrew that same day. I checked at the tax offices and you have not paid Whitehall's taxes this year, but I did the math," John said icily. "You should have a mighty good chunk of change sitting around here somewhere, darling."

Polly lifted her sherry glass and finished the warming liquid. Not sure of how John would take her next lie, she decided to use it anyway. She was running out of excuses.

"Actually," she said confidently. "I left the tax money with my attorney, Harrison Legarre. After the fiasco with my inheritance, which he also handled, he holds that money for Whitehall taxes. In fact, he suggested it." She looked at John evenly. "He will pay the taxes on our behalf. As far as hands, I can spare some Whitehall hands. We can send men to Mr. Roper tomorrow. We'll get River Wood back to work again, with Whitehall's help. You helped me with my cotton." She smiled. "I will return the favor."

John belched. He absentmindedly wiped his mouth with his napkin and winced with pain. "I don't know what you are up to, Polly. But I am feeling sick and don't want to listen to your excuses tonight. Have Kate draw me a bath. We will discuss this tomorrow." He dropped the chair to all four legs with a loud thump, stood, and tossed his napkin on the table. "I'm going upstairs."

Polly rested her chin in her hands and exhaled, the tiniest victory in hand. John believed that Wilkins had abandoned the farm. Her next moves would be crucial. How to explain Kate and Ben's disappearance. How to keep Reg safe. She drained the contents of her glass and stood up. *Maybe the sherry really is a form of courage,* she mused. She rang the small silver bell at her right hand and Cissie appeared.

"Thank you for dinner, Cissie. Can you have George bring up hot water? Mr. Stone wants a bath. Take his whiskey upstairs. He'll ask you about Kate," she warned. "Tell him that she is washing dishes. Tell him that I asked you to prepare his bath. Do not tell him anything more. And for heaven's sake, not a word about Reg."

— • —

POLLY WOKE THE NEXT MORNING TO murmured voices in the next room. She heard John and a woman speaking and jumped out of bed quickly despite the chill. Her fire had died down in the night. She leaned to stir it back to life with the poker. She padded across the floor in bare feet and crouched quietly by the door to John's adjoining bedroom, shivering in her flannel gown.

She listened at the keyhole as Ona prattled on about the breakfast Cissie was preparing for him. "Bacon and eggs and a stack of hotcakes smothered in sorghum syrup." Ona chuckled. "Yes sir, Mr. Stone, after what you prob'ly been eatin,' Cissie's cookin' gone soothe yo' upset stomach fo' sure! It be ready in about fifteen minutes or so, suh."

Polly heard John let out a sigh of contentment and she smiled. Ona was a sly one. She would do her best to ease the man's temper before he even stepped out of bed. "If you drink yo' hot tea I be right back with yo' meal."

Polly heard Ona leave John's room and she quickly hopped back into bed. Ona knocked on her own door and came in chattering loudly. "Mornin' Miss Polly!"

Polly smiled. "Good morning, Ona."

Ona crossed the floor and stooped to add a log to the fireplace. "It a beautiful day, ma'am," she said loudly. She winked at Polly conspiratorially and continued, "I tol' yo' husband that Cissie whippin' up a big breakfast fo' him. What can I get you, Miss Polly?"

"Just tea, thank you, Ona," Polly said. "Did Mr. Stone tell you that he is going into town today?"

"Yes he did." She leaned closer to Polly and whispered, "He asked me to send Kate up with his breakfast. I jes' nodded. You best tell him soon or we all in a worser state. I try to stall a while so's you can talk to him." Ona's wide eyes betrayed her fear. She patted Polly's shoulder and left the room quietly.

Polly tossed the quilts back and sat on the edge of her bed. She closed her eyes and tried to gather her courage. She reached around and began to unwind her braid until her chestnut hair hung loosely around her shoulders. When she stood, she slowly unbuttoned the row of buttons on her flannel nightgown with shaking hands and let the gown slide off her pale shoulders. She stepped out of it and quickly crossed the wooden floor, afraid that any pause would mean losing her nerve. She placed her hand on the doorknob and inhaled deeply. She exhaled a long and slow breath before turning the knob and stepping through the door. It was the only way.

Chapter Forty-Four

JOHN LOOKED AT POLLY WITH HOODED EYES. The lovemaking had been quick and one-sided as usual, for which she was grateful now. His touch sickened her. Her face was sore where his beard had bruised her still-tender cheek. She felt his stare as she sat up in the bed and turned away modestly, plaiting her hair into a hastily done braid.

She felt his fingers on the small of her back and she tried hard not to flinch. "I should go. Your breakfast will be here soon, and I know you have a busy day," she said. She was eager to tell him about Kate while he was in a good mood. "Oh, but I do have something I need to tell you."

"Or you could stay in my bed," he murmured, pulling playfully on her braided hair. "Do your wifely duty again." He rubbed her back and then pulled her towards him.

"I need to tell you—Kate and Ben are no longer here," she blurted.

"What do you mean, no longer here?" John asked, dropping his hands.

She sat up tall and tried to cover her legs with the bed sheet. "John, please do not be upset with me. I allowed Ben and Kate to marry. They were in love. And then, when my dear friend in Alabama married, I gifted them to her. It's a tradition. Your own father gifted Ona to my parents at their wedding, so I thought it would be a fine idea. You gave me Zee and Kate. And now my friend and her new husband have two slaves they can rely on. Do not be upset," she said. "I hoped you'd be pleased."

Polly sensed the heat of John's anger, even with her back turned. Naked and afraid, she realized how vulnerable she was. She pulled the bed sheet around her middle to cover herself. She turned slightly and his ice-blue eyes narrowed as he looked at her.

"You gave away two good slaves without asking me, when River Wood has lost so much. Do you know how much money those two would have fetched at auction?" He scratched his beard and glared at her. "I don't give a shit about your boy, Ben. He was an uppity nigger anyway. But you gave away my Kate. My present to you. Without my consent."

Polly felt a wave of dread surge through her body. "I did not know the state of things at River Wood," she said softly.

"Bullshit!" John sat up and pulled on the bed sheet.

"Let go, John. I need to dress before Cissie comes with your breakfast."

Polly tried to stand but John grabbed her long braid and yanked with all his might. "You knew exactly what you were doing," he said. "You went over there and took Kate away from River Wood. You were jealous. Damn you, Polly. Damn you."

Polly felt as if her scalp might very well pull loose, he pulled so hard. She saw stars in her vision and tried not to cry out. Cissie was surely almost there with his breakfast. "John, please stop it. You're hurting me." She gasped.

John slowly wrapped Polly's long hair around his wrist as he continued to pull her closer. Polly cried out, sure that her hair would rip from the roots. The pain was excruciating. When her head was close to his mouth, she felt his breath in her ear. "You had no right to send her away," he growled. "Why do you continually vex me?" He jerked the braid hard.

Polly's anger burned under the fear in her chest. Through clenched teeth, she said, "You raped her. And Wilkins did, too. Why wouldn't I have sent her away? No one deserves that." She twisted to look back at

John. "Even a slave woman doesn't want your disgusting and vile body on top of her."

Polly felt the hard punch to her kidney and groaned, doubling over. John wrenched her hair, jerking her neck backward as she tried to scramble off the bed. She slapped at his hands but he wouldn't release her hair.

Suddenly she felt the thick braid loop around her neck and tighten. She tried to pull on her own hair, to gasp for breath, but John held the twisted coil tight, cutting off her air supply. He pushed her down on the edge of the bed and sat on her waist, pinning her, as her bare legs dangled off the mattress. He stared into her eyes as he choked her with her own braided hair. The weight of his body on her cracked ribs meant that Polly couldn't expand her lungs to breathe, and she knew that she would soon lose consciousness.

With all her might, she inhaled a bit of air and cried out. "God help me! Please!" The field of exploding stars in Polly's vision turned to black.

— • —

JOHN LET GO OF HIS WIFE'S NECK and she crumpled to the floor, unconscious. He grabbed his pants and quickly put them on. He looked at Polly, lying in a heap on the floor and bent to cover her with the sheet before putting on his boots. He stared for a long minute at his wife, curled now into a fetal position, pale skin bruising already from his violent punch to her back. The curve of her hips and her pale breasts were there in front of him—his for the taking. His.

He heard a muffled sound at the door and crossed the room quickly. He pulled the door open and saw his breakfast tray set down neatly at the threshold. Hotcakes, eggs, a steaming china teapot with cup and saucer had been placed there, along with an autumn rose in a crystal bud vase, all silent witnesses to what he had done.

John kicked the tray angrily and headed down the stairs. Mary Burgiss's precious rose-patterned Limoges shattered into jagged pieces across the rug, while sticky sorghum syrup dripped down the wall and pooled on the floor.

— • —

POLLY AWOKE TO FIND ONA CROUCHED BY HER SIDE, crooning softly as she held a cold cloth to Polly's back. A spreading purple bruise wrapped itself around her midsection. She tried to speak, but her throat hurt too much to get a word out. She tried to move but a wave of pain, like an electric current, shot down her spine. She gasped in agony.

Through blurred vision, Polly saw Cissie on her hands and knees, whimpering, picking up shards of glass in the hallway.

"Shh. Shh. Don't move now, Miss Girl. Cissie done called George. He gone get you back to your own room. Wait till he comes to try and move," Ona said softly.

Polly's eyes grew wide with fright. Ona pulled the sheet tighter around her mistress's small frame. "He ain't gone see you naked. I'll fix this sheet up snug when he's here to carry you. I get my comfrey salve and treat yo' bruises. Lawd, that man 'bout tore up yo' neck, too. My Jesus . . . ," Ona muttered, stroking Polly's hair.

"Where—where is he now?" Polly whispered, despite the painful effort to speak.

"He took off on yo' horse again. I 'spect he headed back to River Wood or to town. Did he do this because you tol' him about Kate? Or Reg?" Ona asked gently.

Polly nodded and closed her eyes. "About Kate. He is sick." She winced as she inhaled. "He will kill me next time. I know it. Then he will take my land." She tried to swallow. "And if he finds Reg here, he will beat him senseless."

They heard George's heavy footsteps ascending the stairs. Ona tucked the sheet around Polly's torso and legs modestly. George spoke quietly to Cissie before entering the room, hat in hand.

Ona swaddled Polly tightly before George crouched down and

wrapped a quilt around his mistress's shoulders. He gently lifted her and carried her into her own room. He bent to lay her on her bed, while Ona busied herself with the quilts to quickly cover Polly's bare legs. George quickly retreated, but not before shaking his head angrily and exchanging looks with Ona.

Ona closed the door behind George and came to sit at the head of Polly's bed. She leaned close to Polly's ear. "Jes' listen. I can take care of this fo' you. I ain't talkin' about the bruises he left on yo' body." Ona gazed at Polly knowingly. "But I can make this stop. Ain't no one else able to he'p you, Miss Girl." She stroked Polly's hair with her calloused hands and waited patiently.

The clock on Polly's mantle ticked loudly in the silence. Finally Polly whispered, "How?"

"How I do thangs ain't what you need to know about right now. Jes' say the word. Else he gone kill you before he leaves to go back up north. He ain't right in the head."

"Your potions? You have something to poison—"

Ona cut her off with an index finger to her lips. She turned to look at the closed door between the two bedrooms and leaned closer to Polly. "There gonna be a meal I fix. There gonna be somethin' I tell you not to eat. That yo' sign, Miss Girl." She squeezed Polly's arm and nodded.

Polly swallowed, wincing in pain. "Yes. Do it."

Chapter Forty-Five

October 31, 1861

ONA STOOD IN THE WARM KITCHEN, STIRRING A LARGE pot of bean soup, the savory aroma making her mouth water. She added extra chunks of smoked fatback, stirred, and held the wooden spoon to her lips. Silas sat on the floor, eating a small bowl of the soup placed in front of him. Outside, cold rain beat down on the tin roof.

The screen door squeaked a warning and Ona jumped, dropping the spoon on the floor. Cissie entered and asked, "What got you spooked, old woman?" She frowned and placed two jars of deep purple on the table. "Here dem' preserves you wanted from the cellar." She leaned down and kissed the top of her son's head before removing her wet shawl.

Ona bent to pick up the spoon and pointed it toward Cissie. "Ev'rything has me spooked all the time now," she grumbled. "Here—go ahead and take this pot. It's fo' the hands' dinner tonight. Mr. Stone wantin' a venison steak and cornbread. Poor Miss Polly still ain't got no appetite. She jes' wants collards."

Cissie looked at Ona warily. "He seem to be behavin' hisse'f today," she remarked. "He was in the library readin'."

Ona sighed heavily. "He leavin' Miss Polly alone for a while . . . thank God. I ain't surprised, but he has hisself some mouth cankers. Complains of fever . . . I jes' know he been with whores and got hisself sick with a pox." She waved the spoon toward the big house. "He mighta gave it to her. Maybe she ain't gone be able to have no chillun 'cause of that evil man. She pissin' red blood after that punch he gave her." She stooped to open the stove and pull out a hot pan of cornbread.

"Maybe his pecker'll fall off." Cissie cackled.

Ona laughed and nodded. "From yo' mouth to God's ears."

Outside, the drumming of rain on the tin roof began to subside.

"Mmm, that cornbread smells mighty good. Guess we jes' gettin' the soup." Cissie sighed.

"You got your own rations. Make yo' family some cornbread. This cornbread here's for Mr. Stone."

"Lawdy." Cissie shook her head. "I cain't make it like you. You always was a better cook than me. You sho' have a way with a piece of meat, too." She watched as Ona speared the slab of venison and slapped it into the hot skillet. The skillet sizzled and smoked, spitting lard. "I 'spect Mr. Stone want you to fix all his meals till he goes."

Ona backed up and turned to Cissie. "That's a good idea. I don't mind. I'll fix them both breakfast tomorrow mornin' too, Cissie. You fix somethin' fo' George and the men goin' to work. I heard tell they goin' to help Mr. Roper at River Wood tomorrow."

Cissie nodded. "Thank ya, Ona." She paused and then asked, "You think Mr. Roper knows what happened to Miss Polly? He seems awful fond of her lately. Don't think he'd take it well to see her so beat up."

"Until Mr. Roper can come back to Whitehall, I don't think he knows anything. Maybe it best that way. If he see what Mr. Stone done, he'd as likely kill him." Ona shook her head.

Cissie nodded. "How is Reg? Has he seen Miss Polly all beat up?"

"Lawdy, no." Ona shook her head vehemently. "I got him hid away in my cabin fo' now. He ain't even doin' chores—jes' hidin'. In a week's time, Mr. Stone's got to go back to the war. Then we can all breathe—least for a while." She forced a smile and held the screen door open. Cissie picked up the heavy soup pot and lugged it out into the gathering dark, Silas following close behind his mother.

Ona shivered and let the screen door slam. Then she closed the wooden door firmly and turned back to her work. The night was a chilly one, anyway, and no one needed to surprise her for the next few minutes. She turned her attention to the charred steak and lifted it from the pan. She plated it and added a heaping spoonful of turnip greens and a hefty slab of the hot cornbread. She added a little milk, salt, and pepper to the frying pan drippings and began to make gravy.

Ona grabbed the stool and carefully stepped up on top of it. On wobbly tiptoe, she reached high into the cupboard and felt for the packet with trembling fingers. The paper rattled and she lifted it, careful not to spill its contents. She stepped down and laid the small envelope on the table, opened the folded paper gently, and tried to decide her next step. It was too risky. Polly could change her mind and ask for some of the cornbread and gravy. She would have to wait. She folded the packet back into a small square and climbed up on the stool. She slid the paper back onto the top shelf and climbed back down. Another day, she thought.

She placed the dishes on a large tray and began the laborious task of getting the meal over to the big house.

— • —

POLLY SHIFTED IN HER CHAIR AND pulled the quilt around her shoulders. It was nice to doze in front of the fire. Her back had stopped throbbing whenever she moved, but the black and blue bruise was quite tender. She was worried that when she passed water, it was tinged pink. The ring of bruised skin around her neck was hidden under a high-necked lace collar.

There was a tap at the parlor door and Ona peeked into the lamp-lit room. "Dinner's ready, Miss Polly. You sho' you don't want nothin' but greens? I made a pan of cornbread and there's blackberry jam alongside. It's delicious." She nodded.

Polly looked at the woman curiously. So far, Ona had not had the courage to do what she had offered. Still, Polly wondered what had kept the woman from poisoning her entire family over the years. She clearly had the knowledge and the means.

Polly smiled. "Thank you, Ona. Can you help me stand up, please?"

Ona hurried to Polly's side and held onto her arm as Polly struggled to her feet, wincing as her back spasmed. She helped her to the dining room and held Polly's chair as she seated herself gingerly. Ona scurried to the library and knocked, relaying the same message to John Stone.

John limped to the table and sat down. The couple had not spoken since the beating. In the soft glow of candlelight, Polly put her napkin in her lap and began to pick at the bowl of turnip greens. John speared his steak and began to saw at it with his knife indelicately. Ona bustled at the sideboard, cutting the cornbread into squares.

"Mr. Stone, I made somethin' tasty fo' ya," Ona began in a sing-song voice. Miss Mary used to have me stir in some whiskey to Mr. Burgiss's jam. He liked it fine on cornbread. Thought y'all might want to try it too." Ona chuckled. "Mr. Burgiss use to say everythin's better with whiskey in it!"

John swallowed a mouthful of steak and said, "That does sound good. What else is in it?"

Ona shrugged and murmured, "Jes' whiskey, blackberries cooked down, and sorghum sugar." She placed the jar in front of Stone, along with a plate of cornbread.

"Whiskey jam, Miss Polly. Have some. Yo' daddy thought it was mighty fine."

Polly watched as John smeared a spoonful of jam on a square of cornbread. John took a large bite of cornbread and chewed and swallowed it before he spoke. "My God, Ona, that is delicious."

Ona looked at her and said again, "Try some, won't ya?"

Polly dipped her spoon into the jam jar and lifted it to her lips. The sweet tang of the berries was complemented by the warm zing of the alcohol. "It is good, but a little much for me," she said quietly. "I don't take much to whiskey."

John finished his square and then smeared jam on another one while Ona looked on.

"I'm glad you like it, Mr. Stone." She chuckled and added, "I can make some tomorrow for breakfast, too, on a stack of hotcakes. It's even better that way. And it sho' makes the kitchen smell good. Boy, did Mr. Burgiss like it. He called it the Massa's Breakfast," she simpered.

John smiled warily at the woman. "That sounds fine. I appreciate the kindness. Have those hotcakes ready for me at dawn, though. With ham steak. I need a hearty breakfast early before I ride to River Wood."

"Yessuh." Ona nodded as she bustled behind John at the sideboard. "Miss Polly? What about you? Hotcakes and whiskey jam for breakfast?" Her face was turned away, but she quickly glanced across John's head toward Polly, shaking her head. "Although—if you don't care fo' whiskey, I can serve yours plain if you like?" Her question was subtle but her eyes bored into Polly's.

Polly caught the expression that quickly crossed Ona's face and then disappeared.

"You know I am not a big breakfast eater. An egg and tea will be fine. Thank you," Polly said, dabbing her lips with her napkin.

"Yes'm." Ona nodded and bustled out of the room and into the butler's pantry to wait for the meal to end.

John watched her go and then put down his knife and fork and laid his napkin on the table. He sipped water and then cleared his throat imperiously. "I will probably keep your hands over at my place tomorrow night. It depends on how much Mr. Roper was able to get done already. I haven't had anyone but ne'er-do-wells apply for this overseer position and I won't be here but a few more days. He will go into Anderson to look for an overseer if we can't find one soon. At any rate, I have closed my house. But I will need someone to oversee the acreage and the outbuildings."

Polly kept her eyes on her plate and toyed with her food.

John cursed under his breath. "I was overly harsh with you and I apologize."

Polly nodded and said, "Thank you for that at least."

"I will not come into your room anymore while I am home. Since I disgust you, I will take my . . . needs elsewhere."

Polly breathed a silent prayer of thanks that there were no slave women left at River Wood but wondered if Cissie was even safe. She sighed and looked up from her plate, propping her chin on her hands.

She began quietly, "It is difficult to believe that we have not been married even a year. So much has happened. I realize that I did not really know you. We should not have married. But we are both still young. You can find someone else . . . refined, rich, and beautiful. Will you consider annulment?"

The color rose in John's face but he stayed seated and merely shook his head. "I refuse to let that happen. You are my lawful wife and when this war is over, we can build a life together. We will build a life together, with River Wood and Whitehall combined."

"Sounds like a business deal and not a marriage." Polly's hopes fell. "You tried to strangle your lawful wife." She pulled the collar away and ran her fingers tenderly around the ring of bruised flesh at her neck.

John did not look at her bruises. He tossed back the remains of his drink. He winced as the alcohol stung the oozing canker on his lip. "It was not my intention to hurt you like that. You are a headstrong woman, and prone to making ill-informed decisions in my absence, which exasperates me. There will be no more of that. I will make the decisions. I am the head of this family now."

Polly did not take the bait and wisely chose to ignore John's taunt. She wondered about the sores on John's lips and shuddered at the memory of his mouth on hers. "When can I get my overseer back here?"

"Dammit, Polly!" John slapped the table with his palm, knocking over his empty glass. "I leave in three or four days. Mr. Roper will be needed there until I leave, if not afterwards. I will interview another man soon. If he works out, you'll have your overseer back here when I go. But get this through your head. This war will end and when I come home, we will make a go of it. Don't even think I will give you an annulment. I will not. I may not be welcome in your bed, but you are still my wife. You will do what I say." He stood and glared at Polly before stalking from the room. Polly heard him climb the stairs and slam his bedroom door violently.

Ona appeared in the doorway and leaned against the frame.

Polly looked at her sadly. "You heard him."

"Yes, I heard him. Let it be fo' now, Miss Girl. Let it be." Ona sighed. "If you bait him, he beat you again." She pointed a bony finger at Polly. "Don't go to confrontin' him about Caleb and Joshua. I jes' know you been wantin' to say yo' piece about that. Don't do it." She crossed the room and began to clear the table, humming softly to herself as she stacked plates and dishes. "Jes' bide yo' time."

— • —

THE GRANDFATHER CLOCK DOWNSTAIRS STRUCK TWO. Polly was awake in the dark, a plan forming in her mind. She had mulled over the details. She would ride over to River Wood with a picnic lunch, and somehow let Tom know what had happened. He had been at River Wood for five days and she had heard nothing. In the morning, John would load her hands into the wagon again and take them back to River Wood, a feeble attempt to restore order. She knew she had no recourse about the beating. A husband could beat his wife into next year, she knew, and no one would do a thing. *But Tom will help,* she reasoned. He would know what to do. He was a kind man.

Her thoughts went down a different path and she imagined Tom as her husband instead of John Stone. She remembered Tom's hand on the small of her back at the dance and his strong arms carrying her out of the field after the colt's death. Tom's even white teeth behind a graying beard and the tender way he gazed at her with his blue eyes when he thought she wasn't looking. She smiled and closed her eyes, her arms wrapped around her pillows, imagining the secret things a loving husband and wife might share in the nighttime.

— • —

November 1, 1861

AN OWL HOOTED OUTSIDE Ona's cabin and she stirred and stretched. Across the room, Reg still slumbered, his breathing almost a man's snore. Ona threw back her quilts and put her stocking feet on the cold floor. She poked the embers to life and added a log. The dry wood caught fire, and soon a warm blaze heated the cold cabin. For a minute, she considered waking Reg just to tell him to stay put until after John Stone had collected the men at Roper's cabin but shrugged and decided to let him sleep. Reg knew to avoid the field hands' area and his snore was deep and even.

Ona smiled at the sleeping boy and tugged on her boots. She stepped outside, wrapped in her quilt. She closed the door quickly behind her. A heavy frost had settled on the ground around Whitehall overnight, and Ona crunched through the brittle grass as she headed for the outhouse in the darkness, her breath sending plumes of moisture into the cold, dry air.

As she approached the outhouse, its door squeaked open and someone stepped out. Ona was not startled. The slaves shared one privy, and there was always someone there before her in the mornings. "Mornin,' Ona," said a deep voice that Ona recognized as George's.

"Mornin' to you, George," Ona murmured. "Y'all headed to River Wood shortly?"

"Yeah, Mr. Stone wants us to meet him at Mr. Roper's cabin around sunrise." He peered toward the eastern sky and added, "Guess that gives us about an hour."

"It's Sunday." Ona snorted. "Mr. Roper ain't never made field hands work fields on a Sunday mornin'. It's the Lawd's day."

George grunted. "Mr. Stone don't strike me as a man has much to do wit' the Lawd." He grunted and moved on past Ona into the dark.

— • —

AFTER SHE HAD DONE HER PRIVATE BUSINESS, Ona walked toward the kitchen house, her lips moving in silent prayer. She pulled open the kitchen door and went inside the dark building. She felt for the kerosene lamp and lit the wick. As the lantern dispelled the darkness, she heard the scuttle of mice fleeing into their secret cracks and holes in the floorboards.

"You ain't worth the breath God gave ya," she said crossly to the tabby cat that stretched and yawned before yowling to be let outside, its guard duty done for the night.

She set Polly's egg to boil and started tea. She quickly pulled together the ingredients for hotcakes and set a rasher of bacon in a cast iron frying pan. Soon the heady aroma of sizzling bacon filled the kitchen. She measured and poured flour and soda into a bowl, cracked eggs, added butter and milk, and began to stir the batter. Her eyes went to the corner shelf where the packet was hidden. She placed the stool and stepped up, retrieved the packet quickly, and then moved the stool back to the table.

The door opened and Ona startled. "Jesus Lawd, you scared me!" she said, her hand on her heart, as Cissie stepped inside. She tucked the packet into the pocket of her apron.

"Who else you think was comin'?" Cissie grumbled. "I lit the fires in the house. Mr. Stone is up. I got these men to feed breakfast before they head off to River Wood. Cracklins and cornbread is what I say. I already tol' George they's got to fend fo' theyselves fo' lunch and dinner over yonder. Else we got to take it there . . ."

"Don't go borrowin' trouble," Ona murmured, stirring batter until small bubbles began to form. "I'm to feed Mr. Stone hotcakes and bacon, but you can get cornbread goin' in the big pans." Ona set her mouth firmly and ladled batter into the hot skillet. Now was not the time. Too much could go wrong if she tried to use the packet now.

She turned to watch Cissie slice long slabs of pork skin for the cracklins and said, "Woman, you want to get us beat? Them slices is way too thick," she scolded. "Cut 'em in half and serve twice't the cornbread. Ain't needin' nothin' else to make Mr. Stone angry."

"He ain't gonna see," Cissie retorted with a shrug. "They gonna be over there all day, this is they breakfast, lunch, and dinner. George tol' me Mr. Stone shut the big house. Ain't no one to cook or clean over that way. Lawd, I pray he don't decide to send us back to River Wood." She began to mound the slabs of ham on a large plate, as the door's hinges creaked again and a sleepy-eyed Reg entered.

"Reg! What are you doin,' boy? Get back to the cabin till I come git ya," Ona snapped. She flipped the first batch of golden-brown hotcakes.

Reg's mouth watered. "Ona, I cain't he'p it. I smelled bacon. And dem hotcakes looks real appealin' too." He laughed, rubbing his belly.

Ona shook the spatula at the boy. "You go now, you uppity thing. I'll bring you cracklins and cornbread, same as the men, soon as I feed Mr. and Mrs. Stone." She lifted the cakes and placed them on a platter, grabbed the jar of blackberry jam, and turned to find a tray. Reg stuck his finger into the jam jar and then scooped a fingerful of preserves into his mouth.

Suddenly the door flew open. "Hello girls!" a voice called out and the three slaves turned to see John Stone filling the doorway, hat in hand. His smile faded when he saw Reg sitting at the table, his mouth covered in blackberry jam.

"You," he whispered, confusion clouding his face. "Reginald? What are you doing here?"

Reg stood, tears welling in his eyes. "Miss Polly. She took me in, suh. I ain't runned away. I swear. Miss Polly, suh, she took me in. I been a good worker here, suh." He extended a hand to plead his case, but Ona stepped in front of the boy.

"Mr. Stone, I got yo' hotcakes and whiskey jam all ready. I got a heap o' bacon and a pot o' hot tea. If you'd be so kind as to hold the door open fo' this ol' woman, I can bring up this hot breakfast I promised. Surely you talk to Mrs. Stone later on 'bout this here little boy. You a busy man." She smiled at Stone, silently willing him to drop his focus on Reg. John's gaze turned to Ona, who did not look away.

"Mr. Stone, ol' Ona can't guarantee these hotcakes'll stay pipin' hot in this cold weather, but this jam will be twice't as strong as last night. I declare I think it doubled in whiskey taste overnight." She laughed gaily and waited for his response, her heart pounding like a hammer.

John's eyes narrowed and went from the tray to the boy and finally settled on Ona's lavish breakfast. "Very well, Ona. Bring the tray to the dining room." He opened the door and allowed Ona to step down and outside. He turned back to Reg.

"Come here, boy." Reg stepped closer, tears sliding down his cheeks. John cupped his chin in his hand. "You will not stay here, boy. You head out with the others in the wagon this morning. If I see your face at Whitehall ever again, I'll beat the hide off you. You hear me? Your place is at River Wood." He squeezed Reg's chin and then dropped his hand. The door slammed behind him.

Reg sank down onto the stool and put his head in his hands, sobs shaking his thin shoulders.

Cissie came over to him and patted his back affectionately. "You gone and did it now, son. I don't know what gonna happen next, but you gone and did it."

— • —

ONA CONTINUED IN THE ROLE OF fawning cook and chattered noisily as John sat to eat his breakfast. She poured tea and watched as the man spooned the thick preserves over the buttery stack of hotcakes. When she was satisfied that he was well into his meal, she tried to slip out of the dining room but John stopped her.

"Ona, what's Reginald doing at Whitehall?" he asked evenly, as he finished the last bite of hotcakes. "I know that my wife tells you everything. Be honest now and avoid a whipping."

Ona thought quickly and answered, "Mr. Stone, your wife has a kind heart, suh. I don't know a lot of things goin' on around here. . . . Best I can remember, when your overseer man disappeared at River Wood, the boy came over here by way of the sheriff's deputy, Mr. McBee." She paused. "Maybe Mr. McBee didn't want to leave a boy over there alone. Mebbe Miss Polly took pity on him 'cuz he were hungry. But he been a hard workin' boy, suh. He a real good one with the livestock and especially Miss Polly's horse."

"I see," Stone said, sipping his tea. "And how did you feel about the mistress giving away your boy and Kate to an old friend of hers far away in Alabama?"

Ona's lower lip trembled and she shook her head, forcing tears.

"You'll never see your son again. Hah, Miss Polly isn't so tenderhearted after all, is she?" He snickered, popping the last bit of bacon into his mouth. "Tell my wife that I will be here for dinner tonight. I expect to see her at my table. And Ona, that boy is not staying here. Have him meet me at the overseer's cabin in thirty minutes, same as the others. Miss Polly will have to tend her own damn horse for a while." He leaned back in his chair and belched loudly. "Woman, you do make a fine breakfast."

"Yessuh." Ona nodded and scurried back to the kitchen house. Dawn was breaking pink and gold across the eastern sky. Overhead, she heard the honk of wild geese as they flew in a vee formation across the fields to the river. She wiped welling tears from her eyes and threw open the kitchen door impatiently.

"You stupid chile!" she cried, rushing to enfold Reg in her arms. "You gonna hafta go with the men now. Get yo'se'f washed up and head to Mr.

Roper's cabin. Do what the other hands do, and fo' God's sake, stay by George or Mr. Roper as much as you can."

She pulled back and looked at the boy. "Do what he tells you and work hard. Mr. Roper is there so I cain't think Mr. Stone gonna beat you."

Reg nodded, his thin body shaking like a leaf

"I tol' him that you came over with that deputy, because you was hungry. That Miss Polly took pity on you." Ona patted Reg's cheek. She looked at Cissie and said, "Let George know what happened. If he can stick by George, maybe this will be alright."

Cissie lifted the heavy platter of cracklins and cornbread and said sadly, "Come wit' me, boy. Let's go find George." Reg held the door while Cissie passed through, his eyes on Ona the entire time.

"I'm sorry," he murmured, as he stepped out into the dawn.

— • —

POLLY STRETCHED AND SAT UP. Morning sunshine streamed into her room, and the warm fire crackled in the hearth. She had finally gone to sleep and slept so soundly that she did not even hear Cissie come in to stoke the fire. As she stood to retrieve her chamber pot, she was happy to find that her back pain was greatly diminished and her urine clear.

She pushed her arms into her flannel dressing gown and crossed to her windows. She watched the frost melt and drip from the trees, then transform into steam rising from the ground where the sun shone brightest. It would be a beautiful day. Crisp and clear. There was a knock on the door.

"Come in," she called. Ona entered shakily with Polly's breakfast tray, worry etched on her face. "What's wrong?"

Ona set the tray down. "Reg was in the kitchen house when Mr. Stone came in. He wants the boy back to River Wood. Today. He was real mad." Ona looked to her mistress for strength and said, "Please tell me he ain't gone hurt him." She wrung her hands in despair.

Polly stood up and stripped off her dressing gown. "Get a dress for me, quickly, Ona. I can run down there and stop him before they leave."

"No," Ona said. "If you go down there in front of all the slaves, and try to take Reg, what do you think Mr. Stone will do?" Her red-rimmed eyes searched Polly's face.

Polly's mind flashed to the plan she had hatched in the night, the idea of a picnic for the men working at River Wood. "Ona, I am going to take lunch to the men working at John's place. After all, they are my men. Not his. I will be able to check on Reg and get word to Tom about him being there. Can you start a batch of ham biscuits and gather enough apples from the cellar for the whole crowd? Tell Zee I will need him to accompany me. We will leave late morning." She placed her corset across her waist and turned to let Ona lace it.

"Are you feelin' up to a drive in the wagon all the way to River Wood?" Ona asked. "An' you ain't worn a corset since the beatin'."

"The thought of seeing Tom makes me happy enough," Polly said. "Don't lace it too tightly. I hope that I don't say anything else to bring John's wrath down on me again. I will just try to avoid him."

Ona put her hands on Polly's pale shoulders. "Miss Girl, that might be a good idea. I think the man has the whorin' sickness."

Polly turned to face Ona. "What do you mean?"

"Dem blisters on his mouth? Fevers, too?"

Polly groaned. A fresh wave of revulsion swept over her. "I–I was with him twice," she murmured, frowning.

"Did you wash?" Ona asked bluntly.

Polly reddened.

Ona huffed and shook her head. "Never mind, we deal wit' dat another time. I don't have no salve fo' dat. Oh, an' he said fo' you to be at supper tonight." Polly turned away and Ona pulled on the corset laces gently.

Polly lifted her hair out of Ona's way.

"He asked me how I felt 'bout you givin' away Ben," Ona said. She noticed the purple ring that ran around Polly's neck like a collar. "He about lynched you with yo' own hair." She shook her head.

Polly felt her blood turn cold. *He plans to get rid of Reg*, she thought. She dropped her hair. "He is an evil, angry man, Ona, and I fear this war has made him worse. He wants to hurt me. We have a few days left before he leaves. Pray that we get through it—all of us."

Chapter Forty-Six

POLLY GRITTED HER TEETH AS THE WAGON BOUNCED OVER every wheel rut and gully in the dusty road to River Wood. Zee tried to avoid the bigger potholes but the road was in bad shape. With so many men off fighting, the district had let the roads languish after heavy summer rains.

The wagon bed was filled with jugs of water, ham biscuits, and a crate of apples. Polly knew that John would be angry, but she was well within her rights to feed her slaves. She tugged on the ruffled neck of her blue silk gown, keenly aware that the neckline of the gown revealed her bruised throat. Both John and Tom would see the evidence of her beating. *And then what?* she wondered.

The wagon neared River Wood's property line. Zee maneuvered through the broken gates, where Polly recognized Cyrus, patiently working to repair the rusted hinges. He tipped his hat as Zee pulled the wagon to a stop.

"Hello, Cyrus," Polly said, pointing to the back of the wagon. "I have lunch for you." Zee stepped into the wagon bed and pulled out one of the ham biscuits and several apples. He hoisted the jug to pour water into a tin cup and handed it to Cyrus.

The man drank deeply. "Thank you, Miss Polly." Cyrus smiled. "I sho was gettin' thirsty out here. Thank you fo' the food." He handed the cup back to Zee.

Polly smiled and Zee hopped back into the driver's seat. He clicked the reins and the wagon moved on. They rode past the house, shuttered, with the front door boarded up. The front porch posts sagged unevenly.

"Goodness, that is a sorry sight," Polly murmured. "Zee, go on until we find Mr. Roper," Polly instructed. "He will know what to do with this food." Zee clicked the reins again and they moved on toward the fields.

A cluster of slaves gathered at the edge of a cornfield, where a few remaining stalks were all that remained of Stone's meager corn crop. Without overseer direction, his hands had planted what seed corn they had, and then plundered it for food when tiny ears emerged. Polly did not recognize any of the men as hers. "Can you tell me where I can find Mr. Roper, the Whitehall overseer?" she called out.

One of the men stepped forward and pointed toward the tree line. "He pullin' down a fence with his boys over to the property line," the man said. "Mr. Stone is over to the barn, back the way you came."

Polly thanked the man and the wagon lurched forward toward the line of trees in the distance. Polly recognized the area as the property line shared with Colonel McQueen's acreage. As they approached, Polly was relieved to see more of her hands, including the small figure of Reg chopping at a felled tree alongside George. She held up a hand to shade her eyes and scanned the group of men. There was no sign of Tom.

Zee helped Polly down carefully and she called out to the men. "I have lunch, boys!" The men put down tools and wiped sweaty brows and came forward slowly.

Zee dispensed water in tin cups, before passing out sandwiches and apples. George approached Polly worriedly. "We got time to eat, Miss Polly?"

Polly put her hands on her hips and said, "I brought a noon meal to my men, working hard on a Sunday. Who would dare fault me?" George smiled and joined the others near the wagon. She knelt by Reg and handed him an apple. "Are you alright?"

Reg looked around quickly before nodding his head. "He tol' me I got to stay here tonight when the Whitehall men go on home, is all. He ain't hit me yet."

"Reg, in a few days, he will leave again and you can come back," she offered. "Just stay out of his way. I know that he plans to come back to Whitehall tonight himself, so don't do anything to rile him up over the next two days of work and you should be fine." She wanted to reach out, to pat the boy's cheek, but knew better.

"There's a sight for sore eyes," murmured a deep voice.

Polly smiled with relief. "Mr. Roper!" she said, as the man extended his hand to help her up. Polly dusted off her skirts self-consciously and squeezed Tom's hand before releasing it. "I am so glad to see you."

When Tom grinned, the corners of his blue eyes crinkled. "Not as glad as I am to see you," he said. His gaze quickly settled on Polly's bruised throat and his smile faded. The purple ring around her neck was quite obvious in the bright sunshine.

Tom put his hand to Polly's elbow and quickly steered her away from the slaves.

"What the hell did he do to you?" he asked through gritted teeth.

Polly saw the anger in his eyes and panicked. "No. Please don't say anything, Tom. I can handle him for just a few days more of his leave. Right now I am worried about Reg."

Tom removed his hat. He wiped his forehead with his handkerchief. "Aside from barking orders, your husband has not had much to say to me. For which I am thankful. When he arrived this morning with Reg in tow, I got the picture pretty quickly. I asked him to let me use the boy to tear down this fence he wants gone."

"He was quite angry to find Reg at Whitehall," Polly said.

"Is that why he tried to wring your neck?" Tom snapped.

Polly put her hand on Tom's arm and said softly, "Shhh. Please watch out for Reg. He is just a boy." She paused. "He is also John's son."

Tom stepped back and cocked his head. "His son?"

"Yes. By a slave girl who was sold away years ago, apparently. He has suffered at John's hands. I don't want him to get separated from our men, but John told him he must stay here tonight. What can we do?"

Roper looked at the small knot of slaves eating lunch quietly in the shade and said, "I will stay in Wilkins' cabin tonight. I'll make up an excuse to stay. He will be safe here."

Polly squeezed Tom's arm gratefully. "Thank you. Thank you so much."

The man looked at Polly tenderly. "You stay away from him, Polly. Don't provoke him or raise your voice to him, do you understand?"

Polly sighed. "I only have to look at the man cross-eyed to get what's coming, I suppose. He has promised to let me be for the rest of his leave." She looked into Tom's eyes and added sadly, "He says he will not give me an annulment, though. And he wants money for his land deal."

Roper crossed his arms and kicked at the ground with a dusty boot. "Right now, I'm more worried about him hurting you if you say or do something he doesn't like. Be careful." Polly's heart skipped a beat. Tom added, "So give him the damn money."

Polly smiled and said quietly, "You forget that I gave everything to you for safe keeping after we went to the bank and sold the cider. So when I told him I have no money, I was not a liar."

Tom looked up and nodded his head in the direction of three men on horseback coming from the outbuildings. "That'll be him, now. Give me your word that you won't tell him what you know about your brothers. We can take that information to the law after he leaves. Don't spit it out in a fit of anger, however righteous that anger might be. Your word?"

Stone and his slave foreman, a pockmarked man called Neary, approached Tom and Polly, an unfamiliar white man riding behind them. Polly watched John's approach and leaned toward Roper. "Is he the new overseer?" she murmured.

Polly inched back a few steps and regarded the trio warily as Tom stepped forward and said, "Mr. Stone."

The three men dismounted and came to stand with Tom. "What brings you to River Wood, dear wife?" John asked curtly, as he looked past Tom to Polly.

"A noon meal for my men," Polly answered cheerfully, pointing to the group of slaves eating under the tree. "They are out here working hard for you on a Sunday. I thought they should eat. I do have enough for your own men if you'd like to call them in."

John took a puff from his cigar and turned to Neary. "Call 'em in. Give 'em fifteen minutes to eat and then back to work," he said sharply. "I don't have weeks to do what needs to be done today."

Neary nodded and jogged back to his horse.

Tom turned to the quiet man standing next to John, extended his hand, and said, "Roper. Tom Roper. Have we met?"

The stranger was slight and young, judging by his clean-shaven cheek. Polly thought he looked kind enough, younger than she, but experienced in the ways of the world. He looked familiar, too. The man looked up with one eye covered under his black hat and shook Tom's hand vigorously. His left arm hung limply. "The name's Stevens. I met you two at the harvest dance in town. When I delivered the letters from Captain Stone."

"Private Stevens. Of course." Tom smiled. "Good to see you, son. Will you be taking the overseer's job then?" he asked warmly.

Stevens glanced at John Stone and said, "I surely would be honored to oversee Captain Stone's place. My bad arm won't slow me down none. No man will work harder, and that's a fact. I am here to apply for the job."

Stone exhaled a cloud of cigar smoke. He clapped Stevens on the back. "Easy there, Stevens. I have another man interested, coming out later this afternoon. After that, I will make a decision." He glared at Tom and added, "I didn't realize that you all met at a soiree. So you took my wife out dancing." He nodded, his blue eyes cold.

Tom returned the icy stare but said nothing.

Polly broke the awkward silence. "Mr. Stevens, thank you for your help today. I know how anxious my husband is to get the farm in good repair."

John tossed his cigar butt on the grass. "Stevens, go ahead and get my wife's boys up from their luncheon. Take them out to the fence line and get the rest of those posts down. After that, you can go home. I will be in touch."

Stevens nodded and shook hands with John. "Thank you, sir. For the opportunity to come out. I could surely use this job. Ma'am." He tipped his hat toward Polly and headed to the group of slaves waiting nervously under the tree. Polly watched as Reg stood. He hovered close to George as the men moved back toward the fence line.

John looked at Tom. "We are clearing brush between my property and Colonel McQueen's. We have a land deal that will go through at some point and I aim to add corn acreage next spring."

Tom nodded but did not speak.

Polly wondered if John had secured the funds needed, or if he would be after her later to get the money. "Will I be able to bring my men home tonight?" she asked pointedly.

"I don't care where they bed down. I'll need them back tomorrow though. I've got my boys on the outbuildings that needed repair. The fields are in better shape, finally. After I get the new overseer in place, they'll go to winter chores. I will be well away by that point," John said.

"I like that Stevens boy," Tom mused. "He'd be a good one to work with."

John bristled. "Stevens is lame. Bum hand and leg. Missing an eye. I only extended the opportunity as a kindness. The fellow coming out this afternoon is older, wiser, up from Camden, and has kin nearby. Name of Gentry. He left a cotton plantation of over 5,000 acres. Whispering Pines, I believe."

Tom nodded. "I've heard of it. They struggled this past season. After the burn order . . ."

John ignored Tom's comment and spoke to Polly. "I will send your boys home at sundown. But I want them back tomorrow, same as today," he paused and added sarcastically, "If you would oblige me, dear wife."

Tom shifted his weight uneasily and clenched his fists. "I can send Miss Polly's hands home tonight and stay here to watch your men while you get your overseer sorted out."

John regarded Tom with suspicion and then nodded. "I would appreciate you staying here tonight. Whether it'll be Stevens or Gentry, I aim to have him here, ready to work, before I leave town."

Polly wanted to ask about Reg but caught Tom's eye and decided against it. "I will leave you men to your work." She picked up an empty basket and asked, "You want supper at Whitehall tonight, then, John?"

John pulled another cigar from his vest pocket and took his time to light it, puffing on it for several moments before answering. "Yes, I would like supper at home with my loving wife," he said, his eyes boring into her.

"I will let Ona know," Polly said, looking away. She hurried toward the wagon, grateful that River Wood would soon have a new overseer and Tom would come home.

— • —

POLLY DRESSED HERSELF FOR DINNER EARLY, fumbling with buttons and hair combs with shaking hands. Then she waited on the front porch in the gathering dark for any sign of John and her field hands to appear. In truth, she was nervous about his reasons for wanting to eat with her but was comforted by the fact that Reg would stay at River Wood with Tom.

The temperature was warm for early November, and Polly draped her shawl on the porch railing. She sat in a rocking chair and began to rock back and forth nervously. A small breeze blew and a smattering of orange sourwood leaves drifted slowly toward the earth. Polly found herself saddened as she watched them fall.

She heard the door behind her open and she turned to see Ona. "Supper be ready in about fifteen minutes," she said. "I brought you a lamp." She handed Polly a kerosene lantern, glowing brightly.

Polly nodded. "Thank you. I will be in as soon as they arrive." Her thoughts ran to Reg, and whether he was safe with Tom at River Wood.

"You hungry?" Ona asked. The sound of a wagon and horses approaching interrupted the women. Polly stood up and stared across the dark front lawn.

"It's them," she said with trepidation. She clutched her skirts and stepped off the porch. John arrived first, on his horse. As he dismounted, George followed close behind, driving the wagon loaded with slaves. He tipped his hat to Polly and clicked the reins, continuing past the big house toward the barn. Polly tried to scan the wagon bed for any sign of the boy, but it was too dark to distinguish faces.

John removed his hat and used it to swipe the dust from his trousers.

Polly smoothed her hair nervously and held the lamp high to see John's face. "Supper is about ready. Did the men get that fence pulled down?"

John sighed wearily. "They did. And I have hired the Gentry fellow as my overseer. He starts tomorrow."

"Oh, I was hoping you'd hire Private Stevens," Polly said. "He is a decent young fellow, a wounded man who needs a job."

"It is not my duty to play nursemaid to a wounded soldier," John said evenly. "Nor is it yours."

"I was only saying, with you leaving soon—"

John cut Polly off. "I know what you were saying. I hired the best man I could find on short notice. I'll not hear another word on the subject. Now find someone to get my horse cared for. I will wash up for supper."

They waited as Zee approached the front of the house at a jog. Zadoc took the reins from his master with a quiet nod and led the horse into the darkness.

Polly turned to go indoors and John followed. He passed her in the hallway and headed up the stairs, his dirt-caked boots heavy on the treads.

Polly registered the savory aroma of roast chicken and wondered which of the birds had been slaughtered. She knew that Reg was prone to naming the fowl, despite Ona's discouragement of the practice for obvious reasons. She walked into the dining room and heard a small commotion in the adjoining butler's pantry.

Peeking inside the tiny room, Polly gasped. "Reg! What are you doing here? I thought you were to stay with Mr. Roper tonight," Polly said, looking from Ona to Reg. "What happened?" The boy looked pitiful, a swollen cheek and split lip were bad omens. He sat on a low stool, making him look even more pathetic.

Tears shimmered in the boy's eyes. "Mr. Stone said I's to come back to Whitehall tonight after all. Told me to come here." His lip quivered. Ona crouched to press a wet cloth to his face tenderly. She looked over Reg's head toward Polly and mouthed a quick prayer.

Polly bent down and looked into Reg's eyes. "Reg, tell me why he hit you," she whispered.

Reg's eyes did not leave hers as he answered, "Because he can."

His expression was so like Ben's that Polly felt her stomach lurch. She shook her head and stood slowly. "Did he say why he wants you in the house tonight?"

"No ma'am. In the wagon, I was tryin' to stay near big George, like you tol' me. But he called me down from the men and asked me why I left River Wood without his permission. I tried to answer. . . . I jes' got a facefull of his hands beatin' on me befo' I could explain."

Polly heard John's boots on the stairs and put her finger to her lips to silence the boy. "Wait here and be quiet." She left the pantry but not before looking back at Ona. The two women locked eyes and Ona nodded, her mouth set in a grim line.

Polly went to the long sideboard and uncapped the whiskey decanter. She poured herself a shot and downed it quickly. Then she poured a drink for John in the same glass and turned to see her husband enter the room. "There you are. Here's a drink." She handed him the glass and stood by her chair.

John pulled Polly's chair out without comment, took the glass, and downed the whiskey as Polly sat. He poured himself another and then grabbed the bottle as well. He scowled as he watched Polly pick up the silver bell and ring for Ona.

Ona bustled out from the pantry, carrying a tureen of soup. She set it down carefully and backed away from the table.

"What is this, Ona? It smells delicious." Polly tried to smile.

"Onion soup. You gave me the recipe last month. I thought it was special enough to make while Mr. Stone was still home," she said. Ona motioned for Polly to taste it.

Polly dipped her soup spoon into the broth and sipped delicately. "Oh my. That is delicious." She ladled the savory broth into John's bowl. "And what will be the main course tonight? I smell chicken."

"Yes, ma'am. Roast chicken and potatoes, with brown herb gravy. Succotash and some pickled beets."

Polly nodded. She placed both hands in her lap to hide their shaking.

John sipped the warm broth. His face showed no emotion but he said, "Ona, thank you for your good cooking. It's one of the few things I will miss while I am away."

Ona smiled awkwardly and said, "Thank you, suh. I'll get the chicken now."

"Just a moment." John wiped his mouth with his napkin. "Is the boy in the house?"

Ona glanced toward the pantry. Polly's pulse pounded in her temples as she weighed her options. "John, please—" she began.

"Ona, get the boy. Send him in here and then you may get the damned chicken." Ona nodded slowly and retreated from the room. John swallowed a mouthful of soup and put down his spoon. He replenished his whiskey and leaned forward, his elbows on the table.

Polly heard whispering from the pantry. And then Reg appeared, eyes rimmed red.

Polly pushed her chair back and stood up haltingly. Her midsection throbbed. She went to Reg, and stood beside him, her hand on his thin shoulder. "John, he is just a boy," she said defiantly.

John regarded Reg and Polly, standing as a united front. "This boy is a slave who left my farm without the master's permission." He lifted his glass and drained the contents. He wiped his mouth with the back of his hand. "He thinks he is better than the other field hands and shirked his duties to run away, like a scared little girl."

Reg shook his head, tears trickling down his brown cheeks. "No suh, I come here and work real hard. Ask Miss Polly—"

John slammed his hand down on the table and shouted, "Enough! Enough, dammit. How dare you interrupt me, boy?"

Polly stepped in front of Reg. "John, calm down and let's enjoy our meal. We can talk about what to do tomorrow. You have only one day left at home. Send Reg away now and let Ona bring the chicken." She forced a weak smile. "Please. Let's enjoy our meal."

John regarded Reg with a smirk. He poured two fingers of the amber liquid into the cut crystal and raised his glass. "To my wife. She runs her household without a damn thought for me." He tipped the glass back and swallowed the entire contents. He slammed the glass down hard and wiped his mouth with his sleeve.

"And so I will run my house without a damn thought about her," he said to no one in particular. He pointed to the boy and continued. "That is why I have sold Reginald here to Colonel McQueen." John's ice blue eyes narrowed. "Boy, you will be leaving day after tomorrow with me. You're going to war."

Reg's knees buckled, but Polly caught the boy. "John. You are doing this only to spite me," Polly said between clenched teeth. "Punish me if you must. Reg did not do anything wrong. He is a good worker—but he is a child."

John twisted his mouth into a malicious smile. "He is a good worker. That is what I promised the Colonel. In trade for that land."

"For God's sake, he is your son!" Polly exclaimed. At those words, John's expression soured and he stood abruptly, knocking over his chair.

"What the hell did you say?" He grabbed Polly by the arm and pulled her away from Reg.

Polly thought quickly and said, "Clay Wilkins told me. Before he left town," she said, grimacing as John wrenched her arm behind her back. "Please, let Reg go back to quarters and we can talk," she said, flinching as his other hand came forward to grasp her chin roughly. John squeezed his fingers into the soft flesh of Polly's chin.

"Please," she begged softly. "Is this because you need money? We will get money. I can get money," she offered.

John pinned Polly's body into the wall. She closed her eyes.

John turned his face to Reg, cowering in the corner. "Boy, get out of here. You come back at dawn. Be on the back porch. You're going to River Wood with me, and then you'll go to your new master from there. Now git!"

Reg stumbled from the dining room. Polly heard the back door slam as he went. She closed her eyes, expecting John's fist to smash into her face. Instead, she felt his hot breath in her ear. "You have embarrassed me, humiliated me, and refused me. I will sell a nigger of mine, or beat a nigger of mine,"–he paused, pressing his knee between her legs–"or fuck a nigger of mine, whenever I want to. Do you understand me?" He squeezed his fingernails into Polly's chin until she cried out.

They heard the back door open. A draft of cold air blew through the room and the candles flickered. John's hands released Polly abruptly and she coughed to catch her breath.

Ona chuckled from the pantry and called out cheerfully, "I got the roast chicken and fixin's fo' y'all now. Let me plate it. I be right in."

John straightened his collar and returned to the table. Polly's fingers touched the tender welts on her chin, before taking her seat. She refused to look at John, who leaned back in his chair, thrumming his fingers on the table impatiently.

Ona scurried into the dining room carrying two fully laden dinner plates. She looked at John and asked, "You like that soup, Mr. Stone? We had some good yellow onions this fall. I thought y'all would like it." She set down his plate. "And this here bourbon gravy I been saving fo' when you came home."

Polly marveled at Ona's calm demeanor, but John did not notice her false cheer.

"Bourbon gravy? Ona, you spoil me." John tucked his napkin into the collar of his shirt.

"It smells pretty strong, suh. I prob'ly poured in more drink than I s'posed to." She cackled. "Mizz Calhoun's cook gave me the recipe when we was in Charleston. I was savin' it fo' you, when the war is over, but it seem like we never gone get you home fo' good, suh."

John seemed taken in by Ona's charmed words. "It's nice to have a good, home-cooked meal, Ona, I cannot deny."

The woman set a plate down in front of Polly, who noticed the dark gravy already smothering John's half chicken and red potatoes. She watched as Ona set the gravy boat near John's plate and then set a small loaf of crusty brown bread at his left hand. "I's jes' glad to have someone to cook for, suh," Ona simpered. "Sop up that good gravy with fresh bread. Miss Polly don't like it, but I knew you would. Mr. Burgiss used to love my cookin'. He called it man food."

With a growing dread, Polly looked up as Ona passed behind John. Something was strange. She glanced at Polly and nodded imperceptibly. Ona turned away and continued to busy herself at the sideboard. Polly looked down at her own plate and began to pick at her food, unsure of what was safe to eat. John cut a piece of chicken and dipped it in gravy, before putting the forkful of food into his mouth. He rolled his eyes as he chewed before swallowing. "Ona, that's some fine gravy."

Ona beamed, "Thank you, suh. Hope you eat it all up. The man of the house should eat like a king." She chuckled, before retreating to the pantry.

Over John's head, Polly could see Ona standing in the shadows, hands motioning to the gravy boat. Polly began to eat her own meal, the plain chicken and vegetables a far cry from John's rich meal. Out of the corner of her eye, she watched as John sliced a thick slab of the brown bread. He tore off a large chunk and dipped it into the gravy. They continued to eat in silence.

Polly picked at her food nervously, occasionally looking up to sip water. She watched as John finished every morsel on his plate and used the remaining bread to soak up the last of the rich gravy. He tipped his chair back on two legs and belched.

She spoke hesitantly. "Is there anything I can do to convince you not to sell Reg away?"

"Not a damn thing." John sighed, blotting his lips with his napkin. "You gave away my Kate, a slave I valued. I am only doing the same thing to you." John reached into his vest pocket and produced a cigar. He struck a match and lit it, puffing a few times before exhaling a plume of smoke. Despite several whiskeys, John showed no signs he'd had too much to drink.

Polly could not help herself. "You never loved me, John. You have used me all along. It seems you live to hurt me," she said sadly. "You could find someone else and let me go."

John cocked his head and looked at his wife warily. Before he could speak, Ona emerged from the pantry with an iron skillet and set it down on the sideboard. "Mr. Stone, I made ginger cake with the last of the sugar and spices. Anyone care fo' a slice with some cream?" she said eagerly. "It's still warm."

She cut a wedge and turned as if to serve her mistress. "Miss Polly, it real tasty but it won't keep yo' waistline tiny," she chuckled. "I remember you tryin' not to eat desserts."

"I'm quite full, Ona." Polly couldn't help but notice the faintest show of relief in Ona's expression. Did it mean what she hoped?

"Mr. Stone? Can I serve you some ginger cake with cream?" Ona held the dark slice of cake in front of Stone. "I know you like a Charlotte Rousse, but we's lucky to have even what we need fo' a ginger cake," she said with a grin.

The man smiled and stifled another belch. "I stuffed myself, for sure, but I think I still have room for dessert. I won't eat like this when I go back to Virginia. That's a fact. A small piece will do," he said.

Ona beamed and set the plate down in front of him. "Cream, suh?" Stone nodded and Ona set the bowl of whipped cream down in front of the man. She quietly retreated to the pantry while Stone finished his meal.

John served himself some of the sweet cream and began to eat the simple dessert. Polly stayed silent and watched him eat. He seemed fine, and Polly wondered if Ona had changed her mind.

When he finished eating, he placed his napkin on the table and picked up the smoldering cigar. He inhaled and blew the smoke across the table, before leaning forward to speak. He pointed the cigar in Polly's direction, and said, "The trouble with you, Polly, is that you assume you are in charge. You are not. You're just a woman. No education. No experience in the world. Nothing."

Polly bit her lip but knew not to take John's bait. If she were going to save Reg, she would need to play the dutiful wife a while longer. She noticed a movement behind John and knew then that Ona was still listening from the butler's pantry.

"You own Whitehall outright as you so clearly pointed out, and so it may be. For now. But as your husband, I have the right to use farm income as I see fit."

He paused to flick ashes into an ashtray, and continued, "I see fit to purchase the McQueen land. Yet you tell me that we had no income this season." He shrugged. "So I will hand over a slave boy, a fine young farm hand, to the Colonel, in exchange for that small parcel that will finally connect River Wood and Whitehall. The deal is done." His blue eyes, once able to make Polly's heart leap, now bored into her own with such malice. He crushed out the remains of the cigar and waited. "You simple-minded woman. I will get this land."

Polly felt a surge of anger but demurred. "John, I can only appeal to any shred of kindness that you may have. He is just a boy." She swallowed hard and added, "Your flesh and blood."

John frowned and picked up his glass. "He's a goddamn slave, Polly. His mother was a slave. My father sired half a dozen half-breed children. Sold them all away. Reg is my property. To be used as I see fit." He drained the last sip of whiskey, before putting a hand to his chest. He grimaced. Polly noticed the small gesture and the tremble in his hand but said nothing.

"Suppose I give you another piece of land," Polly offered. "Or I can sell something of my mother's."

"I've made the decision." John cleared his throat. His eyes narrowed and he touched his chest again with a trembling hand. His face grew quite flushed and he coughed. He stood abruptly, coughed again, and shook his head. Polly noticed that his breath was becoming labored and he stumbled back from the table. She remained seated and watched as John reached out to grip the table for support.

"Are you alright?" she finally asked, feigning concern, in case he was merely having digestive upset after such a heavy meal. "Shall I get the bicarbonate?"

John's face glistened with perspiration and twisted into a grimace. He tried to move toward the doorway but had to grip the chair with both hands to keep from falling. "What did you do?" he rasped. "What did you do?"

Polly stood up and backed away, shaking her head, thankful that John did not wear his sidearm in the house.

"Let me get you some bicarbonate," Polly suggested again, although her feet stayed firmly planted. So Ona had done it. She wanted to watch this play out. After all the times that John had caused her physical pain and injury and replaying the scene of Caleb and Joshua's grisly deaths over in her mind, she leaned against the breakfront and stared, tight-lipped.

John was clearly ill. He gaped at her, open-mouthed, and tried to speak. "What . . . ?" His red face turned ashen and he registered that something bad was happening. Foam flecked the corners of his mouth and his right arm began to twitch. He reached out to her and then sank to the floor, knocking the chair over, his right leg joining the seizure. Polly slowly walked around the dining table and stood over John.

His body became rigid in its seizure; his back arched in a spasm and then shook again. His fists curled. His eyes reddened and bulged. He stared at Polly, tongue thick in his mouth, drooling and gasping for oxygen, right there on Mary Burgiss's oriental carpet.

Polly leaned over John and watched the poison take effect. How similar this is to watching the colt die, she mused. But while the colt lay in agony, she had cried.

John tried to speak, but he could only mouth words. Polly slid down against the wall and regarded her husband, entranced by the macabre dance going on with his arms and legs.

A strange calm descended on her. She began softly. "I know what you and Wilkins did to my brothers, John. I saw you that day. I was just a little girl . . . and I blocked it out for so long. Oh, I repressed it for years, but a stroll through my orchard to that very spot this past spring brought it all back. I remembered what you and Wilkins did that day, to Caleb and Joshua. To the Kemps. What were you after, John? Was it a drunken spree? A botched robbery?"

John stared up at Polly with bloodshot eyes, his chest heaving dramatically as the poison slowed his heartbeat and his ability to breathe.

"You are a murderer. A piece of human filth. I watched you lock Nancy Kemp in the burning building. And you want to buy that same land, where you and your Mr. Wilkins bashed my brothers' heads in for sport? And pay for it with the sale of your own son?" Polly felt the weight of years lift away. "No, that cannot happen."

John tried to reach for Polly's skirt hem but his own trembling fingers would not cooperate. She watched as the foam-flecked spittle traced a path down into John's beard. His eyes were wild with fright, and Polly smirked. She pushed away from her tormented husband and backed right into Ona's legs.

"Ona," Polly said, her voice shaking. Ona crouched down and put her arm around Polly's shoulder. "What do I do now?" she asked.

"He goin' to his maker soon enough, Miss Girl. Or maybe straight to hell." Ona smoothed Polly's hair. "For all the wrong he done to you and to your family . . . and to mine."

Polly nodded solemnly. "Will it be enough?"

Ona chuckled as if the two women were in on a private joke. Ona leaned her forehead against Polly's. "That's the same nasty oleander killed your little colt," she whispered. "An' all the laudanum Dr. Adger left here when yo' Mama was on her deathbed. It should take down the likes of John Stone fo' a while. Maybe not permanent. . . . You hafta see it through. It's part of the plan, remember?" She kissed the top of Polly's head and left the room quickly.

Polly gained strength from Ona's words and finally stood to her feet. She was free. She crossed the room and opened the breakfront drawer. Withdrawing her father's pistol, she turned, and crouched once more by her husband's rigid body. He gasped for breath and Polly couldn't help but notice the blue tinge spreading around his lips.

"You took my entire family from me, John. My dear brothers . . . and if you think about it, you killed my mother and my father. You went after me, only for my land. You didn't love me. I was so naive. You deceived me all these years . . ." She watched as foam flecked John's lips.

"Yes. I went back for Kate. I shot Clay Wilkins. I sent Ben and Kate and Solomon away to their freedom. They're in Canada, safe. The little girl Lydia is with them, safe from your wretched hands. The others will follow, including your own son, Reg. I will keep this land. I'll own no slaves. And you will molder in hell for all that you've done."

John's face had turned to a dull gray-blue and his pupils were fixed. Finally, she lifted the pistol, placed the barrel against John's temple, and squeezed the trigger. She watched as the last bit of life force ebbed from her husband's body in a spreading pool on the carpet.

— • —

November 10, 1861

POLLY REMOVED HER WEDDING BAND and pulled the ebony veil down over her face. She paused at the top of the staircase. She thought of her brothers, her mother, and father, and of all that John Stone had done to her, and when a few tears finally shimmered in her brown eyes, she began to descend the stairs slowly. She wore the same black crepe as when her mother died, although her emotions were decidedly different.

As with her brothers and parents before, the front of the house and the windows were draped in black. Cissie had stopped the clocks and the mirrors were covered. There was no body to speak of, thanks to the fire. John's scant remains were shielded from view inside the closed pine coffin. The fragrance of Meyer lemons and herbs scented the parlor, and the few mourners mingled in hushed tones as they waited for the widow to enter the room.

There was much gossip in town about the mysterious cause of the River Wood fire, but all agreed it was almost too much to bear for the young Polly Burgiss Stone, a widow at twenty-one. Hadn't the poor woman been through enough?

Rumor had it that Captain Stone, afflicted with the Soldier's Heart, had fallen asleep drunk and knocked over a lamp. Whatever the cause, if not for Tom Roper and the River Wood hands in a bucket brigade, the whole place, outbuildings, and all, would have gone up in flames. As it was, only the big house was destroyed.

Polly entered the parlor and the guests quieted. She was met by Dr. Adger, who escorted her to her chair. Polly noticed the younger Adgers were seated behind her, even though Ward Adger had been expected to leave for Virginia days before. Lucinda reached forward and patted Polly's shoulder with a gloved hand.

The minister began to intone his sermon. *Dearly beloved and ashes to ashes and dust to dust . . . John has gone to a better place, having departed this mortal coil, although some hinted at suicide . . . but all are forgiven if they place their trust in Jesus . . . he was a*

good man and bad things do happen to good people . . . this war has claimed many good men
already . . . Amen and Amen.

Polly closed her eyes and saw a warm summer day and grasshoppers
buzzing in the tall grass. Silvery crawdads skittered under the rocks in an
icy creek. There was the high-pitched laughter of children at play, as yellow
sunshine played on their tanned skin. The young boys splashed, full of life
and love, trusting in the sure expectation of adventure in the days to come,
as only children can. Dandelion puffs floated on the breeze. Polly beamed
at the boys from across the broad creek, the sun so bright she could barely
make out their freckled faces. "You go on, brothers. You go on. You're free
now. I will catch up later!"

Chapter Forty-Seven

November 13, 1861

POLLY STOOD WITH ONA AT THE RAILROAD STATION as Tom waited in line at the ticket counter. The depot crawled with soldiers leaving for deployment. Ona loosened the drawstring of the small pouch Polly had placed in her palm and found several large gold coins nestled in the folds. She gasped and looked at Polly. "What are these?"

"Twenty-dollar Liberty pieces. My mother gave them to me when I turned eighteen. She knew I would need them one day. That day has come. I gave Ben the rest of them." Polly shrugged and leaned in. "They are Union currency anyway. I dare not use them here." She laughed and then dropped her voice to a whisper. "There is enough gold there to take care of expenses you will incur after Tom leaves you. If you're lucky, you'll have money left over to help with expenses up north. At the very least, you will need warm clothes for you and Reg."

Ona looked in both directions before standing on her tiptoes to embrace Polly tightly. "Miss Girl, you know that bein' free is a dream I have had since you gave me my paper years ago. My heart's burstin' at the thought of seein' Ben and my new gran'baby. I thank you fo' this. Please don't cry."

Polly tried to focus through her tears. She was grateful for the dark veil that hid her face. "I am crying happy tears, Ona. I cannot thank you enough—for everything."

Ona nodded. "We did what had to be done."

Polly called to Reg, who leaned against the wagon, looking dejected. The boy sidled closer. "You behave on the trip, Reg. Follow Mr. Roper's instructions and do what Ona tells you. You will be just fine. I promise." She extended her gloved hand.

Reg reached out his thin right hand and shook Polly's politely, his face glum. "Yes ma'am."

Ona tapped Reg on the shoulder and said, "Go wait with Zee, Reg. I got to say some words to Miss Polly." The boy nodded solemnly and walked toward the wagon, where Zee sat slumped in the driver's seat.

"I am sorry. It's better if he thinks you're both being sold." Polly shrugged. "For his safety. But I surely hate to part this way."

Ona sighed. "Mr. Roper said that Reg'll figure it out soon enough, though. He a bright boy."

"Like his uncle." Polly smiled. "But he won't be traveling through a dark tunnel under a crate of peaches," she added with a laugh. "Now, I know you have rehearsed our story a hundred times. Do you know it by heart?"

Ona nodded and began her recitation. "If anyone asks on the train, you sendin' us to the big auction in Charlotte. We to be sold together. Mr. Roper has papers. He will be sittin' in the white folks' car. At the Charlotte depot, though, we don't even leave the station. Mr. Roper will claim us from the slave car. A man with a red beard an' a grey hat with a quail feather in it gonna come up and tell Mr. Roper he want to buy us both. Right then and there. Name of Mr. Blake. They gone talk a bit. Mr. Tom gone sell us to Mr. Blake. It s'posed to look like Mr. Roper done sold us right there in the depot. Mr. Blake gonna take us away to New York."

Polly nodded and wrung her gloved hands nervously. "Yes, but remember. Mr. Blake is really a friend of Tom's. He is a conductor on the Underground. He has done this several times. He will see that you both get to Ontario. Mostly by train, ironically. You'll pose as his slaves all the way to New York."

"I understand." Ona fidgeted with her new bonnet nervously.

"Oh, Ona, please write to me when you can. I don't think I can bear not knowing when you'll get to where you're going. Do you remember how to sign your name once you're free?"

"My signed name to be Mary Rodgers 'til the war ends." She shivered and pulled her new woolen cloak closely around her shoulders. "I practiced it fo' days. It a lot harder than a X."

Polly nodded, "That's right. I am sure I will not get any more letters through the U.S. mail until this war is over. I'll pray for you every day."

Ona looked around before reaching out and squeezing Polly's hand quickly. "It was a needful thing. You keep that in mind. The bad times is over fo' you now." She paused and added, "Mr. Roper is a kind man. A good man who is gonna be there for you and love you if you let him. I pray for that to be so. I surely do."

There was a trace of a rueful smile behind the dark veil. "I wonder if the bad times are really over, Ona? A war on our doorstep, the economy in shambles, growing cotton will be out of the question next year . . ."

Ona gathered her tiny self up to her full height. "What do people gain from their labors; from their toil under the sun? Generations come and generations go, but the earth remains forever."

Polly regarded her slave woman with admiration. "That's beautiful, Ona."

"I didn't make it up, Miss Girl. It's from Ecclesiastes. I don't think I said it 'zactly right, but Martin said it every mornin' before he'd leave the cabin. It reminded him that not a one of us is in control. White people might think they's the boss, but they ain't. Not really. Only God knows where he's takin' us all, and what's gonna be is gonna be."

She reached out furtively and squeezed Polly's gloved hand. "It'll all unfold the way it should, if you let Him handle it, Miss Girl."

From the corner of her eye, Polly noticed two women approach them on the platform.

Ona looked at the women and quickly stepped back, dropping her head.

Lucinda Ward pushed a pram ahead of her and waved at Polly. Her mother stepped forward and cleared her throat. "Why, Mrs. Stone! Lucinda attended your husband's funeral only recently, and now we find you here at the depot. Mercy! You are in deep mourning for your husband but I suppose these days it is acceptable to be out and about . . ." She paused. "Even after what happened," she said, looking at Polly with a pained expression.

"Thank you, Mrs. Davis," Polly said stiffly.

Mrs. Davis glanced in Ona's direction and held a lacey handkerchief to her nose. She sniffed daintily. "Killed in a fire at River Wood, was he? How tragic. My deepest sympathies. After all your family has been through."

"Yes," Polly said politely. "Thank you for your condolences."

Mrs. Davis continued, "Your poor mother never stepped foot in town after she became a widow. I suppose this war has changed all the rules and conventions. . . . But surely you cannot be traveling so soon?" the woman asked.

"No, Mrs. Davis. That would be terribly gauche," Polly agreed.

She winked at Lucinda and smiled. Peering into the pram, she said, "And how is little Emmeline?"

Lucinda gazed at her infant daughter. "She is very well. We came to see her father off and soon we are on a train to Atlanta ourselves. Mother has secured a lovely place in the city to wait out the war. Until Ward is home for good, of course."

"Yes!" Mrs. Davis harrumphed. "I told Lucinda that she simply cannot stay here with a baby. Atlanta will have everything we need and is probably much safer."

Lucinda rolled her eyes. "Mother feels that Atlanta will be a better place to raise Emmeline than here. My husband disagreed, but Mother won the day."

Polly sighed. "I will miss you, Lucinda."

Lucinda stepped forward and embraced Polly warmly. She whispered in Polly's ear. "I will miss you too. I feel that I am abandoning you after all that's happened, and I am so sorry."

A train whistle shrieked. "Safe travels to you. Now, if you will excuse me, my overseer is taking these slaves to auction and I must see him off." The words stuck in Polly's throat.

"Oh my goodness!" Mrs. Davis clutched her bejeweled throat dramatically. "You are selling your own mammy away?"

"Actually, she deserves better than I can give her. I am a poor widow now. And I need the money," Polly said with sarcasm. "If you will excuse us, they have a train to catch."

"Well," Mrs. Davis began, leaning in conspiratorially. "I might be in need of a good house woman in Atlanta. My Edna is getting old and forgetful. She will not be with us much longer. How much will you sell this one for?"

"Mrs. Davis, I may be poor, but I would not sell Ona to you for all the money in the Confederate treasury!" Polly sniffed.

The woman gasped. Lucinda exploded with laughter. Polly smiled at her friend and turned away with a wink. Ona followed, trying to contain her own laughter.

Tom returned from the ticket counter. "What did that old biddy want?" He smiled and gazed down at Polly with tender concern.

"Oh, she doesn't bother me anymore. It might actually help us. Word will be all over town by this afternoon that I am so destitute that I am selling my mammy days after my husband's funeral." Polly chuckled.

Tom removed his hat and his face became serious. "Everything is in order. I should be home soon, the day after tomorrow at the latest. I will get them to their destination and take the very next train back."

Polly read the worry in his face. "I'll be fine."

"I hate to leave you right now, Polly. There is so much to do with River Wood," he murmured.

Polly smiled up at the man warmly from behind her veil. "Thank you, Tom. I will be just fine and it is important to me that Ona leaves now. She will be well away should . . . should anything come up."

Tom's brow furrowed in concern, and he exhaled audibly. His breath was visible in the chilly morning air. "I cannot see your face behind that veil, Polly, but if you think I can't read your voice—"

Polly spoke quietly. "Don't worry. He certainly isn't coming back." She glanced at Ona and back to Tom, as the train whistle pierced the air. "Let me say my goodbyes to Ona quickly, since the town witch is so close by, and then you three will be off. It will be good for me to be alone for a day or two." A cloud of released steam hissed and chuffed. "I have some thinking to do. Pray for me?" she said hopefully.

"I always do," Tom answered softly. He turned and handed a ticket to Ona. "Your compartment is in the last car, Ona. You have the letter I gave you. The conductor will know you are with me. You'll be given a privy break in Greenville. Reg is on your ticket. I will see you both in Charlotte." Ona nodded. Tom stepped away to give the women some privacy.

"Ona, I will pray for your safety every day," Polly whispered. "I would not have survived had you and Ben not cared for me so. And for what you did with John? I can never repay you for that. I love you dearly." She extended her hand and Ona looked around before reaching to shake it politely.

"I love you too, Miss Girl." Ona squinted in the bright sunlight. "One day, maybe we can see each other again. The world has to wake up and realize it cain't go on like this, all divided." She squeezed Polly's hand and turned away quickly, following Tom and Reg toward the slave compartment at the back of the train.

— • —

ZADOC URGED THE WAGON SLOWLY DOWN the long drive, his demeanor quiet. Polly dare not tell him the truth. For all of their sakes, the slaves would have to believe that Ona and Reg were sold away like Ben and Kate before them. The ache of it all made it difficult for Polly to breathe, and she could not look at Zee. He slowed to a stop in front of the house and came around to help Polly down. Her eyes were too full of tears to see his face clearly, especially from behind the veil. Jack yipped and yapped, jumping for attention.

"Stop it, Jack. Down," she said, too sharply. "Thank you, Zee. I'll not ride Delightful today. Could you please give her a good canter around the property later?"

"Yes ma'am," Zee said somberly.

"Zee, thank you again for your help. With . . . everything." Polly removed her bonnet and veil, clutching them to her chest.

Zee nodded. "Ona tol' me not to ask questions. So I won't. Don't matter how he died. He was a bad man," he said simply.

"He was indeed." Polly walked up the steps, and the crushing weight of Ona's departure hit her as she opened the front door. The house was as quiet as a tomb. She left her bonnet and veil on the hall table and began to unbutton her coat.

Cissie appeared from the back rooms, wiping her hands on her apron. She asked, "You back already. What time you want lunch, ma'am?"

"No lunch, Cissie. I think I will lie down. If I get hungry, I can make something on my own." She began to ascend the stairs but heard Cissie's footsteps behind her.

Polly turned around. Cissie looked up at her mistress and pointed her finger at her. "Miss Polly, we know what you did." A knowing smile played at Cissie's lips.

Polly gripped the newel post.

Cissie continued, "You didn't sell Ona and Reg away. Ona tol' me and George last night about what a kindness you doin' fo' her. And fo' Ben

675

and Kate and the chillun. . . . You and Mr. Roper done a good thing getting they family together. Ain't sure where they gone, but now we know you ain't sold our folks away somewhere bad. That's a relief, ma'am. Me and George ain't gone say nothin' to the others. But you a good white woman, Miss Polly."

Polly smiled at the woman gratefully and climbed up the stairs.

— • —

POLLY WOKE TO A LEADEN SKY and the muffled stillness that hinted at coming snow. She had slept deeply and well into the morning, without waking, when Cissie came to stoke the fire. The weather had turned cold, but Polly relished the chilly weather. A brilliant cardinal sat on a branch outside her window and sang. She watched the bird for some minutes. She finally swung her legs out of bed and grabbed her dressing gown. There was a gentle knock on the door and the bird took flight.

Cissie entered with a tea tray and set it down on Polly's nightstand. "Good mornin,' Miss Polly. The man you sent a note to is downstairs. I tried to put him off, but he said you sent fo' him."

Polly stood up quickly. "Gracious! I did sleep long. Let me dress and I will come right down. Tell him I will only be just a minute and offer him tea." She hurried to the armoire for a day dress. Forgoing the shabby black crepe, she grabbed her comfortable blue calico and rushed to lace her corset and throw her braid up into a messy coil. After a sip of hot tea and the frustration of a broken bootlace, she hurried down the steps to find Private Stevens standing at the bottom of the stairs, his hat clutched in his good hand.

"Private Stevens! I am so glad that you have come," she said. "Please—come in and sit down." She showed the young man into the parlor and was relieved to see that Cissie had a warm fire blazing in the hearth and the tea tray sitting nearby.

The young soldier tried to suppress a smile as he studied Polly's attire.

Polly felt a rush of embarrassment. "I am sure that you are wondering why I am not in black. After all, my late husband was your commanding officer." She smoothed her dress self-consciously.

"Not at all, Mrs. Stone, not at all. My mama lost my daddy, and then my little sisters, to the influenza in '56. My twin brother, Joel, died at Manassas. After that, Mama was so weary of wearin' black that she told me if I died in battle, she was goin' to wear a red dress to my funeral just to bear the pain," he said. "You remind me of her, only younger."

His face regained its solemnity and he added, "I was sorry to hear of Captain Stone's death. The Soldier's Heart 'bout to take more men than the fightin'."

Polly regarded the young man warmly. "Thank you for your kind words. Your mother must be a very strong woman to have lived through so much suffering."

Stevens nodded. "She is that. I am all the family she has left."

Polly began tentatively. "Mr. Stevens, I asked you here because I have an idea that might benefit both of us. I wondered if you meant it when you said you could oversee River Wood."

Stevens' eyes brightened. "I heard you'd be sellin' it . . . after what happened."

"The rumor mill is wrong on that account. Honestly, I have no plans to rebuild the main house. That is where John's body . . . was found. But I would like to maintain the acreage and the outbuildings. I would like you to consider overseeing that portion under the direction of my manager, Tom Roper."

Stevens nodded enthusiastically. "Yes, ma'am. I liked Mr. Roper. He seemed a good man."

Polly smiled. "He is. He liked you, too. You would report to him but oversee the hands we still have there. There is a small overseer's cottage for you that must be cleaned out and I hope we might count on your mother to come. She could cook for you and manage your kitchen garden, take care of the chickens. My girl Cissie and her small son will continue to keep house here. The two properties will be run separately at first, but I do plan to extend my peach orchards that way in time. No more cotton. We will teach the men how to care for peach trees instead."

Polly's eyes grew brighter as she spoke. "You could take one of the slave cabins and repair it—fix it up nicely for your mother—add onto, even."

Private Stevens grinned and Polly continued enthusiastically. "It would be up to you to decide who takes care of the draft horses and other livestock at River Wood. My husband's last overseer left in haste, as you know, and both the men and animals suffered for it. You would assess the men and assign tasks accordingly."

Stevens nodded. "I will speak to Mother, but I surely think I will take the job, Mrs. Stone."

Polly smiled. "You haven't even heard the salary, Private. And the one important caveat."

Stevens looked at Polly with confusion. "One what, ma'am?"

"One important condition," Polly explained. "I will not have my slaves mistreated. They shall be treated fairly or your employment will be terminated. You may not whip them or beat them." She lifted her chin and continued, "In fact, you should know that if it were not for rules against manumission, I would free them all." Polly stared at the young soldier defiantly.

Stevens shrugged and said quietly, "Ma'am, I fought alongside two Negroes, when I was up north. They was fightin' for the Confederacy too. I don't know how they ended up with our unit." He paused. "When I was wounded, an' draggin' myself back behind the lines, it was one of them that carried my dying brother Joel off the battlefield—a Negro man named Earl. He picked Joel up and ran through cannon fire—jes' barreled right through. Joel's blood was all splattered across Earl's clothes. He got Joel back to our camp though. Didn't leave him in enemy hands." Stevens closed his eyes, lost in thought. "I got to say my goodbyes before Joel died. Don't know what happened to Earl . . ."

His eyes opened abruptly. "Beggin' your pardon, ma'am. I'm so sorry.

I get lost sometimes myself. You have no quarrel with me. I'll respect your wishes. This job is savin' my life."

"I can pay you $40 a month to start and a five percent share of the crops. Do we have a deal?" Polly stood up expectantly.

Stevens nodded and stood quickly. "I am grateful to have a job, ma'am. Thank you."

"Can you begin tomorrow? Mr. Roper is away, but I want to finish clearing that patch of land behind my orchards. I have purchased it outright from Colonel McQueen. We will extend my orchards that way. An old trading post once stood there but it burned down years ago." For a moment, Polly's mind took her down a dark path. She shivered and then looked up at the young man.

"Are you alright, Mrs. Stone?" Stevens asked.

"Ghosts, Mr. Stevens. One mustn't spend too much time with ghosts." She smiled and walked him to the door.

— • —

POLLY USED THE SLENDER WALKING STICK to clear briars from her path. The hem of her dress was torn, and her fingertips blue from cold, but she could barely contain her joy. Jack ran through the orchard in front of her, the fruit trees bare, their branches reaching claw-like into gray skies.

She paused to catch her breath, exhaling a plume of moisture into the dry cold, before heading into the dense and overgrown tangle. Grapevines devoid of leaves twisted and coiled over charred bits of lumber that still dared to poke through. The only evidence of where Ben had buried Wilkins' body was the slight depression in the earth, for the forest had reclaimed the grave quickly.

She stood and surveyed the scene. Soon, George would have the men out burning the few remnants of the old trading post down to ash. The harrow would be dragged across the soil. Saplings would be planted in the groomed earth, where they would sleep until spring.

Spring would come. Tiny emerald buds would unfurl under blue and cloudless skies. Pale pink and white blossoms would perfume the air, and the grass under each tree would be a carpet of green. Honeybees would buzz their hymn to the Creator, and gentle rains would nourish tender roots. She smiled. It would be a fitting tribute.

The grass crunched behind her and Polly whirled to see Tom approaching, his tall frame bent where limbs were low.

"Tom!" she cried and could not stop herself from running into the man's strong arms. He smelled of wood smoke and pipe tobacco, earthy and warm. He held her tightly, murmuring into her hair. She pulled back and put her hands on either side of his face. "They are safely away?"

His eyes told her what she needed to know.

"Your hands are like ice, Polly. You should come home now." His blue eyes crinkled, and he kissed her forehead. Jack danced at the man's feet, pawing at Tom's pants, and begging for a scratch on the head.

Polly laughed, pulled Tom's face toward hers, and kissed him tenderly. "I am home."

— • —

June 18, 1865

Dear Miss Polly,

We heard the war is over and the mail is running again. I know that you probably gave up on hearing from me after nearly four years, but we are all doing well. Ben says I don't have to use the name of Mary Rodgers as we planned because the war is really over and the slaves is free. Praise God. But I was saddened when that wonderful President Lincoln was shot. Oh, the evil in the world.

Ben is a blacksmith here in Hamilton. He does a fine business with the white folks and the freemen alike. Kate is a maid in a white woman's home. I never seen such finery as in that woman's home. I care for the younger grandchildren and it is the joy of my life. We share a house that Ben owns outright. I am so proud.

Reg is a tall young man now, fifteen years. He works with Ben in the shop and is in school too. They favor each other so much and are close as brothers. Lydia is a very smart girl of seven years now. She remembers you fondly and sends her love to her Aunt Polly. She helps me with the little ones after school.

The children go together to a school for negro children. Ben and Kate say they all will go as long as they can. Solomon will begin school in the fall. He is a busy boy now and keeps me worn out each day.

Ben and Kate had a baby girl before I arrived. They named her Polly Caroline, and she is now a beautiful girl four years old, bossy like I remember you at that age. Kate is expecting another child this summer. What a blessing. We is happy here. So happy and cannot thank you enough for seeing us to freedom. Please write to me. Mrs. Ona Burgiss, 12 Shaker Street, Hamilton, Ontario. I want to hear all the news of Whitehall. I pray for you and Mr. Roper, Cissie and George, and all the men there every day.

Fondly,

Ona

— • —

August 22, 1865

Dearest Ona,

I was overjoyed to receive your letter after nearly four long years. We had news from Mr. Blake right after you left us that you were safely on your way to New York to meet another contact, but nothing after that. I worried that you'd been discovered. My prayers have been answered. I am amazed at your writing. Clearly Ben taught you well.

The war was devastating to us. Tom and I married in 1862. Tom was called up to serve as a prison guard at Andersonville that year and served until the war ended. He still has nightmares about what he experienced there and his health has deteriorated somewhat. Luckily, our orchard and sorghum carried us through difficult times. Zee made a fine overseer in Tom's absence. Did you know that Columbia and Atlanta were burned to the ground by General Sherman's march to the coast? We were all relieved that he did not destroy beautiful Charleston. We had a few stray Yankee troops come through here, but since we had little to offer, there was little to take. I was so thankful that they did not destroy our peach trees.

I am overjoyed to hear of Ben and Kate's children and honored beyond words to be the namesake of their daughter, Polly Caroline. I know that you must be so proud of each of your grandchildren. I am unable to bear children, but Tom and I are very happy.

Cissie and George and the other men all stayed through the war. We gave them their freedom after we married, albeit in secret, since it was against the law until the Emancipation Proclamation. They have rewarded us by staying with us and by working hard for Whitehall and for themselves.

We had a number of weddings amongst the former slaves in the area right after the war ended. Zadoc met a lovely young woman, Sarah, and married her just weeks ago. George is quite ill now and Cissie spends her days caring for him. They live in a cabin Tom built for them near the river. Zee has stepped up as farm manager of our property and does a fine job. We have over five hundred acres in fruit now. This means that Zadoc stays busy managing the orchards from our backyard all the way to what was once River Wood. It is all part of Whitehall Fruit Company now.

We could not have managed the orchards or other crops without Meenie, Cyrus, and the others. Many farmers in South Carolina lost everything when both cotton and slavery collapsed. Floride Calhoun was driven nearly to her version of poverty! But of course, she rallied after the war ended and has come home to Mi Casa, for which I am thankful. Her children continued to fight over what remains of Fort Hill until her son Andrew died earlier this year. She is my truest friend beside you, and at her age, she astounds us with her energy and strength.

Give my fond regards to the entire family and be at peace, my friend.

Your dear Miss Girl,
Polly Roper

— • —

December 19, 1872

Dear Polly,

Thank you and Mr. Roper for the package of winter clothing and books for the grandchildren. Glory be! It is so very cold this winter, so the extra clothes will be helpful. The snow is already as high as my waist. Christmas morning will be more exciting with these gifts. Reg invited a young lady friend to come for Christmas dinner, and I believe he plans to propose to her if Ben approves. I will write in the new year and tell you about her.

Fondly,
Ona

— • —

February 14, 1896

Dear Polly,

It is with great sadness that I write of my mother's death. She died peacefully in her sleep after a brief illness. She was a good mother, grandmother, great-grandmother, and a strong woman. We will miss her very much. She spoke highly of you to our grandchildren until her dying day. She asked me at the end to write to let you know of her passing.

I was glad to hear that your orchards are a leading peach producer in South Carolina, and I am not surprised. You must be very proud. My smithy shop and livery continue to do well. Nephew Reg has been my partner for many years. He and his family live next door. Lydia married a local farmer who reminds us of Zee and they also live nearby with their four children. Solomon is our wild child. He moved out to Alberta years ago and homesteads a small cattle ranch. He writes of bulls and hard work and a young wife we have not met. Our youngest, Martin, followed his big brother westward and works on the ranch. One day, Kate and I hope to go west and visit them, and to see the great Rocky Mountains I used to wonder about on Martin's map.

Daughter Polly Caroline is a nurse in Hamilton. I believe that she is my pride and joy, as you can imagine. She works at a hospital for freedmen. Her husband, Ronald Cole, is a teacher. Polly Caroline is a reader like me and has opened my eyes to many wonderful books. I gave her your copy of Uncle Tom's Cabin. *I wonder if you knew it had gone missing again from your father's library? Polly Caroline has just given us a beautiful baby granddaughter, after we'd given up on her ever having children! Her name is Elizabeth. Mama would be so proud of her new great-granddaughter.*

We send our best wishes for continued health and happiness to you. We were all saddened to learn of Mr. Roper's death in your last letter to Mama. He was a good man. I am glad that you had many wonderful years together after the early evil you endured.

The image I will forever hold of him in my mind was when we prepared to cross through Middle Tunnel into the mountains those years ago. A Confederate soldier challenged him on the peach crop that he carried while we hid in terror under the floorboards. The young man commanded him to unload the wagon. Mr. Roper leaped up on top of the crates (and directly onto my hidden and compressed body) and proceeded to jump up and down at the ridiculous idea of unloading a whole wagonload of ripe peaches. His ploy worked and we were allowed to pass without a search. This was a story I told my children through the years and they came to see Mr. Roper as our own version of Buffalo Bill. Tom was an American hero of sorts. As are you, Polly.

I look in the mirror and see the grey in my beard and feel the age in my bones and I wonder where the time went. I have had a good life beyond my imaginings because of you.

Kate and I will ever be eternally grateful for what you did for us.

Warmest Regards,

Ben Burgiss

— • —

SEPTEMBER 5, 1922

TELEGRAM

MANOR REST NURSING HOME
PENDLETON SOUTH CAROLINA

    RECEIVED TELEGRAM UPDATING OUR FAMILY
RE AUNT POLLY'S DECLINING HEALTH. (STOP)
    APPRECIATE YOUR GOOD CARE LAST TWO
YEARS AS REMAINING FAMILY IN CANADA (STOP)
    SENDING NURSE COMPANION ELIZABETH
JONES TO BE WITH HER IN FINAL DAYS (STOP)
    ARRIVES GREENVILLE SEPTEMBER 9 TRAIN
FROM DETROIT (STOP)

MRS. POLLY CAROLINE BURGISS COLE

— • —

September 1922

CURTAINS FLUTTERED GENTLY AT THE window as soft rain fell outside. Thunder rumbled in the distance and Polly stirred in her sleep. A cool breeze brushed her skin and raised goose flesh. With her left hand, she tried to pull the quilt close around her tiny shoulders. Old bones refused to warm.

The wound had turned septic, and neither homemade salves and tinctures nor the doctor's hasty amputation of her right hand had slowed the old woman's raging infection.

So, it comes to this, she thought. When she had avoided so many more interesting ways to go. The irony made her smile. A snapping turtle was hiding in the rhubarb, nowhere near the muddy pond. Its crushing bite had nearly severed two fingers, and the bacteria in its mouth quickly colonized her bloodstream. She should have listened to Reg years ago and killed the lot of them.

"Ma'am?" murmured the young nurse, rising sleepily from her rocking chair in the corner. "Miss Polly, do you need something? Are you chilly?" She crossed the room to close the open window and returned to lay a dark hand on the woman's forehead. Damp wisps of snow-white hair clung to the old woman's fevered brow, and perspiration beaded her upper lip.

"Miss Polly? I'm Elizabeth," the nurse leaned close and whispered. "I'm Ona's grand-daughter. Remember?"

Polly opened her eyes, confused. It was the remembering which frustrated her. The memories came unbidden now; the good mixed up with the bad. She felt as if she was seeing her life from outside her own skin, hovering just close enough to watch it happen all over again, with a softness over it, like a veil. She longed to call out, to keep the little girl safe. To warn the young woman of danger ahead. But it was too late.

"No need to worry yourself, Ona. I just had a bad dream . . ." Her shaky voice drifted off as she turned in her bed. She had no regrets. She had atoned for her sins, at least the deeds she credited as sin. Some of the things that had been done she would never ask God to forgive.

Polly tentatively touched the bandaged stump with her left hand, willing the ghost of her right hand to flex and bend. To feel. She squeezed her eyes shut tightly and tried to think on happy times.

Whitehall. There was Mother, fussing around the lawn, the roses her pride and joy. The view looked far to the north, to hazy green hills folding into the mountains of the Blue Ridge. Pink roses climbed over the veranda railings in profusion and sweetened the summer breezes. The veranda was always swept clean and welcomed visitors with comfortable rocking chairs and a ceiling painted pale blue to keep the "haints" away. Bright orange daylilies lined the long drive. Every evening, Ona rang the brass bell on the post to call the children in for supper. Polly's brothers always beat her home, stiff boots, and ankle-grazing skirts no match for their own bare feet and long legs.

Father raised cotton, although his heart was elsewhere. He was an entrepreneur of sorts, working to bring the railroad further into upstate South Carolina. His dream of a tunnel through the Blue Ridge Mountains kept him away much of the time. When he came home, his warm embrace smelled of fine tobacco and leather. He always brought Polly a paper sack of penny candies after lengthy trips to Columbia and Charleston.

The old woman clambered after another recollection. Perfect summer days, cornfields waving emerald green. Cotton was high. In the distance, the men stooped to their hard labor. Polly balanced precariously on the split rail fence post, eating a ripe peach with childish abandon. Sweet juice dribbled down her chin as she lifted her face to the warm sun.

She blinked and saw gentle Duke, ebony arms and torso glistening with sweat, hard at the plow with the mules, slicing furrows in the rich bottomland. She lifted a sticky hand to wave, and he waved back. She tossed the peach pit towards the mules and the nearest animal flicked his ear in irritation.

The overseer rode up, tall in the saddle. With a wink and a smile, he told her to get on home. "A young lady doesn't exactly belong in the fields when the slaves are picking," he'd said. As if that were where the danger lay.

The clear creek where she waded with her brothers on hot August afternoons tumbled over smooth grey rocks on its way to the river. Barefoot, dark braids undone, she remembered wading in the icy water, her eyes alert for the smoothest stones. Mother chastised her for spoiling another good dress; creek mud and peach juice stained her smock front a dull brown.

Another memory. She watched with satisfaction as Ben kissed his bride. Ah, she had done a fine thing then. Maybe the most important thing in her life. But my, how she missed him still.

And there was her beloved husband, long gone. His handsome face was so hard to summon. Their time together wasn't long enough, but it was fair, she supposed. A life for a life. God's idea of justice confounded her.

The hot summer morning at the trading post, the most vivid image in a lifetime of memories, brought her fully and instantly awake. It wouldn't stay down. It was less painful now, more than seventy years later, but no less unjust. Why was that picture clear as day? Why not the warm kiss of her husband or dear Father's smile?

Elizabeth bent to offer her a sip of water, which Polly took gratefully. She lay back, exhausted from the effort. At the edge of sleep, John's blue eyes followed her, wide and questioning. Not angry really but surprised to find Polly capable of her own crimes.

Her rheumy eyes closed. Nothing would stay down anymore. The memories seeped out of her very marrow and into her blood and breath. With every exhalation, she released another fragment of her life into the ether. Here was her last chance to have her say and set things right before she left this earth. She tried to speak but no words came from her dry throat.

Elizabeth pressed a cool cloth onto Polly's fevered cheek and said, "No need to talk, Miss Polly."

Polly squeezed the woman's brown hand and said with great effort, "Thank you, Ona. For everything. I did so many bad things, but I always loved you. You saved me, you know."

Elizabeth smiled. "And you saved me right back." She did not try to explain that she was not her great-grandmother.

Polly relaxed into her pillow and released Elizabeth's hand. The creek burbled and splashed and in the very middle of the current, Jack barked and wagged his tail, urging Polly to follow. The sky was a brilliant blue. Puffy clouds changed shape and moved on in the warm breeze. She squinted in the bright sunshine and saw her brothers laughing and calling to her from the distant shore. She lifted her skirts and ran barefoot into the crystal stream, giggling and filled with joy.

Epilogue

Law Offices of Legarre, Peterson, White

September 30, 1922

Mrs. Polly Burgiss Cole
22 Linden Street
Hamilton, Ontario

Dear Mrs. Cole,

I wish to offer my personal condolences on the death of your aunt and namesake, Mrs. Polly Caroline Burgiss Roper. Our office is in the process of carrying out the instructions in her will. As you know, Mrs. Roper's property at Whitehall Road, Pendleton, was passed to you, her remaining next of kin. The property consists of five hundred acres of producing orchards, outbuildings, and the old house on the main road.

I received your telegram and understand that your family has decided to gift this valuable property to the Negro sharecropping the land now, a former slave who belonged to her during the war, now known as Zadoc Roper. While I applaud your generosity, I have cautioned you that without white management, the orchards may fall into neglect.

Nevertheless, I understand that you wish to move forward with the transfer. Mr. Roper can indeed pay the taxes due on the land. Therefore, since you desire the agreement to go forward with haste, I have enclosed documents to that effect and sent them for your signature. The entire estate will therefore become the legal property of Zadoc and Sarah Roper and their four adult sons, effective October 15, 1922.

Sincerely,
Jacob White
Jacob White, Esquire

Acknowledgments

Many pairs of eyes looked at drafts of this novel and helped to make it the best it could be. Thank you to my sweet husband, Ed Burchfield, for believing in me. Thank you to my brilliant daughters Dr. Holly Whitson and Dr. Emily Burchfield for offering valuable feedback. Thanks also to my son, Sam Burchfield, who never failed to ask "How is your book coming?" every single time he visited or called. Thank you to my friend, fellow author, and unofficial first editor, Marty Duckenfield. Marty read the chapters I delivered to her door during the early months of the pandemic, and returned each chunk with wonderful notes and ideas, corrections, and instructions on the proper use of Oxford commas.

Thanks also go to one of my favorite Southern authors, Ron Rash, whose writing has inspired me all the way back to his children's book, *The Shark's Tooth*. His willingness to give this first-time novelist some good advice will always be greatly appreciated. Thank you to TouchPoint Press for giving this story a chance. To my fabulous official editor Jenn Haskin, I know your eyes were probably bleeding after working on this story as hard as you did, for as long as you did, but your ideas and edits made it so much better. Thank you for giving life to Polly and Ben, and especially Ona.

Lastly, as I researched my own family trees, I found several documents that pointed to the horrific fact of my own southern ancestors owning slaves prior to the Civil War. While I can never know what happened to these people, I hope that in the tiniest of ways, this story lets them know how incredibly sorry I am for the atrocity that is slavery and the part that my ancestors played in it.

About the Author

Shelley Burchfield is a writer, mom, and former teacher with deep Southern roots. She enjoys writing "what-if" fiction that flips notorious events upside down. She lives in the beautiful South Carolina Upstate with her husband and a menagerie of cats and dogs.

www.shelleyburchfield.com

CPSIA information can be obtained
at www.ICGtesting.com
Printed in the USA
LVHW112153120522
718684LV00004B/19